Prior to taking the decision to write full time, Sheila O'Flanagan pursued a very successful career in banking, becoming Ireland's first woman Chief Dealer. She writes a weekly column for the *Irish Times* and in her spare time plays badminton at competition level.

SUDDENLY SINGLE

ISOBEL'S WEDDING

Sheila O'Flanagan

headline

SUDDENLY SINGLE first published in Great Britain
in 1999 by HEADLINE BOOK PUBLISHING

ISOBEL'S WEDDING first published in Great Britain
in 2002 by HEADLINE BOOK PUBLISHING

First published in this omnibus edition in 2004
by HEADLINE BOOK PUBLISHING

10 9 8 7 6 5 4 3 2

ISBN 0 7553 2261 4

Typeset by Palimpsest Book Production Limited,
Polmont, Stirlingshire
Printed and bound in Great Britain by
Clays Ltd, St Ives plc

Papers and cover board used by Headline are natural,
recyclable products made from wood grown in sustainable
forests. The manufacturing processes conform to the
environmental regulations of the country of origin.

HEADLINE BOOK PUBLISHING
A division of Hodder Headline PLC
338 Euston Road
London NW1 3BH

www.headline.co.uk
www.hodderheadline.com

Suddenly Single

To: Carole Blake for her support and friendship through thick, thicker and thickest. I could not have found a better agent.

Anne Williams – ever patient, always encouraging.

The Survivors' Group – especially Patricia – for everything!

Damien O'Gorman of BRC Shooting Club for his advice.

My family once again – every one of you.

Colm. As always.

Chapter 1

Alix Callaghan stood up and snagged her tights on the corner of her desk.

'Shit!' She examined the run which was progressing down the side of her leg. 'I just took these out of the packet this morning! Why does this always happen when I'm about to go to a meeting?'

'It's one of those laws of nature things,' Jenny Smith told her. 'Whenever a woman has something important to do, her tights let her down.'

Alix grinned and opened the desk drawer. 'And the other law is, be prepared,' she told Jenny as she rummaged through the drawer and fished out another pair. 'Especially if you work in Europa Bank and you know that the managing director calls meetings at every available opportunity. If he's looking for me, tell him I'll see him downstairs in five minutes.' She picked up her bag and the tights and opened the door of the dealing room. 'He probably *will* ring. You know how much he enjoys cracking the whip. Oops!' She nearly collided with Dave Bryant, the senior dealer, as he walked in carrying a brown paper bag with his lunch for the day – two filled baguettes, a slice of banoffi cake and a tin of Diet Coke.

'I'm off to the management meeting,' she told him. 'There's

no change in our positions. We're holding some dollars but not much and I think we should stay that way. I don't think I'll be too long, I can't imagine that our glorious leader has anything new to tell us.'

'OK,' said Dave. 'Are Marks and Spencer up for discussion?'

Alix stared at him. 'What are you talking about?'

'Why are you bringing tights along to the management meeting?'

She looked at the packet in her hand. 'These are my emergency pair,' she told him sternly. 'And they are *not* Marks and Spencer. They're a ridiculously expensive pair of Donna Karan which I bought in the duty free last time I came back from Paris.'

Dave laughed. 'I obviously don't know as much as I thought about women's lingerie.'

'Just as well,' said Alix. 'Otherwise I'd be worried about you.'

'Oh, I'm good on stockings,' Dave told her. 'I'm an expert on stockings – it's tights I can't stand. I'm against them on principle.'

'Stockings have their place,' Alix agreed. 'But not during office hours. Not for me, anyway.' She grinned at him. 'See you later.'

She was the last to arrive in the boardroom. She apologised for delaying them and sat down in her usual seat opposite Des Coyle, the managing director of Europa Bank Dublin.

'I thought we'd discuss profitability,' said Des. 'I know that Pat has a few things he'd like to bring up.'

Pat Enright, the bank's chief accountant, began his presentation. Alix half listened to him. Although she was obviously concerned about the bank's overall profitability, her priority was the profitability of the dealing room. She'd been Europa's head of treasury in Dublin for the past few years, and each year, she had exceeded her targets. She had a reputation for spotting trouble, for finding new ways of making money and for concluding deals that no one else managed to complete. While Pat talked about the profitability of the credit department (down because of a problem with a syndicated loan), Alix was planning a strategy for a customer to borrow yen and switch the proceeds into euros.

'And the dealing room?' Des broke into her thoughts. 'Another good month last month, Alix.'

'Yes,' she said. 'We did a couple of nice trades for Inico and Constant Images. We stayed long of US dollars and US bonds, both of which have performed well for us.'

'Excellent.' Des smiled at her. 'Keep up the good work.'

She nodded. Nobody ever made comments about the dealing room and what the team of four traders did. Nobody understood enough about it and, anyway, every one of the five men around the table was slightly in awe of Alix Callaghan and didn't want to ask her a question that might appear stupid. Alix had a habit of exposing someone's lack of knowledge – something that nobody at Europa Bank could afford to have happen to them. Least of all at a management meeting.

When the meeting was finally over, Alix ran back upstairs to the dealing room. Dave hurriedly closed the sports page of the *Irish Times* as she opened the door.

'How's it going?' she asked.

'Boring,' said Dave. 'We bought a few more dollars but the rate hasn't changed. It's a dull, dull day.'

'Never say that!' She slid into her seat. 'It's tempting fate. And we've had a good week this week so let's not mess things up.' She looked around. 'Where's Gavin?' Gavin Donnelly was the newest and youngest member of the dealing team.

'He's at lunch with Alfonso in Banco Andalucia,' Jenny told her. 'You know how much he loves lunching with the opposition.'

Alix laughed. 'He keeps trying to find out who's earning more than him. He's obsessed with status.'

'I know,' said Jenny. 'Who are you telling?'

'Oh, don't worry about him,' said Dave. 'It's just youth and exuberance.'

'I'll give him youth and exuberance,' said Alix. 'He knows perfectly well he should be back by now.'

~

Gavin arrived back from lunch at four o'clock. Alix looked pointedly at her watch when he walked in the door.

'I know it's Friday,' she said. 'And I know that it hasn't been a particularly busy day. But *you* know that you're meant to be back here by two thirty, Gavin. Where the hell were you?' She didn't really need to ask. It was obvious that Gavin and Alfonso had decided to go for a liquid lunch. Gavin's eyes were bleary.

'I was with Alfonso Moya. We were talking,' he said defensively. 'It's good to know what our opposition are doing. They gave the five-year sterling swap this week.'

'That's fascinating information,' said Alix dryly. 'In how much?'

Gavin burped gently. 'I didn't ask. It's not the sort of question you ask, Alix. You should know that.'

'You're so right,' she said sweetly. 'So they're making money in five-year sterling, are they?'

4

'Yes,' said Gavin.

'The same position that you lost six thousand on last week?'

Gavin stared at her. Jenny busied herself with the phones and Dave immersed himself in the paper again.

'Gavin, it's time for you to grow up,' said Alix. 'Don't believe everything that everyone tells you. Don't ever spend four hours at lunch without my permission again and do your trousers up properly. They're a dead giveaway on the alcoholic lunch.' She got up and walked out of the room.

Dave and Jenny tried to smother their grins.

'She's a bitch!' Gavin tugged at his flies. 'She thinks she's so fucking high and mighty. Well, she's not! There are plenty of people out there better than she is. I suppose she thinks she's smart and witty! Well, one day I'll pay her back.'

'You *were* rather late,' said Jenny mildly.

'Oh, I might have known you'd stick up for her,' said Gavin. 'Well, you won't get very far, Jenny Smith. She won't do another woman any favours, you know. She likes to be in control. But one day she won't be and I'll be right there laughing at her!'

⌇

Alix went downstairs to Dermot Cullen's office. She couldn't have stayed in the dealing room because she would have laughed out loud at the injured look on Gavin's face when she told him to do up his trousers. Gavin Donnelly had lots of potential, Alix thought, but he had to channel it properly. And four-hour lunches in the pub were not the best way.

She knocked on Dermot's door and walked in. He was the

head of settlements and a settlement problem earlier in the week had cost them money.

She sat down opposite him. 'Was it a simple mistake or is there something wrong with our system?' she asked.

'It was a mistake,' said Dermot. There was no point in bullshitting her. 'Noleen should have caught it. She's very apologetic.'

'It was an expensive mistake. Someone should have spotted it.' Her eyes glittered green.

Not a good sign, thought Dermot. It was common knowledge in the bank that Alix's eyes appeared grey when she was relaxed but green when she was angry or excited. He didn't want her to get really angry. Dealers were notoriously temperamental. And, thought Dermot, women dealers were worse than men.

'It'll be sorted,' he told her. 'It shouldn't happen again.'

'I hope not,' said Alix. 'It's hard enough making money without someone else pissing it away.'

'I appreciate that,' said Dermot. 'But you have to acknowledge the fact that Noleen is still relatively new at the job and things were very pressurised last week.'

Alix grimaced then smiled. 'You're right,' she said. 'But you know how it is, Dermot, we're all under pressure.'

'Who are you telling?' Dermot sighed. 'I need more staff. But the budget doesn't allow it.'

'I know.' Alix got up and walked to the door. 'How are things otherwise?'

'Oh, fine.'

'Good.' She smiled at him and her eyes were grey again. 'I'd better get back upstairs.'

'See you, Alix,' said Dermot. He sighed with relief when

she'd gone. It annoyed him whenever she interfered in the settlements area but she was right. They should have spotted the mistake.

'Any change?' asked Alix as she walked back into the dealing room.

'No.' Jenny shook her head. 'It's quiet. Wyn rang to remind you about baby-sitting for her. It's not for a while but she wanted to be sure it was in your diary. She said, "My sister forgets family duties if I don't remind her."' Jenny grinned as Alix made a face. 'And your friend Sophia phoned. She wanted to know if you were going to the forex seminar in London next month.'

'I've better things to do,' said Alix as she picked up the phone and hit the speed-dial button. 'The last one I went to was such a waste of time! I could have given the course myself.'

'This is Sophia Redmond,' said a voice. 'I'm not at my desk at the moment but if you'd like to leave your name and number I'll call you back as soon as I can.'

'Bloody voice-mail,' muttered Alix. 'Hi, Soph! It's me, returning your call. I'm not going to the London seminar but I might just go over to do some shopping. Talk to you soon.' She hung up and looked at her watch. 'I think I'll head off early,' she told Jenny. 'Give Paul a shock!'

'You haven't forgotten about Eimear's drinks, have you?' Dave looked at her in surprise.

'Oh, God!' Her hand flew to her mouth. 'I had forgotten. How could I? Especially since I've just been talking to Dermot Cullen.'

'A much more exciting weekend in prospect?' asked Dave wickedly.

'I wish!' Alix laughed.

'So you'll come to the pub?'

'Of course I will. I can't let our only decent settlements person leave without saying goodbye. If she'd been around on Tuesday there wouldn't have been a problem on the dollar account.'

Alix dialled her home phone number but there was no answer. Paul was obviously out but why, she thought crossly, doesn't he ever switch on the bloody answering machine? She tried his mobile, but that was switched off too. Oh well, tough, she muttered. Just because he couldn't be bothered to stay in touch. She knew Paul, though. He'd be pissed off with her for being late home.

∽

Eimear Flaherty, the girl who was leaving, was having her booze-up in O'Reilly's bar. The dealing-room staff arrived together and Eimear ordered a round of drinks.

'You look as though you've been here a while.' Dave grinned at Eimear who blinked at him.

'I can hardly stand up,' she confessed.

'A few drinks at lunchtime?' asked Alix unsympathetically.

'Afraid so.' Eimear's eyes were glazed. 'But fun.'

'You didn't bump into Gavin Donnelly, did you?'

'Gavin? No. Why?'

'He also had a liquid lunch,' Alix told her. 'Staggered back into the dealing room at four with his flies undone!'

Eimear laughed. 'Poor Gavin.'

'What do you mean, poor Gavin?' demanded Alix.

'I bet you chewed him up and spat him out,' said Eimear.

'No I didn't,' said Alix. 'I was very moderate.'

Eimear was still laughing when Jenny joined them.

'So, Flaherty, what are you going to do with your life?' asked Jenny.

'I am going to devote myself to my children,' replied Eimear. 'Although they'll never appreciate the sacrifice I'm making, giving up the glory that is working for Des Coyle and Europa Bank!'

The girls laughed.

'I think you're lucky,' said Jenny. 'It must be wonderful to chuck in your job.'

'I'm not sure.' Eimear took a mouthful from her bottle of Budweiser. 'It's such hard going rushing out and back and trying to be there at the right time and everything. And I know I'm wracked with guilt every time I kiss Tom goodbye at kindergarten. And even more wracked with guilt when I leave Cliona at the crèche. But I'm afraid my mind will go.'

'Go where?' asked Alix.

'Just go. That all I'll want to talk about is nappies and playschool and shit like that.'

'I'm sure they'll be the last things you want to talk about,' said Jenny.

'Maybe.' Eimear looked worried. 'But perhaps they'll be the only things I *can* talk about.'

'Oh, I don't know.' Alix laughed. 'You can chat about FedWire and Euroclear and Cedel to all the other parents.'

Eimear grinned at her. 'That'll wow them at the PTA meetings, I'm sure. I need to be able to chat about Barney and Postman Pat, not the best way to send a million dollars to the States.'

'You are so lucky, Eimear Flaherty.' Linda Crossan, one of the bank's accountants, waltzed over to them. 'Not having to

9

get out of bed at the crack of dawn every morning. Not having to stay in the bank until all hours at night. I tell you, one day I'm going to chuck it in myself.'

'You'll have to have a nice doctor husband like Eimear has before you can afford it,' said Jenny sternly.

'I supported him through college,' said Eimear. 'It's the least he can do now.'

Alix was starving. There had been delicately cut sandwiches at the lunchtime meeting but she hadn't bothered to eat any. Now there was a guy standing in front of her with a tray of cocktail sausages and she speared three of them at once.

'Ow!' she cried. 'They're bloody hot.'

'They're meant to be.' Dave Bryant took four. 'I love them.'

'I'll have blisters on my tongue,' complained Alix.

'Might shut you up for a few minutes.'

'Very bloody funny.' Alix gulped some beer to cool her mouth.

'Any better?'

'A bit.'

'We had a good week this week,' said Dave.

'Not bad.' Alix blew on a sausage before biting into it. 'It's just as well. Pat was going on about overall profitability at lunchtime.'

'Not good?' asked Dave.

'Could be better,' said Alix.

'At least we're making money,' Dave told her.

'I know,' said Alix. 'That's what we're paid for.'

'What are you paid for?' asked Des Coyle, the managing director.

'Making you money,' replied Alix.

10

'Absolutely,' said Des. 'And you do it so well!'

She grinned at him and he ruffled her hair. He had to reach up to do it because Alix, in her low shoes, was still taller than he was.

'Cigarette?' Jenny's eyes were unfocused.

'No thanks,' said Alix automatically. 'I've given them up.'

'No, I meant d'you have a cigarette?'

'I told you, I've given them up.'

'Don't give me that guff,' said Jenny. 'I've seen the packet in your desk drawer.'

'They're only for emergencies,' said Alix. 'And I really and truly don't have them with me.'

Alix looked at her watch. Almost ten o'clock. She supposed she should leave. She'd tried to ring Paul at six to tell him that she'd be a bit late and to go ahead and have something to eat without her. But he still wasn't in and he still had his mobile switched off. So she didn't give a toss any more about Paul. Even though she knew he'd be annoyed at her for getting drunk. Paul didn't drink, which was one of the things about him that both appealed to her and appalled her. It was great having someone who could drive everywhere and on whom she could depend. It was awful having someone who looked disapprovingly at her when she wobbled her way up the stairs.

'Eimear!' She waved at the settlements clerk. 'I gotta go. Things to do, people to see, all that sort of stuff.'

'OK, Alix. I'll be in to see you all, I'm sure.'

'Have a great life,' said Alix. 'Don't miss us too much.'

'I won't.'

Alix walked unsteadily down the stairs. She'd drunk much more than she meant to and it was stupid because she actually

11

didn't like getting drunk. She enjoyed having a few drinks, but usually stopped at three or four bottles of beer. She'd had a lot more than that tonight.

The night air made her feel dizzy. She waved at a taxi and got in. Lucky to find one free, she thought, as she closed her eyes. Although it was late the city was crowded with people. All the tourists in T-shirts and shorts because the weather was exceptionally mild made Alix feel overdressed in her coffee-coloured business suit and brown court shoes. In her last job the dealers had worn jeans and casual tops. But not T-shirts. She wished it was the same in Europa Bank.

The taxi edged its way through traffic that was almost as busy as during the day. It was blocked solid at St Stephen's Green.

She leaned forward to the driver. 'You can let me out here. I'll walk the rest of the way.'

'If you like,' he said.

Baggot Street was quieter. She yawned as she walked past the Georgian houses and wondered, as she always did, what it must have been like when the owners had lived on the street and it had been residential. Wonderful to have all that space, she thought. The apartment on Percy Place – despite its duplex status and the fulsome praise of the estate agent who had sold it – was sadly lacking in space by comparison.

She walked up the steps and rummaged in her bag for her keys. She wished she didn't always carry a bag so jam-packed with stuff that it was impossible to find anything. She shook it a couple of times to make the keys rattle but she couldn't hear them.

'Oh, bugger,' she muttered and pressed the bell.

'Hello,' said Paul.

'Hi! Sorry I'm late,' she called. 'I can't find my keys.'

She heard the buzzer and the door to the block opened. She took off her shoes and walked along the corridor in her stockinged feet.

Paul had already opened the door to their apartment.

'Hello, Alexandra.'

'Mrs Hunter.' Alix blinked at the sight of Paul's mother. 'How are you?'

'I'm fine,' she said. 'And how are you?'

'I'm fine too,' said Alix. 'I didn't know you were calling around tonight.'

'Of course you did,' said Paul grimly. 'I told you about it on Wednesday. You said you'd nothing planned.'

'Well, I hadn't really.' Alix looked embarrassed. 'I'm very sorry. One of the girls left the office today and there was a bit of a booze-up for her. I tried to ring you earlier, Paul, but you were out and the machine was off.'

'I was collecting Mum,' he said.

'I realise that now,' Alix said contritely. 'I'm sorry.'

'It doesn't matter.' Mrs Hunter's smile didn't reach her eyes. 'I understand you had better things to do.'

'I didn't have better things to do,' said Alix. 'Honestly. If I'd remembered . . .' She didn't say anything else. Paul's eyes warned her to be quiet.

'Would you like a coffee?' he asked.

'Not unless you're having one.'

'We've just finished,' said Mrs Hunter. 'But I'm sure Paul won't mind making some more.'

'It's OK,' said Alix hastily. 'Don't worry about it, Paul.'

But he was already rinsing the percolator.

Alix was beginning to get a headache. Bloody hell, she thought. How could I have forgotten about the battleaxe?

Paul's mother didn't like her. Had never liked her although Alix wasn't sure why. Maybe it was because Paul was her only child – she'd disapproved of all his girlfriends. Maybe it was her job – Mrs Hunter had seen *Wall Street* and *Other People's Money* and strongly disapproved. Or maybe it was simply the fact that Alix and Paul had never quite got around to actually getting married despite having lived together for the past three years. Whatever the reason, the antipathy was, by now, mutual.

'Here you are.' Paul handed her a mug of barely filtered coffee.

'Thanks.'

'How was your day?' he asked.

'Busy. Yours?'

'Equally busy,' he said dryly.

Paul was a freelance journalist. She'd met him when he interviewed her for a piece entitled 'Career Girls – on the up and up'. It was, as she admitted to him later, lust at first sight. They'd moved in together a couple of weeks later and she still thought he was the sexiest man she'd ever known. Pity about his mother though.

She drained her mug and smiled at him. 'Thanks, Paul. I'll just head off to bed.'

'OK,' he said shortly.

'Goodnight, Mrs Hunter.'

'Goodnight, Alexandra.'

I really hate that woman, she thought as she opened the bedroom door. She knows my name is Alix. Plain and simple. Not short for anything. Just Alix.

She closed the door sharply behind her.

Chapter 2

It was three o'clock in the morning when she woke up. The bedroom was hot and stifling and her mouth was dry. She hadn't heard Paul come to bed, but he lay beside her, sleeping soundly, his arm flung across the duvet.

Alix slid gently out of the bed and padded down to the kitchen. She poured herself an orange juice and opened the balcony doors.

The night air was pleasantly warm. She stepped out onto the balcony and leaned over the rail. Beneath her, the water of the canal was dark and murky. She could never understand how people could swim there in the summer, but they often did. The canal had been another one of the estate agent's selling points. He'd waxed lyrical about sitting beside the water while the sun sparkled off the surface. He hadn't mentioned the water rats which she sometimes saw scurrying along the banks.

Alix sat on the wicker patio chair and sipped her orange juice.

She wished she'd remembered about Paul's mother. She knew that Paul was furious with her and she didn't blame him. She was furious with herself. She hated the idea that smug Mrs Hunter would go home to her empty house on the Stillorgan Road and sigh deeply over the fact that her beloved only son was living with someone like Alix Callaghan. Deirdre Hunter wanted someone better for Paul. Someone who would support him and look after him and look up to him.

Alix drained her glass. Well, she did support Paul. Not in the way his mother would have wanted, of course, not by being there every minute of the day and sympathising with him when he was stuck in the middle of a piece with no idea where it was going. Alix supported him by earning four times as much as he did. By walking into the office most days so that he could use the BMW if he wanted. By not hassling him when he was working. And she looked after him. She went shopping with him and made him buy decent clothes instead of chain-store jeans and sweatshirts. She didn't cook for him because she was a rotten cook and he was much better at it than she was. Besides which, he enjoyed cooking, whereas she'd be lost without Marks and Spencer and a microwave oven. So that didn't count. And she looked up to him. Despite what Mrs Hunter might think. She was in awe of his ability to make the most uninteresting subjects sound interesting or to find a new way of looking at an old subject.

Alix loved Paul. But she wished he had a different mother.

∽

'Alix?'

She opened her eyes at the sound of his voice and blinked a couple of times in the dawn light.

'Alix. Are you OK?'

'Yes. I – ouch!' She rubbed her neck which hurt badly. She couldn't believe that she'd fallen asleep on the patio, wearing nothing more than the silk top of her pyjamas.

'What on earth are you doing out here?' Paul looked at her in amazement.

'I woke up and I was hot. So I came out for a breath of fresh air.'

'Honestly, Alix!' He raised his eyebrow. 'Dressed like this?'

'It was darker when I came out,' she said. 'Anyway, nobody can see me up here.'

'I wouldn't be so sure of that. Any old busybody could be looking out.'

'At four in the morning?'

'You never know.' He stood at the balcony rail and peered across the canal.

'Paul, I'm sorry about being late.'

'I said it didn't matter,' he told her tightly.

'I know what you said. But you didn't mean it, did you?'

He was silent.

'I really do try to get on with your mother,' continued Alix. 'It's just that she doesn't like me. She doesn't understand me.'

'My mother is OK,' said Paul. 'Maybe she's old-fashioned.'

'I can't be the sort of person she wants me to be.' Alix got up from the chair and stood beside him. 'I can only be the sort of person I am.'

'And what sort of person is that?'

'Oh, I don't know.' She slid her hand under his T-shirt. 'Wicked, wanton, sexy?'

'Not now, Alix,' he said.

'Oh, fine!' She withdrew her hand. 'Fine. Your mother's thoughts about me are more important to you. Great. Be like that!'

'It's not that at all,' said Paul.

17

'Of course it bloody is! You dance attendance on the old bat as though she was the only woman in your life. It's time for you to grow up, Paul!'

'Really?' His voice was cold. 'I don't think I'm the one who needs to grow up. I'm not the one who drinks myself stupid and loses my house keys, am I?'

'I wasn't drunk,' protested Alix. 'And I didn't lose my keys. They were at the bottom of my bag.'

'You were pissed as a newt,' snapped Paul. 'And you can't find anything in that bag.'

'Why are we arguing?' she asked. 'This is silly.'

'Yes,' said Paul, 'it is.' He turned round and walked back into the apartment. Alix stayed where she was and clenched her fists.

~

He'd left a note to say he'd gone to Carlow to do an interview. Alix had gone back to bed and was still asleep when he left. It was nearly eleven by the time she woke and she couldn't be certain whether she'd really spent half the night on the balcony or whether it was part of a fuzzy dream. But she knew that the bit where she'd arrived home, fairly drunk, to find Paul's disapproving mother sitting in the apartment had been real. She groaned. That woman was a real pain. If there was one good reason for not marrying Paul, it was his damned mother!

To make up for her forgetfulness the previous evening, she booked a table at Dobbins for dinner. Paul liked Dobbins and they hadn't eaten out in ages. It would cheer him up, she thought. No man could resist being stuffed with food.

It was nearly eight by the time he arrived home.

'Hard day among the celebrities?' asked Alix brightly.

'Yes,' said Paul.

'I've booked Dobbins for half eight,' she told him. 'You'll just have time to hop under the shower.'

He stared at her. 'Why did you do that?'

'I thought you might like to go out. We haven't been out to dinner in such a long time. Save you having to cook or me having to pretend!'

'I don't want to go out,' said Paul.

Alix smiled at him. 'Of course you do. You're just tired and . . .' Her voice faltered as she looked at him. He was still angry, she realised. Far too angry to simply forget about it. 'Look, I'm really sorry about your mother,' she said. 'I've said it about a hundred times already and I mean it. I won't do it again. But there's no point in smouldering with anger about it, Paul. That doesn't help.'

'I know,' he said.

'Well, then.' She smiled at him. 'Let's forget about last night and go out to dinner.'

He pushed his fingers through his jet-black hair. 'No,' he said.

She shrugged. 'If you don't want to, that's fine. I'm sorry. I should have asked you first. I thought it was a good idea.' She turned away from him.

'Alix, it's not that.' He reached out and touched her shoulder. 'It's nothing to do with last night. Not really. Well,' he sighed, 'maybe it is, partly.'

She turned to him. His blue eyes were troubled. 'What's the matter?' she asked.

'We need to talk,' said Paul.

Alix was astonished. Paul wasn't one of life's talkers. Paul did things or wrote about doing things. Alix had never sat down with Paul and had a meaning-of-life conversation. She wasn't sure she wanted to now.

'OK,' she said finally. 'What do you want to talk about?'

'Us,' said Paul and she nearly choked.

'What about us?'

'It's not really easy to say this,' said Paul. 'I've thought about it a lot, but saying it is something quite different.'

'Say what?' Alix didn't like the tone of his voice.

'I care about you a lot, Alix. I know you've been good to me. In the way that you know best – materially – but there's more to it than that.'

'I know there's more to it than that!' Alix stared at him. 'And I don't just look after you in a material way. That's a horrible thing to say.'

'I know. It came out all wrong. That's what I mean about this being difficult to say.'

'Look, Paul, are you trying to tell me it's over or something?'

'I . . .' He looked uncomfortable.

Alix couldn't think of anything to say. She loved Paul. She'd thought he loved her. She couldn't believe that he was just going to walk out on her.

'But why?' she asked.

'We've been together for three years,' said Paul. 'And we haven't really gone anywhere, have we?'

'Where did you plan on us going?' she asked tartly.

'You know what I mean.' His voice was harder. 'We're still living here. You're still doing the same thing. We're getting older but not behaving any differently.'

'How do you want to behave?' Alix was truly surprised. She couldn't understand what was troubling Paul.

'I want to get married and have a family,' he said. 'I want to change jobs. I want to settle down.'

'Settle down?' She looked at him in astonishment. 'You're the most settled person I know. You're not like the stereotypical journalist who spends his time in pubs. You work all day and you come home and write all night – how much more settled can you be?'

'I like doing it,' said Paul. 'But it's not my whole life. Not the same way as the bank is yours. I'm not a career person, Alix. I enjoy the work and I enjoy writing but I don't have this great ambition to win Pulitzer prizes or be a media mogul. Which is what you'd be like if you were a journalist!'

Alix looked sheepish. He was probably right. 'So what do you want to do?' she asked.

'I've accepted a job offer from RTÉ,' said Paul. 'It's a salaried job – no more freelancing.'

'But that's great!' She smiled at him. 'Really great. Although you could've told me you'd applied.'

'I didn't want to. In case I didn't get it.'

'But you have.' She kissed him lightly on the cheek.

'Yes,' he said. 'And it's the start of a new way of life for me.'

'Is this where all the family thinking is coming from?'

'Maybe.'

'So what do you want?' she asked. 'For us to get married? For me to get pregnant? To leave work? We couldn't afford this place if I left work. Not unless they're paying you an absolute fortune in RTÉ!'

'It's your apartment, not mine,' said Paul. 'I have the house near Malahide. But you wouldn't live that far out of town.'

'It's not that I wouldn't,' said Alix. 'It just seemed silly when I already had this place.'

21

'You see,' said Paul. 'We always do things your way, Alix. You never think about what I want or what I'd like.'

'But it doesn't matter where you live!' she cried. 'It's just as easy for you to live here! Plus it's quicker for you to get into town.'

'This is silly,' said Paul. 'Arguing about who should live where.'

'If you want to get married and start a family then we should sit down and talk about it properly,' said Alix. 'Not have a silly row like two teenagers.'

'That's the whole point,' said Paul. 'Sometimes you act as though you were still twenty-two. Alix, you're thirty-two years old. I'm thirty-four. We can't go on living our lives like twentysomethings.'

She sighed. 'I don't live my life like a twentysomething.'

'Yes, you do,' said Paul. 'You do this crazy job that has you high as a kite most evenings. You enjoy going to the pub on a Friday night – Friday being the one evening I like to be at home – and you spend half your life trotting off to London or Paris for meetings. It's not the lifestyle of someone who's ready to settle down.'

'We *are* settled,' said Alix tightly. 'And I go to London and Paris on business. I don't spend the time out on the piss, you know. Of course I go for a drink on Fridays. But it's usually only one drink. And I didn't know that you missed me. You're usually locked away with the computer. Which I bought, by the way.'

'I knew it would come down to this at some stage,' said Paul. 'That you'd throw your superior earning power at me.'

'Don't be absolutely ridiculous,' snapped Alix. 'We have a joint account, for goodness' sake.'

'You don't put everything into it,' said Paul.

She stared at him. 'I'm going to forget you said that.'

'Yes, do.' He sighed. 'I'm sorry. I didn't mean it.'

She walked to the sofa and sat down. She hoped that by sitting she would diffuse some of the tension in the room. She couldn't understand Paul tonight. His sudden desire to 'settle down'. His totally unexpected need to have children. It was extraordinary.

'So how come you've decided all this?' she asked.

'I've been thinking about it for a long time,' said Paul.

'And you haven't said anything?'

'There never seemed to be a good time.'

'Paul.' Alix smiled at him. 'We've gone through the odd bumpy patch before. We can work this one out. Can't we?'

He was silent.

'We can work it out, Paul.' She watched him carefully.

'I don't think so,' he said finally.

'Why not?'

He looked uncomfortable and Alix felt a cold band suddenly wrap itself round her heart.

'Why not?'

'Because I'm not sure about us,' said Paul.

'Why?' asked Alix dangerously.

'I – might have met someone.'

'You might have met someone?'

'I've met someone and I like her a lot.'

Alix swallowed. 'And do you love her?'

'I don't know. How can I know?'

'So you've met someone and because of that you don't want to give us a chance, is that what you're saying?'

'No, it's not.' Paul glared at her. 'Don't twist things around,

23

Alix. I've met this person and she's the sort of person I'd like to spend more time with.'

'What's her name, this person?' asked Alix.

'Sabine.'

'Sabine?'

'Sabine Brassaert.'

'Sounds French to me.' Alix wrinkled her nose.

'She is French,' said Paul.

'Where did you meet her?'

Paul exhaled slowly. 'In Paris.'

'In Paris?' echoed Alix. 'When did you meet her in Paris?'

'When do you think?'

Alix stood up. 'You mean you met this Sabine person when we were on that trip to Europa Bank for the opening of their new office? You met her there?'

Paul looked uncomfortable. 'Yes.'

'I don't believe you.' Alix stared at him. 'I brought you on that trip. And you got a great lifestyle piece out of it too!'

'I know,' said Paul.

'And you met a French woman with whom you now want to set up a love nest and make babies.'

'Alix, it's not like that.'

'Well, what's it like?' she demanded.

'I met her. I talked to her. I got on with her. Being with her made me look at you and me in a different light. That's all.'

'Being with her,' repeated Alix. 'How long were you with her? Who was she? I don't remember her. Was she one of the dealers? One of the dealers' wives, maybe? It was Paris, after all.'

'Alix, stop it.' Paul's voice was harsh. 'She wasn't a dealer. She was a designer.'

24

'A designer!'

'Yes,' said Paul. 'The colour schemes, that sort of stuff. And she did the quotations.'

Alix remembered the quotations. They were painted on the walls of the dealing room and she couldn't make up her mind whether they were clever or simply pretentious. Certainly *De l'audace, encore de l'audace, et toujours de l'audace!'* (boldness, and again boldness, and always boldness) was apt, although Alix wasn't sure that dealers needed much urging towards boldness. A bit more caution might be more appropriate, she thought.

'How on earth did you manage to chat up the designer?' she asked.

'I didn't chat her up,' said Paul. 'I went outside for a breath of air and she was there too. We got talking.'

'And on the strength of a fifteen-minute conversation with this Sabine person you've decided that our relationship is over and you want to marry her and have babies. Is that it?' Alix's eyes glittered. 'Or have I missed something along the way?'

'It wasn't just a fifteen-minute conversation,' said Paul.

'Well, what then?' Alix demanded. 'When else could you have spoken to . . .' Her voice trailed off. 'The next morning,' she said slowly. 'That's it, isn't it? When you allegedly went jogging. While I was in bed. You met her.'

Paul looked uncomfortable. 'Yes.'

'You bastard!' Alix could hardly speak but she managed to get the words out. 'You complete bastard! While I was asleep you were shagging Miss Parisienne.'

'Alix, don't be ridiculous,' said Paul. 'I certainly wasn't shagging her, as you so delicately put it. We met, we chatted, that's all.'

'And what happened? Did she say to you that she wanted

25

to have babies and suddenly that was it, you fell for her? Is that it?'

'No,' said Paul.

'Then what?' cried Alix. 'Because I can't believe this situation, Paul. Honestly I can't. Last night you're mad with me because I'm not home in time to meet your awful mother who absolutely hates me and tonight you're telling me that actually you want to leave me and marry a girl you've known for a few hours and have babies with her.'

'Alix, you're twisting it all around.'

'I don't think so.'

'Yes, you are,' said Paul. 'I don't know whether I want to marry Sabine or not. I hardly know her. But I do know that our relationship isn't working and I need to get my life together.'

'Oh, good for you,' snapped Alix.

'You don't want to get married and have babies, do you?' asked Paul. 'I mean, it's not exactly on the great Alix Callaghan five-year plan, is it?'

'I don't have a five-year plan,' said Alix.

'Don't you? What about your comments that very night to Guy whatsisname, the French treasury bloke? I want to be a director before I'm thirty-five? That doesn't exactly fit in with marriage and babies, does it?'

'Guy Decourcelle is thirty-six. He's married. He has two daughters. It hasn't been a problem for him,' said Alix grimly.

'Oh, come on, Alix. You know it's different for you.'

'Why?'

'Because you'd have to take time out to have kids. And you're not ready to take time out. You don't hear your biological clock ticking, but it is! And so is mine. I want to have kids now, when I can enjoy being with them and play with them and have a good time with them. I don't want them to be a carefully crafted part of my executive lifestyle, thank you very much.'

'Paul, I do want to have kids. Some time. Not exactly now, I'll admit. That's a choice I have to make. I thought that when the time came I'd be having them with you. I love you, Paul.' Suddenly Alix's eyes were full of tears which she did her best to hold back. Alix prided herself on not being the sort of woman who cried during an argument. She hated crying women.

'Maybe we will,' said Paul. 'Alix, don't you see? I just don't know any more. That's why I need some time to think about things. That's why I have to move out for a while.'

'And where are you going to move to?' she asked bitterly. 'Paris?'

'No.' Paul sighed. 'The lease on the Malahide house runs out next month. I'm going to move back there.'

'And in the meantime?'

'I'll stay with my mother.'

Alix stared at him. 'Was that why she was here last night? Were you both going to spring this on me then?'

Paul shook his head. 'No. I'd already asked her over, remember? But we talked about it – when you didn't come home and she started to ask me what I saw in you.'

'And you told her nothing much and that you were thinking of shacking up with some French tart instead.'

'Alix! Sabine is not a French tart. I'm not going to shack up with her. She was just the catalyst.'

'So have you seen her since the reception?' asked Alix. 'That was – how long? Two months ago?'

'I've spoken to her on the phone,' said Paul.

'And when is she coming to Dublin?' asked Alix.

'Not yet,' said Paul. 'We haven't decided. I haven't decided. It's not about you or Sabine, Alix. It's about the future.'

'It's a crock of shit,' said Alix and walked out of the room.

Chapter 3

S he hadn't expected him to be still there but he was. She'd stalked out of the apartment, got into the BMW and driven across the toll bridge and along the coast road to Dollymount. She parked the car and walked along the old wooden bridge of the Bull Wall until she was sitting beneath the huge and ugly statue of Our Lady Queen of the Seas. Alix liked it out here. It helped her to think.

She couldn't believe the scene that had just taken place. It was as though it had happened to someone else. She hadn't known about the job, hadn't known about Sabine, hadn't known that Paul suddenly wanted to join the ranks of people whose weekends were spent in Mothercare and DIY stores. It wasn't what they had planned when they moved in together. Then, it had been strawberries and cream in bed. Brunch in Café Java on Sunday mornings. Weekends in Cork or Galway, or London or Paris.

It had been wonderful then.

Alix wrinkled her nose as she thought of morning sickness, smelly nappies and sleepless nights. It was a phase he was going through, she decided. He'd change his mind quickly enough.

'I didn't want to walk out without saying goodbye,' he told her when she got back.

She looked at the suitcases and the plastic bags beside him. 'This is absolutely ridiculous,' she said. 'I can't believe you won't sit down and talk about it properly. I thought you loved me, Paul.'

'I thought I did too.' He looked puzzled. 'But now I don't know, Alix.'

She grimaced. 'Cuttingly honest. Journalistically honest, in fact.'

'I'm sorry.'

'Yes, well.' She had decided to be practical. So that he could see that she wasn't the sort of woman to crumple and cry and fawn over him. 'If that's the way it has to be. You're going back to Stillorgan then?'

'For a few weeks.'

'I'm sure your mother is delighted.'

He smiled faintly. 'Pleased, I guess.'

'She never liked me, did she?'

'No.' He smiled again.

'Have you ordered a taxi?'

'I was waiting until you got back.'

'I'll drive you,' said Alix.

'Really, Alix—'

'Come on. It won't take long.'

'But—'

'Oh, for God's sake, Paul. There's no point in arguing with me now, is there?'

He shrugged and lifted the cases. Alix grabbed the plastic bags.

They were silent during the ten-minute drive.

Alix pulled up outside the house. 'Give me a call sometime,' she said.

'Oh, Alix—'

'I'd better rush. There's a programme on Channel Four I want to see. About the UK and the euro. Starts in half an hour.'

His eyes caught hers and she hated the fact that there was sympathy in them.

'See you,' she said quickly and rammed the car into gear.

‿

She was sitting on the balcony staring unseeingly over the canal when she remembered the photographs. The night that they'd gone to the reception in Paris for the opening of Europa's new headquarters had been one when numerous photographs were taken. She remembered posing with Paul as they'd entered the building. And more photos in the marble and glass foyer. And still more in the state-of-the art dealing room. The one where Sabine Brassaert's selection of quotations adorned the walls. She'd been given some of the photos and she'd shoved them into a folder somewhere.

She pulled a box from the wall unit and rummaged through it. Photographs spilled out onto the floor.

She bit her lip as she looked at them. They were mainly photos of herself and Paul the first time they'd gone to Paris together, a month after he'd moved into the apartment. She was standing outside a patisserie, looking wide-eyed at the cakes. And standing beside the Seine trying to look graceful but, in reality, looking big and healthy. And sitting in the gardens at Versailles, still looking big and healthy but surrounded by its manicured beauty. The kind of photos you take on your first romantic weekend in Paris.

Eventually she found the ones she was looking for. There was the photo of herself and Paul as they entered the building. There was a group photo of everyone in the dealing room, with herself standing beside Guy Decourcelle and smiling broadly. And there was a photograph of the crowded room.

Alix picked up the one of the crowded room and looked at it closely. In the top right-hand corner was a splash of red. Almost everyone had worn black that night. She'd worn black herself, a stunning silk dress by Jasper Conran. Everyone had remarked how lovely she'd looked in it. But the designer had worn red. She remembered someone pointing her out. So that must be her, fuzzy and out of focus, but in red all the same, with cropped blonde hair.

Alix could remember her more clearly now. Guy had introduced them and she'd smiled – smiled – at the bitch and told her that the quotations were great. *'De l'audace, encore de l'audace, et toujours de l'audace!'* she thought again.

Sabine had shown boldness, though. Alix sighed as she turned the photograph over. Sabine had been bold enough to whip Paul from under her nose and she hadn't even noticed it being done.

She stared at the photograph. Even out of focus Sabine Brassaert looked very pretty and terribly young. 'Bloody French women,' she said out loud. 'Bloody, bloody French women.'

∼

She was first into the dealing room on Monday morning. She called a trader in London and sold ten million dollars. Then she checked her appointments for the week. Although Alix liked trading more than she liked anything else, her diary was full of meetings with clients and prospective clients. Some weeks she was lucky and could spend the week at the desk. This wasn't one of those weeks. She was going to be out of the office for most of it.

'Good weekend?' asked Jenny as she hung her jacket over the back of her chair.

'OK,' replied Alix. She wasn't going to talk about Paul. She didn't talk about her personal life in the office very much anyway.

'You look tired.' Jenny switched on the terminals in front of her. 'Hard night last night?'

Alix had gone to bed early but hadn't slept much. She'd kept rolling into the space where Paul's body should have been.

'No,' she said. 'Jenny, will you get some background on the next G7 meeting for me?'

Jenny looked at her in surprise. 'What sort of background?'

'Background,' snapped her boss. 'Just background.'

⁓

'Alix, I need to buy twenty million dollars,' said Charlie Mulholland. 'For settlement next week. Against euros. And, Alix, I need a good rate.'

'You always need a good rate,' Alix laughed as she checked her screens. 'And don't I always get you one?'

'You usually beat the competition,' admitted Charlie. 'But that could just mean that the competition is lousy.'

'What a thing to say!' Alix pressed the mute button on her phone so that Charlie couldn't hear her next words. 'Gavin, get Don Jones, will you? I think they're long dollars, they might show us a good price. Jenny, will you get a price from Nikki Brown? She was a seller earlier this morning.'

'In the full amount?' asked Gavin.

'Yes,' said Alix. 'We're short ourselves or hadn't you noticed?' She wasn't making any money on the ten million she'd sold an hour earlier. The price hadn't moved at all.

'Alix, what's keeping you?' asked Charlie plaintively. 'You know I have to get two quotes. The other guy is showing me a price already. Where's yours?'

'Just a second, Charlie.' She clicked out of the line again. 'Come on, guys, what's happening?'

'Slow at making the price,' said Gavin.

'Nikki wasn't there,' said Jenny. 'Her sidekick's quoting me.'

'Oh, bloody hell.' Alix glanced at the screen. She clicked into the line again. 'Charlie? I can offer them to you at eighty.'

'Eighty!' Charlie sounded disgusted. 'I can get them better than that.'

'How much better?' asked Alix.

'Much,' said Charlie.

She looked at the screen again. Dougherty Brewing, the company for which Charlie worked, was a good client. Twenty million dollars was a big trade to lose. She thought about improving the price for a moment but rejected the idea. She was already short dollars, the market wasn't moving in her direction and she really couldn't afford to throw money down the drain.

'Sorry, Charlie,' she said firmly. 'Eighty's the best I can do.'

'Forget it,' he said.

She put the phone down. 'He got better away from us.'

'You could've stalled him,' said Gavin. 'I had two ticks better.'

'I don't think so,' said Alix. 'And I didn't like how long it took to get those prices. The market hasn't been doing anything. They should've been quicker.'

'Being short ourselves didn't help,' said Gavin.

'I know,' said Alix.

Gavin made a face. 'Why did you sell first thing?' he asked. 'You didn't want to stay short more than five million over the weekend. The rate has barely changed. Why bother?'

'I thought it was a good idea at the time,' said Alix tiredly.

Gavin looked at her in surprise. Normally, she'd have chewed him out for asking questions that made her look stupid.

Dave answered the phone. 'It's for you,' he said. 'It's Charlie Mulholland again.'

Alix clicked into the line. 'Hi, Charlie. Need to do some more?'

'No.' Charlie sounded annoyed. 'The other guy dropped me. When I went back he pulled the price.'

'Oh?' Alix raised her eyebrows. 'So you didn't deal?' Gavin and Jenny stopped talking about the missed trade and looked at her. 'What price had he shown you?'

'Eighty-five,' said Charlie.

'Charlie, I'd love to help but I'm not going to be able to show you anything better than eighty.' She gesticulated to Gavin and Jenny who both got on the phones again while Alix called up a dealing screen.

'If you can show me the twenty at that I'll do it.' Charlie sounded resigned.

The screen prices were changing but Alix was confident that she'd be able to buy the dollars she didn't have back at at least the same price as she was selling them to Charlie. And, if she was lucky and the price was right, she'd buy back the ones she'd sold earlier, as well as the five million they'd stayed short over the weekend. She'd lost her belief in this position.

'OK, Charlie. That's done.'

'Great. Thanks, Alix. Gotta rush.'

'No problem. Anytime.'

'I can get ten at eighty-one,' said Jenny.

Alix nodded at her as she cancelled Charlie's line. 'Take them.'

'Eighty is my best,' said Gavin. 'No, sorry, change – eighty-three for ten, Alix!' His voice rose, knowing that the price was moving in their direction.

'Do it,' said Alix. 'And ask for a price in another fifteen.'

'Where are you left?' Gavin nodded that the deal was done.

'Alix, Nikki Brown is on,' Jenny cut across the conversation. 'She has up to twenty to go at eighty-six!'

'Done in fifteen,' said Alix. 'Gavin, we're off that!'

'OK,' he said.

'Yes, thanks, Nikki.' Jenny tapped the trade into her computer. 'That's great. You too.' Jenny smiled. 'OK. We're all done.'

They sat back in their seats.

'Well done, everyone,' said Alix. 'Good work.'

Jenny and Gavin grinned.

'Just as well.' Dave Bryant, who'd been talking to a customer about the current situation in Australia, hung up the phone and pointed at the screen. 'Look where the price is now!'

Alix had sold dollars to Charlie at a rate of 1.2280. That meant for every million euros Charlie gave her, she gave him one million, two hundred and twenty-eight thousand dollars.

They'd bought the dollars in the market themselves at a higher price, which meant that they received more dollars per euro. But, as quickly as it had gone up, the price had gone down again. Right now, it was 1.2270.

'Timing is everything,' said Alix as she picked up the phone to answer the next call. 'Always remember that, Jenny. Timing is bloody everything.'

Alix's first meeting was at ten o'clock. It was with the financial controller of a large supermarket chain which had recently started doing business with Europa Bank. She didn't really need to go to the meeting – James Clark, their business development manager, had organised it – but she was going in case treasury business was discussed.

'Keep as flat as you can in the dollar,' she told Dave before she left. 'I was very bearish on it, now I'm not sure.'

'OK,' he said. 'Are you all right, Alix? You look tired.'

'Anyone would be tired in this madhouse,' she said. 'I'll see you later.'

'She looks awful,' said Gavin. 'I bet it's because of the dollar position. We were bloody lucky to get out of that! It's higher than where she sold it this morning. If Mulholland hadn't come in she probably wouldn't have covered them back and we'd be offside now and—'

'Give it a rest,' said Jenny. 'You never shut up, do you?'

'I'm just pointing out that—'

'Gavin!' Dave's tone was dangerous. 'Leave it, will you.'

'But you're right about her looking awful,' said Jenny after a couple of seconds. 'She was white as a sheet earlier.'

'She isn't pregnant, is she?' Gavin's eyes lit up. 'Maybe she's up the pole and she'll have to take three months off!'

'Gavin!'

'Well, she will if she's pregnant,' he said stubbornly.

⌒

William Taylor, the financial controller of the supermarket chain, had the most boring voice that Alix had ever heard. She couldn't concentrate on what he was saying and it wasn't very relevant to her anyway. She really didn't care about the shelf life of whole-wheat products.

She was thinking about the dollar/euro. It had been a mistake to sell this morning. One which she'd just managed to get out of, but a horrible mistake all the same. Given that the dollar hadn't weakened in New York on Friday, she should have reappraised things when she'd come in this morning. But no, she'd just barged in and sold them without thinking about it. And it could have been a disaster. Gavin had been right.

She rubbed the back of her neck. She had a headache. She was tired. She didn't want to be at this meeting. And she couldn't stop thinking about Paul.

It was ridiculous. The man had made it perfectly clear that he didn't see a future for them together. But she couldn't accept that. She couldn't simply let him walk away and into the arms of that blonde bimbo from France. She'd invested in him, for God's sake. She'd invested three years of her life and she'd told him that she loved him. He'd told her that he loved her. And now, because of some kind of male midlife crisis (he was too young to have a midlife crisis surely!), he'd decided that he was walking out.

Well, she wasn't going to give in. She'd been too shocked to think things through properly when he'd first told her. But what she needed to do now was to sort out her priorities, think about her life and work out how to get Paul back. Because that was what she was going to do. She wasn't going to let him waltz off into the sunset with this designer woman who, let's face it, was hardly going to start giving him babies straightaway. A woman who wore a red dress to a reception where everyone else was in black was hardly home-baking and baby material. It wasn't a settling down thing at all. That was just an excuse. It was probably sex.

She gritted her teeth at the thought of Paul having sex with Sabine. He'd denied it, but then he'd hardly admit it, would he? And Paul was good at sex. She bit her lip. Very good at sex. She remembered—

'What do you think, Alix?'

She flushed as she looked up at William Taylor. She'd heard that men thought about sex on average every six seconds. She wondered if it was true. She hauled her mind back from her first night with Paul and smiled at William. She'd been listening to the conversation in the background and it took a second for her to replay his question in her mind.

'It shouldn't be a problem,' she said, hoping she was answering the right one.

'Excellent.' He smiled broadly at her.

'OK, then, William. We'd better be off.' James stood up.

'Nice to see you,' said William. 'And you, Alix.' He leaned across the desk and shook her hand. He had a dead-fish handshake. She immediately allocated his account to Gavin.

'Went well,' said James as they got back into the car.

'Good,' said Alix.

'Are you OK?' he asked. 'You were unusually quiet, I thought.'

'Busy,' she said.

He glanced at her but she was looking out of the car window. He made a face and drove back to the office.

She had another meeting, this time with a dealer from Dresdner Bank, who called in to her office. They discussed limits for dealing with each other and looked through some outstanding trades. She couldn't keep her mind on the conversation. She kept seeing Paul and Sabine in bed together. She kept thinking about strawberries and cream. She thought she was going mad. When the dealer from Dresdner Bank left, she opened her desk drawer and rummaged around. Then she stepped out into the dealing room.

'Who took my cigarettes?' she asked sharply.

'No one.' Dave looked up from the article he was reading on the likelihood of a sharp fall in the Dow Jones Index.

'Someone must have. They were here last week.'

'I thought you'd given them up,' said Jenny. 'You told me you'd given them up!'

'I have,' snapped Alix. 'I just wanted to know where they were, that's all.'

'Why should you care?' asked Dave.

'Look, quit hassling me and just tell me where they are.'

'Honestly, Alix, I haven't seen them,' Jenny told her. 'I've got some chewing gum if you like.'

'No thanks.' Alix stalked towards the door. 'I'll be back in a few minutes.'

'Oh, Alix, don't give in!' Gavin joined the conversation. 'If you can't stay off them, who can?'

'Shut up, you little runt,' said Alix and walked out of the room.

The other dealers stared at each other.

'What the fuck's wrong with her?' Gavin asked.

Dave shrugged. 'Time of the month.'

'Oh, Dave!' Jenny made a face at him.

'Or else Gavin's right and she's pregnant.' Dave grinned at her.

'Either way it's hormonal,' said Gavin. 'And she needn't think she can talk to me like that.'

'Let's leave it.' Dave picked up the phone. 'We've other things to worry about. Come on, let's see how things are in the FRA market.'

Alix took the lift down to the ground floor and walked out of the Europa Bank building. She squinted in the bright light of the sun which reflected off the white flagstones outside the door. Then she walked the few yards to the small newsagent's.

'Hi, Marty, twenty of the usual, please.'

'Alix!' Marty Stephens, the manager of the shop, looked surprised. 'I thought you'd given them up.'

'I have,' she said. 'But I need one now.'

'That's not the way to go about it,' he told her. 'Look, why don't you have some chewing gum instead?'

Alix gritted her teeth. 'If I wanted chewing gum I'd have asked for chewing gum. I want a cigarette, Marty, and I want it now.'

'OK.' He sighed and reached for the packet. 'But it's a shame to go back. What's the matter, markets giving you a hard time?'

She shook her head, suddenly close to tears. 'No. Nothing like that.'

'You OK, Alix?'

'I'm fine.' She handed him the money and walked out of the shop. She wasn't going to burst into tears in a newsagent's store.

There was a no-smoking policy in the office building. Alix sat on the steps outside and inhaled deeply. She felt the soothing sensation of the smoke hit her and almost instantly relax her. She was annoyed at herself for giving in to the urge, but she couldn't help it. She'd almost lost it in the dealing room earlier. Both dealing with Charlie Mulholland – the deal had been OK but she'd handled it badly, she thought – and then later with Gavin. She felt uncomfortable, lacking in the authority she normally had. It was as though being without Paul had somehow lessened her belief in herself. And she couldn't understand why that should be the case because she'd had buckets of self-belief before she'd ever known him. So why should she feel vulnerable now?

'You should give them up, you know.' The man approaching the building grinned at her as she finished the cigarette and ground it out under her heel.

'I *have* given them up,' she told him.

'That was the last?' he asked. 'I've witnessed someone actually putting out their last cigarette?'

'Perhaps,' she said. She wasn't in the humour for this kind of chitchat and, although he was obviously a customer of the bank, she didn't feel like being nice.

'Don't you feel totally marginalised having to smoke outdoors?'

'I don't have to smoke at all. And it's a nice break from inside.'

'Why? Difficult day?'

'Look,' Alix smoothed her skirt, 'I'm really not in the mood for this kind of thing. I know that smoking might kill me. I know I'm totally anti-social. But I don't want to talk about it. OK?'

'OK,' he said.

'Fine.' She pushed open the glass door and walked back into the building.

He went to the reception desk. 'Matt Connery of Anatronics to see Alix Callaghan.' His voice carried across the foyer to where she waited for the lift to arrive.

She groaned. It was turning into another bad day.

Chapter 4

A lix walked back over to the reception desk.

'I'm Alix Callaghan,' she said, extending her hand. 'I'm sorry, I didn't realise who you were.'

Matt Connery grinned at her. 'No problem. I'm a bit early. I'm afraid I caught you off guard.'

'Not at all,' said Alix briskly. 'Just taking some time out.'

'Busy day?' he asked sympathetically as he followed her to the lifts.

'As usual.' She pressed the button for the third floor.

She said nothing as the lift moved upwards. She was furious that a client had seen her sitting on the steps like some careless clerk with nothing better to do. She was also annoyed with herself for getting into a tit-for-tat spat with him. She was supposed to be a professional person and she knew that she hadn't acted in a professional way. But he'd arrived just as she was imagining Paul and Sabine's hurried meeting in Paris while she had been asleep in bed after the Europa Bank reception. She'd been visualising them running towards each other, holding each other, Sabine asking if he was sure it was OK to meet and Paul telling her yes, absolutely, Alix was safely sleeping in the luxury of the Georges V and there was no chance of her waking before noon.

She hadn't guessed, that was what hurt her the most. She hadn't thought that Paul had any doubts about their relationship. She knew that she was sometimes impatient and often self-centred about how she lived her life, but she'd honestly believed that Paul was happy about things. How could she have been so stupid?

The lift sighed to a stop.

'This way,' said Alix shortly. She led Matt past the dealing room and into the small meeting room on the corner of the building with its views over the Liffey and back towards the city.

'So what did you want to discuss?' She was brusque to the point of rudeness. Usually when she met a new client she was courteous and helpful. She'd try to find out a little about them, their likes and dislikes. She'd engage in some meaningless conversation just to get the measure of them. But she didn't feel like that right now.

Matt Connery opened his briefcase and took out a sheaf of documents which he passed across the table to her. 'This is some background on the company. This shows growth projections. These are our receivables – as you can see they're mainly in dollars but we have payments in a variety of other currencies, including the Far East. I want to streamline the way we look after things. I've also been talking to your credit guy, John Collins. We should have a facility in place soon.' He smiled at her. His eyes were blue but not the same deep blue as Paul's. Matt Connery's eyes were a lighter blue, a product of what seemed to Alix to be Scandinavian ancestry, because his hair was wheat-coloured and his skin was golden brown.

She skimmed through the papers. Anatronics was a computer

animation company and, if the figures were to be believed, it was growing very quickly. It could be an interesting account.

'OK,' she said. 'Here's the way I think you should play it.'

She talked for ten minutes, going through a range of products, becoming more and more confident as she spoke. She forgot about the less than fortunate meeting with him on the steps of the building. She forgot about the fact that she thought her heart was broken. She talked about spot rates and forward rates and futures and options while he listened carefully, stopping her once or twice for clarification.

'Thank you,' he said when she'd finished. 'Obviously we've thought about some of this already. I need to chat to my people back at the office and talk through these scenarios with them.'

'That's fine,' said Alix. 'If you need anything else or if you want me to come and give a presentation to your board, just give me a call.'

'I will.' He smiled and looked at his watch. 'If you're not busy would you like to join me for lunch?'

'Lunch?' She looked at him in surprise.

'It's after one,' he said. 'And I'm hungry!'

'Thank you, but I'm busy.'

'That's a shame.'

'I've been out of the office a lot this morning,' she said. 'I need to get back to the desk for a while.'

'I see.' He smiled at her. 'Some other time, perhaps?'

'Well, yes. Maybe. Let's see how you get on with your people. Perhaps we could all meet up, have lunch here.'

Matt sighed. 'Perhaps.'

She looked at him quizzically. 'Did you intend to see John Collins or anyone else while you were here?'

He shook his head. 'Only you. And I'm delighted to have met you at last.'

'At last?'

'Oh, I mentioned to a guy I met at a corporate treasurers' dinner that I was meeting you today. He was full of praise. Charlie Mulholland.'

She smiled. 'Charlie's a good customer.'

'He told me you were the nicest trader he ever dealt with.'

'Did he really!' She smiled, remembering Charlie's abruptness earlier in the day.

'Anyway, I'd better get going. Let you get on with the churning and burning or whatever it is you do.'

'Thank you,' she said. 'I'll see you out.'

～

Gavin was shouting 'Done, done!' when she walked back into the dealing room.

'What's going on?' she asked Dave.

'I know you said to stay flat in dollars,' he said, 'but Gavin heard of a couple of buyers coming out of New York. So we picked up a few and we're just squaring the position now.'

She glanced at the price. The dollar had strengthened considerably since the morning. Thank God she'd covered back the ten million she'd sold earlier. Otherwise she'd be licking her wounds by now.

'How'd you do, Gavin?' asked Dave.

'Out at fifty.' Gavin grinned, pleased with himself.

'What did you make?' asked Alix.

'Ten grand,' replied Gavin.

'Well done,' she said.

'Thanks.' He grinned again. 'Took your advice, Alix. I didn't get too greedy. Though it'll probably strengthen a bit more. There's talk that Soros is buying.'

'Oh, really?'

If George Soros, one of the world's biggest investors, was buying dollars, then Gavin was probably right. But deep down Alix still thought that dollar rates would fall and so would the value of the currency. The Federal Reserve Bank in the US was having its monthly meeting on Thursday and an announcement about rates could be made afterwards. Alix thought they might cut because one of the members of the board, who'd always been against a fall in rates, had recently resigned. But Janis Kerrigan was only one member of the board and George Soros had much better contacts than Alix Callaghan! Soros was more likely to be right.

'You should go to meetings more often,' said Gavin. 'I do better when you're not here!'

'I'll bear that in mind,' said Alix dryly and picked up the phone.

⁓

There was a different feeling in the apartment. When Paul had lived with her she never really felt lonely, even when he wasn't there. In fact she liked being alone. But this wasn't the same at all. This was knowing he wasn't coming back this evening. This was loneliness. She took a bottle of Miller out of the fridge and walked into the second bedroom, the one where Paul had done so much of his work.

It was almost frighteningly tidy. Paul was a neat and tidy person when he worked, there were never huge mounds of paper scattered around the place, but there had always been lots of it – newspapers neatly stacked by the desk, back copies of magazines in which he'd had articles published, reference books piled against the wall. He'd taken almost everything.

She gulped some of the beer and placed the bottle on the desk. Then she switched on the computer.

Although Paul had used it a lot, the computer was actually connected to her terminal at work. She couldn't execute trades from home, but she could monitor prices. The dollar was even stronger. Once again she breathed a sigh of relief that luck had been on her side today.

The phone rang and startled her so much that she knocked over the beer. She swore as it formed a golden puddle in the middle of the desk.

'Hello,' she said.

'Hi, Alix. It's me.'

'Paul.' They'd only been apart a couple of days and yet it seemed like forever. 'How are things?'

'Not bad,' he said. 'And you?'

'Fine.'

He cleared his throat. 'I rang because I left some stuff in the apartment.'

'Really?' She looked around. It didn't seem like there was much left to her.

'Yes. In the filing cabinet. Some papers and some disks. Remember that series on Georgian houses that I did? Also, the CD-ROM set. Sorry about this but I wondered, could I come and collect them sometime?'

'When did you have in mind?'

'Some afternoon.'

'I won't be here in the afternoon,' said Alix.

'I know.'

'How will you get in?'

'I have keys. I left mine there but I forgot about the ones we left with Mum. I'll leave them behind.'

'Why don't you come over now?' asked Alix.

'Can't,' said Paul.

'Why not?'

'Just can't.'

'Whenever,' said Alix. 'I don't care.'

'Alix?'

'What?'

'Look – I'm sorry.'

'Oh, sod off,' she said and hung up.

She got a cloth and wiped up the beer. He wouldn't call now because he was afraid of seeing her. Afraid that he'd suddenly realise that he'd treated her badly. And she knew that, even if he didn't think he loved her, he still did. They worked together. She knew it.

She went into the living room and curled up on the sofa. What would it be like to have children? she wondered. It wasn't something she'd thought about before now. Not since she'd been at school, anyway, and they'd played at being parents. Children were something that grown-up people had, that demanded time and attention. Children went with houses and gardens, not apartments along the canal. Children were other people. Messy people. Noisy people. People with their own agendas.

What would their children be like? Would they be dark and have navy-blue eyes like Paul's? Or would they look like her? She got up and stared at herself in the wall mirror. Grey-green eyes in an oval face. Dark brown hair with glints of red, pulled back, as she always wore it. Generous lips. Kissable lips, as Paul had once told her.

She leaned closer to the mirror and gasped. She couldn't believe it. She undid the tortoiseshell clip that held her hair and pushed her fingers through the strands. But she hadn't been mistaken.

Clumps of grey! Not just the occasional grey that had amused her in the past. Not the solitary silver thread running through dark tresses. These were real grey hairs and there were at least half a dozen. She pushed her hands through her hair again. There were more. Not clumped together now, more occasional, but still more.

She had grey hair. She was getting old. Paul was right. There must have been something wrong with her when she hadn't heard the ticking of her biological clock before now. The alarm bell was about to go off! You are a woman in your thirties, she told herself. You are getting too old to have your first child. You have grey hair!

Was this why Paul had left her? Had he noticed the grey and decided that she, Alix, was getting too old for him? Was that why he'd lusted after the Lolita-like Sabine? She shook her head. She was being paranoid now. Paul had the odd grey strand in his thick black hair. Although on men grey looked distinguished. On women it just looked old.

She pulled her hair back from her face again. You didn't really notice the grey unless you were actually looking for it. You'd have to be staring at her to be certain it was there.

She'd get it coloured as soon as she could, all the same.

Chapter 5

G avin yawned and leaned back in his chair. It was Thursday, the day of the Fed meeting, but the markets were quiet. There wouldn't be any news from the States until later and nobody in Europe was trying to move bonds or currencies dramatically one way or another. Alix was meeting a client for lunch, Jenny had gone for a walk, and only Gavin and Dave were in the dealing room.

'Peaceful,' said Gavin.

Dave glanced up from the copy of *The Phoenix* he was reading. 'What?'

'Peaceful. Here. Without Alix ranting and raving and without Jenny backing her up.'

Dave closed the magazine. 'You really hate her, don't you?'

'No,' said Gavin. 'But she's such a fucking prima donna. And I hate it when she starts snapping.'

Dave laughed. 'Snapping?'

'Reminds me of one of the teachers in school,' said Gavin. 'Always nagging, nothing ever done right.'

'You're being a bit unfair,' Dave said. 'She actually gets a lot right.'

'Not this week.' Gavin tapped on the computer keyboard

and called up the profit and loss account. 'She's done some shitty trades this week.'

'It hasn't been one of her best,' admitted Dave. 'Although Monday was OK.'

'That was me,' retorted Gavin. 'My call on the Soros buying. We made money on my trade and then she called a couple of clients and we made money on the back of their trades. But it was me that set the whole thing going. Left to her, we'd still be short dollars with our arses hanging out the window!'

Dave laughed. 'So what do you want me to say? Well done, Gavin?'

'No,' said Gavin. 'I just think you should back me up a bit more. I can't understand how you can side with that woman when she's probably taking home twice as much money as you although you're easily as good as her. You're so passive about it!'

'She'll burn herself out,' said Dave. 'I know I'm not a knife-in-the-back type of operator – not like you'll be! But she's getting on a bit now and I'll bet you anything you like she'll get married to her boyfriend and start producing babies by next year.'

'You think?'

'Absolutely. I met Paul a couple of months ago. He was muttering about settling down and families and all that sort of stuff. So she might be throwing her weight around a bit now but it'll be a different story in a few months.'

'Make me a price,' said Gavin.

Dave grinned. 'In what?'

'Weeks before she gets engaged.'

Dave considered for a moment. 'Ten/fifteen. A fiver a week.'

'You're reading me,' Gavin complained. 'And you could drive a bus through that price.'

'It's not an easy market to read.'

'I thought you were convinced.'

'I know what I think.' Dave grinned at him. 'What do you think?'

'Oh, all right, you're done at fifteen,' said Gavin. 'If she gets engaged before fifteen weeks are up, you win. After, I collect.'

'Done. But you'll be paying me, Gavin.'

'It's worth it,' he said. 'If some bloke takes her off our hands before fifteen weeks are up, I'll pay gladly.'

Dave laughed. 'She might get engaged. But she won't leave.'

'If she gets engaged she'll get married soon afterwards. Why wait? And if she gets married then it's lots and lots of lovely snotty-nosed kids! I can almost believe it myself.'

'Believe what?' Jenny walked into the room and draped her jacket over her chair.

'Nothing,' said Gavin.

'Nothing,' said Dave.

Jenny looked from one to the other. 'It's a man thing, is it?'

The two guys laughed.

'Hopefully,' said Gavin. 'Hopefully.'

~

It was nearly three o'clock by the time Alix got back. She went directly to her small office in the corner of the room and took some paracetamol from a packet in the desk. She had a raging headache. Lunch had taken longer than she'd expected and

Fergus Reilly, the client she'd met, had insisted on ordering a second bottle of wine and telling her not to worry, he was picking up the tab. Fergus was a good client and normally she enjoyed a boozy lunch with him. But she hadn't been in the humour today, she'd found it difficult to laugh at the off-colour jokes he told, which normally amused her, and she couldn't help wondering why she was there in the first place.

If I was married with children, she'd thought as the wine waiter topped her glass with Pinot Noir, I'd be sitting in the garden playing with them right now. I'd be laughing and having real fun instead of pretending to laugh at jokes that aren't even halfway funny.

Are you mad? she asked herself as she thought about it again. She sat up straight and flexed her hands behind her head. You'd hate to be sitting in the garden with a brace of children.

'Line four, Alix!' Dave's voice carried through. 'It's Christie Reardon.'

'I'll take it out there,' she replied.

Christie, a treasurer in a manufacturing company, wanted to talk about interest rates. While Alix chatted to her she massaged the back of her neck and wished she'd kept off the red wine.

'What do you want to do about this evening?' asked Dave when she finally hung up.

'What do you mean?'

'Our positions. We're flat on the currency book but we're holding some treasuries. Do you want to leave it like that?'

Alix rubbed the bridge of her nose. She still had a sneaking feeling about rates. And the dollar. But she wasn't as convinced as she'd been before she'd heard about Soros.

'What do you think?' she asked.

Dave leaned back in his chair. 'Stay flat currencies. Lose the treasuries. It doesn't look like the Fed'll do anything, despite Kerrigan. I know you think they'll cut but they might not want to do it straightaway.'

Alix sighed. 'Whatever you think, Dave. I'm heading off now anyway.'

'Now?' Dave glanced at his watch. It was only four o'clock. Alix rarely left the office before five.

'Yes, now. I have a headache.'

Jenny looked at Alix in surprise. A headache had never sent Alix home before.

'Gavin, even if you have some good information from your US friends, stick to whatever Dave says, will you?' Alix pulled on her Mondi jacket and picked up her bag. 'Don't go trying to be a hero. OK?'

'OK,' said Gavin. 'But someone might have—'

'Gavin!' warned Alix.

He sighed.

'See you guys tomorrow,' said Alix and walked out of the room.

The three remaining dealers stared at each other.

'I'm telling you,' said Gavin, 'she's up the pole.'

'Gavin!' Jenny looked angrily at him.

'She must be,' he said, unabashed.

'I doubt it very much,' said Jenny dryly. 'Alix wouldn't drink or swallow paracetamol if she was pregnant. You know her, everything by the book.'

Gavin looked disappointed. 'You might be right. But there's something wrong and that spells opportunity for all of us.'

'You make me sick,' said Jenny. 'You're like a vulture. And you,' she turned to Dave, 'you're not much better.'

'I haven't said a word.' Dave looked at her innocently.

'You don't need to,' she snapped.

～

Paul's compact discs were still on the table where she'd left them. Alix was pretty sure he'd arrive today – his Thursday schedule was usually light. She hadn't set out with the intention of being in the apartment when he arrived, but she'd suddenly thought about it as she was talking to Christie Reardon. And from that moment she'd wanted to be back in the apartment, to see him.

She rubbed her eyes. She was tired. She hadn't slept properly since he'd left and she was annoyed with herself for caring so much.

Her feelings about Paul fluctuated wildly from one moment to the next. Sometimes she thought that it was a good thing he was gone – he could be demanding, fussy, disapproving and make her feel like an irresponsible adolescent. Other times she missed him so much it physically hurt her. But she needed to see him. If she saw him face to face she might be able to decide how she really felt.

It was almost five o'clock when she heard the key in the door. Her heart beat faster and she could feel adrenaline coursing through her body. He walked into the living room and looked at her in surprise.

'What are you doing here at this hour?'

'Headache,' she said. 'I had lunch with a client, drank too much wine, couldn't concentrate.' Almost immediately she wished she hadn't mentioned the wine. He disapproved strongly of her drinking at lunchtime.

'I've never known you to come home before,' said Paul.

'The screens were making it worse,' she told him. 'And I need to be OK for tomorrow. There's the bank reception tomorrow night.'

'Oh, yes.' Paul made a face. 'I'd forgotten about that.'

'Why should you remember?' asked Alix. 'You're not going now, are you?'

'Are you serious?' asked Paul.

'No,' she said. 'Despite the fact that your name is on the guest list.'

The reception, to be held in the bank the following night, was to celebrate its ten years in Dublin. All bank employees and their partners, together with a select client list, were to attend.

'Haven't you told them I won't be there?' asked Paul.

She shrugged. 'It doesn't make any difference. It's a buffet and I expect half the people who said they'll turn up probably won't. They won't miss you.'

'Thanks,' he said wryly.

She smiled slightly at him. 'Sorry, that sounded worse than I meant.'

'Doesn't matter.' Paul gestured to the table where the CDs were stacked. 'Is this all of them?'

She nodded, even though it made her headache worse.

'I thought I'd packed them all,' he said as he put them into a box he'd brought with him. 'I completely forgot about these.'

'Doesn't matter.' She watched him. He looked well, she thought. He didn't look as though he'd spent an almost sleepless week. He was clean-shaven and his eyes were clear. He was wearing a denim shirt and jeans and he looked fit and healthy.

Alix had changed into a pair of figure-hugging blue trousers and a white lycra sports top when she'd come home because she knew he liked them. But she regretted it now, not wanting him to think she'd made an effort.

'Have you been talking to Sabine?' The words were out of her mouth before she could stop them.

'Yesterday,' he said. 'Just for a couple of minutes.'

'And has she decided if she's coming over?'

'Why?' asked Paul.

'I just wanted to know.' She shrugged. 'I'm sorry, it's none of my business.'

'Not yet,' said Paul shortly.

Alix bit her lip. 'Would you like a drink?'

'No, thanks.' He shook his head. 'I'm in a hurry.'

'Anything important?'

'This and that.'

'I see,' said Alix.

'I'd better be off,' he said uncomfortably. 'I've a few other things to do.'

'Sure.' She stood up.

Paul held out his hand. 'The keys to the apartment,' he said. 'Better not take them away with me.'

'Better not.' She smiled at him.

'Alix – you've been great about this,' he said as he picked up the box of CDs. 'And I am sorry if I've hurt you.'

'If?' she said.

He grimaced. 'OK, I've hurt you. And I'm sorry.'

'Oh, I'll get over it,' she said. 'You know me.'

'It's one of the things I admire about you,' said Paul. 'You're a strong woman, Alix. You don't let things defeat you.'

'But you don't want a strong woman,' she said. 'You want a feeble little one around the house having babies.'

'That's not true,' he said sharply. 'Just because a woman is at

59

home it doesn't make her feeble! My God, Alix, if your female friends heard that they'd lynch you.'

'I didn't say women who stayed at home were feeble,' said Alix. 'I just said *you* wanted a feeble one.'

'Alix, we're having a row,' said Paul. 'And we don't need to have a row, do we?'

'No,' she said. 'I just wanted to clarify things in my mind.'

'Look, Alix.' He reached out and took her hands in his. 'It's not that I don't care about you, I do. It's not that I think you're too strong and too self-sufficient. It's just that I want someone who depends on *me*. And you don't depend on anyone!'

'But what if I did?' she asked. 'What if I gave up my job and depended on you? What then?'

'Then you wouldn't be Alix Callaghan,' said Paul.

'But I'd be someone you'd settle down with.'

'You'd be a different person.'

She smiled. 'I can be a lot of different people – you should see me at work.'

'I'd better go.' He let go of her hands.

'Yes, sure,' she said. She leaned towards him and kissed him lightly on the cheek. 'I'll look out for your articles.'

'I'll look out for you,' he said. 'See you, Alix.'

'Goodbye, Paul.'

～

She walked into town. It was warm and the evening sun reflected off the pavement and hurt her eyes. Her headache still nagged at her just behind her right eye.

The city was crowded. Mainly, she noticed, with couples.

Grafton Street was infested with men and women holding hands, gazing at each other, whispering to each other.

She walked into Break for the Border and ordered a bottle of beer. She'd chosen it because it wasn't really a couples sort of place, but there were lots of couples there all the same. And a group of girls, laughing hysterically as they fitted a mock veil to one of their number and hung a sash round her which said 'Official Hen Night'.

'It'll be you next, Lisa!' cried the bride-to-be. 'I'll throw the bouquet at you for extra special luck.'

Lisa laughed and kissed her friend but Alix thought that the girl had actually looked despairing.

It was a whole different world, she thought. You belong when you're part of a couple. It doesn't matter how great your job is or how well you cope with your life or how much money you earn. When you're a woman, people expect you to be part of a couple. And when you're part of a couple, they expect you to be a family. She sighed. The idea of starting all over again was horrible. She didn't want to spend nights in bars looking over the available talent. She didn't want to look at each new man she met and wonder if he was the one. She didn't want to be single. She wanted Paul.

She finished the bottle of beer and caught a cab back to the apartment. Her headache was still there and she knew that she shouldn't have drunk any alcohol.

She opened the fridge door. There was a large carton of Häagen-Dazs ice cream in the freezer. Cookies and cream, one of her favourites. She took a spoon from the drawer and then walked out onto the balcony with the ice cream.

She ate it all and felt marginally better. Then she went back inside, lay on the sofa and closed her eyes.

It was nearly ten o'clock when she woke. With a shock, she realised that she'd forgotten all about the Fed meeting. Dave was probably right though, she thought as she logged on to her computer. The Fed wouldn't cut rates so soon after Kerrigan's announcement.

'Oh, shit!' She looked at the headline on the screen. 'Shit, shit, shit!'

The Fed had cut rates by twenty-five basis points. She should have stuck with her instincts. The dollar had fallen just as she thought it would.

Chapter 6

S he was at her desk by seven the following morning. The dollar was still weak. She checked their position to see if Dave had sold the bonds. Naturally, he had. Because of the rate cut, bonds had increased in value. Dave had sold them at a price which was fair for yesterday but which was way below the price she would have got today.

Alix sighed. It could have been worse, they could have been holding dollars and be sitting on a huge loss this morning, but she absolutely hated the idea that she could have made money if she'd stuck with her gut feeling. In the end, though, she'd bottled out. Why? Because she was tired, because her mind was on Paul and not on her job.

Did this happen to blokes? she wondered. If she'd dumped Paul, would he sit at his computer, a blank screen in front of him, and struggle to find the words for an article? Would he miss deadlines, not concentrate and turn in a piece that was absolute rubbish? Or would he be able to push his misery to the back of his mind while he was working so that he could write just as well as he ever did?

Somehow she didn't really want to know the answer.

Dave's hurried entry into the office made her shelve her thoughts.

'Bloody hell,' he said. 'I didn't think they'd do it.'

Alix grimaced. 'I suppose I didn't either. Otherwise I'd have told you to short the dollars and hang on to the bonds.'

'It was the right decision,' said Dave. 'Odds were in favour of them doing nothing. It would have been risky to run both positions.'

'I should have taken the risk on one of them,' said Alix. 'I was so certain when I heard the news about Kerrigan. It was stupid not to.'

'But if they hadn't done anything the dollar would probably have strengthened and the bonds would have fallen and you'd have been losing money. As it is, we haven't lost. We just haven't made anything.'

'I know,' said Alix. 'But I hate making nothing. It's nearly as bad as losing.'

She lost again that afternoon. She sold sterling to one of her retail customers, thought that the currency would weaken, and then realised that it was going stronger. She lost two thousand pounds on the deal and she was furious with herself.

Gavin, on the other hand, had made five thousand dollars on a swap deal with a new customer and had celebrated his second good trade of the day by exchanging high-fives with Dave and generally exuding a sense of confidence which Alix didn't feel.

By five o'clock their overall profit for the day was around ten thousand dollars, not a particularly good day, but good enough.

'I'm heading off now,' said Alix. 'I'll see you guys back here at seven for the reception. Don't be late – you know how Des is if we're late.'

'We're going to the pub for a couple and coming straight back,' said Dave.

'All of you?' Alix looked around at them.

'I'm having a quick one and then off home to change,' said Jenny.

'Oh. OK.' She picked up her bag. 'See you later then. Don't be absolutely plastered by seven.'

They watched her as she walked out of the room.

'She's not happy about us going for a drink without her,' said Jenny.

'She's been a pain in the neck all day,' said Dave. 'Sulking over the rate cut. It's much better that she goes home and gets over it.'

'What she needs is a good seeing-to from that boyfriend of hers,' said Gavin.

'Oh, Gavin, that's a revolting thing to say.' Jenny made a face at him.

'That's her problem,' said Gavin. 'She's not getting it enough.'

'I thought you decided the other day that she was pregnant.'

'I did. But I bow to your superior knowledge on that issue.' Gavin grinned at her. 'You're probably right. She wouldn't be downing Pinot Noir and Hedex in equal measures if she was up the spout.'

'She shouldn't be doing that anyway,' said Jenny.

'Why don't you have a nice little girlie lunch with her and find out what's wrong?' suggested Dave. 'We can't operate in this room without all the facts. And Alix is certainly keeping something from us.'

'Maybe the bloke has dumped her,' said Gavin. 'That's what happens to you women when you're dumped, isn't it, Jen? You get all mopey and wistful and you can't concentrate.'

'I wouldn't know,' said Jenny acerbically. 'I'm always the

one that does the dumping. Why don't you use your own experiences, Gavin? How did you feel when that girl you were hanging around with left you for someone else?'

'She was a stupid cow,' said Gavin. 'And I went out, got pissed and met someone much, much nicer.'

Jenny laughed. 'There's no putting you down, is there, Donnelly?'

'Nope.' He laughed too.

'Come on,' said Dave, 'let's hit O'Reilly's.'

❦

Alix sat in the hairdresser's and explained that she wanted a colour to hide the grey.

'It's not that bad.' Tina examined her client's hair.

'It's bad enough,' said Alix. 'And I need it to look good tonight, we have a reception in the bank. I don't want to be some dowdy middle-aged crone in the corner.'

'Alix, you could never be dowdy,' said Tina. 'You're getting this out of proportion, don't you think?'

'No,' said Alix. 'I can't afford grey hairs. Dealing is a young person's game. I start turning up looking like someone's grandmother and I'm toast.'

Tina laughed. 'Well, why don't you do something else?'

'Like what?' asked Alix.

'I don't know,' said Tina. 'Surely you should be in charge of something that doesn't depend on the colour of your hair! You're not a bloody supermodel, after all.'

'You can say that again.' Alix peered at her reflection. 'I look like shit, Tina.'

'You'll look great after this,' the stylist promised. 'I'll stick close to your natural colour and then lift it with some red tones. It'll be lovely.'

'Thanks.' Alix sat back in the chair and waited to be transformed.

It looked perfect, she decided later as she stood in front of her bedroom mirror. Tina had delivered on her promises and now Alix's hair glinted reds and russets in the evening sunlight. Because of the reception tonight she'd asked Tina to put it up, which immediately made her look even taller and more elegant. If only my eyes didn't match the red, she said to herself, I'd actually look OK.

The redness in her eyes was due to both a lack of sleep and looking at the screens all day.

She went into the bathroom and put some Optrex drops into them. She blinked a couple of times. At least she looked less exhausted now. It took her ten minutes to do her make-up. Alix wasn't the sort of person who spent a lot of time on cosmetics, and mostly she didn't need to. She slid her emerald earrings into her ears and hung her matching gold necklace with emerald stone round her neck. She'd bought the jewellery with her last year's bonus.

She took her black silk Jasper Conran out of the wardrobe. The same dress she'd been wearing the night Paul had met Sabine. That had been the first time she'd worn it. Some women she knew would probably never wear it again. But she liked it and it was just right for tonight. All the same, she felt a surge of rage as she zipped it up. Paul had zipped it up the last time. She gritted her teeth. It's only a bloody dress, she told herself. It doesn't mean anything.

❧

The reception area of the bank was already quite full by the time she arrived. Des Coyle kissed her on the cheek and looked around.

'Where's Paul?'

'Couldn't make it, unfortunately,' said Alix. 'He sends his regards.'

'Right.' Des steered her through the crowds. 'Have a word with Norman Keogh, will you? He's on his own and I don't think he knows anyone.'

'OK.' Alix grabbed a glass of wine from a passing wine waiter and walked over to the customer. 'Norman!' she exclaimed. 'I haven't seen you in ages. How are you keeping?'

She drifted from customer to customer, always saying how pleased she was to see them, exchanging a few words about the markets and asking about their families. Alix knew that she was good with the clients. They liked her and the majority of them trusted her. Usually, at functions like this she'd be aware of Paul's slightly condescending presence. Paul wasn't a crusading journalist, nor did he have vehemently socialist beliefs, but he would always have a gently mocking word for the business functions she dragged him along to.

'It's all a sham,' he'd say. 'You pretend you like these guys and they pretend they like you and everyone is wondering if they're making more than everyone else. It's sad really.'

'You talk such bullshit.' She'd snuggle up to him and kiss him on the cheek. 'You know that we're keeping the wheels of commerce turning.'

'And you're all trying to outdo each other and make more money than each other.'

'Give it a rest, Paul.' And then he'd kiss her on the lips

and sometimes they'd end up late for whatever the function was.

She missed him tonight. She'd hardly spoken to him on the night of the Europa Bank reception in Paris but she'd been glad that he was there. Glad that when Rolf Schwimmer of the Swiss office had sidled up to her and asked her where she was staying the night, she was able to point to Paul and tell Rolf that she was staying with that man over there. And she was pleased that Paul was in the traditional tall, dark and handsome mould whereas Rolf Schwimmer was short and pudgy and had beads of perspiration on his brow.

'Hi, Alix.'

She turned round, the voice vaguely familiar. Matt Connery grinned at her. 'How are you?'

'I'm fine,' she said. 'And you?'

'Great.'

'It's a good evening, isn't it?'

'Absolutely. You guys certainly pushed the boat out. Imagine importing the Eiffel Tower!'

Alix smiled. The centrepiece of the buffet table was a huge ice carving of the Eiffel Tower which had drawn admiring gasps from everyone.

'It does a special party trick,' she said solemnly.

'Oh?'

'Turns into the River Seine at midnight.'

Matt laughed. 'It's beginning to lose its shape a bit.'

'It's hot in here.'

Alix was right. There were nearly two hundred people swarming around the reception area and it was becoming increasingly difficult to move.

'It's warm outside too,' said Matt.

Alix nodded but she'd been distracted by the sight of Gavin Donnelly deep in conversation with Des Coyle. Both of them were laughing. Alix didn't like to see someone as keen and aggressive as Gavin hobnobbing with the managing director. It sent a frisson of worry through her. She looked around to see if she could spot either Dave or Jenny but it was impossible to identify them in the crowd.

'I'm sorry?' She looked at Matt. 'I didn't catch what you said.'

'I asked if you'd eaten yet.'

Alix shook her head. 'To be honest I'm not hungry. Never am at these sort of events.'

'That's a shame,' said Matt. 'I thought it might be nice to sit outside with a plate of something.'

'Feel free,' Alix told him. 'Eat as much as you like!'

'With you, I meant.'

She looked at him. 'I think I'm supposed to circulate,' she told him.

'Not attend to the every whim of your clients?'

'Certainly not.' But she smiled to show him that she hadn't taken offence.

'I spoke to our managing director,' said Matt. 'We were wondering if you'd be free either next week or the week after to call in to the company and go through some of your proposals.'

'Sure.' She smiled brilliantly at him and he realised that her eyes were an amazing shade of green. 'Give me a call on Monday and we'll fix it up. Can you excuse me a moment? There's someone I need to talk to.' She moved away from him and tapped Jenny on the shoulder. 'Hi.'

'Oh, Alix, isn't it just the pits in here – so bloody crowded.'

'Yes.'

'You look great,' Jenny told her. 'How is it you can look so wrecked at five and so sophisticated now?'

'Probably because I didn't spend a couple of hours in O'Reilly's.'

'I wasn't there long,' said Jenny. 'Just had one and left.'

'And what was going on while I wasn't there?' asked Alix. 'What are the two boys hatching?'

'Hatching?' Jenny raised an eyebrow.

'Don't look at me like that,' said Alix. 'I've seen the two of them huddled together. They're up to something and I want to know what it is.'

'They're not up to anything,' said Jenny. 'Nothing.'

'You sure?' asked Alix.

'Certain. You know them, they're probably just putting bets on horses or something.'

'You think so?' Alix wasn't sure, Jenny could see that.

'Yes,' said Jenny as convincingly as she could.

'Alix! Hi, haven't seen you in ages!'

Jenny breathed a sigh of relief as Stuart Phillips, a client, waved at Alix. Another second and she'd have told Alix about Dave and Gavin's dreams of changing the dealing room. Jenny felt uncomfortable about the situation. Alix had given her the opportunity of a dealing career. She didn't like to think of her being stabbed in the back by the other dealers. But if she was, maybe there'd be greater opportunities in store. You couldn't be grateful forever.

Jenny waited until her boss was talking to Stuart and then made her way over to the bar area where Dave was chatting to one of the girls who worked in the settlements department.

'Got to talk to you for a minute, Dave,' she said, hauling him away. 'Sorry, Jackie, you can have him back shortly.'

'What?' asked Dave. 'I was getting somewhere with her.'

'Don't be ridiculous,' said Jenny briskly. 'Jackie Walshe has no interest in you whatsoever.'

'How do you know that?' he demanded.

'Because she's going out with Richard Cornwell in Chase.'

'Well, she may be going out with Richard but she was having second thoughts while she was talking to me,' Dave told her. 'We'd just got onto our favourite pub.'

'Oh, forget about her,' said Jenny impatiently. 'I was talking to Alix. She wants to know what you and Gavin are up to.'

'Up to? We're not up to anything,' said Dave.

'Oh, come on, Dave. After all the conversations we've had this week? You know perfectly well that you're up to grabbing her job.'

'Only if she makes a complete tit of it,' said Dave. 'Let's face it, Jen, so long as she's making money, there's nothing we can do.'

'But she knows you have something in mind,' said Jenny. 'She knows—'

'She knows nothing,' said Dave. 'Because there's nothing for her to know. If she trades well then there's no hope of either me or Gavin managing to dislodge her. But if she has another week like this week . . . We're paid to make money and she didn't do it.'

'She would have if she'd shorted dollars last night,' said Jenny.

'It was her call. She could have opened a position and made the money. But she didn't.' Dave shrugged.

'You were the one to suggest selling the bonds.'

'She asked my opinion and I gave it. Look, you can't blame me because I told her to stay out of the market.'

'No,' said Jenny, 'but would you have stayed out if it had been your own decision?'

Dave sighed. 'Maybe. Maybe not. It was a messy week. It could have been a lot messier. And she wasn't a bit confident about her call. So I gave her a conservative opinion.'

Jenny looked at him uncomfortably. 'I like Alix,' she said.

'So do I,' said Dave. 'And I'm not going to hang her, Jenny. But if she hangs herself then I'll step into her spot. And I don't have a problem doing that.'

～

Alix wandered up to the dealing room. She liked being there on her own. She turned on the monitor to see how markets were trading in Tokyo time. The dollar was still falling. She'd been such a fool not to go with her gut instinct. Just because she'd felt tired and headachy and not in form for making constructive decisions. She'd never felt like that before and it was stupid. Really stupid.

She sat down in her high-backed chair and closed her eyes. Everything had been so right until Paul dropped his bombshell. Now she felt as though her life was disintegrating and she couldn't understand why. She'd been ambitious before she met him. She'd been successful before he'd moved in with her. So why did she suddenly feel scared when she looked at the screens? Where had the confidence gone?

She looked at her watch. Almost midnight. The crowd downstairs would be thinning out.

A sudden shadow across the flickering screen made her look

up. Matt Connery was standing outside the glass wall of the dealing room and looking in at her. She got up and opened the door.

'I know it sounds like a bad spy movie to say this,' she told him, 'but this is a restricted area. You shouldn't be here.'

'I know,' he said. 'But I was heading home and I wanted to say goodbye. One of your colleagues said you'd probably be up here.'

'Really?' She smiled slightly. 'I didn't realise I was that predictable.'

'Why are you sitting in the dark?' he asked.

'No need for the lights.'

'How are the markets?'

'Dollar is down again,' she told him. 'The yen is staging quite a good rally in Tokyo.'

'Do you love it?' he asked curiously. 'All this?'

'It's all I've ever wanted to do,' said Alix. 'When I was in college everyone talked about banking and finance as though it was some sort of huge mysterious subculture. I always wanted to be involved. And when I studied finance I just loved the idea of capital markets, moving money around the globe, financing trade deals – all of it.'

Matt smiled at her. 'And have you burned out yet?'

'Do I look burned out?' she laughed.

'No,' said Matt. 'You look lovely.'

Alix hadn't blushed in years but she felt the sudden surge of colour in her cheeks and was grateful for the semi-light of the room.

'Flattering the dealer is not necessarily going to make the pricing of your trades any better,' she told him.

He smiled. 'Shame, and I thought I was so irresistible.'

'I can resist everything except chocolate,' she told him as she switched off the monitor again. 'Come on, I'd better go down. If people are leaving I suppose the least I should do is say goodbye.' She waited for him to leave the room first and followed him to the lifts.

'What do you do when you're not working?' asked Matt.

'I go to the gym a couple of times a week,' she said. 'I know that sounds terribly boring. And I shoot.'

'You what?'

'Shoot,' she said.

'You mean hunt? Foxes and rabbits, that sort of thing?'

She grinned. 'No. Target shooting.'

'What sort of targets?'

'Ordinary ones – rings. And silhouettes.'

'Silhouettes?'

'It sounds awful. But little shapes. Like chickens and rabbits and rams. They're at different distances. And you get points for shooting them.'

'My God.' He stared at her. 'Are you good at this?'

'Not bad,' she said. 'I've won a couple of competitions.'

He looked at her with a new respect. 'I guess I'd better not get on the wrong side of you.'

'I guess you'd better not.' She smiled at him and stepped into the lift.

∽

Dave, Gavin and Jenny plus a handful of the settlements staff were going to the Riverside Club.

'Are you coming, Alix?' asked Jenny.

'Why not?' she said. She noticed that Dave and Gavin had

exchanged glances. Those two bastards were up to something, she knew they were, no matter what Jenny might say.

She looked around to say goodbye to Matt Connery but he was nowhere to be seen. Probably giving her a wide berth after her revelations about the shooting club. She smiled to herself. She'd call out there tomorrow, she hadn't been shooting in nearly a month. And it relaxed her.

The nightclub was crowded and the music was loud. Alix bought two bottles of wine and poured for everyone. Dave and Jackie disappeared into the crowd. Gavin Donnelly and Peter Strong, one of the settlements people, began chatting up a couple of extraordinarily attractive girls who were standing at the bar.

It reminded her of her life before Paul, when she'd gone to nightclubs almost every night and wondered (without really believing) whether that night she'd meet the man who would change her life completely.

Why did I do this? she wondered as she looked around her. I don't really want to be here.

'You OK?' asked Jenny.

'Fine,' said Alix. She smiled half-heartedly at Jenny. 'I'm beginning to think I'm a bit old for this, that's all.'

'Not at all,' said Jenny.

'I'm glad you think so.' Alix sipped her wine. 'I just sometimes wonder about it, Jen. Whether or not it's worth the struggle.'

'What d'you mean?'

'Look at them.' Alix nodded at Dave and Gavin. '*They're* my struggle. Wondering if they're about to shaft me.'

Jenny took a gulp of wine. Not again, she thought. Alix was far too good at spotting trouble.

'You'd tell me, Jenny, wouldn't you?' said Alix. 'If they were plotting anything.'

'I – well, sure.' Jenny looked at Alix uneasily.

Alix gazed at her younger colleague. Jenny's face was flushed.

'They're up to something, aren't they?' she demanded. 'Those fucking bastards are up to something.'

'Not really,' said Jenny. 'Honestly, Alix. Not really.'

'Then what?' asked Alix. 'Don't lie to me, Jenny.'

'It's just that – that they think there's something wrong with you and they're wondering if it might be to their advantage.'

'Something wrong with me?' Alix stared at her.

'You've been acting funny all week. They thought you were pregnant.'

'What!' Suddenly Alix began to laugh, the first time she'd really laughed since the previous week. Jenny grinned uncertainly. 'I'm not pregnant,' said Alix. 'Not at all.'

'Good,' said Jenny.

'Why?'

'Gavin made me a price. I dealt. He owes me twenty quid.'

Alix laughed again. 'You see, young Jenny,' she said. 'Stick with me and I'll make us both money.'

It was two o'clock by the time she got home. The apartment was deadly quiet. No Paul to nag at her for drinking all night. No Paul to shove her out of her spot in the bed.

She poured herself a glass of orange juice and drank it. She'd never liked going to bed on her own.

Chapter 7

Alix adjusted her position and looked through the gun scope. She breathed slowly and easily, allowing herself to fall into a gentle rhythm so that she knew exactly when the sight would be perfectly aligned on the target. She squeezed the trigger gently and was pleased when she saw the bullet hit the ring nearest the bull. You had to be relaxed when you were shooting which was why she enjoyed it so much. She wasn't very good at sitting around doing nothing, but forced relaxation was something else altogether. She squeezed the trigger again.

'How'd you do?' asked Niall Rourke, the chairman of the club, when she'd collected the target.

'Hundred and eighty seven,' she said.

'You should come more often.' Niall grinned at her. 'We could make you two hundred out of two hundred.'

'I like to think I'm not perfect.' She smiled. 'I'm going to have a go at the rams.'

She moved to the silhouette area and took aim at one of the small metal rams two hundred metres away. The bullet hit it and sent it spinning off its stand.

'Poor innocent creature,' whispered Niall in her ear. 'You looked positively malevolent that time.'

'Me?' she murmured. 'Never.'

She hit nineteen of the twenty rams. 'You're right,' she told Niall. 'I need more practice. I was slow.'

'You're shooting well,' he said. 'Are you going to enter the next competition?'

'Perhaps.' She slid the scope from the rifle. 'I don't have much time, Niall. I'm supposed to go to Paris for a meeting and I'll be in London soon too.'

'Oh, for the life of executive stress,' he said.

'I bet you have a much nicer life than me,' she told him. 'London and Paris are very dull when you're at meetings all the time.'

'Paris could never be dull,' said Niall. 'I haven't been there in years and I'd love to go back.'

'I'll send you instead of me the next time.' She looked at her watch and gasped in dismay. 'Is that the time? I'd better dash, I'm supposed to be baby-sitting for my sister tonight.' She kissed him on the cheek. 'I'll be out again soon.'

'Bring the boyfriend the next time,' said Niall. 'I thought he was keen to join.'

'Oh, you know these journalist types,' she said lightly. 'They'll say anything and all they want is a good story.'

'I hope not,' said Niall. 'I'd be completely disillusioned if that was the case.'

Alix got into the BMW and drove off. She didn't want to talk to Niall Rourke about Paul who'd been flattering and charming when he'd been at the club and told Alix afterwards that he thought that target shooting was for weirdos. 'So I'm a weirdo?' she'd asked and he'd smiled and told her that she was the best sort.

When she got home she changed into another pair of jeans and sweatshirt and grabbed some earplugs to take to her nieces. Nessa, who was eight, and Aoife, aged four, loved the brightly coloured squashy earplugs and always demanded some when Alix turned up.

◆

Wyn's house was in a small terrace of three near the Merrion Gates. It had spectacular views of Dublin Bay from the upstairs bedrooms and Wyn had said that it was the views which had clinched it for them, outweighing the fact that the garden wasn't as big as they would have liked. 'Although,' she told Alix wryly one day, 'I don't get any time to sit in the bedroom and look at the view any more. I'm too busy running after my lunatic children.'

The lunatic children were watching a cartoon video when Alix arrived and looking the picture of innocence.

'Have you got anything for us?' demanded Nessa.

'No,' said Alix.

'You must have, Alix. You always have.' Aoife looked distraught.

'You should be glad just to see your aunt,' said Wyn, 'and not always expect her to be bringing you things.'

'But she always does,' Nessa said firmly. 'Always.'

'Oh, here!' Alix laughed and handed her the earplugs. 'And these are for you and Aoife too.' She gave her niece a bag of jelly sweets.

'You spoil them rotten,' said Wyn as her daughters flopped in front of the TV and began doling out the sweets. 'They only associate you with someone who brings them garbage!'

'I like indulging them,' Alix smiled. 'And I don't always bring rubbish.'

'Wait until you have your own.' Wyn led the way into the kitchen. 'You won't be indulging them!'

'I don't think I'll ever have kids,' said Alix. 'It isn't me, somehow.'

'But what about Paul?' asked Wyn. 'Doesn't he want them?'

Alix said nothing.

'Why didn't he come with you tonight anyway?' asked Wyn. 'Is he working?'

Alix pushed her hair out of her eyes. 'I don't know.'

Wyn, who had been rummaging through her handbag looking for a lipstick, paused and looked at her sister. 'Why don't you know?'

Alix sighed. 'Paul and I have – aren't living together at the moment.'

'Alix!' Wyn stared at her. 'Why? What happened?'

'Oh, this and that.'

'Alix!'

It was harder to tell Wyn than she'd thought. She'd imagined mentioning it casually to her sister, saying that it was temporary and that they were just working things out, but now that it came to saying the words her throat was dry and she was afraid that she'd burst into tears.

'When did it happen?' asked Wyn.

'Last week.'

'And was it his decision or your decision?'

Alix shrugged. She didn't trust herself to speak.

'Hi, Alix!' Terry, Wyn's husband, barged into the room.

'Hi, Terry.' She smiled faintly at him.

'We're talking,' said Wyn. 'I'll be with you in a minute.'

Terry looked at both of them and joined his daughters in the living-room.

'So, are you going to tell me about it?' demanded Wyn.

'There's nothing much to tell,' said Alix quickly. 'We weren't going anywhere. We weren't sure what we wanted. So we're giving each other a bit of space, that's all.'

'Spare me this "space" nonsense!' Wyn made a face at her sister. 'You've split up, haven't you?'

'For the time being,' admitted Alix.

'So he's left the apartment?'

'That's usually what happens when you split up. One of you leaves. And it *is* my apartment.'

'And is it over for good or is it really just a "space" thing?'

'I don't know,' said Alix. 'I think we'll get back together again. He loves me. He's just having a bit of a midlife crisis, that's all.'

'You sure?'

'Pretty sure,' she said.

'Is there someone else?'

The image of Paul and Sabine together almost made her throw up.

'No,' she said, deliberately misinterpreting Wyn's question, 'although there's a corporate client who keeps asking me out.'

Wyn looked at her shrewdly. 'I meant has Paul got someone else?'

Alix shrugged. 'I knew what you meant. Not really. He met this French girl in Paris and I think meeting her made him question what he wanted out of life, all that sort of stuff. But he's not living with her or anything.'

'Hardly, if she's in Paris,' said Wyn dryly.

'Anyway,' Alix smiled brightly at her, 'it's no hassle. We'll work something out.'

'Are you sure?' asked Wyn. 'And are you OK? If it only happened last week—'

'I'm fine,' interrupted Alix. 'Honestly, Wyn, it's no big deal. We'll probably be back together next month.' She opened the kitchen door. 'Come on, you'll be late.'

When Terry and Wyn had left, Alix sat down beside the two girls.

'Can we play doctors and nurses?' asked Aoife. 'I like being a nurse.'

'And I'm the doctor,' said Nessa bossily. 'You're sick, Alix, you have a pain in your head.'

'I certainly have!' exclaimed Alix as Nessa pulled at her hair. 'Let go, you little horror!'

&

'It sounds serious to me,' said Wyn as Terry turned the car onto the Strand Road. 'She didn't want to talk about it.'

'Who does, if they've split up with a partner?' asked Terry. 'She probably still feels upset.'

'But you know Alix.' Wyn shook her head. 'She never gets upset.'

'This is bound to upset her.'

'With a normal person, yes. But Alix isn't normal, Terry. She doesn't let things upset her. She seems to shrug it off and then she does some brilliant deal in the office and everything's OK.'

'I've never seen her upset,' admitted Terry. 'But that doesn't mean she doesn't get upset.'

'Not when it comes to boyfriends,' said Wyn.

'Well, maybe not now,' said Terry. 'She probably feels that she's too old to start sobbing in our kitchen.'

'She was never upset about boyfriends,' said Wyn. 'Never. When we were teenagers and going out with blokes I was always distraught if someone dumped me. But she just shrugged it off. Used to say that she needed to study more and it had come at a good time. Not that she cared much about guys anyhow. If they asked her out, fine. If not, it didn't seem to bother her.'

'I thought you told me she had loads of boyfriends.'

'Loads of blokes asked her out,' said Wyn, 'but she was very choosy about the ones she actually went out with.'

'She *is* very picky, your sister,' said Terry. 'You can see it in everything she does. It has to be the way she wants it all the time. I suppose she couldn't stand chopping and changing boyfriends and having to get used to different people all the time.'

'I never thought about it like that.'

'She's a control freak.' Terry slowed down as they came to the booth on the toll bridge. 'She's a nice girl, Wyn, and good fun. But only on her terms.'

'You're not being very fair,' said Wyn. 'She lived on her own for a long time. She got used to doing things her own way.'

'I'll tell you something about Alix.' Terry glanced at his wife. 'Remember ages ago she gave me a lift out to the airport?'

'When you were going to Scotland?'

'Yes,' he said. 'On the way I asked her to switch on the radio. So she switched on a CD.'

'And? What was wrong with it?'

'There was nothing wrong with the CD. But when I asked her what radio stations she listened to, she told me that she never listened to the radio in the car except Radio Four for the business news.'

'So?'

'I asked her why she didn't listen to FM104 or 98FM or something a bit more cheerful than Radio Four or the Patsy Cline stuff she was listening to. She said that she preferred listening to CDs because that way she knew what track followed what. She said that she didn't like listening to a mixture of stuff and that's what you got on FM104. She said that she preferred to control her own listening.'

'Well, that's fair enough,' said Wyn defensively.

'Come on, Wyn!' Terry turned into the Point Depot car park. 'Imagine not listening to the radio because you want to listen to songs in sequence. Patsy Cline at that! There's something seriously wrong with your sister.'

Wyn sighed. 'I think it was because of Dad. I think—'

'Don't let's worry about Alix now.' Terry reversed the car into the nearest space. 'She's got her own life to lead. And we've got a night out together. Don't let's spoil it by talking about your father.'

'OK.' Wyn smiled at him.

'That's my girl.' Terry leaned towards her and kissed her gently on the cheek. 'Come on, let's get a drink before the concert starts.'

⤳

Alix would have liked a drink herself. It wasn't that the girls were particularly difficult or disobedient, but they were full of high spirits and insisted on her sharing all their games, most of which involved chasing around the house. Alix often wondered if Terry and Wyn's other baby-sitter, a girl who lived in Blackrock, ever spent as much time playing with Nessa and Aoife as she did. Because she didn't enjoy the games very much,

Alix tried doubly hard to get involved and usually ended up either injured, when one of the children accidentally poked her eye or tripped her up, or covered in paint or crayon or glue if they were going through one of their creative phases. Tonight they played hospitals (Alix suffered a number of painful injections administered by Wyn's basting syringe), followed by jewellery making (hoist by her own petard, Alix told herself, since she'd given Nessa the kit the previous Christmas).

An hour after she first proposed it, the girls were finally bathed and in bed, and looking angelic. She read them a couple of stories and – amazingly, given their excitement of earlier – the two of them had fallen asleep before she finished an instalment from *The Secret Seven*.

She tiptoed downstairs and poured herself a gin and tonic. She honestly didn't know how Wyn coped with two children. She knew that they were in school during the day and that Wyn didn't spend every waking moment with them, but they seemed to take up so much effort. Nessa went to ballet classes and music lessons twice a week. Both girls went swimming. And Wyn had to be there to take them wherever they needed to go. She had to organise her life around them.

Alix never ceased to be amazed at how Wyn had adapted so easily to the role of wife and mother, happily abandoning her career to do so. And Wyn had been the really clever one, Alix thought as she sipped her drink, Wyn had been the one with the string of As in her Leaving Certificate, including higher-grade maths. Alix had only got a B in maths, yet she was the one shifting money around the world while Wyn had given up her actuarial job with one of the country's most prestigious life assurance companies. Wyn could have had a really good career. Alix stretched her legs out in front of her.

She wondered if her sister thought that the sacrifice had been worth it.

She checked on the children an hour later. They were both sleeping peacefully. She felt a surge of affection for them. How much would it change her life? One baby, one child?

She walked quietly out of their bedroom and into the spare room. She stood in front of the wall mirror and looked at her figure sideways on. She leaned back as pregnant women did. It was amazing how different it made you look. Then she picked up a cushion from the cane chair in the corner and shoved it under her sweatshirt.

The effect was frightening. Alix stared at her reflection in horror. She actually looked pregnant! Not like a woman with a cushion at all – a real, live, pregnant woman.

She whipped the cushion out from under her sweatshirt and threw it back onto the chair. If only the rest of it was that easy.

⁓

The final credits for *Terminator 2* were rolling up the TV screen when Alix heard the car pull into the driveway. She went into the kitchen and switched on the coffee filter.

'We're home.' Wyn pushed open the kitchen door. 'How were the girls?'

'Fine.' Alix took some cups from the cupboard. 'They were very good. We played hospitals.'

Wyn sighed. 'Ever since Nessa cut her arm and we had to bring her to casualty they've been playing hospitals.'

'But that was over six months ago!'

'I know,' said Wyn. 'But they don't forget. Things that mean absolutely nothing to me get stored in their brains and regurgitated when I'm least expecting it.'

'But you love them all the same.' Alix's tone was light-hearted.

'I can't imagine life without them,' said Wyn. 'I'm not exactly sure it's the same thing.'

Alix loaded up the tray and carried the coffee into the living room where Terry was stretched out on the sofa.

'Coffee?' she asked.

He nodded. 'So what's all this Wyn tells me about you and Paul?' he asked, ignoring Wyn's glare. 'That's a bit of a surprise, Alix.'

'I guess so.' Alix sat down beside him. 'I don't know whether it's for good or not yet, Terry.'

'He's probably not good enough for you anyway,' said Wyn loyally.

Terry snorted. 'He's a decent bloke!'

'I know.' Alix smiled at him. 'We're just working things out, Terry. That's all.'

'What happened?' he asked. 'Did he fall at the commitment hurdle?'

Alix raised an eyebrow.

'Did you want to get married and have kids?' asked Terry. 'I know a lot of men get cold feet about marrying and having kids.'

'As it happens,' said Alix calmly, 'it was him that wanted the kids. I wasn't sure about it.'

There was a taut silence.

'Oh,' said Terry.

'Do you want more coffee?' asked Wyn.

❧

Even though it was nearly one o'clock in the morning, Alix drove home with the sunroof open to let in the air. It was oppressively hot and her sweatshirt was sticking to her back.

She thought about babies again. She kept seeing herself standing in front of the mirror with the pillow stuffed under her top. It was a freaky kind of picture and it terrified her. But she couldn't let it go. The same way she couldn't let Paul go. She wanted to let him go but she couldn't stop thinking about him and it frightened her.

Surely the Sabine thing was a symptom, nothing more. He wouldn't actually be happy living with a Parisienne who floated around doing arty kinds of things with swathes of muslin and pots of paints. Paul was a practical sort of person. That's why he did journalism and not creative writing. He couldn't see the sense of made-up stories when there were so many real ones to be told. Besides, Sabine was a child. She'd probably just graduated and was barely out of her teens. She'd got the design job for Europa because she knew somebody, Alix was sure of that.

Did Sabine love Paul? Did Paul love Sabine?

Alix ground her teeth as she listened to Patsy Cline tell her she was crazy.

Chapter 8

Alix flew to Paris on Tuesday morning for a meeting with Guy Decourcelle and the treasury managers of some of the other Europa Bank branches. It was one of the regular quarterly meetings when everyone talked about their perspective on markets and which trading strategies they currently preferred.

'The problem with Canada is the lack of confidence in the government,' said Jaques Martin. 'Nobody can believe a word they say. They've had more fiscal reform packages than they know what to do with – and they don't know what to do with them most of the time anyway.'

'It's like Japan a few years ago,' Remy de Valmy agreed with him. 'Too little, too late.'

'It's a market I want us to stay out of,' Guy told them. 'Concentrate on what we know best. What do you think, Alix?'

She looked at him. She knew he didn't think she'd been listening, but she had.

'I have never traded Canada as a market, as you should know, Guy,' she told him. 'We've occasionally transacted Canadian dollar foreign exchange for our clients, but we've never run any positions ourselves. We've always passed them on to Remy.' She smiled at the tall, muscular Canadian trader. 'And I'm sure you did very well out of them too.'

He grinned at her. 'Never well enough.'

'Oh, come on! What about the time I sold you Canadian dollars just as the market went up?'

'What about the time you bought them from me and the market went even higher?'

'What about—'

'OK, OK.' Guy looked at them both irritably. 'Come on. Lunch is no doubt waiting for us.'

The dining room of the bank's headquarters was on the tenth floor of the building and had wonderful views over the city. Alix chose a seat where she could look at the Eiffel Tower. She remembered standing at the top with Paul, holding him tightly, afraid to look down.

'Are you going back to Dublin tonight?' Guy sat down beside her.

'Yes,' she replied.

'Why don't you ever stay?'

'What for?' she asked.

'Why does anyone stay in Paris? The food, the nightlife – whatever!'

She smiled and delicately attacked a shrimp. 'I don't like rich food. I'm quite happy with a burger and chips. As for the nightlife, I get that at home.'

'How is your partner?' asked Guy.

'Fine,' replied Alix.

'Don't you ever tire of him?'

She turned to look at Guy. 'No, I don't.'

'Are you always faithful to him? You are not married, are you?'

'Guy!' She glared at him. 'It's really none of your business. Are you always faithful to your wife?'

91

Guy took a sip of Chablis. 'Not always. But it doesn't mean I do not love her.'

'I'd forgotten,' said Alix sourly, 'about the French way of doing things.'

'It's often the best way,' said Guy.

'Well, it's not my way,' Alix snapped.

'Such a shame,' Guy murmured. 'You miss out on so much.'

Alix swallowed a whole cherry tomato and almost choked. By the time she'd regained her composure, Guy had turned to the trader from the Madrid branch and was ignoring her completely.

⌇

She'd forgotten to buy milk. She was dying for a cup of coffee, there was no milk in the fridge and it was almost midnight. If she'd stayed in Paris she could have gone to a fashionable restaurant, drunk fine wine courtesy of Guy Decourcelle's expense account and then had brilliant and wonderful sex with him. Well, maybe not the brilliant and wonderful sex, although he'd given her the distinct impression that it was a possibility. It was flattering to think that he might be interested, all the same. She needed to think like that right now. If I was any good at being single, she thought, I'd have stayed in Paris and flirted madly with Guy. It might have even been good for my career! Instead of which I'm in this bloody apartment drinking black coffee which I absolutely hate and I'll be sleeping on my own which I don't much like either.

Tomorrow, she promised herself, as she slid between the sheets, I'll get my act in gear tomorrow.

But she woke up late the following morning. She blinked

sleepily in the morning light and realised that it was already eight o'clock. She swore softly, hopped out of bed and under the shower.

She walked to work. It was infinitely quicker than driving through the rush-hour traffic although by the time she'd reached the office she had a blister on her heel and felt hot and bothered.

'YO! SUSHI!' Gavin was standing on his chair exchanging high-fives with Dave while Jenny sat on the edge of her desk and laughed at them.

'What on earth is going on?' demanded Alix.

'Oh, hi.' Gavin beamed at her and jumped from the chair. 'How was Paris?'

'Fine,' said Alix. 'What were you doing just now?'

'Trading,' Gavin replied. 'What do you think I was doing?'

'It looked like you were standing on your chair to me,' she said.

'Celebrating,' said Dave. 'As we've every right to.'

'Oh?'

'Gavin landed a new account,' Dave told her. 'We did their first trade this morning and we've just bagged a few grand.'

'What's the account?' Alix took off her chocolate-brown Jil Sander jacket and hung it over the back of her chair.

'A crowd called Anatronics,' said Gavin. 'He was selling yen.'

'Matt Connery?' Alix looked at him. 'Was it Matt Connery that called?'

'Yes,' answered Dave. 'D'you know him?'

'Don't be bloody stupid, Dave. I had a meeting with him about ten days ago! And he was at the reception on Friday. It's hardly a new account.'

'We haven't dealt with them before,' Gavin pointed out. 'That makes it a new account.'

'It's an account I was handling,' said Alix. 'I'm supposed to be making a presentation to them next week.'

'They obviously don't need you to do anything,' said Gavin. 'And Matt whateverhisname was perfectly happy to deal with me. So I'd call it a new account and I'd call it my account. Anyway,' he added, 'wouldn't have done much good if he had asked for you because you weren't here.'

Alix could feel the acid churn in her stomach. Because she'd been in a bad mood when Matt had called she hadn't bothered to set up Anatronics as an account on their internal system. Usually she would have entered all the relevant details on the computer and assigned someone to look after the account. Anatronics, with its base of business both in the Far East and the States, looked very interesting and profitable and she had wanted to look after it herself.

But they had an unwritten code in the dealing room that if someone did a deal for an unallocated account, they were given the job of looking after the client. It was her own fault that Gavin was trying to pinch the Anatronics account.

'I'll talk it through with them at the meeting,' she said finally. 'They might have other ideas about their account manager. *Did* Matt Connery ask for me?'

'No,' said Gavin rudely. 'Why should he? I told you he was perfectly happy with the pricing of the deal.'

'Good,' said Alix and stalked into her office without even checking the screens.

Gavin and Dave exchanged glances. Dave shrugged and Gavin grinned. Jenny sat down in her chair and picked up the telephone.

Alix opened her copy of the *Financial Times* and stared at the top story without seeing it. Her heart was pounding and now she had a pain in her stomach. That bloody pup, Donnelly, she thought furiously. He's so fucking pleased that he's pinched a deal from under my nose. 'You weren't here,' he'd gloated. The little shit. And Dave Bryant had said nothing, just looked faintly pleased with himself.

Well, she thought, if I somehow end up leaving this place, Dave won't last very long. Not with Gavin breathing down his neck. Gavin is the kind of bloke who wants to go straight to the top. And he'll probably do just that. But not, she muttered, without a lot of work. And not over me.

She walked back into the room, sat down at her desk and started calling clients. But business was slow and she hadn't done a single trade by lunchtime.

'Want to join me for a sandwich?' she asked Jenny at midday.

Jenny glanced anxiously at Dave who studiously ignored her look.

'Well, OK.'

'You don't have to if you don't want to,' said Alix. 'If you've something planned—'

'No, nothing,' said Jenny hastily. 'I'd love to have a sandwich with you.'

'Great,' said Alix. 'I've got to pop down to settlements for a couple of minutes. Meet you in reception at a quarter past?'

'Fine,' said Jenny.

Gavin stuck out his tongue at Jenny and licked the air as Alix left the room.

'Oh, give it a rest,' Jenny snapped at him.

'Have a sandwich with me!' said Gavin in a falsetto voice.

'And tell me what those nasty boys in the dealing room are up to.'

'Stop it.' But Jenny giggled.

'You better come back with more information than you impart,' said Dave. 'Because we'll be quizzing you in the pub afterwards.'

'Not tonight you won't,' smirked Jenny. 'I've got a date!'

'Don't forget he'll definitely respect you in the morning,' Dave said.

'Thanks for the advice.' Jenny got up from the desk. 'I'm off to meet the boss for lunch. See you later!'

She stood in the reception area and waited for Alix to arrive. Part of her felt sorry for Alix who was obviously going through some kind of crisis these last few days. Jenny had never seen her boss look uncertain, or go home early, or arrive at the office late. And she couldn't believe that Alix hadn't already set up an account for Anatronics! What had she been thinking of?

She smiled as Alix strode through the swing doors.

'O'Reilly's?' asked Alix.

'Fine,' said Jenny.

It was another glorious day. The sky was clear blue and the sun was hot. The smell of the city's traffic hung in the air and mingled with the odour of the Liffey as it wound its way to the sea.

'I hope it's like this for Anna's wedding,' said Jenny brightly as they walked along the quays. 'She needs it to be warm because she's wearing a dress that's almost indecent it's so low cut.'

'What date?' asked Alix.

'Next month,' said Jenny. 'The eighteenth.'

The eighteenth. Paul's birthday. Last year they'd gone to

Paris for his birthday. Absolutely nothing to do with work, she hadn't gone near the Europa Bank building. They'd stayed in a small but elegant hotel near Montmartre and they'd had a loving and romantic weekend. Alix had bought a bottle of Dom Perignon and a huge punnet of strawberries and they'd brought them back to the bedroom and—

'Are you OK, Alix?' Jenny looked at her curiously.

'I'm fine,' Alix replied. 'Come on, there's a break in the traffic!'

They ran across the busy road to the pub and sat down at one of the outside tables.

'At the reception the other night I got the impression from you that Dave and Gavin were out to get me,' said Alix after they'd ordered baguettes and beer. 'How badly are they out to get me?'

'It's not that bad at all.' Jenny shifted uneasily in her seat. 'I told you. They thought you were pregnant. I told them you weren't – I had to so's I could collect on my bet.'

'And why did they think I might be pregnant?'

'You've been acting strangely. Going home early. Missing trades. Being in late this morning. Not setting up the Anatronics account – Alix, why on earth didn't you set it up?'

Alix shrugged.

'But it could be worth a lot of money,' said Jenny.

'I'm the boss,' said Alix. 'I allocate the accounts. And even if I let Gavin keep it, that doesn't mean all the profit will be matched against his name.'

'But that's not fair,' protested Jenny. 'Matt Connery wasn't going to deal until Gavin persuaded him that we could show him the best price.'

'And why wasn't Matt Connery going to deal?'

'Because—' Jenny sighed and shifted in her chair again. 'Because he told Gavin he didn't know him.'

'And Gavin said?'

Jenny fiddled with a paper napkin.

'Jenny?'

'Gavin said that he looked after your accounts while you were away and that since you'd been in Paris he wasn't expecting you back until tomorrow at the earliest and he wouldn't advise Connery to wait in case the rate went against him.' Jenny's words tumbled out in a rush.

Alix said nothing. She knew that if she'd been Gavin she would have done exactly the same thing. She could hardly fault him for enthusiasm and for hanging on to the client. Matt Connery might have tried a different bank if Gavin hadn't been so pushy. But, she thought, Gavin had lied when he said Matt hadn't asked to talk to her. She would never have lied about that. Never.

'Alix?' Jenny spoke tentatively. 'Alix, what's the matter?'

Quite suddenly, Alix wanted to cry. She wanted to put her head on the table and sob her heart out and tell Jenny that Paul had dumped her for some French nymphet who was dying to have his babies. She wanted someone to put their arms round her and tell her that it didn't matter, that Paul was a shit and that there were other fish in the sea. She sat up straight in her seat.

'Nothing's the matter.'

'But it's not like you,' protested Jenny. 'Being late, or being caught out – any of it.'

'I've just had a rough week or so,' said Alix. 'I am entitled to the occasional off week, don't you think?'

'Of course you are.' Jenny smiled at her. 'But it's unsettling,

Alix. And I hate it when I think the guys are ganging up on you.'

Alix laughed. 'You sound like my big sister when you say that.'

'I didn't mean it like that. It's just that there are so few women doing really well in this profession. I'm really proud that I work with you and that you're so good at the job. I hate to think that you'd let someone get the better of you.'

I've been dumped by my boyfriend, I'm making a mess of my career and I'm still a role model for Jenny Smith. Alix sighed. Some bloody role model.

'I won't let anyone get the better of me,' Alix promised. 'And when they debrief you on the result of lunch with me, you can tell them that I'm not pregnant and that I'm entitled to be late occasionally and that I haven't got any dreadful disease. You can tell them that I'm perfectly in control.'

'Great!' Jenny beamed at her although she still wasn't convinced that everything was OK.

'So, come on,' Alix pulled her chair closer to Jenny, 'tell me all about Anna's wedding. What are you going to wear?'

Chapter 9

The letter in the postbox was addressed to Paul. Alix could see at once that it wasn't an official letter that could be thrown in the wastepaper basket and ignored. This was a bulky letter, but it was personal. The envelope was pale blue and Paul's name and address had been handwritten. It wasn't a woman's writing, though, she decided. And it wasn't from Sabine Brassaert because the letter had been posted in Cork. Alix turned the envelope over and over in her hand. There was no return address. Whoever had sent it obviously didn't know Paul well enough to know he wasn't living in the apartment any more.

She picked up the phone and dialled the number for RTÉ. It just might be important for Paul to know about the letter – it could be information for a piece he was working on and he might need it urgently.

'I'm sorry,' said the guy who answered the phone. 'Paul isn't available right now.'

Alix glanced at her watch. After six. 'When will he be available?'

'He's working on something. I guess he'll be finished in about an hour.'

'Thanks,' said Alix.

She hung up and stared into space. There had been countless times when Paul had been waiting impatiently for original documents or certain correspondence to arrive by post – he'd always grabbed the envelope immediately and spilled its contents onto the table. He'd want this letter right away no matter what else he was working on.

She went into the bedroom and opened the wardrobe door. The one good thing about Paul's departure, she thought bitterly as she looked through the rails, was that she finally had enough room to hang up all her clothes.

She selected a wraparound skirt in vivid purple and a shocking pink T-shirt. She undid her hair from its clip and shook it loose around her head. Without her hair tied back and wearing the clashing T-shirt and skirt, she looked infinitely younger. Could almost pass for early twenties, she said to herself as she leaned towards the mirror to check for more grey hairs. As long as you didn't get too close.

She sprayed herself liberally with Escada Sport and slung her canvas bag over her shoulder.

The traffic through Donnybrook was terrible. She tapped the steering wheel impatiently as the Fiesta in front of her stalled on Morehampton Road. Oh, for God's sake, she muttered as the hapless driver failed to restart the engine, what the hell are you doing on the road if you can't drive? She glanced in her mirror, flicked the indicator and roared past the Fiesta.

Alix had been in the RTÉ complex a couple of times before. Once she'd been on a radio programme talking about interest rates and the need for a tighter fiscal policy. She'd been the only woman on the panel and the presenter had discriminated very positively in her favour so that she'd received loads of airtime while the men around the table glared furiously at her.

The second time she'd appeared on a television current affairs broadcast, talking about the impact of a change in China's foreign policy on European markets. Everyone in Europa Bank had watched the TV interview and had told her that she looked great. Feminine, Des Coyle had told her, but professional. And she'd made it sound interesting. Alix had laughed and told him that Chinese foreign policy could never compete with *Coronation Street* but she'd done her best.

Alix parked her car and walked up the steps to the radio studio.

'I'm looking for Paul Hunter,' she told the receptionist.

'Who shall I say?'

'Alix Callaghan.'

The receptionist dialled a number.

'He's in a meeting,' she told Alix. 'He might be a while.'

'Can you make sure he's told I'm here and waiting for him? It's urgent.'

'Sure. Would you like to take a seat?'

Alix nodded and sat down.

'. . . and now for financial news. Currency markets were quiet today with little activity. The US dollar . . .'

Alix didn't want to listen to RTÉ's financial report. She picked up a magazine and tried to ignore the radio broadcast.

'Alix! What's the matter?' Paul hurried into the reception area looking hassled.

'Hi.' She smiled at him. 'How are you?'

'I'm OK,' he said. 'But busy. What's the problem?'

'There's no problem,' said Alix.

'But they told me it was urgent.' Paul stared at her. 'I've just come out of a very important meeting because I thought there might be something wrong.'

'How sweet.' She smiled again. 'It might be urgent but I don't think there's anything wrong.' She took the envelope out of her bag. 'This arrived for you today. I know how you always have to rip your letters open so I thought—'

'But you dragged me out of a meeting!'

'How was I to know which was more important, your letter or your meeting? I just went on past experience. I'm sorry if I've upset you.'

'No.' Paul shook his head. 'You didn't upset me. Just surprised me.'

'You'd better get back to your meeting,' she said.

'Oh, it can wait a moment now,' said Paul. 'How are you, Alix?'

'Me? I'm fine.'

'You look great.'

'Thank you.' She smiled at him. 'I'd say the same but you look tired, Paul.'

'Oh, busy day, that's all.'

'I can imagine,' she said sympathetically. She ran her fingers through her hair. 'We've been pretty busy ourselves lately.'

'And how are things in the dealing room?'

'Not so bad,' she told him. 'That little shit Gavin Donnelly is getting a bit too big for his boots.'

'I'm sure you'll find a way to stamp him down,' Paul laughed. 'You generally do.'

'I'm much more mellow these days,' said Alix.

'Don't try to fool me,' said Paul. 'Mellow is something you'll never be.'

'Maybe not mellow,' she conceded. 'But I do my best. Anyway, I'd better go. I simply thought I should give you this in case it was something vital.'

'Thanks,' he said. 'It was thoughtful of you.'

'Anytime. Well, not anytime, I can't spend my life hurtling out here. Traffic was awful.' She pushed her hair back from her face again.

'Why are you wearing it like that?' asked Paul.

'Sorry?'

'Your hair? You usually tie it back.'

'A change,' she said. 'I told you, I'm trying to be mellow.'

'Oh, I see.'

'I bet you don't!' She grinned. 'Look, Paul, water under the bridge and all that – why don't we go for a drink?'

'I can't,' he said. 'I told you, I'm in a meeting.'

'I didn't mean straightaway.' She grimaced. 'You don't have to take me so literally. I meant some evening. You and me.'

'I'm pretty busy most evenings,' he said. 'As you can see.'

'Indeed.'

He met her eyes. 'But you're right. Water under the bridge, as you said.'

'How about tomorrow?'

'Tomorrow?'

'Why not?' She shrugged. 'It doesn't matter. Forget it. Maybe it's not a good idea.'

'No, Alix, wait. It is a good idea. I think we need to have a civilised drink together.'

'You sound like your mother.' She smiled wryly at him. 'A civilised drink. Like we were going to have two glasses of sweet sherry!'

'God forbid I should sound like my mother,' he laughed. 'OK, tomorrow.'

'Seven o'clock?' she suggested. 'Kiely's?'

'That would be great.'

'Absolutely,' she said. 'I'll see you then.'

'OK,' said Paul. ''Bye, Alix.'

She strolled down the stairs of the radio centre. He still fancied her. At least that was something!

～

For the first time since Paul had left, Alix didn't wake up heart thumping and throat dry in the middle of the night. She went to bed at eleven and woke, refreshed, at six o'clock, just before the alarm went off.

She was at her desk by seven, flicked through news reports on overnight trading and had just completed a study of the last fortnight's profit and loss account for the dealing room when Dave Bryant walked in. He was surprised to see her.

'Morning,' he said as he dumped a bundle of newspapers on the desk. 'You're early.'

'Thought I'd make a head start.' She grimaced. 'I've been a little later than usual these last couple of weeks so I decided I'd better get myself back on track.'

'Everything OK?' asked Dave.

'Not a bother,' she told him. 'What on earth were we doing when I was in Paris? We seem to have been churning the sterling/euro book.'

'Just trading it,' said Dave.

'But so many trades.' Alix scratched her head. 'I know we ended up in profit at the end of the day, but you must have had a few dodgy exposures in the meantime.'

'We had some interests—'

'But these are all professional trades,' Alix interrupted him.

105

'None of them are on the back of corporate interests. You didn't have any customers calling, only other banks.'

'It was very volatile,' Dave said. 'And we thought we should take advantage of it.'

'I see.' She gazed at him for a moment and eventually he looked away.

Jenny arrived with some hot croissants from the shop across the road and prevented further discussion.

'Good morning!' She beamed at them. 'How are you all this morning?'

'Wonderful,' said Alix. 'Is one of those for me?'

'Of course, my leader!' Jenny smiled at her. 'You're looking very chirpy this morning.'

Alix knew that she looked good. She'd brushed her face with Christian Dior, her eyelids with Estée Lauder and her lips with Chanel. Despite her lack of interest in make-up she was forever buying it in the duty free and she normally wore it to work. But since Paul's departure she hadn't bothered. Now she was pleased she'd made the effort again.

She took a croissant from Jenny and poured some coffee from the pot. Everything was getting back to normal, she thought to herself. She felt OK again.

Gavin burst into the room. 'Sorry I'm late, Dave! I got stuck in – oh, Alix, hello.'

'Good morning,' she said. 'It doesn't matter that you're late. We hadn't started the morning meeting yet.'

Gavin flushed to the roots of his hair. Alix smiled at him. 'But now you're here, let's start.'

She outlined the strategy for the day, listened as Jenny gave a rundown on some interests their customers had, and reminded them that a guy from the New York office was dropping by that afternoon. 'So I want us to look smart and efficient and at least make him think we know what we're doing!'

It was a busy morning. Alix talked to her customers, completed a few trades, felt good about things. At eleven o'clock she answered one of the flashing lines.

'Alix?'

'Yes,' she said. 'This is Alix Callaghan.'

'How are you? It's Matt Connery.'

'Hi, Matt. Sorry, I didn't recognise your voice.'

'That does my ego a lot of good,' he laughed. 'You're still meeting us here on Friday?'

'Absolutely,' she said. 'Eleven o'clock.'

'Looking forward to it,' he said. 'In the meantime, it's just small, but I have a quarter bar euros to put on deposit for a month. What can you pay me?'

A quarter of a million euros was a small amount in terms of interbank dealing.

'Three per cent,' she told him.

'OK, that's fine. Deutsche Bank will be paying them.'

'Great,' she said. 'Thanks for the call. And I believe we did a foreign exchange trade for you while I was away.'

'Yes,' he said. 'I was sorry to miss you. But the guy told me you were in Paris and mightn't be back this week.'

'I was in Paris all right, but I was back the next day.' She laughed although her eyes glittered green as she looked at Gavin.

'I'm glad I caught you this time,' said Matt. 'Though Gavin was very efficient.'

'All my team are efficient,' said Alix, 'especially Gavin.'

'I've got to go,' said Matt. 'My other line is ringing. One

107

day I'm just going to pull the plug on the phone! I'll see you Friday.'

'See you.' Alix clicked out of the line. 'Gavin?'

He met her eyes. 'What?'

'Why did you tell Matt Connery I'd be away this week?'

'I didn't,' said Gavin. 'He's getting it wrong.'

'I see.' Alix nodded. 'Thank goodness the customer isn't always right.'

She was pleased to see Gavin's face turn an interesting shade of red.

⌒

'Alix, it's Paul for you. Line two.'

'Hi, Paul.' She sounded bright, breezy, confident.

'Alix, it's about tonight.'

'Oh?'

'I'm not sure I can make it. I'm really busy.'

'It's four o'clock,' she told him. 'Surely you'll be free by seven?'

'I hope so,' he said. 'It's just that I have a deadline of ten tomorrow morning for the piece I'm working on, and I'm nowhere near finished.'

'Ten in the morning is hours away!'

'Look, my work isn't like yours. I have to spend a lot of time thinking. I can't just write something straightaway.'

'I can't just execute a trade straightaway either,' she said. 'Not always.'

'You know what I mean,' he said. 'Anyway, I just thought it might be a good idea to leave it tonight. We can meet another time.'

'When?' asked Alix.

'Next week?' he suggested.

'OK.' She called up her electronic calendar. 'How about next Wednesday?'

'It looks OK,' said Paul. 'But it'll depend on how things are.'

'Paul, have you taken a job that allows you no social life whatsoever?' demanded Alix. 'Because it seems to me—'

'Wednesday's fine,' said Paul hastily. 'Sorry about this, Alix. If I'd been here longer maybe I wouldn't worry about it so much. But I want to get everything just right. Surely you, of all people, understand that? You're such a perfectionist yourself.'

'I'm not a perfectionist,' she said.

He laughed, a genuine laugh. 'Don't be utterly ridiculous. Of course you are.'

'Maybe,' she conceded. 'Thanks for ringing.'

'See you next week.'

She walked out of the dealing room and into the toilets. He was backing out of the deal, she thought with rage. He'd said he'd meet her and now he was backing out because – because why? He was afraid of her? That didn't make sense, he couldn't be afraid of her. Because he was afraid of himself? Because he knew that if he saw her again he'd want to move back in with her and have everything the same as it was before? Or was it simply that he didn't want to see her at all? But he'd been nice yesterday, she thought, they'd behaved in quite an adult way.

She leaned her head against the frosted glass window and sighed.

She wished she knew what she wanted from her life. At the moment, all she knew was that she didn't want it to be like this.

The light on the answering machine was blinking at her when she got home. Maybe Paul had rung, she thought, maybe he'd changed his mind and wanted to meet her after all. She kicked off her Bruno Magli slingback shoes and padded across the room.

'Alix? I suppose you're not there. I didn't want to ring you in the office. It's Carrie. What's all this about you and Paul? Ring me as soon as you get in.'

Alix groaned. She really didn't feel like having a long and involved conversation with her mother about her relationship with Paul. And any conversation with Carrie Callaghan became long and involved because Carrie had an opinion on everything and insisted on sharing it with whoever she was talking to.

I'll get changed, then call, Alix decided. She picked up her shoes and went into the bedroom. She took off her suit and hung it in the wardrobe, all the time wondering what Wyn had told their mother about her split with Paul.

Because the only way that Carrie knew was from Wyn. The two of them had always been close, much closer than Carrie and herself. Wyn and Carrie enjoyed long and intimate heart-to-heart discussions with each other, eagerly sharing the latest gossip about national and international movers and shakers. And Carrie was perfectly placed to find out lots of things about people. She ran a small but very exclusive beauty salon at the Grafton Street end of Chatham Lane and she also had a stake in a health farm just outside Wexford town. Her clients were rich and successful women and the wives of rich and successful men. Carrie never talked to anyone other than Wyn about them, but she had to talk to someone. And Wyn enjoyed being part of it all.

Alix knew that she had inherited her mother's business sense while Wyn had inherited her love of people. She often wondered what either of them had inherited from the father who had walked out on them when she was three years old. His academic skills was the obvious answer, yet Alix didn't want to think that her brains were the gift of someone who'd abandoned her.

She remembered her mother holding Wyn and herself closely to her and promising that she'd never leave, they were all strong women in this together.

It was after John Callaghan walked out that the two girls started to call their mother by her name. Neither of them ever referred to her as Mum again.

Alix pulled on a loose T-shirt and a pair of Levi's. She walked into the bathroom and sprayed Evian water onto her face. Then she went into the kitchen and took a bottle of Miller from the fridge.

She was just about to pick up the receiver when the phone rang.

'Hello,' she answered.

'Alix! It's me.'

'Hi, Carrie.'

'Did you get my message? I rang earlier.'

'Of course I got your message. I was just about to call you back.'

'Huh.' Carrie sounded disbelieving. 'I bet you didn't want to call! Have to tell me all about your love life.'

'I don't mind telling you.' Alix sat in her favourite armchair and tucked her legs beneath her. 'Paul and I are spending some time apart.'

'Why?' asked Carrie.

'I'm sure Wyn has already told you why,' said Alix acidly.

'Come on, Alix. Don't be like that. She's your sister. She's worried about you.'

'Oh, for heaven's sake! If she's all that worried she should have called me.'

'She just wanted to let me know.'

'So that you could spend ages talking about me behind my back.' Alix's voice trembled.

'Alix, darling, don't be ridiculous,' said Carrie gently. 'We just want to be sure you're OK. That's all.'

'I'm sorry,' said Alix. 'I didn't mean to get ratty. Sure, I'm OK.'

'You don't usually get ratty,' Carrie pointed out. 'So it's obviously having some effect.'

Alix sighed. 'I'm still upset, of course. I'm not sure how things are going to work out.'

'Do you want to get back together? Is there someone else?'

'No,' said Alix cautiously.

'How do you know?'

'I – it's – Paul is having a bit of a midlife crisis,' she told her mother. 'He wants to settle down and have kids.'

'Actually, a midlife crisis is usually where the man thinks having a wife and kids was a mistake,' said Carrie. 'And he has a messy affair with a girl who usually looks like a younger version of his wife.'

They were both silent for a moment.

'Did Dad have a midlife crisis?' asked Alix.

'Your father's life was one long crisis,' said Carrie. 'And we were well rid of him.'

Alix undid her hair so that it fell in front of her face. 'Are you sure?' she asked.

'What?'

'Are you sure we were well rid of him?'

'I don't want to talk about it,' said Carrie firmly. 'It's in the past.'

She never wanted to talk about it. The day he'd left, Carrie had bundled all the things he'd left behind into a bag, driven straightaway to the dump at Dunsink and thrown them in.

John had rung the house one day to ask when he could pick up his stuff and Carrie had laughed wildly and told him anytime but he'd have to be quick before it all rotted away completely. Wyn had told the story to Alix one night when Carrie had gone out and left them with a baby-sitter who spent the entire time reading a romantic novel and wiping tears from her eyes.

'So what are you going to do about Paul?' asked Carrie.

'I don't know.'

'Do *you* want to marry and have children?'

Alix bit her lip.

'Just because it didn't work for me doesn't mean it won't work for you.' Carrie said the words she'd said to her daughters a thousand times before. Wyn had believed them so much that she'd married at twenty-one.

'I'm meeting Paul next week,' she told Carrie. 'We'll have a chat then. I'll let you know.'

'Why don't you come into the salon beforehand?' suggested Carrie. 'I'll do you up, make you look so wonderful he won't know what hit him.'

Alix laughed. 'He'd get a fright if I suddenly turned up

113

in full metal jacket make-up. Thanks, Carrie, but I don't think so.'

'Come in anyway,' said her mother. 'I'll give you a massage. Then, no matter what happens, you'll be ready for it.'

'Maybe,' said Alix.

'Absolutely,' said Carrie.

'Thanks for calling.'

'Look after yourself.'

Alix replaced the receiver and finished her beer.

Chapter 10

Alix peered at the laptop on the desk in front of her and wondered if she needed glasses. She needed to make the print on her slides much, much bigger. But that meant cutting down on the information on each one.

She sighed and rubbed the bridge of her nose. She'd been working on the presentation for Anatronics all afternoon and she was tired. She looked through her glass window at the dealing room. Dave and Jenny were both reading the newspapers. Gavin was on the phone.

He worked hard, she thought ruefully. He was keen and he was arrogant but he worked harder than the other two put together. Dave was quick-witted and good at analysing trends. Jenny was methodical and got on well with the customers. But Gavin was all of those things as well as possessing a drive that neither Jenny nor Dave seemed to have. Alix knew that it wouldn't be long before Gavin would be looking for a promotion. Or another job.

She bit the tip of her finger. This was the first time she'd ever felt threatened by anyone in the dealing room. This was the first time she'd ever balked at giving someone extra responsibility because she knew that they wanted it. If she gave Gavin too much opportunity he could simply walk all over her. And she'd worked too hard to let someone walk all over her.

He was gesticulating as he spoke, obviously making the case for whatever trade he was trying to get the customer to do. His face was intense as he concentrated on the prices on the screen in front of him.

Of course he could always fly too high, Alix mused, as she watched him nod vigorously and begin tapping details of a trade on the keyboard. He could take one risk too many and end up out on his ear. She'd seen it happen before. It had almost happened to her.

She shuddered as she remembered. She'd been working in London at the time, dealing Kiwi, which was slang for New Zealand dollars. She'd been building a long position in them, confident that the New Zealand dollar was going to appreciate in value. She was almost at the limit of the amount she was allowed to hold when Rik Johnson, the financial controller of a beef processing plant, had called her saying that he needed to buy a million US dollars and sell Kiwis. The trade would push her over her limit but she knew that she could sell Rik's Kiwis easily enough and return to her correct position.

She bought the Kiwis, and almost straightaway the US dollar had roared upwards because a headline appeared on her Reuters screen saying that the US had fired a missile at Iraq. People were buying US dollars and selling other currencies because they always did whenever there was the faintest threat of military action. The value of the Kiwi had plummeted as the dollar soared.

Even remembering it now made Alix feel sick. She'd known that she should just cut the position and at least get back inside her limits but she couldn't believe that the US had really fired a missile at Iraq. She sat there for a minute as the profit and loss spreadsheet in front of her assimilated the new exchange rates. The numbers all turned red. What had been a small profit was turning into a significant loss before her very eyes.

And then, just as she was about to call another trader and cut the position, a US official's denial of the alleged missile-firing flashed across the screen. As quickly as it had gone up, the dollar came down again. The numbers in front of Alix had turned from red to black. Not only that, but the dollar fell lower than it had been before the news story broke. She cut the position straightaway.

Afterwards, Logan McDonald, the chief dealer, had called her into his office and asked her why she'd gone over her limit. She'd explained but he was furious.

'Those limits are for our protection. You can't just choose to break them whenever you like. You know the rules. I can fire you for this, Alix.'

She'd stared at him. 'But I made money for us.'

'That makes no difference. You broke the rules.'

She couldn't believe it. 'Are you going to fire me?'

He'd gazed at her for a moment, then shrugged. 'Not this time. Maybe you've learned something. But if you break a limit again, Alix, you're out.'

She hadn't broken a limit again, even though there were times when she wanted to. Whenever she felt really strongly about anything she talked to Logan about increasing the limit. Sometimes he did, sometimes he didn't. But she'd played by the rules every time.

She walked out into the dealing room.

'How are things going?' she asked.

'Not bad,' said Dave. 'Couple of late trades, nothing too exciting.'

'And you, Gavin?'

He looked up at her in surprise. 'What about me?'

'What was the last trade you did?'

Suddenly, he looked very uncomfortable. 'Me?'

'Yes, you.'

'Small foreign exchange,' he said. 'Nothing much.'

'Tell me about it.'

'We bought some dollars. We were a little bit short anyway. It was only a hundred thousand.'

She nodded. 'Who was the client?'

'Anatronics,' said Gavin.

She regarded him thoughtfully. 'Did they ask for me?'

Gavin looked even more uncomfortable. 'Yes,' he admitted eventually. 'But I said that you were busy. You did say that you didn't want to be disturbed and I thought that, for a hundred thousand dollars, you probably didn't.'

'You made a decision,' said Alix. 'It was entirely up to you.' She smiled at him and walked back into her office.

'Shit,' said Gavin as she closed the door behind her.

'I told you you should have called her,' said Jenny. 'She wants that account.'

'Well, let her fight for it,' said Gavin defiantly.

'Who d'you think would win?' Dave asked Jenny lazily. 'Our lovely leader or the young Turk?'

'Fuck off, Bryant,' said Gavin.

'Evens?' suggested Jenny.

Dave raised his eyebrows. 'You're that negative on our boss?'

Jenny flushed.

'I won't deal,' said Dave. 'I might be tempted to swing things one way or the other if I did.'

'Dave.' Alix opened the door. 'Can you find the report on the Far East that Guy sent over last week? I want to rob some info out of it.'

'Certainly,' said Dave. He grinned wickedly at Jenny and at Gavin. 'I always follow orders.'

❧

Alix took the laptop home and practised her presentation in front of the bedroom mirror. She never used notes when she spoke and she hated it when other people did. She liked to give the impression that she was simply talking to the people in the room, with each topic flowing easily from the one before. The slides helped to keep her focused and the graphs helped to keep her audience focused too.

She ran through the presentation three times. When Paul had lived with her, she'd always do the last practice run in front of him. He understood enough about finance to ask occasional questions and he would tell her whether or not the whole thing was boring. But she didn't need him to listen to the presentation. It would simply have been nice to have had his encouragement.

She picked out her purple suit before she went to bed. She knew that the purple was striking and that people remembered it. The skirt was calf-length and narrow and the jacket fitted to her waist. The suit made her look tall and commanding and gave her confidence.

❧

The meeting with Anatronics was at eleven o'clock. The markets weren't busy, and by the time she was leaving, Dave was already reading the sports supplements while Jenny was leafing through the *Guardian*. Gavin was doing a technical analysis study on the future direction of the South African rand.

'I'll be back by lunchtime, Dave,' she told him as she slung the laptop over her shoulder. 'This shouldn't take too long.'

'See you later,' said Dave. 'Have fun.'

She made a face at him then turned to Gavin. 'By the way, have you any particular recommendations for their yen cash flow?'

Gavin looked up from the graph. 'Not really.'

'Why? I thought you wanted this account.'

He glared at her. 'I want what's best for the company.'

'Oh, I see.' She beamed at him. 'That's great news, Gavin. I'm so pleased to hear it.'

Alix opened the sunroof of the BMW as she turned onto the M50. It had been cloudy until now but suddenly the sun had come out and she was hot. Alix looked enviously at the planes parked around the airport terminal buildings as she drove by and wished that she was heading off herself. A holiday would be nice, she thought, as she pressed harder on the accelerator. A relaxing, sun-soaked holiday where she could read a good beach book and forget about Paul and Gavin, Carrie and Wyn.

Anatronics shared a modern building in an industrial estate just off the motorway – a couple of miles past the toll plaza, Matt Connery had told her, the second exit and then to the left.

She could see the building, as he'd described it, from the motorway. She indicated and took the exit, then slowed down to find the entrance to the industrial estate.

This was one of the things she really liked about going to meet clients. When she was in the bank, using the telephone and the Reuters screens to trade, the reality of what she was doing always seemed remote. But when she went to see a client, when she walked around their offices or their factories, it all became more real to her and she knew that finance wasn't just about shifting money all around the world. She could help these companies be more profitable. If her advice was right, both the company and the bank would benefit.

She pulled into a space marked 'Visitors' and pushed open the glass door of the building. She gave her name to the receptionist and sat down on one of the steel and canvas chairs. She picked up the *Irish Times* business supplement and began to read it.

The jobs pages were crammed with advertisements. 'Head of Treasury for World Name in Banking,' she read. She wondered who that could be. The ad had been placed by a leading recruitment company.

'Surely you're not thinking of moving?' Matt Connery had appeared behind her and she jumped. She'd been half watching the lifts opposite, expecting to see him arrive from there.

'I just like to keep aware of what's going on.' She smiled at him and folded the newspaper. 'I'm already the head of treasury for a world name in banking.'

He laughed. 'We're in the boardroom. It's on the second floor.'

She picked up the laptop and her briefcase and followed him across the small reception area.

'We're hoping to move from here in a few months,' said Matt as he pressed the button in the lift. 'We're sharing this building with three other companies and it's getting rather crowded.'

'Is that because you're expanding or because the others are?' asked Alix.

'Both.' He gestured to her to step out of the lift before him. 'We've taken on some more people but so has everyone else here. It's good news for industry generally, though.'

'Absolutely.' Alix followed him into a room dominated by a large chrome and glass table. There was a projection screen at one end.

'Is this all you need?' asked Matt.

'It's fine.' She nodded.

'Let me round up the posse and we can get underway.'

She stood in the boardroom and stared out of the window. She could see the motorway where cars, lorries and freight containers whizzed past. It was busy, she thought. The economy was still strong.

She attached a lead to the projector, switched on the computer and called up the presentation. She experienced the usual frisson of fear that somehow it wouldn't work, that the disk had been corrupted and that she'd look like a complete fool. But Power-Point whirred into action and the Europa Bank logo appeared on the screen.

Her heart was beating faster now. It always did just before she made a presentation. She could never decide whether she was nervous or excited. She wiped the palms of her hands against her skirt.

'Alix, this is Michael Hollis, our managing director.' Matt re-entered the room followed by four other men. 'And this is Josh Redmond, another director. We also have Peter Carmody and Declan Barr with us today.'

'Gentlemen.' Alix shook hands with them in turn. 'Thank you so much for coming along.'

'Thank you,' said Michael Hollis, 'for taking the time to come across the city to see us.'

'No trouble,' she said. 'My pleasure.'

She cleared her throat and looked at the men sitting round the table. She wanted to make them all believe in her and her ability to deliver. The fact that they'd done a few small deals with her was incidental. There was a lot more business that Anatronics would be in a position to do and she wanted to make sure that Europa Bank got all of it.

Matt Connery smiled encouragingly at her. He imagined that she must be nervous. It couldn't be easy, he thought, for such a beautiful girl to walk into a room of five men and start talking about forwards and options, caps and collars. He'd heard most of this from her already, from the time he'd called in to see her in Europa Bank. He smiled a little at the memory of her sitting on the steps to the bank, puffing away at her (last) cigarette. She'd been embarrassed, he knew. As though she'd been caught out doing something she shouldn't. That had made her seem more vulnerable and she'd compensated, he thought, by being incredibly businesslike in the meeting with him.

There was no doubt that she knew her stuff. Michael Hollis had just interrupted her and asked her to explain the pricing of an option. And she hadn't faltered for a moment, she broke it down into steps so simple that a school child could have understood.

Matt was fascinated by her. She looked absolutely wonderful in the purple suit with the unbusiness-length skirt and the tight jacket which was cut a tiny bit lower than he would have expected. Her green eyes glittered as she spoke and the sun caught the auburn tones in her hair.

Was she always this cool? he wondered. Was she the sort of

girl who put her career before everything or was she, secretly, a homebird who only wanted to meet the right man before she settled down into a life of suburban bliss?

He couldn't see her settling down into a life of suburban bliss somehow. But he really wanted to know what she was like outside of working hours.

He remembered her on the night of the Europa Bank reception. Still cool, still professional, even when he'd wandered up to the dealing room and found her sitting there in the dark.

There had to be more to her than he was seeing now, he thought. Then he remembered her words when he asked her what she did in her spare time. 'I go to the gym and I shoot.' She looked like a woman who went to the gym. She looked toned and healthy although Matt thought that there were dark smudges under her eyes. But that could always be make-up, he told himself. You never know with women and make-up. He wondered what she was like when she was shooting. Did she wear camouflage gear and paint on her cheekbones? Did she stand up in front of the target or shoot lying down?

He shifted in his seat. It wasn't a good idea to think of her lying down.

'Any further questions?' Alix looked around at them. 'Matt?'

He dragged his mind back to the meeting. 'I don't think so.'

'Michael? Josh?'

'Tell us about the people in your team,' said Josh. 'I know you're the person in charge, but what about the people who work for you? How good are they?'

'Excellent,' said Alix briskly. 'Dave Bryant, who's the senior dealer, has nearly ten years' experience in the markets. He worked in London and Frankfurt before coming back to

Dublin. Jenny Smith has been with the bank for seven years. She's hugely experienced in all types of corporate business. Gavin Donnelly was with Hypo Bank before he came to us.'

'That's the guy I've been speaking with,' said Matt. 'I thought he was the senior dealer.'

Alix regarded him calmly. 'Gavin is a very experienced member of the team.'

Michael Hollis stood up. 'Thanks again, Alix. We'll look over the stuff you've left with us and decide what to do about forward cover in both the Far East and the States. But we're really happy with what you've done for us so far.'

'Great.' She unplugged the laptop. 'Anytime you have any questions, give me a call.'

They shook her hand and filed out of the room until only Matt Connery remained.

'You were good,' he said.

'It's my job.' She zipped up the holder for the laptop.

'You get so passionate about it.'

'Not passionate,' she said. 'It makes sense for companies to manage risk. That's all I do. Talk to you about managing risk.'

'What sort of risks do you take yourself?' he asked.

'Me? Personally?' She raised her eyebrows. 'I'm not a risk-taker. I take risk for the bank, of course, but that's entirely different.'

'What about the shooting?' asked Matt.

'The shooting?' She grinned at him. 'Very, very risk-free. There's a range officer to make sure no one walks out onto the firing range by mistake. I have a special sling to protect my arm. And I always wear my earplugs.' She picked up her bags.

'Would you like to go to lunch?' asked Matt.

She looked at her watch. It was a quarter past twelve. 'I told them I'd be back by lunchtime,' she said.

'Surely this very experienced team can manage without you?' Matt's blue eyes twinkled at her.

'Touché.'

'So you'll lunch with me?'

'I'm hungry,' she confessed. 'Talking always makes me hungry.'

She rang the office before she left. The markets were still quiet. Both Dave and Gavin were out and Jenny was looking after things.

'But I might as well be out too,' she told Alix. 'It's boring.'

'Not to worry. If it's still like this when I get back you can head home.'

'Great, Alix, thanks.'

'I won't be too late,' said Alix. 'I think we're only going to the pub for lunch. There isn't much else around here.'

She followed Matt's black Audi to the Spawell leisure complex which offered food and drink as well as a par-three golf course, go-karting, tennis and snooker.

'Gosh,' said Alix. 'Everything for the busy executive.' She looked out to the driving range where all the booths were occupied despite it being a Friday.

'It's always busy,' said Matt. 'What would you like to eat?'

'Soup and a sandwich is fine,' Alix replied. 'I'm hungry, but I couldn't eat much more.' She sat down at a table near the window.

'Are you sure that's all you want?' Matt looked at her doubtfully.

Alix nodded. 'Truly. I don't eat a lot during the day.'

'OK.' He ordered the same for both of them and sat down beside her.

She caught the faint smell of Polo aftershave. She had bought Paul some Polo aftershave once. She suddenly missed him with an intensity that hurt.

'Alix? Are you all right?' Matt looked at her anxiously.

'Of course,' she said. 'Why?'

'You looked – strange.'

'I'm fine,' she said dismissively. 'Do you come here often?'

'Pardon?'

'For lunch, I mean.' She looked around the crowded bar area. 'Is this a local for you?'

'Sometimes,' he replied. 'We're not exactly in the same class as the financial services sector when it comes to flashy restaurants.'

'I try not to spend too much time in flashy restaurants,' she told him. 'Not good for the waistline.'

'You seem to have a pretty good waistline from where I'm sitting,' he said. 'All that time in the gym, I suppose.'

'You remember a lot about me,' said Alix. 'The gym, the shooting. You don't need to know all that.'

'I like knowing the people I deal with,' said Matt. 'I like the relationship to be more personal.'

She looked at him thoughtfully. 'What do you mean by personal?'

'Not personal,' he said hastily. 'Friendly. I mean friendly.'

'That's OK,' she said. 'I want to make sure we have everything straight. I don't do personal with my clients.'

'Who do you do personal with?' Matt could have kicked himself. The question had formed in his head and spilled out before he had a chance to stop it.

'I don't think that should matter to you.'

'I know,' he said. 'I'm sorry.'

A barman arrived with their food. Alix sprinkled salt onto her soup.

'It's bad for you,' said Matt. 'Too much salt.'

She put down her spoon. 'If we gave up everything that's bad for us we'd never do anything. I like salt.'

'What else do you like?'

'You really do want to know personal things, don't you?'

Matt shook his head. 'Sorry, forget it. You rang the office, didn't you? What's going on in the markets?'

Alix felt more comfortable now that they'd switched back to business talk. 'It's quiet,' she told him. 'Although the European Central Bank will be releasing their monetary policy statement next week. Should have a bit of action then.' She outlined her view on the European Central Bank's monetary policy.

Matt Connery listened to her but the words went over his head. He was too busy wondering what Alix Callaghan would be like in bed.

⌒

She got back to the office at three o'clock. Neither Gavin nor Dave were back from lunch. Jenny was playing Solitaire on the computer.

'How did the presentation go?' asked Jenny.

'Pretty good.' Alix sat down in her chair and put her feet up on the desk. 'They didn't ask anything I couldn't answer and they liked some of the hedging ideas.'

'Where did you go for lunch?'

'The Spawell. A soup and sandwich with Matt Connery.'

'Is he the tall, blond guy that was at the reception?'

Alix nodded.

'No wonder you don't want Gavin to have the account.' Jenny grinned wickedly at her. 'Why should you give up a hunk of muscle like that!'

'What?'

'Alix! He's absolutely gorgeous. Don't tell me you hadn't actually noticed!'

Alix frowned. 'Of course I noticed he's good-looking, Jen. I'm not blind. But he's not my type.'

'He's probably married,' said Jenny gloomily. 'The gorgeous ones always are.'

'He might be.' Alix shrugged. 'I didn't ask.'

'Was he wearing a wedding ring?'

She shrugged again. 'Don't think so.'

'Oh, Alix, you're absolutely hopeless. If you're going to be like that you might as well just marry Paul and have done with it!'

Marry Paul. If he'd asked her to marry him instead of bleating on about settling down and having babies, what would she have said? Alix sighed. She would have said yes, because she always imagined she would marry him someday. And she would have expected life to go on exactly as before.

'Alix? You OK?'

'Yes, absolutely.'

'Is everything all right between you and Paul?' asked Jenny. 'I thought that maybe—'

She broke off as Dave walked into the dealing room carrying a new golf club. 'Dennis gave it to me to try out,' he said. 'Looks good, doesn't it?'

'Great,' said Alix, relieved that she didn't have to talk to Jenny about Paul. She wouldn't have been able to lie to Jenny about him. She'd almost told her anyway. 'Who's Gavin lunching with?' she asked.

'Dunno.' Dave took a couple of practice swings with the club and almost put it through one of the screens. 'Oops, sorry, Alix.'

'Dave, how much have you had to drink?'

'Not much,' he assured her. 'We shared a bottle or two of Faustino and had a couple of beers.'

Alix sighed. 'Why don't you head off, Dave? It's quiet here anyway and there's no point in you hanging around.'

'They're still in the pub,' he told her. 'I was going to stay but I thought I'd better come back.'

'Decent of you,' she said. 'But feel free.'

'In that case, I'll see you on Monday.' He left the room whistling cheerfully.

'You might as well go yourself, Jenny,' said Alix. 'There's nothing happening.'

'OK, if you're sure.'

Alix nodded. 'Go ahead.'

She liked being in the room on her own. She liked knowing that information from all over the world was being concentrated on the screens in front of her.

She couldn't imagine giving it all up and having babies. Despite her grey hair and her biological clock. But she couldn't imagine doing both either. She didn't really believe it was possible to have it all. A lot of the time, she thought, it was difficult enough to have the part of it she had.

It was nearly half past four when Gavin returned. He looked surprised to see her there.

'I thought you'd stay out to lunch,' he said. His words were slurred.

'Just as well I didn't,' she said, 'since you decided to.'

'If I'd been you I would have stayed,' he told her. 'I would have stayed and I would have made sure that the Anatronics guy only ever wanted to talk to me.'

'I know,' said Alix.

Gavin blinked at her. 'How do you know?'

'I've seen people like you before,' she said. 'I know how you work.'

'Roy Dunphy offered me a job,' said Gavin. 'Corporate trader in Banco Andalucia.'

'And are you going to take it?' asked Alix.

Gavin shrugged.

'After all, there aren't so many corporate trader jobs these days. Since the euro, half of us have been wiped out. We're having to concentrate more and more on other options.'

'I might take it,' said Gavin. 'Or I might wait for your job.'

'It'll be a long wait,' said Alix. 'And you still have to think about Jenny and Dave.'

'Write off Jenny for a start,' said Gavin. 'She doesn't really care. And Dave wants to get out of trading.'

'Does he?' Alix kept her voice calm but she was surprised. She thought that Dave liked what he was doing.

'Ultimately,' said Gavin. 'He wants to be head of compliance.'

'Poacher turned gamekeeper.' Alix smiled.

'But I'm good,' Gavin told her. 'I'm the best dealer here.'

'Do you think so?'

'Yes,' said Gavin. 'I know I am.' He swayed a little on his feet.

'Why don't you go home,' said Alix. 'Or go back to the Harbourmaster – I think that's where Dave is. You and he can keep hatching your great career development plans. And when you've sobered up a bit, you can remember this conversation and feel embarrassed.'

'You could never embarrass me.' He stared her straight in the eye. 'Never.'

'We'll see,' said Alix.

～

She went to the gym after work and pumped iron until she was lathered in sweat. Then she went home, watched *Die Hard with a Vengeance* on TV and went to bed.

Chapter 11

Someone was chasing her. The road was long and straight and there was nowhere to hide. She could hear the sound of her attacker gaining on her and she tried for one last, desperate surge. But her legs were tired and someone seemed to have wrapped them up in heavy sacking because it was getting more and more difficult to move. And her pursuer was closing in now, she could hear the sound of his breathing over the bell ringing—

It was the phone. Alix emerged, tousle-headed, from the duvet which had wrapped itself around her as she slept. She was trembling with tension from the dream, from the fear of being caught.

'Hello.' Her voice shook.

'Alix? Are you OK?'

'Of course I am, Carrie.' She sat up in bed. The summer sun streamed through a chink in the curtains. 'I was asleep.'

'For heaven's sake!' Carrie sounded disgusted. 'It's ten o'clock on a glorious Saturday morning. What are you doing in bed?'

'Do you really want to know?' asked Alix.

'Oh! Alix! Don't tell me that you've actually—'

Alix laughed. 'I was having a nightmare, to tell you the truth. I'm kind of glad you called.'

'What sort of nightmare?'

'The chasing one,' said Alix.

Carrie murmured some words of sympathy. Alix had always had the chasing nightmare, even as a little girl. Carrie remembered her daughter coming into her bed, shaking with fright, terrified to go back to her own room and the shadowy someone who was running after her.

'It's OK,' said Alix impatiently. 'I'm fine now.'

'Well, get your ass out of bed and get in to the salon,' ordered Carrie. 'I have a cancellation for a twelve o'clock aromatherapy massage and it'll do you the world of good.'

'I don't need a massage,' said Alix. 'I need to do some shopping.'

'You've plenty of time for shopping,' said Carrie. 'Come on in. My God, loads of other women would kill for a free massage.'

'I'll pay you,' said Alix automatically.

'Not this time,' said Carrie. 'I want to give it to you. Cheer you up a bit.'

'I don't need cheering up,' Alix told her. 'I'm great. Honestly.'

'Everyone needs cheering up,' said Carrie. 'Twelve o'clock, Alix. See you then.'

Alix sighed as she got out of bed. She knew her mother was trying to be kind and supportive and she truly appreciated it. But she wasn't sure that she was ready for Carrie's questions yet or for her undoubted sympathy. She still hadn't got over the feeling of wanting to cry whenever she thought of Paul, even though she knew that she was being ridiculous.

She had a quick shower and pulled on a T-shirt and jeans. She'd been telling Carrie the truth when she said she needed to go shopping – there was virtually no food left in the apartment. She'd eaten the half-dozen Marks and Spencer dinners over the past couple of weeks – at least, she'd heated them up then discovered that she wasn't really hungry. There was no powder for the dishwasher (or maybe it was the washing machine), she needed toothpaste and dental floss, and, above all, she needed more beer and more wine.

Paul had always done the shopping. Paul was an efficient shopper who knew the prices of things and who always made sure that they didn't run out of any essentials. Even beer and wine.

Alix hated supermarkets. She felt ridiculous pushing a trolley around when she was only shopping for one, but those wire baskets weighed a ton when you put washing powder in them. She wished she'd checked whether it was dishwasher or washing-machine stuff that she needed. Not knowing meant that she had to buy both.

'Are you a club card holder?' asked the girl at the checkout.

Alix looked at her in bewilderment. 'Club card?'

'Do you have an in-store card?' the girl asked patiently.

'I don't think so,' said Alix. She shook her head. 'No, I don't.'

'Would you like to apply?'

Alix knew that there was a queue of impatient people behind her.

'Next time,' she said hastily. 'When I've more time.'

She paid for the purchases and carried them to the car. Were they club card holders? she wondered. Paul had never mentioned it to her. Not that it made any difference, she told herself. But it would have been nice to know.

She parked her car in Drury Street car park and made her way to Carrie's salon. She was dreading meeting her mother. She was afraid that she'd cry and, after the awful day when John Callaghan had walked out, she'd never cried in front of her mother again. Carrie had wanted them to be strong. Alix had wanted to be strong for her mother. She didn't want Carrie worrying about her, thinking that she couldn't cope. Besides, Carrie didn't cry. Carrie hadn't sat around and wondered what she should do with her life. Carrie had got on with things, worked at her business, earned success.

But it would be nice, Alix thought wistfully as she pushed open the door of Destressed, to have the kind of mother you didn't mind seeing you cry.

'Alix! You look . . .' Carrie Callaghan regarded her daughter thoughtfully, 'not as bad as I expected.'

'Well, thanks.' Alix gave her mother a peck on the cheek. 'You look wonderful, as always.'

'Thank you.' Carrie glanced at her reflection in the wall mirror. 'I do my best to advertise my work.'

She was a good advertisement. At fifty-five she was an elegant woman, fine-boned, with ash-blonde hair and eyes which were the same intriguing shade as her daughter's. Carrie's white shirt and navy trousers emphasised the trim body of a woman who looked after herself.

'Hi, Alix!' Samantha Sullivan, Carrie's twentysomething assistant, opened the door of one of the treatment rooms and glanced over the reception area. 'Having the works, are you?'

'Just a massage,' replied Alix.

'Nice,' Samantha smiled. 'Carrie, I forgot to mention that

Mrs Burton will be in at three for her facial. She changed it this morning and I knew you wouldn't mind.'

'Of course not,' said Carrie. Bernadette Burton was the wife of a senior government minister but, as Carrie said to Alix while she lay on the massage table, she was as nice as anything and wouldn't change an appointment without good reason.

'So is there anything I should know about government policy?' asked Alix.

'Nothing I could tell you,' said Carrie primly. She poured some oil onto Alix's back and began to knead her muscles. 'Good God, Alix, you're even more tense than usual!'

'Yeah, yeah.' Alix heard this every time her mother gave her a massage.

'I mean it,' said Carrie. 'Your shoulders are completely knotted. This business about Paul must be getting to you.'

'It's because I was busy yesterday.' Alix shifted a little to make herself more comfortable. 'I had a presentation to do and it took up a lot of time. The others left the office early and there was a settlements problem with some Greek drachma.'

'So that's why you're tense and that's why you had the chasing dream? A piddling little presentation and something wrong with Greek drachma?'

Alix sighed. 'It wasn't a piddling little presentation, it was a very important account. And three billion drachma had been paid into the wrong bank. Could have been very costly.'

'So the Paul thing isn't upsetting you at all?' Carrie's tone was neutral.

'Of course it's a bit upsetting,' Alix mumbled. 'Naturally it's making me a little tense.'

'Tell me about it.'

'I've told you already.'

'Not about the French woman, you haven't.'

I will *kill* Wyn, thought Alix viciously. I will tear her limb from limb. 'Honestly, Carrie,' she said mildly, 'haven't you and Wyn anything better to do than talk about me?'

'I told you before, we worry about you.'

'Worry about me!' Alix snorted. 'What's there to worry about? I have a good job, a nice apartment and a decent car. There's no need to worry about me. Ouch!'

Carrie prodded her daughter just below her shoulder blade. 'Very tense,' she said. 'Very, very tense.'

'You're making me tense,' said Alix. 'Look, I know you and Wyn love your gossipy evenings and telephone conversations and everything but there's nothing wrong with me and it's up to me to decide what I want to do about Paul.'

'Are you sure that it's not up to Paul to decide what he wants to do about you? Or his French girl?'

'Will you *stop* talking about this French woman,' snapped Alix.

'But she must be part of the equation.'

'She was a catalyst,' said Alix. 'Paul admitted that. But he hasn't run off with her or anything. She isn't even in the country.'

'Is he?'

'Yes,' said Alix shortly. 'He is.'

She hoped he was. She hoped he was at home tapping away on a keyboard, writing something against a deadline. She didn't like to think that he might be in Paris with Sabine. He couldn't be in Paris with Sabine. He didn't have time. He was working too hard – too busy to meet her earlier in the week.

138

'Tell me about her anyway,' Carrie said.

'Her name is Sabine,' Alix sighed. 'She's a designer. He met her in Paris.'

'And?'

'What?'

'What did they do in Paris?'

'For heaven's sake, Carrie!' Alix tried to turn over but her mother's hands on her shoulders prevented her. 'I don't bloody know.'

'You should,' said Carrie. She tipped some oil onto Alix's thighs and began to massage them.

'Maybe I don't want to know,' Alix admitted.

'It's hard for a man living with a successful woman,' said Carrie. 'And when he gets to Paul's age and starts thinking about a family, maybe it gets harder.'

'He could have talked to me about it.' Alix buried her head in the towel at the top of the table. 'We could have worked it out.'

'And now?'

Alix was silent for a moment. 'If I decide he's worth it, then I'll get him back,' she said.

'You're done,' said Carrie. 'Lie there for a couple of minutes and relax.'

She walked out of the room and Alix closed her eyes. She hated to think about Carrie and Wyn talking about her. She hated the fact that she was the object of their concern. Of their sympathy. She didn't want to be the object of anyone's sympathy. She was OK. She could cope.

The piped music was restful. She stopped raging at her mother and her sister and let Dvorak's New World Symphony soothe her.

'What are you doing for the rest of the day?'

Alix jumped, she hadn't heard Carrie open the door. 'I'm going to dinner with Terry and Wyn tonight,' she said. 'Where I will tell my bloody sister to stop gossiping with my bloody mother about me.'

'I told you, we weren't gossiping.' Carrie stood beside her daughter. 'Going anywhere nice?'

'I don't know,' said Alix. 'They want me to make up the numbers. Some business thing of Terry's.'

'Let me give you a facial,' suggested Carrie. 'You might as well look good anyhow.'

Alix screwed up her face. 'You mean I don't?'

'Let's just say that every little helps.'

Alix enjoyed facials. She decided to let her mother have her way.

~

It was still warm by the time Alix was dressing for dinner. She chose a long, floaty dress in burnt sienna by Ghost, which emphasised her willowy frame and made her look both serene and elegant. She wore the gold earrings and gold necklace that Paul had bought her the previous Christmas. She'd intended to wear the emerald jewellery that she'd bought herself but had suddenly wanted something that Paul had given her. She sprayed herself with Dune which was her favourite evening perfume.

She wondered about tonight's dinner party. Wyn enjoyed entertaining and would happily cater for dozens of people, given the opportunity. Paul had never really liked going to Wyn's parties, although he always seemed to enjoy himself once he was there. At least, thought Alix as the taxi she'd ordered turned into Wyn's driveway, I won't have to worry if he's having a good time.

Nobody else had arrived. The only other car in the drive was Terry's.

'Hi, Alix! You look lovely!' Wyn smiled at her as she held open the front door.

'Hi, Wyn.' Alix kissed her on the cheek. 'So do you.' Wyn was wearing a pastel-pink linen dress and looked cool and refreshed in the warmth of the evening. 'Am I the first?'

'You're the only,' Wyn told her. 'We're not eating here tonight.'

'We're not?'

Wyn shook her head. 'Terry's booked Roly's.'

'Oh.' Alix was surprised. She rarely went out to dinner with her sister and her husband.

'We felt it would be best,' said Wyn. 'Otherwise Cathal might feel overwhelmed.'

'Overwhelmed?' Alix looked at her sister suspiciously. 'Who is this Cathal person? And who else is coming along?'

Wyn was saved from answering by Nessa and Aoife hurling themselves out of the kitchen and along the hallway to wrap their arms round Alix.

'Yes, yes, of course I brought you something,' she said in response to their eager questions. 'Don't I always?' She handed them each some sweets. 'Only for heaven's sake don't eat them all in one go. You know your mother doesn't approve.'

'Oh, she doesn't mind really,' said Nessa calmly. 'She never lets us eat sweets normally, that's why we like it when you come, Alix.'

'It's so nice to be wanted.' Alix grimaced.

'Terry! Are you ready yet? Alix is here!' Wyn shouted up the stairs to her husband.

'Of course I am,' he answered as he came downstairs. 'No need to yell, Wyn.'

'I thought you were beautifying yourself.' She smiled at him and kissed him on the lips.

'OK,' said Terry. 'Are we ready?'

'Sure.' Wyn opened the living-room door. 'Girls, see you later. Behave yourselves and do what Miranda tells you. Miranda,' she looked at the baby-sitter, 'get them to bed by ten.'

'OK, Mrs Mitchell.' Miranda looked up from the book she was reading.

'See you.' Wyn blew a kiss at her daughters. 'Be good.'

Alix followed her sister and brother-in-law outside. Terry unlocked his Audi and held the door open for Alix.

'Tell me about tonight,' said Alix as Terry started the car. 'Why are we going to a restaurant? Who else is going to be here? What does this Cathal bloke do?'

She saw Wyn and Terry exchange a quick glance.

'Wyn!' She leaned forward. 'What is tonight all about?'

'It's not about anything,' said Wyn. 'It's just dinner, that's all.'

'But who else is going to be here?' asked Alix urgently. 'Who—'

'The four of us,' said Terry. 'You and Cathal. Wyn and myself.'

'Is this some sort of set-up?' demanded Alix. 'You've never had a dinner party for one person before. What exactly is all this about?'

'Cathal Moran is a really nice bloke who works in our finance department,' said Terry quickly. 'You'll like him, Alix. You'll have a lot in common with him.'

'Will I?'

'Absolutely,' said Wyn. 'Truly, Alix, he's really sweet. And he's just come back from two years in Brussels. He doesn't know anyone.'

'Wyn.' Alix's voice was dangerously low. 'Is this some kind of blind date?'

'I wouldn't put it like that,' said Wyn.

'How exactly would you put it?'

'It's just a dinner engagement.'

'Is this a business dinner or a social dinner?' asked Alix.

'A bit of both.'

'I don't believe it.' Alix flopped back into the seat. 'I don't believe you two! You're setting me up with some bloke I've never met before. What on earth has got into you?'

'Oh, come on, Alix.' Wyn turned to look at her. 'I told you, Cathal's a decent guy. He's lonely. We thought it would be nice if—'

'Well, you bloody thought wrong!' said Alix angrily. 'I'm not going to dinner with someone I haven't met before and I'm not taking part in some ridiculous dating game you've set up.'

'Alix, be reasonable,' said Terry. 'It is partly business. Cathal is an up-and-coming member of the company. I want to take him under my wing a bit.'

'Terry, I don't want to get involved with up-and-coming people,' said Alix. 'I know enough of them already.'

'Oh, be a sport, Alix. Besides, you might like him.'

Alix gritted her teeth. 'I don't want to like him.'

'That's being silly,' said Wyn. 'You're cutting off your nose to spite your face.'

I wish I'd cut off yours, thought Alix, seething with rage, then you wouldn't keep sticking it in my business.

She was still angry as she followed Terry and Wyn up the stairs into the restaurant. Normally she liked the buzz of conversation, the chink of glasses, the clatter of crockery. But all she wanted to do now was to go home. She hated being manipulated like this.

Cathal Moran was already at the table. He stood up as they arrived and Alix guessed he was around six feet tall. He had sandy hair, grey eyes and a light tan that covered a cheerful, freckled face.

'Hope we didn't keep you waiting,' said Terry.

'Not at all.' Cathal smiled at them. 'Nice to see you again, Wyn. And this must be Alix.' He held out his hand to her.

Alix grasped it firmly and shook it. 'Hi.'

'I've heard so much about you,' said Cathal.

'I've heard so little about you,' said Alix wryly as she sat down.

'What do you want to know?'

'I haven't decided yet.' Alix took a menu from the waiter and opened it.

'Anyone like a drink?' Terry asked.

'Gin and tonic,' said Alix.

'Same for me,' Cathal nodded.

'Martini,' said Wyn.

'And I'll have a gin and tonic too,' Terry told the waiter.

The four of them studied their menus in silence. Alix peeped over the top of hers and quickly looked away when she realised that Cathal was observing her. I'll kill them, she thought again. They'll wish they'd never been born! What on earth was Wyn thinking about, agreeing to this charade?

144

She kept her menu open until well after the others had closed theirs.

'How were the markets this week?' asked Cathal when she finally put the menu down on the table.

'Quiet,' said Alix.

'Are the Brits going to cut interest rates?' he asked.

Alix shrugged. 'Hard to say.'

'Is it likely? Do you think they should?'

'Since none of the economists agree, it probably doesn't matter an awful lot what I think.' God, she thought, you sound so petulant. It's not his fault he's been dragged out here too. 'But yes,' she added, 'I think they should.'

'So is it as exciting working in a dealing room as everyone says?' asked Cathal. 'I remember when I was in college, so many of the guys wanted to give financial services a go.'

'It's a job,' replied Alix. 'I enjoy it.'

'But what about the male-dominated part of it?' Cathal asked. 'Don't you find it difficult giving orders to a load of men?'

'No.'

Wyn stifled a giggle and Cathal sighed. 'That's me put in my place.'

Alix shrugged. 'I'm sorry, but people ask me that all the time. It doesn't make any difference to me whether I work with men or women. Men are more confrontational, certainly. Women try to be more helpful. But at the end of the day you either make money or you don't and it doesn't matter whether you're a man or a woman then.'

'I worked for a woman once.' Cathal buttered a slice of tomato bread. 'She was pretty good. But she gave it up to have babies.'

Alix tensed. She didn't want to get into this particular debate.

'But Terry tells me that you've no interest in children.'

She flicked an angry glance at her brother-in-law who was unconcernedly looking around the restaurant.

'Alix is very good with children,' said Wyn. 'She treats my two daughters like they were her own.'

No, I don't, thought Alix. If they were my kids I wouldn't bring them Bertie Bassett sweets every time I came home. I wouldn't play hospitals with them and let them inject me with the meat baster!

'I like children,' said Cathal. 'Although I'm certainly not in a rush to settle down and have any!' He beamed at Alix who smiled weakly in return.

The waiter came with their drinks and took their dinner order. Alix gulped some gin and tonic.

'Have you ever made a whole heap of money?' asked Cathal. 'Or – worse still, I suppose – lost it?'

'I've done both at various points,' replied Alix. 'And making it is certainly better fun.'

'You make a lot of money, don't you?' said Wyn.

'For me or for the bank?' Alix asked.

'For the bank, of course.'

'I suppose I do.'

'And what do you do for recreation?' asked Cathal. 'I knew a dealer in Brussels who was into hang-gliding. He'd jump off the edges of cliffs on his hang-glider! Had dreadful trouble with his life assurance.'

Alix smiled slightly. 'I don't do anything half as hazardous.'

'What about the shooting?' asked Terry.

'That's not dangerous,' Alix laughed. 'Unless you're a piece of paper!'

'Remember when you took up judo?' Wyn made a face at

Alix. 'And you did some throw and dislocated your shoulder? Poor Carrie nearly had a fit.'

'That was years ago,' Alix reminded her. 'And someone threw me. I just didn't land properly.'

Cathal smiled and leaned back in his chair. 'At least it means that you can look after yourself, Alix,' he said. 'And whoever you go out with too. No worrying about muggers at any rate.'

'I guess not,' she said as the waiter put her roulade of crab in front of her. 'I guess not.'

～

He wasn't bad, she admitted to herself as she touched up her make-up in the ladies'. He kept quizzing her about her life but she couldn't blame him if he was a direct sort of guy. And, during the meal, he'd lightened up a bit, related some stories about his work in the European Commission in Brussels. But she didn't find him remotely attractive. They'd both reached for the salt at the same time and his hand had brushed against hers and she felt absolutely nothing. He'd smiled at her then, a kind of complicit smile, but it had left her cold.

She wished Terry and Wyn hadn't set this whole evening up. It wasn't fair on her and it certainly wasn't fair on Cathal who seemed to have been living the life of a monk in Brussels, if his stories were to be believed. No time for anything but work. No wonder he was pleased to be home.

She ran her fingers through her hair and leaned towards the mirror. The roots were beginning to show a little grey again. She bit her lip. She wondered what Cathal thought about grey-haired women.

He lived in Ranelagh and offered to share a taxi home with her.

'Good idea,' said Wyn.

'I was going to walk,' said Alix. 'It's not far. And it takes Cathal out of his way.'

'Not really,' he said. 'But if you want to walk, I'll join you as far as your apartment. Make sure you get home safely.'

Alix groaned to herself. She'd realised, almost as soon as the words were out, that she'd made a mistake to talk about walking. 'Don't feel as though you have to,' she told him. 'I walk quite fast. As exercise.'

'I could do with some exercise myself after that meal.' Cathal patted his stomach. 'Terry, it was great. Thanks very much.'

'No problem,' said Terry as he signed the Amex slip. 'We like to make sure everyone feels welcome in the firm.'

'I feel very welcome now,' said Cathal. 'Wyn, thanks for giving up your Saturday night.'

'Cathal, it's not like my Saturdays are a riot of entertainment.' She grinned at him. 'It's dreadful to need an excuse for my husband to take me out.'

It was warm outside. The gentle breeze drifted along the road and rustled through the trees of Herbert Park. Alix pushed a strand of hair out of her eyes.

'We'll be off then,' she said. 'I'll give you a call, Wyn.'

'Yes, do.' Her sister kissed her. 'Safe home.'

'It's OK, Wyn, she has me to look after her,' Cathal said. 'And she *is* a judo expert, isn't she?' He grinned at them. 'See you Monday, Terry.'

'See you, Cathal.' Terry and Wyn walked hand in hand to their parked car.

Alix wished she had pockets so that she could shove her own hands into them.

'I like your brother-in-law,' said Cathal as they began to walk. 'He's friendly. So's your sister.'

'Yes.'

'I thought you would be more outgoing,' he said candidly. 'I always thought that dealers were the in-your-face sort.'

'And is that the sort you prefer?' asked Alix.

'Not at all.' Cathal took her arm. 'I like you, Alix.'

She felt herself flinch. 'I like you too,' she said. 'But I've got to be honest with you, Cathal, I'm not looking to go out with anyone right now.'

'Why not?'

'I'm really still in a relationship.'

'Not according to Terry,' said Cathal calmly. 'According to Terry you've split up with your boyfriend.'

'Have you been talking to him about me?' she demanded.

'Only chatting.' Cathal steered her across the road. 'So don't get uptight about it, for heaven's sake!'

'Look.' Alix stopped walking and turned to him. 'I don't know exactly what Terry's agenda is, or yours, or Wyn's. But the truth of the matter is that I haven't yet split with the man I've known for the past three years. And even if I had I'm not ready to go out with someone new yet. And even if I was, I don't know if that person would be you.'

Cathal raised his eyebrows. 'Don't tell me I fall down on all your requirements?'

She smiled at him. 'Of course not. But I'm not ready to jump into the whole going-out thing again. Honestly, I'm not.'

'Hey, I'm not ready for any great commitment either,' said Cathal easily. 'Let's wait and see, OK?'

'OK,' she said.

They walked in silence back to her apartment. She didn't ask him in for coffee and he didn't try to kiss her goodnight.

She was still going to kill Wyn. And Terry. And anybody else who tried to mess with her life.

Chapter 12

Alix unlocked the apartment door, went straight into the kitchen and rummaged in the bottom drawer of the fitted unit to find her emergency packet of cigarettes. Despite the fact that she'd left all the windows open, the apartment was like an oven. She opened the patio door and stepped out onto the balcony. The air was milky-warm on her bare arms.

Alix lit a cigarette and breathed in the smoke. Part of her was disappointed in herself for lighting it in the first place. Another part of her was grateful for its soothing properties. She inhaled again and the tip of the cigarette glowed in the darkness.

She thought about Cathal Moran as she leaned on the balcony rail and stared into the inky blackness of the canal. He definitely wasn't her type. She wasn't exactly sure what her type of man really was, since all of her boyfriends had been very different. But she knew, somehow, that it wasn't Cathal.

There'd been quite a few boyfriends when she was still at school, but none of them had lasted very long. It wasn't that she'd had any problem grappling with them in the laneway beside her home, or that she'd been shy about trying alcohol or cigarettes or doing any of the things that Carrie hoped she wouldn't do, it was just that she grew bored with them very quickly. What was the point, she'd once asked Wyn, in wasting time with blokes that just weren't interesting? Practice, Wyn had told her, but Alix had shrugged and said she didn't need any.

Sophia Redmond, who'd been her best friend at college and who had worked with Morgan Stanley in New York for a couple of years before being headhunted back to London, had once told her that she never let men get close enough.

Alix had retorted that she'd let far too many of them get close. But she knew that Sophia wasn't entirely wrong. There was always a point in her relationships when she panicked, when someone wanted more commitment than she was prepared to give. And that was the point at which she would call it a day. She had always been the one to call it a day.

'You definitely have a problem,' Sophia told her the day after she had split up with yet another boyfriend, a solicitor named Christopher Symmons. 'You just can't hack togetherness.'

'Not at all,' she'd replied briskly. 'I just haven't met my type yet.'

And now, standing alone on the balcony of the apartment which she'd bought herself five years earlier, she wondered if she ever would.

She thought it had been different with Paul. She hadn't expected to fall for a journalist who thought her job was a heap of rubbish even though the subsequent article made her sound like a cross between Margaret Thatcher, Kate Moss and Ulrika Jonsson. *'Callaghan needs very little sleep. She hits the hay around midnight and is up before six most mornings. But you wouldn't know it to look at her. She is tall and slender with an arresting face and eyes that glitter like a pair of emeralds. But it's not all work for Callaghan. Friday nights see her drinking pints with the lads and she never once during this interview complained about sexism in the workplace.'*

She'd had to endure a lot of stick from her colleagues in the bank after that had appeared. But she hadn't cared. For the first time in her life she liked someone ringing her in the office, or waiting for her in reception or cooking her dinner at night. Paul had seen her as someone to take care of and she'd enjoyed the way he looked after her. She'd *allowed* him to look after her. She'd let him get close and she'd opened up to him and now it looked as if that had been a terrible mistake.

So now she was supposed to start all over again. Meet new men. Find out about their likes and dislikes. Learn what made them tick. She shuddered. She wasn't ready for all that. She didn't want to do it all over again. She'd been right never to get involved before. And she wasn't going to become some manic thirtysomething looking for a man, any man.

Was this how people saw her now? A solitary, ageing female for whom they would have to trawl their lists of acquaintances to find a remotely suitable man? Instead of Alix Callaghan, have-it-all, successful, envied financial dealer who lived with an attractive, articulate man, she would now be Alix Callaghan, single, depending on her job for fulfilment but never quite finding it. She was an Alix Callaghan that deserved sympathy because she was thirty-two and had wasted three years of her life on a bloke who was quite prepared to run off with the first available blonde that came into his life. Alix Callaghan, the odd number at dinner parties. Alix Callaghan who'd probably end up looking through the lonely hearts columns of newspapers and afraid to ring up any of them in case they were sickos.

She finished her cigarette and flicked it over the balcony and into the canal. She was ashamed of herself for doing that because she was firmly anti-pollution as far as the canal was concerned, but she'd felt like doing something bad. She recognised the feeling from her childhood, when she'd deliberately drop a plate when drying the dishes or splash a tidal wave of water over the side of the bath when she was getting in. Carrie would look at her impatiently and ask her if she was born clumsy and Alix would stick out her jaw and say, yes, she was.

She could see Carrie now, in her imagination, standing in the living room looking out at her and asking if she just wanted to stay alone forever. Because, she could almost hear Carrie say, you'll have to make an effort, Alix. Most of the good ones have been snapped up by now.

The phone rang and startled her. She went back inside and picked up the receiver.

'Hello?'

'Hi, Alix.'

'Who's that?'

'How quickly they forget!' The man's voice was amused. 'It's me. Cathal.'

'Cathal! How did you get my number?'

'I got Wyn to write it on the back of the business card you gave me,' he told her. 'I really didn't want to call you at work.'

God, thought Alix, Wyn was really pushing it. She was going to have a real heart-to-heart with Wyn. Tell her that she, Alix, was perfectly capable of looking after her own love life, thank you very much. And stop bloody interfering.

'I rang to say that I enjoyed tonight,' said Cathal.

'Did you?'

'Oh, absolutely. I like Terry and I like Wyn. But, obviously, it was you I liked the most.'

Alix made a face at the phone. This was the corniest line she'd ever heard. She said nothing.

'So I was wondering if you'd like to get together again sometime?'

She sighed. 'I thought I told you—'

'You said you weren't ready for commitment. I understand. Neither am I. But there's nothing wrong with us being friends.'

'I'm not a great believer in the theory that men and women can be good friends,' said Alix wryly. 'Sex usually complicates matters sooner or later.'

'Hey, it was you that brought up sex, not me. Just remember that in the future, will you?' Cathal sounded amused, and despite herself, Alix smiled.

'Thanks for ringing,' she said. 'But I've got to go, Cathal. I'm very tired.'

'So what about another night?'

'Maybe,' she compromised. 'I'm honestly not sure.'

'How about I call you next week?' suggested Cathal. 'Give you a bit of time to think about it.'

'Yes, fine.' Suddenly Alix wanted the conversation to be over. 'I've got to go, Cathal. 'Bye!'

'Goodbye,' he said, but he was already talking to a dialling tone.

She poured herself a gin and tonic and went back outside.

∽

Cathal stood on the pavement opposite her apartment and wished that he could see the balconies on the other side of the block. He was sure she'd be sitting on the balcony. He'd hoped she'd ask him up. The fact that she hadn't made him feel very uncomfortable. He was beginning to lose his touch.

He sighed and put his mobile phone back in the pocket of his jacket. Then he flagged down a taxi to take him home.

～

Alix couldn't sleep. She turned over in the double bed and pushed the light summer duvet away from her. She'd never been so warm in her life, not even on the holiday in Greece when there'd been a heat wave that had sent everyone, tourists and natives, scurrying for cover.

She wondered what Paul was doing now. It was difficult to imagine that, at the exact same moment, he was living his life, not even thinking about her, not caring about her. When she tried to picture him, the images of Sabine cluttered her memories so that she couldn't separate the pictures of Paul from the visions of his latest love.

He doesn't love Sabine, she told herself fiercely. And he isn't going to move in with her and have babies. It's a revolting concept. If he wants babies, he can have them with me.

But she found that concept even more revolting.

～

She started to sneeze at three o'clock. She sat up in the bed and reached for a tissue. Her eyes hurt and her head throbbed. Though it was still warm in the room, she shivered. Bloody hell, she thought, don't tell me I'm coming down with a cold. We've had the hottest summer in living memory and I might have a cold. Bloody wonderful!

She pulled on a T-shirt and went into the kitchen. Her throat was hurting now and every bone in her body ached. She poured herself some orange juice. She peered blearily at the carton as she closed it again. Best before 15 July. Out of date. If the cold didn't kill her, the orange juice probably would.

She got back into bed and pulled the duvet around her. She was shivering now, really cold. She wished that she had some-one – anyone – to cuddle her. Selfish bitch, she told herself, wrapping herself even more tightly in the duvet. Whoever it was wouldn't thank you for giving them the flu.

She tossed and turned, alternately cold and hot, before falling into a fitful sleep around six o'clock. She opened her eyes again at seven, wished that she had her gun handy so that she could shoot the magpie that was screeching outside her window, and then suddenly fell into a deep and dreamless sleep.

The phone woke her. She was tired of the phone waking her, she thought, as she reached for the receiver.

'Hello?'

'God, Alix, you sound rotten.'

'Thanks, Wyn.'

'What on earth did you and Cathal get up to last night?' Her sister chuckled. 'It wasn't that late when we left you.'

'It wasn't late when he left me either. Hold on a second, will you?' Alix dropped the receiver on the bed and reached for another tissue. Her nose was sore. She bet it was red.

'You OK?' asked Wyn.

'More or less,' replied Alix. 'I've got a cold.'

'Poor thing.' Wyn didn't sound in the slightest bit sympa-thetic. 'Do you need anything? Will you be OK?'

'I need peace and quiet,' said Alix. 'And I'll be fine.'

'I just called to see how you and Cathal got on,' said Wyn. 'But I'll phone back if you like.'

'No need.' Alix lay down, holding a tissue to her nose

and the phone to her ear. 'There was no getting on, as you put it.'

'Alix, he's a perfectly nice guy. What's wrong with him?'

'Nothing,' Alix told her. 'Absolutely nothing.'

'Didn't you have a decent conversation as you walked home? Did you ask him in for coffee?'

'Really, Wyn, don't be ridiculous. Of course I didn't ask him in for coffee. What d'you take me for? If I'd asked him in for coffee we would have ended up in bed and I didn't want to go to bed with him.'

'You don't have to go to bed with everyone you invite into the apartment for coffee,' said Wyn waspishly.

'Well, Cathal Moran would have expected it,' said Alix.

'Not necessarily.'

'Yes necessarily.'

'But—'

'Look, Wyn, he's a perfectly decent bloke and all that but there's really no need for you to try and fix me up with someone. I'm capable of looking after myself.'

'We weren't trying to fix you up.' Wyn sounded hurt. 'Terry had asked Cathal about dinner ages ago. We would have invited you and Paul if you'd been able to hang on to him.'

'What do you mean, "hang on to him"?' demanded Alix.

'Oh, come on,' said Wyn. 'You've got to face facts. He's dumped you for some French crumpet and he's not coming back. All this shit about space and everything is just a sop to his conscience.'

'Actually,' said Alix as she burrowed even deeper beneath the duvet, 'Paul and I are meeting for a drink on Wednesday. So you can just forget about your stupid matchmaking plans with Cathal. Thanks all the same!'

'A drink? You and Paul?'

'I told you but you didn't believe me.' Alix blew her nose. 'It *is* all about space and time and working things out.'

'He'll probably just tell you it's all over,' said Wyn.

'Gee, thanks for your support!'

'These on-again-off-again things seldom work out,' Wyn told her. 'And I'm not trying to be mean to you, Alix. All I'm saying is that you can't hang about any more. You've wasted your three best years with Paul. You need to get out there and find someone else before it's too late.'

'For Christ's sake!' Alix was so annoyed that she sat up, even though it made her head ache. 'You're talking as though I was on my last legs, Wyn. I'm thirty-two years old, not a candidate for the Sunnyside Home for Retired Gentlewomen. I have a great life as it is. I don't need someone in it. I might choose to have someone in it, but that's entirely different.'

'You're nearly thirty-three,' Wyn told her. 'Terry and I didn't manage to have kids straightaway. It might be the same for you. Next thing you know you're in your late thirties, childless and struggling to conceive. And don't tell me that's rubbish because it isn't. It's exactly what'll happen. You just don't hear your bloody clock ticking because you're obsessed with that stupid job!'

'I don't need to hear any clock ticking,' said Alix furiously. 'And who says I want any kids anyway? And even if I did, it's up to me to decide when to have them.'

'No, it's not,' said Wyn. 'You might decide when you'd like to have them and your body might disagree. You've got to face facts, Alix. You can't control everything.'

'I don't need to control everything.'

'Of course you do,' said Wyn. 'You plan, you manipulate,

you do exactly what you want when you want. You control, Alix. But you can't control your biological clock. It's doing its own thing and it isn't waiting for you.'

'You can be a real bitch sometimes.' Alix blew her nose again.

'I'm just telling you stuff you don't want to hear,' said Wyn.

'Well, thanks for waking me up and reminding me that I'm an ageing single woman with nothing to look forward to.'

'You can look forward to another date with Cathal.'

'No, I can't.'

'Why not?'

'Because he's not my type.'

'Oh, for crying out loud!' Wyn's tone was sheer exasperation. 'Of course he's your type. Corporate. Businesslike. Works out in the gym. Exactly like you, Alix. Exactly.'

'Then maybe that's why he isn't my type,' said Alix triumphantly.

'Alix,' said Wyn gently, 'believe me. One day you'll wake up and there won't be any of your type left.'

'Goodbye, Wyn,' said Alix.

'I'm only trying to—'

'I'm going back to sleep,' said Alix. 'I want to get rid of this cold by tomorrow. I have a busy day at the office ahead of me.'

But her cold got worse, not better. By four o'clock in the afternoon she'd gone through an entire box of Kleenex for Men and her nose was like a red beacon. Her throat was sore and her eyes continually watered.

She sat, shivering, on the sofa and watched black-and-white movies on TV while trying to read the business section of the *Sunday Times*. The last time she'd had a cold like this, Paul had brought her hot toddies and made her stay in bed. But she didn't like staying in the double bed on her own. She wished he was here now, to rub her aching shoulders and tell her that she'd be better before she was twice married. Huh, she thought miserably, how right he was.

She found a bottle of Night Nurse in the bathroom cabinet and took a dose at seven o'clock. Then she went back to bed and fell asleep.

～

For the third day in a row, the phone woke her. She picked up the receiver and tried to say hello, but a strangled croak was all that came out of her mouth.

'Alix, is that you?'

'Yes,' she rasped.

'It's me, Jenny. When you weren't in by eight I thought I should ring. You know you have a meeting with Des and the finance guy from Sorrento Products at ten, don't you?'

Alix glanced at the alarm clock. She'd forgotten to set it the previous night. But she never slept as long as this. Thirteen hours! It must have been the Night Nurse.

'I've got a slight cold,' she said.

'What?'

'A cold,' said Alix.

'You sound terrible,' said Jenny. 'Do you want me to cancel the meeting? Or let Dave go instead?'

'No,' Alix croaked. 'I'll be in. I have a lot of stuff for that meeting.'

'Are you sure?' asked Jenny doubtfully. 'It sounds like more than a cold to me, Alix.'

'I'll be there,' said Alix painfully. 'Don't worry.'

She hauled herself out of bed and into the shower. The hot water helped but she still felt rotten. She stood in the bathroom, wrapped in a blue-and-white striped towel, and wished, for the first time ever, that she didn't have to go in to the office.

She dried her hair and pulled it back and secured it with a tortoiseshell clip. Her face was blotchy, as though she'd spent the night crying. Her skin was sensitive and stung when she applied some foundation.

But the make-up made her look less haggard. She sprayed herself liberally with Issey Miyake perfume. She hoped she hadn't been too heavy-handed. Her nose was so blocked that she couldn't smell a thing.

∽

There was an air of quiet efficiency about the dealing room. Jenny was on the phone to a dealer in London, Dave was chatting to one of their customers and Gavin was plotting a moving average graph of sterling two-year bond prices.

Alix went into her small office and logged on to her computer. She opened the file with the material for this morning's meeting. The light of the screen made her eyes water. She took out her compact and checked her nose. Despite the foundation, it was still red.

'Line two, Alix,' said Jenny over the intercom. 'Charlie Mulholland for you.'

'Can you take it?' Alix whispered. 'I'm trying to save my voice.'

'Sure.'

Alix took an Extra-Strong Fisherman's Friend lozenge from the box she kept in her drawer. The menthol taste nearly blew her head off but didn't unblock her nose.

She printed some graphs for the meeting and went through the notes she'd made the previous week. She knew what she needed to talk about.

Then she sat back in her chair and read the *Irish Times*. She didn't have the energy to care about anything else.

Eileen Walsh, Des's secretary, called Alix to tell her that Brian Nicholls of Sorrento Products had arrived and the meeting was in the boardroom.

'I'll be right there,' said Alix.

'Are you OK?' asked Eileen. 'You sound awful, Alix.'

'Just got a sore throat,' Alix told her. 'I'll be fine.'

She gathered up her notes. As she stood up, the room seemed to spin round her and she had to grab the edge of her desk to steady herself. Her heart was pounding. She flashed an anxious look through the glass wall at the other dealers but they hadn't noticed anything. Alix blew on her palms which were beginning to perspire. She still felt dizzy and light-headed as she walked into the dealing room.

'I'll be in the boardroom,' she told Dave. 'Give me a shout if anything dramatic happens.'

'Nothing dramatic will happen,' said Dave confidently. 'Martin Dardis is thinking about taking a five-year swap – that'll suit our position if he deals. But it's the only imminent interest we have at the moment.'

'OK,' said Alix. 'I'll leave things in your capable hands.'

'You should be at home,' said Jenny. 'You look terrible, Alix. Have you got a temperature?'

Alix shrugged. 'I feel a bit odd,' she admitted. 'But I'll be OK.'

She left them and walked downstairs to the boardroom. She knew that she should have stayed at home. If this had happened a couple of weeks ago, Paul would have made her stay at home. He'd have brought her honey and lemon and medicinal alcohol and told her to stay in bed.

But she couldn't have stayed in bed today. It was vital that she didn't miss any meetings with clients, especially any that involved the managing director of the bank too. She wasn't going to give Dave Bryant or Gavin Donnelly or even Jenny Smith the slightest opportunity to show how brilliant they were. She was the head of treasury. She was the one in command. And she was going to make sure it stayed that way.

'Hello, Alix.' Brian Nicholls got up when she walked into the room. 'It's nice to see you again.'

'And you,' she said as firmly as she could.

'Are you all right?' he asked.

'Touch of a sore throat,' Alix replied. 'So don't expect me to do too much talking!'

'That'll be a change,' said Des Coyle. 'Usually we can hardly shut you up.'

'How unfair.' She smiled at him.

'OK,' said Des. 'Let's go through the proposal with you, Brian. I think you'll find we've covered all your concerns.'

Alix listened while Des outlined the scheme whereby Brian's company borrowed cheaply in the US market and then swapped the proceeds back into euros. Every so often Des asked her a question and she supplied the right answer. But it seemed to her as though he was talking to her from a huge distance and his words were fuzzy and indistinct.

She yawned.

'Tired?' asked Des tersely.

'Of course not,' she answered quickly. 'My sinuses are blocked. I'm just trying to unblock them.'

'I've got a great spray at home,' said Brian. 'You should try it. I can't remember the name – my wife buys it for me. I'll check it out, though. Let you know.'

'Thanks, Brian.' She smiled at him.

'Now,' Des brought the meeting back to business, 'about the three-year borrowings . . .'

Alix could hardly keep her eyes open. It wasn't that she was tired, she simply wasn't able to concentrate. Des's words became more and more indistinct.

Her eyelids were like lead. They were closing and there was nothing she could do about it. Her whole body was relaxing. The boardroom seemed to recede into the distance.

She tried to keep conscious but it was slipping away from her. She slid, slowly and inexorably, from the chair and onto the boardroom floor.

Chapter 13

When she came to, the first person she saw was Eileen Walsh who was kneeling beside her, holding a glass of water.

'Oh, Alix!' she cried. 'Are you OK?'

'Of course.' Alix tried to sit up. 'I don't know what came over me. I'm perfectly all right.'

'You're certainly not perfectly all right,' said Eileen sharply. 'You gave everyone a terrible fright.'

'I just fainted,' protested Alix. 'It's not such a big thing.'

'Would you like to sit with your head between your knees?' asked Des. 'That's what you're supposed to do.'

'No, honestly.' Alix was burning with embarrassment. 'It's just this cold. My head was so blocked up that I got dizzy. That's all.'

'You're dreadfully pale,' said Brian Nicholls.

Oh God, thought Alix. He's still here. I collapsed in front of a client. Des will never forgive me. 'I guess I'm not as well as I thought.' Alix tried grinning at him but it took a lot of effort.

'You shouldn't have come in if you felt like this,' said Des.

'I didn't want to miss seeing Brian,' said Alix.

'That's very flattering.' Brian smiled at her. 'But Des is right. You should be at home in bed, Alix.'

'You're right,' she agreed. 'As soon as we're finished here, I'll go home.'

'You'll go home right away,' said Des. 'You're not fit to be here.'

'Honestly, Des—'

'Alix,' he said firmly. 'We can finish this meeting without you. We've already covered the foreign exchange swap anyway. There isn't anything else major, and if we need something, we can give Dave a call.' He turned to Eileen who was still holding the glass of water. 'Phone for a taxi, will you? Tell them to be here as soon as possible.'

'Des, I—'

'No arguing, Alix.'

She managed to get up from the floor and sit on a chair.

'Des is right,' said Brian. 'You should put your head between your knees.'

'I'll just sit here quietly,' said Alix. 'I'm much better now.'

The three of them sat in silence. Alix wished she could think of something bright and witty to say so that she could distract them from the fact that she'd keeled over in front of them. Fainting in front of the managing director and an important customer was awful. How could she appear efficient and commanding when Brian Nicholls had seen her spread out on the floor? It was hardly the image of an executive woman in control of her life. She was prepared to bet that Brian had never before been at a meeting where one of the participants had fainted. He might well, she supposed, have been at drinking sessions where a business colleague had collapsed, but that was an entirely different situation. She sighed. This was a catastrophe. It just underlined how absolutely crap the last few weeks had been.

'Taxi's here!' Eileen poked her head round the door and smiled brightly at Alix.

'Take your time,' warned Brian. 'Don't rush things.'

'I'm much better now, Brian,' said Alix, although the floor felt unsteady beneath her. 'I probably just need a few more hours in bed.'

'Don't come in tomorrow,' said Des. 'In fact, you might be better off staying out all week.'

'Absolutely not,' said Alix. 'I'll be right as rain tomorrow.' She followed Eileen out of the room and to the taxi.

'Are you sure you're OK?' asked Eileen. 'You really are as white as a ghost.'

'I'm OK,' said Alix. 'Thanks, Eileen. I'm sure I gave them a bit of a shock.'

Eileen laughed. 'Poor Des nearly collapsed himself! He came running out of the boardroom and I thought someone had died.'

'He hasn't quite got rid of me yet.' Alix smiled feebly. 'Apologise to him for me, will you?'

'Why should you apologise?' Eileen stared at her. 'You're sick, Alix. You should be at home in bed. You shouldn't have come into the office in the first place.'

Alix nodded.

'Why on earth did you?' asked Eileen. 'Any of the others could have stood in for you. Des would have understood. And I'm sure Dave wouldn't have minded meeting Brian.'

I'll bet he wouldn't, thought Alix miserably. Dave would have sat there and talked about golf and rugby and they would have had a very convivial meeting, everything would have been sorted out and it wouldn't have ended with Dave conking out on the boardroom floor.

She got into the taxi and closed her eyes. She could just imagine Des and Brian back in the office, talking about her. Thinking that she wasn't up to the job. Des would be wondering if it was all getting too much for her. She rubbed her eyes and put her hand to her forehead. It was burning hot. She'd better get the taxi to drop her at the doctor's. She hated going to Dr O'Neill but if she'd picked up some sort of bug then she'd better just get some antibiotics to shift it.

She leaned towards the driver. 'Can you drop me on Baggot Street, please. Near the bridge.'

'Sure.' The driver glanced in his mirror. The woman looked haggard, he thought. Her face was white and her hair, damp and escaping from the clip that held it back, snaked across her face. He hoped to God that she wasn't going to pass out in his taxi.

❧

Des asked Eileen to bring coffee for himself and Brian.

'She didn't look very well,' said Brian. 'I thought as much even when she came into the room.'

'She hasn't been one hundred per cent for the last few weeks,' said Des. 'I was chatting to Dave – you know Dave, don't you, the senior dealer? He said she'd had to go home early a couple of times.'

'She's not pregnant, is she?' asked Brian. 'You know the way they get when they're pregnant. Theresa kept falling asleep when she was having James. Couldn't take her anywhere without her eyes closing.'

'I don't think Alix fell asleep,' Des said dryly. 'It was more dramatic than just falling asleep!'

'She could be pregnant all the same,' Brian laughed. 'Either that or she's got a new bloke and she's spending so much time in the sack that she's not getting any sleep. He might have her completely worn out.'

Des laughed. 'She's been living with the same guy for a few years. Maybe he's been taking Viagra.'

'Or maybe she has!' Brian laughed too. 'Actually, she's not at all bad looking, is she?'

'She's a bit of all right,' nodded Des.

'Have you— ?'

Des shook his head. 'I wouldn't dare. To be honest, I thought she was one of those chic lesbian types at first. Didn't seem to even notice men and *so* cool. But I was wrong about that.'

'Could be a ruse,' said Brian. 'Maybe her bloke's gay. Maybe it's all a cover! And the strain of this double life caused her to collapse.'

Des chuckled. 'You've been watching too many TV soaps. Anyway, she'd better not keel over again. I'm running a bloody bank, not a hospital.'

'Well, since you're running a bank you'd better give me those facility documents to sign. Might as well get the formalities over and done with.'

'Great,' said Des. He passed over a sheaf of paper. 'Always nice to do business with you, Brian.'

'And you, Des,' said Brian as he signed on the dotted line.

⌒

Alix sat in Dr O'Neill's waiting room. She'd thought that it would be a quick visit to the doctor – nip in, collect a prescription, and nip out again. She hadn't counted on the number of

170

people who were there ahead of her. She'd been waiting nearly an hour already and she was beginning to feel as though she would collapse again. She flicked through the year-old copy of *Cosmo* but, much as she wanted to, she couldn't concentrate on the article about 'Getting a Man and Keeping Him'.

'Alix Callaghan?' The receptionist was bright and cheerful and ushered Alix into the doctor's surgery.

'Hello, Alix.' Geraldine O'Neill smiled at her. 'Haven't seen you for a while. How are you keeping?'

'Not very well, obviously.' Alix's throat was absolutely killing her now and talking was even more painful than it had been earlier.

'My goodness!' Geraldine raised an eyebrow. 'How sore is that?'

'Very.'

'OK,' said Geraldine briskly. 'Let's have a look at you.'

Alix let the doctor listen to her chest and look at her throat and take her blood pressure. It was nice to have someone worrying about her and someone else in charge.

'Have you felt sick at all?' asked Geraldine as she took Alix's temperature.

Alix shook her head and immediately felt dizzy again.

'It's a virus,' said Geraldine. 'I know that isn't awfully helpful, Alix. But there is a bug going around. I'm surprised you haven't been sick, most people tend to throw up as well as everything else.'

'Charming,' murmured Alix.

'I'll prescribe something for you. But you really need to rest. Take a couple of days off and stay in bed.'

'I can't do that,' said Alix. 'We're busy in the office now and I—'

'Don't be ridiculous,' Geraldine told her. 'You're not indispensable. What do they do when you're on holiday?'

'That's different,' protested Alix feebly. 'We have time to organise and plan things then.'

'Well, you can organise and plan three days at home. Minimum,' said Geraldine firmly. 'What's your diet been like lately? Leaving aside the bug, you look rundown, Alix.'

'There's nothing wrong with my diet.'

'Plenty of fresh fruit and vegetables?'

Alix thought of the straw basket on the kitchen counter where a couple of dusty apples (bought by Paul) lay uneaten.

'Yes,' she replied.

'It doesn't look like it to me,' said Geraldine. 'Do you cook a meal in the evening?'

'I eat out at lunchtime quite a lot,' said Alix.

'And what do you eat when you're not lunching?'

Alix shrugged. 'It depends.'

'Eat properly,' said Geraldine. 'Especially now. Come back to me in a few days. You should be feeling a lot better by then, but I want to have a look at you again.'

'You don't think there's anything seriously wrong with me?' Alix was suddenly alarmed by the look of concern on the doctor's face.

'Of course not,' said Geraldine. 'I just want to give you another check, that's all.'

'OK.' Alix opened the door.

'Look after yourself,' said Geraldine.

'I will.'

Alix walked slowly to the chemist and handed in her prescription. She felt utterly exhausted now, hardly able to stand up. The walk back to the apartment was even worse. But when she got inside she immediately phoned the dealing room.

'Yo, dealers.'

Alix grimaced. 'Hello, Gavin.'

'Alix? Is that you?'

'Yes,' she said. 'And if I ever hear you answer the phone like that again—'

'Sorry,' said Gavin, though he didn't sound very sorry. 'We're having a good day, Alix. Although you're not, I hear. Are you OK?'

'I'm fine,' she said. 'Put Dave on, will you?'

'Hi, Alix.' Dave sounded very cheerful. 'What's all this I hear about you throwing yourself at Brian Nicholls?'

Alix smiled faintly. 'It wasn't deliberate, I assure you. Is everything OK there?'

'Great,' said Dave. 'We did the swap trade with Martin Dardis. Markets are trading in tight enough ranges but we've executed a few client orders and everything is under control.'

'Good,' said Alix. 'I was supposed to meet Steve Pearson for lunch. Will you call and cancel for me?'

'Sure,' said Dave. 'I guess you'll be out for the rest of the week.'

'Depends on how I feel,' Alix said. 'I've got some anti-bs from the doc. If I'm OK tomorrow I'll be in.'

'Don't rush,' Dave told her. 'Everything's fine here. Take your time.'

'I will,' she said and hung up.

Take your time, she thought as she crawled into bed. They'd want her to take her time, of course they would. Dave – despite Gavin's protestations to the contrary – would be only too pleased to have an opportunity to prove himself. Gavin would be delighted to have her unexpectedly out of the picture for a couple of days. And Jenny . . . Alix sighed. She thought she could count on Jenny but she couldn't be certain. Jenny never said anything about wanting to have more responsibility or moving on within the dealing room. But if the opportunity was there, Alix was sure that the younger girl would take it. Hell, she'd take any opportunities she could if she was Jenny. But she doubted, somehow, that Jenny wanted to be the one in charge. At the same time, the girl was good at aligning herself with people of influence. She was very friendly with all of the other managers and Des Coyle liked her a lot.

Alix rolled over in the bed. Bloody body, she thought angrily. Letting me down at a time like this.

⤳

She woke up later that afternoon. Her throat still hurt but she didn't feel quite as light-headed as earlier in the day. She had a raging thirst, though, and it was still an effort to get up and go into the kitchen for a drink. There was only the out-of-date orange juice in the fridge. She drank it anyway. It couldn't make her feel any worse.

The sheet on the bed was damp with sweat. She wished she had the energy to change it but she just moved to the other side of the bed.

She lay on her side and thought of Paul. She wished he was here now to look after her. She didn't want to be in the apartment all by herself when she felt so miserable. She couldn't remember when she'd last felt like this. A tear slid down her cheek and plopped onto the pillow.

Damp sheet and damp pillow, she said to herself. Not a good idea. I'll probably catch pneumonia.

The next time she woke up it was dark. She had to blink a couple of times before she could focus on the digital clock. Four a.m. People died at 4 a.m., she reminded herself. Your body is at its lowest ebb then. She reached for the clock to check that she'd set the alarm. Despite what everyone said, she didn't want to stay out of work for another day. She didn't want to leave Dave and Gavin and Jenny to plot against her. And she didn't want to spend a whole day on her own in the apartment, feeling miserable.

But when the radio clicked on at six o'clock, Alix couldn't drag herself out of bed. She'd go in for the afternoon, she told herself as she hit the off button. She needed to sleep.

∾

Gavin answered the phone. He almost said 'Yo, dealers' but at the last minute realised that it could be Alix and instead gave the preferred 'Europa Bank, dealers' greeting.

'Hi, can I speak to Alix Callaghan?'

'Who's calling?' asked Gavin, although he recognised the voice.

'This is Matt Connery, Anatronics.'

'Hi, Matt. It's Gavin Donnelly here.' Gavin hit a couple of keys on his computer terminal and a graph of the dollar/yen exchange rate for the past two days appeared. 'Alix is out of the office today. Can I help?'

'Is she ever in the office?' Matt sounded aggrieved.

'She's a very busy person,' said Gavin. 'She tends to be out a lot. Although this time, I'm afraid, it's just a common or garden cold that's laid her out.'

'She's off sick?'

'Probably just as well she didn't come in,' said Gavin. 'Even if you don't feel that bad in yourself, you hate to infect other people in the room.'

'I need to sell some yen buy dollars,' said Matt. 'It's not huge, forty million yen.' Forty million yen was less than three hundred thousand dollars. Small money in foreign exchange terms.

'One fifteen forty-five,' he said.

Matt hesitated. 'Actually, I—'

'I can do forty-four and a half,' said Gavin swiftly. He'd pitched the price a little on the expensive side. He wanted to see how in touch Matt Connery was with the current exchange rate. The difference was less than a thousand dollars, but it was the principle that mattered.

'OK,' said Matt. 'Can you pay the dollars to our account at Chase. The yen will be coming from Bank of Tokyo.'

'That's fine,' said Gavin. 'Thanks for the trade, Matt.' He paused for a moment. 'We should get together for a bite to eat sometime.'

'Perhaps,' said Matt.

Gavin called up his Microsoft Outlook calendar. 'I'm free on Thursday. Would that suit you?'

'I can't meet you this week,' said Matt. 'I'm busy every day.'

'Tell you what,' Gavin said, 'I've got some tickets to the pro-am golf tournament in Portmarnock on Friday next week. I'm taking a few clients. Why don't you come along to that? It should be a good day.'

'I'd like to,' Matt told him. 'But I'm not sure about my schedule. Let me get back to you.'

'Fine,' said Gavin. 'I'll keep a place for you anyway. You can let me know next week.'

'OK,' said Matt. 'When do you expect Alix back into the office?'

Gavin gritted his teeth. 'Not certain,' he said lightly. 'To be fair to her, she doesn't usually stay out for very long if she's ill. But that's not always a good idea. You know yourself, you think you're fine and the next thing you've relapsed and you're out for another few days.'

'Does she get sick that often?' asked Matt. 'I didn't get the impression she was a sick kind of person.'

'Oh, you know women!' Gavin laughed. 'There's always something.'

'If she rings in, tell her I'd like a chat,' said Matt.

'Sure,' replied Gavin. 'And in the meantime I'll book up this trade. If there's anything else you want, don't hesitate to call. And let me know about Portmarnock.'

'Of course,' said Matt.

Gavin disconnected the call and looked at Dave and Jenny who were staring at him.

'What?' he demanded.

'That was really mean,' said Jenny. 'You've made Alix sound like some hypochondriac.'

'It's not my fault she flaked out.' Gavin was inputting the dollar/yen trade.

'It's more than just a cold,' objected Jenny. 'And she hasn't been out sick in years. Listening to you, anyone would think she's out every couple of weeks!'

'Hey, it's business, that's all.' Gavin looked at her impatiently. 'She'd do exactly the same thing.'

'I don't think she would,' said Dave. 'But who cares. Anyway, it was a good idea to offer him the Portmarnock tickets.'

Gavin grinned. 'I know. I'll have to bump someone off the trip if he accepts, though. Right now, I don't have any spare.'

'I can get you one if you're stuck,' said Dave. 'But you'll owe me.'

'Great, thanks.'

'Alix will be pissed off at you,' Jenny told him.

'Oh, come on, Jen! He's turning into a good customer. Looks like we're getting his trades exclusively. She'd want me to look after him.' Gavin pressed the 'enter' button on the keyboard to commit the trade to the system. 'And that's all I'm doing.'

'I know,' said Jenny. 'And looking after yourself too.'

Gavin shrugged. 'We all have to look after ourselves. It's the business, after all.'

~

Alix still felt as though she was detached from reality but she thought her temperature had come down and she didn't feel as shaky as she had earlier. She'd spent the entire day in bed, drifting in and out of sleep, and she had to admit that it had been the best thing for her. It was now half three and she leaned across to pick up the phone.

'Europa Bank, dealers.'

'Hi, Jenny.' Alix was pleased to find that her throat wasn't quite as sore either. 'How are things?'

'Alix! You feeling any better?'

'Improving, thanks,' replied Alix. 'I thought about coming in this morning, but I couldn't stand up.'

'You poor thing.' Jenny was sympathetic. 'It's one thing to

feel like that after a night on the beer, it's quite another when you're actually sick!'

'My doctor told me that there's a bug going round,' said Alix. 'So you'd better take care. She's been advising me to overdose on fruit and vegetables.'

'I'll keep it in mind.' Jenny laughed.

'Anything happening?' asked Alix. 'Is it busy?'

Jenny glanced at Dave and Gavin who were watching her intently. 'Busy enough,' she said. 'The dollar is trading in a very narrow range but the bond has been doing well and we picked up some five-year treasuries which are in profit.'

'Great,' said Alix. 'Any decent client trades?'

'No,' answered Jenny. 'All less than half a bar.' Less than half a million was considered small by the dealers, though some of their clients thought even fifty thousand was a huge sum.

'Nothing I should know about?' asked Alix.

'Not a thing,' said Jenny uncomfortably. 'We're all slaving away for the good of the bank.'

'That's what I like to hear,' said Alix. 'How's Gavin?'

'Gavin?' Jenny looked at him and he made a face at her. 'He's fine. Do you want to talk to him?'

'No,' said Alix. 'I'm sick. I don't want to jeopardise my recovery.'

Jenny laughed. 'I'll tell him you were asking for him. Will you be in tomorrow?'

'Absolutely,' said Alix. 'There's a management meeting at lunchtime. I really need to be there for that.'

'Don't push yourself,' cautioned Jenny. 'If you're still feeling shaky you should stay out. Dave can go to the management meeting.'

'I'm sure he can,' said Alix dryly. 'But I'd like to be there myself.'

'It's up to you,' said Jenny. 'We might see you in the morning.'

'You will.'

'Take care, Alix.'

'You too.'

Alix hung up and lay back on the pillows. The simple conversation had exhausted her. And she felt sure that Jenny was being reticent about something. She hoped she'd feel better tomorrow. There wasn't a chance in hell that she was going to let Dave go to the management meeting.

In the dealing room, Dave looked at Jenny. 'Well?' he asked.

'She might be in tomorrow,' said Jenny.

'What did she say?' Gavin's tone was truculent.

'Just asked what was going on. You heard the conversation.'

'You didn't say anything about Matt Connery.'

'Why should I?' asked Jenny. 'It was a small trade, Gavin. It doesn't matter in the great scheme of things.'

Gavin grinned at her. 'You're not bad,' he said. 'For a woman.'

Jenny threw a bottle of Tipp-Ex at him but he ducked just in time and it hit Mike Keogh, one of the settlements people, as he opened the dealing-room door.

～

At four o'clock, all of the TV stations were showing variations on cookery programmes. Alix sat in front of the screen, the duvet wrapped round her, while she watched someone concoct a cordon bleu meal out of a couple of squashed tomatoes and some herbs. Paul could do that, she thought. Paul could rummage around in the fridge and come up with the ingredients for something wonderful. Although even Paul would be hard pressed to find anything worth eating in the fridge right now. Despite her shopping expedition, the contents of Alix's fridge were still sparse. The freezer was packed to capacity with meals for one, but the fridge only contained the remains of the out-of-date orange juice, an almost out-of-date jar of mayonnaise, half a carton of milk and a packet of Easi-Singles cheese. There was some beer and some wine, of course, but beer and wine weren't exactly what she needed right now.

The intercom buzzed and Alix jumped in surprise. Who was looking for her? The thought that Paul might have rung the office and discovered she was ill flitted through her mind. And when he discovered that she was sick, he'd rushed to be with her! She tried not to think like that but she couldn't help it. It almost made her feel better.

'Who is it?' she asked.

'Delivery for Callaghan, Apartment 2A.'

'Come on up.' She pressed the door release, and while the delivery man was coming up the stairs, pulled on a pair of jeans. She'd only been wearing a T-shirt beneath the warmth of the duvet. She pulled a brush through her hair.

She looked through the security window of the door. The delivery man was holding a bouquet of flowers.

'Sign here,' he said when she'd opened the door.

'Thank you.'

She took the flowers into the apartment and ripped open the envelope on the card that accompanied them.

'Sorry you're ill,' said the message. 'Get well soon.' It was signed Matt Connery, Anatronics Industries.

Chapter 14

The next morning Alix woke at her usual time of six o'clock. She shook her head experimentally to see if she still had a headache, but it seemed OK. She swung her legs over the side of the bed and stood up. A little shaky, she thought, but at least she didn't feel as though she was going to fall over.

She got ready for work slowly, not wanting to provoke any sudden feelings of dizziness. By the time she'd dressed in the checked Chanel suit that she'd bought in Paris the previous year, she felt more like her old self. She wore more make-up than usual to hide the pallor of her cheeks. She looked at herself in the mirror and was pleased with the reflection. Not perfect, she thought, but at least she'd lost the haggard look.

She picked up her car keys and closed the bedroom door behind her. There was no way she would be able to walk to the office today and anyway, for the first time in weeks, it looked as though it might rain.

The living room was full of the scent of Matt Connery's flowers. Even though her sinuses weren't completely clear, she could still smell the combination of carnations and tiger lilies. She looked at them in the porcelain vase, hurriedly shoved in so that the beautiful arrangement of the florist had been ruined. She'd rearrange them when she got home.

What had the man been thinking of? she wondered. Why on earth would he send her flowers? She knew that he was attracted to her – God, she told herself, at thirty-two (nearly thirty-three, as Wyn had reminded her) she could tell when a man was attracted to her. But sending flowers! Completely over the top. Besides, he was a client. And she knew nothing about him. He could be married, for all she knew. Probably was. At her age, the pool of unmarried, available, heterosexual men diminished substantially.

Flowers! It was such an old-fashioned thing to do. And sweet, but she had never been turned on by sweetness. She liked her men with a touch of iron. She wondered who had given Matt her home address. Not the bank – it was strictly against their policy to give out telephone numbers, let alone addresses. Perhaps he'd looked her up in the phone book. She wondered if he'd sent flowers to the other A. Callaghans too. It seemed an awful lot of effort. He must be married, she decided. Unmarried blokes wouldn't bother. 'Anyway,' she said out loud, 'I am not ready to start all this new relationship stuff. If that's what I wanted, there's always Cathal Moran.'

Traffic was light at that hour of the morning. She turned into the car park under the Europa Bank building. Because she often walked to work, she'd told people in the bank that they could use her space if it wasn't occupied by eight thirty. She was surprised to see it already occupied by a five-year-old green Mazda coupé. She glanced at her watch. Twenty-five to eight. But maybe nobody had expected her in today – the story of her collapse at the meeting had probably gone through the bank like a dose of salts. All the same, it was infuriating. There was a very limited number of spaces and she didn't want to rob someone else's. She drove back out of the complex and parked on a double yellow line outside the building, her hazard lights flashing. She ran up the steps and told the security guard at reception to keep an eye on the car. 'I'll be back to move it in a couple of minutes,' she promised. 'I know it's early and there shouldn't be any of those clamping maniacs around, but please watch out for me.'

'Sure,' he said. 'But I won't be able to stop them, you know.'

Dave and Gavin were already in the dealing room.

'Do you know who owns the Mazda in my space?' asked Alix as she walked in. 'I know everyone has assumed I'm at death's door, but robbing my space is a bit much to take.'

'Actually, it's mine.' Gavin shrugged. 'Sorry, Alix, I didn't think you'd be in today. I knew you wouldn't mind.'

'I mind the fact that you decided I wouldn't be in,' she said waspishly. 'Now you're just going to have to move it.'

'Give me five minutes,' said Gavin. 'I'm waiting on a call from Hans Mueller in Frankfurt. He was checking some data for me. He said he'd call back before eight.'

'I'm sitting on a double yellow outside,' said Alix. 'I don't want to be clamped.'

'You won't,' said Gavin.

'Forget it,' said Alix. 'I'll take it round to the public car park.'

'I'll pay for your day's parking,' said Gavin without looking up from his computer.

'It's OK,' said Alix. 'It doesn't matter.'

She hurried down the steps of the building. As she reached her car, she saw a van marked 'Ace Security Services' approaching. The bloody clampers, she thought, and rammed the BMW

184

into first. If she'd been clamped then she'd certainly have made Gavin pay.

She would have to do something about Gavin. He was becoming more and more arrogant. She should really do something about Dave and Jenny too. Both of them were senior to Gavin but neither of them seemed prepared to show any authority over him. Jenny didn't have the killer instinct that would drive her to the top, but she couldn't understand why Dave allowed his subordinate so much leeway. Maybe Gavin had been right when he'd told her that Dave didn't want her job. Maybe Dave didn't care any more. But she did! And she would have to confront Gavin sooner rather than later.

She was about to leave the car park when the threatened rain began to fall. Not a soft, drizzling rain as she had expected, but a torrential downpour. Fat raindrops bounced off the pavement and rivulets of water ran along the gutters. She groaned. She didn't have an umbrella in the car. She looked up at the sky. It didn't look as if it was going to stop and it was only a five-minute walk back to the office. But she'd be soaked in five minutes.

She stood, undecided, for another couple of seconds before she decided to make a run for it. By the time she reached the bank she was drenched and the Chanel suit was clinging to her.

She went into the ladies' and tried to dry her soaking hair under the hot air dryer. Although she kept a second suit in the office, she didn't want to walk into the room looking like a wet rag. Her efforts with the dryer had a limited effect but she was marginally more comfortable when she walked into the dealing room.

By then, Jenny had arrived and the three dealers were chatting about the day ahead.

'The futures position is at our target level,' Dave was saying as she pushed open the door. 'But I think we can run it a little more.'

'No technical resistance,' said Gavin. 'Should be good for another ten ticks anyway.'

'What futures position?' asked Alix.

'Hi, Alix!' Jenny beamed at her. 'Good to have you back. How are you feeling?'

'Great,' she said. 'Especially after walking back from the car park in a bloody monsoon.' At least Gavin looked a little guilty, she thought. Though not half guilty enough.

'I'm sorry,' he said as he looked at her wet clothes. 'I really didn't think you'd be here today. And I would have moved my car.'

'It's OK,' she said. 'I can change into my other suit. But first of all, what futures position?'

'We're long some gilt futures,' said Dave. 'The gilt crapped out yesterday afternoon and we thought it was time to buy. It picked up in late trading and we ran with it. We're up twenty-five grand at the moment.'

'Excellent,' said Alix. 'What else did we do?'

'Not a lot, to be honest,' said Dave. 'A few client trades. We put a couple of swap prices into the market but no one dealt. Fairly routine stuff.'

'Leave the report on my desk, will you?' she said. 'In the meantime I'll change my clothes.'

Her emergency suit was a black Donna Karan that she'd bought in New York but which she hadn't liked when she got it home. It was good as a standby and had been called into use a couple of times, notably the day Dave had accidentally dumped a full cup of coffee into her lap five minutes before she'd had a meeting with Guy Decourcelle and the rest of the Paris management team who'd flown to Dublin on one of their infrequent but nerve-wracking fact-finding missions. She kept a pair of black shoes in her office too. The day the French managers had come over, she'd been wearing her favourite office colour of chocolate brown. Unfortunately she'd also been wearing brown shoes which had clashed horribly with the black Donna Karan. She'd noticed Guy looking at her shoes and imagined him thinking that no French girl would dream of wearing a black suit and brown shoes. Even if they'd cost her a fortune in Milan.

She felt better once she was wearing dry clothes, although her teeth had chattered alarmingly while she was peeling off the damp Chanel. But now, dry and with her make-up retouched, she felt able to face the day.

They were on the phones again when she returned. She smiled briefly at them and walked into her glass-panelled office. They were still running Dave's futures position, she noted. Very profitable. She picked up the list of yesterday's trades and looked through it.

Dave had been right, most of them were small client trades. The biggest had been Martin Dardis's swap, but none of the foreign exchange deals had exceeded half a million. She turned over the page and saw the name Anatronics at the top. She couldn't believe it. Matt Connery had dealt again. And she'd been out again. She looked at the figures. Not a big trade. They wouldn't have made much on it.

'Gavin!' she called, and he indicated that he was still on a phone call. 'When you're finished,' she mouthed.

187

It was nearly five minutes before he came into her office.
'Yes?'

Alix ignored the aggression in Gavin's voice. 'I see our good friend Matt Connery dealt yesterday.'

'It was another small deal,' said Gavin.

'That's fine.' Alix smiled at him. 'He didn't ask you anything about swaps, did he?'

'No,' replied Gavin. He looked at her anxiously. 'Should he have?'

She shrugged. 'Not necessarily. I just wondered. Did we make much out of the deal?'

'Not a lot,' admitted Gavin. 'It's too small.'

'If only these bloody clients knew how little we make out of them,' said Alix. 'That's OK, Gavin. Thanks.'

He turned to walk away but she stopped him. 'Did Connery ask for me?'

'I told him you were sick,' said Gavin. 'It was true.'

'I know,' she said. 'That's fine.'

He turned again and she stopped him for a second time. 'He didn't ask you for my address by any chance?'

'Your address?' Gavin swivelled around. 'Your home address?'

'Yes.'

'No,' he said. 'Why should he?'

'Don't mind me,' she said. 'It's nothing.'

'He didn't ask for anything.' Gavin regained his composure. 'But I've asked him to the pro-am in Portmarnock. I'm sure he'd enjoy it.'

'I thought you'd used up all your invitations,' said Alix.

'Dave had one spare.' Gavin grinned. 'I owe him but it's worth it to get Connery for a day out and check out exactly what sort of business he has to do.'

'Great idea,' said Alix.

'It's my account,' Gavin said abruptly. 'I've done all the work and all the small, shitty deals. When the big one comes, it's my account.'

'Let's wait for the big one, shall we?' said Alix. She was getting tired of being nice to Gavin.

'When it comes, I'll be ready,' he told her.

'Fine,' she said.

～

She was finding it hard to concentrate. Her head was buzzing and her eyes were tired. The computer screens made them water and she constantly had to wipe them with a tissue. Jenny giggled and told her that she looked as though she was going to burst into tears at any minute. Alix muttered that you never knew, she just might.

At twelve o'clock, Eileen Walsh called to say that the management meeting had been cancelled. Des was stuck in another meeting, she told Alix, and he wouldn't be back in time.

Alix gritted her teeth. She could have stayed at home after all and done some more recuperating. She'd really only come in because of the management meeting.

The rain had stopped and the sun was beating down again so she decided to stroll downtown and buy herself something new to wear for her drink with Paul. She wanted him to know that she'd had time to go shopping and look after herself and that she hadn't gone into some kind of decline.

She spent significantly more than she meant to on a canary-yellow dress in Debenhams. As she brought it (and the earrings, silver chain and bright red Lancôme nail varnish which she'd also bought) back to the office she thought, ruefully, that Paul wouldn't even notice that it was new. Paul never noticed what she wore, unless it was a particularly short skirt.

She phoned RTÉ when she got back. 'Paul Hunter, please.'

'Paul's desk.' The girl who answered sounded young and busy.

'Is Paul there?'

'No, he's out for the day.'

'When will he be back?'

'Not until tomorrow,' said the girl. 'Can I take a message?'

'No,' said Alix slowly. 'It's OK.'

'Sure?'

'Yes. Thanks.'

Shit, she thought. Where was he? Had he forgotten about their drink? Or was she supposed to meet him in Kiely's like the last time? Her head was beginning to ache. She rubbed her temples. As she glanced downwards, she saw the trading report with the Anatronics deal listed on it. She should phone Matt Connery and thank him for the flowers. But really, she thought angrily, he'd put her in a dreadful position. It was far too personal a thing to have done. Maybe she should stop thinking of the account as one she wanted to handle and just tamely hand it over to Gavin. But she couldn't do that. Not now. Not when the account had become something of a battle zone for them.

She smiled as she thought of Gavin's expression if she rang Matt now and started thanking him profusely for his thoughtfulness. Poor Gavin would have a coronary. It'd almost be worth it just to watch him.

But she didn't want to phone Matt Connery. She didn't want

to have to thank him for doing something she hadn't needed or wanted him to do in the first place.

She was uncomfortable with the idea of a man sending her flowers. Paul had never done anything like that. Paul wasn't into romance very much and that was one of the things that Alix liked about him because she wasn't into romance either. They'd never bought each other Valentine cards, or had candlelight dinners or walked hand in hand along the beach. Theirs had been a practical relationship with lots of very exciting sex thrown in. But just because they didn't waste time on heart-shaped boxes of chocolates, it didn't mean that they didn't love each other.

Or maybe it did. Alix picked up a pencil and snapped it in half. Maybe Paul had only pretended not to be interested in flowers and champagne and jewellery and silly cards. Maybe he'd already sent Sabine hundreds of exorbitantly priced stupid gifts. Like furry teddy bears with 'I love you' stamped across their stomach. Alix had told him that if he ever sent her a furry teddy bear with something ridiculous stamped on its stomach she'd leave him.

She pushed Paul to the back of her mind while she decided what to do about Matt bloody Connery and his bloody bouquet of flowers.

Eventually she went into her office and dialled the Anatronics number.

'Matt Connery,' she said when the phone was answered.

'I'm sorry,' said the receptionist, 'Matt is out of the office today. I don't expect him back until Friday.'

'Right!' Alix exclaimed.

'Pardon?'

'I'm sorry. I – can I just leave a message for him?'

'Certainly.'

'Could you say that Alix Callaghan called to say thank you?'

'Of course. Does he have your number?'

'It's Europa Bank,' said Alix. 'He has the number.'

'Fine, Alix. I'll pass on the message.'

'Thank you.'

'No problem.'

Great, thought Alix as she hung up. Now he knows I got the flowers and called him. So I've gained kudos for ringing, without having to talk to him. An outcome which she decided was very satisfactory.

⁓

She left the office at half four. By that time her eyes were smarting and she was feeling light-headed again. She wanted to go home and sleep before meeting Paul. Or before he called. Or before she decided that she had to call him. I won't, she told herself. I won't call. I'm not going to demean myself by running after him.

'If Paul phones, will you tell him I've gone home?' she asked Jenny as she picked up her shopping.

'Of course,' said Jenny. 'Are you sure you were right to come in today, Alix? You look awfully pale.'

'I'm just tired,' Alix told her. 'I'll be OK.'

'See you tomorrow,' said Jenny.

'Yeah, Alix. See you tomorrow. Look after yourself.' Dave's voice was sincere and, unaccountably, Alix felt tears prick at her eyes.

'Thanks.'

'If you're sick again, don't come in tomorrow,' said Gavin. 'I really don't want to catch whatever it is you're harbouring.'

If I cry, thought Alix looking at him, it'll be tears of rage before I tear you limb from limb!

Des Coyle rang the dealing room fifteen minutes after Alix had left.

'She's gone home, Des,' said Dave. 'She was feeling tired.'

'If she wasn't better she shouldn't have come in at all,' said Des. 'Are you busy, Dave? I need to talk to someone about Polish zloty.'

'What I know about Polish zloty could be handwritten on a microchip,' said Dave. 'But I'll give you the benefit of my expertise. Do you want me to drop down to your office?'

'Yes, good idea,' said Des.

Dave left the dealing room and strolled down to the managing director's office. In Europa Bank, the dealing room was on the third floor. Somewhat unusually, Des Coyle had his office on the floor below but it was a significantly bigger office than he otherwise would have had. It was L-shaped and had a view across the Liffey as well as down towards the port. Unlike the dealing room where everything was utilitarian, Des's office had a thick-pile blue carpet, blue-grey wallpaper and modern pine furniture. He also had some original paintings by a local artist (who the bank's design consultant said would one day be very famous) hanging on the wall.

'Hi, Des.' Dave strode across the office and sat in the grey leather chair in front of the desk. 'How's it going?'

'Jim Rothwell has asked me about this zloty thing.' Des pushed a piece of paper in front of Dave. 'What d'you think?'

Dave skimmed through the paper. 'Looks OK to me,' he said. 'Who are you getting to do the swap?'

'Don't know,' said Des. 'Who do you advise?'

'Don't you want Guy Decourcelle's mob to do it?'

'Do you trust them not to go after the client? Try to nab the whole deal for themselves?'

Dave made a face. 'I'm not sure. It's possible but I don't think they'd deliberately shaft us. Let me talk to Guy.'

'OK,' said Des. 'Tonight?'

'Not a chance,' Dave laughed. 'They're an hour ahead of us, you know. Guy is doubtless sitting in a brasserie with some French tart as we speak. He's certainly not in the office.'

'And tell me,' Des leaned back in his chair, leather, like his visitor's chair, but with a higher back and much more padding, 'what's the story with Alix?'

'Alix?' said Dave carefully. 'What kind of story do you want, Des?'

'This bloody so-called cold. Keeling over in the boardroom. Going home early. What's behind it?'

'I don't know.' Dave stretched his hands over his head. 'Maybe it is just a virus. But, I have to be honest with you, Des, we were wondering if there was something wrong with her before this. Remember I mentioned it to you? She left the office early a couple of times. She's forgotten one or two meetings. And she's giving poor old Gavin a terrible time.'

'What d'you mean?'

'Nothing he does is right,' said Dave. 'He's made some pretty decent calls, following some tips he's got from guys he knows in the States. She wouldn't let us position ourselves on the back of some of them, and we would have made money. She doesn't like him very much and it's clouding her judgement.'

'Is she broody?' asked Des. 'God knows, she's in her thirties.

194

Even the most career-minded of them get broody in their thirties.'

'She hasn't said anything,' Dave replied. 'But she could be. Des, you know how it is with women. They think they want it all – the career, the promotions, the management positions. But do they really understand what it's about? Let's face it, if she is getting broody she'll drop this job like a hot potato.'

'Do you like her?' asked Des.

Dave considered the question. 'I respect her,' he said eventually. 'But people have to earn respect and they can lose it just as quickly.'

'Is she coming in for the rest of the week?'

'It doesn't much matter about tomorrow. But she has to be in on Friday because Gavin is taking some clients to the pro-am and I have a meeting with Arnie Daly in the afternoon. So there won't be enough cover if she doesn't come in.'

'I'll be at the pro-am myself,' said Des. 'Who's Gavin taking?'

'About half a dozen people,' Dave said. 'Including that new guy, Connery, from Anatronics. Gavin's doing really well with that account.'

'Great,' said Des. 'Tell him to keep up the good work. He's not a bad golfer himself, is he?'

'Plays off twelve,' said Dave, 'but he could be better. If he spent more time on the course he'd get down to single figures.'

'Encourage him to take guys out for golf,' said Des. 'It always pays off.'

'Sure.' Dave smiled. 'Anything else?'

'No,' replied Des. 'That'll do for now. Let me know what you think about Decourcelle and the zlotys.'

'Will do,' said Dave. 'I'll give you a call tomorrow.'

'Great. Doing anything interesting this evening?'

Dave shook his head. 'I'm working on some technical analysis charts. Good time to get them done, when the markets are closed.'

'It's all nonsense to me,' said Des cheerfully, 'but if we make money out of it, I don't care whether or not you read tea leaves.'

'Sometimes I think they'd tell us just as much,' joked Dave as he got up from the chair. 'Talk to you tomorrow.'

'Sure thing,' said Des and returned to the folder in front of him.

Dave whistled lightly as he ran up the stairs. A good evening's work, all told, he thought. He looked at his watch. He'd hang around for another twenty minutes in case Des called again. Then he'd go home. He hated technical analysis and Gavin had done the charts hours ago anyway.

Chapter 15

The phone was ringing as Alix opened the door to the apartment. Paul! she thought in relief as she dropped her shopping on the floor and rushed to pick up the receiver before the answering machine clicked in.

'Hi, Alix! It's me. What on earth are you doing home at this hour?'

Alix's heart sank as she recognised Sophia's voice. 'Hi, Soph,' she said, trying to sound enthusiastic. 'I left the office early.'

'You guys sure have it easy in Dublin,' joked Sophia. 'It's a nightmare over here. I'm up to my tits in work and London is like an oven.'

'Poor thing.' Alix smiled despite herself. 'Plenty of securitisation going on then?'

Sophia also worked in financial services. Her job was to repackage a range of small, individual loans into one big loan, turn it into a single bond and sell it to institutional investors. The concept of securitisation had first emerged in the States where nobody was sure how successful it would be. But securitisations had been very successful and, because many financial institutions had hedged their bets and shunted women into their securitisation departments, it was one area in financial services where women could do sensationally well. Sophia was one of those women. She earned almost three times as much as Alix, and if you took her bonuses into account, almost three times that again. She lived in a small but perfectly located townhouse in Chelsea, took three holidays a year, and loved her work.

'We put together a very exciting ship leasing package,' Sophia told Alix. 'Excellent yield, AAA rating, was a blow-out. Everyone wanted a piece.'

'Good for you,' said Alix.

'So – why are you at home?' asked Sophia again. 'I rang your office and some very rude bloke told me you'd skived off early!'

'Probably Gavin,' said Alix. 'If that's all he said, I'm lucky. Gavin and I aren't exactly seeing eye to eye at the moment.'

'Oh, dear.'

'I'll tell you about it sometime,' said Alix. 'But not today. It wouldn't do my blood pressure any good.' She flopped into the armchair. 'I'm home because I caught some kind of bug over the weekend and I've been off work for a couple of days. We were supposed to have a management meeting today so I went in. But I was wrecked by four, that's why I came home.'

'Poor you,' commiserated Sophia.

'Why are you calling?' asked Alix. 'Any news?'

'Well . . .' Sophia paused teasingly. 'A bit.'

'Come on, Soph, tell me.'

'It's so funny really.'

'What is?'

'Richard and me. We're getting married!'

'Sophia!' Alix nearly dropped the phone. Her friend had been seeing Richard Comiskey since the beginning of the year. Alix knew that Richard and Sophia were practically living together but she'd never thought about them actually getting married. 'Congratulations,' she added.

'That's not all.' Sophia giggled.

'What?' asked Alix, although she felt a tremor of suspicion already.

'We're going to have a baby!'

Alix said nothing.

'Alix? Are you still there?'

'Of course I am,' she replied. 'It's just – I'm shocked. I mean, is congratulations the right word? Did you want the baby?'

'If you'd asked me this last year, I would have said no. But, oh Alix, yes – I'm thrilled.'

'Then I guess it's congratulations again.'

'I know it sounds really hormonal and stupid and everything. But I haven't felt so wonderful in ages.'

'That's great,' said Alix.

'I know I'm supposed to be feeling tired,' Sophia went on, 'but I don't. I feel terrific.'

'That's great,' said Alix again. 'I'm really pleased for you.' To her, the words sounded incredibly banal.

'Thanks.' Sophia giggled. 'I know I'll probably hate it when I swell up and can't see my toes, but right now all the good things have happened – like my hair shines and my skin is ultra-clear!'

'So what you're saying is that I should cancel my membership to the gym and get pregnant instead?'

'Somehow I can't imagine you pregnant, Alix,' said Sophia. 'But I couldn't imagine me pregnant either, so I guess if you and Paul want to go ahead . . .'

'I doubt it,' said Alix dryly.

'Is everything OK?' Sophia caught the tension in her friend's voice. 'You and Paul are all right, aren't you?'

Alix sighed. She didn't like keeping things from Sophia. Theirs was the kind of friendship where they didn't speak to each other for ages but when they did, it seemed like the time between calls had never existed.

'We're struggling,' she said finally.

'Oh, Alix!' Sophia was full of sympathy. 'What's the matter?'

'Paul's going through a phase,' said Alix. 'He's changed jobs – full time in RTÉ now – and he's talking about settling down and starting a family ourselves.'

'But isn't that what you want?' asked Sophia. 'I know you love your job, Alix, but I thought that maybe by now you'd feel as though you can let go a little.'

'Having babies doesn't mean I have to give up work,' Alix said sharply. 'Are you going to?'

'I'm not sure,' said Sophia honestly. 'Sometimes I think it would be so wonderful, not having to buy the kind of clothes I hate wearing just because I'm supposed to look businesslike, not having to get up at five thirty in the morning, not having to argue all the time with the sharks on the twenty-second floor – oh, yes, sometimes it sounds great.'

'But . . .'

'It's been my life,' said Sophia simply. 'It defines who I am. Since I left college, Alix, I've been like you, living for my work. And now I don't know if I want to do that any more.'

'I still do,' said Alix. 'But I don't know if I could do it and have kids. And I know Paul wouldn't want it. It'd mean such a change in our lives . . .' She faltered as she realised that she'd been speaking as though she still lived with Paul. As though he hadn't walked out on her. She wanted to tell Sophia the truth. But she couldn't. Besides, she reasoned, Paul might come back. What was the point in telling her if Paul came back in the end?

'I know exactly how you feel,' said Sophia. 'And financially the whole thing is a non-starter. But sometimes you need to look beyond the money, don't you? You need a jolt to make you decide. Mind you, this isn't a jolt I'd recommend for everyone!'

Alix laughed. 'So what are you going to do? Give up? Get a nanny? Make Richard give up?'

'I haven't decided yet,' Sophia answered. 'But I feel as though my life has moved on to a whole new level. The things that mattered to me before don't matter as much. I can't explain it, Alix.'

'When are you due?'

'End of January,' said Sophia. 'Poor little mite will demand to go back in because it'll be so cold.'

'Are you going to have it there or come home?'

'Oh, here,' said Sophia. 'We're getting married here too.'

'When *are* you getting married?' The news about the baby had pushed Sophia's wedding plans out of Alix's mind.

'As soon as we can. Probably next month.' Sophia laughed. 'I know it's terribly sudden and I thought about coming home for it, but we've decided to just get it done here then come home and celebrate. Mum and Dad are coming over but we're keeping it a small event, Alix. I'm not really into all this wedding schmaltz.'

'I'm in shock,' Alix told her. 'This morning you were my only other unmarried, living-with-someone, childless friend. Now you're defecting!'

'I feel terribly grown-up,' said Sophia. 'I know it's weird, Alix, but suddenly I remember all the mad things I've done and they seem so trivial and silly.'

'Remember the night of Cliona O'Brien's party?'

'Don't remind me,' said Sophia. 'Do you know, I never even spoke to that bloke afterwards? I could have got pregnant then, Alix – I was so bloody careless!'

'I guess God was looking out for you.'

'So was my mother,' Sophia said. 'And she gave me a right earful. And what about that rave we went to with Josie and Tara? Remember, in Southampton?'

'I will never forget it,' said Alix. 'And every time I see anything about Ecstasy on TV, I wonder if I did myself irreparable damage.'

'I think if anything was going to happen to you, it would have happened by now.' Sophia sighed 'It was eight years ago.'

'I've never taken anything since,' said Alix. 'Part of it was great, but it wasn't me, somehow.'

'That's because you lost all your inhibitions and just had a good time,' said Sophia. 'I haven't seen that happen before or since.'

'I have good times,' said Alix. 'I go to the pub. I drink. Sometimes I smoke – though I'm trying not to. I might have inhibitions but I'm not repressed, you know.'

'I know, I know.' Sophia was surprised at the vehemence in Alix's voice. 'Listen, I'd better go. I'm supposed to be at a marketing meeting in fifteen minutes and I need to run through some details with the troops first. But I wondered if you'd like to come over, Alix. I'd love to see you.' She laughed. 'Before I get married!'

'I'd love to come over,' said Alix, although it was the last thing in the world that she wanted to do. 'Maybe next week, Sophia. I've been putting off a few London meetings for a while. I could set them up and then meet you.'

'Perfect,' Sophia told her. 'Give me a call when you get things sorted.'

'OK,' said Alix. 'I'm glad you rang. And I'm really glad about you and Richard. And the baby.'

'Thanks,' said Sophia. 'Take care of yourself, Alix. Get rid of the cold! And give my love to Paul.'

'Yes, sure,' said Alix. 'I will.'

She replaced the receiver and stared into space. Sophia! The one person she always felt she understood. The one person who definitely understood her. Sophia had now joined the ranks of the disposable nappy and breast-is-best brigade. Sophia was already thinking in terms of her future life outside financial services. Why, thought Alix, why do we have to make a bloody choice?

She glanced at her watch. It was after five o'clock. She wondered what she should do about Paul. She really didn't want to ring him at RTÉ again. And she certainly didn't want to phone him at his mother's home. Besides, if she called him, he'd know that it mattered to her. She didn't want him to know how much it mattered. So she'd wait for him to phone. If he did.

I don't believe it, she said to herself as she curled up in the chair. I'm sitting beside the phone like some lovesick adolescent. I never did this when I was sixteen.

She sat beside the phone for almost an hour but it didn't ring. She was annoyed with herself for caring so much, and furious with Paul for not calling. Maybe she should ring after all, she thought. She was a mature adult, for heaven's sake. There was no need to sit around and wait. If she knew whether or not she was meeting him, then she could plan what she wanted to do for the rest of the evening. Go to the gym, perhaps. Or the shooting club.

She couldn't go to the gym, of course. She was far too exhausted to lift weights or pound the treadmill. And she wasn't feeling strong enough to go to the shooting club either. She'd never be able to support the weight of the gun.

She decided to take a shower. One of the rules of waiting for the phone to ring was to be doing something else. Preferably something that made it difficult to answer straightaway. The shower would be perfect for that.

But in case he called, she switched on the answering machine.

Actually, she thought as she shampooed her hair, it would be good if he rang while she was in the shower. Getting the machine would teach him that she didn't need to hang around and wait for him. Not that he probably cared either way. She stood under the jet of water. Her emotions were all over the place. She didn't know what she wanted him to feel. She didn't even know how she felt.

She was wrapping a towel round her when the phone rang. She stubbed her toe on the bathroom door as she hurried into the living room.

'Hi, I'm sorry we can't take your call but don't hang up. Leave your name. Leave a number. We'll get back to you.'

'Hi, Alix, it's me. Have you got someone else living with you? Who's the "we" on the machine? I just—'

'Paul! I'm here!' she interrupted him. 'Sorry, I was busy, that's why the machine was on.'

'Always busy,' he joked.

'You know how it is,' she said noncommittally.

'Are we still meeting tonight?' he asked.

'Whatever suits.'

'I'm in Dundalk at the moment,' he told her. 'Had to interview someone up here so I'm on the way back right now.

I can meet you if you want, but I've got to see someone else at around half nine.'

'You sound busier than me.'

He laughed. 'It's been all go since I took this job.'

'Why don't we meet for a quick drink,' she said. 'After all, it wasn't ever going to be anything else, was it? What about seven thirty in the Beggar's Bush? It's convenient for me, and for you if you're coming over the toll bridge.'

'That sounds OK,' said Paul. 'I'll see you then.'

'OK,' said Alix. 'Looking forward to it.' It was amazing, she thought, how she was talking to him as though he was a client all of a sudden. Looking forward to it! She'd never talked to Paul like that before.

She went back into the bathroom and rubbed down with the towel before hanging it neatly on the towel rail.

Once she'd dried her hair, she did her nails with her new Lancôme varnish. Alix rarely wore varnish because her nails weren't really long enough. She used the computer terminal so much that it was impossible to have long nails, and whenever she was particularly tense, she bit the nail of her little finger so that it was usually shorter than all the rest. But right now, they were almost uniform in length, the little fingernail a couple of millimetres shorter but not so much that Paul would notice.

~

She arrived at the pub early. It was only a five-minute stroll from her apartment, but she couldn't sit around any longer. The rain that had persisted on and off for most of the day had stopped and the clouds were beginning to break up. Quite suddenly, it was warm and humid.

There were a few people sitting outside the pub when she arrived. She looked inside for Paul without any real hope of seeing him, and when he wasn't there, she ordered a bottle of Miller and took it outside. She knew that she wasn't supposed to drink with the antibiotics, but she was only going to have the beer. She couldn't sit on her own in a pub and drink mineral water.

It was nearly fifteen minutes later before a blue Rover drew up at the pavement and Paul got out. Alix felt her heart miss a beat as she saw him. He looked even more handsome than before – his hair was shorter, he was wearing a pair of stonewashed Levi's which she hadn't bought him and didn't recognise, and a blue Nike top. Paul had always hated branded clothes.

She was glad that she'd decided against wearing the yellow dress she'd bought at lunchtime after all. She hadn't wanted to look dressed-up for Paul and that was exactly how the yellow dress had looked. So she'd chosen a black Kookai top and her black tight-fit denims which she normally had to squeeze into but which, following her loss of appetite over the past few weeks, were now easier to wear. They made her look thin, she knew, and much younger. She'd pulled her hair back into a loose ponytail, unlike the more severe look she used for work, and she was wearing the new silver earrings and chain.

'Hello!' She waved at Paul and he walked over to her and kissed her on the cheek.

'Hi,' he said. 'Can I get you a drink?'

'Let me get you one,' said Alix.

He shook his head. 'What do you want?'

'A bottle of Miller, please.'

'OK.' He smiled at her and his eyes turned vivid blue. 'Back in a jiffy.'

She sat back in her seat, aware of the relief she felt that he'd shown up. She'd had a horrible feeling he might phone and say that he was sorry, he'd been delayed, he couldn't make it. She took her mobile phone out of her bag and switched it off.

'Here you are.' Paul put the drink in front of her. 'God, it's hot again, isn't it?'

She nodded. 'I got caught in the rain earlier. It's hard to believe it's so nice now.'

'Hottest summer since I can remember.'

'Makes it very hard to work,' said Alix. 'You see the blue skies outside and it seems such a shame to be cooped up indoors.'

'Not something that ever worried you before,' said Paul casually.

'It hasn't been this hot before.' Alix was determined not to argue with him. She'd planned her strategy in the time since he phoned. She was going to be relaxed and composed. She wouldn't let him ruffle her and she wouldn't try to score points off him. Serenity would be her watchword.

'So how is the new job?' she asked.

'It's great,' replied Paul. 'I wish I'd taken the plunge before now, Alix. I really do. I know people knock RTÉ and say that national radio and TV is bland and boring – and maybe sometimes it is – but we're working on some really interesting stories and there's so much more in terms of resources! I'm doing stuff I would have liked to do before but didn't have the backup myself. Best thing I ever did. Honestly.'

'That's great,' she said.

He told her about the interview in Dundalk and how he'd had to work to get the confidence of the interviewee and how, eventually, he'd got the story he wanted to get.

'Sounds like you're really enjoying things,' said Alix.

'I am.'

'New car?' She nodded at the Rover.

'Yes.' He looked a little guilty. 'I know I've been anti-car in the past, but I need it now.'

'You never minded borrowing the BMW,' she reminded him.

'But I felt bad about it,' he said.

She laughed. 'Not so's I noticed.'

They were silent for a moment.

'So how have you been?' asked Paul. 'How are things in the big bad world of capital markets?'

'It's been busy,' she answered. 'I'm still having arguments with Gavin Donnelly. Little shit is getting cockier by the day. We've had a few really good days but a few truly horrible ones as well. I'm a little behind budget for the year, but I guess I'll be able to make it back.'

'I admire you,' he said.

'Pardon?'

'I admire you. I always have. You're so – so much in control of yourself. Of your life. Of the people around you.'

She stared at him. 'No, I'm not.'

'You are, Alix. Of course you are.'

'Wyn says that too.'

'There. You see. We can't both be wrong.'

'Of course you can. I'm not in control of anything.'

'You know exactly what you want from life and you've got it,' said Paul. 'If that's not control, I don't know what is.'

'How do you know I've got exactly what I want from life?'

'Because you light up every time you talk about work.

You should see yourself – animated, knowledgeable. I envy you.'

You're just saying that, she thought. You're saying it so that I can't burst into tears and beg you to come back.

'I've been sick,' she said.

'You don't look it,' he told her. 'You look wonderful.'

She was glad he'd said that. It had taken Rimmel concealer, Clarins fake tan and Dior face bronzer to look healthy. She'd sat in front of the mirror and thought that she looked like shit earlier.

He grinned suddenly. 'But you must have been ill. You're wearing your crotch-cutting jeans and you haven't squirmed in your seat once yet.'

She blushed. Paul had always called them crotch-cutters but she hadn't expected him to notice that she was wearing them. 'How come you spotted I was wearing them without the giveaway wriggling?'

'I'm clued in to fashion at the moment,' he explained. 'Doing a piece on double-dealing in the rag trade.'

'Does that explain the Nike top and Levi jeans?' she asked.

'No.' He looked abashed. 'I just thought I should treat myself.'

'Do you miss me?' The question was out before she had a chance to stop it and she was furious with herself. She hadn't meant to ask.

He looked uncomfortable. 'I hate living with my mother. Maybe you were right about her, Alix. She's dreadfully over-bearing. And she asks me when I'm going to be home!'

Be serene, she told herself as he avoided the question. Don't push it.

'I miss you,' she told him. 'Are we in the Superclub?'

'What?' He looked at her in amazement.

'Superclub. Or whatever it's called. Club card. In the supermarket. They asked me when I went shopping and I didn't know.'

He roared with laughter and people at the next table turned to look at them. 'Only you could ask a question like that, Alix.'

'I just wanted to know.'

'Yes,' he said. 'We – or at least I – have a club card. It's in my name but it's the apartment's address. Do you want it?'

'No,' she said in annoyance. 'I just wanted to know if it was something you'd joined.'

'Take the card.' He took his wallet from the pocket of his jeans. 'I don't need it. Mum is doing the shopping. I'm just giving her a fortune in cash.'

'No,' she said. 'You'll need it when you move to Malahide.'

'It's probably a different supermarket out there.' He grinned at her. 'You might as well have this.'

She shook her head. 'I hate that bloody supermarket. I think I'll just buy things as I need them.'

'That's hopelessly uneconomic,' said Paul.

'I don't care.' She was trying very hard not to sound petulant but she knew she did.

Paul drained his glass.

'Do you want another?' she asked.

He hesitated.

'I do,' she said. 'You've plenty of time.' She got up and walked inside. She shivered. Her eyes were beginning to water again. Maybe she shouldn't have drunk two bottles of beer.

She carried his pint and her mineral water outside.

'Water?' He looked at her drink in surprise.

'I shouldn't be drinking any alcohol,' she explained. 'I'm on antibiotics.'

'What exactly is wrong with you?' he asked.

'Don't know,' she said laconically. 'It's not too bad. Wasn't good the first day but I feel OK now.'

'Are you really sick?' he asked. 'Have you been throwing up?'

'No,' she answered. 'But I've had headaches, scratchy throat, that sort of stuff. I'm much better.'

'Have you been off work?'

She nodded. 'Couple of days.'

'You must have been really bad,' he said. 'I don't remember you ever staying off ill.'

She grinned at him. 'What about the night we went to Drogheda?'

'Close,' he said. 'But it doesn't quite cut it.'

It had been when they'd first started living together. Paul had taken her to the Boyne Valley Hotel for dinner and then shocked her by saying that he'd booked a room for the night.

'You can't do that,' she'd told him. 'I've got to go to work in the morning.'

'So what?' he'd said. 'Take a day off.'

'I can't just take a day off.'

'Why not?'

'I just can't!'

But when the phone had rung at half five the following morning, she'd replaced the receiver and snuggled up to him. They'd only been asleep for three hours. After dinner, they'd gone to the room and made love. Just as she'd been falling asleep, Paul had rung room service and ordered a bottle of champagne. He'd insisted on making love while drinking champagne. It hadn't been a very successful exercise in terms of champagne consumption, but it had been hugely erotic. And then they'd taken a bath together because both of them were covered in champagne and that had led to another bout of lovemaking. Alix had told him that she'd never believed a bloke could do it three times in one night. Paul had told her that he hadn't expected to!

So she'd been in no mood to get out of bed at the crack of dawn the next morning and drive to work. She'd tried to drift back to sleep again but she couldn't. So she'd slid out of bed.

'Where are you going?' Paul had woken up just as she was slipping into her shoes.

'Work.'

'Alix! Forget about work! Come back to bed.'

'I can't,' she'd told him. 'I have to go in. I'll be late as it is.'

'Phone in sick,' he'd mumbled. 'God knows, after all the wine and champagne you should feel a little under the weather.'

'I feel great.' She'd kissed him on the forehead and gone to work, even though it had been impossible to concentrate on anything all day.

'Why don't you take some time off?' Paul broke in on her thoughts.

'Too busy,' she said.

'Always too busy.'

She could hear the coolness in his voice. She said nothing and the silence between them became awkward. Paul looked at his watch.

'Before you go,' Alix put her hand on his arm, 'I need to know. Have you been talking to Sabine?'

'Of course,' he said simply.

'What – what is your relationship with her?' Alix hated herself for asking.

'I told you before. And it hasn't changed.'

'When are you moving out to Malahide?' She changed the subject.

'Ten days,' he said thankfully. 'Weekend after next.'

'It'll seem strange, I guess.'

'Not as strange as living with my mother.'

'I suppose not.'

'Alix.'

'Yes?'

'I don't know about Sabine. I truly don't. But I know that I want something different from a relationship than what we had.'

'You liked what we had in the Boyne Valley.'

'I know,' he said. 'And I never stopped enjoying that part of our lives. It's just that there's more to it than making love.'

'I know,' she said.

'I care about you a lot.'

'Do you?'

'Of course I do. Alix, there's so much about you that I love. It's just that I think your priorities are different to mine.'

'What makes you so sure?'

He shrugged.

'You don't really know me at all,' she said. 'You only think you do.'

'I'm pretty certain I do,' he told her. 'Look, I'd better go, Alix. I have to drop home before I go out again.'

'OK.'

He stood up but she stayed where she was.

'It was nice meeting you but I don't think we should see each other for a while,' he said.

'Sure.'

'Do you want a lift back to your apartment?'

'No,' said Alix. 'I'll sit here for a little longer.'

'Are you certain?'

'Yes.'

'OK.' He kissed her on the cheek again. 'Take care of yourself.'

'And you.'

She watched him as he walked to the car and unlocked the door.

If he waves before he gets in, she said to herself, he still fancies me.

She held her breath as he opened the door. He looked back at her, waved, and got in.

She waited until he'd driven away before lighting a cigarette.

Chapter 16

Alix didn't know whether it was the result of the drinks or the cigarette or whether it was simply meeting Paul again, but she felt wretched by the time she got back to the apartment. Her head was pounding, her palms were sweating and every so often she shivered violently.

She sat in her favourite armchair and turned on the TV. Why was the scheduling so bad during the summer? she wondered. Why did producers assume that anyone actually watching TV at nine thirty in the evening was either mentally subnormal or had the memory of a goldfish? The episode of *Friends* they were showing was one that she'd seen at least three times already on this station.

It would be nice though, she thought tiredly, as she watched Jennifer Aniston serve cups of coffee, to have a job where you didn't have to think. And people who cared about you no matter what. She couldn't see Jennifer's character having to worry about junior members of the café plotting to take over her best clients. And if Jennifer was feeling sick with some ridiculous virus she'd happily stay at home while her charming and reliable friends called around to make her cups of coffee and hand out slices of comfort cake.

The thought of coffee and cake made Alix feel ill. She jumped out of her chair, sprinted to the bathroom and was sick in the shower tray.

Oh, God, she groaned as another wave of nausea hit her. Please don't let me puke again. Please.

Better out than in. She clutched at the shower door and tried to tell herself that she was better off for having dumped her granary roll and two bottles of Miller. Dr O'Neill had been surprised that she hadn't thrown up already. At least she was now conforming to the symptoms of the bug. Geraldine O'Neill had also told her to take a minimum of three days off work.

Alix ran her fingers through her damp hair and leaned against the relative coolness of the tiled wall. She should have done what the doctor ordered and she shouldn't have had anything to drink. Haven't you got any bloody sense? she asked herself as she rinsed out the shower.

She dragged herself back to the armchair. Her head, which had felt as though it was going to explode while she was actually being sick, wasn't pounding quite so much now. But she still felt horribly shaky and was shivering violently.

'This is what it would be like if you were pregnant,' she said out loud. Running to the bathroom and puking your guts up every morning. That's what it's like and you'd absolutely hate it. This is what's going to happen to Sophia and she'll regret every minute of it. So, Alix, you've no regrets. You're better off. You'd be hopeless, useless, absolutely dreadful at being pregnant.

But – if it meant having Paul back in her life? Would it be worth it then?

She turned off the TV. She could hardly focus on the screen. She'd be better off in bed. Besides, a decent night's sleep would make all the difference.

It didn't. She tossed and turned all night. At three o'clock she was sick again.

~

She phoned Wyn at seven the next morning.

'I'm really sorry,' she said. 'But I feel terrible. I got up to go to work but I couldn't even stand up without wanting to be sick. I think I should go to the doctor again, but I'm afraid I wouldn't make it to her surgery without passing out.'

'For goodness' sake, Alix!' Wyn was alarmed by the desperate tone in her sister's voice. 'Why didn't you ring me last night? I would have come straight over.'

'I thought I'd be better by now,' said Alix. 'I thought I'd be OK once I got to sleep.'

'I never heard anything so ridiculous in all my life,' said Wyn sternly. 'Why don't you ring the doctor, get her to make a house call? I'll be over as soon as I get the girls to school.'

'Will she do house calls?' Alix was rarely ill – the last visit she'd made to the doctor was for her regular smear test.

'Of course she'll do a house call,' said Wyn impatiently. 'She probably has set times for them.'

'I thought you had to go to doctors,' Alix muttered. 'I didn't think they'd come to you any more.'

Dr O'Neill began her surgery at eight. Alix phoned at a quarter to, and was astonished when the receptionist said that Dr O'Neill did house calls from ten-thirty to twelve. But it would be nearer twelve when she got to see Alix. She had a number of other calls first.

My God, Alix thought as she hung up. Half of the country is obviously down with this bug.

She lay on her back and closed her eyes. She didn't want to feel like this. She wanted to be better. She wanted to be back at work. She wanted to see Gavin Donnelly licking her boots. She smiled weakly at the thought of Gavin licking her boots and then reached out for the receiver to phone the bank.

'Not again, Alix!'

Dave's tone made her flush. She didn't like the implication that she was making it up. 'I was throwing up all night,' she said. 'I feel awful. The doctor is calling around twelve. I'll give you a shout afterwards.'

'It doesn't much matter today,' said Dave. 'There's no news out and no one has meetings. But you know that Gavin is going to the pro-am tomorrow and I have a meeting at half two. That'll leave Jenny on her own.'

'I'm perfectly well aware of the situation tomorrow, Dave,' she said with an authority she didn't feel. 'And I'll be in the office in time to cover for you, so don't worry about it.'

'It's not me that's worrying,' said Dave. 'If you're not here, you're not here. But you know Des. He'll burst a gasket if he finds out that you're out again.'

'Dave, the last time I was out sick you didn't even work for the bloody bank,' she snapped. 'So just don't give me all that shit. I've said I'll be in and I will.'

'OK, OK. Keep your knickers on,' said Dave. 'Although I suppose it should be keep your pyjama bottoms on, shouldn't it?'

She smiled weakly. 'If I wore pyjamas.'

He laughed. 'See, you're getting better already.'

She'd only just hung up from her conversation with Dave

when the buzzer to the apartment sounded. She walked unsteadily to the monitor and peered at it.

'If you gave me a bloody key I wouldn't have to get you out of bed,' said Wyn. 'Hurry up and let me in.'

Alix released the entrance door and waited for her sister to reach the apartment.

'Hi,' she said as she opened the door. 'Come in.'

'Jesus, Alix. You look like shit.'

'Thanks.'

'I mean it.' Wyn's eyes were troubled. 'What's supposed to be the matter with you? I thought you just had a cold.'

'According to the doctor it's some sort of bug. I went on Monday because I felt bad at work. It's doing the rounds apparently. So I suppose I'm giving it to you by making you fuss over me. I'm sorry.'

'There's no need to be sorry,' said Wyn. 'I'm your big sister. I'm supposed to fuss over you.'

'Like you did when I had chickenpox?'

'Most kids would have been happy that their sister loved them enough to try and pick off their spots,' said Wyn. 'Now get into bed! Did you phone the doctor?'

'She'll be here around twelve.'

'Fine,' said Wyn. 'I'll stay with you until then.'

'You don't have to.' Alix was already feeling better now that there was someone with her. 'I think I'm over the worst.'

'Get into bed,' said Wyn again. 'And try to get some sleep. I'll make myself coffee.'

Alix made a face. 'I don't think I have any milk,' she said. 'I came home in a bit of a hurry last night and I forgot to call into the shop.'

'How could you forget milk?' Wyn stared at her. 'Why don't

219

you stock up when you go to the supermarket? It lasts long enough.'

'Wyn, don't panic about milk. Maybe there's some there.' Alix crawled beneath the duvet and pulled it round her.

'I won't panic,' said Wyn dryly. 'Now, go to sleep.'

Alix closed her eyes and listened to the sound of her sister pottering around in the kitchen. It was nice to have someone here to look after her. To worry about things. She definitely didn't feel as ill now that Wyn was here.

Wyn filled the kettle and plugged it in. She looked around the tiny galley kitchen and sighed. Alix didn't seem to use the kitchen for cooking. A week's supply of newspapers (including four Sunday papers all with a range of supplements) were stacked up on the counter. A bundle of Bloomberg financial magazines were piled onto the cooker. A sheaf of bills was in imminent danger of floating down from the top of the microwave.

The kettle boiled. Wyn opened a cupboard door and took out the silver tea caddy that she'd given Alix as a present when she had moved into the apartment. It contained one crumpled tea bag. Wyn sighed and opened the fridge. There was just enough milk for one cup of tea.

After she'd drunk the tea, and when she'd looked into the bedroom to find Alix sleeping soundly, Wyn emptied the remainder of the best before 15 July orange juice down the sink and dumped the carton in the refuse sack, as well as the Easi-Singles (which were also past their best before date) and the half-empty jar of mayonnaise.

The only other items in the fridge were two cans of Miller and a bottle of Chardonnay.

Had Alix any food in the house at all? Wyn asked herself.

Whenever she'd visited in the past, there'd seemed to be plenty of fresh fruit, edible cheese and enough milk for as much tea and coffee as you could drink.

She opened the door of the freezer and leaped out of the way as two frozen Beef Byrianis fell out and almost hit her on the head. She picked the packets off the floor and squashed them back into the freezer alongside four Thai green curries for one and a spinach lasagne.

Honestly, Alix, she thought crossly. You should be eating better than this. It's no wonder you've caught a bug.

She took an envelope from the pile on the fridge and wrote 'Gone to shops – won't be long' on it. She propped it on the bedside locker where her sister would be sure to see it, took the keys from the worktop and let herself out of the apartment.

She'd been gone about fifteen minutes when Alix woke up. She blinked a couple of times and rolled over very slowly. It took her a few minutes to focus on Wyn's note.

Shit, she thought. Wyn would no doubt have done a complete snoop around the kitchen, found it to be completely devoid of food and was now marching through the supermarket looking for fresh produce to counteract the scurvy which Wyn was no doubt assuming she had contracted. She'd meant to do a proper bout of shopping this weekend. She'd even written some things down on a list. But now Wyn would think that she'd gone to pieces completely and she'd start lecturing her on not letting herself go simply because she'd been dumped by her boyfriend. Wyn was a great lecturer about how to get over being dumped by your boyfriend – probably because she had so much practice at it when we were younger, thought Alix viciously, as she thumped her pillow.

She lay on her back and stared at the ceiling. It was nice to have mean thoughts about Wyn who was so irritating when she got into her elder sister mode. Meddling elder sister mode, thought Alix as she recalled last Saturday's blind date with Cathal Moran, organised by her brother-in-law and aided and abetted by his wife.

Wyn was so happy in her marriage and so happy with her kids that it sometimes drove Alix to distraction. She seemed to have found exactly the right person in Terry. How had they known? wondered Alix. How had Wyn been so sure that it was right to marry Terry when she was only twenty-one? And when it was right to start a family? Was everything always bloody perfect for her? Wyn never stopped telling her that it was all very well being a modern career woman but that sooner or later she would want to settle down. Her sister had made such an easy transition from potential high-flier to wife and mother, thought Alix. But she knew she couldn't be like that herself. Yet people seemed to expect it. If you didn't want a horde of screaming children, there was something wrong with you. Even Sophia had sold out. Alix groaned.

The apartment door clicked open.

'Are you OK?' Wyn pushed open the bedroom door.

'I'm fine,' said Alix.

'I thought I heard you moan.'

'You did.' Alix smiled faintly at her. 'But not because I felt bad. Just because I'm stuck here and haven't the bloody energy to get up.'

'You can stay there until the doctor comes,' said Wyn. 'I'm going to fill your fridge. Honestly, Alix. Miller and Chardonnay!'

'Life's little essentials,' said Alix.

'Well, I've bought you milk and eggs and cheese and fruit. I got you some bread and sliced ham. And some tomatoes. And tea bags.'

'Thanks,' said Alix. 'There's some money on the worktop.'

'It wasn't expensive,' Wyn told her sternly. 'It's a lot cheaper to buy decent fresh produce than half a dozen Marks and Spencer's Thai curries.'

'Are there really half a dozen there?' asked Alix. 'I didn't see any before I went shopping.'

'Don't be facetious.'

'Don't be disapproving then.'

'Ungrateful wretch.' But Wyn smiled at her before she went back to the kitchen.

∽

Geraldine O'Neill arrived at half past eleven.

'I didn't think you were that bad, Alix,' she said as she sat on the bed beside her.

'I wasn't,' said Alix. 'I felt miles better yesterday. Then it suddenly came over me again and I was sick.'

'Thought you should have been sick.' Geraldine shoved a thermometer under Alix's tongue. 'Any aches and pains? Neck? Joints?'

Alix shook her head. 'Not specifically,' she mumbled.

'Shivering and sweating?'

Alix nodded.

'Feeling light-headed again?'

Alix nodded.

'Did you stay in bed like I told you?'

Alix shrugged.

Geraldine took the thermometer out of her mouth and looked at it. 'Don't tell me you went to work.'

'I came home early,' said Alix defensively.

'And then you went to bed?'

'I had to meet someone.' She felt herself blush. Wyn, who'd been sitting in the chair by the window, gazed at her sister speculatively.

'Did you have anything to drink?'

'Like?'

'Like alcohol,' said Geraldine.

'Just a bottle of beer.'

'For goodness' sake!' Geraldine looked at her angrily. 'You had to be carted from your office to my surgery. I tell you that you have a particularly nasty bug and to stay in bed for three days. You proceed to go back to work and meet friends in the pub. Honestly, Alix. Are you actually surprised you've had a relapse? Not that you were ever really better in the first place.'

Alix looked at her sheepishly. 'Sorry.'

'So you should be.' Geraldine strapped a blood-pressure pad round Alix's arm. 'When I say stay out of work I mean stay out of work. What is it with people that they feel this need to rush back to the office? You work in a bank, don't you? Surely there's plenty of people who can cover for you.'

'I'm a dealer,' said Alix. 'I'm in charge of the dealing room, Geraldine. I had to go in yesterday. It was important.'

'Don't be stupid,' said Geraldine. 'Your health is far more important than jumping up and down and shouting buy and sell and whatever other rubbish it is that you do.'

'It's not rubbish,' said Alix. 'It's—'

'Relax, relax. You'll burst the monitor.' Geraldine grinned at her and Alix made a face. 'OK,' said Geraldine finally. 'You *are* taking the tablets I prescribed already?'

'Yes,' said Alix.

'I want you to take these as well.' She scribbled another prescription and handed it to Alix. 'Start today. Finish the course. Also, stay in bed today and tomorrow.'

'But I can't stay in bed tomorrow,' protested Alix. 'Honestly I can't.'

'Of course you can.' Wyn got up from the chair and walked over to the bed. 'You're staying there and you're not getting up. I'll make sure of that.'

'You don't understand.' Alix wished she could get through to them. 'I can't just stay out. I'm needed.'

'No you're not,' said Geraldine brutally. 'If you were run over by a bus they'd have to get on without you. And that's exactly what they'll do tomorrow.'

Alix bit her lip. She had no doubt that they could get on without her, but she didn't want Dave Bryant telling Des that she had let them down. She felt herself grow even hotter at the thought.

'Come to the surgery on Monday evening,' said Geraldine as she repacked her bag. 'Five thirty until seven.'

'OK,' said Alix.

'And do what I said. Your immune system is weakened. I don't want you to pick up anything else.'

'What exactly is the matter with me anyway?' asked Alix.

'Viral infection,' said Geraldine. 'Covers a multitude, I know. But that's what it is. You'll be fine in a few days but you really must stay in bed and rest. I mean it, Alix. Even Saturday and Sunday you should take it easy.'

'I always take it easy at the weekends,' said Alix.

Wyn showed Geraldine out then came and sat on the edge of Alix's bed. 'What did she mean, carted to her surgery?' she asked.

Alix made a face. 'I was ill at work. They sent me home.'

'How ill?'

'I felt bad,' said Alix. 'I fainted.'

'Alix!'

'Lots of people faint,' said Alix. 'It wasn't a big deal.'

'You're not pregnant or anything, are you?' asked Wyn suddenly.

'Don't be absolutely ridiculous,' retorted Alix. 'How the hell could I be? Paul doesn't live here any more.'

'I thought, perhaps, that before he left—'

'Give me some credit,' said Alix. 'When I told him I didn't want kids, I meant it.'

'Did you meet Paul last night?' asked Wyn.

'Of course. I told you I was going to meet him.'

'But you were ill.'

'So what?'

'It was bloody stupid to meet him if you weren't feeling well!'

'Don't be ridiculous,' said Alix. 'You sound like the sort of mother Carrie isn't.'

'She'd want to know if you were being stupid.'

'Oh, give me a break,' Alix snapped.

'It's your business, I suppose,' said Wyn. 'But why don't you make a clean break of it? What's the point in clinging to him? You're not the clinging type, Alix.'

'I think he's making a mistake, that's all.'

'Do you love him?' asked Wyn.

'Of course I do.'

'Are you sure?'

'Don't give me that shit.' Alix closed her eyes. 'I can do without the lectures, thanks.'

'No one ever broke it off with you before, did they?' continued Wyn. 'You were always the one.'

Alix shrugged.

'I just wonder if you're trying to hang on to him simply because you can't believe that anyone would want to leave you,' said Wyn.

'Wonder all you like,' said Alix. 'I'm sick, I don't want to talk about it.'

'I'm sorry,' said Wyn. 'Honestly I am.'

Alix opened an eye.

'I'm so used to seeing you up and about and in control of things that I can't imagine you don't feel well enough to argue with me.'

Alix smiled weakly. 'I enjoy arguing with you. Usually.'

'Oh, Alix. I just want you to be happy,' said Wyn. 'Really I do. But it seems to me that Paul has a point. After a certain age people's priorities change. They did with me.'

'Come on, Wyn. You always wanted a husband and kids.'

'Yes, but not straightaway. It was just that when I met Terry—'

'Love's young dream.' Alix yawned.

'A career isn't everything,' Wyn continued. 'And everyone says that yours is a young person's game. And you're not as young as you were, Alix.'

'Thirty-two is hardly old, Wyn.'

'But it's different to when you're twenty-two.'

Alix sighed. 'I really don't want to talk about this any more. I'm tired.'

'I'll let you get some sleep,' said Wyn. 'I want to wash out your fridge anyway.'

Alix closed her eyes. Arguing with Wyn had exhausted her. She tried to think about Paul and babies, but she was asleep within five minutes.

❦

When Wyn had finished cleaning Alix's kitchen she tiptoed into the bedroom, took the prescription and went to the chemist to get it filled. Although she was sorry that Alix was ill, she couldn't help enjoying her role in looking after her. Alix was so damned independent, she thought as she crossed Haddington Road. She hated the idea of not being able to do everything for herself. Wyn remembered her when they were children, pulling her tricycle up the hill at the back of their house, determinedly trying to keep up with her elder sister and her friends. Alix's four-year-old legs struggled to keep up, but when Wyn (in a sudden fit of sibling duty) turned round to help her, Alix struggled away from her. 'I can do it myself!' she'd cried, tugging at the handlebars of the bike and pushing Wyn out of the way. And she had.

But Wyn couldn't understand why Alix always seemed to want to test herself. The high-pressure job in a male-dominated industry. Taking part in shooting competitions at the shooting club. Pushing herself to the limits in the gym. Alix had once invited Wyn along to the gym with her. Wyn had agreed, looking forward to a gentle jog on the treadmill and a leisurely swim afterwards. She'd been astounded to see her sister push herself through what seemed to Wyn, at least, a punishing regime of bike, treadmill, rowing machine and weights.

'You're not training for the bloody Olympics,' Wyn commented sourly as she watched Alix use the shoulder press.

'I like it,' her sister said. 'It makes me feel good.'

But there had to be something wrong with someone who felt that they needed to push themselves all the time, thought Wyn. There wasn't any need for Alix to do everything she did.

The chemist was busy and Wyn had to wait for Alix's prescription. She'd lecture Alix about taking the tablets, she said to herself. She knew that her sister would be just as likely to forget about them once she felt the slightest bit better.

And she'd better make sure that Alix didn't even consider going in to work in the morning. Perhaps she should call round, just to be certain.

'I said I wouldn't go in and I won't,' Alix said when she woke up two hours later. 'Though I do feel a lot better now.'

'Maybe you do, but you won't if you go to work tomorrow.'

'I told you, I'll stay home.'

'Fine,' said Wyn. 'The doctor said that you should stay in bed. I'll call round at nine, see how you're doing.'

'There really isn't any need,' Alix protested.

'I'd like to,' said Wyn. 'If you give me a spare set of keys you won't even have to get up.'

'Really, Wyn—'

'It's no trouble at all.' Wyn smiled sweetly at her. 'I wouldn't be much of a sister if I left you to suffer all on your own, would I?'

❧

Alix waited until after three to phone Dave.

'I'm sorry,' she said. 'I'm not going to be able to make it in tomorrow.'

'Fuck it, Alix!' Dave sounded annoyed as she knew he would. 'You know I'll be out in the afternoon. And you know Gavin's taking people to Portmarnock! We need you here.'

'It seems that my bed needs me more,' said Alix dryly. 'I'm sorry. I feel a lot better but my doctor – and my sister – have both absolutely forbidden me to get up. So you'll have to manage without me. Is there any chance you can reschedule your meeting?'

'Are you crazy?' asked Dave. 'You know what it's like trying to get to see Arnie. He's put me off twice already.'

'I'm really sorry, Dave. But Jenny can cope and you could ask Mike Keogh to help with the phone lines. It probably won't be that busy anyway. There aren't any economic releases due and it'll probably be one of those quiet Fridays where everyone goes home early.'

'You know that's rubbish,' said Dave gloomily. 'You know how it's always when you're short of people that something really major breaks and it's a complete nightmare.'

'I'll phone in the morning,' said Alix. 'See how things are.'

'Things are fine, to be honest,' said Dave. 'It's not that we can't manage, Alix. It'd just be nice to have the bodies around.'

'It's great to feel wanted,' she muttered. 'Look, if there's a problem, just call me. The phone is right beside me.'

'Sure,' said Dave. 'We'll see you on Monday.'

'Absolutely,' said Alix. 'Monday.'

She lay back and closed her eyes again. She wondered which was worse for her health, work when she was ill or to be away from the office when she just knew that those bastards were waiting for an opportunity to shaft her.

It was Carrie, not Wyn, who called round the following morning. Alix was in the kitchen inspecting the new contents of her fridge when her mother rang the bell.

'Where's Wyn?' asked Alix as Carrie walked into the apartment.

'I told her I'd call to see you this morning. She rang me last night.' Carrie picked up the kettle and began to fill it. 'You should be in bed.'

'I'm much better,' said Alix. 'And there wasn't any need for Wyn to ring you.'

'You're my daughter,' said Carrie. 'I need to know these things. And Wyn was right to tell me.'

Alix sighed. She supposed that Wyn had enjoyed ringing Carrie and telling her that she was sick and alone. They probably had a nice girly discussion about poor, solitary, deserted Alix who was doomed to a life of single womanhood.

'Go back to bed,' said Carrie. 'I'll bring you in a cup of tea.'

'Coffee,' Alix told her. 'I was going to make coffee.'

'Tea is better for you.'

Alix gritted her teeth and went back to bed. There wasn't any point in arguing.

She was watching CNN on the portable TV when Carrie brought a mug of tea and a slice of toast in to her.

'Thanks.' Alix took the tray from her.

Carrie picked up the remote control and turned off the TV.

'Oh, switch it back on!' Alix cried. 'I was watching a piece about the Tokyo markets.'

'Nothing you can do about the Tokyo markets from your

bed,' said Carrie briskly. 'So there's no need for you to be watching it.'

Alix said nothing.

'So.' Carrie sat on the edge of the bed. 'What the hell is all this about?'

'All what?' asked Alix defensively.

'Collapsing at work! Too ill to get to the doctor's surgery.' Carrie's eyes were full of concern. 'Alix, I'm worried about you.'

'I have a bug,' said Alix. 'According to the doc, lots of people have it. It's no big deal. I know I was very sick, but you know me, Carrie, I always had a flair for the dramatic when it came to illness. Remember all my stomach upsets as a kid? Puking everywhere and right as rain next day. There's no need to fuss. It's the same now.'

Carrie looked at her daughter thoughtfully.

'But I was worried yesterday,' Alix conceded. 'I knew I was pretty shaky and I thought I should go back to the doctor. So I did what you have to admit was the most sensible thing I could have done and asked Wyn to come over.'

'How come you were so susceptible to this bug?' asked Carrie.

'Who knows?' Alix shrugged.

'I'll tell you,' said her mother. 'You were as tight as a drum when you called into the salon. You looked tired and unwell. And it's all because of this thing with Paul.'

'Oh, Carrie, for God's sake! It's nothing to do with Paul.'

'You miss him, don't you?'

'Well, of course I miss him,' snapped Alix. 'It's only been a few weeks.'

'But according to Wyn you're convinced he'll come back.'

'He might.'

'What makes you say that?'

'I just know.'

'And if he does, what then?'

'What do you mean?'

'Are you going to change for him?'

'Change?'

'Alix. Cop on. Paul wants to settle down and have a family. A reasonable enough desire at his age. And at yours. So it seems to me that the only way you're going to get back together is to settle down and have a family.'

Alix put her half-empty mug on her bedside locker. 'Maybe. Maybe not.'

'Alix, when you want to have children it's a really strong desire. If Paul feels like this now, there's nothing you can do to change him.'

'I never said anything about changing him.'

'I can see it in your eyes,' said Carrie. 'You're thinking that somehow you can get him back and make him forget this children nonsense. Maybe promise to do something about it next year.'

Alix squirmed uncomfortably in the bed.

'It's not like that,' Carrie continued. 'You can't just put him off. If you truly don't want kids, then you should forget about Paul.'

'Thanks for your support,' said Alix tartly.

'I'm only trying to help,' said Carrie. 'Make you see how things are.'

'And if I give in to Paul and have a kid before I'm ready, then everything will be OK.' Alix laughed shortly. 'It sure worked for you, didn't it?'

'Alix!' Carrie went white. 'You don't know anything about that. Anything at all!'

'Oh, come on,' said Alix. 'You're a businesswoman, Carrie. You settled down and had kids. And he still walked out on you. Lot of good that did you.'

'First of all,' said Carrie, keeping her voice as steady as she could, 'both of us wanted children. I wasn't a businesswoman. I worked in a beauty salon. I had to change when he walked out on us. That was nothing to do with you or Wyn. It was about him and me.'

'And who wanted children in the first place?' asked Alix. 'Him or you?'

'We both did,' answered Carrie.

'But, like most men, he couldn't take it once we were born.'

'Alix, you weren't the reason he left.'

'We weren't enough reason for him to stay,' she said.

Carrie rubbed her temples. 'It was nothing to do with you,' she said again. 'Or Wyn.'

'But the point is,' said Alix, 'men are not necessarily the best people to decide that they want kids. I've heard them in the office, you know. Blokes who talk about the wife and kids as though they were talking about some encumbrance. Having to go home is a duty to them half the time. And any time there's a crisis, it's the wife who has to run around picking up the pieces. She's the one who takes time off if one of the children gets sick. She's the one who has to make sure they've got the right stuff for school. She's the one who remembers birthdays and is rushed to a frazzle at Christmas. Meanwhile blokes stay late at the office and go for pints after work and look at Christmas as one long party season! And as

234

soon as their wives get pregnant they're ogling every girl in the office.'

'It's not like that,' said Carrie.

'Yes it bloody is,' snapped Alix. 'If you're a working mother you're guilty for working and guilty if you give it up. Nobody looks at you in the same light any more. Actually, even if you're not pregnant, once you get married they're waiting for the announcement almost straightaway. I've worked really hard, Carrie. Really, really hard. I've had to do all they do and more. I'm not ready to give it up to have kids.'

'So you're not ready to spend the rest of your life with Paul.'

'He's started a new job,' said Alix. 'He's really happy there. I bet he's not quite so eager to start a family too.'

'I wouldn't bet on it,' said Carrie.

'You hardly know him,' Alix told her.

'I know people,' said Carrie. 'Most men like to have a wife and family. You might not think that, but they do.'

'They like to have a wife and family so that they have something to moan about in the office,' said Alix.

'Why are you so bloody cynical?' demanded Carrie.

'I'm not. I'm just practical.'

Her mother sighed. 'Don't you ever want to have kids?'

'Maybe,' said Alix. 'But I'm still young.'

'Not getting any younger.'

'Oh, don't you start! Listening to Wyn you'd swear I was ready for HRT.'

'You get more pleasure out of your children than anything else,' said Carrie softly. 'More than work, more than anything.'

'I'll take your word for it.' Alix leaned back against the pillow.

'It's true,' said Carrie.

Alix closed her eyes.

Carrie watched her for a moment, then took the tray back into the kitchen.

Chapter 17

When Alix woke up again it was midday and she felt a hundred times better. She slid out of bed and wrapped her towelling robe round her.

Carrie was sitting in the living room watching Jerry Springer on TV.

'How on earth can you look at that rubbish?' asked Alix.

'It makes me laugh.' Carrie turned to look at her. 'How are you feeling?'

'Much better,' replied Alix. 'I've stopped shivering and my head doesn't hurt any more.'

'Good.' Her mother smiled. 'But you should still stay in bed, Alix. There's no point in rushing things.'

'I feel fine,' Alix protested.

'You probably felt fine the other day,' said Carrie. 'Please, Alix. Just for once do what someone else tells you.'

Alix sighed. 'OK. But I need to ring the office and check how things are going.' She ran her fingers through her hair and wrinkled her nose. 'And I want to take a shower. I feel so grubby.'

'Go ahead,' said Carrie. 'It's a good idea. You'll feel better.' She reached for her red and white striped canvas bag. 'Here. Use this. Aromatherapy shower soap. It'll relax you.'

'Thanks.' Alix took the sample bottle her mother gave her. 'You don't need to stay with me. I know Friday is a busy day for you.'

'I told Samantha that I'd be in around three,' said Carrie. 'I'll make you some lunch and then I'll go.'

Alix sat down on the sofa beside her mother and hugged her. Carrie looked at her in astonishment.

'We don't hug very often,' said Alix. 'And I do love you, you know.'

'Don't be an idiot,' said Carrie, but she hugged Alix back.

Before she showered, Alix logged on to her computer to check on markets. It looked as if it was a quiet day, the graphs were all within very narrow ranges. She picked up the phone and dialled the office.

Jenny answered.

'How are things, Jenny?' asked Alix.

'Great,' said Jenny. 'Actually, you've picked a reasonable enough day to be out. Forex markets are quiet and there isn't too much going on in fixed income. The Footsie's up ten, so nothing much there either.'

'What have you done for cover this afternoon?'

'Mike will sit in for the afternoon,' said Jenny, 'though, to be honest, he probably won't have anything to do. The phones haven't been ringing much this morning.'

'Good,' said Alix. 'Can you put me on to Dave for a second?'

'Sure,' said Jenny. 'He's just finishing up a call. How are you feeling, Alix?'

'Much better,' she replied, 'but the doctor was adamant that I shouldn't come in. So I thought I'd better listen to her for once.'

'You were right,' said Jenny. 'Hang on, I'll pass you on to Dave now.'

'Hi, Alix. How are things?' asked Dave.

'Not bad. Listen, Dave, did you send the table of historical rates to Gary Hafford? I left it on my desk and I completely forgot about it.'

'He rang yesterday,' said Dave. 'I didn't know it was on your desk so I re-ran it and sent it by e-mail.'

'Thanks,' said Alix. 'Anything I need to know about?'

'Nope,' said Dave dismissively. 'It's been pretty quiet so you don't have to worry too much. Did a nice five-year swap with Charlie Mulholland yesterday. We were going to run it because the market was moving slightly in our favour and I liked the position. Then we were asked for a price in the interbank market and dealt. So we picked up ten basis points on five million.'

'That's great,' said Alix.

'Gavin did a trade with Christie Reardon and we made another four grand on that. So, even though it's been quiet, it's been profitable.'

'Excellent,' said Alix. 'I presume he's got everything organised for the pro-am this afternoon.'

'Yes. He's sent them the tickets and they're meeting in the clubhouse for a pint and sandwiches first. I told Gavin to order toasted bacon, egg and sausage. Portmarnock is famous for it.'

'Ugh,' said Alix. 'I was feeling OK until you said that.'

'Will you be back on Monday?' asked Dave.

'Absolutely,' said Alix. 'I'm much better.'

'See you then,' said Dave.

'Right,' Alix said. 'Tell Gavin to have a good time. And you have a good meeting with Arnie.'

'Sure.' Dave clicked out of the line.

Gavin looked up from his monitor. 'So, how is she?'

'Sounds OK,' said Dave. 'Hard to tell. She said that you're to have a good time today.'

'Huh,' said Gavin, 'bet she hopes it's a disaster.'

'She's not like you.' Jenny stretched her arms over her head. 'She probably *does* hope it goes well.'

'It will,' said Gavin. 'It will.'

～

He'd been afraid that some people wouldn't show up, but by half past one they had all arrived. Even Matt Connery, whom Gavin had been the most doubtful about.

'Hi, Matt,' he said as the taller man was shown over to their table. 'Nice to meet you. Gavin Donnelly.' He extended his hand.

'Hi, Gavin. Nice day for it.' The sun was shining from a clear blue sky and the breeze was from the south-west.

'Sure beats the hell out of sitting in the office,' said Gavin.

'Wouldn't mind being on the course myself.' Matt sat down beside him. 'Though they'd have me arrested for wanton destruction. I like watching golf, but I'm not a great player.'

'Member anywhere?' asked Gavin.

'We've got corporate membership in the K Club,' said Matt. 'But I don't usually use it. Too embarrassed.'

'Can I get you a drink?' asked Gavin. 'And a sandwich? We're on toasted bacon, egg and sausage.'

'Sounds good to me.' Matt grinned. 'And a pint of Carlsberg, please.'

'Coming up.' Gavin was pleased at how the day was going

so far. Some of the clients knew each other already, but those that didn't were getting along well and Matt Connery looked pleased to be there. Gavin knew that the right sort of corporate entertaining was worth its weight in gold. Some clients liked gold-card-style entertaining – brash and obviously expensive. Others preferred events like today's, a relaxed day out in an informal atmosphere. And as long as they didn't have to put their hands in their pockets they were happy. Everyone enjoyed being entertained.

'Feel free to follow whoever you like,' said Gavin, after they'd finished the sandwiches. 'I thought what we could do is to meet up in the tent for a beer around four, four thirty, and then we could head back to Gibney's in Malahide for a few more. For those of you who drove here, if you want to leave your cars in Malahide later, I've organised drivers to drive you and your cars home.'

'Sounds good,' said James Morrissey, one of Gavin's best clients. James was twenty-four and worked in an insurance company. He got on well with Gavin and both of them often went on drinking binges together.

'Excellent.' Niall Baldwin added his approval.

'Great,' said Gavin. 'Let's go.'

They split up as they walked towards the course, James and Niall electing to follow Darren Clarke and his partner, a minor television celebrity. Joe Fitzgerald, Martin Dawson and Eddie Byrne wanted to camp at the ninth. 'I come to grief here every time,' said Martin. 'I want to see how the celebs get on.'

'Any preference?' Gavin asked Matt Connery and Dermot Doyle. He would have liked to go with James and Niall but today was work and both Matt and Dermot were his newest accounts.

'Think I'll just watch a few of them teeing off,' said Matt.

'Good idea,' said Gavin.

'I'll join you shortly,' Dermot told them. 'I see someone I know over there – won't be long.'

Gavin and Matt strolled to the first tee where Padraig Harrington was chatting to his caddy.

'Do you play much?' asked Matt.

Gavin shrugged. 'Not as much as I'd like, to be honest. I used to play every day but I don't get the time these days.'

'Busy at work?'

'Yes,' said Gavin. 'We're doing really well right now. Got a lot of new clients, fresh interests.'

'What's Europa Bank like as a place to work?' Matt applauded a long, straight drive from Harrington.

'It's good,' said Gavin. 'Lots of freedom, flexibility. If you think something is worthwhile you're encouraged to go for it. Most of the time.'

'And Alix Callaghan? It must be unusual to work for a woman in the dealing area.'

'Oh, Alix is a legend,' said Gavin easily. 'She's very committed to the job. At least, she used to be.'

'Used to be?'

'I suppose people's attitudes change as they get older,' Gavin mused. 'I don't think she has as much time for it as she used to have. But maybe I'm wrong.'

'What makes you say that?'

'Hard to define,' said Gavin. 'Just an impression I got. Between ourselves,' he leaned towards Matt, 'I think there's a bit of boyfriend trouble. And you know how the girls get when things aren't going smoothly in that department.'

'What sort of boyfriend trouble?'

'I don't know.' Gavin laughed. 'We were putting bets on her getting either pregnant or married in the next few months. But Jenny – she's our other female dealer – Jenny thinks that Alix's current relationship might be going through a rough patch.'

'Why is that?'

'Womanly intuition, I suppose – oh, great shot!' Gavin applauded the club pro's drive.

'She did a great presentation for us,' said Matt.

'What?'

'Alix. She did a great presentation to the board.'

'She's good at that,' Gavin conceded.

'Why didn't she come out today?' asked Matt.

'She's not really into golf,' said Gavin, 'which is a huge disadvantage in this business. Also, she has a feminist thing about Portmarnock's non-lady membership. It's stupid, really. Half the major deals get done on the golf course. Anyway, she's still out sick.'

'She's been out all week,' said Matt.

Gavin shrugged again. 'That's what I mean about not being as interested.'

'What is she interested in?' asked Matt.

'Do you know, I haven't a clue,' said Gavin. 'She goes shooting, that's all I know. Hi, Dermot. Did you see that drive? Brilliant, wasn't it!'

'Wish I could do that,' said Dermot Doyle glumly. 'I always hook mine. Always.'

⌣

Alix was glad that Carrie had left. She was pleased to be on her own again, feeling reasonably OK and checking the computer every so often to see how the markets were doing. She felt incredibly guilty to be out of the office when she was feeling so much better. It wouldn't have done her any harm to sit at the desk simply to answer phones as necessary. But Jenny was right. The markets were quiet and it probably was a good day to be out.

She turned on the TV. Another one of those cookery programmes! Why did they go to all that bother with garnishes and colours and making everything look so attractive when it all tasted pretty much the same in the end? Alix thought about the business lunches and dinners she attended where the waiters brought the food to the table with such a flourish and hovered around anxiously checking whether or not everything was OK when nobody really cared what it tasted like. All they wanted to do was to talk about the bigger, better and more important deals that they'd done. Sometimes the stories they told were even true!

Food was for refuelling, Alix thought, as she watched the chef slice vegetables at an incredible speed. She was a burgers and chips person really, not a timbale of crab with cherry tomatoes and fresh basil.

The phone rang and she jumped.

'Hello,' she said.

'Alix. How are things?'

'Who's that?' she asked.

'Oh, come on! Don't tell me you've forgotten already!'

'Cathal?' she guessed.

'Exactly. I said I'd call this week and I left it until the very end of the week so that you wouldn't think I was pressuring you. I gave your office a buzz but they said that you were out today. Doing anything nice?'

'Actually I've been out sick,' said Alix. 'I caught some kind of bug at the weekend and it pretty much flattened me all week.'

'Hope it wasn't anything you ate in Roly's!' Cathal laughed.

'No, more of a flu thing,' said Alix.

'Are you feeling better now?'

'Much,' said Alix.

'I was wondering if you'd like to go to dinner tonight?'

'Oh, Cathal, that's nice of you. But the doctor said I was to stay in bed for the next couple of days.'

'That doesn't sound too good,' said Cathal. 'Are you sure you're OK?'

'I'm fine,' said Alix impatiently. 'But I went back to work when I shouldn't have and I relapsed. So I'm following her instructions to the letter this time.'

'Maybe I could drop round for a while,' suggested Cathal. 'I could bring some pizza or Chinese or Indian food, if you like?'

'That's really good of you, but I'm not hungry,' said Alix. She laughed. 'One good thing about being ill. You lose weight without having to try.'

'You don't need to lose weight,' said Cathal. 'You're perfect the way you are.'

'Thanks,' said Alix. 'But even so, Cathal, I'd prefer to be on my own right now.'

'Are you certain?'

'Yes,' she said. 'Besides, I might still be infectious. Wouldn't like to be the cause of you catching anything.'

'It'd almost be worth it,' said Cathal.

'I've got to go,' Alix told him. 'It's time for my tablets.'

'OK,' said Cathal. 'I'll give you a call next week, see how you are. Monday, maybe.'

'I – oh, OK.'

'Take care, Alix.'

'Sure.'

Shit, she thought, as she stared unseeingly at the TV. Cathal Moran was a nice guy but definitely not for her. Wyn, of course, didn't see that. Carrie wouldn't see that either. Alix sighed. She didn't want a new relationship. New relationships were far too much trouble. Finding out about someone. Discovering their likes and dislikes. Having to endure an evening of country music or heavy metal simply because some bloke thought it would be fun! Then having to decide whether or not to go to bed with them afterwards.

No, she decided. Far too much trouble.

❧

Gavin had managed to stick with Matt Connery for most of the afternoon. He'd discovered that Anatronics was thinking about taking over another animation company and that, if so, they'd be looking for new financing facilities. They might borrow on the US private placement market, Matt told them. They hadn't decided yet.

Gavin had asked about their future foreign exchange and interest rate business. Matt said that they were happy with their current arrangements – foreign exchange was shared between Europa and another bank, with Europa getting the lion's share. Borrowings were mainly with an American bank at the moment. Deposits were shared.

'Are you happy with what we're doing for you?' asked Gavin.

'Sure,' Matt replied. 'Otherwise I wouldn't call.'

'What about other business?' Gavin asked him. 'Options, perhaps?'

'Haven't decided which route we're going down,' said Matt. 'Alix left some pretty good information packs with us after her presentation. We're still thinking about it.'

'She goes into everything pretty thoroughly,' said Gavin.

'I liked her.' Matt grinned at him. 'Nothing fazed her. Our MD asked some ridiculous question about pricing something and her answer was so clear and precise that even he understood it. And all without blinking an eye!'

'Sounds like she really impressed you.' Gavin knew that he was gritting his teeth.

'I like women with brains,' said Matt.

'She's only part of the Europa Bank team,' said Gavin as lightly as he could.

'Oh, I know,' said Matt. 'And don't worry, Gavin. I appreciate all you've done for us.'

'Great,' said Gavin. 'Thanks. Can I get you another drink?'

Des Coyle, the managing director of the bank, was at the bar.

'Hi, Gavin,' he said. 'Having a good day?'

'Yes.' Gavin beamed at him. 'They're all enjoying it. Weather's been great, everything's working well.'

'Who's that guy I saw you with?'

Gavin glanced back towards Matt who was chatting to James Morrissey. 'Matt Connery, Anatronics. We've been doing some small forex trades for them. A little bit of deposit business too. But they'll be much bigger, Des. And I'm working hard to make sure that when they deal in size, we'll be ready.'

'Excellent,' said Des. 'In the meantime, fill 'em with food and drink and keep 'em entertained.'

'Exactly.' Gavin smiled.

'I believe you're a bit of a demon on the golf course yourself.' Des took a sip from his beer.

'Oh, could be better,' said Gavin.

'Dave told me you play off twelve.'

'As I said, could be better.' Gavin laughed.

'Where are you a member?'

'Here, actually,' said Gavin. 'My father's a member too.'

'I'm in Woodbrook,' said Des. 'We must have a round together sometime.'

'That would be great.' Gavin nodded at him.

'I'll look at my diary on Monday. Let you know.'

'Thanks, Des.' Gavin gathered up the drinks he'd ordered.

'Have fun,' said Des.

'Absolutely.'

Yes, thought Gavin as he walked back towards the group of clients, yes, yes, yes!

Chapter 18

Alix felt nervous as she took the lift to the third floor on Monday morning. She couldn't understand why she should feel this way, she'd never felt anxious on her return from her fortnight's holiday which she took every May, or her week's skiing at the end of January. Those times she bounded enthusiastically back into the office, eager to know how things had gone in her absence. Now she was nervous.

She was in before anyone else. She sat at the dealing desk and called up the deals for the previous week. It had been busy enough, she thought ruefully, and a lot of trades had been done for her own clients. Charlie Mulholland had dealt. So had Christie Reardon. So had a number of her smaller accounts. And so had Matt Connery. Another foreign exchange deal, less than half a million dollars again, executed by Gavin Donnelly.

She should let him have the account. It didn't matter in the scheme of things. She was still the head of treasury. She was the one who called the shots. She was in control. So why was it, she thought, biting her lip, that she felt as though she was the one who was being outmanoeuvred at every turn?

'Good morning, Alix. Are you better?' Jenny smiled at her as she walked into the room.

'Completely,' Alix assured her. She watched in surprise as

Jenny came round to sit at the desk beside her. 'What are you doing?'

'Dave thought it would be a good idea if we switched,' explained Jenny. 'He's going to sit beside Gavin. He said that he'd be able to keep an eye on him that way.'

'Did he?' Alix tapped her pen on the edge of the desk. 'And Gavin said?'

'Gavin was delighted. Oh, Alix, you know he and I don't get along that well. To be honest with you, I wanted to move.'

'And nobody thought of waiting until I was back to ask me?'

'We didn't think you'd mind,' said Jenny. She looked quizzically at Alix. 'Do you? We could always switch back, I suppose.'

Do I mind? Alix asked herself. Or am I being paranoid? Are those bastards really out to get me?

'No, I don't mind,' she lied. 'How was business in my absence?'

'Oh, fine,' said Jenny. 'No traumas. Dave is working on some Polish zloty deal with Guy Decourcelle at the moment. It looks like it's actually going to work! The bank gets fees and the dealing room ends up with cheap six-month dollars.'

'Really.'

'Yes. Dave wasn't too sure about the mechanics of it but he had a long conversation with Guy who pretty much set him straight and the whole thing will be closed this week or next, we hope.' Jenny beamed at her.

Now I'm praying that the zloty deal will go wrong, Alix realised. I'm hoping that the whole thing will blow up in their fucking scheming faces and that we lose a fortune! This is not me, she tried to tell herself. I believe that when one of us makes money, we all make money. Don't I?

'Good morning!' The door banged open and Dave walked in. 'How's the patient?'

'Better, thanks,' said Alix.

'Good. Not infectious any more?'

'Hopefully not.'

'We had a good week while you were out.' Dave took off his jacket and hung it over the back of his chair. 'Did you see the profit and loss?'

'Yes.'

'Pleased?'

'Of course.'

'You don't sound very pleased,' said Dave peevishly. 'If I'd been out and the room had ended up making the guts of a hundred grand on the week, I'd be pretty pleased.'

'Would you?' asked Alix. She looked up and caught Dave's eye. They stared at each other for a couple of seconds before he looked away.

'Profit is profit,' he said abruptly.

'And I see you've done a bit of moving around the place too,' said Alix.

'It was a good idea,' said Dave. 'I thought it would be helpful if I sat next to Gavin for a while. Keep an eye on him, that sort of thing. He's awfully bright, Alix, but inclined to lose it a bit sometimes.'

'So I noticed. We'll see how it works out. Anything on the agenda for today?'

'Morning all!' Gavin walked in carrying a bag of doughnuts. 'Anyone want breakfast?'

251

'Jesus, Gavin, doughnuts?' Jenny wrinkled her nose. 'At this hour?'

'Why not?' he asked. 'Very nutritious they are too. I think. Alix, would you like one?'

'Thank you.' She took one covered in pink icing and sugar strands. 'How did it go for you on Friday?'

'Absolutely fucking brilliant.' Gavin grinned broadly at her. 'Great day, Alix. Super weather, course was playing great, everyone had a good time.'

'And they all showed up?'

'Oh, yes. We walked around for a while, followed a few of the matches. Then we had a couple of beers. A couple of them left after that but Niall, James and Matt came back to Gibney's where we had a few more.'

'And what time did you finish up?' asked Alix.

'Around eleven.' Gavin smirked. 'I tell you, those blokes will be eating out of the palm of my hand. I was so good to them. They won't dream of dealing anywhere else.'

'I don't want to disillusion you, but most of us feel like that after corporate outings,' said Alix dryly. 'And the gratitude lasts only as long as it takes to get a competing quote that's better than the one you gave them.'

'She's right,' said Dave. 'But I must say, I thought Matt Connery enjoyed himself.'

'How do you know?' asked Alix.

'Because I called out to Gibney's myself,' said Dave. 'But of course Paul wouldn't have told you.'

She stared at him, aghast. 'Paul?'

'He was there,' said Dave. 'We were both talking to him. Gavin and me. He was telling us about his new job in RTÉ.'

Alix felt her throat constrict. 'He's mad about the job.'

'Bloody hell, yes. So I said that you must hardly see him at all these days and he said not bloody likely since he was moving out to Malahide. He'd been doing some DIY around the house. You didn't tell us anything about that, Alix. That he'd given you the boot.'

Alix stared wordlessly at Dave.

'Still, he's not with some other woman,' Dave assured her. 'At least he wasn't on Friday night. He was with a gang of very arty types!'

'What's the story, Alix?' Jenny looked at her wide-eyed.

'There isn't a story,' said Alix briskly.

'But why have you and Paul split up? Is that what was wrong with you? You were upset about it and didn't want to come in?'

'Don't be absolutely ridiculous,' snapped Alix. 'I certainly wasn't upset about Paul. I had the flu.'

'Psychosomatic,' said Gavin.

'I was at the doctor,' said Alix. 'I had to take antibiotics.' God, she thought, why am I even telling him this?

'Probably brought on by stress, though,' said Jenny. 'After all—'

'Jenny, forget it,' said Alix. 'It doesn't matter.' She punched a few letters on her keyboard. 'We've work to do. Dave, you'd better give us a rundown on last week. And don't leave anything out.'

The three dealers exchanged knowing glances while Alix stared unseeingly at the screen in front of her. She felt humiliated. She should have told them before now so that they would have found out on her terms. By keeping it quiet, by pretending it hadn't happened, she'd made herself look a complete fool. She scrolled through the computer worksheet, ignoring Jenny's sympathetic glances.

'The main thing for this week is the zloty transaction.' Dave didn't look directly at Alix. 'I'm going to Paris tomorrow morning to tie up some details with Guy.'

'Tomorrow?' Alix glanced up at him.

'Flight out tomorrow morning,' he told her. 'We're meeting in Europa Bank at two.' He grinned. 'I'm looking forward to that – I haven't been in the new dealing room yet and you said that it was fabulous, Alix.'

'Yes,' she said. 'It is.' *De l'audace, encore de l'audace, et toujours de l'audace!* she thought wryly.

'Anyway, I'll be back Wednesday and I have a meeting with Des and Jim Rothwell at lunchtime to go through the whole thing.'

'How about me?' Alix looked at him. 'Am I involved in this meeting?'

'If you like,' said Dave. 'It's up to you.'

'We'll see,' she said.

'Apart from the zloty . . .'

But Alix didn't hear the rest. She was thinking about Dave and Guy in Paris working out the deal, dividing up the profit, being pleased at how things were panning out. She could see Dave chatting expansively to Guy and maybe going to some club with him later that night – something that she couldn't (and wouldn't) have done. And she could almost hear them swap stories about her. Guy would probably tell Dave that she must be frigid because he, Guy, had offered her a good time and she'd refused. And Dave would tell him that Paul had dumped her and that she'd been off work for a week with an imaginary illness. She felt herself grow hot and cold at the thought.

'Are you all right?' Jenny looked at her anxiously. 'You're

very flushed, Alix. Are you sure you should be back in the office?'

'I'm fine,' she snapped. 'Come on, let's get to it.'

At eleven o'clock, when the markets were quiet, she called down to Des Coyle's office.

'Alix!' He stood up as she entered the room. 'How are you feeling?'

'Much better, thanks, Des.'

'What was wrong with you?'

She shrugged. 'Some kind of viral infection, according to my doctor. I thought I'd shaken it off but she was right. I needed to stay in bed for a few days.'

'Everything went OK in your absence,' Des assured her. 'You've built up a strong team, Alix.'

'Yes,' she said, 'I have.'

'You know Dave is involved in the zloty transaction?'

'Sounds like a good deal,' said Alix. 'We'll end up with cheap dollars and Jim ends up with cheap funding. Good for both of us.'

'Dave worked hard on it.'

'He tells me he's going to Paris tomorrow.'

'Yes. He needs to go through the final details with Guy and he thought it would be better if they could sit down and look through the papers together.'

'I agree,' said Alix.

'Anything else on the cards for this week?' asked Des.

'Not yet,' she said. 'I have to reschedule a few meetings, that sort of thing.'

'Don't push yourself too hard,' said Des. 'These viruses are hard to shake off. You might think you're OK and the next thing you know you've relapsed. Take it easy.'

'Sure,' she said.

Not a chance, she thought, as she walked back upstairs. She was going to work even harder. The current trauma in her life was caused by her work. If it was causing her pain personally, she was damn sure she was going to make it pay dividends professionally. She certainly wasn't going to let anyone in the dealing room push her out of her job.

The others were all on the phone when she walked back into the room. Another line rang and she picked it up.

'Europa Bank, dealers. Alix Callaghan,' she said.

'Hello, Alix. Feeling better?'

'Matt?' she said cautiously. Because so much of her work was done on the phone she was adept at recognising voices. But it seemed like ages since she'd last spoken to him.

'Yes,' he said. 'How are you?'

'A lot better,' she said. 'I believe you had a good time on Friday with Gavin.'

He laughed. 'It was fun.'

'I rang,' she said uneasily. 'To thank you.'

'For what?'

'The flowers.' Her voice had dropped to almost a whisper. The others were too busy to listen to her anyway.

'Oh, you're welcome. Gavin told me you were sick and I just thought – it was probably very silly of me.'

'No,' she said. 'It was nice.'

'Nice,' echoed Matt. 'That sounds – boring.'

Alix laughed. 'Sorry.'

'And are you feeling better?'

'I'm fine,' she said.

'Good.'

There was a moment's silence.

'What can I do for you?' asked Alix.

'Actually, I didn't ring to trade,' said Matt. 'I rang to invite you to lunch.'

'Lunch?' said Alix.

'Yes.'

'I have to tell you I'm not a great lunch person,' she said. 'I get a bit edgy. Want to get back to work, you know.'

'It's not any old lunch,' Matt assured her. 'We're having a preview screening of a new animated movie we've been working on. A few of our other business partners will be there. I thought you might like to come along.'

'Oh.' Alix smiled. 'That sounds interesting.'

'It'll be fun,' said Matt. 'Next week. I'll send you a formal invitation but I thought you'd probably forget about it if we just did that. So I wanted to ask you personally.'

'I wouldn't have forgotten,' she protested. 'Not if you sent a formal invitation! What d'you take me for? But I'm glad to come.'

'Good,' said Matt. 'You should get the invitation by tomorrow. I'll look forward to seeing you.'

'In the meantime, is there anything we can do for you?' Alix laughed. 'Spot, forward, interest rates?'

'No,' he chuckled. 'I think I did the month's dealing while you were out. Sorry about that.'

'No problem,' she said. 'I'm sure Gavin looked after you very well.'

'He did.'

'Well, thanks for the call,' said Alix.

'See you next week,' said Matt.

She disconnected the line. Gavin was looking at her suspiciously.

'Who was that?' he asked.

'Matt Connery.' She smiled at him.

'What did he want?'

'To ask me to lunch,' said Alix.

Gavin stared at her.

'But he did mention that he'd had a great time on Friday,' she told him. 'It sounded like he really enjoyed it.'

'Good,' said Gavin shortly and Alix suddenly felt a lot better.

&

'Would you like to go for a sandwich?' Jenny asked Alix at twelve thirty. 'I'm starving.'

'Depends on what the guys want to do.' Alix looked across the desk at Gavin and Dave. 'Anything planned?'

Dave shook his head. 'I want to do some work on the zloty transaction for tomorrow,' he said. 'I'm going to order a roll or something. I can stay here.'

'And you, Gavin?'

'I'll stay here too,' he said.

'OK.' Alix smiled at Jenny. 'A sandwich it is.' The smile didn't reach her eyes. She still felt under pressure. Dave was going to Paris instead of her; Gavin was undoubtedly raging that Matt Connery had asked her to lunch and was probably plotting his revenge; and Jenny was going to pump her for information about her break-up with Paul.

'My treat,' said Jenny as they sat at one of O'Reilly's outside tables.

'If you like,' said Alix.

'So, how are you feeling?' asked Jenny.

Alix sighed. 'If anyone else asks me how I'm feeling I'll scream. You've asked me already. I'm better.'

'I didn't mean about being sick,' said Jenny. 'I meant about Paul.'

'I'm fine about Paul,' said Alix.

'What happened?' asked Jenny. 'If you don't want to talk about it, that's fine, but I thought you and Paul were for life, Alix. You always seemed so close. If I had to make a price on anyone splitting up, it wouldn't have been the two of you.'

'How sweet,' murmured Alix.

'So what went wrong?'

'First of all,' Alix unfolded her paper napkin, 'nothing went wrong, as you put it. Paul and I are going through a difficult patch. We both want different things from the relationship. We decided it would be a good idea to live apart for a while.'

'So he hasn't dumped you?' asked Jenny.

'When you get to my age you'll discover that relationships are more complicated than dumping or being dumped,' said Alix.

'Says who?' Jenny cut her roll in half.

'Says someone who knows,' said Alix.

'But don't you think it would be better to work things out together?' asked Jenny. 'I mean, it seems to me that being apart is a backwards step.'

Alix regarded her thoughtfully. 'Maybe it is. But we took it anyway. And I think it's a good idea. Besides, it's not as though we're not speaking or anything like that. I met him on Wednesday.'

'Maybe that's why you were sick on Thursday!' Jenny giggled. 'Couldn't stand the sight of him.'

'It wasn't like that.' Alix smiled.

'But you have to admit that it's odd that you got sick after he – after you decided to live apart.'

'Not at all,' said Alix.

'But you're never ill,' protested Jenny. 'I don't remember the last time you were out of the office.'

'I do.' But it had been a long time ago. 'Anyway, Jenny, it doesn't matter, it's a personal thing and nothing to do with work.'

'I wasn't even suggesting it had anything to do with work.' Jenny looked surprised. 'I just thought you might like to chat about it, that's all.'

'Thanks, but I'm fine,' said Alix.

'Just because you're my boss doesn't mean I don't care if you're upset,' said Jenny.

'I'm fine,' repeated Alix firmly. 'What I'd really like to know is how the blokes reacted to my being out for another couple of days.'

'I thought they'd argue more,' said Jenny, 'but actually they worked quite well together. I suppose because Dave was doing the zloty thing and Gavin was all fired up about his golf outing.'

'Which went well,' said Alix.

'I guess so.' Jenny emptied a sachet of sugar into her coffee. 'He was pretty happy about it this morning, wasn't he?'

Alix nodded.

'You're still the head of treasury,' said Jenny. 'Nobody is as good as you.'

'Thanks for the vote of confidence.'

'Dave isn't as assured. Gavin is too reckless.' Jenny took a sip of coffee. 'You're still better than both of them.'

'And if I wasn't, would you tell me?'

Jenny made a face. 'I don't know,' she answered honestly. 'I suppose I would.'

'If you think I'm losing it, I want you to tell me,' said Alix. 'It's important to me, Jenny.'

'OK.' Jenny nodded. 'I'll tell you.'

~

'She's pissed off at you.' Gavin propped his feet up on the desk and looked at Dave.

'Maybe.'

'She wants to go to Paris.'

'Tough,' said Dave.

'We've rattled her.'

Dave grinned. 'I know.'

'What do you want?' asked Gavin. 'You said you didn't want her job, but you do, don't you?'

'It'd be good on my CV,' said Dave. 'I don't necessarily want it forever, but head of treasury sounds a damn sight better than senior dealer.'

'And senior dealer sounds better than dealer,' commented Gavin.

'We haven't got rid of her yet,' said Dave.

'But if she leaves?'

'Actually,' Dave clasped his hands behind his head, 'this Paul thing makes it a bit less likely, don't you think? After all, we were assuming that she was getting broody and thinking of settling down, which might have made her chuck it in. If she's finished with Paul it seems to me a lot less likely.'

'Bugger!' Gavin took his feet off the desk. 'I never thought of that!'

'Of course, she might be so distraught that she'll blow it anyway,' mused Dave.

'Perhaps she'll want to move abroad,' suggested Gavin. 'She might ask for a transfer to Paris.'

Dave looked at his colleague thoughtfully. 'That's an idea. Maybe I should suggest it to Guy. Ask him if he thinks Alix would work well there.'

Gavin's eyes brightened. 'Brilliant idea.'

'That's me.' Dave grinned at him. 'Planning ahead.'

﹋

Alix sat on the balcony and sipped a glass of water. She was still on a no alcohol regime. She'd called into Geraldine O'Neill's surgery on the way home and the doctor had told her that she was much better but that she should still take it easy. Geraldine had suggested that Alix take a week off. Alix had laughed and told her that she'd just had a week off.

'Somewhere hot and sunny,' Geraldine advised. 'Relax, Alix. You're awfully tense.'

Alix was fed up with people telling her she was tense. Anyone would be tense if they had to go into Europa Bank every day and face the concerted effort that was Gavin and Dave. It was funny, she mused, how she now thought of them as Gavin and Dave not Dave and Gavin. All of the pressure was coming from the younger man. Until Gavin had arrived, Dave had been happy to work with her and for her.

She flushed as she remembered their comments about Paul. They must be thrilled to think that he'd dumped her. To them it was a sign of strength. Poor, feeble Alix, distraught at her lover's departure, gets sick. Poor, feeble Alix spends the best part of a week at home sobbing her eyes out. She gritted her teeth. They could think what they liked. She knew the truth. She knew that she could get Paul back. If she went about it the right way.

If she knew what the right way was.

Chapter 19

Alix had learned the art of travelling light years earlier. For her trip to London she packed a pair of black trousers, a silk blouse and a white shirt – a combination which covered either a dressed-up night out or a sloppy night out. She also packed a very fine cashmere top just in case. Including her toilet bag, underwear and a pair of very light black leather Italian shoes she'd bought in Florence, everything fitted into a small overnight bag which she could carry onto the plane. Alix hated having to wait for luggage after a flight. Given that a part of her day was taken up with work, she wore a simple Principles suit which made her look efficient and businesslike. Alix quite happily mixed designer labels and multiple-store clothes. If they looked good she didn't care where her clothes came from.

Alix knew that she should feel guilty about using a trip to London to see her friend, but she didn't care. At least, not much. She could justify the journey, though, because she had two meetings lined up before she was due to meet Sophia and she knew that she could make it worthwhile.

She took a cab from City Airport to Chase Bank's wonderful building at London Wall, where she had a very agreeable meeting with Colin Harper, a dealer she'd known for years.

Then she strolled back to Bishopsgate for her second meeting, this time in NatWest.

Russell Cobham, the specialist US company where Sophia worked, also had a building in Bishopsgate, so after another successful meeting, Alix walked up the street to meet Sophia.

'You can go up.' The security guard handed Alix an ID badge. 'The fourteenth floor.'

Alix waited for the lift while she fiddled with the tag. It always irritated her that so many of these security badges were designed to clip onto the top pocket of a suit. Very few women's suits had top pockets. As usual, Alix ended up clipping the badge to the waistband of her skirt where, she thought, it looked absolutely ridiculous.

Russell Cobham had redecorated the offices since Alix had last visited Sophia a year earlier. Gone were the ultramodern clear plastic seats, chrome uplights and glass tables that had been in the reception area before. They'd been replaced with maroon leather seats, green shaded lamps and heavy mahogany tables. In a period of recent market volatility, Russell Cobham were clearly trying to look serious and long-term. She sat in one of the leather seats and waited for Sophia.

'Alix! How are you?' Sophia beamed at her. 'How was your day? You look fantastic!'

'Thanks.' Alix kissed her friend on the cheek. 'My day was fine. And you, Soph, you look absolutely wonderful.'

Sophia Redmond was almost as tall as Alix, with honey-coloured hair coiled into a loose knot on the back of her head, and hazel eyes.

'I feel wonderful.' Sophia's eyes sparkled. 'Well, I do now. This hasn't been an exactly great week for me. I've got the most wretched heartburn and I haven't slept a wink.'

'You'd never guess.'

'I fake it,' said Sophia solemnly. 'That Christian Dior face stuff you gave me last Christmas is a godsend!'

Alix laughed. 'Glad you found a use for it.' She stepped back and looked at her friend. 'Sophia, are you sure you're pregnant? Only you don't seem to have put on an ounce of weight.'

Sophia turned a circle so that Alix could look at her. 'It's all in the cut,' she said. 'The jacket hides the bump so well. It's vital, you know, not to look as though you're going to pop at any minute. It scares them if they think you might go into labour during office hours!'

'Well, you don't. You look as efficient as ever.'

'Thanks,' said Sophia. 'Do you want to come into my office? I just need to finish something on the computer and then I can leave.'

'OK. If you don't mind having someone hanging around while you work.'

'It's nothing much,' said Sophia. 'But I want to get it finished. You know how it is.'

Alix nodded and followed her along the corridor. To her right was a huge dealing room where men, mainly dressed in jeans and casual shirts, were shouting prices at each other. Occasionally, someone in a suit joined the fray. There were no women.

'We decided on a dress-down policy for Fridays,' said Sophia as they walked past the room and into an adjoining office. 'But I couldn't be bothered to get casual maternity outfits for the office. It was bad enough having to buy the more formal stuff. And my leggings are too scruffy. Anyway, sit down anywhere. I'll only be a couple of minutes.'

Alix sat in one of the visitor's chairs and picked up the *Wall*

Street Journal. One of the things about working in financial markets was that she always wanted to read everything she possibly could about what was going on in the world. However, she rarely had the time to read anything. Her news was gleaned from the TV and the radio and the constant headlines that scrolled up on the Reuters and Bloomberg screens in her office. It was nice to simply sit back and read newsprint for a change.

Sophia's phone rang and she swore softly. 'No, Ramon,' she said. 'I can't come to a meeting at six . . . yes, I know it's vitally important but only to you . . . of course we'll still be able to do it on Monday . . . if anything goes horribly wrong you can e-mail me at home . . . yes, I believe you can handle it yourself . . . I wouldn't have suggested it otherwise . . . OK, Ramon . . . have a good weekend.'

Sophia was warm but efficient, thought Alix. She wondered if she was warm enough herself. Sophia had been sympathetic and friendly with Ramon. It was a long time since Alix felt she'd been sympathetic and friendly with anyone in Europa Bank.

Her friend sounded so much more at ease than she did.

'Finished,' said Sophia with satisfaction a couple of minutes later. 'I think that package will be pretty impressive for my presentation next week.' She logged off her computer and rubbed her eyes. 'I wish they'd invent a screen that didn't tire you out.'

'Are you supposed to sit in front of that all day?' asked Alix. 'In your condition, I mean?'

Sophia grinned. 'I don't sit in front of it all day. I used to. But actually, I spend more of my time at meetings than anything else these days.'

'And do you prefer that?' asked Alix.

'Sometimes,' Sophia admitted. 'But I like doing the research. More fundamental.' She smiled at Alix. 'Ready to go?'

Alix nodded.

'Do you want to go straight back to the house?' asked Sophia. 'Get rid of the travel stuff, freshen up?'

'Yes, please,' said Alix.

'And after that, do you want to eat posh or homely?'

Alix laughed. 'Oh, homely, I think. I'm not really a posh person, Soph. You know that.'

'Come on, then.' Sophia smiled. 'Let's grab a cab and book something homely.'

~

'Richard won't be home for ages,' said Sophia as she unlocked the door of the house. 'He never gets in before seven and he plays indoor soccer on Friday nights with a gang from work.' She rubbed the base of her spine. 'Just thinking about indoor soccer makes my back ache. Do you want to bring your stuff upstairs? The usual room, Alix.'

'Thanks.' Alix carried her bag up the stairs to the pretty blue and white painted bedroom while Sophia went into the living room and poured herself a Malvern water. She really wanted a gin and tonic but she was trying very hard to be a good mother to her unborn child.

'Drink?' she asked as Alix walked into the room. 'I'm on water myself but there's loads in the cupboard. Although there are plenty of things Richard will share with me, abstinence isn't one of them.'

'I see his point of view.' Alix poured herself that gin and tonic that Sophia would have liked. 'Cheers.'

'Cheers.' Sophia raised the glass of water. The two friends smiled at each other.

'So.' Sophia placed her glass on the coffee table. 'Do you want to have a shower and all that sort of thing and hit the restaurant early? Or do you want to fall into intimate gossip straightaway and send out for food when you're too drunk to walk?'

'I haven't been too drunk to walk in a long time,' said Alix. 'And I'd really love to have a shower.' Now that she was here, face to face with her friend, she found that she wasn't ready to spill her guts about Paul. Not yet.

'Fine,' said Sophia calmly. 'I'm glad you said that because I'm going to wallow in the bath for twenty minutes. It's soothing. I'll give the restaurant a call and book us in for seven. It's only a five-minute walk.'

'Sounds good to me,' said Alix.

She sipped her drink while Sophia made the reservation. It was good to be somewhere different, she thought. Good to be away from Dublin, even for a couple of days. She suddenly realised how sick she was of being alone in the apartment every night and how poor her social life had been in the last few weeks. Except on the occasions she'd met Paul, she hadn't been to a pub or to the cinema since he had left. The only other events she'd been to were the bank's tenth anniversary night and the blind date that Terry and Wyn had so ridiculously organised for her. She gritted her teeth as she remembered it. Other than that, she'd been to the shooting club once and the gym once. And that was all. The rest of the time she'd sat around and wondered when Paul was coming back. Of course, she had been sick. She had to allow herself a whole week of being unable to go anywhere. She drained her glass and stood up.

'See you here in about half an hour?'

Sophia nodded. 'Take your time, Alix. We're not in a rush.'

Alix laughed. 'You used to be a very rushed kind of person as far as I remember, Sophia Redmond.'

'I still am.' Sophia grimaced. 'But I'm trying to chill out a bit more. For the sake of junior. My gynaecologist tells me to be calm. And you know how it is, Alix. Women are always supposed to do what their gynae tells them.'

'I don't know how it is exactly,' Alix grinned, 'but I'm pretty sure that your gynaecologist is terrified of you.'

'I wish.' Sophia finished her water. 'I was hoping for a sympathetic woman. I got a man who is wonderfully reassuring but talks to me as though I have a mental age of about ten.'

'Never mind,' said Alix. 'I'll ask you lots of hard questions later. Get your intellectual level back to its peak again.'

⌒

They strolled down the road to the Italian restaurant, enjoying the warmth of the evening sun on their backs.

'Wonderful Indian summer,' remarked Sophia.

'Fabulous,' agreed Alix. 'Remember last year? Rain and hurricanes and all sorts.'

'You went to Mexico, didn't you?'

Alix smiled wistfully. 'Cancun and Playa del Carmen. It was wonderful.'

'Where did you go this year?'

'Majorca. Pollensa. We had a good time.' She flicked an imaginary strand of hair out of her eyes. 'We always had a good time on holidays.'

Sophia was silent.

'And all the time I didn't know that he was yearning for a suburban house, a dog, a cat and two point four children.'

'Cross over here,' said Sophia. 'That's the restaurant.' She pointed at a green and white striped awning over a huge picture window.

'Looks good,' said Alix.

'But homely.' Sophia grinned at her as they walked inside.

Although it was early, the restaurant was almost full. Alix and Sophia sat at a table near the window and looked at the menus.

'I get ravenously hungry,' remarked Sophia. 'But as soon as I start to eat I feel full. I'll just have a pizza.'

'Same for me.' Alix closed the menu.

'Wine?' asked Sophia.

'Only if you're having a glass.'

Sophia shook her head. 'As an incubator I'm not supposed to drink. And although I had a few glasses before I realised that Sophia junior was on the way, I've decided I'd better do things properly.'

'Fine by me,' said Alix. 'We'll just have Pellegrino.'

Sophia gave the order to the waiter who returned a moment later with the mineral water.

'Cheers.' Sophia raised her glass.

'Cheers.'

'So, Alix.' Sophia looked thoughtfully at her friend. 'Do you want to tell me what the story is with Paul?'

Alix exhaled slowly. 'I – suppose so.'

'It's really upset you, hasn't it?'

'More than I thought,' admitted Alix.

'Why?'

'I don't know.' Alix ran her finger round the rim of her glass.

'We don't have to talk about it now,' said Sophia. 'We don't have to talk about it at all if you don't want to. We're supposed to be having fun!'

'I think that was part of the problem,' said Alix wryly. 'Paul thought I was having too much fun.'

'Too much fun?' echoed Sophia.

'He complained that I was still living my life as though I was twentysomething when, in fact, I should be settling down and thinking of starting a family.'

'And you don't want to?'

'Settle down and start a family?' Alix smiled at Sophia. 'It's a bit callous of me to say no when that's exactly what you're doing.'

'Starting a family yes, settling down no!' Sophia laughed. 'Do I look settled down to you?'

'You looked very efficient in the office,' said Alix. 'And you look almost normal now.'

Sophia was wearing a loose denim shirt over a pair of jeans. 'Maternity jeans,' she hissed earlier when Alix had expressed surprise that her friend could fit into jeans. 'They have an elasticated waist.'

'Anyway it's not how you look, it's how you feel,' Sophia said. 'I didn't think that I'd ever feel maternal, Alix, but I have to confess that I do now.'

'You see,' Alix sighed. 'That's what everyone says. That if you get pregnant you suddenly change. But Soph, I'm not ready to change yet. And I didn't think Paul was either.'

'But he has changed,' said Sophia. 'So what are you going to do about it?'

'It's what he's done about it,' Alix told her. 'He's moved back into his house in Malahide and he's got some French bird who's going to move in with him.'

'Alix!' Sophia stared at her. 'You didn't tell me all this before!'

Alix didn't reply as the waiter arrived and placed their Quattro Staggione pizzas in front of them.

Sophia made no attempt to pick up her knife and fork, but continued to stare at Alix.

'Don't look at me like that,' said Alix uncomfortably.

'Alix, you've split up with your boyfriend of three years and you've waited until now to tell me? When did this happen?'

'About a month ago,' said Alix.

'Had he moved out when I phoned?'

Alix nodded.

'And you didn't say anything?'

Alix squirmed in her seat. 'I wasn't sure about it. Whether or not he'd come back. I . . .' She didn't finish the sentence and looked miserably at her plate.

'You'd better tell me the whole lot now,' said Sophia. 'And don't leave anything out.'

So Alix told her. Her voice wavered when she said that Paul and Sabine had met at a Europa Bank bash in Paris. 'If I hadn't brought him along he'd never have met her,' she finished bitterly. 'And everything would still be OK.'

'Well, maybe not.' Sophia finally ate a piece of pizza. 'I mean, he can't have suddenly decided he wanted to rush off and start procreating.'

'I suppose not,' said Alix tiredly. 'But I didn't know he was thinking like that. And Soph, she doesn't even look like the sort of woman who wants to jump into the whole family scene. I only vaguely remember her, but in the photo – admittedly not a very clear photo – she looks about seventeen and she has that blonde spiky look that school kids have. Part of me thinks the baby thing is just an excuse. But he didn't need that sort of excuse.'

'This Sabine is a designer?'

'That's what Paul told me. But afterwards I remembered meeting the designer. I'd say she's more of a decorator or painter or something.'

'Arty,' said Sophia.

Alix nodded.

'Maybe not very businesslike.'

'Possibly not.'

'And therefore not as threatening as you.'

'Oh, for heaven's sake, Sophia! I'm not threatening.' Alix placed her knife and fork firmly on her plate.

'In the business sense,' said Sophia. 'In the money stakes, Alix.'

Alix shook her head. 'I can't believe it's all about money.'

'But Paul said so,' Sophia told her. 'You said that he threw it in your face that you earn more than he does. He obviously resents that.'

'But it's so silly,' objected Alix. 'It was never an issue before.'

'So maybe it's an issue now because he's older and you're still doing better than him.'

'I don't see why,' said Alix mutinously. 'I loved him, Sophia. I thought he loved me. If there was a problem, why couldn't he talk about it?'

'I don't know,' answered Sophia. 'But talking isn't exactly what most men are good at.'

Alix smiled faintly. 'I suppose you're right.'

'So what are you going to do now?' asked Sophia. 'Now that you're single all over again?'

Alix pushed her half-eaten pizza away. 'I don't feel single all over again,' she said. 'In fact, I don't want to be single all over again. I want to work it out with Paul.'

'But, Alix, what can you work out? Unless you've decided that you want your career to take a back seat to your relationship?'

'Have *you*?' asked Alix fiercely. 'Is that what you're planning, Sophia? To give up the struggle at Russell Cobham and stay at home with the baby?'

Sophia took a sip of Pellegrino. 'No,' she said honestly. 'But that's not an issue between Richard and me. And maybe I'll feel differently about it when the baby is born. Maybe there are other things besides boardroom battles and avoiding getting stabbed in the back.'

'Not for me,' said Alix.

'Why?'

She stared at Sophia. 'Because that's the way it is. I like my job. I want to keep doing what I'm doing. Maybe in five years or ten years or something I'll change.'

'Maybe in five years or ten years it'll be too late,' said Sophia.

'Oh, don't you start!' Alix banged her fist on the table. 'Wyn's already had a go at me about my bloody biological clock! I expected something different from you.'

'I can't tell you anything different,' said Sophia reasonably. 'And I'm only stating a fact, Alix. In ten years you'll be in your forties. It's not exactly easy to start conceiving in your forties.'

'Why is it so hard to have what you want?' asked Alix.

Sophia shrugged. 'I don't know.'

'But you have what you want.'

'I didn't know I wanted it until I had it,' said Sophia gently. 'And I still don't know if I can have it all.'

Alix rubbed her eyes. 'I don't want it all,' she said miserably. 'I just want it to be the way it was before. I was happy, Sophia. I truly was. Paul and me – we just seemed to work, you know? And Europa Bank was such a good place for me too.'

'Was?'

Alix sighed. 'They're having a go at me in the dealing room,' she said. 'I haven't been on top form lately, Soph. Obviously. And they scent blood. Dave Bryant – remember him? You met him last year – Dave is supposed to have said he doesn't want my job, but I know he does. And he's aided and abetted by Gavin Donnelly. We hired him last summer. He's a good trader, or at least he will be, but he's so ambitious! He brokes clients into deals that they probably shouldn't do and it's made us lots of money but one day it'll all go wrong. And I'll be caught in the crossfire.'

'Don't be silly,' said Sophia.

'And there's an account that we're fighting over,' said Alix. 'I mean, it's crazy, Soph, it's only a small account. It has the potential to be big, but it's peanuts at the moment. But it's become a kind of symbol of the clash between us. Gavin keeps booking trades with them and I'm keeping tabs on him and I won't allocate him the account even though I probably should. It's so stupid. And I can't help myself!'

Sophia looked at her sympathetically. 'But that's business, Alix. It happens all the time.'

'I know,' said Alix. 'But I could cope with it when Paul was around. I just can't seem to cope now.' To her surprise and horror she started to cry. She rubbed at her eyes with her napkin.

'Are you all right?' asked Sophia.

She wanted to say yes, she was, but the tears were flowing freely now and she couldn't speak. Sophia watched her in silence. She had never seen Alix like this before. In all the time that she'd known her, Alix Callaghan had been the most self-contained person she'd ever met. Even on the occasions when she'd got blazingly drunk, Alix had never truly lost control of herself. When, for the one and only time, they'd taken drugs and Alix *had* let herself go, she'd been embarrassed afterwards and refused to take anything ever again.

'You just want to draw experiences in,' Sophia said to her the next day. 'And you don't let anything out.'

Alix had laughed and told her friend not to be so stupid. But Sophia was right. She didn't let herself go. Yet now she was sitting in a restaurant, a public place, and crying as though she was never going to stop.

'Here.' Sophia pushed a clean tissue at her.

Alix took it wordlessly.

'What's upsetting you more?' asked Sophia. 'The situation with Paul or the situation at work?'

Alix scrubbed at her eyes. 'I don't know,' she muttered. 'They're entwined, Sophia. Don't you see?'

'Maybe.'

'As long as I was with Paul everything was OK. Since he moved out, my life has been a disaster. Work is a shambles, my social life has fallen apart. I've had the flu – and you know me, Soph, I'm never ill. I can't seem to control anything any more.'

'And controlling things is important?'

'Don't try to psychoanalyse me,' said Alix sharply. 'It's not all about control. It's about your life moving the way you expected.'

'So what do you want to do?' asked Sophia.

'I wish I knew.' Alix smoothed her hair. 'I have no idea what I want to do.'

'Do you love Paul?'

'Of course I bloody love him,' she said. 'Christ, Sophia, what do you think this is all about? I'm a basket case because I hate him?'

'I'm only trying to help,' said Sophia.

'I know. I'm sorry.'

'So you love Paul and you want him back. But to get him back you have to oust Sabine. And you have to want children. And give up your job.' She looked at Alix. 'Is that it?'

Alix sighed. 'Probably.'

'Are you ready to do all that?'

'Why does it have to be one thing or the other?' she asked. 'Why can't I have Paul, keep my job and think about babies?'

'Did he ever talk about it before?' asked Sophia. 'Was this a complete bolt from the blue?'

Alix considered the question. 'We talked about it,' she admitted. 'I told him that I wasn't ready.'

'When?'

'Last January.'

'So you had some idea.'

'I didn't think he was serious.' She began to cry again. 'I'm a fucking idiot, Sophia. He was trying to tell me stuff and I wouldn't listen. He's right. I *am* selfish. I *am* self-centred. I *don't* care enough about other people. As long as I'm happy I don't think about anyone else's happiness.'

'That's not true,' said Sophia.

'It is.' She buried her face in her hands while Sophia gazed at her in disbelief.

'Stop crying, Alix,' said Sophia.

'I can't.' The tears were streaming down her face and she was shocked by them. She was crying in a crowded London restaurant where people could look at her and point their fingers at her and wonder what on earth was wrong with the girl in the white shirt. This wasn't her. It wasn't.

'Alix,' said Sophia gently. 'Please stop crying.' She reached out and took her friend's hands from her face.

'I want to, but I can't.' Alix gulped.

'It's probably really good for you but you'll make yourself sick.'

'I hate my life,' she blurted. 'I've got it all wrong, Sophia. I was so fucking smug about my job and my boyfriend and my lifestyle. And now it looks as though I've lost them all.'

'Don't be utterly ridiculous,' said Sophia sternly. 'You may have lost Paul but you haven't lost your job. And what's a lifestyle except something in the Sunday supplements?'

Alix smiled through her tears. 'You're right, I suppose.'

'Come on.' Sophia let go of her hands. 'Let's settle the bill and go back to the house.'

'OK,' said Alix.

Sophia gestured to the waiter who brought the bill.

'Let me.' Alix handed her credit card to the waiter. 'Cheap counselling,' she said to Sophia. 'I'd have to pay a lot more to a professional.'

'We have until Sunday to sort out your life,' said Sophia. 'Don't worry, it'll cost you a fortune.'

Chapter 20

Alix had regained her composure by the time they got back to the house. Which was just as well, because Richard had returned from his indoor soccer match and was watching TV, his feet propped on the coffee table in front of him.

Alix smiled at him, told Sophia that she was tired and wanted to go to bed, and disappeared upstairs before either of them could object.

'What's wrong with her?' Richard asked in surprise.

'Man trouble.' Sophia sat down beside him. 'Oh, Richard, I'm so glad I found you!'

'Me too,' he said. He pulled her closer to him. 'I love you, Sophia.'

'I love you.' She snuggled into the crook of his arm.

He kissed her gently on the eyes. 'I love every single bit of you.'

'Even the new, fatter bits?' she asked.

'Especially the new, fatter bits.'

She sighed with pleasure as he opened the button of her jeans. 'She's broken up with Paul.'

'Oh?' Richard didn't care about Alix.

'And she doesn't know what she wants any more.'

'I know exactly what I want,' said Richard. 'And it's right here beside me.'

∽

Alix could hear them. She tried not to listen but she couldn't help it. She hid her head under her pillow and thought about the dollar/yen rate and how the dollar had strengthened again following its weakness after the rate cut and concentrated fiercely on American economic policy for the months ahead.

∽

Her eyes were puffy the next morning, the lids still red.

'You look like you have hayfever,' said Sophia. 'Wear your sunglasses, nobody will notice.'

Richard had gone out for the day.

'I feel like I'm driving him out of your home,' said Alix. 'I didn't mean to come over here and just dump everything on you, Soph.'

'You didn't,' said her friend. 'He's gone to a cricket match, and let me tell you, he's delighted not to be dragged around Mothercare or its equivalent this morning!'

'All the same—'

'All the same nothing,' said Sophia. 'I thought you might like to go shopping. A little bit of retail therapy never did anyone any harm. And we didn't get to Harvey Nics last time you were here.'

Alix smiled at her. 'No, we didn't.'

'So what are we waiting for?'

∽

281

It was certainly true that buying things helped. When they returned to Sophia's house later that day, Alix had inflicted serious damage to her credit card and was surrounded by a mound of shopping.

'I'll never fit all that into my bag,' she told Sophia. 'I think I lost my reason this afternoon.'

'You lost your misery anyway.' Sophia was glad to see that Alix no longer looked pale and drawn. 'Who cares, Alix. It was fun.'

They had fun that evening, too, when Richard insisted on taking them to dinner and booked a table in Orrery, Terence Conran's fashionable restaurant which, Alix remarked, was falling over itself with modern chic.

'Thanks for everything,' she told Sophia the next day as she got into a cab to go to City Airport. 'I had a good time and I feel miles better.'

'Anytime you feel you're on the verge of a breakdown, just let me know.' Sophia grinned at her.

'All I need now is to figure out what I want to do with my life,' said Alix. 'Shouldn't be too difficult, should it?'

Sophia shook her head. 'The day any of us knows what we want to do with our lives will be the day! I wanted fame and fortune as a prominent female investment banker. What am I going to get? Nappies and regurgitated milk, that's what.'

'But you're happy with it,' said Alix. 'Which is what matters.'

'You'll be happy once you've sorted yourself out,' Sophia told her. 'Just get out there again. Be single! Have fun.'

'Sure.' Alix smiled at her. 'That's exactly what I'll do. And I'll think of you when I'm having it!'

'I rather hope you'll think of more exciting things.' Sophia's eyes were full of amusement.

'Goodbye, Soph. I'll give you a call next week.'

'Take care, Alix.' She waved at the cab until it had turned the corner and was out of sight.

～

It was bedlam at Dublin Airport. A dozen flights seemed to have arrived all at the same time and the arrivals area was a seething mass of irritated and tired travellers. Alix was glad that she'd managed to squeeze so many of her new purchases into her bag and had managed to get away with carrying a couple of Harvey Nichols bags onto the plane too. At least she was able to avoid the hysteria that was the baggage hall and walk straight out into the terminal building.

It was equally crowded. A young girl with an enormous rucksack banged into her and Alix turned round in annoyance. The girl smiled and shrugged apologetically. 'I'm sorry,' she said in heavily accented English.

Alix bit back the angry words that she'd been about to snap. Be cool, she told herself. Peaceful. Relaxed. Don't drive the tourists away. Sophia had told her that she was too tense. Carrie was forever telling her that she was too tense. Perhaps, only perhaps, they were both right.

The backpacker walked towards the exit and Alix stared in front of her. Because only a few yards away was Paul, scanning the new arrivals for someone. He looked great, she thought, dressed in jeans and sweatshirt but looking fashionable rather than scruffy. She almost went over to him but some instinct stopped her. She stood, indecisively, clutching her bags.

'Sabine!' She didn't hear him but she could see the name on his lips. And then a blonde girl pushed her way through the throng and almost threw herself into his arms.

Alix thought she was going to be sick. She stood, rooted to the spot, while Paul kissed Sabine on both cheeks and then, more passionately, on the lips. She felt uncomfortable as she watched them. Sabine was holding Paul's head, pushing her fingers through his hair, pulling him closer to her. Alix could almost feel the heat of Paul's fingers through her own clothes, could almost taste him on her own lips.

The pair finally parted. Alix moved out of sight, blending in with a group of holidaymakers who had just returned from Spain. But, she thought, even if she'd been standing right beside him, Paul wouldn't have noticed her. His eyes had been only for Sabine. His embrace had been only for Sabine.

Had he ever looked at her like that? As lovingly, as intimately as that? She wasn't sure. She swallowed and felt sick again.

They were walking out of the building now. Alix followed at a distance and watched while Paul paid for his parking ticket. She moved towards the machine as soon as they had left. She wondered where he had parked, whether she would see them leave.

She paid for her own ticket and walked to her car in a daze. Her hands were shaking as she unlocked it and threw her bag and her shopping inside. The retail therapy had worn off already. She felt as awful as she had the night Paul had told her that it was over between them.

She started the engine and drove slowly out of the car park. It was ridiculous to think that she would see them leave and there was no reason to. She knew where they were going.

Back to Paul's house in Malahide. Where they would make love. Passionately, as she and Paul had once done.

Alix's grip tightened on the steering wheel. She couldn't get the image of them out of her mind. Paul tracing his fingers from Sabine's throat to the blonde hair between her legs. Perhaps she wasn't a real blonde, thought Alix suddenly. Maybe Paul would discover that the collar and cuffs didn't match – something that, if it was there to be discovered, he'd probably discovered already. He'd implied that he hadn't been to bed with Sabine in Paris, but how did she know that for sure? Perhaps he'd been sampling Sabine's delights even while she lay sleeping in the comfort of her room in the Georges V.

The car behind her blasted her with the horn as she veered out of her lane. She corrected instantly, her heart pounding.

At the roundabout leading onto the motorway, Alix saw the blue Rover. She knew that it was Paul's car. She recognised the registration instantly. Paul used to tease her about her ability to remember a car's reg even if she'd only seen it once before and they would laugh at the fact that she found it so much easier to remember numbers than names. She'd seen the registration of the Rover when he'd waved goodbye to her outside the Beggar's Bush.

Without knowing why, she turned left at the roundabout and, at a careful distance, followed the Rover.

Although Paul's address was in Malahide, his house was in a development that stretched between the pretty harbour town and the inland town of Swords. When they'd first met, he'd wanted her to move into the house with him. But it was two miles away from the train station and the faster, electric trains didn't run as far as Malahide which meant that she would have had to get a lumbering diesel train to the office. Since the town had grown so rapidly over the past few years the traffic into the city was dreadful. That was why she had persuaded Paul that it was a much more practical proposition to rent out his house in Malahide and move into the apartment with her.

But Paul had loved living in Malahide. Alix had teased him, told him that he was, after all, living in a suburban semi not a bijou cottage beside the sea. And he'd laughed, said she was right and agreed to rent out the house.

The Rover indicated left and turned into the estate. Alix, a good distance behind, indicated too. She wasn't too worried about Paul noticing the BMW. He never recognised cars, never mind their registration numbers.

She turned right, then left and slowed down to a crawl as she saw Paul and Sabine get out of the Rover. Paul lifted Sabine's case out of the car and carried it up the path. As Alix drove slowly by, he opened the door and the two of them disappeared inside the house.

Alix was horrified to find that she was crying again. This is ridiculous, she told herself as she wiped the tears from her eyes. I worked all of this out. I'm a single girl with nothing to worry about. So what if he wants to live with somebody else? Why should I care?

But I want him back, she moaned out loud. I don't want him to be living with her. I don't want him doing the things to her that he used to do to me. I don't want him to forget about me. I want him back!

∽

'How was the trip?' asked Jenny as Alix walked into the office the next morning.

'Good,' she said briefly.

'Any news from our pals in London?'

'Like what?' asked Alix.

Jenny shrugged. 'I don't know.'

'Then don't ask stupid questions.'

Dave and Jenny exchanged glances.

'Get out of the wrong side of bed this morning?' asked Dave cheerfully.

'Oh, shut up, Bryant,' snapped Alix. 'I'm not in the mood for your brand of humour this morning.'

'You're never in the mood for anything these days,' said Dave. 'Is it because of Paul?'

Alix glared at him. 'It's absolutely nothing to do with my personal life whatsoever, Dave. And I resent the implication that I can't cope with something as trivial as a bloke moving out of my apartment.'

'Keep your knickers on, Alix.' Dave stared at her in amazement. 'I was only trying—'

'Yes, well, don't try,' she said. 'If you want to do something useful you could go to the forex meeting for me this morning. I'm sure their particular brand of humour and innuendo will suit you.'

'Alix, fuck off,' said Dave.

'Don't talk to me like that,' she said furiously.

'Alix, fuck off,' said Dave again.

'Alix,' said Jenny gently. 'Lighten up, can't you?'

Alix exhaled slowly. She knew that she was being ridiculous but she couldn't help it. She felt as though she was a pot about to boil over. She clenched her fists and bit her lip.

'I'm sorry, Dave,' she said. 'I'm a bit preoccupied today. I didn't mean to snap at you.'

'That's OK,' said Dave guardedly.

Alix pulled her hair back from her face and refastened her tortoiseshell clip. 'Where's Gavin this morning?' she asked, trying to keep her tone friendly.

'He had a dentist's appointment,' said Jenny.

'Oh, yes.' Alix nodded. 'I remember.'

She took a copy of the *Financial Times* from the bundle of newspapers on the desk and opened it. Her hands were still shaking. They hadn't stopped shaking since she'd seen Paul and Sabine at the airport. She'd lain awake for most of the night thinking about them and, when she'd finally fallen asleep, it was to dream about them. She felt utterly exhausted.

❧

'Europa Bank, dealers.'

'Hi, Alix.'

'Cathal?'

'Yes. I left a message on your machine. Didn't you get it?'

'I'm sorry, Cathal,' said Alix. 'I was away for the weekend and I didn't get back until late last night.'

'I said you could ring anytime until midnight.'

'I know. But I was really tired.'

'How about tonight?' asked Cathal. 'I wondered if you'd like to go for a drink.'

'It's good of you, Cathal, but—'

'Listen, Alix, I understand you don't want some long-term thing. That's fine by me. But, come on, you've got to live a little.'

'I know,' she said.

'Quick drink,' urged Cathal. 'You choose the venue.'

She didn't want to go for a drink with Cathal. 'Smyth's,' she said, naming the pub that was practically next door to her apartment.

'Great,' said Cathal. 'See you there, half eight?'

'Half eight,' she agreed tiredly.

Jenny grinned at her. 'Got a date, Alix?'

'Oh, nothing special,' said Alix.

'You're a fast worker,' said Jenny. 'Paul just out the door and you've got someone else already. Alix, you're incredible.'

'I haven't got someone else.' Alix couldn't help smiling a little.

'Sounds to me like you have. How do you do it?' Jenny looked at her ruefully. 'When I split up with Ruairi I didn't go out with anyone for months. Not that I didn't try!'

'How did you try?' asked Alix.

'Clubs, pubs, dinner parties – I did the lot.' Jenny laughed. 'I even went to evening classes because I thought there might be a few eligible men there.'

'What sort of evening classes?' asked Alix.

'Computer studies,' said Jenny.

'But you know everything there is to know about computers,' said Alix.

Jenny made a face. 'I know. I thought I could impress them with my knowledge. But they were all teenage wimps.'

Alix chuckled. 'Too young for you?'

'Too young, too boring.'

'And now?' asked Alix.

'I've had a couple of dates but there's nobody special,' said Jenny. 'You know that.'

'What are you doing about it?'

'Nothing,' said Jenny. 'I'm kind of enjoying things the way they are.'

❧

Alix examined her hair for grey as she stood in front of the bathroom mirror. A few strands, nothing too serious, although she was due to visit Tina again soon. She gathered her hair and pulled it back into a knot.

Alix the confident, she thought, as she looked at her reflection. Alix the poised. Alix the control freak. She let her hair go and it swung in front of her face. She'd wear it loose tonight even though it irritated her like that. She pulled on a pair of grey trousers and a black T-shirt. She looked dull. But that was the way it was going to be.

Cathal was already in the pub when she arrived, a pint of lager in front of him. Alix smiled at him and he stood up and kissed her on the cheek.

'What can I get you?' he asked.

'White wine, please.'

He went up to the bar and got her a drink. 'So,' he said as he sat down again. 'Where were you for the weekend?'

'London,' said Alix. 'Business mainly.'

'You look tired,' said Cathal.

'Thanks,' she said.

'I'm sorry.' He looked at her in contrition. 'I didn't mean—'

'It's OK.'

They sat in silence for a moment.

'Would you mind if I smoked?' asked Alix.

'Well, sure, no problem.' Cathal looked at her in surprise. 'I didn't think you smoked.'

'Only sometimes,' she said as she took the packet of cigarettes out of her bag and lit one. 'Do you?'

He shook his head. 'How are you feeling after your bug?' he asked.

'Oh, much better,' she told him. 'It was pretty awful at the time but I seem to have shaken it now.'

'Lots of people seem to have had it,' he said awkwardly.

'I guess.' Alix inhaled deeply. 'Though no one else in the office managed to catch it from me.'

Cathal drained his glass. 'I'm going to get another. Would you like one?'

Alix looked at him in surprise. 'I've hardly started this.'

'I'll get you another anyway,' said Cathal and went to the bar.

༄

It wasn't a good evening. Alix didn't feel like talking and Cathal was finding it heavy going. Every so often he'd light upon a topic that she was interested in and he thought that he'd finally managed to reach her, but she'd close up again and sit silently, waiting for him to think of another conversational gambit. She is very attractive, he thought as he watched her, but attraction can only do so much. She doesn't seem to have any life in her at all.

This was a mistake, thought Alix. It wasn't fair on Cathal and it wasn't fair on her. She wasn't ready for an evening in the pub with a bloke she hardly knew.

'Would you like one for the road?' asked Cathal.

She shook her head. 'I truly am tired,' she told him. 'I think I should get to bed.'

'OK.' He sounded relieved and that amused her. 'I'll walk you home.'

'Not that it's much of a walk,' she observed as she slipped on her jacket.

He laughed. 'Do you like living here?'

'Oh, yes,' she told him. 'I can walk to almost anywhere – although I have to confess that I usually drive. I'm not really the most environmentally friendly of people. I just throw glass jars into the rubbish which I guess is probably high up on the list of environmental crimes.'

'I'll have to report you to the green police,' Cathal warned her as he took her by the arm. She almost pulled away from him but she didn't.

'Here we are,' she said apologetically. 'Thanks for the drink.'

'Anytime,' said Cathal.

She looked at him and said uncomfortably, 'Would you like to come in for a coffee?'

He smiled at her. 'I don't think so, do you?'

'No.' The relief in her voice was clear.

'I'm sorry I wasn't the man you were looking for,' said Cathal.

'I'm sorry,' said Alix. 'I was a horrible person to take out tonight. I should have said no from the start.'

'Oh, I probably wouldn't have listened,' said Cathal. 'I needed tonight to get you out of my system.'

'And I'm out now?' She smiled faintly at him.

'I think so.' Cathal grinned at her.

'That's something,' she said.

'Goodnight, Alix.' He kissed her lightly on the cheek.

'Goodnight, Cathal.'

She watched him for a moment as he turned and walked towards Baggot Street. Then she took her keys from her bag and let herself into her empty apartment.

Chapter 21

'So the complete upgrade will cost us around twenty-five thousand.' Mike Wallis, Europa Bank's chief accountant, looked around the boardroom table. 'But I think it's worth it. It'll increase our processing speed enormously.'

'What do you think, Alix?' asked Des. 'You've been using that system for the past six months.'

Alix continued to stare out of the window at the mountains in the distance.

'Alix,' repeated Des. 'What do you think?'

'Oh, sorry.' She blinked and looked at the five men present. 'I didn't realise you were talking to me.'

'Alix, you've been out of it for nearly the entire meeting,' said Des. 'What on earth is wrong with you?'

She couldn't tell him that she was thinking about Paul and Sabine. She couldn't say that she hadn't been able to get them out of her mind for the past two days, ever since she'd seen them together. When she was least expecting it, when she felt sure that she was engrossed in whatever she was doing, she would suddenly imagine them together and she wouldn't be able to stop thinking about them. She'd been picturing Sabine telling Paul that she was pregnant and Paul's ecstatic response. Him telling her that it was the best moment of his life. That he loved her more than anything. And then she'd imagined another scenario, one in which Paul suddenly realised that the whole baby thing had been the most awful mistake and he cursed himself for ever leaving her in the first place.

She dragged her mind back to the conversation the management group had been having about computer upgrades.

'Twenty-five thousand sounds fine,' she said, glad that she could absorb a conversation while thinking about something else.

'You haven't had any problems?' asked Mike.

She shook her head. 'No. We had a few crashes at the start but that was due to the defaults on the software package we were using. When we changed some of the settings, everything was OK.'

'Right.' Des closed the folder. 'That's the lot. I'm stopping at the Galloping Green for a pint on my way home. Anyone heading in that direction is free to join me.'

The rest of the group stood up. 'I will,' said John Collins, the credit manager, as he looked at his watch and saw that it was nearly seven. 'I'm gasping for a drink.'

'Me too.' Kieran Dougherty slipped his jacket on.

'I can't,' said Alix. 'I promised the others I'd meet them in O'Reilly's. We're celebrating the closing of the zloty deal at last.'

'What was the problem?' asked Des. 'I was getting worried.'

'Nothing serious,' Alix told him. 'It was a settlement thing, nothing intrinsically wrong with the deal.'

'It was a great deal,' said John. 'And the client is delighted.'

'The best sort of deal is one where we're all happy.' Des patted John on the shoulders. 'And you did well to come up with the client, John.'

'I think Dave deserves some of the credit,' said Alix. 'After all, he did all the hard work.' What am I saying? she asked herself. Why am I praising him? Would he give me the credit for it if our roles were reversed?

'I've spoken to Dave already,' said Des.

'Oh.' Alix wondered what the managing director had told her senior dealer. That one day he would have her job? That they'd move her somewhere else? Transfer her to London? Or Paris? Don't be paranoid, she told herself. You don't have to imagine conspiracies in everything.

'By the way,' said Des to the room at large, 'don't forget about the Institute dinner next month. It's in the Shelbourne. Black tie. Boring, I know, but it has to be done.'

'Hilary will kill me,' said Mike Wallis. 'I seem to be out at something every night.'

'She won't kill you this time,' said Des. 'This is the one where you get to bring your wife.'

'I don't *have* to bring her, do I?' Mike looked horrified.

'Actually, yes,' said Des. 'We're trying to make things a little less stuffy. We thought that spouses would be a good idea.'

'It's a dreadful idea,' said John.

'Tough,' said Des firmly. 'The decision was taken at the spring general meeting. There are two dinners a year. One will be without partners, the other with.'

'We can come on our own if we want, though, can't we?' asked Alix.

'Oh, I'm sure Paul will have a good time,' Des told her. 'He can write about us if he wants.'

Alix had assumed that Des would know. She was certain Dave would have told him. In a man-to-man-type conversation, Dave could have said that the reason she was behaving like a basket case was that Paul had walked out on her. And that she was in denial about the whole thing.

I *am* in denial, she told herself as she walked across the Matt Talbot Bridge. I don't want to believe he's with Sabine. I don't want to accept that it could possibly be over between us.

The pub was heaving with people. They'd spilled outside the building onto the tiny patio in front and onto the pavement outside. You'd swear they were serving free beer, thought Alix as she pushed her way inside. And it was only Wednesday.

'Alix! Over here!' Gavin waved at her.

'Why is it so crowded?' she gasped. 'I thought we'd be able to have a quiet kind of celebration but this is bedlam.'

'There's a twenty-first party going on,' Gavin told her. 'A gorgeous bit of stuff, Alix. Legs up to her armpits. Look at her, over there.'

'I'm sure she hasn't noticed you,' Alix said as she turned to look at the object of his admiration. The girl was striking, with jet black hair that hung to her tiny waist, piercing blue eyes and legs which, as Gavin had said, were long and shapely and shown to best advantage in the short skirt she was wearing.

'I'm pretty certain she has.' Gavin winked at her.

'What would you like to drink?' she asked.

'Heineken,' said Gavin.

'And you?' She turned to Dave and Jenny.

'Same,' said Dave.

'Miller,' said Jenny.

Alix ordered the drinks. 'It's warm enough outside,' she said. 'Do you guys want to stay in here or go out?'

'Oh, stay here,' said Gavin. 'We've got a much better view of the action here.'

Jenny made a face. 'You're so bloody childish, Donnelly.'

'She wants me,' he told her. 'I can see it when she looks at me.'

'Are you out of your mind?' asked Alix. 'She's probably seen you flashing your gold card around or something and thinks that you have money. Little does she know!'

'After this year's review, I'll have a lot more.' Gavin looked at Alix, the challenge in his eyes. 'I deserve it.'

'You deserve something, all right,' said Alix.

'Money talks,' said Gavin. 'I work hard, I'm entitled to the reward.'

'We're here to celebrate Dave's deal tonight,' Alix said firmly. 'Not talk about future bonuses.' She raised her glass at Dave. 'Well done, Mr Bryant.'

'Thanks,' said Dave.

'I never asked what you thought about the Europa building in Paris?'

'Fantastic,' said Dave. 'It's exactly the sort of place that makes you feel the money flowing.'

'I know what you mean. What did you think of the dealing room?'

'Pretty neat,' he said. 'I liked the way the desks are grouped. And so far it hasn't got the complete bombshell look of most dealing rooms. But give it time.'

'What about the quotations?' asked Alix.

'Bloody silly.' Dave made a face. 'I wouldn't want to be sitting with a losing trade looking at some tripe spouted by Napoleon Bonaparte.'

Alix grinned. 'My sentiments exactly.'

She felt almost normal again. The tension between herself and her colleagues seemed to have disappeared. She told a joke and even Gavin laughed. They weren't so bad, she thought, it was just that she was so sensitive right now. But she'd get over it. She had to face the fact that Paul was out of her life forever. She could do that. But she wasn't going to let anyone else in.

'Alix?' Jenny's eyes were glazed.

'Yes?'

'What happened?'

'What do you mean, what happened?'

'Between you and Paul.'

'It's really none of your business, Jenny.'

'I know,' said Jenny. 'But I wanted to ask anyway.'

'We were getting on each other's nerves,' said Alix. 'We decided to live apart for a while.'

'So it's not a permanent split?'

Of course it was a permanent split. She'd seen him walk up the pathway to his house carrying Sabine Brassaert's suitcase. How much more permanent could it be?

She shrugged. 'Who knows?'

'Will you bring him to the Christmas party this year?' asked Jenny.

'I might.'

'I like him,' Jenny told her. 'He's a decent kind of bloke.'

Oh really, thought Alix. Decent enough to be tearing the clothes off that French bitch while I was asleep in my hotel bedroom. *Our* hotel bedroom. That was pretty decent, all right.

'He's not the worst,' she said.

'Anyway, I hope you two get back together,' Jenny sighed.

'Thanks,' said Alix dryly. 'And what about you?'

'I'm working on it.' Jenny made a face. 'I have a date for tomorrow night.'

'Really?'

Jenny nodded. 'I met him at Anna's wedding. He was a friend of the groom. I wasn't expecting to meet anyone there, so maybe it's a good sign.'

'Maybe it is,' said Alix. 'Love is funny like that. When you're looking for someone he never comes along.'

'I think that's a watched pot you're thinking of.' Jenny grinned at her.

'Whatever,' said Alix. 'I'll await your detailed report with interest.'

Gavin and Dave had joined in the twenty-first birthday celebrations. Gavin had his arm round the exotic-looking birthday girl, while Dave was chatting to someone else in the group.

'How do they do it?' asked Jenny.

'I don't know.' Alix smiled at her. 'You're surprised because you know them. You can't understand why anyone would be bothered with them. But girls that have never met them before probably think they're attractive and rich.'

'Gavin certainly gives that impression.' Jenny watched him as he bought a bottle of champagne.

'He's young,' said Alix.

'You're very understanding all of a sudden.'

'Maybe I'm mellowing in my old age.' She grinned at Jenny.

'You? Mellow?' Jenny laughed. 'That'll be the day, Alix. That will definitely be the day.'

∽

She'd only had three bottles of beer because she'd driven in to work. The security guard at reception smiled at her as she walked into the building. 'Can't stay away?'

'I love it so much,' said Alix. 'I'll be in the dealing room for about ten minutes and then I'll leave.'

'Fine,' said the security guard.

She went upstairs and let herself into the room. She switched on the screens. The Nikkei – the index of the Japanese stock exchange – was higher. The yen was stronger. That was OK, they were running a small position in yen and an upward move suited them. She sat at her desk and watched the numbers change in front of her – red if the price was lower than the previous price, blue if it was higher. The market would end a lot higher, she thought as she watched the blue numbers outweigh the reds.

She closed her eyes. It was comfortable here. She felt contented. She liked the rise and fall of the numbers on the screen, the muted bleep every time an important news item was announced, the feeling that she was connected to the entire world. It was better than being in the pub. Better than being at the gym. Better than being at the shooting club. And much, much better than being at home on her own.

~

She kicked off her shoes, flopped on the sofa and flicked the remote control. She pressed the buttons in quick succession but there was absolutely nothing worth watching on TV. Even the news was boring – Sky was running a piece about a dog who'd walked over a hundred miles to get home when his family had accidentally left him behind at the seaside. How could you accidentally leave a spaniel behind? she wondered.

Didn't anyone miss him drooling all over the back of the car? She switched off the TV and opened the balcony doors.

It was cool tonight. Until now the summer had been hot and stifling. For the first time in weeks the breeze that blew across the balcony had the chill of autumn in it. Alix shivered and rubbed her arms.

She walked back into the living room and closed the door behind her. She picked up her jacket and slipped on her shoes again. She had to go out.

She pretended to herself that she didn't know where she was going, but of course she did. She didn't bother with the toll bridge but drove through the city centre and Fairview and turned left for Malahide. It was about eight miles to Malahide from Fairview. She passed through a variety of suburban developments before emerging onto the narrower, more countrified part of the road at Kinsealy where the enormous detached houses reminded her that a number of seriously wealthy people lived around here. She drove by the estate of the ex-Taoiseach, the disgraced Charlie Haughey, and wondered if all the wealth he had accumulated over the years compensated for ending up in court. Money isn't everything, she muttered as she overtook a bright orange Nissan Micra.

If she'd had less money maybe Paul would have cared about her more. She shook her head. It wasn't as though she was loaded, for God's sake! She was well-off, but that was a completely different thing. She couldn't afford to chuck in her job and become one of those half-envied, half-despised people, the ladies who lunch. She smiled to herself. If she gave up work she wouldn't get out of bed early enough to lunch!

The traffic lights were red at the junction to Paul's house. She glanced at herself in the rear-view mirror as she waited for them to change. She looked OK. A bit tired, maybe, but OK.

The lights turned green.

The house was in darkness. Alix hadn't expected it to be dark. She glanced at the clock on the dashboard. Nearly half eleven. Maybe they'd gone to bed. She grimaced. Paul had never been keen on going to bed early. That had been one of the things they argued about, her complaining that she had to be up early and needed to be asleep before midnight, Paul telling her to go ahead, he'd join her later. But if she went to bed before him, she'd invariably wake up when he slipped under the duvet beside her and slid his hand between the warmth of her thighs. She'd wake up and she'd say 'not now' but he'd know that it didn't take much to make her change her mind and she'd already be moving her body closer to him, warm with desire herself.

He made her feel that way. He was the only man who ever had.

And now he was doing it with Sabine. She couldn't let it go on like this. He needed to be told that it was a mistake. Shown that it was a mistake.

She got out of the car and slammed the door. Her footsteps echoed loudly on the pathway. She stood in the pool of light cast by the lamp in the porch. He should have turned off the porch light before going to bed, she thought. He was careful with money, he wouldn't want to waste electricity like this.

She took a deep breath and pressed the doorbell. Her mouth was dry but her palms were sweating.

She could picture them, stopping in the very act of making love, faces shocked, wondering who could be calling to the house this late at night. And worried, because people only called late at night if there was something wrong.

She waited for the lights to come on but nothing happened. Perhaps they were hoping that the caller would go away. Perhaps they'd been asleep and were only now waking.

She pressed the buzzer again, holding it down for longer this time.

Nothing stirred.

They must be out. She clenched her fists in annoyance. She was ready to confront them and they weren't there to be confronted! Where were they? Had Paul taken Sabine away for a few days? A kind of honeymoon in Ireland? A few nights at a luxury hotel in the country where they'd be waited on hand and foot?

She banged on the door in her frustration and the house alarm went off.

Shit, she thought, as her heart thudded in her chest. She ran down the pavement and jumped into the car, praying that nobody had seen her, that the residents of Marina Cove didn't have a neighbourhood watch scheme. If she started the car now perhaps some interfering old biddy with nothing better to do, who was already looking out of the window, might take down the registration. And then the police would call to her apartment. Her imagination ran riot as she thought of the police coming round and warning her for – what? Breaking and entering? Well, hardly. Causing a disturbance? Possibly. Being a total fucking idiot? Definitely, if that was at all possible.

She crouched down in the driving seat and hoped that no one had seen her.

Of all the bloody stupid things you've ever done, this has to rate as the most stupid, she muttered as she banged her head on the steering column.

Now that she was bent down like this, she wondered when she could get up. She couldn't see anything. Maybe there were people already peering into the car to find out who the potential burglar was. She groaned.

It seemed like at least half an hour, but was in fact only ten minutes later, when the alarm stopped. She sat up cautiously and peeped out of the window.

The front door was open. Paul and Sabine had obviously arrived home from an evening out.

'I can't see anything.' Paul's voice carried across the road.

'Are you sure?' It was the first time she'd heard Sabine speak. The French accent was unmistakable.

'It was probably the cat from next door,' Paul told her. 'Sometimes he manages to set it off.'

'You don't think there is a need to worry?'

'Of course not, *ma chérie*,' he said.

Ma chérie. Alix nearly threw up.

'OK, then. You are coming inside?'

'Yes. In a moment.'

Alix ducked down again as Paul walked to the side of the road. She held her breath but there was no furious rapping on the window of the car. He didn't wrench the door open and haul her outside. She was right about his inability to recognise cars.

Alix heard the front door close and she sat up again. The light was on in the front bedroom, the blue curtains drawn. She saw Paul's silhouette as he walked across the room, then the main light was turned off and the fainter glow of a bedside lamp was all that was left.

You're such a bloody, bloody fool, she told herself as she started the car. They'd be right to lock you up and throw away the key. You shouldn't be let out on your own. You crazy, stupid cow.

Chapter 22

When she finally got to sleep that night Alix had the chasing dream again. She was grateful when the radio alarm clicked into life the next morning even though she was still exhausted. The dream always made her feel tired the next day, as though the chase had been for real, as though she'd run throughout the night.

She pushed back the duvet and then she remembered Paul. Surely she hadn't driven out to Malahide for some ill-defined showdown. Surely she hadn't set off the alarm on his house by banging on the door. And surely she hadn't been hiding in her car while he checked for nonexistent burglars.

She felt a wave of guilt and embarrassment wash over her. I'm acting like some neurotic teenager, she thought. If any of them in work ever got to hear about last night – she shuddered at the idea.

I will put it out of my mind, she told herself firmly. It was mad, impetuous and incredibly silly but no harm has been done. Forget about it, that's the best thing.

❧

'Alix, it's your sister on line two,' Jenny called.

'Thanks.' Alix picked up the phone. 'Wyn, how's it going?'

'All right,' said Wyn. 'And you?'

'I'm fine.'

'Good.'

Alix waited for Wyn to say something else.

'Wyn? Are you still there?'

'Yes,' said Wyn.

'Is something wrong?'

'Not exactly wrong,' said Wyn.

'What then?' Alix was impatient. It had been a busy day, she had lots of paperwork to do and she didn't have time to waste in roundabout conversations with Wyn. That was the worst thing about her sister, she could never get to the point quickly.

'I had a phone call from Carrie,' said Wyn hesitantly. 'At lunchtime.'

'And?' Alix glanced at her watch. It was almost five o'clock.

'Dad's back.'

The numbers on the screen in front of Alix blurred.

'What did you say?'

'I said that Dad's back.'

'Back where?'

'Back here, of course. Don't be so bloody silly.'

'I'm sorry.' Alix cleared her throat. 'I didn't mean – I just said the first thing that came into my head.'

'It's OK,' said Wyn. 'I was a bit dazed myself.'

'What does he want?' asked Alix. 'And how's Carrie?'

'I don't know. I wanted to call over but she said no. She phoned from the house. He was there.'

'In the house? She let him into the house?'

'Apparently so,' said Wyn.

'Is she mad?'

'I suppose she thought it'd be OK. Alix, do you realise that they're still married?'

'I know they're still married,' snapped Alix. 'Of course they're still married. Didn't I have a row with her last year about getting a divorce?'

'Yes. I remember.'

'So because she's still married to him she feels that she can let him into our house.'

'Her house,' said Wyn.

'We both lived there too,' said Alix. 'It's our house. It's not *his* house!'

'Calm down, Alix,' said Wyn.

'I am calm. I just don't want him barging in on our lives and upsetting Carrie all over again. Why is he back? What does he want?'

'I don't know,' said Wyn. 'Carrie wants us to call over to her tonight.'

'And will he be there?'

'No,' Wyn answered. 'I asked that. He's staying in a guest house. He won't be anywhere nearby.'

'OK,' said Alix. 'Just so long as she doesn't think that there's going to be a great family reunion or anything.'

'I hardly think so,' said Wyn. 'I don't think she wants him back in her life either. Alix, it was nearly thirty years ago. Everything is completely different now.'

'I know.' Alix sighed. 'It's a shock, Wyn.'

'Yes,' said her sister.

'What do you think? How do you feel?'

'To be honest?'

'Yes, to be honest.'

'I don't know how I feel.' Wyn sounded bewildered. 'I

don't know why he's back. What he wants. I don't know how I should feel.'

'What time?' asked Alix.

'Sorry?'

'What time does she want us to come over?'

'I don't know. Some time after tea, I suppose. I didn't ask.'

'That's not like you.' Alix laughed shortly.

'No. I know. Alix, do you want to come here first?'

'Yes,' said Alix. 'I'll go home and change and then come over.'

'OK.' Wyn sounded relieved.

'See you then,' said Alix.

'See you,' said Wyn.

Alix stared at the screens in front of her. The numbers and the graphs were just meaningless whirls. A news headline, giving details of the Federal Reserve's latest monetary policy comments, scrolled past her without registering in her consciousness.

Her father was back. Dad. She hadn't thought of him as Dad for a long time, hadn't thought of him at all. She didn't want to think about him. She bit her lip.

'Are you OK, Alix?' Jenny looked at her in concern.

'What?'

'Are you OK?'

'Yes, fine, Jenny. I'm sorry. Just a domestic problem. Nothing serious.'

'Sure?'

'Of course.' Alix smiled at her. 'I was miles away there for a moment.'

'I know,' said Jenny. 'Alix, is it all right if I head home now?'

'Sure,' said Alix. 'Everything has gone through to settlements?'

Jenny nodded.

'You seem very cheerful.' Alix suddenly registered Jenny's eagerness to be off. 'Anything special planned for tonight?'

'Yes.'

'Oh?'

'I'm going out,' said Jenny.

'Anywhere nice?'

Jenny shrugged. 'I don't know. I'm meeting Mike.'

'The guy you went out with last night? You're seeing him again?'

'Yes.' Jenny looked defiant.

'Go for it,' Alix told her. 'Have a good time. Obviously you like him.'

'We got on,' said Jenny simply.

'What does he do?'

'He's an electrician. He has his own company.'

'That'll be useful when the fuses blow,' Alix grinned.

'Well, hopefully we'll generate enough electricity of our own.'

'Jenny Smith!' But Alix was laughing. 'Enjoy yourself tonight.'

'Thanks.' Jenny picked up her bag.

Alix finished the report she'd been writing then stood up. 'I'm off myself, Dave. See you tomorrow.'

'Fine,' said Dave. 'I'll be heading home shortly.'

She glanced at Gavin's empty seat. 'I thought he was coming back this afternoon.'

'The client's offices were in Stepaside,' said Dave. 'I guess he thought it was too much hassle to come back.'

'He should have phoned,' said Alix. 'I couldn't care less

whether he was here or not, Dave, but he should have phoned.'

'Normally he would.'

'Perhaps.' Alix stretched her arms over her head. She didn't know why she was bothering about Gavin. She didn't know why she'd had a conversation with Jenny about her new boyfriend. She didn't know how she could be thinking about anything else other than the fact that her father was back. And she didn't want him in her life.

❧

Wyn opened the door before Alix had time to ring the bell.

'Terry's taken the kids over to his mother's,' she said as Alix walked into the living room. 'I told him to bring them home in about an hour. I didn't want anyone here, Alix.'

'That's OK.'

'D'you want tea?'

Alix shook her head.

'Coffee?'

'Wyn, this isn't a social get-together,' she said. 'I don't want anything to eat or drink. I couldn't drink anything anyway.'

'I know.' Wyn pulled at the bottom of the sweatshirt she was wearing. 'I can't help myself. It makes things more normal.'

Alix sat on the sofa and motioned her sister to sit beside her. 'Everything is normal,' she said. 'There's nothing for us to get frazzled about. The man is in Ireland after spending most of his life in the States. As far away from us as he could possibly be.' She looked at Wyn. 'There's no need for us to get upset about it. He means nothing to us. He wasn't there when we were kids and now we don't need him. If Carrie wants us to meet him we can say no. We're not under any obligation to him.'

'I remember it,' said Wyn blankly. 'The day he left. I remember Carrie screaming and crying and throwing his things into bags. I remember she wouldn't take a tissue from me. I remember her tearing a photograph of him in half.'

Alix reached out for her hand. 'It was a long time ago.'

'What do you remember?' asked Wyn.

She hadn't wanted him to leave. She'd known there was something dreadfully wrong. She'd seen Carrie crying and she'd started to cry too. And she'd held on to him. And Carrie. And she hadn't wanted him to leave.

'Being afraid,' said Alix slowly. 'Knowing that there was something awful happening. Knowing I couldn't do anything about it.'

Wyn squeezed her hand. 'Carrie called him an uncaring bastard,' she said. 'That's what I recall the most. "Get out, you uncaring, selfish bastard," she said.'

'It doesn't matter why he left,' said Alix. 'The point is that he did.'

'But why wouldn't Carrie ever talk about it?' asked Wyn. 'I questioned her over and over and she just wouldn't say anything. And then, I suppose, I got tired asking.'

'Anyway, you could never be sure she'd tell us the truth,' said Alix.

'Is there something wrong with us that we didn't ask?' wondered her sister. 'That we never tried to find out?'

'Carrie didn't want us to find out,' said Alix. 'And I didn't want to hurt her by delving into the past.'

'But he's our father,' Wyn said. 'We should want to know about him.'

'Why?' asked Alix fiercely. 'What did he ever do for us?'

Wyn drove them to Carrie's house, one of a small red-bricked terrace in Ranelagh. They'd lived in Clontarf when John had been around and for a few years afterwards until Carrie, who needed the money for the salon she'd decided to open, sold the rambling old seafront house and brought them across the city to Ranelagh. Alix liked Ranelagh but she always remembered the sound of the sea in Clontarf.

∽

Carrie saw the car pull up outside the house. She took a couple of deep breaths and closed her eyes. She waited until the doorbell rang before going to open the door.

'Hi, Carrie.' Alix dropped a kiss on her mother's cheek and walked past her into the front room.

'Hi, Carrie.' Wyn did the same.

'I'm glad you came over.' Carrie sat down on one of the newly re-covered armchairs. She smoothed her already smooth hair and looked from one to the other of her daughters who sat side by side on the sofa.

They were angry, she could see. And confused. Alix stared back at her, eyes like emeralds. Wyn's gaze was more troubled, less aggressive.

'Your father was here today.' Carrie's voice wavered a little and, for a moment, she was afraid she was going to cry. She took another deep breath and exhaled slowly. The two girls watched her carefully. 'He wanted to know how you were.'

'Huh,' snorted Alix. 'First time in his life he cared.'

'Alix.' Wyn placed a warning hand on her sister's arm.

'No,' said Carrie. 'Alix is right.' She sighed. 'Almost right.'

She smoothed her hair again. She wasn't good at this. She'd never been good at talking to them. Not about serious things anyway. Especially with Alix. At least with Wyn she could have easy, gossipy conversations about the salon and about her clients. And sometimes about Alix. But they never talked about each other.

Carrie had never felt like a real mother to her girls. She'd encouraged them to call her by her Christian name and to think of themselves as partners in her life. And so they talked to her as an equal, but they never came to her with their troubles. And she never shared hers with them. It had seemed right until today. But now she wasn't certain.

'I was very angry when your dad left,' she said. 'Really angry.'

'I remember,' said Wyn.

'I thought he'd betrayed us.'

'Why?' asked Alix.

'Leaving us was a betrayal,' said Carrie cautiously, 'of everything I thought we were.'

'What did you think we were?' asked Wyn.

'Happy,' said Carrie simply. 'I was happy. I had the two of you, I had your father. I worked a couple of days a week in Sheri's salon. I was happy about things.'

Alix gripped the edge of the sofa.

'I didn't know that John wasn't happy.' Carrie looked carefully at both of them. 'Truly I didn't. I knew that there were *times* when he wasn't happy but that's not the same. I thought it was because of work – you know how it is with work, sometimes you hate it, sometimes you love it.' This was hard, she thought. She'd practised this talk for hours but it was still hard when the two of them were sitting in front of her, staring at her. 'So I didn't know that he was really unhappy.'

'Why was he really unhappy?' asked Wyn.

'Because he'd met someone else.'

They sat in silence.

'Who?' asked Alix eventually.

'John worked for IBM,' said Carrie. 'At that time, of course, it was business machines not computers. He sold accounting machines, ones that posted items to ledgers. He was good at it. He was good at the mechanical end and he was good at the numbers end.' She smiled faintly. 'He was better at the numbers than the machines. He could total a column of figures almost just by looking at them.'

'Like you, Alix,' said Wyn.

Alix said nothing.

'He sold them to a company called Addtrex. I've no idea what they did. But there was a girl in the ledgers department called Imogen Hogan. He started going out with her.'

'Going out with her!' spluttered Wyn. 'He was married to you! What was he playing at?'

'Imogen Hogan was beautiful,' said Carrie. 'Really beautiful. I saw her photograph. She had dark hair and huge eyes and I could see why he'd fall for her.'

'But he shouldn't have fallen for her,' said Alix. 'What about us?'

'Don't be naïve,' Carrie snapped at her. 'How many of your married friends are completely faithful to their husbands?'

'I don't have that many married friends.' Alix thought about Guy Decourcelle who'd offered dinner and maybe more in Paris. And of Des Coyle who, though in his view very happily married, had conducted an affair with one of the temps in the accounts department for six months until she left Europa Bank.

'How did you find out about her?' asked Wyn.

'The photograph,' replied Carrie. 'Stupid sod had left it in his shirt pocket. I knew straightaway even though he tried to deny it at first. But he admitted it eventually.'

'So you threw him out,' said Alix.

'I think these things can be worked out,' said Carrie. 'I told him that. I said he could stop seeing her and we'd forget about it.'

'That was decent of you,' said Wyn.

'It was probably very stupid,' said Carrie. 'But, you know, it's really easy for people to tell you what to do in those circumstances. To say that you should throw him out and never see him again. To say that you shouldn't trust him any more. I was married with two small children. I didn't want to throw him out.'

'So why did you?' Alix closed her eyes and remembered it more vividly than ever before. She was sitting at the dining-room table, doing a jigsaw of a cow. She could see it clearly, big wooden pieces coloured black and white. And blue pieces for the sky. She'd put a piece of sky in place when she heard her mother begin to cry. She'd sat, frozen, on the chair. Wyn had been sitting on the floor, playing with a set of Dinky cars. She jumped up and hurt her foot when she stepped on one of the cars. They'd run into the hallway together and John had been standing there with a suitcase in his hand.

'Where are you going?' Alix had asked. 'Where?'

And then the shouting and screaming had started and Carrie was crying and Wyn had shoved tissues at her but Carrie hadn't even noticed.

'She was pregnant,' said Carrie.

Alix and Wyn stared at their mother.

'What?' whispered Wyn.

Carrie was silent for a moment. She'd practised this bit too but it was hard to stay calm. It was history now, she reminded herself, and she could cope with it. It didn't have the power to hurt her as it had before.

'She was pregnant,' repeated Carrie. 'And he wanted to be with her.'

'And us?' asked Alix. 'Didn't he want to be with us?'

Carrie got up from the armchair and walked to the window. 'Of course,' she said. 'He offered to take you with him. So that you could be a family together.' She stared out at the quiet cul-de-sac.

Alix and Wyn exchanged glances.

'I'm glad you didn't give us away,' said Wyn shakily.

'I thought about it.' Carrie continued to look out of the window. 'Because I thought that maybe it would be better. I was trying to be rational about it, but how can you be? And I said to myself, come on, Carrie, think about what's best for the children.'

'And you told him to sod off,' said Alix.

Carrie smiled. 'Actually, yes, I did.' She turned to face them again. 'I told him that he was a bastard to even suggest it and that if he thought he was getting his mitts on my beautiful children he could think again.' She sighed. 'I don't want to be truly horrible but I think he was relieved in the end.'

'So he left,' said Wyn.

'Yes,' Carrie sighed. 'He left and he went to work for IBM in the States and Imogen went with him.'

'And the baby?' asked Alix. 'Our father's daughter?'

'Yes,' said Carrie. 'She looks just like her mother.'

'You've seen her?'

'Only a photograph,' said Carrie. 'She's very pretty.'

'What's her name?' asked Wyn.

'Kate.'

I have another sister, thought Alix in wonderment. A half-sister, but still someone connected to me. By blood. It felt strange.

'So why is he here?' asked Wyn. 'Is there some drama with Imogen and Kate? Has one of them got a terminal disease or something? That's usually the way with the long-lost mother or father or son or daughter, isn't it?'

Carrie smiled faintly. 'Only in the movies, dear. Both Imogen and Kate are in perfect health.'

'So what does he want?'

'A divorce, for starters,' said Carrie. 'They didn't bother about getting married before but they want to now. Because Kate was married last year and she's having a baby. And they want to be legitimate grandparents.'

Alix laughed. 'You're not serious?'

'Oh, I am,' said Carrie. 'You know, when he left to be with Imogen, it was all very romantic as far as he was concerned. She was so lovely and fragile and waif-like he couldn't help himself. That's what he told me, anyway. And they thought it was even more romantic to live together and not get married because it meant that they were together for love and not for the piece of paper.'

'Oh, for heaven's sake!' exclaimed Wyn. 'That's so bloody old-fashioned.'

Carrie smiled. 'That's John.'

'But why did he insist on leaving us for her?' asked Alix. 'It might be romantic to have an affair, but afterwards?'

'He said that he cared about me a lot and he loved both of you immensely,' said Carrie. 'But he said he couldn't live without Imogen.'

'What shit.' Alix grunted.

'Her parents didn't talk to her for months,' said Carrie. 'Actually, I felt sorry for her. He took the job in the States and dragged her with him. She didn't have a job and she was quite sick with the baby. I guess it wasn't so romantic then.'

'Have they been back here before?' asked Wyn. 'In Ireland?'

'A few times, apparently,' said Carrie. 'To see her family.'

'And he wasn't in touch?'

'He phoned,' said Carrie. 'But I didn't want to see him.'

'Did he want to see us?' asked Alix.

Carrie sighed. 'Of course he did. But he didn't come back for five years. So he wasn't exactly pining, was he? And I thought it would be too upsetting for both of you. The next time he came was when Alix was in hospital with appendicitis. I didn't think it would do you any good, Alix, to see him appear in the ward carrying a bunch of grapes.'

'I'd have thrown them at him.'

'You were only thirteen, Alix,' said Wyn.

'That wouldn't have stopped me.'

'Anyway,' said Carrie, 'he stopped asking after that.'

'But he never sent cards or anything,' said Wyn. 'Never.'

'He did the first year,' said Carrie. 'And after that, no, he didn't.'

'And now he wants to see us?' asked Alix.

'If you like,' Carrie said.

'I hate him,' said Alix. 'I've always hated him.'

'You don't know him,' Carrie told her. 'You hate what you think he is.'

'How do you feel?' asked Wyn suddenly. 'You met him here. In this house.'

'I didn't mind,' said Carrie. 'It's my house. I was OK.'

'Does it upset you?' asked Alix.

Carrie bit her lip. 'I'd be wrong if I said it didn't. But you don't feel it so much after time. And I've been happy since.'

'But you haven't had anyone else,' said Alix.

'Biblically, you mean?' Carrie smiled at her daughter.

Alix blinked. 'Oh!'

'To love,' said Wyn hastily. 'A partner.'

'I've been happy,' said Carrie. 'Honestly I have. I have both of you and a business that's very successful. I don't need a partner.'

'All the same.' Wyn shrugged expressively.

'I know you've been very lucky with Terry,' said Carrie. 'And I think it must be the most wonderful thing in the world to have a happy-ever-after kind of marriage. But it's worked out for me. I like the way my life is.'

'I don't want to see him,' said Alix.

'Don't rush into it,' Carrie said. 'Think about it.'

'I do,' said Wyn. 'I need to see him.'

'You should think about it too,' said Carrie. 'We can set it up in a couple of days.'

'OK,' said Wyn.

Carrie heaved a sigh of relief. 'Does anyone want a drink? I'm gasping for some vodka.'

'Great,' said Alix.

'Yes,' said Wyn.

'Right,' said Carrie.

Chapter 23

They left Carrie's house at nine o'clock. Because she was driving, Wyn had drunk only one glass of vodka. Carrie had had quite a few and Wyn thought that Alix had too.

The sisters were silent as Wyn drove down the narrow road where Carrie lived to join the steady stream of traffic in Ranelagh village.

'Are you all right?' asked Wyn as they waited for the lights to go green.

'Fine,' said Alix.

'What do you think?' asked Wyn.

'Of what?'

'Oh, for God's sake, Alix! Of everything.' The lights changed and Wyn crunched the gears.

'Take it easy,' said Alix. 'You'll destroy the car.'

'I know what I'm doing.' Wyn gritted her teeth and shoved the gearstick into first.

'She seemed OK,' said Alix.

'Carrie?'

'Wyn, there wasn't anyone else there.'

'I know, I know.' Wyn thudded the car into third gear. 'I'm sorry. I'm kind of distracted.'

'Are *you* all right?' asked Alix.

Wyn glanced in her rear-view mirror, indicated and pulled the car in to the side of the road. 'I don't know.' She bit her lip.

'Do you want me to drive?' asked Alix.

'Are you out of your mind?' Wyn said. 'You and Carrie were knocking back vodkas. We'd be stopped for sure.'

'I wasn't,' said Alix. 'I had one but I kept topping it up with lemonade. Carrie didn't notice.'

'Neither did I,' said Wyn.

'If you want, I'll drive,' Alix said. 'Honestly, Wyn, I'm fine.'

'It's OK,' said her sister. 'I can do it. It's just – oh, Alix, I don't know! How could she not have told us! He left her because of a woman he'd got pregnant. And he preferred her to us. And that other baby to us.' Wyn's face was contorted with pain. 'Why?'

'I don't know,' said Alix gently. 'I don't know.'

'I loved him,' said Wyn. 'He used to bring things home for me. He called me his princess.' She laughed shortly. 'I suppose all fathers call their daughters princesses. But I thought he meant it. I though I was special. *We* were special.'

'Yeah, well, we weren't,' said Alix.

'I know.' Wyn turned to look at her. 'You probably don't even remember him very well.'

'Well enough,' said Alix. 'Well enough to have wanted him to stay.'

'I could understand it if she was young and beautiful and not pregnant,' said Wyn. 'I could understand that! At least he'd be running away for something more glamorous than Carrie and Wyn and Alix. But he was just exchanging us, Alix. Exchanging us for someone else with a kid.'

'Stop,' said Alix. 'I don't want to talk about it any more.'

'But we have to talk about it.' Wyn wiped her eyes. 'We have to figure it out.'

'I don't want to figure that bastard out!' Alix clenched her fists. 'I don't give a shit about him. No more than he does about you or me. I'm not going to meet him and I couldn't care less about his wife or his daughter or his bloody granddaughter either.'

'Oh, God,' said Wyn. 'I'd forgotten about the grand-daughter. We're related to that child. I've never been an aunt before.'

'It's great.' Alix smiled wryly at her. 'You get to be real nice to them and then leave them if it becomes too hectic. Anyway, Wyn, you're only some kind of step-relation to the kid and you're never likely to see her anyway so I don't know what you're worrying about.'

'But the other one. Kate. She's our half-sister, Alix.'

'I don't care what she is,' said Alix. 'She means nothing to me. I didn't know about her before and I don't know about her now. Come on, Wyn. Either drive or let me drive. I don't want to sit here all night.'

'OK, OK,' said Wyn. She put the car into gear and moved off. 'Aren't you curious, though?' She shot a glance at Alix. 'Don't you want to know what she looks like?'

'No,' said Alix.

'Or what *he* looks like now?'

'Definitely not,' said Alix.

'Maybe he's sorry,' said Wyn. 'Maybe he regrets it.'

'Like shit he regrets it,' snorted Alix. 'He's back to sort out his affairs. Get a divorce from Carrie. Marry the lovely, fragile, has-to-be-looked after Imogen. Play happy fucking families with his granddaughter! You think he cares about us? Think again, Wyn.'

'But you can't just blot people out of your mind,' said Wyn. 'I mean, Alix, he must have thought of us sometimes. Carrie said he wanted to see us.'

'After five years! He obviously wasn't all that gutted, was he?'

'How do you know? Maybe he was.'

'Wyn, you live in a fantasy world, didn't anyone ever tell you? Where fathers love their children and mothers love their husbands and everything is happy ever after.'

'Don't be stupid.' Wyn rubbed her eyes and slowed to let a car out in front of her.

'You've been lucky,' said Alix. 'You married Terry and you had the kids and everything has worked out for you. So you think that everyone should be like you.'

'No, I don't,' said Wyn. 'And I resent the implication that I'm so one-dimensional that I can't see outside my own family. I'm not stupid, Alix.'

'No, you're not.' Alix smoothed back her hair in a gesture that was a carbon copy of Carrie's. 'I'm sorry, Wyn. I'm pretty thoughtless sometimes.'

'I love Terry,' said Wyn. 'He's been good for me, Alix. And I love my kids more than anything else in the world. I don't know how anyone could ever leave their children, I really don't. And I can't see how you could ever stop thinking about them if you did. But I know that some people can. And maybe, for whatever reason, it's easier for men to leave them. I just wish it hadn't been our father that had done it.'

'We're better off without him,' said Alix.

They drove the rest of the way in silence. Alix leaned back

in the seat and closed her eyes. She had a thumping headache. She was glad that Wyn was doing the driving.

She remembered him coming into the bedroom one night. Walking lightly because he thought they were asleep. She should have been asleep but something had woken her. Alix hadn't been the sort of child to cry when she woke up. Usually she just lay in her bed and looked around her, not afraid of the dark.

He leaned over the bed and saw that her eyes were open. 'Why aren't you asleep?' he whispered.

'I am,' she said.

'With your eyes open?'

'They're nearly closed.'

He smiled and kissed her on the cheek. He pulled the sheet up to her neck. 'Sleep well,' he whispered.

'I love you,' she said.

She didn't want to remember things like that. They weren't real. She'd probably dreamed it anyway.

∽

Terry was in the living room. He looked up when they walked in.

'How was it?' he asked.

'OK,' said Wyn uncertainly. Then she began to cry.

He jumped up from the sofa and put his arms round her. Gathered her close to him and stroked her hair. 'It's all right,' he murmured. 'It's OK.' He looked at Alix who was standing at the door watching them. 'What happened?' he mouthed silently.

She shrugged.

326

Terry kept his arms round Wyn who leaned against him. Alix sat on the sofa and said nothing as he held her tightly and comforted her.

I want someone like that, she thought. The pain of wanting seared through her. I want someone to care about me the way Terry cares about Wyn. I want someone who'll comfort me when I feel bad, who'll be there when I need him the most. She shivered.

Terry led Wyn to the sofa. She sat down beside Alix, her face tear-stained.

'Do you want to tell me about it?' asked Terry.

'The news from the front is that good old Daddy, who abandoned us and Carrie, left us for another woman who was pregnant with his child,' said Alix lightly. 'He's returned to the old sod because he wants a divorce from Carrie – not that she has much say in it anyway, I suppose. The reason for this sudden desire to disentangle himself from her is because he wants to marry his girlfriend. Her name's Imogen. The daughter, their daughter, is pregnant and they want to be legitimate grandparents.' She laughed shortly. 'He also claims to want to see us. But I guess that's just to make things sound good.'

'Your father has another child?' Terry stared at her in amazement.

'Hardly a child at this point,' said Alix. 'She must be at least twenty-nine.'

Terry held Wyn's hand. 'I'm not surprised you're upset,' he said. 'You're probably in shock.'

'It's only hitting me now.' Wyn's voice was shaky. 'I just can't believe it. I thought that he'd left because of work. Because he thought it was so important. That's what Carrie used to say when we were small. That he'd left us for work. She wouldn't ever say anything else. Eventually we stopped asking. But even when I didn't believe that any more I still never thought he'd left us because of another child.'

'If it was another woman I could understand,' said Terry. 'But a woman and a kid.'

'His kid,' said Alix.

'How do you feel about it?' Terry asked her.

She shrugged. 'What's there to feel? The man obviously didn't give a shit about us. Why should I get upset about things now? He only wants to see us as some kind of sop to his conscience, I guess. He never really cared about us.'

'Perhaps he did,' said Terry.

'Oh, don't you start!' Alix looked at him in disgust. 'Carrie, despite refusing to talk about him when we were kids, was trying to make excuses earlier. He's a shit, he always was a shit and he always will be a shit. And I'm not going to waste any emotions feeling sorry for him or wondering about him or even remembering any of it.'

'He's your father,' said Terry gently.

'A biological accident,' Alix told him. 'Who cares who our father is? The facts of the matter are that Carrie brought us up and Carrie did everything for us and she made us stand on our own two feet and accept nothing from anyone and she was right. So I won't get mushy and sentimental over someone who had no more than a bit part in my existence.'

Terry was silent. Wyn blew her nose.

'You're so strong, Alix,' said Wyn. 'I'm your older sister. I should be the strong one. But it's you. You could always stand up for yourself.'

'No one else will do it for you,' said Alix harshly. Then she smiled. 'Well, for you, Wyn, I suppose Terry will.'

Terry patted Wyn on the hand and got up. 'I'll put the kettle on,' he said. 'I think you could both do with some tea.'

'Thanks,' said Wyn. She leaned back in the seat. 'I feel exhausted.'

'Me too,' said Alix.

'Do you think he ever thought about us?' asked Wyn.

'I couldn't care less,' said Alix.

'But what if he regretted it?' Wyn looked anxiously at her. 'What if he used to sit at home and think about us and wish he hadn't left Carrie.'

'His loss,' Alix said shortly.

Terry brought tea and biscuits in to them. They sipped the hot drinks, cupping their hands round the bright red mugs. He switched on the TV but it was only for background noise. None of them watched it.

Alix closed her eyes. She wished that John hadn't come back to Ireland. She wished Carrie had never told her about Imogen and Kate. Despite not wanting to think about them, she couldn't help imagining what they were like. The fragile Imogen and her equally fragile daughter. So unlike herself and Wyn, both of whom were tall and strong and healthy-looking. Unlike Carrie who, in many ways, looked fragile too. Alix gritted her teeth. Did they get their sturdy bodies and dark hair from John? She remembered him, of course, but only as the sort of memory that floats into your head when you're not trying to find it. Whenever she really tried to think about him, she couldn't visualise him at all. But he was dark, she remembered that much. And Carrie was fair. At least, Alix conceded, she was fair now. Perhaps she hadn't been quite so blonde when she was younger.

Thinking of Carrie's hair colour made her think of her own grey strands. Visible signs of being older. Wiser. But she didn't feel either of those things. She felt exactly the same as she'd always done. She yawned.

'Tired?' asked Terry.

She shook her head. 'Not really. I suppose it's been a long day.'

'You should go to bed early. Get some sleep,' he told her.

'I should do that every night.' She smiled faintly at him. 'Never quite manage it, unfortunately.' She stood up. 'You're right, though. I'll head off. Leave you two in peace.'

'You don't have to rush away,' protested Wyn. 'Stay the night if you like.'

'Don't be daft,' said Alix. 'I haven't even got a change of things with me. I'm fine, Wyn. Besides, I have a busy day at work tomorrow.'

'You sure?'

She nodded. 'Absolutely.'

Wyn stood up and kissed her on the cheek. 'We'll always have each other,' she said.

'Don't be so dramatic,' Alix grinned. 'What you mean is we're stuck with each other.'

Wyn made a face. 'Sure. That's exactly what I mean. But I love you, Alix.'

'And I you.' Alix gave Wyn a hug. 'Take care.'

'Safe home,' said Wyn. 'Sleep well.'

Terry and Wyn stood at the door and waited until Alix had turned out of the driveway before they went back inside.

'Was it really difficult?' asked Terry.

'It's just that your life isn't what you thought it was,' said Wyn falteringly. 'I always thought there was just Alix and me. And Carrie. As far as I was concerned, John existed, and I suppose I assumed that he'd have another relationship, but I never, ever thought of children. How naïve could I be?' She looked at him in puzzlement. 'I mean, it was odds on that he'd have another family. But it just never occurred to me.'

'It's not something I'd think about either,' said Terry. 'How do you think Alix is taking it? She seems pretty OK.'

Wyn shrugged. 'You know Alix. Shocked at first and then she kind of made a joke of it. Dismissive. Light-hearted. Said it didn't matter.'

'And is that what she really thinks?'

'I wish I knew.' Wyn leaned her head against her husband's shoulder. 'I really wish I knew.'

~

Alix turned the key and walked into her empty apartment. She went over to the computer and checked the level of the dollar. Slightly stronger. She wrinkled her nose. She didn't want it to be slightly stronger. But then, nothing was as she wanted it these days. So it wasn't entirely surprising that the dollar wasn't doing her any favours either.

She pushed open the bathroom door and peered at her face in the huge mirror over the sink. She could see Carrie in it. In the shape of her eyes. In the lift of her mouth. In her cheekbones. All of that was Carrie. But her thick dark eyebrow, weren't like Carrie's. Carrie's were finely arched and their shape had as much to do with nature as with their owner's skill with tweezers. The green and grey colours of

331

her eyes weren't Carrie's either. Carrie had blue eyes. Like Wyn.

He was a shit, she told her reflection. A complete and utter shit who walked out on us and who wouldn't stay. Even though Carrie begged him. He didn't love us then and he doesn't love us now.

She switched off the bathroom light and went to bed.

❧

It was five o'clock when she woke up, heart thumping. She hadn't had the chasing dream. She didn't know why she was suddenly sitting upright in the bed, trembling with fear. She listened for the sound of someone in the apartment but everything was quiet.

She slid out of the bed and pulled her dressing gown round her. She peeped out of the window but there was nothing to be seen. She tiptoed out into the living room and checked the patio doors but everything was closed. Then she head a muffled thud and a stifled laugh from the apartment next door.

Three girls shared the apartment next door and it looked as if at least one of them was having a very late night. She sighed. Lucky Fiona or Meredith or Yvonne.

She looked at her watch. She was wide awake now and she knew that she would never get back to sleep. She might as well get dressed. She could go into the office early. Get a few things done.

But an hour later she didn't feel like going into the office. It seemed a suddenly pointless exercise to sit in the dealing room for an hour and a half ahead of everyone else. She could do some early trades, perhaps, but she didn't feel in the right frame of mind for trading.

What does Kate do? she wondered. Besides being married and being pregnant. What is her career? And is she going to give it up now because of her child? John's grandchild.

Why had he walked out? How could he walk out?

Alix picked up the keys to her car and let herself out of the apartment. The sky was lighter as she slid behind the wheel and turned the key. She drove down Haddington Road and towards the toll bridge. Then she took the coast road northwards, round the estuary, until she was in Malahide village.

This is crazy, she told herself. You're being stupid.

She drove through the village and turned towards Paul's estate. You are not to drive past his house, she told herself. He could be up. He could see you. Although Paul was never out of bed before eight. But Sabine might be. Doing whatever arty thing it was that she did. She might like to paint in the early morning.

Alix slowed down as she drove past his house. It was silent, curtains closed, a pint of milk on the doorstep.

A pint of milk. It looked so bloody domesticated.

The tears stung her eyes as she accelerated past the house and back to the main road.

Chapter 24

In the end, Alix was late getting into the office. She hurried up the stairs, too impatient to wait for the lift. The others had started the morning meeting without her.

'Sorry,' she said as she slipped into her seat. 'Traffic.'

'We were just talking about the UK unemployment data,' Dave told her. 'Lots of talk that they'll be worse than expected. The gilt market looks like it'll open lower.'

'Fewer people out of work and it's bad for the market,' sighed Alix. 'I can never quite get my head around that.'

Jenny smiled. 'You're not meant to get involved in the moral dilemma.'

'I don't,' said Alix. 'But I think it's crazy that we say that the numbers will be "worse". They're not worse for the people who've got a job for the first time.'

Dave and Gavin exchanged glances.

'I didn't realise you were a bleeding heart,' said Gavin.

'Now you know,' Alix said. 'So if you ever lose your job, Gavin, you'll take comfort from the fact that I'm feeling very sorry for you.'

'Thanks. But I won't lose my job,' he told her. 'I'll only ever move onwards and upwards.'

She laughed suddenly. 'I believe you, Gavin. I truly do.'

An hour later she opened her diary and sighed. Meetings, meetings and – she'd almost forgotten – her lunch date with Matt Connery. Not a lunch date, she told herself, a viewing of their computer-animated movie. It would be interesting, she thought, if it wasn't for the fact that the idea of being around Connery was an uncomfortable one. She wished he hadn't sent her those damned flowers. How could she sit near a man who'd sent her a magnificent bouquet of carnations and tiger lilies and not feel uncomfortable? It messed up the whole basis of a business relationship to have one party sending the other flowers.

At least Paul had known better.

She flushed as she thought about having driven out to Malahide this morning. Of all the stupid things she'd done, that was the most stupid. Well, no, it wasn't, she reminded herself. Her previous trip to Malahide when she'd set off the house alarm had been even more stupid. In fact, she thought, her behaviour over the past few weeks had been littered with stupidity.

Her first meeting of the morning was with Des Coyle. She walked into his office and sat down in the visitor's chair, stretching her long legs out in front of her.

'You look a lot better,' Des told her. 'You've got some colour in your cheeks again.'

'Thanks,' she said, although she was acutely aware that the colour in her cheeks was more to do with the embarrassment she still felt about her early-morning activities than anything else.

'Completely recovered?' he asked.

'Of course,' she replied. 'It wasn't all that bad, Des. I should have taken the time off earlier, that's all.'

Des leaned back in his seat. 'You work hard,' he said.

'You pay me to work hard,' said Alix. 'And I try to do my best.'

'I'm sure you do.'

She was suddenly aware of an edge in his voice. 'Is everything all right?' she asked.

'Why wouldn't it be?'

'Because I know you,' she told him. 'And it sounds to me like you have something to say to me and you're not quite sure how to say it.'

Des sat up straight. 'Why don't you beat about the bush?' he complained. 'Why do you always have to come to the point so quickly?'

'Beating about the bush just wastes time,' said Alix. 'What's the matter?' She kept her eyes focused on his face, something she knew made him feel awkward.

'I was chatting to Dave while you were out,' said Des cautiously. 'He tells me that there have been some problems in the dealing room lately.'

'Problems?' Alix stared at him. 'What sort of problems?'

Des shrugged. 'Between you and young Gavin Donnelly.'

'Oh, for heaven's sake!' Alix looked at him in disgust. 'Gavin Donnelly is an ambitious young bloke who wants to barge his way to the top. Fine, I can understand his point of view. But it's my job to run the dealing room in the best and most profitable way possible. And letting Gavin do exactly what he wants all the time doesn't achieve that objective.'

'Dave says that you won't listen to Gavin.'

'Rubbish,' Alix snorted.

'He says that you resent him.'

'Give me a break!' Alix sighed. 'I don't resent him, Des. I just want to keep him under control, that's all.'

'What about the Anatronics account?' asked Des. 'What's the problem there?'

'There's no problem,' said Alix. 'It's an account that I put a lot of work into but Gavin did the first trade. And he wants to keep looking after it. I just haven't allocated it to him, that's all.'

'Why?'

'Do you know, Des, I'm not certain,' answered Alix slowly. 'Maybe it's because I'm not sure he'll deal with it in the best possible way.'

'But he gets on well with the finance guy – what's his name?'

'Matt Connery,' said Alix.

'Exactly. Connery. He invited Connery to the pro-am in Portmarnock and they had a great time.'

'I'm glad,' said Alix.

'So if he's prepared to put the time in entertaining this guy, why shouldn't he get any of the rewards?'

'I never said he wouldn't get any rewards,' said Alix. 'I just said I haven't allocated him the account yet. I might. I might not.'

'It's not like you to be undecided,' said Des.

'I'm not undecided,' said Alix. 'Anyway, I'm meeting Mr Connery for lunch today. He's invited me to a showing of their latest movie.'

'Oh.' Des looked slightly abashed.

'So, don't worry, Des. We have the account well covered and it shouldn't matter to you whether Gavin or I talk to Matt

Connery because either of us is perfectly capable of dealing with the business.'

'Sure,' said Des hastily. 'I just wanted to make certain that everything was OK, that's all.'

'Anything else bothering you?' asked Alix.

Des sighed. He'd wanted to bring up the subject of a possible transfer to Paris for Alix but he didn't feel that this was the most appropriate time. He'd given Guy Decourcelle a call while Alix was out sick and Guy had been quite positive about the idea. 'We can use a girl like Alix,' he'd said enthusiastically. 'There are plenty of areas where her experience would be a tremendous asset.'

Des had told Guy that he'd have a chat with Alix, see how she felt about the whole idea. He couldn't imagine she'd feel anything but elated at the idea of working in Paris. Particularly since she'd been dumped by her boyfriend.

Dave Bryant had told him about that the previous evening when they'd bumped into each other in the car park. As far as Des was concerned, Paul's departure explained a lot. It explained Alix collapsing at the meeting with Brian Nicholls. It explained her absences from work. It explained the slightly distracted air that she'd had at the last few meetings. Des knew that women fell to pieces whenever their relationships broke up. It was the way they were. And Alix, despite her efficiency and her desire to be the best dealer in the world, was still a woman who'd been dumped by her boyfriend. She'd be better off working somewhere else for a while. But he wasn't going to suggest it today. He had a feeling that she might hit him if he did.

Alix knew that there was still something bothering Des. She could see it in his eyes and in the false cheerfulness that he showed throughout the rest of the meeting. She knew that it was something to do with the dealing room. She just didn't know what. What she did know was that she was going to kill Dave Bryant. Going behind her back to Des like that! Just as she'd anticipated he might. They were so bloody predictable, she thought angrily, and so bloody male!

∼

Her next meeting was with Linda, one of the bank's accountants. They went thought the profit numbers for the first half of the year and Alix's estimates for the second half.

'I hear you were sick,' said Linda when they'd finally finished going through the accounts. 'Keeled over in the boardroom.'

'I'm never going to live that down,' sighed Alix. 'No matter what I do in the bank now, the defining moment of my career will be collapsing in front of Des.'

'Eileen tells me that he was white as a sheet when he came rushing out of the room looking for her.' Linda chuckled. 'I bet he hadn't a clue what to do.'

'It was more embarrassing than anything else,' said Alix. 'He was embarrassed, I was embarrassed and I'm sure Brian Nicholls will never deal with us again!'

'He signed the facility letter,' said Linda practically.

'That's true.' Alix smiled then yawned.

'How's Paul?' asked Linda idly as she closed the folders on her desk.

Alix glanced at her. Linda wasn't even looking at her, had asked the question casually, with no ulterior motive.

'We're not together right now,' said Alix.

'Oh?' Linda looked up from the folders. 'I'm sorry, Alix. I didn't realise.'

Alix shrugged. 'It doesn't matter.'

'But you were living with him for ages, weren't you?'

'Three years,' said Alix.

Linda smiled sympathetically. 'Plenty more fish in the sea.'

'Right,' said Alix.

'No point in settling down with one person too soon,' said Linda brightly.

'Absolutely,' said Alix. 'How about you and Michael Devlin?'

'Still together,' Linda told her. 'Just about.'

'Really? Or are you saying that to make me feel better?'

Linda laughed. 'No. We fight like cats and dogs. But I like it really.'

'And you've no plans to settle down and have kids?'

'Not yet,' said Linda blithely, 'but I'm only twenty-five, Alix. I've buckets of time.'

Alix returned to her office and stared at the Reuters screen. She'd be thirty-three in less than three weeks. Turning thirty hadn't bothered her. Why did she now feel older when she'd always thought of herself as young?

~

The reception area of Anatronics Industries was crowded with people. A woman wearing a badge with her name, Maria, welcomed Alix and handed her a glass of champagne.

'I wasn't expecting to see quite so many people,' said Alix.

'It's a big event for us,' said Maria. 'This is the first piece we've done in Ireland. We're very happy about it.'

'Great,' said Alix. She looked around. 'Is Matt Connery here?'

'He's about somewhere,' Maria told her. 'But I haven't seen him in a while. He's probably with the banking blokes – they were chatting about money earlier.'

Alix smiled. 'I'm sure I'll find him.'

She wandered through the crush of people, sipping her champagne appreciatively. Alix liked champagne. Especially Moet. She stood beside one of the large windows and gazed at the cars and trucks whizzing along the motorway. It would be interesting to work in a manufacturing company, she thought. It must be very satisfying to develop a product, produce it, sell it and make a profit. Sometimes financial services seemed very mundane in comparison.

'Alix Callaghan! How are you?' She turned to see Thomas Hewitt, who'd once worked for Europa Bank but had left to join one of their competitors the previous year.

'Thomas. Nice to see you.' She smiled at him.

'I didn't expect to see you here,' said Thomas. 'I thought John Collins might be, since we did a joint facility for Anatronics.'

'Maybe he is.' Alix glanced around. 'Although he didn't mention it to me.'

'Much nicer to see you,' said Thomas. 'Are you keeping well?'

'Yes, thanks,' she said. 'And you? How are Evelyn and the kids?'

'Oh fine,' Thomas told her. 'Actually, Alix, we're expecting number three any day now.'

'You're not!' She looked at him in surprise. 'I thought Evelyn said that she wasn't going to have any more.'

'You know women.' He sighed. 'As soon as Greta started in

Montessori, Evelyn came over all broody again.' He laughed. 'I didn't mind, actually. I love the kids.'

'Give her my regards,' said Alix.

'Of course,' Thomas said. 'What about you, Alix. Any news?'

'What sort of news?'

'You know. Wedding bells, that kind of thing.'

'Not at all,' she said firmly. 'I'm not that kind of girl.'

'Not what kind of girl?' Matt Connery appeared at Thomas's shoulder and looked from Alix to Thomas. 'Welcome, by the way,' he said. 'Sorry I didn't get to you earlier but more people came than we thought.'

'Good turn-out,' said Thomas.

'Yes.' Matt looked pleased. 'Do you two know each other? I thought rival bankers would spit at each other or something.'

Alix smiled. 'You have the completely wrong impression of financial people,' she told him. 'And Thomas and I are old friends.'

'Ah,' said Matt. 'So what kind of girl are you, Alix?'

'Pardon?'

'As I arrived you were saying you weren't that kind of girl. What kind of girl are you?'

'A very ordinary kind,' she said, 'who has to go to the ladies' room and freshen up.' She handed her empty champagne glass to a waiter who was hovering nearby. 'If you'll excuse me, gentlemen.' She strode across the room, leaving Matt and Thomas together.

'I like her,' said Thomas. 'I used to work in Europa. Lots of the dealers had no real time for what went on in credit, but Alix was always interested. She was one of the most helpful people I knew.'

'I like her too,' said Matt, 'although I don't seem to be able to have a conversation with her for more than ten seconds at a time.'

Thomas looked at him speculatively. 'And what conversation would you like to have?' he asked.

Matt grinned. 'Keep your filthy thoughts to yourself, Hewitt. My motives are entirely pure.'

'Oh really?' Thomas raised an eyebrow. 'I'm not sure how successful you'll be if you're interested in her. She's been living with some bloke for a few years.'

'So I believe,' said Matt. 'Still, you never know.'

'He's a journalist,' Thomas told him. 'A bit pretentious, like most of them. He wrote some awful guff about Alix in one of the business magazines. She really struggled with her credibility for months afterwards. Everyone in the bank gave her such a hard time.'

'Why?' asked Matt.

'Oh, it was all about how good-looking she was and how wonderful and how talented.' Thomas laughed. 'And, of course, by the time it was published they were actually living together. So they gave her an even worse time. Didn't bother her, though. She toughed it out.'

'She's tough all right,' said Matt.

'Heart of gold, though,' Thomas told him. 'And, according to her boyfriend, she's a wow between the sheets.'

⁓

Alix undid her hair and brushed it. She peered at it in the mirror. Definitely more grey again. It seemed to reappear with indecent haste. She'd colour it later in the week with the colour she'd bought while in the chemist to pick up vitamins. She was trying to take Geraldine O'Neill's advice and look after herself more but she kept forgetting to take the vitamins. She repinned her hair at the back of her head. They grey wasn't really noticeable. Then she did her lipstick and sprayed herself with Tommy Girl. Though I should probably be wearing a more mature perfume, she told herself. As befits my elderly creaking body. She fastened up the jacket of her maroon silk suit and walked back into the room.

Michael Hollis, the director who'd been at the presentation she'd done for Anatronics, was giving a speech. Alix listened idly as she leaned against the wall. She glanced at her watch. She was feeling tired and very slightly light-headed from the champagne. She hoped that Michael wouldn't talk for too long.

Fortunately he didn't. He invited them in to see the movie, which lasted half an hour. Alix thought it was very clever and she could see how it would achieve Michael's objective of being both educational and entertaining for its target six- to eight-year-old audience.

When the movie was finished, they were ushered into another room where a buffet lunch was being served. Alix was starving. She hadn't eaten since lunchtime the previous day. She hadn't felt like eating last night and of course she'd skipped breakfast in her ridiculous flight across the city to Malahide this morning.

What was going through your head? she asked herself as she queued up for some chicken fricassee. Did you actually want to see Paul? Or Sabine? And do you want to see Dad? The thought came into her head before she could stop it. She tried to push it away but she couldn't. Right now she could remember him again. More clearly than ever before. Images hurtled into her head. Of him picking her up after she'd fallen from the swing in the back garden. Dusting the dirt from her knee and kissing her on the forehead. 'You're OK, my little angel,' he said. 'Daddy loves you.'

She closed her eyes. It was too real. Too close.

'Alix?'

She opened her eyes again. Matt Connery stood beside her, a look of concern on his face.

'Are you all right?' he asked.

'Yes,' she said hurriedly. 'I'm fine.'

'You looked as though something had upset you,' said Matt.

'Not at all,' she told him.

'I thought perhaps you were feeling unwell again.'

'Everyone keeps going on and on about my so-called illness,' she said impatiently. 'I had a bug, that's all.' She handed her plate to the chef who piled it with rice and chicken.

'But you've regained your appetite.' Matt grinned as he looked at her plate. She laughed and he was pleased to see that it was a genuine laugh.

'You've probably told them to feed everyone up so they'll go away thinking nothing but nice thoughts about the company.'

'Maybe,' said Matt. 'I can't take the credit or otherwise. The organisation was nothing to do with me.' He led her to one of the small tables.

'The organisation was excellent.' She sat down. 'And so was the movie.'

He nodded. 'The guys here know what they're doing. All I have to do is to make sure that we keep the financing on an even keel and don't do anything stupid.'

'I won't let you do anything stupid,' said Alix.

'Thank you.' He smiled at her and held her gaze until she suddenly busied herself with her food.

'I should thank you again myself,' she said without looking up.

'Oh?'

'For the flowers. You really shouldn't have done that, you know.'

'I know.'

She glanced up at him.

'It was crass of me really. I don't know why I did it. It must have been embarrassing for you.'

'Embarrassing?'

'I know that you live with someone. I didn't think of that possibility. I'm sorry.'

'It's OK,' she said. She smiled faintly at him. 'Actually, I thought you were married.'

'Married!' He looked at her in astonishment. 'Why on earth would you think that?'

'It was such a – a – gesture,' she said. 'It's the kind of thing a guy who's trying to seduce a woman does.'

'Well, yes, maybe,' admitted Matt. 'But it doesn't mean he has to be married.'

'It's like you've done it before,' she said.

'Bloody hell.' He put down his fork. 'You really see the worst in me, don't you?'

'Not at all,' she said cheerfully. 'I'm just covering all the angles.'

'And have you been living with this guy for long?' Matt picked up his fork again.

'Why?'

'Curiosity,' he said.

'None of your business,' she responded.

'I guess not.'

'Absolutely not.'

'I like you,' he said and smiled at her.

Their eyes met and Alix was the first to look away.

She liked him too. Sitting at the table chatting to him she realised that he was an interesting person to talk to. He'd only been with Anatronics a few months. Before that he'd worked in the States and in Malaysia.

'I was lucky,' he told her. 'When the Asian economy went down the toilet I thought I might have to take any job that came along. But then our parent company in the US offered me something in California and off I went.'

'Must be nice to have worked in a number of different places,' she said.

'Yes. Good experience. But eventually you want to come home.'

'Why?' she asked.

'I don't know.' He considered the question. 'Roots maybe? I've no idea. But I was delighted to have the chance to get home.'

'And you don't miss California or Malaysia?'

He shook his head. 'Not in the slightest.'

Her mobile rang and she jumped. Matt turned away while she took the call.

'You asked me to call if you weren't back by half three,' said Jenny. 'It's half three now. Are you having a good time?'

'It's fine,' said Alix.

'Are you coming back?'

'I have to,' Alix told her. 'I'm supposed to meet that guy from Dresdner Bank at half four.'

'What guy from Dresdner Bank?' asked Jenny. 'You haven't got an appointment in your diary. Oh!' she said. 'There's someone with you.'

'Got it in one, Ms Smith,' said Alix. 'I'll be back shortly.' She ended the call and put the phone back in her bag. 'I've got to go,' she told Matt.

'That's a pity,' he said. 'I was enjoying our conversation.'

'So was I,' said Alix. She stood up. 'But I really must be off.'

'Let me see you to the lift,' said Matt.

'It was a very enjoyable lunch,' she said as the lift doors opened. 'And anything we can do to help, just let us know.'

'Sure.'

The doors began to close and Matt suddenly pressed the button again. Alix looked at him in surprise as he got into the lift beside her.

'I could do with some fresh air,' he said. 'I'll see you to your car. You're OK to drive, aren't you? Or would you prefer me to order you a cab?'

Alix shook her head. 'I had a glass of champagne when I arrived, that's all.' She yawned and put her hand over her mouth. 'Oh, I'm sorry.'

'Late night last night?' asked Matt.

'Late enough.'

You'll always be my best little girl. Her father had held her over his head. Why could she suddenly remember all this stuff when she'd never been able to remember it before? And she'd only been three years old. It wasn't as though people remembered much of their life at the age of three.

The lift stopped at the ground floor and Matt followed her out.

'Goodbye, Matt.' She held out her hand.

'Goodbye.' His handshake was firm and confident.

'Don't forget to call us with your next trade,' she said.

'I won't. But will I be dealing with you or with Gavin?'

'Does it matter?' she asked.

'I suppose not,' said Matt. 'He's efficient. And I enjoyed myself out in Portmarnock.'

Alix nodded. 'I believe it was a good day.'

'Yes, it was,' said Matt.

'I'm glad you enjoyed it.' She unlocked the car.

'Drive carefully,' said Matt.

'I will.' She got into the car and drove swiftly away.

Matt watched as she indicated and moved onto the main road. He rubbed his chin thoughtfully. What was it about the girl that attracted him so much? Her looks? Her brains? The fact that she was living with someone else?

Forget about her, he told himself. It's not worth the grief.

Attractive and uncomplicated, thought Alix. But I'm not interested.

Chapter 25

For the first time in weeks, Alix didn't feel tired when she woke up the following morning. She got out of bed as soon as she awoke and pulled open the bedroom curtains. The sky was clear blue and cloudless, marred only by the long white streak from a plane thirty thousand feet higher. She stood at the window and wondered where the passengers in the plane were going. Somewhere nice, she hoped. Not somewhere boring and businesslike. Somewhere people could have fun.

She needed to have fun again. She'd go to the shooting club which was always fun. When Paul had lived with her she used to go most Saturday mornings. She missed the discipline. And she felt, very strongly, that she needed some discipline in her life right now.

She dressed in a pair of loose cotton trousers and pulled on her long-sleeved T-shirt followed by a sweatshirt. Even on the warmest days it could be cold at the shooting club, located on the north-facing side of the mountains. She pulled her hair back from her face and into a tight plait so that she wouldn't be distracted by stray wisps floating into her line of vision. Right, she thought, ready for the fray.

There were a lot of cars already at the shooting club grounds. A surprising number, thought Alix as she locked the BMW and walked towards the clubhouse. There must be a competition on. Shit, she thought. If there was a competition she might not get the opportunity to shoot. And now that she was here, she desperately wanted to shoot.

'Hi, Niall,' she said as she walked into the small room that was the clubhouse. 'How are things?'

'Alix!' He smiled at her. 'I thought you'd given up.'

'I've been busy.'

'You said that the last time you were here. You mentioned trips to Paris and London and other exotic destinations.'

'London, exotic?' She raised an eyebrow.

'Maybe not exotic,' he conceded. 'But different.'

'You're right, though,' she said. 'I've been away quite a bit and there's been lots of things going on. So I haven't had the time to be here. Sorry.'

'I don't mind,' said Niall. 'But you'll be a bit rusty for this morning.'

'I didn't realise there was a competition today,' she said.

'But you'll enter for it?'

'Is there space for me to enter?'

'Of course. But I'd better warn you that Darren Sherlock is shooting so you'll have stiff competition.'

She shrugged. 'It's not the winning, it's the taking part.'

'Oh, Alix!' Niall laughed. 'You know quite well that as far as you're concerned, it's always been the winning!'

He was right, of course. Alix collected her ammunition and walked outside. Winning was important. What was the point of competing if you didn't think you had a chance?

'Hi, Alix.' Darren stood beside her. 'Haven't seen you in a while.'

'Been busy,' she said laconically. 'I believe you're tipped to win today.'

He laughed. 'They always tip me to win. That's just to put the pressure on.'

'You won't be getting much pressure from me,' she told him.

'You should practise more,' said Darren.

She shook her head. 'I enjoy it and I want to win. But I can't afford the time.'

'Pity,' he said. 'You could be really good.'

'Bet you say that to all the girls,' she teased and Darren blushed.

Alix smiled as she watched him walk back to the clubhouse. She liked Darren; he was only nineteen but he was a skilled shooter. He wanted to compete in the Olympics one day.

She was one of the first to shoot. She pushed her earplugs into her ears, took up her prone position and sighted the paper target. She allowed her breathing to become slower and settle into a steady rhythm. Her mind was clear of everything except the target. The faces that had haunted her dreams over the past few weeks disappeared. There was nothing but herself and her rifle and the target.

Her first shot was high and to the left. She was surprised. She adjusted her sight. The first five shots didn't count as part of the competition. After that, she had five shots at each of four targets. The maximum score was 200. Her best ever was 196. She knew that there was no hope of beating Darren Sherlock today but she wanted to give him a run for his money. She kept her breathing slow and steady as she aimed at her first target.

She was shooting well, despite her lack of practice. When

she'd completed all four targets she estimated her score to be around 190. There were a couple of shots she wasn't sure about.

'How did you do?' asked Darren as she walked back to the clubhouse, removing the single point sling she used to help steady her aim.

'Your title is safe,' she told him. 'Unless you were out on the town last night.'

'I wish,' he said.

'How's Angela?'

Darren made a face. 'I haven't seen her in a few weeks. We've decided to cool it a bit, Alix.'

'Oh. I'm sorry to hear that.'

'No need.' He beamed at her. 'It was getting too involved, to be honest with you. She wanted to know where I was every minute of the day. It's kinda nice to be cut loose again.'

'I suppose it is,' said Alix.

She walked to the observation point to watch the other shooters. Why couldn't she think of how nice it was to be cut loose again? Why was it that the thought of Paul still had the power to hurt her so much? Why couldn't she just bloody well get over him?

'Dad!' She heard Darren call to his father who was also a member of the club.

'Hi, Darren. Have you shot yet?'

She looked round at them. Father and son stood beside each other, discussing the event, completely at ease in each other's company. Darren was laughing at something his father had said and the older man clapped his son on the back. Alix gritted her teeth. Fathers were a sensitive subject with her. She wasn't going to think about hers. She'd successfully kept him out of her mind all day. She wasn't going to allow him to invade her thoughts now.

Darren won the competition with a score of 198. Tony Leehy was second with 193. And Alix was third with 191.

'Are you coming for a drink?' asked Niall. 'We're going down the road for one.'

She shook her head. 'I don't think so. I've things to do.'

'Are you sure you're OK, Alix?' he asked. 'You've seemed – oh, I don't know, unlike yourself all day.'

'What am I supposed to be like?' she asked lightly.

'I don't know,' admitted Niall.

'Your imagination is getting the better of you,' she said. 'I'm fine. I just don't have time to go for a drink, that's all.'

'No problem,' said Niall easily. 'Hope you'll start dropping by more often again.'

'I will,' said Alix. 'I had a good time today.'

~

After the noise at the shooting club, her apartment seemed unnaturally quiet. I should have gone for a drink with them, thought Alix, as she leafed through the *Irish Times*. I'm becoming completely anti-social.

The phone rang and she jumped.

'Hello,' she said.

'Hi, Alix. How are you?'

'I'm fine, Wyn.' Alix put the paper to one side. 'And you?'

'I'm OK. I rang earlier but you didn't answer.'

'Sorry,' said Alix. 'I forgot to switch the machine on.'

'I was worried about you.'

'Worried?'

'On your own. I thought maybe – well, I don't know what I thought really.'

'Oh, Wyn, don't be such an idiot,' said Alix crisply. 'What on earth did you think I was doing?'

'I just thought you might be upset.'

'Well, I'm not,' said Alix. 'Are you?'

'Of course I am,' said Wyn. 'I don't understand you, Alix. You seem to shrug off life's great events as though they mean absolutely nothing.'

'What the hell are you talking about?' demanded Alix.

'Things like Dad. Things like Paul. Nothing seems to bother you.'

Alix almost laughed out loud. Just as well my darling sister didn't see me running down Paul's driveway and diving into my car after banging on his door and setting off his alarm, she thought. 'Of course things bother me,' she told Wyn. 'I just get over them quicker.' She felt as though she should cross her fingers at the lie.

'I don't know how you can sweep Dad out of your life so easily,' said Wyn.

'As easily as he did it to us,' Alix told her. 'Nothing to do with him is ever going to bother me.'

'But what about Imogen and Kate?'

'What about them?' asked Alix. 'They won't interfere with me and I won't interfere with them. Simple.'

Wyn sighed. 'I can't just put it to the back of my mind, Alix.'

'Don't,' said Alix. 'Just don't complain because I can.'

'We're different, I suppose.'

'Yes,' said Alix. 'And it's a good thing.'

'There was something else I wanted to ask you,' said Wyn.

Alix grimaced. She wasn't comfortable with this conversation. 'What?' she asked.

'Any chance you could drop over tonight and baby-sit?'

'Sneakily done, Wyn Mitchell,' Alix laughed. 'You ring up and pretend to be all concern for me when in reality you only want to know if I'll be fit enough to look after your kids!'

'It's not like that,' protested Wyn.

'Oh, isn't it?' Alix chuckled. 'But, yes, I'll come over. Seven o'clock be OK?'

'Perfect,' said Wyn with relief.

'See you then.' Alix replaced the receiver and picked up the paper again.

When she'd finished both the Simplex and Crosaire crosswords she went into the bathroom to investigate the hair colour she'd bought. It was an auburn shade, close enough to her own. She opened the box and read the instructions. Alix had always liked messing with paints when she was a child. She put colouring her hair into the same category – plenty of messing around with tubes and bottles. She hoped that they were telling the truth when they said that the eventual colour of her hair was nothing like the purple mess on top of her head now. She looked at her watch and timed twenty minutes.

The phone rang with a minute to go.

'Bugger,' she said out loud as she wiped some colour off her ear and picked up the receiver. 'Hello.'

'Hi, Alix.'

She felt herself freeze on the spot. She said nothing.

'Alix? Are you there?'

'Yes, yes. I'm here. How are you, Paul?'

'Great,' he said cheerfully. 'And you?'

'I'm great too.'

'Good to hear,' he said.

She waited for him. She wanted to talk, to gabble at him, to find out why he'd called. But she waited.

'You're probably wondering why I phoned,' said Paul.

'Yes,' she said.

'I hope you don't mind.'

'Why should I mind?'

'It's just that I was wondering if you'd do me a favour.'

'A favour?' she repeated.

'I'd really appreciate it,' he said. 'And it's not as though you haven't done it before?'

'Done what?' she asked suspiciously.

'Been on TV.'

'On TV? You want me to go on TV?'

'It's a programme about women who've made it,' said Paul. 'It's right up your street, Alix, and you know you're good at interviews.'

'Women who've made what?' she asked acidly.

'You see, that's exactly the kind of thing they're looking for,' said Paul. 'Wit, sarcasm, a bit of a putdown with a sense of warmth.'

'A sense of warmth!'

'Oh, be a sport, Alix. Say you'll do it.'

'What sort of format is it?' she asked. 'What do they want to talk about?'

'Business,' explained Paul. 'The series is about women in business, or any successful women. The idea is to try to go for women who aren't in traditional roles but who are successful in more male-dominated areas. Like finance. Or engineering.

We've nabbed a wonderful engineer named Anastasia Moran. Does anything sound less like an engineer to you than someone called Anastasia? And we've got a woman who runs a trucking company and used to drive articulated lorries, plus a woman who's a flying instructor. So it's not boring old suits, Alix, these are good women.'

'In fact, I'm the boring suit,' she said.

'Well, yes, I suppose so.'

'Thank you for those words of comfort.'

'So what do you think? Will you do it?'

'What show?' she asked.

'New show. Twenty-minute interviews. Different one each time,' he said. 'Not me this time, unfortunately. Haven't quite managed to get myself in front of the camera yet.'

'If that's what you want, I'm sure you will,' said Alix dryly.

'Maybe,' said Paul. 'To tell you the truth, I'm not sure what I want.'

Was he happy? she wanted to ask him. He sounded happy about work. But he was asking for a favour from her when she was sure he'd rather not. Was he happy at home? Or had his dreams of domestic bliss begun to evaporate? Did he suddenly realise that work could be even more fulfilling?

'When?' she asked.

'Fairly soon,' he said. 'We'll broadcast before the end of the year.'

'And the questions are all about work?'

'About what it's like,' Paul told her. 'You know, dealing with macho blokes all the time. Putting up with the harassment.'

'I've never been harassed,' she told him. 'Unless it was by you, looking for something to eat.'

He laughed. 'People would be afraid to harass you,' he said. 'I never did, Alix. I was far too scared.'

'I don't believe that for a moment,' she said. 'OK, I'll do your interview thing. Where do they want to do it?'

'I'm not sure,' said Paul. 'I'll get back to you on that.'

'OK.'

'Alix – thank you.'

'Anytime,' she said.

She was glad he'd asked her. He could have suggested Sabine as a successful arty, interior design sort of type, but obviously she wasn't successful enough. So it was all very well for her to wander around the house in Malahide looking blonde and babyish and pretty but that wasn't much good to Paul when he was putting together a successful women show. He'd come to her. He'd come back to her. She smiled and leaned back in the chair. Then she remembered the hair colour. She leaped out and scrubbed at the upholstery with a tissue. It was an interesting shade of purple and orange.

'Shit!' She ran into the bathroom. Talking to Paul, thinking about him afterwards had knocked her schedule out of the window. Her hair would be some ridiculous shade by the time she'd rinsed off the colour and dried it.

But it was OK. A little more purple than she'd expected, perhaps, but all of the grey was successfully covered which was the main thing. And it was gleaming under the high-intensity bathroom light. She looked good, she thought. Good and healthy and OK with her life. Maybe things were finally getting better again.

∽

Wyn opened the door before Alix rang the bell. She looked tired, thought Alix, even though she was dressed up and wearing more make-up than usual.

'Saw the car pull up,' explained Wyn.

'Are you going anywhere nice?' Alix hung her linen jacket on the coat stand.

'Terry is taking me to dinner,' said Wyn as she led Alix into the kitchen. 'I think he feels it would be good for me to get out.' She laughed shortly. 'As though I'm going to stay indoors and never move again.'

'He probably thinks that if you're out and about you won't be brooding on the John and Carrie situation,' said Alix.

'Probably.' Wyn sat on a stool at the breakfast bar. 'But I honestly don't feel like it, Alix. He doesn't have to drag me out like this. I know he's probably worried because I was so upset – and I'm still upset – but he's carrying it a bit far.'

'He worries about you.' Alix sat beside her. 'And I think it's nice that he does.'

'Have you spoken to Carrie?'

Alix shook her head. 'I thought about ringing but I wasn't sure what to say. I don't want to meet him and I couldn't think of anything else to talk to her about. Have you?'

'Of course,' said Wyn. 'But I call her a lot more than you anyway, Alix. She's fine.'

'I assumed she *was* fine,' said Alix. 'After all, she's known everything all along. It's only you and me who've been taken for idiots.'

'I said that to her.' Wyn sighed. 'I got quite ratty with her. Said that she should have told us everything before now. That it was unfair to keep it from us.'

'And she said?'

'That she was trying to protect us.'

'What utter bullshit.' Alix slapped her hand on the counter. 'Protect us from what?'

'Feeling hurt, I suppose.'

'And she thinks this way is better? Give me a break.' Alix looked disgusted.

'It wasn't her fault,' said Wyn forcefully.

'I know. I know. And I'm not blaming her or anything like that. But I'm not going to fall in with her wish that we can all bury the hatchet.'

'Do you think that's what she wants?'

'I haven't a clue,' said Alix. 'But I think she feels bad about not telling us everything before now. So she wants us to do something she'll feel better about.'

'But I can't see her feeling better about us meeting Dad.'

Alix shrugged. 'You know her better than I do, Wyn. You've always been closer to her. You figure it out.'

Wyn said nothing.

'Do you still want to meet him?' asked Alix eventually.

'I think we have to,' said Wyn. 'I think we owe it to ourselves.'

'Go ahead,' Alix said. 'I don't mind whether you see him or not. But I won't. And that's final.'

'Why?'

'I just won't,' said Alix obstinately. 'I've no interest in seeing him either to please Carrie or to please you.'

'I think you're making a mistake,' said Wyn.

'I don't,' Alix said.

❧

Terry brought Wyn to Jacob's Ladder for dinner. They sat near the window and watched the crowds of people bustle through the city streets.

'She won't meet him,' said Wyn suddenly.

Terry replaced his glass of Beaune on the table. 'Why?'

'She says she's not interested in meeting him.'

'In that case there's nothing you can do about it, Wyn.'

'But she's his daughter. He's our father! Surely that means something.'

'Doesn't have to,' said Terry.

'It does to me.' Wyn's eyes were bright.

'You can't make her meet him,' Terry told her. 'And you shouldn't try.'

'I know.' Wyn sighed. 'I just think it would be the right thing to do.'

'Maybe. Maybe not.' Terry reached over and took her hand. 'People have to make up their own minds, Wyn. And what's right for you might not be right for your sister.'

'I worry about her,' said Wyn.

'For heaven's sake! What do you need to worry about Alix for?'

'Because she's on her own. Because she's lonely. Because she has a tough job and sometimes I think she takes on too much.'

'What about Paul?'

Wyn shook her head. 'I can't see anything coming of that. He's living with the French tart now.'

'Wyn!'

'Come on,' said Wyn angrily, 'they got together on a business trip to Paris. That French girl probably threw herself at him.'

'That's a bit judgemental, don't you think?'

Wyn shook her head. 'The French think differently about things.'

'Really and truly, Wyn, you're getting very insular. That's completely untrue. This French girl was no more likely to throw herself at him than any Irish girl. Or American. Or English. It's more likely that, bored out of his mind listening to Alix gibber on about swaps and options, he threw himself at the French girl. What's her name?'

'Sabine,' Wyn snorted.

'If the relationship was OK it wouldn't matter how many Sabines were in the room,' said Terry. 'A whole army of them could walk in here right now and I wouldn't take my eyes off you.'

'Oh, Terry.' Wyn smiled at him.

'Don't worry about everything so much,' he said. 'You decide what you want to do about meeting your Dad. Let Carrie solve Carrie's problems. Let Alix make her own decisions. Don't take it all on yourself.'

'You're right.' Wyn began to butter her bread roll. 'I can't help it sometimes.'

'You know, you and Alix are really very alike,' said Terry thoughtfully. 'Both of you have very set ideas about what you want from life. And both of you want things to go as you plan them.'

'I'm not as bad as Alix!' Wyn looked at her husband in horror and he laughed.

'No.' He leaned across and kissed her on the forehead. 'You're unique, Wyn. And I love you.'

∽

Alix sat in the children's bedroom and read Enid Blyton to Aoife and Nessa. She wished the two girls would go asleep. But they'd been full of energy, running around the house, playing hide and seek and fighting with each other over the slightest thing. And when she'd finally got them to bed they insisted on a story. And another. And another. Now, finally, Nessa's eyes were closed although Aoife was struggling to stay awake.

Were we like that? wondered Alix. Did we scream and fight and give Carrie all sorts of grief? She couldn't remember. She remembered Carrie shouting at her occasionally. She remembered giving Wyn a black eye (justified at the time because Wyn had robbed her Fuzzy Felt game). But she didn't remember running out of the house when bedtime came around, or hiding behind the sofa and refusing to come out or clutching a chair and forcing her mother to prise her fingers loose one by one.

But, she thought, as Aoife finally closed her eyes, they probably had done all those things. Time just changed your perspective on them.

Chapter 26

There was something comforting about the fact that it was a busy day in the dealing room and that she was about to have a row with Gavin Donnelly. The last few days had been far too full of emotional stuff for Alix's liking. Every time she tried to push the situation about her father to the back of her mind, Wyn would phone begging her to meet him. And when she wasn't wrestling with that particular dilemma, she kept musing about Paul and the TV interview.

She couldn't help hoping that he'd asked her to do it so that he could get closer to her again. She tried to tell herself that she was mistaken, but she didn't think so. His tone had been so different when he talked to her, friendly and caring rather than simply polite. She felt certain that she could get him back if she really wanted to. She just needed the right set of circumstances.

But neither John nor Paul was her foremost thought right now. She had to deal with the fact that Gavin had gone to lunch with Niall Matthews without booking a trade. And that he hadn't arrived back until three o'clock. And that nobody had known about the trade until he returned in high good humour – having consumed a bottle of Cabernet Sauvignon. And, worst of all, that because Gavin hadn't booked the

365

trade nobody knew that they were long dollars and Jenny had bought more.

Very unusually, this hadn't cost them any money. Normally if a trade was booked incorrectly or somehow overlooked, they always lost money on the position. But foreign exchange markets had been quiet and the dollar stable, so it hadn't mattered.

That, as Alix said sharply to Gavin, was hardly the point.

'I've said I'm sorry,' said Gavin stubbornly. 'And I am. But anyone could have made that mistake.'

'No they couldn't,' retorted Alix. 'You're the only one who's bloody careless about inputting your deals. When was the last time anyone just "forgot" to put one in?'

Gavin sighed. 'Cut me a bit of slack here, Alix. I work hard. I contribute. No need to treat me like a child.'

'I'm not treating you like a child,' she said. 'I'm merely pointing out that if everyone walked off without checking what they'd done we'd lose a fortune.'

'But, hey, we didn't lose anything, did we?' He beamed at her. 'So we got away with it. Lucky, I know, but better to be born lucky than smart, don't you think?'

She gritted her teeth. 'Gavin, I have to tell you that your attitude is getting right up my nose. And not only that, it's bloody unprofessional. Now, I'm telling you that I want you to shape up, take more care, cut back on the boozy lunches and the afternoon golf outings and get your act together.'

'Des told me to take clients golfing,' said Gavin truculently.

'Perhaps he did,' said Alix. 'And I'm telling you to cut back.'

'How do you think he'll feel about that?' asked Gavin.

'Gavin, I don't give a fuck how he feels,' said Alix. 'I'm your boss and I'm telling you what I want. OK?'

He shrugged. 'Suit yourself.'

'I will,' she said. She got up and walked to the door. 'I'll be in the accounts department if you're looking for me.'

She walked out of the dealing room and exhaled slowly as she closed the door behind her. She was shaking. That little shit, she thought. 'Des told me to take clients golfing.' I'll kill him. I'll kill him and I'll kill Des and I'll fucking kill Dave Bryant too who's probably laughing his head off right now.

She walked down the corridor and into the ladies'. She needed to cool down for a minute. She hated having to reprimand anyone. She did it when she had to, but it left her feeling drained afterwards. Maybe, she thought, this is why men are supposed to be better at the cut and thrust of office politics. They don't mind yelling at each other.

When she'd calmed down she went to see Linda Crossan. The accountant was looking through a bundle of reports when Alix walked into her office.

'Hi.' Linda pushed the papers to one side. 'What can I do for you?'

'Nothing,' said Alix. 'I just came for a spot of refuge.'

'Refuge?'

Alix sighed. 'I needed some peace and quiet. I've had to yell at Gavin Donnelly for not inputting a trade and I couldn't stay there.'

'You don't like him, do you?' asked Linda.

'It's not a question of liking or disliking,' replied Alix. 'And what makes you think I don't like him?'

'Common knowledge,' said Linda.

'Common knowledge?'

'Yes.' The other girl shrugged. 'You know how people talk. The word is that you and Gavin don't get on.'

'And why aren't we supposed to get on?' asked Alix.

'Because he's supposed to be so brilliant.' Linda grinned at her.

'For God's sake!'

'So they say,' said Linda.

'He's good, I'll grant him that. But brilliant? Where did the word get around that he's brilliant?'

'I don't know,' said Linda. 'He probably spread it himself. But I've heard the guys in settlements say so.'

'What the fuck would they know?' Alix rubbed her forehead.

'Getting to you?' asked Linda sympathetically.

'A bit.' Alix sighed. 'Sometimes I don't know why I put myself through all this, Linda. Sometimes I just think it would be so nice not to have to worry about the office politics and hanging on to my job and all of the other shit.'

'And what would you do instead?' asked Linda. 'I can't visualise you as the stay-at-home type.'

'Maybe I can become the stay-at-home type,' said Alix.

'At least you don't have to worry about hanging on to your job,' said Linda. 'Your profits were good last month.'

'Not the best,' said Alix.

'They don't have to be the best,' Linda told her. 'They just have to be on target.'

⌒

She met Des Coyle as she walked along the corridor.

'Hi, Alix.' He smiled at her.

'Hi, Des.'

'Making money?'

'Yes,' she said.

'Great.' He stood in front of her, blocking her.

'Did you want me?' she asked.

'Want you?'

'You look as though you want to ask me something,' she said.

'Oh. Well. Yes. Sort of.'

'Sort of?'

'Come into my office,' said Des.

She followed him into the office, her high heels sinking into the deep pile of the blue carpet. She sat down in the leather visitor's chair.

'So what's the problem?' she asked.

Des fiddled with the cap of his Mont Blanc fountain pen. 'I was talking to Guy Decourcelle the other day,' he told her. 'Guy thinks a lot of you.'

'Does he really?' she asked dryly.

'Well, yes, he does.' Des glanced up at her. 'He's very complimentary about you, Alix.'

'How nice,' she murmured.

'And he was telling me that they're looking for people in Paris.'

She sat upright in the chair. 'Oh?'

'Yes. They're looking for experienced people. Highly rated people.'

'And?'

'Your name was mentioned.'

'Was it?'

'Yes,' said Des. 'Absolutely. Guy asked me if we had any

talented people in the dealing room, and of course I said Alix Callaghan.'

'Really?'

'Yes. And he thought it'd be a great idea if you were in Paris.'

'Did he?'

'So I said to him that I'd ask you about it. After all, it's such a great opportunity.'

'To do what?' asked Alix.

Des stared at her. 'To work there. In the dealing room. In Paris.'

'As what?' asked Alix.

'Well, as a dealer, of course.'

'What title?'

'We didn't discuss titles,' Des told her.

'How senior a position?' asked Alix.

'Very senior,' said Des.

'Guy's job?' asked Alix

'I don't know,' said Des. 'I didn't ask. But he didn't imply—'

'So you don't think he's hiring for his job.'

Des looked at her uncertainly.

'Because it wouldn't make a lot of sense for me to go to Paris unless it was an upward move, would it?' she asked. 'Georges' job could be considered an upward move because he has about twenty people working for him. Guy's job would be an upward move because he's head of European Trading. But any other job would be a backward step for me, wouldn't it?'

'Don't be silly,' said Des. 'Paris is such a big organis-ation! Anywhere in their dealing room would be exciting, wouldn't it?'

'You think so?' asked Alix. 'Would I have staff of my own?'

'I – don't know,' said Des.

'If Guy was talking about it, surely you do know.'

'It was just something he mentioned in passing,' said Des.

'But you thought I'd be suitable for a job that you don't really know the description of? Is that it?' Alix's eyes were glinting dangerously.

'It's not like that,' said Des. 'I just thought that maybe you'd like a change. What with the upset about Paul and everything.'

'The upset about Paul,' said Alix slowly. 'What upset about Paul?'

Des looked uncomfortable. 'I heard that he's left you.'

The phone rang and startled both of them. Des answered it. 'I'll call her back in a couple of minutes, Eileen,' he said in response to his secretary's message. 'Thank you.'

'It's true that Paul and I aren't together any more,' said Alix. 'But that certainly doesn't mean that I want to run away to Paris.'

'It's not running away,' protested Des. 'It's just an opportunity to have a change of scenery.'

'Oh, I see,' said Alix. 'I didn't realise that. For a moment I thought you were trying to shift me out of my job.' She smiled sweetly at him. 'Sorry, Des. I misinterpreted your motives.'

'Of course, if you don't want to go—'

'Do you know, I don't think I do,' said Alix. 'I like it here too much.'

Des screwed his fountain pen back together. 'And how are you getting on with everyone?' he asked.

'With everyone?'

'Generally,' said Des.

'Fine,' Alix told him. 'Absolutely fine. Couldn't be better, in fact.'

'Great,' said Des. 'Great. Good.'

They sat in silence. Alix didn't take her eyes from his face. Finally Des stood up.

'I'd better – I was going to drop something up to John Collins,' he said. 'You probably have to get back to the desk.'

'Yes,' she said. 'But it was nice chatting to you, Des.'

'Good. Yes. You too,' he said.

Alix walked out of the room and up the stairs. Her heart was thumping in her chest. They wanted to get rid of her. They were plotting to get rid of her. She wouldn't let them. She wouldn't let anyone force her out of her job.

∼

'Alix, it's Paul for you.' Jenny raised her eyebrows inquiringly as she looked at her boss.

'Thanks,' said Alix calmly. She clicked into the line. 'Alix speaking.'

'You know, I always feel like you're about to spank me when you say that,' said Paul.

'Really?' asked Alix. 'I didn't realise.'

'It's a very provocative way to answer the phone.'

'You think so?'

'Sure do.'

'Well, not in my book it's not. What's the matter?'

'Nothing,' he said. 'I just wanted to say that the interview will probably be next week. How does that sound to you?'

'Sounds fine,' said Alix.

'Can they do it at the office?' asked Paul.

'Here? Oh, Paul, that's so embarrassing.'

'It won't be,' he said. 'It'll be simple.'

'I'm not convinced,' she told him.

'I'll get Colin Willis to give you a call,' said Paul. 'He'll sort everything out with you.'

'What have I let myself in for?' she asked.

'Nothing,' Paul promised her. 'It'll be a doddle, honestly, Alix.'

Jenny stared at her as she disconnected the call.

'What?' asked Alix. 'Why are you looking at me like that?'

'Well?' Jenny said. 'What did he want? Are you guys back together again?'

'Not exactly,' said Alix. 'But I think I'm in the driving seat right now.'

&

The dealing room was quiet. The others had gone home. Gavin had stayed the latest, intent, Alix thought, on being the last to leave. But she'd sat at her dealing desk, called clients and gone through piles of research until finally he got up and left. She smiled to herself as he walked out the door.

Gavin should be the one to go to Paris. That is, if Guy Decourcelle really did want anyone there. Alix was pretty sure that this was a plan dreamed up by Des because he knew that there was friction in the dealing room. She knew that the previous holder of her job – a guy called Tony O'Connell – had left after a bust-up with Des. She didn't know the rights and the wrongs of the situation, but she knew that Des could be tough when he wasn't on your side. She wondered exactly whose side he was on now.

The phone rang. She glanced at her watch. Not many people called the dealers at a quarter to seven in the evening.

'Alix Callaghan,' she said.

'Alix? How are you? It's Matt Connery.'

'Hi, Matt. What has you calling us so late?'

'It's early in New York,' he said.

'It's post-lunch in New York,' Alix told him. 'Did you want to do a dollar trade?'

'No,' said Matt. 'I wasn't sure you'd be still there.'

'Do you make a habit of calling the office when nobody's here?' asked Alix.

He laughed. 'No, I don't. Actually, I'm ringing to invite you to a function we've organised.'

'Another one?'

'I know. It sounds as though we do nothing else. But this was arranged months ago. I didn't think to ask you before – goodness knows why because it's right up your street, Alix.'

'Really? You're intriguing me.'

'It's a clay pigeon shoot,' said Matt triumphantly. 'On Saturday. It should be great fun and I thought you might enjoy it.'

'Clays aren't really my thing,' Alix told him. 'I'm more a paper person myself.'

'Paper?'

'Targets,' she explained. 'Clays are completely different.'

'But you'd still enjoy it?'

'I – I suppose so.'

'You'll join us then?'

Gavin Donnelly would have a breakdown, she thought.

She'd mention it tomorrow. Nonchalantly. Bring it ever so casually into conversation. He'd be fuming. She grinned. 'OK, I'd love to.'

'Great!'

'What time and where?' asked Alix.

'It's near the Glen of the Downs,' said Matt. 'But we've organised transport.'

'Oh, it's OK, I'll drive,' Alix told him.

'Don't do that,' said Matt. 'We're bringing people down by helicopter.'

'What? How many people are going?'

'About twenty,' said Matt. 'We've got choppers departing from the Point Depot and Clonskeagh. The Point is probably nearest to you.'

'You're some flash bastards,' Alix laughed.

'We've made a lot of money from the animated film,' Matt told her. 'This was organised before then but it's turned into a celebration. And we think that it's good for people to feel appreciated.'

'I haven't done much for you,' said Alix.

'You've given us some good advice,' Matt said. 'And you helped on the foreign currency credit facility.'

'Anyone could have done that,' said Alix.

'But you did it.'

'Flattery is nice,' Alix said. 'You can keep going.'

Matt laughed. 'Four o'clock on Saturday. How does that sound to you?'

'Fine,' she said. 'I'll look forward to it. But don't expect me to be any good at shooting.'

'You're the only woman I know who does it,' said Matt. 'You'd better hit at least one of them.'

'I'll do my best.'

'Oh, and there's dinner afterwards,' said Matt. 'You'll stay for that, won't you?'

'We'll be filthy after the shoot! Where on earth are you having dinner?'

'In the Glenview Hotel. You can use the facilities in the leisure centre to shower and change,' Matt told her. 'It's all organised.'

'What can I say? You seem to have it all worked out.'

'That's Anatronics,' said Matt. 'We think of everything.'

'Thanks for asking me,' said Alix.

'I'm looking forward to seeing you,' said Matt.

She thought about him as she drove home. He definitely fancied her. Flowers, business lunch invitations, corporate outing invitations – he must be attracted to her. And he was nice. Uncomplicated. And unmarried.

A chilling thought struck her. Matt Connery was in his thirties. Still unmarried. Maybe he was looking to find someone to marry and have babies with. Maybe he was feeling exactly the same as Paul. Maybe he thought of her as a good bet.

But he thought she was living with Paul, didn't he? Well, maybe that didn't bother him. She pulled into the car parking space beneath her apartment. She wasn't going to get involved with Matt Connery. Especially as she thought that Paul was just ripe to come home.

&

She was drinking hot chocolate when Wyn phoned.

'Hi,' said Alix. 'Any news?'

'I'm going to see him,' said Wyn.

'What?'

'I'm going to see him.'

Alix put her cup on the coffee table in front of her. 'Our father, you mean?'

'Who else?'

'Nobody else, I suppose.'

'Carrie has invited him to dinner on Saturday night and asked me if I wanted to come. I said yes.'

'Why on earth do you want to meet him in some social setting with Carrie?' asked Alix. 'If you have to meet him, wouldn't it be better to do it on your own?'

'I don't want to meet him on my own. And you won't come with me,' said Wyn.

'Fair enough,' said Alix.

'Are you going to come along?' asked Wyn.

'No.'

'Oh, Alix, for goodness' sake! It would do you good to meet him.'

'No it wouldn't,' she said.

'Please, Alix.'

'Look, Wyn, I've said no. Anyway, Carrie hasn't invited me. It's her dinner party, after all.'

'She asked me to tell you about it,' said Wyn. 'Of course she wants you there, Alix.'

'I'm not going,' said Alix.

Wyn heaved a sigh. 'Why not?'

'Because I don't want to. Because Carrie should be the one to ask me. And because I'm out on Saturday night anyway.'

'Out where?' asked Wyn.

'Business,' replied Alix.

'Alix, that job isn't worth missing dinner with Dad over,' said Wyn. 'People will understand.'

'Don't be ridiculous,' snapped Alix. 'If I want to see that man I'm sure I'll have plenty of opportunities. I doubt very much that it has to be this Saturday or nothing. But it wouldn't matter what Saturday it was. I'm not going to see him.'

'You're so bloody obstinate!' cried Wyn. 'What harm would it do to meet him?'

'I've made a decision and I'm sticking to it,' said Alix. 'And that's final.'

'Alix, he's our father.' Wyn's tone was persuasive.

'I couldn't care less whose father he is,' said Alix sharply. 'I'm not going, Wyn. And I'm not saying it again.'

She was rinsing her cup when the phone rang again.

'Yes?' she said.

'You're in a bad mood,' said Carrie.

'No I'm not,' said Alix. 'I've had Wyn on the phone trying to persuade me to go to your dinner on Saturday night and I've told her I won't go. She keeps trying to force me.'

'I won't force you,' said Carrie. 'But I'd like you to come.'

'I can't,' said Alix. 'I have a business engagement all day Saturday and we're having dinner afterwards. So it's absolutely impossible.'

'You could skip the business thing,' said Carrie.

'I couldn't,' said Alix.

'Oh, Alix, you can't go around all your life feeling bitter,' Carrie told her. 'Resenting him. Blaming him.'

'Resenting him for what?' asked Alix. 'Blaming him for what? You two have been reading some God-awful self-help books, haven't you? And you're supposed to confront your feelings or something. I don't resent or blame anybody. I just want to get on with my life.'

Carrie was silent for a moment. 'And how is your life?' she asked finally. 'Anyone in it?'

An image of Matt Connery slid into Alix's mind, followed immediately by a picture of Paul.

'Plenty of people,' she told Carrie. 'And it's working out fine.'

'Seven o'clock on Saturday,' said her mother. 'It would be great if you could make it.'

'Have a good time,' Alix said. 'But I won't be there.'

∽

He was chasing her down the street. She ran as fast as she could. She was almost tripping over her own feet she was running so fast. And her arms were pushed out in front of her, waving people out of her way. She fell as she stepped off the pavement. She felt herself falling and she tried to cry out but she couldn't.

She opened her eyes. It was 4 a.m.

Alix pulled the duvet round her and went back to sleep.

Chapter 27

Alix wasn't sure about the clay pigeon shoot. She stood indecisively in the hallway of her apartment and wondered whether or not she should simply stay at home. People sometimes didn't turn up at corporate events. Any number of things could prevent them. She could phone Matt on Monday, apologise to him and say that something had cropped up. He'd understand. She didn't know exactly why she was uncertain about going. Even though she'd only once shot clays before she knew that she would enjoy it. And yet – she sighed. She wished she understood what was going through her own head.

She couldn't not turn up. All very well on a week day to say that business had prevented you from attending, but on a Saturday there was very little excuse. And Matt Connery knew that she liked shooting. That was why he'd invited her.

She picked up her padded jacket and her keys. She'd go. If she felt really uncomfortable she didn't have to stay for the dinner later on. Although she had a bag with a change of clothes just in case.

Because it was a pleasant afternoon, Alix decided to walk to the Point Depot. It took about half an hour from her apartment but it was an enjoyable stroll. The water of the Liffey glittered and sparkled under the sun and even the distinctive river smell wasn't as unpleasant as usual.

There were about ten people already at the Point when she arrived. She spotted Matt Connery among them – his tall, fair-haired figure stood out among the crowd.

'Alix!' He smiled at her. 'I thought you weren't going to make it.'

'I was a little delayed,' she lied. 'But I wouldn't miss it.'

'Paddy is just about to take the first batch down now.' Matt nodded over to a bearded man with a clipboard in his hand. 'You'll have to wait for the second run.'

'That's OK,' she said.

'I'll be on the second run too,' said Matt. 'Want to make sure that nobody is left behind.'

'Fine,' said Alix.

She stood on the edge of the group while Matt and Paddy exchanged a few words and then led half of them towards the silver and blue helicopter which was waiting for them.

'Nice, isn't it?' one of the remainder of the group said to her.

'Yes,' she said. 'I'm looking forward to the flight.'

'You ever been on one before?' asked the man.

'On a trip,' said Alix. 'Over some Caribbean islands.' With Paul. The thought stabbed at her. The first year they'd been together when she'd received a huge bonus and blown as much of it as she could on a dream holiday with him. They'd cruised around the Bahamas and then taken a helicopter trip to see it all from the air. It had been wonderful.

'I haven't,' said the man. 'I'm not even a good air passenger. I don't like flying.'

'It's different to a plane,' said Alix. 'You'll probably enjoy it.'

'I doubt it,' he said gloomily. 'But it seemed like such a good idea at the time.'

Alix smiled sympathetically.

'My name is Dermot Donoghue,' he said. 'In case you need to identify me.'

'If we go down, we go down together, Dermot,' she said solemnly. 'We'll be on the same flight.'

'That's some comfort,' he said. 'What's your name?'

'Alix Callaghan. I'm a dealer. My bank looks after Anatronics' foreign exchange business.'

'Really?' Dermot looked at her with interest. 'And have you ever gone shooting before.'

'I do some,' she said cautiously. 'But not usually clays.'

'I went on an outing a couple of weeks ago,' he told her. 'Great fun. I only hit about two but I sure as hell terrified the instructor. Mind you, my shoulder was so bruised afterwards I could hardly move my arm.'

'That's why I have the jacket.' Alix nodded at her bag with the padded jacket neatly folded on top. 'There's a lot more kick from those guns than you expect.'

They both looked upwards as the helicopter lifted gracefully into the sky and clattered overhead.

'You'll be fine,' said Alix.

Matt Connery strolled over to them. 'All prepared?' he asked.

'Absolutely.' Dermot beamed at him. 'I can't wait.'

～

Alix had forgotten how noisy it was inside a helicopter. Although people could talk to each other through small mikes and hear the conversation through their earphones it was almost impossible to make out what anyone was saying.

Beside her, Dermot Donoghue was clutching at his seat and staring straight ahead. She thought she'd heard him praying earlier but she wasn't certain. She leaned her head against the window and gazed down. She loved the sensation of flying in the helicopter. So much more real than being in a plane at thirty thousand feet.

It didn't take long for them to arrive at the Glen of the Downs. Dermot Donoghue bent almost double as he left the helicopter. 'In case it chops my head off,' he told Alix. 'Now that we're here safely, I don't want to be injured by the bloody thing while I'm on the ground.'

She smiled at him. She couldn't help liking him.

'Right, everyone!' called Matt. 'Can you follow me, please?'

He strode through the long grass towards a wooded area. Alix slapped at some midges that instantly surrounded them.

The rest of the group was already in the clearing waiting for them and drinking cans of Coke.

'We wanted beer,' said one of them. 'But Richard here wouldn't let us.' Richard was the instructor, a thick-set man with blue eyes and a weather-beaten face.

'Safety is paramount,' said Richard. 'And alcohol and guns don't mix.'

He began to lecture them about the guns and safety and explain what they'd be doing that afternoon. Alix half listened to him as she looked around at the rest of the group. They were all men. She didn't feel uncomfortable in a group of men, she was used to it, but she couldn't help feeling that a solitary woman among them would cramp their style. Alix was very pragmatic about men and women. In single-sex groups both behaved very differently to mixed groups. Without her presence, she was sure that the clay pigeon shoot would be a much bawdier affair.

'OK, who's first?' asked Richard.

'Me,' said a short, red-haired guy with glasses whom Alix remembered having seen at the film presentation. 'I'll have a go.'

'Fair play to you, Andy!' called one of the others. 'Give 'em hell!'

Alix watched as Andy stepped up and took the gun gingerly. Richard helped him to get comfortable and pulled the clays. Alix stuffed her earplugs into her ears.

The bright orange clays fell back to earth unscathed as Andy fired and missed. Everyone roared with laughter and Andy's face coloured to match his hair.

'It isn't as easy as it looks,' said Richard. 'Wait until the rest of you have a go.'

Andy clipped one of the next targets to much applause but he failed to hit any more.

'You'll do better than that.' Matt stood beside Alix.

She took one of the earplugs out of her ears. 'Pardon?'

'You'll do better than that,' repeated Matt.

'I wouldn't bet on it,' said Alix. 'Stationary targets are fine. But I'm not sure about this.'

'You'll be great,' said Matt confidently.

Alix wished she could be so certain. She was definitely regretting her decision to come now. She felt as though the weight of women everywhere was on her shoulders. She wanted to do well so that the blokes knew that whether you were male or female, you could still do just as good a job. She didn't want them to look on her as a token, included out of a sense of duty. Shooting in the club was different. They were her friends. These people were other business people. And in front of them she desperately wanted to do well.

Three of the others had shot with varying degrees of success before Alix was bundled forward.

'Have you ever shot before, young lady?' asked Richard kindly.

'Yes,' she said firmly. 'But not clays.'

'What do you shoot?' he asked.

'Targets. And silhouettes.'

'OK,' he said. 'Of course this is different. What rifle do you use?'

'An Anschutz .22.'

'Nice gun,' he said. 'You'll be using a Beretta today. It's a double-barrel and we'll be using twelve-gauge cartridges.'

'OK,' said Alix.

'Just take it nice and easy,' said Richard. 'Squeeze the trigger.'

'I know the theory,' said Alix. 'I'm just not sure about the practice!'

She loaded the gun and brought it up to her shoulder. She tried to breathe as evenly as she could.

'Pull!' she called.

She winged the first clay and caught the second cleanly.

'Well done,' said Richard. 'Ready again?'

'Pull!' she called.

She got the next two dead centre.

'Pull!' She called again.

Orange fragments fell into the trees.

'Jesus,' whispered one of the guys in the group. 'You wouldn't want to get on the wrong side of her, would you?'

'Let's make it a little harder,' said Richard.

'Pull!'

Another two targets, another two hits.

'Pull!'

Everyone was quiet as Alix demolished another two clays. And another. And another.

'That was exceptional,' said Richard. 'Well done!'

She broke open the gun and handed it back to him. 'I enjoyed it. Thank you.'

The group applauded her as she turned round. She grinned at them. 'Thanks.'

'When you said you shot I didn't quite realise what you meant,' said Matt as she walked back to her place beneath a tree. 'I thought you might miss something from time to time.'

'I was lucky,' she confided. 'Normally I would miss.'

'You never thought about doing this professionally?' he asked.

'My body wouldn't manage it.' She massaged her shoulder. 'It's hard work.'

'You've put us all to shame,' said Matt. 'You'll have destroyed everyone's confidence.'

She laughed. 'I doubt it.'

But no one else came near Alix's accuracy.

'It's only reasonable that I should have done better than anyone,' she told Matt as he walked back having missed all but three of his targets. 'I do have experience of it, after all.'

'Most of these guys have done clays before,' said Matt. 'That was why I invited them.'

'It's different,' said Alix. 'The occasional event isn't the same as being in a club.'

'Why are you making excuses for us?' he asked. 'You were better.'

She grimaced. 'I was lucky.'

⁓

She sat in the sauna in the leisure centre and allowed herself to relax. She'd enjoyed the afternoon. She enjoyed being the best at something, at having everyone appreciate her skills. She'd stopped saying that she had some experience as a shooter and allowed them to praise her and it had been very, very satisfying.

Sweat trickled from her forehead and down her nose. She ladled more water over the coals and revelled in the sizzle of heat.

Afterwards she stood in the shower and pepped herself up with one of Carrie's aromatherapy gels. And then she thought of Carrie and John and Wyn sitting down to dinner together that evening. She felt suddenly sick.

She turned off the shower and wrapped a white towel round her. Would they expect her to show up? Would Carrie set a place for her even though she had refused to go? She towelled her hair vigorously. How dare he come back. How dare he try to insinuate himself into their lives again, having had his time with Imogen, having been a father to Kate. How could he even bear to face Carrie and Wyn again? Especially as he was asking for a favour. For divorce and forgiveness. Well, he was asking the wrong person if he was asking her. She'd been so secure in her three-year-old world. Everything had been perfect. Her father, her mother, her elder sister. And he'd ruined it all by leaving them. By walking out to have babies with someone else.

She bit her lip until she tasted the salty tang of blood.

She left the sauna, had a quick swim, followed by a shower, and got dressed. She wore her black Jasper Conran dress with a soft grey cashmere cardigan over it. She unplaited her hair and put it up, secured by a silver clip.

'Alix, you look wonderful!' Matt smiled as she entered the bar.

'Thank you.'

'What will you have to drink?'

'Beer would be nice,' she said.

'You look far too lovely to drink beer,' he said. 'I feel as though you should be sipping a cocktail. Although I'm not going to argue with a girl who can stop a clay at five paces.'

She grinned at him. 'I'm thirsty.'

'Have a seat, Alix.' Brian Dolan, one of the other guests, pushed a bar stool over to her.

'Thanks.'

'So, Alix, how often do you shoot?' asked Peter Morgan.

'I used to do it once a week,' she told him. 'But not so much in the last few weeks, unfortunately.'

'And what do you shoot?'

She went through it all for them again. They stood around and listened to her.

'Just as well my wife doesn't have a gun,' said Pat Riley. 'I'd be dead by now.'

The others laughed.

'What about you, Alix?' asked Dermot. 'Is there a Mr Callaghan?'

She shook her head.

'Young, free, single and with a rifle,' said Pat. 'It's a heady combination.'

'But there is someone,' said Matt casually.

She shot him a glance. 'There is – was – is a Mr Hunter,' she told him.

'Is or was?' he asked.

She sipped her beer. 'I'm not exactly sure at the moment.'

'God, hope he didn't do something awful to you,' said Dermot. 'I mean, Alix, let's face it, who'd want to have you hating them? You'd be walking around in terror for the rest of your life!'

'I'm not that bad!' she laughed.

'All the same.' Dermot winked at her. 'Better be on the safe side.'

It was another hour before they went in to dinner. Alix had drunk three bottles of beer and was feeling light-headed. She looked at her watch. It was half eight.

They'd have started dinner in Carrie's house by now. Alix knew what her mother would have cooked. Roast lamb with garlic and rosemary. Rosemary for remembrance, Carrie used to say. Garlic for remembrance, Alix would laugh.

What was John telling them? That he'd never meant to hurt them. That he'd always cared about them. That he'd meant to come back and see them but that things hadn't worked out that way.

'Excuse me, madam.' A waitress put Alix's starter of smoked salmon in front of her.

'Thank you.'

Carrie would have done cheese soufflés for starters. Carrie had found the recipe in a Delia Smith book and had thought that it was the most wonderful starter ever. Simple but effective, she'd told the girls as she produced it three Sundays in a row. And for dessert? Carrie wasn't a dessert person. Neither were her two daughters. She'd probably just have cheese.

'Alix?' Matt Connery, who was sitting on her left, leaned towards her. 'Don't you want your food?'

'What?' She glanced around. Everyone else had started. 'Of course. I was daydreaming.'

'What about?' he asked.

'Nothing in particular.' She picked up her lemon and squeezed it over the slices of salmon.

'You were miles away,' said Matt.

'Not really.'

'Thinking about Mr Hunter?' he asked.

She smiled faintly. 'No.'

'What's the story about Mr Hunter?'

'Why?'

'I just wondered.'

'I've known him for a long time,' said Alix simply. 'Things don't always go smoothly.'

'It really can't have helped when I sent you the flowers.' Matt looked almost contrite.

'It didn't make any difference.'

'So – what do you think will happen?'

'I don't know,' she said.

'Do you love him?'

'Really and truly, Matt, that's a very personal question for an accountant to ask a banker.'

'I was hoping we weren't just accountant and banker,' he said.

'What were you hoping we were?' she asked.

'Friends?'

'Not a good idea, really. I might not give you the rate you want and you'll feel put out by that because we're supposed to be friends. I might give you the best advice I can but you mightn't want to act on it and I'll get pissed at you because we're supposed to be friends. It doesn't work, Matt.'

'I see.'

She applied herself to her food. He watched her as she cut some salmon and popped it into her mouth. A strand of hair fell across her cheek. He had to fight the urge to brush it away. He had never felt like this before. Not with Emma or Grainne or Helen or – not with any of them. He'd never felt both admiration and a desire to protect at the same time. He'd never seen someone who looked so capable and yet so vulnerable. And so incredibly sexy. He'd hardly been able to take his eyes off her earlier when she was sitting on the bar stool, her long legs crossed demurely at the ankles but encased in shimmering black stockings. And he was pretty sure that she was wearing stockings, not tights. He'd seen a glimpse of lace as she'd got down from the stool.

Maybe they were all laughing together, thought Alix. Maybe Carrie and Wyn had forgiven him for leaving. Maybe they were playing happy families. In Carrie's house. She took a sip from her glass of wine.

'What do you think about the new administration in the White House?' asked Matt.

'What?' She looked startled.

'The new administration. Do you think that their economic policies are better than the last lot?'

She smiled at him. 'Economic policy varies so little from administration to administration these days it's hardly a cause

391

for either elation or depression when a different person is in the White House.'

'Is it likely that the dollar will begin to appreciate against the yen?'

'Possibly,' said Alix. 'Although Japanese policy has been more expansionary of late which is why the yen is stronger than it has been.'

'And interest rates?'

'In the States?' She put her knife and fork neatly on her plate. 'Will continue to have an easing bias.'

'Oh, come on, Alix.' He looked at her in exasperation. 'Why don't you tell me to sod off?'

She laughed. 'Because I enjoy talking about politics and economics.'

'What else?' he asked.

'Oh, anything. I talk a lot whenever people let me.'

'How do you get on with the guys in the dealing room?' asked Matt. 'Don't you find that they resent your authority?'

'Why should they?' A mental image of Gavin Donnelly's sullen face flashed before her eyes. 'I'm the boss.'

'But do they—'

'Matt, I'll talk about anything. But not the internal politics of Europa Bank.'

'Fair enough,' he said. 'I guess I wouldn't want to talk about the internal politics of Anatronics Industries.'

'Hey, Alix!' Pat Riley called across to her. 'What kind of gun do you shoot with?'

'Mine is an Anschutz,' Alix told him. 'But there are lots of different types – Brno, Marlin, Lakefield.'

'How much would one cost?' he asked.

'Second-hand you can pick up something for under five

hundred,' said Alix. 'Mine was more expensive. And I have a lovely little scope, a Tasco dot scope, which helps. My rifle is very different to what you were using today, though, because I shoot targets.'

'What made you take up shooting?' asked Dermot, who was sitting on her right-hand side.

She shrugged. 'I don't know. I was always interested.'

'What else do you do in your spare time?'

'What spare time?' She smiled at him. 'I go to the gym.'

'Definitely not worth getting on the wrong side of you,' said Dermot. 'If you couldn't shoot me, you'd probably knock me out.'

∽

They went back to the bar after dinner. The men told ribald jokes and Alix laughed with them. Then she told some ribald jokes of her own. Matt ordered a round of tequila slammers.

'I can do this, but I'm not going to,' said Alix.

'Oh, come on.' Dermot urged her on. 'You've been one of the lads all day. The least you can do is finish a drink with us now.'

She looked at her watch. 'Actually, I have to get home. I was just about to order a taxi.'

'I'll order a taxi for you,' said Matt. He walked off towards reception.

'Come on,' said Peter. 'Down the hatch, Alix.'

She sighed and drank the tequila in one gulp. The men applauded her.

Matt returned to the bar. 'There's a taxi already outside. He'll take us to town.'

'Us?' Alix looked at him. He was coming in and out of focus. Tequila always did that to her.

'I'll see you home,' he said.

'Way to go, Matt!' called Ronan Hogan, another of the Anatronics people.

'It's the least I can do,' said Matt.

'Fine,' said Alix. 'Do you remember where I left my bag?'

'It's here.' Matt picked it up. 'Are you ready?'

'Yes,' she said. She slid off the stool and stood unsteadily beside him. 'See you, guys!'

''Bye, Alix. See you again.'

'Cheers, Alix!'

'Listen, Alix, if you're ever looking for a spot of drinking company . . .' Dermot handed her his business card.

Suddenly lots of business cards were being thrust at her. She shoved them all into her bag. 'Thanks, guys. I've got to go.'

Matt walked beside her. 'Are you OK?'

'It's the tequila,' she told him. 'I can't drink tequila.'

'Why did you?' he asked.

'I couldn't let you all down,' she said. 'You all so desperately wanted me to drink it.' She got into the car and yawned. 'It was a good day, though. Thanks for asking me.'

'I'm glad you enjoyed it,' said Matt. 'I wasn't sure you'd come.'

She glanced at him in the darkness. 'Neither was I.'

The car moved slowly down the road. She closed her eyes and felt herself drift into sleep. She didn't really want to sleep, she was too aware that Matt was in the car with her and he was a business contact and it wasn't a great idea to fall asleep beside him, but she couldn't keep her eyes open.

He wanted her to fall asleep on his shoulder. He thought it

would be a good sign if she fell asleep on his shoulder. But she was leaning in the opposite direction, her head against the car window. As he watched, she heaved a sigh.

What was she really like? he wondered. When she wasn't dealing or working out or shooting? What went on inside her head? And what was the inside track on that boyfriend of hers? Was it worthwhile making a move, or would it be something he'd regret forever?

The taxi pulled up outside Alix's apartment.

'Will I wait?' asked the driver.

'I'll see her home. It's OK,' said Matt.

'Best of luck, mate!' The driver grinned knowingly at him.

Alix prised her eyes open. 'Oh! We're here.'

Matt got out of the taxi and opened the door for her. 'Come on,' he said. 'I'll see you safely in.'

'I'm quite all right,' she told him. 'I've had a sleep.'

'I know,' he said. 'You snored.'

She stared at him. 'I did not!'

'Just little snores,' he told her. 'Nothing too awful, honestly.'

'I don't snore,' she said firmly. 'I know I don't.'

Matt paid the taxi driver who pulled away.

'He's gone!' exclaimed Alix. 'He should have waited for you.'

'It doesn't matter,' said Matt. 'I'll call another one.'

'Do you want to come in for coffee?' Alix looked at him doubtfully.

'Great,' said Matt. 'I'd love to.'

He followed her up the steps to the apartment building. She fumbled with the key but eventually got the door open.

'This way,' she said as she walked along the corridor. She

stopped in front of her door and turned to him. 'Just coffee,' she said firmly.

'Absolutely,' said Matt.

She was glad that she'd tidied the apartment that morning. They stepped inside.

'Wow, Alix, what a wonderful place!' Matt stood in the living room and looked around.

'I like it,' she said.

'It's great.' He took in the wooden floors, the white walls and the lack of clutter. 'Makes my place look a complete mess.'

'It's not always this neat,' she confessed. 'I cleaned up this morning.'

'I love it,' he told her. 'It's almost Nordic in its neatness.'

She grinned at him. 'I'll make coffee.'

He opened the doors to the balcony and stepped outside while Alix spooned coffee into the percolator. She still felt unsteady from the tequila and from the beer and wine she'd drunk before then. She wasn't sure why she'd asked Matt to her apartment. She hoped he was the sort of guy who knew that no meant no.

'I like it here.' He stepped back inside. 'Did you do all the decorating yourself?'

'More or less,' she said. 'I like to keep things simple.'

'So I see.' He sat down in one of the armchairs. She bristled. That was Paul's armchair. It was wrong of Matt to be sitting in it. She felt ill at ease about having someone new, someone different in a place that had been their place. But Matt didn't notice how uncomfortable she felt. He leaned back in the chair.

'Love the music system,' he told her.

'Bang and Olufsen,' she said.

'I know,' said Matt. 'I work in a hi-tech industry, remember?'

She opened the fridge door and looked inside. 'Is black coffee OK?' she asked. 'I forgot to buy milk this morning.'

'Sure,' said Matt. 'I love black coffee.' He picked up one of the magazines on the coffee table in front of him. 'Is this your reading matter of choice?' he asked as he flicked through *The Securities Review*.

'Not choice,' she said. '*The Economist* is my reading matter of choice.'

'Don't you ever leave it behind?' he asked. 'Don't you ever just read something for fun?'

'Like what?'

'I don't know. Women's magazines. Books.'

'I'm reading Margaret Thatcher's autobiography at the moment,' she said.

'You're joking.'

'No.' She handed him a cup of black coffee. 'It's interesting.'

She watched him as he settled into Paul's chair again. 'What do you read? *Accountant Monthly*?'

He laughed. 'No. Thrillers mainly. Michael Crichton, John le Carré, that sort of thing. You probably think that's hopelessly illiterate of me.'

'No,' she said. 'I like thrillers myself. Although I'm more of a P.D. James than a Michael Crichton.'

'What movies do you like?' he asked.

She shrugged. 'Depends on my mood. I'm not really into arty movies. Or ones with nothing but special effects. I like plot-driven stuff. If Hugh Grant isn't in it, I'm prepared to give it the benefit of the doubt.'

'Where's your boyfriend tonight?'

The change of subject startled Alix. 'What?'

'Your boyfriend,' repeated Matt. 'The on-again, off-again boyfriend.'

'Not here,' said Alix.

'Where?'

'Mind your own business,' she said sharply.

'I'm sorry.' Matt put the cup on the table. 'You're right. It *is* none of my business.'

'That's OK.' Alix looked at him warily.

'I should get home.' He stood up and so did she.

'Thanks for a great day,' she said.

'I'm glad you enjoyed it. We do our best at Anatronics.'

'We do our best at Europa Bank too. Will I phone for a taxi?' she asked.

'I will,' he said. 'I have the number coded.' He took his mobile phone out of his jacket pocket. 'Ten minutes,' he told her. 'But I'll wait outside. No point in both of us sitting around.'

'If you're sure?'

'Absolutely,' he said.

'OK.'

She walked with him to the apartment door. 'Thanks again.'

'You're welcome.'

They looked at each other hesitantly. Then Alix opened the door and Matt walked away.

Chapter 28

Alix woke up on Sunday morning to the sound of rain beating against the window. She pulled on her dressing gown and padded into the kitchen. The cups with the dregs of last night's coffee were still in the sink. She'd forgotten to wash them.

She turned on the tap and rinsed them under running water. She thought that she might have been rude to Matt but she couldn't remember. The time after she'd drunk the tequila slammer was a hazy blur. She remembered him coming to the apartment and sitting in Paul's chair. She remembered making him coffee and feeling uncomfortable. But she couldn't remember what they'd talked about.

Anyway, coffee was what she needed again now. She spooned roasted Java into the percolator. Bugger, she thought. No milk. She wished she could get her head around remembering the milk. Matt Connery certainly wouldn't have been impressed by her catering arrangements.

The buzzer to the apartment went. Alix walked over to the monitor to see who was there. In a corner of her mind she wondered whether or not Matt was sending her flowers again. But it was Wyn who was standing outside waving at her.

Alix pressed the entry button to let her in.

'You're out and about very early,' said Alix as she opened the apartment door. 'Is anything the matter?'

'No.' Wyn slid out of her wet coat. 'Of course not. I just thought you'd want to know how things went last night.'

'Last night?' Alix was still thinking of Matt Connery and how she'd misjudged his interest in her. As far as she could recall from her jumbled memories, he'd been quite happy to get away from her. She wasn't sure exactly how things had gone.

'With Dad. Alix! Surely you haven't forgotten about dinner last night?'

'No, of course not.' She yawned. 'I was out late myself. I've only just woken up. I'm sorry, Wyn, I'm not with it.'

'I don't know how you can be so blasé about it,' said Wyn.

'I'm not blasé,' said Alix. 'Just sleepy.'

'I thought you were at a work thing,' said Wyn suspiciously.

'I was,' Alix told her. 'But it was late when I got home.'

'Oh. OK.' Wyn sat down on the sofa. 'That coffee smells good. Do you have any more?'

Alix winced. 'Yes. But no milk.'

'For goodness' sake, Alix!' Wyn shot her an exasperated glance. 'Don't you do any shopping any more?'

'Do you want it or not?' Alix ignored Wyn's question.

'Fine,' said Wyn.

Alix brought over two cups of coffee and sat down beside her sister.

'He was there when I arrived,' said Wyn. 'Terry dropped me off. He told me to ring any time I wanted to leave.'

Alix studied the design on her cup.

'He – I kind of remembered him, Alix. I know that sounds crazy but I had a picture of him in my head and he wasn't all that different to it.'

'Older,' suggested Alix.

'Yes,' said Wyn. 'And his hair is grey. And he was wearing glasses. But I could still see him as the father I remembered.'

'How nice,' murmured Alix.

'It was nice,' said Wyn defensively. 'It put me in touch with stuff.'

'So did he fall on you and say "I'm back and I've always wanted to see you"?'

'Don't be ridiculous,' said Wyn. 'It was civilised. We said hello and Carrie gave us some drinks and then he told me that he was sorry about everything but that he'd tried to keep in touch with our lives. Of course, he was out of touch for ages because Carrie wouldn't really speak to him. He understood why and he accepted that.'

Alix yawned again. Wyn didn't notice.

'So he said that he knew it would be difficult for us to understand and that it was a pretty shitty thing that he did and that he never meant to hurt us.'

'People never mean to hurt other people,' Alix interrupted, 'but they usually do a pretty good job of it all the same.'

'He said that every year on our birthdays he used to buy cards and sign them but he never sent them. Carrie had told him not to. So he brought them with him. He gave me mine. He has yours for you.'

'Oh, please.' Alix made a face. 'That's so corny I don't know how you fell for it, Wyn.'

'I didn't fall for anything! I have the cards at home.'

'He could have bought them all just before he came over!'

'No,' said Wyn. 'They were old.'

'OK.' Alix began to plait the ends of her hair. 'So what then?'

'He told us about his life in the States. He's done awfully well, Alix. He's the president of a computer company there.'

'Everyone who's anyone is called president in the States,' said Alix dismissively. 'You know the Yanks, they love titles.'

'He has a home in Connecticut and another on the West Coast,' said Wyn.

'Good for him.'

'He showed me pictures of Imogen. And of Kate. I have them with me.'

Alix got up and took the cups into the kitchen.

'Would you like to see them?' asked Wyn when she returned.

'Not especially.'

'Kate is very like you,' said Wyn. She reached into her handbag and took out an envelope. 'Here. Have a look.'

Alix took the envelope and turned it over in her hand. He had touched this. He had put the photographs inside and closed it. She swallowed.

'Have a look,' said Wyn again. 'You're hardly compromising your principles by having a look, are you?'

'It's not a question of principles,' said Alix. 'I just don't see why I'm supposed to be thrilled that this bastard has come back and wants to be a father to us. What a load of crap! He thinks he's in some American afternoon soap.'

'He's not like that,' said Wyn. 'Really he isn't.'

Alix turned the envelope over again. 'So why did he have an affair with Imogen in the first place? Why did he get her pregnant? Why did he piss off to the States at the first available opportunity?'

Wyn sighed. 'He wasn't making excuses,' she said. 'He knew it was wrong. He feels very guilty about it. He says that sometimes he doesn't know if it was the right thing to do. But Imogen was very different to Carrie. Imogen couldn't have coped on her own.'

'Of course she could,' said Alix dismissively. 'All that fragile maiden stuff is just an act. Carrie had to cope. She wasn't given the choice, was she?'

'But she coped well,' said Wyn.

'I can't believe you're so prepared to forgive and forget,' said Alix. 'And what about Carrie? How does she feel?'

'She talked about it,' said Wyn. 'She said that she used to be very angry but there's no point in being angry all your life. So she's forgiven him.'

'She thinks she's in a fucking soap opera too! What was last night? An orgy of forgiveness?'

'No,' said Wyn. 'You weren't there, were you?'

'Too right I wasn't.' Alix handed the unopened envelope back to her sister. 'And I won't be part of some kind of love fest between you all.'

'Alix, why be bitter about it? You can't even remember him!'

'No,' said Alix. 'I can't. My own father. And I can't even remember him.' But she did. The flashbacks were coming more often lately. Of them sitting at the table together. Of him buttoning her coat. Of him waving to her as he went to work.

'It was good to see him,' said Wyn. 'It helped, Alix. Truly it did.'

'I don't need any help,' said Alix. 'And I don't need to see him.'

'What about pictures of the house?' asked Wyn. 'There are pictures of his house in this lot.'

'Wyn, can't you get it through your head that I'm just not interested,' said Alix sharply. 'I know you've always felt that you wanted to see him and get some kind of explanation from him. I haven't. So I don't need all this crap.'

Wyn sighed. 'How do you know you don't?'

'I just know.' Alix began to plait her hair again. Why did they all want to fall over John? What was so wonderful about him coming back? What did they expect to gain out of it all? A mention in the will? She laughed to herself. Maybe he was stinking rich and maybe he'd leave them all a fortune. But they'd be waiting a long time. He'd only be in his sixties now. Hardly ready to pop off. Unless he was, like so many captains of industry, overweight and underexercised. She didn't care anyway. They could say all they liked. She wasn't going to be taken in by him.

'Where were you last night?' asked Wyn.

'Out.'

'Out where?'

'One of our clients had organised a clay shoot for the afternoon and a dinner afterwards. It was fun.'

'I don't know how you can do that,' said Wyn distastefully.

'You've never even held a rifle and aimed at a paper target,' said Alix. 'But you've probably played one of Aoife's video games where you laser a whole bunch of people to death!'

Wyn looked shamefaced. 'I like video games,' she said.

'Clays are fun,' Alix told her. 'Although I prefer targets really. But it's nice being out in the open on a bright sunny day.'

'How many people were at the shoot?'

'About twenty,' Alix said. 'We got a helicopter down to the event.'

'You're joking!'

'No, seriously.'

'Do you like your life?' asked Wyn.

'Pardon?'

'Do you like it? Whizzing around in helicopters. Jetting to London and Paris. Shouting at blokes down the phone? Pumping iron at the gym and pumping bullets into a target?'

'You've got a completely distorted idea of how I live,' Alix said. 'I've only been in a bloody helicopter twice – the first time was with Paul. I'd hardly describe the free-for-all to London as "jetting" and Paris isn't a lot better. I don't shout at anyone down the phone. And I don't pump iron. Nor do I pump bullets. My gun isn't pump-action.'

'But what about other things? What about a boyfriend?'

'For heaven's sake!' Alix looked at Wyn in exasperation. 'I've only just split with Paul. Why on earth would you want me to jump into a relationship with someone else?'

'So it's definite with Paul, is it?'

'I don't know,' said Alix. 'I'm not certain.'

'Because I heard that he was living with the French girl. Sabine.'

Alix stared at her. 'Who told you that?'

Wyn shrugged. 'Just heard, that's all.'

'He might be,' said Alix.

'You're not seriously thinking that he'll come back to you after a few weeks with the blonde bombshell, are you?'

'She's not a bombshell,' said Alix. 'She's more modern-looking than that.'

'Seriously, though. He's not going to come back to you, is he? And even if he did, you'd hardly have him back.'

Alix sighed. 'I know.'

'It would be embarrassing to take him back.'

'I know,' said Alix. 'It's just that – well, it's an easier option.'

'Easier than what?'

'Starting all over again with someone else,' said Alix.

Wyn looked at her sympathetically. 'I know,' she said. 'I understand, Alix. Honestly I do.'

'And someone else would probably want exactly the same as Paul,' continued Alix. 'A wife and a family and someone to love him.'

'Maybe if you met the right someone?'

Alix sighed. 'Maybe the right someone for me just doesn't exist.'

&

Alix was glad when Wyn left. She hated it when her sister tried to manipulate her into feeling how she felt. That had always been Wyn's way. She tried to twist you emotionally to make you do the things she wanted. But Alix had wised up to her a long time ago. Nobody could make her do anything she didn't want to any more.

She went to the gym and worked out for an hour. She always felt invigorated afterwards. Then she went shopping. She drove to the Merrion Centre and loaded up her supermarket trolley with kilos of fresh fruit and vegetables, cartons of juice, milk and fresh soup, meat that she would freeze, bread, biscuits, yoghurts and an array of cleaning stuff. She was going to advertise for someone to do the cleaning. She hated it.

'Have you a club card?' asked the cashier.

Alix sighed. Her shopping bill was astronomical. She should have taken the card from Paul.

When she got home the message light was blinking on the machine. She hit play.

'Alix, is there ever a time when you are available to take a call? This is Carrie. Phone me when you get in.'

She groaned. She didn't want to call her mother. She didn't want Carrie's requests for them all to be a family again to be added to Wyn's desire to forgive and forget.

She spent ages unpacking her shopping. She looked at the pineapple and wondered when on earth she'd get around to eating it.

She didn't phone Carrie for another hour. She had to steel herself to pick up the receiver and dial the number.

'Hello.'

'Hi, Carrie.'

'Well, about time,' said Carrie. 'Where have you been?'

'Out,' said Alix. 'Shopping.'

'Anything nice?'

Alix laughed. 'Grocery shopping. Nothing more exciting than chicken fillets and Domestos. Wyn was around earlier and she was moaning at me because I didn't have any milk in the house.'

'No milk!' Carrie sounded shocked.

'Oh, don't you start. It's not exactly vital for day-to-day living, you know.'

'For tea it is,' said Carrie.

'You should be drinking herbal tea,' Alix chided her.

'Actually I hate it,' said Carrie, 'Filthy stuff. I like my tea with—'

'Two sugars and plenty of milk,' Alix interrupted her.

'Yes,' said Carrie. 'You remembered.'

'Of course I do,' said Alix. 'I've made it for you often enough.'

'I suppose so.'

'What did you want?' Alix kept her voice light and cheerful. 'Anything in particular?'

'I thought I'd tell you about last night's dinner,' said Carrie.

'Wyn has already given me the gory details,' said Alix. 'You don't have to.'

'I was disappointed you didn't come.'

'I told you I wasn't coming. I was busy yesterday.'

'Too busy to see your own father?' asked Carrie.

'He's been too busy to see me for the last thirty-odd years,' Alix retorted.

'Look, he was my husband. I had a right to be mad at him. But I've managed to live and let live,' said Carrie. 'There's no reason why we can't be adult about it.'

'I know,' said Alix. 'All the best advice pages would tell us that we can get on with each other and put the past behind us. Not to let bitterness take over. Well, I haven't let bitterness take over. I haven't thought of the man for years. Now, just because he feels it's time to come home, I'm supposed to start remembering. I don't want to, thanks all the same.'

'He never stopped loving you.'

'Carrie! We've been through this a hundred times already. I don't give a shit whether he did or not. I don't want to see him and that's that.'

'You're very like him,' said Carrie.

Alix was silent for a moment. 'That's a horrible thing to say,' she muttered eventually. 'I'm very like me. That's it.'

'OK,' said Carrie. 'Have it your way. He's staying for another couple of weeks. Imogen is with him.'

'Imogen!' Alix almost choked. 'Don't tell me you've met Imogen!'

'No,' said Carrie. 'Although it wouldn't bother me if I did.'

'So what about the pregnant daughter?' asked Alix.

'Kate? Her baby is due in November,' said Carrie. 'She's at home with friends.'

Alix thought of the pregnant Kate for a moment. She wondered what she looked like – the baby that her father preferred.

'Alix? Are you still there?'

'Of course,' said Alix.

'If you change your mind about meeting him, tell me,' said Carrie. 'He'd really love to see you, Alix.'

'I'll tell you,' said Alix. 'But don't hold your breath.'

She curled up on the sofa, a glass of wine in her hand. She opened the book she'd bought on her shopping expedition. It was about a thirtysomething who was too fat, hated her job and kept losing her boyfriends.

Why is it that losers are so much more sympathetic? thought Alix. Why can't someone be a successful, happy, single person who doesn't have a weight problem and doesn't mind sleeping on her own?

Probably because such a person doesn't actually exist, she thought later that night as she pulled the duvet round her shoulders and rolled into the space that used to be Paul's. Just like the person for me doesn't exist either.

Chapter 29

Matt Connery didn't ring the dealing room the following week. Alix hadn't really expected him to, yet she couldn't help feeling a frisson of disappointment that he hadn't called. She told herself that she was being particularly silly in wanting a man in whom she had no real interest to phone, simply because she wanted to know that he'd bothered.

On Friday afternoon she went into her office and printed out a list of all the Anatronics deals they'd done. The account was a mid-range account, she decided, as she analysed the profits. But of course the big trade had yet to come. They always wanted the big deal to come from all of their clients.

'Gavin.' She buzzed his desk.

'Yes?'

'Can you come in for a moment?'

'OK.'

He walked into the office and leaned against the glass door.

'I was at a lot of meetings this week,' she said. 'You were busy in my absence.'

He sighed heavily. 'And? Is that a problem?'

'Not at all.' She leaned back in her chair. 'You seem to think I have some agenda as far as you're concerned, Gavin. And, I guess, not a particularly pleasant agenda.'

'You don't encourage me,' he said darkly.

'I try,' said Alix. 'But I also have to keep your trades within our risk limits. I know you haven't been in the market all that long, Gavin. I know that it can be irksome to have somebody tell you that you can't do something when you clearly feel that you can, and that you can make money out of it.'

'That's just the point,' he exploded. 'You spend more time telling me no than yes. Everything I want to do you want to think about first. It's safe, Alix, but is it good dealing?'

'I think so,' she said calmly. 'In all the years I've been doing this I've never presided over some dramatic loss. I've had losses, like everyone, but I've always had limits on them. That's all I'm trying to instil into you. Stick to the limits. Know when to cut your losses. Run with your profits.'

'I do OK,' said Gavin.

'Of course you do,' she said. She sat up straight. 'Anyway, the reason I asked you to drop in was to tell you that I've allocated three new accounts to you. Harris-Gilpin, Constant Images and Anatronics.'

'Oh.'

'I hope you're happy with that,' she said.

'Sure,' he said. 'I get on well with all those people anyway. Jack Harris likes me. So does that dizzy blonde from Images, and Matt Connery had a great time on the golf outing.'

'So he said.' Alix nodded.

'I deserve these accounts,' said Gavin.

'I know you do.'

'Right. Well, I'd better go ring them,' said Gavin. 'Let them know that it's me they should be talking to in future.'

'Sure.'

He shrugged his shoulders. 'Thanks.'

'You're welcome,' said Alix but he'd already left the room.

She was reading the *Financial Times* when Jenny knocked at the door.

'Come in.' Alix folded the pink newspaper and put it to one side.

'I want to talk,' said Jenny abruptly. She sat down in the chair opposite Alix and frowned.

'Something bothering you?' asked Alix.

'Of course there is,' she replied. 'You've given that bastard Donnelly three new accounts.'

'I thought you told me that he was entitled to the Anatronics account,' Alix reminded her.

'That was ages ago,' said Jenny dismissively. 'And whether he's entitled to it or not makes no difference. You gave him Harris and Images as well.'

'He's done a lot of research for both of them,' said Alix. 'I thought it would be a good idea for him to talk to them.'

'I get on with Susan Darcy,' said Jenny. 'I should have got Constant Images.'

'I know you do,' Alix told her. 'But so does Gavin. And he has talked to them more than you.'

'It's not fair,' said Jenny mutinously. 'I work bloody hard here, Alix. But I get passed over for some little shithead with his brains in his arse!'

Alix stifled a grin. 'It's not like that, Jen.'

'Oh, but it bloody is,' retorted Jenny. 'He goes around making so much noise – "I'm Gavin Donnelly, shit-hot trader!" – and everyone thinks he must be great. He pisses off playing golf when there's stuff he could do in the office. But it's put down to entertaining clients. Meanwhile, what do

I do? Plod along talking to accounts, getting trades and not getting rewarded for it.'

'You got a good bonus last year,' said Alix.

'But I don't get any respect!' Jenny thumped her hand down on the desk.

'I respect you,' said Alix. 'I always have.'

'But you don't think I'm as good as them, do you? You don't think I'm as committed because I don't spend my whole life talking about dollar/yen or the operations of the Fed or whatever! Just because I have another life you think that I don't care!'

'That's not true,' said Alix sharply.

'It is,' Jenny insisted. 'They only ever talk about work in the office. Work and the number of women they shagged at the weekend. I talk about other things, like movies I've seen or books I've read. But it isn't enough. You don't think that I have enough drive to get to the top, do you?'

Alix sighed. 'I probably don't feel as though you want to put as much into it as they do.'

'But you'd be wrong,' said Jenny. 'I want to do well, Alix. I try my best. I know I sometimes miss trades because I advise customers against doing something. But I'm usually giving them good advice. I don't want them to lose money – it's not good for us in the long run. Gavin Donnelly doesn't give a shit once he gets the trade. He'll sympathise with them afterwards, but that doesn't help their profit and loss.'

'Helps ours, though,' said Alix.

'And that's what it's all about?' Jenny looked at her defiantly. 'You don't care if a customer loses money as long as we make it?'

'That's not true.' Alix shook her head. 'I do care. But I can see Gavin's point of view too.' She got up and walked to the window. 'When I was in London I used to be really helpful to all our clients. I gave them the best advice I could and I know I saved some of them from making complete fools of themselves. And I thought it was better for us in the long run too. In a lot of ways, I still do. But there was one account, Jeffrie Wallace, and the guy there used to trade almost every day. One day he wanted to buy dollars and I told him not to because I thought that the Fed would move on rates and the dollar would go down. From the bank's point of view, if he'd done the trade and I was right, we could have made a lot. But he said, OK, he'd leave it, and sure enough the Fed made the move. The dollar plunged afterwards. So I rang him up and said that he'd been right not to deal with me. And then he told me, very sheepishly, that he'd called one of my rivals and that they'd done the deal for him. He had to do it, you see, and he felt embarrassed dealing with me after I'd told him it would be crazy. So I lost the deal and the bank lost the money and I never really got back on track with that bloke again.'

'So what are you saying?' asked Jenny. 'That we shouldn't give them good advice?'

'No,' Alix sighed. 'Just that sometimes we're looking at things from a different perspective. And that they always have another bank they can deal with.'

'That's not a lot of help to me,' said Jenny flatly.

Alix sat down at her desk again. 'So what do you want?' she asked.

'I want to be treated like Dave and like Gavin,' said Jenny. 'I don't want you to think of me as someone who's just putting in time.'

'I don't think like that,' said Alix.

'I'd like to believe you,' said Jenny. 'But I think that in some ways you're harder on me because I'm a woman.'

'What!' Alix looked at her in amazement.

'I think that because you're a successful woman you don't want me to be successful too. Because that would diminish your achievements. The only woman head of treasury. But if you have another woman snapping at your heels, it puts more pressure on you.'

Alix gazed at Jenny. 'That's not true, Jenny.'

'But you haven't helped me,' Jenny insisted. 'You haven't made it any easier for me even though it's hard doing this job. You're so concerned that I shouldn't get preferential treatment that you sometimes discriminate against me. Because I don't kick up a fuss like the other two, you don't give me new accounts. I'm sure I don't earn as much as Dave did when he was doing my job.'

'You do,' said Alix.

'But you believe in them more,' said Jenny. 'And I don't feel that I can depend on you to look after my interests.'

Alix was silent. 'I'm sorry you think that,' she said eventually. 'I really don't think it's true, Jenny, but maybe you've got a point. I need to think about it a little more.'

Jenny rubbed the bridge of her nose. 'I'm sorry,' she said. 'I didn't mean to lose my temper. I just felt—'

'Don't apologise,' interrupted Alix. 'Do you think either Dave or Gavin has ever apologised for losing their temper with me?'

Jenny bit the corner of her lip. 'I guess not.'

'I have more rows with Gavin Donnelly than with anyone else in the world,' stated Alix. 'And he's never once apologised for losing his temper.' She smiled slightly. 'Besides, you didn't lose it. You just said a few things.'

'Maybe I should have lost it,' said Jenny.

'I'm glad you didn't.'

'But would it have been better if I had?' asked Jenny. 'You see, I hate having rows. Gavin thrives on them. I hate asking for things. Dave demands them.'

'I hate to admit that you might be right,' said Alix dryly.

'I'm as entitled as either of them to do well,' said Jenny. 'Just because I take a slightly different approach doesn't mean that it's wrong.'

'I know,' said Alix.

Jenny stood up. 'That's all I wanted to say.'

'OK,' said Alix. 'I'll keep it all in mind, Jenny. I understand how you feel.'

'I hope you do,' said Jenny.

'I do. Honestly.' Alix smiled at her. 'Any plans for the weekend?'

Jenny blushed. 'I'm going to Galway with Mike.'

'The new boyfriend?'

Jenny nodded.

'Well, well.' Alix grinned. 'And how serious is this relationship?'

'I don't know,' said Jenny. 'I like him a lot, Alix. He's fun to be with and he's really good to me. At the moment,' she added darkly.

'Maybe he'll always be good to you,' said Alix.

'I'm not holding my breath. But right now, we're having a good time together. And I'm glad I met him.'

'I'm glad for you,' said Alix.

'But just because I've met a bloke it doesn't make any

difference to our discussion,' said Jenny. 'I'm not likely to run off with him and settle into a life of domestic bliss or anything like that.'

'I didn't for one moment imagine you were,' said Alix.

'I just want my cards on the table,' Jenny said.

'Jenny, you've made your position perfectly clear,' Alix told her. 'Don't worry.'

'But I do worry,' said Jenny. 'I worry all the time.'

When she'd gone, Alix sat back in her chair and thought about what Jenny had said. Was it true? she wondered. Did she discriminate against Jenny because she was female? She didn't think so but maybe she was lying to herself. Maybe deep down she saw Jenny as a more potent threat than Gavin. She sighed. She really didn't seem to know her own mind any more. And it bothered her.

∽

It was seven o'clock before Alix left the office. After talking to Jenny she'd had a brief meeting with John Collins, in credit, and bumped into Des Coyle again. The managing director had asked her about the week's trading but hadn't mentioned anything about Europa Bank Paris and Alix hadn't said anything either.

'What are you doing for the weekend?' he asked when she told him that she had to get home soon.

'I'm going to a wedding in London,' she told him. 'My friend, Sophia, is getting married tomorrow afternoon.'

'That's the girl who works in Russell Cobham, isn't it?' said Des. 'I met her when she was over last year.'

Alix nodded.

'Cracking-looking girl,' said Des. 'Wasted in financial services.'

'What do you mean?' asked Alix.

'Body like that!' Des looked pityingly at Alix. 'She'd have made a fortune doing modelling.'

'Do you think so?'

'Absolutely,' said Des.

'I'll tell her,' said Alix and went home to pack.

Alix owned one hat. It was a cream-coloured Philip Treacy that she'd bought when she worked in London and it had cost her over £500. The reason she'd bought it was that she'd been invited to the wedding of one of her best clients at the time, a guy named Ossie Livsey, who worked on Wall Street. She hadn't wanted to appear as though she couldn't afford to get dressed up for Ossie's wedding, but it broke her heart to spend so much money on a hat. Particularly as she hated wearing them.

But, even though she hadn't been very keen on wearing it, everyone had told her – in the warm way that Americans have – that her hat was 'truly fabulous'. She half believed them which was why, any time she went to a wedding, she hauled the hat out of its striped box and bought something new to go with it.

For Sophia's wedding, she'd bought a navy and cream Nicole Fahri suit. She also bought new navy shoes and a navy bag. It could have looked like office wear, but the suit was loose and unstructured and was chic without being too formal.

Richard kissed Sophia and the small crowd of people broke into spontaneous applause. Sophia turned and smiled at them.

She looked lovely, thought Alix, in her peach voile dress with flowers in her hair. Lovely and pregnant. The dress did nothing to hide the fact that Sophia's bump had expanded since Alix had last seen her. But Sophia didn't care.

Her mother did. Mrs Redmond had muttered to Alix that she'd never understand why Sophia hadn't waited until after the baby was born. There was no hurry, Mrs Redmond said. It wasn't as though she needed to get married.

Maybe she did. The thought occurred to Alix as they left the registry office and walked the hundred yards to the restaurant where they were having a celebration meal. Maybe she felt that being married was important when she had her baby.

I wish I knew what it was like to want a child, she thought. I wish that feeling would surge through me so that I would look at every man I saw as a potential mate. I wish I knew what all the bloody fuss was about.

There were about thirty people at the meal. Alix liked the low-key approach to the day. She hated big, fussy weddings where the bride wandered around like a meringue and scattered guests every time she passed by.

'You're Sophia's friend, aren't you?' The girl beside her looked at the place name in front of Alix's plate.

'Yes,' she replied. 'Alix Callaghan.'

'I'm Nicola Rowntree. I work with her.'

'Oh, Nicola! She's talked about you a lot.'

Nicola raised an eyebrow. 'Good, I hope.'

'Naturally.'

'She's mad as a hatter, of course.'

'Sorry?'

'Sophia. Mad. I don't know why she wants to marry him at all.'

'Because she's crazy about him?' hazarded Alix.

'Come on, Alix.' Nicola pushed her heavy-rimmed glasses higher on her nose. 'You can't possibly believe that. Nobody gets to our age and is "mad" about someone.'

'Our age?' asked Alix.

'Thirtysomething. You are thirtysomething, aren't you?'

'Afraid so,' admitted Alix.

'And you know quite well that you'll never be "mad" about someone again, don't you? Not like you were when you were a teenager, for example. And not like you were when you were in your mid-twenties and you wanted someone for life.'

'I don't think I ever wanted someone for life in my twenties,' said Alix.

'Didn't you?' Nicola looked surprised. 'I thought everyone went through that phase. But – and I think you have to agree with me here – when you've reached your thirties you know that the whole thing is a con. What do you need a bloke for anyway? Sexual fulfilment can be found without a phallus, you know.'

Alix almost choked into her consommé.

'Why commit?' asked Nicola. 'Why decide that this one man has to be it? There are plenty of them around. You can even hire them if you want.'

'For sex?' asked Alix.

'For anything,' replied Nicola. 'You can pay a bloke to wallpaper your house, tile your kitchen, fix your car, mend your roof – why the hell do you need one living with you as well?'

'Good point.' Alix was enjoying the one-sided conversation.

'I was married once,' said Nicola. 'But the bastard left me.

420

For a fucking teenage nymphet with massive breasts. I realised then that you can never own them. They're like cats. They do their own thing when they feel like it and then come back to you looking for food and attention. Take it from me, Alix, she's out of her tiny little mind.'

~

'You know you're crazy, don't you?' Alix and Sophia stood in the marble and glass ladies' room and reapplied their make-up.

'Crazy?'

'Your friend Nicola thinks so.'

Sophia laughed. 'I didn't think Nicky would come,' she said. 'She has a thing about weddings.'

'She told me that her husband left her and ran off with a big-breasted woman.'

Sophia nodded. 'Nicky was devastated,' she said. 'She used to go on and on about how Dorian loved her for her mind. She said that theirs was a relationship based on intellect.'

'Was it?' asked Alix, 'At first?'

'Who knows?' Sophia blotted her lips with tissue. 'Although Nicky looked a lot better when she was married to him. She wore contacts and her hair was better styled and she took more care about her clothes.'

'And when he left it all went downhill?'

'I think she decided that the looking good thing was all a con. So she went to the other extreme.'

'She is quite attractive even if she doesn't bother with the clothes.' Alix examined a spot on her chin. 'How is it I have a bloody spot, Soph? I'm thirtysomething, as Nicky pointed out. Why haven't my spots disappeared?'

'Mine have,' said Sophia triumphantly. 'Ever since I got pregnant my skin has been flawless.'

'Just as well there are some compensations.' Alix snapped the top back onto her lipstick. 'Ready to face them all again?'

Sophia nodded. 'Come on, let's go.'

∽

'Nice hat.'

Alix turned to look at the speaker. She'd seen him at the registry office earlier, looking bored.

'You were wearing the cream hat earlier,' he said to her. 'I noticed it.'

'I was,' she agreed.

'And I liked it. It wasn't a fussy hat. No feathers or bits of lace or anything. Just plain. And nice.'

'It cost me a fortune,' Alix told him. 'So I'm glad you liked it.'

He was in his thirties, she guessed. Tall, mid-brown hair, grey eyes. He'd been sitting beside Richard's sister during the meal. Tara Comiskey was flame-haired and gorgeous and regularly broke men's hearts. At least, that was what Sophia had said.

'Where's Tara?' asked Alix.

'Tara?'

'Beside you at dinner. Red hair? Tumbling around her face in little curls. Creamy skin?'

'Large chest?'

Alix grinned. 'That's the woman.'

'I think she got tired of me when she realised that I was a lowly teacher and not a hotshot financier.'

'I don't think she's like that,' said Alix.

'Do you know her?'

'Better than I know you.'

'I'm sorry,' he said. 'My name's Marcus Bridgewater.'

'Alix Callaghan.'

'Nice to meet you,' he said.

'What do you teach?' asked Alix.

'Chemistry,' said Marcus. 'At the local grammar. Nice kids.'

'I liked chemistry.' She smiled. 'I enjoyed mixing stuff together and causing explosions.'

'I thought you might,' said Marcus.

They looked at each other for a moment. He was going to ask her if she wanted a drink, thought Alix. And then he'd steer her to a corner of the room. And he'd probably tell her that marriage was overrated. He looked like someone who thought marriage was overrated. And then he might ask her where she was staying. And, after that, who knew—

'There you are!' Tara Comiskey put her arm round Marcus's waist. 'I thought you'd left me.'

'Would I?' He smiled at her.

'You're Sophia's friend, aren't you?' Tara turned to Alix who nodded.

'Glad you could make it,' said Tara. 'Come on, Marcus. I want you to tell me all about being a teacher . . .' She dragged him away from Alix who sat down at the nearest table.

'That girl needs help.' Nicola lit a cigarette and offered one to Alix. 'She'll never keep him if she hangs on to him like that.'

'I thought you disapproved of the whole idea.' Alix took the cigarette and lit it.

'I do,' said Nicola. 'But I hate seeing women make fools of themselves.'

'Maybe she's not making a fool of herself.'

'We all make fools of ourselves over men.' Nicola inhaled deeply then blew out the smoke in a steady stream. 'They're bastards. All of them. I just hope poor old Sophia knows what she's letting herself in for.'

Chapter 30

Monday morning was very busy but Alix was still feeling tired from the weekend. They'd stayed in the restaurant until after nine, then she, Nicola and a couple of others had gone to a nearby pub. Nicola hadn't stayed long and then Alix, who had drunk far too much, ended up making a pass at Marcus Bridgewater.

He'd been surprised but charming about it. He told her that he was with Tara and that though she, Alix, was undoubtedly a lovely girl, he was staying with Tara. Alix remembered the feeling of humiliation as he smiled at her and then made his way to the other side of the pub where Tara was chatting to some friends. He'd spoken to her and then the two of them had picked up their jackets and left.

Alix felt sick as she remembered. No doubt he'd told Tara that she had made a move and that they'd better leave, she thought, I'm such a bloody idiot!

She hadn't even been all that interested in Marcus. It was just that she was feeling left out of the general feeling of love and contentment that Sophia's wedding had generated. And she was feeling sorry for herself.

I am a sad case, she told herself as she scrolled through a

story about the European Central Bank's economic forecasts.
A sad, sad case of a frustrated single woman.

'Alix!'

She turned to Jenny.

'You were miles away. Paul is holding on line three.'

Alix dragged her thoughts back to the present and clicked
in to the line. 'Paul?'

'Hi,' he said. 'How are you?'

'Fine.'

'Any news?' he asked.

'What sort of news?'

'Any sort.'

'Sophia got married at the weekend.'

'Your friend? The girl in New York?'

'She's been in London for ages, Paul. You know that. The
last time she stayed with us she came over from London.'

'I forget,' said Paul simply. 'Who did she marry?'

'Richard Comiskey.'

'Oh, I remember,' said Paul. 'Dark-haired bloke. Played lots
of sports.'

'That's him,' said Alix.

'I hope they'll be very happy,' he said.

'I'm sure they will.' Alix bit her lip.

'Anyway, I called to see if Friday would be good for the
interview.'

'I thought someone else was meant to organise it,' said
Alix.

'I offered,' said Paul. 'Is Friday OK? Or is it one of those
Fridays when there's a slew of figures coming out and you
can't possibly be civilised with anyone?'

'I'm always civilised,' said Alix tartly. 'And Friday is fine.'

'Great,' said Paul. 'There'll be three of them. One of the new reporters is doing the interview – Damien O'Riordan. I'm not sure who else will be there. There'll be a sound guy and a camera guy and probably someone else.'

'Why on earth don't they have a female interviewer?' asked Alix. 'You said the programme is about women achievers. Well, why haven't they got a woman fronting the programme?'

'Maybe if it was all women, people would find it too boring,' said Paul. 'Perhaps they want some balance.'

'You only ever talk about balance if all the participants are women,' snapped Alix. 'Nobody thinks about it if they're all men.'

'Get out of the wrong side of bed again?' asked Paul. 'There's no need to bite my head off, Alix.'

'Isn't there?'

'No,' he said. 'Fortunately we're just in a business relation-ship here. I don't have to think about your feelings.'

'Don't you?' she asked.

He was silent for a moment. 'I'm sorry. Forget I said that.'

'I will,' said Alix.

'Friday is OK, then?'

'Sure,' she said dispiritedly. 'Afternoon rather than morning if you can arrange it.'

'Of course I can,' said Paul. 'I'll give you a call on the day to remind you.'

'I'll remember,' she said. 'I'll write it down.'

'Take care, Alix,' he said.

'Sure.' She clicked out of the line and walked out of the dealing room.

'What's wrong with her?' Dave looked at Jenny inquiringly.

Jenny shrugged.

'She's in rotten form today,' he continued. 'I thought she went to the UK for the weekend. You'd imagine she'd be in better humour after a weekend away.'

'She was at her friend's wedding,' said Jenny. 'I think she's feeling a bit down after it.'

'For God's sake!' Gavin looked disgusted. 'What is that woman's problem?'

'Maybe the fact that her boyfriend dumped her for a younger, leaner model?' suggested Jenny.

'You have to expect that,' Gavin sniggered. 'You girls don't realise what—'

'Gavin!' Jenny's eyes glittered in warning.

'Oh, come on! Alix is getting on a bit. She had to expect that sooner or later she'd get traded in.'

'Thank you for those words of wisdom, Gavin.' Alix's tone was icy. 'I'll certainly keep it in mind for the future.' She walked round to her desk and picked up the phone.

Gavin got up and left the room.

⇝

Because Europa Bank was a wholesale bank and dealt only with corporate clients, not personal ones, none of the staff had accounts there. Alix was happy with that, she didn't like the idea of anyone she was working with knowing the state of her bank balance! Which might be a bit dodgy this month, she thought, as she queued at her own bank's automated teller machine at lunchtime. The month had seen lots of payments, including some big ones like the house insurance and her gym membership. She sighed as she thought of her gym membership. The number of times she'd been lately was abysmal, it was becoming a complete waste of money. And she knew that she wasn't as fit as she had been. The tightening waistband on her skirt was evidence of that. It was just that all the things that she'd once enjoyed doing didn't have any appeal right now.

'Hi, Alix!'

She turned round. Eimear Flaherty, who had left the bank the same time as Paul had left Alix, walked up to her. She was pushing a stroller with a sleeping baby inside.

'Eimear! It's nice to see you.' Alix smiled. 'How's life?'

'Oh, not so bad,' said Eimear.

'Do you miss us?' asked Alix.

Eimear laughed. 'Not a bit! I thought I would, but I haven't had time, to be honest with you. I'm looking after the two of them at home now, so there isn't a minute.'

'Does she always sleep like this?' Alix nodded at Eimear's daughter while she frantically tried to remember her name. Kate, she thought and grimaced. No, that was John Callaghan's daughter – her half-sister! How could she possibly think of that name right now?

'She's a little pet,' Eimear said, 'and she's really good about sleeping, Alix. Funny, she wasn't great all the time I was at work, but since I've given up she seems to have settled a lot more.'

'And what about her brother?' Alix couldn't remember his name either.

'Oh, Tom's always been a good sleeper.' Eimear laughed. 'Like his father!'

'Where is he now?' asked Alix.

'Tom is at his grandmother's,' said Eimear. 'She loves him,

loves looking after him. I had to bring missy here to the doctor – nothing wrong, just a check-up, so that's why she's with me. I was in Europa earlier – had to pick up some documents for the tax man. You know how it is.'

'And you didn't feel the urge to do a few quick settlements?'

'Not on your life!' Eimear shook her head. 'Honestly, Alix, I don't miss it at all. I miss the people, but you'd expect that. But I don't miss rushing around every morning trying to organise a husband and kids and myself and then rushing around every evening as well. Besides, the kids are fun. I know not everyone would think so, but I get a great laugh out of them. Tom still goes to the kindergarten in the mornings, of course, and I miss him while he's there.'

Alix slid her card into the ATM and keyed in her personal number. Despite the house insurance and the gym membership, her account was still in credit.

'And how are you keeping?' asked Eimear as Alix took her cash and replaced her card in her wallet. 'Not tripping up the aisle yourself yet?'

Alix laughed. 'Not me.'

'Don't you and Paul want kids?' she asked curiously. 'At some stage?'

'Even if I did, I wouldn't be having them with Paul,' said Alix lightly. 'We split up.'

'Oh, Alix, I'm sorry! I didn't know.'

'Of course you didn't. It's no problem. To be honest, I was upset at first, but I'm over it now.'

'So you'll have to find someone else to have babies with,' joked Eimear.

'It's not me,' Alix said. 'I don't have your patience, Eimear.'

'Of course you do,' said the other girl. 'It's instinctive.'

'That's a myth,' Alix laughed. 'I panic around kids.'

'Doesn't your sister have a few?'

'Two,' confirmed Alix. 'And I look after them from time to time. But it's a different kettle of fish when you can go home every night.'

'I think you'd be a great mother,' said Eimear. 'You're smart, you're fair, you're—'

'Going to be late if I don't get back!' interrupted Alix. 'It was nice to see you, Eimear. I'm glad it's all working out for you.'

'I'm sorry, I tend to gabble a bit these days,' said Eimear. 'It's probably because I do spend so much time with the kids. I've lost the knack of adult conversation.'

'Not at all,' said Alix. 'I'd love to chat for a little longer. But we've had a tense morning in the dealing room and I don't want to leave the bruised egos alone for too long.'

'That's something I certainly don't miss.' Eimear pulled the blanket more firmly round her baby. 'All that testosterone around the place. People trying to shaft other people! I lead a much more peaceful existence now.'

'Maybe you're right.' Alix smiled at her. 'Maybe one day I *will* settle down.'

'It's wonderful,' said Eimear sincerely. 'I'd heartily recommend it.' She waved at Alix again as she walked away.

Cliona, thought Alix, as she made her way back to the bank. Her daughter's name is Cliona.

⌒

'Europa Bank, dealers.'

'Hello, Alix. *Ça va?*'

'Guy.' She made a face. 'I'm well. And you?'

'I am well also. I am phoning to say that I will be visiting the Dublin branch on Thursday.'

'Great,' said Alix insincerely. 'What time will you get here?'

'I'm coming from London,' said Guy. 'We expect to arrive in Dublin at around ten.'

'Who's coming with you?'

'Jacques Monet,' said Guy.

Jacques Monet! A high-profile meeting, thought Alix. Jacques was the manager for all of the European branches of the bank.

'I look forward to seeing you,' she said.

'And I look forward to seeing you,' said Guy. 'I know that Jacques will be lunching with Des. But perhaps you and I can have something to eat together?'

'Wonderful,' said Alix. 'I'll book a restaurant.'

'Perfect.'

'See you Thursday,' she said.

'*Au revoir*,' said Guy.

She sat back in her chair and scratched the top of her head with her pen.

'Was that Decourcelle?' asked Dave.

She nodded. 'He's coming over on Thursday. With Monet.'

Dave made a face. 'Wonder what's up.'

'I dunno.' She rubbed her nose. 'Something, for sure. They just don't drop in like that.'

'Maybe they're going to close the branch.' Jenny looked worried. 'Perhaps we're not profitable enough.'

'Don't be ridiculous,' said Gavin, although there was an edge in his voice. 'We're very profitable.'

'The treasury department is profitable,' said Alix. 'But the credit department was down last year.'

'That's because of the syndicated loan,' said Dave. 'Nobody thought that would end up being rescheduled.'

'And Paris was involved with that too,' said Alix. She sighed. 'I don't know, Dave. Maybe they're just visiting all the branches. They're coming from London.'

'Not so bad.' Dave nodded. 'Could be a whistle-stop tour.'

'Could be,' said Alix. 'But let's make sure we're on top form on the day.' Her phone line blinked and she picked it up. 'Europa Bank, dealers.'

'Hi, Alix.'

Her grip tightened on the receiver. 'Matt. Nice to hear from you.'

'I need to buy a tiny amount of dollars. Only fifty thousand.'

She glanced at the screen, then paused. 'I'll pass you on to Gavin, if that's all right, Matt. He's looking after your account and he's the one that should quote you.'

'I know. He rang to tell me. Why did you do that?' asked Matt.

'I don't take responsibility for many individual accounts,' she told him. 'I have overall responsibility for the room. So the accounts are usually allocated among the others.'

'Unless it's a huge account?' guessed Matt.

'I look after one or two,' she agreed.

'So when I have a big, big deal to do I might get to talk to you. Is that it?'

'Don't be silly,' she said.

Gavin looked across the desk at her.

'I thought you might ring me,' said Matt.

'Oh?'

'Yes. To tell me why the dollar has cheapened up so much against the yen.'

'Because people think they'll cut rates again,' she said automatically.

'I didn't know that,' said Matt.

'I think you did,' said Alix.

'Did I say or do anything to offend you?' Matt sounded aggrieved.

'When?' asked Alix.

'After the shooting,' said Matt. 'At your apartment. I thought I must have upset you somehow.'

'Of course you didn't.' She was very aware of Gavin following the conversation. The fact that he could only hear her side of it didn't make any difference.

'I thought you might have got a bad impression of me.'

'Matt, I've no idea what you mean.'

'Maybe it was me,' he said. 'Maybe I'm misreading the situation.'

'You're certainly misreading something,' said Alix.

'Well, look, before you pass me over to the young Turk, how about dinner?'

'Pardon?'

'Dinner. You know. You eat it in the evenings.'

'I know what it is,' said Alix.

'I was wondering if you'd like to eat it with me,' said Matt.

'I should ask you,' said Alix. 'You're the client, after all.'

'I was asking you as a friend. We can talk business, of course, but I wanted to be the one to ask,' said Matt.

Alix bit her lip. 'Remember what I said about that before? The next time you ask for a better rate or don't take advice or anything like that, both of us will get pissed at each other because—'

'I remember exactly what you said,' Matt said. 'But if you're handing over the account to Gavin, it doesn't matter, does it? Because I'll be getting all my advice and all my rates from him. So neither of us will get pissed at each other, as you so elegantly put it.'

She couldn't help smiling. 'When did you have in mind?'

'Thursday,' said Matt.

'I'm sorry,' said Alix. 'That's a really bad day. The European manager and the French head of European trading are both coming over. I'm meeting Guy at lunchtime and I'm pretty sure I'll need to be around later too.'

'Is this an excuse?' asked Matt suspiciously.

'Absolutely not,' she said.

'That's a pity,' said Matt. 'Because I'll be away myself the following week.'

'Oh.'

'Never mind,' he said cheerfully. 'Another time, maybe. You'd better put Gavin on the line, Alix. The dollar could have soared in the time we've wasted.'

'It hasn't,' she said.

'Just as well,' said Matt. 'Or I could sue you for keeping me chatting so that you could give me a rotten rate.'

❧

She never minded being alone. When Paul had lived with her she'd enjoyed the evenings he was away, savoured curling up

435

on the sofa with a bottle of beer and a book. Because she spent so much time talking during the day, she loved not having to speak in the evenings.

But tonight was different. Of all the nights she'd spent since he'd left, tonight was the first night that she felt truly lonely. She wished things had been different. That he'd talked to her about babies. She might have taken more heed of him if he'd insisted on talking about it. She looked around at her white apartment and visualised sticky fingerprints on the walls. She sighed. She couldn't bear to think of sticky fingerprints on the walls.

⌒

She wore her purple suit on Thursday and pulled her hair into a neat chignon. She took time over her make-up, ensuring that she looked perfect when she stepped out of the apartment. Her perfume was Chanel. She remembered that Guy Decourcelle liked Chanel.

Guy and Jacques arrived at a quarter past ten. Eileen Walsh phoned the dealing room and told Alix that they were meeting in Des's office. Pat Enright, the chief accountant, would be there too.

'Here goes,' she told the others as she left the room. 'Let's hope it's good news.'

'Ah, Alix! Good to see you.' Guy kissed her on both cheeks.

'And you, Guy.'

'Alix.' Jacques Monet kissed her too. 'You are looking well this morning.'

'Thank you, Jacques. I hope your flight was enjoyable.'

The older man made a face. 'We were late,' he said. 'Airlines do not seem to understand what "on time" actually means.'

Alix smiled at him as they sat down.

Eileen came in, carrying a tray loaded with cups and a large pot of coffee. She poured for all of them and then left.

'OK,' said Des. 'What brings you to Dublin?'

'Europa Bank in Paris will be making an announcement on a euro loss of fifty million due to unauthorised trading,' said Jacques.

Des, Alix and Pat looked at each other.

'Oh, shit,' said Alix.

'We have discovered the trader took positions in derivative products and was valuing them at a price significantly different to the actual market value.' This was always a nightmare scenario for trading houses. Because there were so many different products that a dealer could get involved in, and because so many of the risk managers and accountants found them difficult to value, there was always the possibility that a trader with a loss-making position could hide the potential loss.

'How did that happen?' asked Pat.

'We have an excellent futures trader,' said Guy. 'Unfortunately he managed to get himself into a position that depended entirely on interest rates going up. As you know, they haven't.'

Alix thought back to the Fed rate cut in July. The problems had probably started then.

'We have visited our European branches so that we can keep people informed ourselves,' said Jacques. 'There will, no doubt, be adverse press reaction and ridiculous stories about rogue traders and high-flying dealers and all the usual stuff that comes out around this time. Obviously this will impact on the share price.'

'Obviously,' said Des.

'So we are also thinking of ways to increase our control on trading,' said Guy. 'Our systems let us down in this instance. We thought that they were foolproof but nothing ever is.'

'No,' said Pat. 'If someone has a shit position they'll find a way to hide it.'

'We hope not in the future,' said Jacques.

'So what does that mean for us in Dublin?' asked Des.

'Increased reporting to Paris,' Jacques told him. 'Also, we are thinking very much of bringing more of the trading function under the Paris umbrella.'

'The Paris umbrella wasn't very effective in the instance you're talking about,' said Alix. 'We haven't had that problem here.'

'I appreciate that,' Jacques said. 'But we are having to make radical changes in the way we operate. We haven't yet decided what way things will go but obviously since Dublin is such a tax-efficient operation for us, it might be worthwhile to take less risk here and channel more business through.'

'Which would make us a booking office and not a trading centre,' said Alix.

'It's only a possibility,' Guy reassured her. 'We haven't made any decisions yet. And nothing will happen before next year.'

'Next year will be here soon enough,' Alix said.

'We will be in constant contact with you,' said Jacques. 'But we will be conducting an audit of all the branches who trade. So that we can be sure there is nothing to hide.'

'That's fine by me,' said Alix. 'I know what's going on.'

'I agree with Alix.' Pat nodded. 'Our operation is relatively small and that means we have a good chance of finding anything untoward.'

'The auditors will come here next week,' said Jacques. 'So I hope you are right in what you say. We cannot afford any unpleasant surprises. As it is, the market will jump on this story.'

'It's tough,' said Des.

'You have to expect it from time to time,' Guy sighed. 'But you always hope that it won't happen to you.'

They discussed the situation for another fifteen minutes then Jacques looked at his watch. 'We have a meeting with ABN-Amro in ten minutes,' he told them. 'I think we had better leave. Des, I am meeting you at lunchtime, yes?'

'That's right.' Des nodded.

'And I am meeting you, Alix?' Guy smiled at her.

'Yes,' she said. 'I've booked Wrights for us. I'll meet you there.'

'Excellent.' Both men stood up and shook hands with their Dublin colleagues.

Des accompanied Jacques and Guy to the main door while Alix and Pat remained in his office.

'This is not good,' said Pat gloomily. 'It's been ages since any shock-horror huge trading loss story hit the market. The share price will take a battering.'

'I hope that fifty million is the whole size of it,' said Alix. 'You know these bloody things. They end up finding all sorts of horrible trades under the carpet.'

'Alix, there isn't anything like this in the dealing room here, is there?' Pat looked at her in concern. 'If there's anything I should know about, I'd appreciate finding out now, before the sharks from Paris descend on us.'

'I promise you there's nothing,' said Alix, grateful that because the room was so small she was able to keep abreast of everything that went on.

'We don't know enough,' said Pat, 'us accountants and risk managers. We take so much on faith, particularly on those structured products.'

'That's why I don't deal them,' said Alix kindly. 'Just to keep you happy, Pat. Anyway,' she smiled at him, 'since the hedge fund debacle in nineteen ninety-eight, a fifty million loss isn't the great disaster it once was. If you haven't lost four billion dollars, like John Meriwether and his friends, you're nobody.'

'I'm quite glad to be nobody, thanks,' said Pat sourly. 'I just hope you're right, Alix.'

The office door opened and Des walked back in. His face was grim. 'Right, you two,' he said. 'Let's get to grips with this. Starting now, Alix. I want to go through all your outstanding positions.'

Chapter 31

Guy Decourcelle was already sitting at the table in the bistro when Alix arrived. She walked through the restaurant to join him.

'I already ordered wine, I hope you don't mind,' he said.

Alix glanced at the bottle. Chablis. Guy only ever ordered French wine although he knew she preferred Italian.

'Not at all.' She sat down opposite him.

'You are concerned,' said Guy.

'Not for Dublin,' said Alix. 'I know everything that's going on here. It's just not good for the bank overall.'

'It's shit for the bank overall.' Guy poured the wine into her glass. 'And, Alix, it is not good for me. I should have known about this trade.'

'I know,' said Alix. 'Do they expect you to fall on your sword?'

Guy laughed. 'Not this time, I hope! The trader and his immediate superior have gone, but I've managed to stay put.'

'You were always good at getting out of a tight spot, Guy. Remember the Thai trade?'

He made a face. Guy had been long Thai government debt, a trade which had been spectacularly profitable for him. He had added to the position until he was close to his limits. And he had cut it in September 1997, a month before the Asian crisis hit the markets and caused spectacular losses. Guy and Alix had been talking about Asia during September of that year. Alix had seen a report on riots in Indonesia and had speculated that there would be unrest in the region. Guy had agreed with her. But not in Thailand, he'd said. He liked the Thai position. So it wasn't any great trading insight that had suddenly made him sell the debt, but a need for capital to fund a different project in the US. Guy had liquidated the entire position and, a month later, he was a hero.

'Better to be lucky than smart.' He chanted Europa Bank's mantra.

'You were always lucky.'

'So are you, Alix.'

'So far,' she admitted.

A waiter approached them and they gave their order.

'We will be looking for replacements in Paris,' said Guy.

'Oh?'

'We will not stop trading derivatives. Sure, they can be very risky but they are also very, very profitable. We will be making some changes in the room after this.'

'Recruiting from outside?'

'Yes,' said Guy. 'We want to shake up some of the teams. Change things around. Bring in new blood.'

'It's a good idea.'

'We would like you to join us, Alix.'

She stopped buttering her tomato bread and looked at him.

'Me?'

'Yes, you. You have experience. You are trustworthy. You're

not some hotshot trying to make a name for himself – or herself.'

'I might not want to move to Paris,' she told him.

'Why not?'

'I like my job in Dublin.' She resumed buttering the bread.

'Oh, come on!' Guy looked at her in disgust. 'It is a small operation, Alix. Surely you must find it very restrictive! I remember when you were in London. You were dealing in big size, running big positions. Lots of potential to make large sums of money and even larger bonuses. You can't get that in Europa Dublin.'

'I know. But it's interesting. I get to do a whole range of different things, not just specialise in one product. We have a diverse client base. I talk a lot to the credit people, the accounts people, the banking people. I get involved in a whole lot more than just trading.'

'And you find this more interesting than running the swaps desk in Paris?'

She sat very still. The swaps desk in Paris, where they dealt in fixed and floating rate borrowings, was a very big and very profitable area. If Guy was offering her the senior position on the swaps desk, it was a very good job.

'Swaps?'

'We're moving Michel Petit to the derivatives desk. That will leave an opening in swaps.'

'It's an interesting thought,' she said slowly.

'And you will accept?'

'I don't know,' she said. 'You've sprung this on me, Guy. I haven't had time to think.'

'You're a trader.' He smiled at her. 'You shouldn't need time to think!'

'About this, I do,' she said seriously. 'It would be a big change for me.'

'You will not have too much time to decide,' said Guy. 'I can only keep this offer open for you for two or three weeks. After that, we will approach someone else.'

'I see.'

'You should accept this,' said Guy. 'It is a good opportunity, Alix. Probably one of the best you'll ever get.'

He was right, she thought, as she listened to him talking about the Paris operation. It probably was one of the best offers that she'd ever get.

$\backsim$

Dave, Gavin and Jenny were eating sandwiches at the desk.

'There's definitely something up,' said Jenny. 'They were at meetings all morning and Alix is late back from lunch.'

'You know Guy Decourcelle, he takes ages over lunch,' said Dave.

'But there was an atmosphere this morning,' Gavin said. 'Didn't you sense it?'

'We were creating it,' said Dave. 'Because we're worried.'

'Do you think we're right to be worried?' asked Jenny. 'Do you think they're going to close us down?'

'I can't see why.' Dave cracked his knuckles and made the other two wince. 'It's not as though we're losing money! Last year was phenomenal.'

'But they might be going to rationalise,' said Gavin.

'We wouldn't be the only place,' Jenny pointed out. 'There've been a number of cutbacks over the last eighteen months.'

'Maybe it's time to dust down the CV,' said Gavin. 'Get out there early before anyone realises something is up.'

'You were offered a job in Banco Andalucia, weren't you?' asked Jenny. 'Why don't you give them a call?'

'It was a crappy position,' admitted Gavin. 'They were looking for a junior.'

'I thought—'

'I know I made it out to be great,' said Gavin, 'but it wasn't what I wanted. Otherwise I'd have gone.'

They sat in silence.

'Maybe it's good news,' said Dave eventually. 'Maybe Europa has taken over another bank.'

'Maybe.' Jenny's face brightened.

A phone line began to ring. They all rushed to answer it.

∽

When Alix walked back into the room after lunch everyone looked anxiously at her.

'Well?' Dave asked.

She sat down at her desk and looked at the screens. The dollar was lower. The bonds they were holding had fallen in value but only slightly. Things were reasonably all right.

'They've made a monumental cock-up in Paris,' she told them.

'What?' asked Dave.

'Some junior managed to lose fifty million on an options trade.'

'Stupid fucker,' said Dave. 'Didn't anyone catch it?'

'Oh, Dave, you know how it is. He was marking it to market

at some totally unrealistic price. The head of derivatives didn't even notice.'

'You'd notice,' said Jenny.

'I hope so,' Alix grinned. 'But the upshot is that they're sending a team of auditors over in a week or so to look at the books. So, please, guys, no mad trades, no unauthorised positions.'

Although there were always strict limits on positions in place, sometimes an urgent customer trade might cause a dealer to breach that limit and ask for a retrospective authorisation. It was what had happened to Alix when she'd been trading Kiwis in London, and when she was almost fired by Logan McDonald as a result.

'They might want to take more control from Paris,' she added.

'Why?' asked Gavin. 'What can they do there that we're not doing here already?'

'They think that they might book more trades through us, but decrease our overall independent limits.'

'That's crap,' said Gavin. 'They'll be handcuffing us if they do that.'

'I know,' said Alix. She thought again of Guy's offer. If Paris did try to take control over Dublin then her job would be a lot less interesting than it was now. It made the offer look even more attractive.

'They just want pen-pushers!' Gavin was disgusted. 'They don't want dealers.'

'It's a reaction to the loss,' said Alix. 'They haven't decided what they want to do yet.'

'What about in Paris?' asked Gavin. 'Will there be more jobs there?'

'What do you mean?'

'I presume they're going to fire a whole bunch of them. They have to fire a bunch of them, Alix, you know how it works. So maybe there'll be jobs in Paris. That'd be more exciting.'

'There could well be,' she said carefully.

'Have they offered you something?' Jenny caught the tone in her voice.

'They might,' said Alix.

Dave, Gavin and Jenny stared at her.

'Guy is talking about a position on the swaps desk. It might not come to anything, of course.'

'What about us?' asked Dave. 'Where would that leave us?'

'They're not talking about losing jobs in Dublin,' said Alix. 'You guys will be fine.'

'But maybe not as busy,' said Jenny.

'Busier, if they start dealing more through Dublin,' said Alix. 'But maybe without as much autonomy.'

'And that's why you'd go, isn't it?' asked Dave shrewdly. 'You don't like people telling you what to do.'

Alix shrugged. 'It might be that they just don't want to keep me here. But I'd prefer to be my own boss, yes.'

'And you don't give a fuck about us,' said Gavin.

'That's not true,' she said sharply. 'Des and I will be having a number of meetings to discuss the future direction of the bank. We are concerned about everyone. Not just the dealing room either.'

'So if you go, there'll be another job here?' Dave looked at her with interest.

'I have no idea whether I'm going or not,' she said. 'I don't even know whether I have a choice in the matter. But if I do then I suppose one of you will become head of treasury. I doubt very much that they'd recruit externally.' She looked at her watch. 'I have to go and talk to Pat Enright. I'll be in his office if you need me.'

'Well,' said Jenny when she'd left the room. 'Food for thought, don't you think?'

'I wonder will she go?' Dave frowned.

'Or will she be sent?' Jenny mused.

'Of course she will,' said Gavin. 'And it's a good opportunity for us if she does. You know how bloody conservative she is. It'd give us the chance to take some meaningful positions.'

'Not if we have Paris breathing down our necks,' said Jenny.

'You can get around that sort of thing,' Gavin said. 'It's easy enough. We could get bigger intraday limits, maybe. Make the trading easier.'

'From all accounts, Paris wants to make trading harder,' said Dave.

'Oh, you're cast in the same bloody mould!' cried Gavin. 'You just don't want to put your balls on the line.'

'I don't mind putting them on the line,' said Dave. 'It's the chopping block I have an aversion to.'

'Either way,' said Jenny hastily, 'we have to consider our own futures. Alix is going to be all over us like a rash making sure we don't do anything crazy.'

'We won't,' said Dave. 'Anyway, the Paris guys will be over soon so we don't want anything out of the ordinary on the books while they're here.'

'So we play it cool,' said Jenny.

'Absolutely,' said Dave.

'OK.' But Gavin looked dissatisfied.

❧

Alix arrived home at six o'clock to find Wyn's car parked outside the apartment. There was no sign of her sister.

She let herself in and changed from her suit into a pair of Levi's and a jumper. She brushed her hair and pulled it into a loose ponytail. Almost immediately, she looked about five years younger.

The doorbell buzzed and Alix looked at the monitor.

'It's me,' said Wyn unnecessarily. 'Let me in.'

Alix let her sister in the main door and opened the door to the apartment. A minute later Wyn appeared.

'I called earlier,' she said, 'but you weren't home.'

'What's up?' asked Alix.

'I dropped over because if I phoned you'd make some excuse not to come,' said Wyn.

'Come where?'

'Dad is going home on Saturday,' Wyn told her. 'We're going out tonight. Carrie has booked a table in Milano. She's booked for four, Alix. You must come.'

'Wyn, does nothing I say penetrate your thick skull?' demanded Alix. 'I've already told you a thousand times that I've no intention of being a sop to John Callaghan's conscience. I'm not going out to dinner with him and that's absolutely final. Besides,' she added, 'I'm meeting Guy Decourcelle from the Paris office for dinner this evening.'

'Oh, Alix, just for once can't you forget about the job and think about your family?'

'He's not my family,' she hissed. 'He never was and he never will be.'

'We really want you to be with us,' said Wyn miserably. 'It doesn't feel right without you, Alix.'

'It doesn't feel right because it isn't right,' snapped Alix. 'He can't just come back and pretend that everything's OK. So I won't be there and I don't care, Wyn, I'm not going to be pressurised by you or by Carrie.'

'So what's the business dinner about?' asked Wyn.

'Guy Decourcelle is head of European trading in Paris,' said Alix. 'They've had a serious loss in the Paris office which has caused them to fire a number of people.'

'How does that affect you?' asked Wyn.

'Guy has suggested a job in Paris.'

'Paris!' exclaimed Wyn. 'Would you go?'

'Why not?' asked Alix. 'It might be fun.'

'I'd miss you,' said Wyn simply.

'What?'

'If you went to Paris. I'd miss you and so would the children.'

'That's nice to know,' said Alix. 'But they wouldn't miss me for long, I'll bet.'

'Why do you always have to pretend that nobody cares about you?' asked Wyn. 'Why don't you feel upset that you might miss us?'

'Of course I'd miss you,' said Alix. 'But it's no big deal. Lots of people work abroad. Anyway, I mightn't have a choice if I want to stay with Europa.'

'What about Paul?'

'What about him?'

'How would you ever get him back if you were in Paris?'

'I don't know if I will ever get him back,' said Alix.

'What about your aversion to finding someone new?'

450

'That doesn't matter at the moment.' Alix rubbed the back of her neck. 'Right now I'm more concerned about Paris. Of course,' she looked at Wyn thoughtfully, 'I could always just change jobs in Dublin. Or go back to London, maybe. Or even New York.'

'Would you?'

'Would I what?'

'Go to New York?'

'Why not?'

'It's so far away.'

'God almighty, Wyn, you're so parochial!' Alix glared at her. 'I've nothing to tie me down here and I don't want to have. Doesn't that make sense to you?'

'I know what you're saying,' Wyn responded. 'I just don't think it's very worthwhile, that's all.'

'So what would make you happy?' asked Alix.

'Seeing you happy,' said Wyn.

'I am happy!' snapped Alix. 'How can I prove that to you?'

'I don't know.'

The sisters were silent.

'Would you like some coffee?' asked Alix. 'I was just about to make some.'

'Yes, please.'

Alix filled the kettle and spooned coffee into the mugs.

'I brought some photographs,' said Wyn.

'Not again!' Alix stared at her. 'What is this, Wyn? Some kind of war of attrition?'

'I just thought that—'

'Don't think,' said Alix. 'Just forget it.'

'But if Carrie can forgive and forget—'

'I doubt very much if Carrie can do either.'

'I think she has,' said Wyn. 'She says there's no point in nursing a grudge for thirty years.'

'If that means you think I'm nursing a grudge, you're mistaken,' said Alix. 'I'm not nursing anything. But what you both seem to forget is that I can hardly remember the man. I was only three when he left. So he wasn't all that much a part of my life. I just don't see the need to fawn all over him now. That's all.'

'But don't you want to know what he's like?' asked Wyn. 'That's what I don't understand, Alix. You're usually so curious about people.'

'Not about him.' Alix opened the fridge. There was just enough milk for one cup of coffee. She poured it into Wyn's cup. 'Here.' She handed Wyn the coffee.

'Thanks.'

'I hope you have a good time at Milano,' said Alix after a few moment's silence.

'I'm sure we will,' said Wyn.

'Tell Carrie I'll call her tomorrow or Sunday,' said Alix.

'OK.'

'Tell me one thing.'

'What?'

'How does Imogen feel about all this togetherness?'

Wyn shrugged. 'I don't know.'

'Because if I was her I'd sure be pissed off about it.'

'Why?'

'She's been his main woman for the past thirty years. Now he's gone all gooey about his wife and kids. If I was her I'd be feeling worried.'

'I don't think she is,' said Wyn. 'I think she accepts it. She's a strong woman.'

452

'I thought she was weak,' said Alix. 'I thought that's why he left us.'

'Oh, Alix.' Wyn drained her cup. 'You just won't accept that people grow up, will you?'

'Don't talk rubbish.' Alix took the cup and put it on the counter.

&

She really wasn't in the mood to meet Guy Decourcelle for dinner. But she had to talk to him so that she could assess the potential job in Paris. And find out more about their plans for Dublin. So she'd booked Les Frères Jacques in Dame Street for nine o'clock. She knew that Guy liked the French restaurant.

Really, she thought, as she applied her make-up, it would be so much nicer to just flop in front of the TV and chill out for the night. It would be much more agreeable to send out for Chinese than eat haute cuisine. Alix's favourite meal was beans on toast but she'd never admitted that to anyone.

Her taxi arrived at a quarter to nine, just as she was beginning to think it wasn't going to come at all.

'Ready for a nice night out?' asked the taxi driver.

Alix muttered noncommittally. She wanted to think about what she needed to say to Guy. What was important for her and for the others in the dealing room.

She arrived at the restaurant exactly on time and was shown directly to her table. The waiter brought her a glass of Perrier and then Guy arrived.

'You look lovely, *ma chérie*,' he said as he took in her simple black dress, the strand of pearls round her neck and her pearl earrings.

'Thank you,' she said.

'I like the way you do your hair,' he told her. '*Très chic.*'

'You think so?' She'd redone the chignon.

'Absolutely,' he said. 'Although I would like it more if it were around your face.'

'I don't wear my hair down when I go out for dinner,' said Alix.

'You never wear your hair down,' said Guy.

'I wear it down in the office,' she told him. 'Although I tie it back.'

'But never loose,' said Guy.

'No,' she said.

'Because you are not truly relaxed.'

'Because it gets in my eyes,' she told him as she handed him the menu she'd been given earlier.

Guy chose mussels and boeuf bourguignonne. Alix ordered salad and chicken.

'Excellent,' said Guy when the waiter left with their order. 'I like this place, Alix.'

'That's why I chose it,' she said.

'So.' He looked at her. 'Are you going to come and work for me?'

'I don't know,' she said.

'It will be a good job,' he told her. 'A senior position, Alix. You will earn more money than you do now. I think you would enjoy it.'

'What about my family and friends?' she asked.

'Pardon?'

'What about my family and friends here?'

'Well, for sure, they cannot come!' Guy laughed at his own joke.

'I know,' said Alix. 'I might miss them.'

'You are not serious, *ma petite*? A woman like you, you do not miss your family and friends. Besides, Des told me, the boyfriend is history!'

'Des told you that, did he?'

'Yes. We were talking about you some weeks ago.'

When Des had first mentioned the possibility of a job in Paris to her, had he known about the losses already?

'We were talking about Paris generally,' Guy explained, as if he sensed her unspoken question, 'and I said we could always do with fresh talent.'

'And I'm fresh talent?'

'For Paris, yes.'

'And Des wanted me to go?'

Guy shrugged. 'He said that he thought you were under-utilised in the dealing room.'

'I see.' Under-utilised my foot, thought Alix. Des was just trying to make life easier for himself. He thought things would run more smoothly with Dave in her job. So, she thought, if she took the Paris job she'd be playing directly into Des's hands. But if she didn't, she could be cutting off her nose to spite her face. She sighed.

'What's the matter?' asked Guy.

'Nothing,' she said. 'I just have a lot to think about.'

'Why don't you come over to Paris soon,' said Guy. 'Have a look around. Get the feel of the place as somewhere you might work rather than just visit.'

She nodded. 'That would be a good idea.'

'Because we do have to resolve things quickly, Alix. The market will expect it.'

'I understand,' she said. 'And I'll come over as soon as I can.'

❧

It was late when she got back to the apartment. Guy had asked her to join him for a drink in his hotel, but she refused.

'I'm tired,' she told him. 'I need to get some sleep.'

'I am also tired,' said Guy, 'but not so tired that I cannot enjoy a brandy with you.'

'I would fall asleep,' she told him. 'It's been a busy week for me.'

'Take the job,' he said as she left him. 'You'll regret it if you don't.'

He was probably right, she thought, as she looked through her wardrobe to select what she'd wear the following day. A good job with a good bank in a beautiful city. Why would she even have to think about it? What was there left for her in Europa Bank Dublin? Where would her career go if she stayed? Would she fade into insignificance?

'Bugger,' she suddenly said aloud, as she took a suit from the wardrobe. It was the bloody TV interview tomorrow! She groaned and selected a different suit. One more appropriate to appearing on TV and telling the world what it was like to be a successful female executive in a male-dominated industry.

She wished she bloody knew what it was like herself!

Chapter 32

Paul rang early to remind her about the interview.

'I hadn't forgotten,' she said testily. 'You don't need to remind me.'

'The crew will be there by half past two.' Paul ignored her tone. 'Be nice to them, Alix.'

'Of course I'll be nice to them!' she exclaimed. 'What d'you take me for?'

'Alix, if you're in a bad mood you can strike a man down at five paces,' said Paul. 'And Damien O'Riordan is new to the job. I don't want him terrorised.'

She laughed. 'I won't terrorise him. It's not in my interests to terrorise him, is it? I'm supposed to be a showcase for the successful woman. You know, caring, sharing but with an edge of steel.'

'It'll take about an hour,' said Paul. 'You can spare him that much?'

'Sure.' She could spare him as much time as he liked. 'Are you still expecting to broadcast it before the end of the year?'

'I think so,' said Paul.

Alix hoped it would be before she moved to Paris. If she moved to Paris.

'Good luck,' Paul said. 'I'll phone you later, see how it went.'

'Thanks.' She noticed Jenny gesticulating at her. 'Got to go. Talk to you later.'

'Charlie Mulholland for you,' said Jenny. 'Line two.'

Alix picked up the line. 'Hi, Charlie. What can I do for you this morning?'

They were busy all morning. Alix tried to imagine what it would be like without her. She glanced at the other three dealers. Dave was chatting to one of his favourite clients about the weekend's football matches, Jenny was talking to another about the potential for world recession and Gavin was trying to explain the theory of Elliott Wave technical analysis to a guy who could hardly add two and two together.

Dave would get the job, even though Gavin probably harboured a secret hope that he'd be promoted. But Dave would run things efficiently. Alix wondered whether or not he'd have the same measure of control that she had. If Paris was going to become more involved, it probably wouldn't matter.

The phone rang again. 'Europa Bank, dealers,' she said.

⁓

The TV crew arrived at exactly half past two. Alix had spent ten minutes in the ladies' reapplying her make-up before they arrived. She knew that she looked good in her olive-green Louise Kennedy suit, her understated jewellery and her hair slicked back into a French plait. She just hoped that she wouldn't make a complete fool of herself.

Rita McDonough, the receptionist, was chatting to Damien

O'Riordan when Alix stepped out of the lift on the ground floor. Damien was promising to interview Rita for a piece called *Unsung Heroes*.

'Alix Callaghan.' Alix extended her hand.

'Damien O'Riordan, nice to meet you.'

He was younger than she'd expected, in his early twenties, with gelled hair and silver glasses. He wore a navy suit, white shirt and red tie.

'I didn't know where you wanted to do this, Damien,' said Alix. 'We have a meeting room on the first floor or we could use my office which is attached to the dealing room. But there isn't a lot of space in my office.'

'I think we should do the interview in the meeting room,' said Damien. 'Then Phil can take a few shots of you at work.' He turned to the cameraman. 'What do you think, Phil?'

Phil nodded. 'Sounds OK to me.'

Alix led them to the meeting room where Phil and his sound technician set up the equipment.

'You're younger than I expected.' Damien smiled at Alix.

'You're younger than I expected too,' said Alix.

'I just look young,' said Damien. 'It's been a terrible curse. People think I should be doing children's TV because I have this youthful face.'

'How old are you?' she asked.

'Twenty-nine.'

She looked surprised.

'You see,' he said. 'Everyone reacts like that. I want to do serious stuff but they see my face and they think I'd do best telling four-year-olds how to make things out of old washing-up bottles.'

Alix laughed. 'Your shelf life will be longer. You can progress as you age gracefully.'

'I want to get on to the meaty stuff now,' said Damien. 'I've done lots of puffball pieces. I think this series will help.'

'So why have they got a male interviewer doing it?' asked Alix. 'Why not a woman if the piece is about women?'

'Because it was my idea,' replied Damien. 'And I wasn't going to hand it over to one of the female sharks, thanks very much!'

'Female sharks?'

'Barracudas,' said Damien. 'Once you get your teeth into something you don't let go.'

'Maybe because it's so difficult for us to get our teeth in in the first place,' suggested Alix.

He laughed. 'This is going to be a good interview. I can feel it.'

'How old did you think I was?' asked Alix.

'Pardon?'

'You said that I was younger than you thought. How old did you think I was?'

'I expected someone in their forties,' said Damien. 'But you're a lot younger than that. I've done a couple of these already and most of the women were older than you.'

'This is a young person's game,' said Alix. 'A few more years and I'll be too old.'

Damien smiled at her as he excused himself to check something with the cameraman. Alix stood at the window and gazed over the Liffey. She suddenly realised that the words she said were true. A few more years and maybe she would be too old for dealing. Everyone said that you burnt out in your thirties. That you had to move on before then. She shivered. This was all she had ever done. All she ever wanted to do. She couldn't accept the idea that one day she wouldn't be able to do it any more. That younger people, snapping at her heels, would push her out of the way.

But they still wanted her in Paris. There was a role for her there. And perhaps, there, she could move higher in the corporate structure. Become part of a management group. Perhaps she could take over from Guy or even Jacques eventually. There was no reason why not. She spoke fluent French and both her Spanish and German were passable. She could easily be a manager for Europe. It might be an interesting job, shuttling between capital cities, devising strategic plans for Europa's branch network.

'Alix, we're ready.' Damien cut into her thoughts.

'OK,' she said. 'Where do you want me to sit?'

The TV camera didn't bother her. Although she'd only ever done one TV interview before, camera crews were part of the lives of people in financial markets. Anytime there was a sudden surge in prices or a sudden fall, camera crews popped up in dealing rooms zooming in on already harassed people trying to salvage something from the mess. During her time in London, when markets went through a particularly volatile phase, Alix was used to seeing herself on TV almost every evening as part of a run-in to that day's news item.

Damien O'Riordan cleared his throat and smiled at her.

'Alix Callaghan, head of treasury at the prestigious Europa Bank in Dublin, successful career woman, welcome.'

She smiled slightly at him, conscious that the camera was focused on her.

'Where do you get your drive?' asked Damien.

I don't know, she thought. I don't know why I get up every

morning to battle with everyone else in the market. I don't know why I want to pit my wits against people I've never even met.

'I've always been interested in financial markets,' she replied.

'But it's essentially a man's game, isn't it?' asked Damien.

Yes, she thought, it is. Maybe that's why I like it. Maybe I enjoy fighting with people like Gavin Donnelly. At the time I don't think I do, but it must be part of me.

'That's changing, Damien. There are more and more women in financial services these days.'

'So is it harder to be taken seriously as a woman in this industry?'

She remembered an argument with Dave Bryant one day when she'd insisted that he cut a position and he'd yelled at her that it was making money and that he was going to run it. And she'd screamed at him, literally screamed, that he was to cut the fucking position now! There'd been a moment's silence and then he'd muttered 'time of month'.

'I think many men still find it difficult to accept women in positions of authority,' she said.

'But not you,' said Damien. 'You have a reputation for being strong.'

Afterwards, she'd gone into the loo and stayed there until she'd managed to get herself under control again. It hadn't been the time of the month. Not even close.

'Everyone has to be strong if they want to do well.'

Damien continued to ask questions and she continued to answer them. What would he say, she wondered, if I told him that I'd spent the last couple of months in a power struggle with one of my junior dealers and that, at the end of it all, it mightn't make any difference?

'So what about your personal life?' asked Damien.

'Pardon?'

'Personal life. When do you get time?' He glanced at his notes. 'You're in the office for ten or twelve hours a day. Is there someone special in your life and, if so, how do you cope with that?'

Had he been talking to Paul? He must have spoken to him, he must know already that her personal life was, currently, nothing to write home about.

'I go to the gym and I'm a member of a shooting club,' she said. 'So that gives me outside interests.'

'But what about a family?' asked Damien. 'Don't you ever feel that the time is approaching when you'd like to settle down?'

She smiled even though she was gritting her teeth. I'll kill Paul, she thought. I'll fucking kill him.

'Sometimes,' she said easily. 'But not yet.'

'But this is a problem for career women, isn't it?' Damien persisted. 'Because you commit so much to your career you have to put the family side of things on hold. And then, suddenly, it's too late. So how do you cope with that?'

'It's not too late for me yet.' She smiled at him. 'So I don't know how women for whom it has become too late actually cope.'

'It's something that must concern you, all the same.'

'I think about it,' she said. 'But it doesn't occupy my waking thoughts.'

'And if the right man came along, would you abandon everything?' asked Damien. 'Would you say, yes, I've had a great career but things have changed now?'

'Would you ask a man that question?' Alix regarded him

stonily. 'Why should I give up my career? If you were interviewing a man you wouldn't ever consider asking him that question.'

'But it's an important issue for women, not for men.'

'I beg your pardon!' She stared at him. 'Are you saying that only women should care about family and children? That the choice is ours alone?'

'No.' Damien looked uncomfortable. 'I'm just saying that most women eventually give up their jobs and I wondered what the catalyst was.'

'Maybe the fact that, at present, so much of business is played by rules that have been set by men,' suggested Alix. 'The workplace is not overly friendly towards women although certain companies have tried. But as long as the route to the top is by confrontation rather than compromise, women will always struggle.'

'Is that because women are hopeless at confrontation?' asked Damien.

'It's because we prefer compromise,' said Alix. 'Because we don't think you have to stamp a rival into the ground. Because we don't feel you have to constantly score points off each other. But men seem to enjoy that.'

'So, at present, you have no plans to give up work and have a family?' Damien returned to his original question.

'I don't think the two are mutually exclusive,' said Alix.

'Alix Callaghan, thank you very much.' Damien grinned at her as the camera was turned off. 'Great interview, thanks.'

'I didn't realise you were going to get so personal,' said Alix.

'Oh, we always have to on the woman-in-work front,' Damien told her. 'It's the great dilemma thing, isn't it? Home and family versus the corporate struggle.'

'I suppose so,' said Alix.

'Anyway, that was great. Can we take a couple of shots of the dealing room now? You know, a few of you answering the phone, jumping up and down, that sort of thing?'

'Of course you can,' said Alix, 'but I can assure you nobody will be jumping up and down.'

∽

In the dealing room Dave, Gavin and Jenny were discussing their futures.

'I bet she'll take that job in Paris and not give a shit about the rest of us,' said Gavin.

'What would you do?' asked Jenny.

'I'd take the job and not give a shit about the rest of you,' Gavin laughed.

'So why are you blaming her?'

'I'm not,' said Gavin. 'I'm just pointing out what she'll do.'

'And what are you going to do?' asked Jenny.

'I'm going to continue to be a valued member of the team.' Gavin grinned at her and Dave.

'If she goes you'll probably get promoted, Dave,' said Jenny.

'And so will I,' said Gavin.

Jenny looked at him. 'Promoted to what?'

'Senior dealer.'

'But you're still only learning,' said Jenny. 'If anyone becomes senior dealer, Gavin Donnelly, it'll be me.'

'Guys, guys!' Dave interrupted them. 'It's all pretty irrelevant at the moment. Let's just wait and see, shall we?'

'Sure,' said Jenny. 'But I don't want you giving any favours to him over me, Dave. Just keep that thought with you.'

'And remember,' said Gavin, 'that I might be the most recent member of the team, but it was me who made ten grand last week out of Harris. So I'm valuable.'

'I'll keep it all in mind,' said Dave, who was beginning to feel very pressurised.

'Here she is.' Gavin gestured to the other two as Alix walked in, followed by Damien O'Riordan and the cameraman.

'Alix! You never said that we were going to be on TV.' Jenny looked anguished. 'I would have done my face again.'

'It's OK,' said Alix, 'it's only a few general shots.'

'All the same,' moaned Jenny, 'if my mother is watching I don't want her to think I look a wreck.'

'We'll only take you from your good side,' said the cameraman. 'Is this unusual – half of the people in here are women?'

'Put like that I suppose it is,' said Alix. 'But maybe it's because we're a relatively small unit. Certainly you wouldn't get half of a thirty-strong room being women.'

'And how do you like it?' Damien turned to Gavin. 'Working for a woman?'

Alix held her breath.

'I'd prefer to work for a man,' said Gavin. 'But I suppose that Alix isn't too bad.'

'I'm not sure whether I'm being damned with faint praise or not,' said Alix.

'It's an interesting idea for a follow-on,' mused Damien. 'Men under women – what do you think?'

'Don't ask me,' she said. 'I always believe in being on top.'

Damien laughed but Gavin's smile barely reached his eyes.

❧

It was almost time to go home by the time the camera crew had left. Alix poured herself some coffee and sat down.

'We're having a management meeting on Monday,' she told the others. 'We'll be going through the accounts and positions and all that sort of thing ahead of the audit. I thought we should have a meeting ourselves at five o'clock on Monday to talk it through. Does that suit everyone?'

'It'll have to, won't it?' said Gavin.

'Yes, it will.'

It would be nice, thought Alix, not to have to worry about Gavin any more. Of course there would still be someone. There was always someone ready to rip your face off when it came to trading.

'Five o'clock Monday,' she repeated.

Her phone rang and she answered.

'Hi, Alix, this is Rita at reception. There's someone here to see you.'

'Who?' asked Alix in surprise. She never scheduled meetings for Friday evenings.

'It's a gentleman,' she said. 'His name is John. He didn't give his surname. He said you'd know what it was about.'

Alix held the receiver in her hand and said nothing.

'Alix? You still there? Are you coming down or do you want me to send him up?'

'No!' she said sharply. 'Don't send him up. I'll be down. Tell him it might be a while.'

'OK,' said Rita.

Alix sat at her desk and stared unseeingly at the computer

screen in front of her. How *dare* he come here! How dare he try to confront her at work. In the place where she felt safe. She'd made her position perfectly clear. She wasn't going to see him.

'Alix, are you all right?' Dave looked at her curiously.

'Yes, sure,' she said.

'I think I'll head off,' said Dave. 'It's nearly five.'

'Fine.' She didn't look up. 'Actually, anyone who wants to go, just go.'

Gavin and Jenny exchanged glances.

'OK,' said Gavin and pulled on his jacket.

'See you Monday.' Jenny smiled at Alix.

'Yes. See you Monday,' said Alix.

She sat in the silence of the room and watched the numbers on the screen change in front of her. The dollar was down again. She'd known it would go down.

She wasn't going down to reception. She wasn't going to see John. Her father. The deserting bastard.

She picked up the phone and dialled Wyn's number but there was no reply. Then she dialled her mother's beauty salon.

'Carrie is with a client at the moment,' said Samantha. 'Do you want me to interrupt her, Alix?'

'No,' said Alix. 'It's OK. It's not important.' She hung up.

He needn't think he could browbeat her like this. He needn't think that she'd come running just because that was what he wanted. How dare he, she thought again. How dare he mess with her life.

She got up from the desk and looked out of the window. Tomorrow he'd be gone back to the States, back to Imogen and Kate and the life he'd made with them. And, if she met him, he'd go back congratulating himself on having smoothed over the cracks of his previous life. He'd feel exonerated. Forgiven. Well, she wasn't going to help him feel good.

She picked up her handbag and her car keys and walked out of the dealing room to the lifts. She got inside and pressed the button for the car park. Let him wait. She didn't care.

～

Rita glanced at her watch and at the man sitting on the uncomfortable seat in the reception area. He was reading the paper, oblivious of the amount of time that had passed. He hadn't hassled her to phone Alix again and find out why she was keeping him waiting for so long.

Rita wondered who he was. She felt as though she should know him, as though she'd met him before. He'd only given his first name and when she pressed him for his surname he'd shaken his head and said that his first name was enough. That was very unusual. And, although he was smartly dressed in suit and tie, he didn't look like the usual businessman that came to Europa Bank. Although, Rita had to admit, sometimes the strangest looking people had business with the bank.

'Excuse me,' she said brightly and he put down the paper to look at her. 'Alix has obviously been delayed. I'll call her to remind her.'

'Fine,' he said.

There was a trace of an American accent, thought Rita. And there was something about the cut of the suit and the shining grey of his hair that reminded her of America too. She dialled Alix's extension. Phones in the dealing room rarely rang for more than a couple of seconds before someone picked them up. But there was no reply from extension 2421.

469

'Excuse me,' she said again and this time he folded the paper and walked over to her. 'I'm really sorry but it looks like Alix has gone home. She must have forgotten you were here. It's so unlike her.'

'I see,' he said.

'Can I give her a message on Monday?' asked Rita. 'Or will you be able to contact her before then?'

'I'm not sure,' he said. He stood hesitantly at the reception desk.

'If you like I can try her number again. She might have just popped out for a couple of minutes.'

He shook his head. 'It's OK. Tell her I waited for her, will you?'

'Of course,' said Rita. 'Can I give her your full name?'

He thought for a moment then smiled at Rita. 'No, it's OK. Just tell her I waited.'

Chapter 33

Wyn opened the bottle of Californian Chardonnay which John had given her and poured two glasses of wine. She handed one to Carrie who was sitting in the armchair, her legs curled up beneath her.

'Thanks.' Carrie smiled at her elder daughter and they clinked the glasses together before Wyn sat down opposite Carrie.

'I wish Alix had met him,' said Wyn. 'I think it would have put a lot of things in perspective for her.'

'Oh, I don't know.' Carrie ran her finger round the rim of her glass. 'She was only a toddler when John left. I guess she doesn't feel any attachment to him.'

'You always feel an attachment towards your parents,' said Wyn. 'Even a parent who has deserted you.'

Carrie sighed. 'Alix isn't like you. She's more detached. More self-contained. Maybe she doesn't feel the same emotional pull.' She took a sip of wine. 'I know she certainly doesn't feel it towards me.'

'That's not true!' Wyn stared at her mother. 'Alix is devoted to you.'

'Wyn, come on, it's me you're talking to! Alix isn't devoted to me.'

'Of course she is,' said Wyn.

'She cares about me,' said Carrie. 'I'm sure, in her way, she loves me. But she's always been difficult to know.'

'Is that because he left?' wondered Wyn. 'Would it have been different if he'd stayed?'

'You don't know how many times I've asked myself that question.' Carrie sighed. 'I don't know. Perhaps it's just the sort of person she is. She can compartmentalise her life so easily.'

'But she's cut up over Paul,' Wyn reminded her.

'Not in the way you'd imagine, though,' said Carrie. 'I called to see her when she was sick, remember? And she was cool as a cucumber about it. Said she might get him back and might not.'

Wyn shook her head. 'I think she was more upset than she let on. When I told her to go out and meet new people she said that she didn't want to. That it was too difficult.'

'She's the hard part of it,' said Carrie. 'She's so unyielding. I always felt sorry for her boyfriends, having to live up to whatever ideal she'd decided. Anyway, she hasn't let it interfere with her work, has she?'

'God, that bloody job!' Wyn put her glass on the coffee table beside them. 'It's a substitute for her. A substitute for everything.'

'Oh, Wyn, that's not fair.'

'It is,' said Wyn fiercely. 'She throws herself into it, wanting to be one of the lads all the time, pretending that it matters. It's a load of rubbish, Carrie! All this shifting money around the place. What does it achieve in the end? Makes a few rich people even richer, that's all.'

'It's made Alix fairly well off,' said Carrie in amusement.

'But she doesn't have a life,' complained Wyn. 'She spends so much of her time in there. Seven in the morning until six in the evening! Why? Surely there's more to life than that. It's no wonder Paul decided to dump her. She was never there for him. And as for kids,' she snorted, 'what chance would any kid of Alix's have? She'd never be there.'

'I worked long hours,' said Carrie. 'When you two were younger and I was setting up the salon I was there morning, noon and night. I remember you giving me grief about it, Wyn. You told me that Daddy spent all his time at work and so did I and it wasn't fair.'

Wyn blushed. 'I remember that too.'

'So you can't blame Alix if she's inherited the work ethic.'

'I don't mind her working so hard,' said Wyn. 'I just don't think it's worth sacrificing everything for.'

∽

Alix switched off the computer monitor and rubbed her eyes. They were always sore after a day's trading which was why she rarely watched TV. After staring at a monitor for ten hours the last thing she wanted to do was to look at a TV screen.

She collected the sheets of paper from the printer. This month's profits were excellent. Two really good trades which accounted for over half the profit and a steady stream of income from the smaller accounts. Although it was always exciting to make a killing from a couple of big trades, it was satisfying to know that the income stream was diverse. You couldn't expect big ones every month and sometimes the big deals ended up losing you money. But not this month. This month was good.

'Still here?' Des Coyle put his head round the door.

'Just going,' said Alix. 'I was doing up the month-end figures.'

'How does it look?'

'Great.' She grinned at him. 'Paris will be pleased.'

'We've always shown them good profits,' said Des. 'And I'll be sorry if you decide to go, Alix.'

'Come on!' She laughed at him. 'You were trying to get me to go before all this blew up.'

Des looked embarrassed. 'Not really.'

'Oh, absolutely.' She looked him in the eye. 'You think that life will be easier with Dave in charge, don't you? You think that he'll get on better with Gavin and there'll be less tension.'

'It's no secret that you and Gavin—'

'That I rein in some of his worst impulses,' interrupted Alix. 'And if I do go, Des, you'd better look after Jenny Smith. She's worth ten of Gavin Donnelly.'

'I might have guessed you'd play the female card,' said Des.

'I'm not playing any card,' said Alix. 'I'm just telling you that Jenny is a smart girl and you'd be mad to lose her.'

'I'll keep it in mind,' said Des. 'Have you decided to go then?'

Alix shook her head. 'No. Not yet. I'm going to Paris to look things over. I won't decide until then.'

'I meant what I said,' Des told her. 'I would be sorry to lose you. But the opportunities are better there and I guess you've always wanted the opportunities, haven't you?'

'Maybe I'll get the opportunity to come back and grab your job.' She grinned at him and he smiled.

'I'll watch out for that.' He opened the dealing-room door. 'By the way,' he said, 'don't forget the Institute dinner next weekend.'

'Oh, God!' Alix stared at him. 'I *had* forgotten.'

'That's the sort of thing you can't forget if you want my job,' said Des and closed the door gently behind him.

Alix opened her desk drawer and rummaged around for her invitation to the dinner. She'd responded to the RSVP and then completely forgotten about it. Or, she admitted to herself, she'd pushed it to the back of her mind because she hated these kind of events. She found the invitation at the back of the drawer, a little the worse for wear. 'The Directors have much pleasure in inviting Alix Callaghan & Partner' it said coyly. She grimaced. They'd have to do with Alix Callaghan on her own. She'd told them she'd be coming on her own. She could do a bit of networking that way. God, she thought, I hate that too!

The phone rang.

'Alix Callaghan,' she said.

'Still there?' Paul's voice was teasing.

'Still here,' she said.

'I meant to ring you sooner,' said Paul. 'Damien says that you did a great interview. He's really pleased with it.'

'They'll probably edit it down to nothing,' said Alix.

'They'll edit it,' admitted Paul, 'but not to nothing. They think you were great, Alix. And you looked wonderful! But you always looked good in that suit.'

'You've seen the interview?' she asked.

'Yes.'

'I was very hassled that day,' she told him. 'Guy Decourcelle and Jacques Monet were over the day before. They were talking about restructuring the bank worldwide. Guy offered me a job.'

'You have a job,' said Paul.

'In Paris,' Alix told him.

'And will you take it?'

'I don't know,' she said. 'Part of me wants to and part of me doesn't.'

'What part doesn't?' asked Paul. 'I always thought you enjoyed the times you've worked abroad.'

'I do,' said Alix. 'It's just . . .' She sighed. 'I like my apartment. I like the way Dublin has developed over the past few years. I enjoy living here now.'

'You always waxed lyrical about Paris,' said Paul. 'I can't imagine your not wanting to live there.'

'I know,' she said. 'It's just something I need to think about, that's all.'

'Sabine is homesick,' Paul told her.

She said nothing.

'She likes Dublin,' he continued, 'but she misses her family.'

'I can understand that,' murmured Alix.

'So I'm sending her back to Paris next weekend,' he said. 'As a treat. For her to see how she really feels.'

'And will you miss her?' asked Alix.

'Of course I will,' said Paul. 'But she'll come back.'

'You're full of confidence.'

'Not really,' he said, 'but I think it'll do her good.'

Alix fingered the crumpled invitation in front of her. 'If you're at a loose end,' she said cautiously, 'you could always help me out.'

'Help you out with what?' asked Paul.

'The Institute dinner?'

'Oh, Alix! Not that stuffed shirt affair! I thought you weren't supposed to bring partners to it. I distinctly remember you telling me the last time you dragged me to one of those events that they never usually invited the spouse.'

'This year they have,' said Alix.

'I don't believe you haven't got someone else you can bring,' said Paul.

'I probably have,' she said, 'but I thought that, if you were doing nothing, you might like to come. It's purely business.'

'Great,' he said, 'you're dragging me to a boring business function.'

'It'll be your way of repaying me for doing that sodding interview,' she told him.

'Oh, well, if that's the case . . .'

'You'll come?'

'I suppose so,' he said. 'You could always wrap me round your little finger. But, Alix, it's just a friendship thing.'

'Of course it is,' she said. 'I'm not interested in you in any other way, Paul. I promise you.'

'I don't know whether I should be pleased about that or not,' he said.

'I'll phone you next week to arrange everything,' she said.

That worked out well, she thought, as she clicked out of the line. Des and Dave would be surprised to see her with Paul again. Dave had made a few pointed remarks about ageing dealers being left on the shelf in the last few weeks. It would be nice to show that she wasn't entirely without male company – even if it was Paul Hunter.

She was feeling full of energy when she got home. She threw her sports gear into her bag and drove to the gym. The changing rooms were full of women in various states of undress.

'Hi, Alix!' One of the aerobics instructors smiled at her. 'Haven't seen you in a while.'

'I've been busy,' she said. 'But I thought I needed the workout.'

'Are you coming to one of my classes?' she asked.

Alix shook her head. 'I'm just going to do some weights and have a run.'

'Good luck.' The instructor smiled at Alix and went off to take her class.

Alix changed into her Reebok top and shorts and pulled her hair back into a ponytail. She stretched a couple of times then walked out into the gym area.

'Don't forget to warm up properly!' called the instructor and Alix made a face at her.

But she stretched again, then warmed up for ten minutes on the bike before beginning a circuit of weights. She liked being at the gym. The only thoughts that came into her head when she was working out were of the number of repetitions she was doing. Even on the treadmill she simply watched the people swimming in the pool below and didn't think of anything at all. But this time, as she ran, she couldn't help wondering about John Callaghan. Had he waited long when he'd come to see her? she wondered. Or had he realised quickly that she wasn't going to waste her time coming down to see him? She gritted her teeth as the incline grew steeper and she had to run harder. It was his own fault, he shouldn't have called in like that. If he wanted to see her, he could have rung her first. And she wouldn't have answered his call.

⌒

'Alix, Matt Connery wants to talk to you.' Gavin glared at her. He'd done a trade with Connery, another small purchase of dollars by the client, and he'd thought that Connery was happy enough with the price. But he'd asked to speak with Alix. Gavin didn't want him to speak with Alix.

'Hello,' she said.

'Hi there.'

'How are you?' she asked. 'How was your trip?'

'Oh, fine.' He sounded tired, she thought.

'When did you get back?'

'Yesterday,' said Matt.

'Profitable?'

'I sure hope so.' He laughed. 'I like the Japanese but I really haven't managed to get to grips with their culture. I feel as though they're all looking at me as a stupid foreigner even though they're smiling at me.'

'I suppose they've finally got something to smile about.' Alix glanced at the dollar/yen exchange rate. 'The economy is beginning to turn around a little.'

'You bring it back to basics so quickly,' complained Matt. 'I was talking about the people and their culture and you've reduced it to economic performance!'

'Sorry,' said Alix. She was conscious of Gavin watching her. Why should he be worried? She'd given him the account, hadn't she? She could chat to a client if she wanted to.

'Have you ever read *Tai-Pan*?' asked Matt.

'By James Clavell?' Alix smiled. 'Actually, I have. And the follow-ons right up until *Noble House*. They were very interesting.'

'They explain a lot,' agreed Matt.

'I had a number of Japanese clients when I worked in London,' said Alix. 'You learn to work differently with them.'

'"He who smiles rather than rages is always the stronger",' said Matt.

'I beg your pardon?'

'It's a Japanese proverb,' he told her. 'And it's one that I try to follow.'

She laughed. 'It wouldn't work in the dealing room, I'm afraid. A little healthy rage goes a long, long way.'

Matt laughed too. 'I don't want you to rage at me,' he said, 'but I did want to ask you something.'

'Sure.'

'Before I went away I asked you to dinner but you couldn't come. You were meeting people from your Paris office.'

'That's right,' interjected Alix, 'Guy Decourcelle. He's the head of European trading over there.'

'So I thought I'd renew the invitation,' continued Matt. 'How about Friday night?'

'This Friday?' asked Alix.

'Yes,' said Matt. 'Actually, I've got tickets to *Phantom of the Opera* at the Point Depot. I know it mightn't be your thing, but I thought it could be fun. Then dinner afterwards? It's just a thank-you for all the help you've given us.'

'Oh, Matt, I'm really sorry,' she said, 'but on Friday night we've got a Bankers' Institute dinner. I can't miss it. I'd be murdered if I did. Besides, I haven't been that helpful. If anything, I should be asking you to dinner as my client.'

'My timing is all off,' he said ruefully. 'Never mind, another night perhaps.'

'Yes, sure,' she said. 'Another night.'

'Do I have to book it in your diary months ahead?' he asked.

'Don't be silly.' She laughed but it was forced laughter.

'How about the following Thursday?'

She looked at her electronic diary. 'Please don't get insulted, but I'll probably be in Paris on Thursday. I'm not sure whether I'll be back at the weekend or not.'

Matt sighed. 'I'm away around then myself. I might have to go back to Tokyo. Maybe I'll give you a call when I get back.'

'That's a good idea,' she said.

'OK,' said Matt. 'Sorry we couldn't have sorted out something first. Next time we should try and synchronise our diaries better. In the meantime have a good night at the Institute dinner and enjoy Paris.'

'If you want to talk about anything urgently we could do lunch,' suggested Alix.

'No. I wanted something more leisurely,' said Matt. 'I'll call you.'

'Fine,' said Alix. 'Talk to you then.' She ignored Gavin's black look as she hung up.

❧

Matt replaced the receiver and leaned back in his chair. He really didn't know why he was pursuing Alix Callaghan.

She was attractive and intelligent, certainly, but she was too damned independent for him. And she hadn't apologised half enough for not being able to go to the theatre with him.

He looked at the tickets on the desk in front of him and sighed. He picked up the phone again and punched in a number.

'Hello,' said a female voice.

'Kats?'

'Hello, Matt.'

'How are you?'

'I'm fine. Haven't heard from you in a while.'

'No. I've been busy. Listen, I was wondering if you're doing anything on Friday night?'

'No,' said Kats. 'I'm not.'

'Great. Would you like to come to *Phantom of the Opera* with me?'

'Who's let you down now, Matt?'

'Why should someone have let me down?'

'Why are you phoning me if it's not a case of someone letting you down?'

'OK,' he admitted, 'it's a woman I met. I thought she might like to come but she's busy that night.'

'Too busy for you?'

'Kats, please!'

'Oh, all right,' Kats laughed. 'But couldn't you find someone else?'

'I don't want to find someone else,' he told her.

'Oh!' She sounded surprised. 'Is this serious, then?'

'How can it be?' he asked. 'I haven't managed to get her out yet!'

'She'll fall for your charms eventually,' said Kats. 'They always do.'

I wish I could be so sure, thought Matt as he hung up on his younger sister. I really wish I could be so sure.

Chapter 34

Alix was torn between the pearl-grey knee-length Jasper Conran dress and the charcoal-grey Kaliko trousers. She stood in front of the mirror wearing the Conran and holding the trousers in front of her. They'd both look equally good for the Institute dinner, she thought, but which would make her look that little bit special?

She wanted to look special. She wanted Paul to look at her and wonder why on earth he had left her for Sabine Brassaert, painter and decorator, homesick Parisienne. She kept asking herself why she wanted to impress Paul, whether she really wanted him back in her life, what exactly her game plan was, but she didn't know the answers.

She slid out of the silk dress and into the trousers. The cut of the trousers was very flattering and she couldn't help wanting them. But the dress was more feminine. She toyed with the idea of buying both. She tried on the dress again.

It would have to be the dress, she decided. And she might buy the trousers but not today. If she bought the trousers she'd need to buy a top as well and she didn't have time to look for the right sort of top. She glanced at her watch. She was already late back from lunch as it was.

She took the dress to the cash desk and handed over her credit card.

'It's beautiful, isn't it?' The sales girl smiled at Alix. 'I want one myself. They've only just come in.'

'It's lovely,' said Alix. 'But I must be supporting that man by now. The amount of money I spend on his clothes is ridiculous.'

'They're classic pieces,' said the sales girl, 'and you get great wear out of them.'

Alix nodded. Actually, she got very little wear out of any of the clothes she bought for evening functions. She attended a few each year but she always felt as though she should be wearing something different each time. On the one occasion when she'd worn the same dress to two events in a row Des Coyle had asked her why.

'Because I like it,' she'd told him, wondering at the same time whether he was wearing a new suit.

She rarely dressed up for events other than work-related ones. At the weekends she wore jeans and sweatshirts, and she always changed into a comfortable pair of trousers and a sloppy jumper when she came home in the evenings.

Maybe that was another reason Paul had deserted her for Sabine, she thought as she walked along Abbey Street to the office. Perhaps he was tired of always seeing her encased in denim. But he was a casual dresser himself, surely he wouldn't have expected her to be wandering around the apartment in slinky dresses.

Or maybe he would. She wondered what Sabine wore. When she'd seen her in the airport, the girl had looked chic and elegant in designer jeans and a well-cut jacket. And at the reception in Europa Bank Paris she'd worn the stunning red

485

dress. And yet – that was such a contradiction. If Paul had really wanted the earth-mother type, why had he ended up with French chic like Sabine?

Alix gritted her teeth then sprinted across the road against the traffic lights.

~

'I can do those for you at fifty-five,' said Gavin.

Dave Bryant glanced at his colleague.

'Yes,' Gavin confirmed, 'fifty-five.'

'Who are you dealing with?' mouthed Dave.

Gavin ignored him. 'Fine,' he said. 'Settlement Monday.'

'Who was that?' asked Dave when Gavin had concluded the call. 'And what exactly have you done?'

'Bought dollars,' said Gavin, 'from Harris.'

'At fifty-five?' Dave stared at him. 'How many?'

'We're short, aren't we?' asked Gavin.

'Yes, but Jenny already bought some from Ronan McMahon,' said Dave. 'And it's on the way down, Gavin.'

'I bought a bar,' said Gavin, using the slang for a million.

'Oh, fuck it!' Dave glared at his colleague. 'Jenny bought a bar too. We were only short half a bar. You knew that.'

'Sure, but Matt Connery was a buyer this morning and he hasn't dealt yet. I'll give him a call, try and lose some at a better level. You can sell the rest in the market.'

'At a loss,' said Dave. 'It's moving against us.'

'I'll ring Connery now.' Gavin pressed the speed dial on his phone.

'Matt Connery.'

'Hi, Matt, Gavin Donnelly here.'

'How are you, Gavin?'

'Fine, thanks. Look, remember you wanted to buy dollars this morning? The market's moved your way and I can show you some now.'

'I said I might be a buyer,' Matt told him, 'I didn't ask you for a firm price this morning. I'm not ready to deal yet.'

'But you'll need to, won't you?' asked Gavin. 'You were pretty definite about it earlier.'

'I know,' said Matt. 'But our US people didn't confirm so I won't know that I need them for sure until tomorrow.'

'That doesn't matter,' said Gavin confidently, 'I can sell them for you forward settlement.'

'It's OK,' said Matt. 'I'll wait until we get confirmations. I don't know what date I might need to settle.'

'But the dollar is moving your way now.' There was an edge to Gavin's voice. 'If you deal now you'll get a much better rate.'

'I'll have to risk it,' Matt told him. 'Anyway, it's been sliding all week. Maybe another day will move it even more in my direction.'

'I thought you were meant to cover risk not run it,' said Gavin.

There was a silence at the other end of the phone.

'Matt?' he said.

'Look, I appreciate the call,' said Matt eventually. 'I just don't need you telling me how to run my business. OK?'

'Of course,' said Gavin hastily. 'I'm sorry, Matt. I didn't mean to imply that you didn't know what you were doing.'

'That's OK,' said Matt. 'Hey, is Alix around?'

'No,' said Gavin shortly. 'She's shopping.'

'No, I'm not.' Alix stood behind him. 'I'm back. Anything the matter?'

He closed his eyes. He hadn't heard her come in.

'Matt Connery wants to talk to you,' said Gavin.

Alix walked round to her desk, dumped her shopping on the floor and picked up the phone. 'Hi.'

'Hi, how are you?'

'Fine,' said Alix. 'And you? Are you dealing with us?'

'Not today,' said Matt. 'Though Gavin was showing me some dollars.'

'Was there something wrong with the price?' asked Alex.

'Not at all,' said Matt. 'He wanted to sell dollars and he thought I was a buyer because I told him I might need some soon. But I don't have the goods yet and I don't want to buy until I do. I know I could do an option trade but I might actually just shift funds between a couple of Anatronics accounts. I think Gavin must really want to sell them – he was very determined!'

'Was he indeed?' Alix glanced at Gavin who was having a muttered conversation with Dave. 'I'm sure he has it all under control.'

'So am I,' said Matt. 'And I'm glad he put you on to me. How's your diary?'

'Still a little frantic,' said Alix.

'So's mine,' said Matt. 'But I'm determined to make a dinner date with you before the end of the year.'

'I'm sure we'll find time eventually,' she said.

'With a bit of luck,' said Matt. 'Enjoy the Institute dinner.'

She hung up and looked over at Gavin. 'What's going on in the dollar?'

'We're long,' said Dave. 'Gavin and Jenny bought some at the same time.'

'No we didn't,' said Jenny. 'I bought them from Coburn's before Gavin took them.'

Both Dave and Gavin glared at her.

'So are we very long?' asked Alix.

'A bar and a half altogether,' said Dave. 'We'd been holding a half.'

'And what are we long at?' asked Alix.

'Fifty-five,' said Gavin.

'An average of fifty-three,' said Dave, 'when you take Jenny's into account.' Alix looked at the screen. If they cut the position now they'd take a thousand-dollar loss.

'How has the dollar been trading?' she asked. 'It looks like it's still on a down trend.'

'It is,' said Gavin, 'but technically it's oversold.'

'What do you think, Dave?'

'It's a small enough loss,' he said. 'We can afford to run it a little, see if the dollar moves up a bit.'

'And why do you think it's going to move up?' asked Alix.

Dave shrugged. 'Gut.'

'Technicals,' said Gavin.

'I'll leave it up to you,' Alix told them. 'But don't run it past a five-grand loss.' She sat down and began to eat the sandwich she'd brought back for her lunch.

⌒

By five o'clock the dollar had hit the stop-loss limit that Alix had imposed and Gavin sold them to the market.

'It shouldn't have gone past ninety-five,' he told her as he wrote the ticket. 'Technically, ninety-five should have stopped it.'

'Technically it doesn't always do what you think,' said Alix.

'Oh, things could be worse,' Dave said. 'At least we made a few grand this morning out of the swap position.'

'And we made a grand out of the sterling position,' Jenny reminded her.

'Hallelujah.' Alix looked at the three of them. 'We've broken even on the day. I'm sure Guy Decourcelle will be very pleased about that.'

'It wasn't my fault,' said Gavin.

'I never said it was.'

'You're implying it.'

'Gavin, stop behaving like a bloody four-year-old.' Alix stretched her arms over her head. 'Go home, have a good weekend.'

Gavin got up and slung his jacket over his shoulder. 'I will,' he said and left the room.

'Why didn't you just cut it, Dave?' asked Alix when Gavin had gone.

Dave shrugged. 'I don't know. I wanted him to make the decision.'

'He won't,' said Alix. 'He's hopeless at cutting losses. He always thinks there's some magic way to turn them into profits again. He needs to learn.'

'You're right,' said Dave. 'And I suppose I should have done something.'

'It was a cheap lesson,' said Alix. 'Maybe it'll rub off this time.' She stood up. 'I'm heading home now, Dave. Got to soak in the bath and all that before the dinner tonight. I'll see you there, shall I?'

'I'll be in the Horseshoe Bar,' said Dave.

'OK.' Alix picked up her shopping. 'See you later.'

❦

She mixed the hair colour carefully. She was getting quite good at this, she thought as she checked her roots for grey. The sprinkling was there, mocking her. She covered it with the purple gel hoping, as she always did, that it would definitely come out the shade of auburn that was on the packet.

Her heart was beating more rapidly than usual. She could feel it pumping away inside her chest and she could feel, too, a frisson of nervous excitement. It was like the first time she'd gone out with Paul – a feeling of mingled anticipation and hope.

'Idiot,' she told herself as she sat on the sofa and painted her nails with fast-drying varnish. 'When you're with him you might decide that you've gone off him completely. Shit!' She swore softly as she painted the side of her thumb with carmine red.

When the time was up she rinsed the colour out of her hair and dried it. Perfect, she thought, as she surveyed it in the mirror. Much glossier than it ever was before she started colouring it in the first place!

She took time over her make-up, not rushing it like she usually did but blending the foundation carefully into her face and blotting her lipstick with a tissue before reapplying it for a more professional finish.

She wore the necklace and earrings that Paul had given her

and they glittered under the bedroom light. The grey silk dress was perfect, she decided. Simple and plain but with a low neck which she knew would draw eyes to her cleavage. And tonight she had a cleavage because she was wearing her Wonderbra. She knew that Paul had always liked the Wonderbra effect!

The doorbell buzzed. She went into the living room and checked the monitor.

'It's me.' Paul was looking directly into the camera. 'Will I come up or do you want to meet me down here?'

'I'll come down,' she said. She didn't want Paul in the apartment. Not yet.

She took her grey coat from the stand beside the door, picked up her bag and keys and went downstairs to meet him.

Paul was standing by his car, his hands in his pockets, when he saw Alix walk down the steps of the apartment. He drew in his breath sharply as she stood for a moment in the light of the doorway. She looked fantastic, he thought. So tall and elegant, her hair swept up into the sophisticated style that he so loved to undo at the end of the night, her coat open, revealing the knee-high dress and her shapely legs. Sabine was very pretty, he told himself, in her young, gamine way, but Alix was truly elegant.

'Your chariot,' he said as he opened the car door.

'We can take mine if you like,' she said. 'I'll leave it in town overnight and get a taxi home.'

'Don't be silly,' he said. 'I'll drive you home. It's the one advantage of being a non-drinker.'

'Sure?' she asked.

'Of course.'

She got into the car without further protest.

'You look lovely,' he said as he turned the key in the ignition.

'Thanks.' She smiled at him. 'So do you.'

'I hate this suit,' he told her, 'as well you know.'

She smiled again. 'So I'm especially grateful to you for wearing it.'

'You're exacting a tough payment for that bloody interview.'

'You know they'll give me such a hard time in the office.' She sighed.

'Don't pretend not to enjoy the attention,' he said. 'You love it really.'

She laughed and he turned on the car radio to listen to live football on Radio 5.

It was nice to sit beside him again, thought Alix, even if it was strange to be in his car. She leaned back and closed her eyes.

'Tired?' he asked.

'Not really. Just chilling out.'

'Hard day?'

She opened her eyes again. 'That Donnelly dickhead lost money. Not much but enough. Trying to be a hero.'

'*You* try to be a hero,' said Paul.

'Maybe,' Alix agreed, 'but I also know when discretion is the better part of valour.'

'And how are things in the dealing room these days?'

'*Comme çi comme ça*,' she replied. 'A bit of trouble in Paris which might have a knock-on effect.'

'Is that why they offered you a job over there?' asked Paul as he drove into the carpark.

'I think it's either go to Paris or leave Europa,' she told him.

'And what have you decided?'

'I haven't.'

'It's not like you to take a while to decide anything,' said Paul.

'I'm trying to be more mature,' Alix told him. 'I'm not going to rush into anything. Maybe I'll go. But maybe someone will offer me a wonderful job in Dublin tonight. Stranger things have happened.'

'It just seems so weird,' he said. 'That you might end up in Paris while I—'

'It does, doesn't it?' she interrupted him.

Paul parked the car and she opened the door and got out. 'Come on, I'd better not be late.' She strode purposefully towards the carpark exit and he had to hurry to catch up with her.

'Would you like to go?' he asked.

'I'm not certain.'

'How long would it be for?'

She turned to him. 'It's a permanent job.'

They stepped out into the side-street and Alix shivered. 'It's suddenly turned very cold.'

'Come on, then.' Paul put his arm round her shoulders. 'Let's walk quickly and you'll warm up.'

But she still felt cold even with the warmth of his arm round her.

Chapter 35

The foyer of the Shelbourne Hotel was crowded. Alix pushed her way through the Friday night throng towards the famous Horseshoe Bar. If anything, it was even more crowded. She stood on tiptoe to see if she could spot Dave but it was futile.

'Would you like a drink?' asked Paul.

'If you can manage to order one,' she replied doubtfully.

'Of course I can,' said Paul. 'Do you want a beer or a vodka?'

'Vodka and tonic, please,' said Alix. 'One cube of ice—'

'And no lemon. I know,' Paul interrupted her. 'Wait here.'

She leaned against the wall as he disappeared into the mêleé and wondered how long it would be before he emerged again. She eavesdropped on snatches of conversations between the other people near the bar. The row between the slim brunette and the overweight businessman was particularly interesting. But Alix missed the remainder of their argument when Paul squeezed by and handed her her vodka and tonic.

'Dave's in there,' he told her. 'With some girl.'

'Do we know her?' Alix swirled the drink in the glass.

'I didn't recognise her.' Paul shrugged.

'Great.' Alix beamed at him. 'Someone for me to annoy him

about. It doesn't happen often enough. Cheers!' She raised her glass to him.

'Cheers,' said Paul as he clinked his glass of 7-Up against it.

'What time did Sabine leave?' asked Alix casually.

'Lunchtime,' said Paul.

'Did you drop her to the airport?'

He nodded.

'When will she be back?'

'Next week, I hope,' he said.

Alix looked at him quizzically. 'Is it OK between you?'

'I don't really want to talk about it right now,' said Paul. 'Dave is about to join us.'

Alix turned as Dave Bryant and his companion stopped beside them. 'Hi, Dave,' she said unenthusiastically.

'Hello,' he said. 'This is Marilyn. Marilyn, this is Alix Callaghan.'

'Hi, Marilyn.' Alix extended her hand which the other girl shook briefly.

'You're his boss,' said Marilyn.

'I prefer to say colleague,' Alix told her.

'But you are his boss.'

'Yes,' said Alix.

'He loves being dominated.' There was a sudden twinkle in the other girl's eye. 'I should know.'

'Marilyn!' Dave looked aghast.

'It's true.' She shrugged and leaned her head on his shoulder.

'Don't you think we should be moving into the function room?' suggested Alix. 'It's after eight.'

'Suits me.' Paul drained his glass.

'You go ahead,' said Dave. 'We'll follow you.'

'See you later,' said Alix.

Paul walked beside her but he didn't take her arm or try to steer her by keeping his hand on the small of her back. She stopped to greet some of the other bankers who all smiled at her and nodded in recognition at Paul.

'I've missed this,' said Paul as she led him to their table.

'What?' she asked.

'These kind of stupid evenings.' He sat down. 'We don't have them in work.'

'I'm sure you do,' she replied spiritedly, 'and not only that but you have much more lovey-dovey arty kinds of things. Think of the Oscars for starters.'

'The Oscars are for movies,' said Paul calmly. 'The Emmys are for TV.'

'Oscar, Emmy, who cares what you call them,' said Alix impatiently. 'They're all the same.'

'Not if you're a winner,' Paul told her.

'Maybe you'll win something for the series,' she said.

'I don't think so,' Paul responded, 'but yours was the best by a mile, Alix. The others were so pushy but you were just yourself.'

'That's because you know what I'm like,' she said. 'The others were probably more interesting than me.'

'Not at all—' He broke off as Dave and Marilyn arrived at the table. 'Hi, there. Sit down.'

They glanced at the name cards then sat down opposite Alix and Paul.

'Paul is just telling me about the Oscars and Emmys,' said Alix.

'Actually we were talking about your TV interview,' he reminded her.

'That bloody thing!' Dave snorted. 'Why did they have to come in and film the place when we were so busy?'

'I thought it was a good time.' Paul glanced at Alix. 'You said it'd be OK.'

'And so it was,' she told him. 'As well you know, Dave Bryant. You guys were in the middle of a heated debate when I walked in. And I bet it had nothing to do with the dollar/yen rate!'

Dave grimaced. He hoped she hadn't overheard any of their discussion on the future of Europa Bank's dealing room without her.

~

The dinner was like every other dinner that Alix had ever attended. Generally stilted or careful conversations but occasionally too much drink leading to the revelation of true feelings. There'd been a bust-up already between Shane Morgan, the very young chief executive of one of the German banks, and Piet Beumer, the much older chief executive of a Dutch bank. Alix had watched with interest as the younger man grew more and more red-faced while Piet Beumer chomped on a huge cigar and looked self-satisfied.

The speeches were particularly boring, with references to recent financial market turmoil and the credit crunch that borrowers were currently experiencing. But, she noticed, the banks were more concerned with eliminating risk than they were about lending to potentially viable customers. Alix knew that banks went with fashionable trends just like everyone else. When it was fashionable (and profitable) to lend money to emerging markets such as Brazil and Korea, the banks rushed around handing out money as fast as they could, although it all went horribly wrong for them later. Renowned figures like Rupert Murdoch found it easy to obtain credit simply by telling one bank that he could get the money cheaper somewhere else. Banks hated to think that their rivals were lending to the tycoons more cheaply. •

Alix fiddled with her napkin while she listened to the same stuff she'd heard the year before and the year before that too. She glanced at Marilyn who was staring into the distance, a glazed look on her face. No wonder she looks like that, thought Alix. I understand what they're talking about and I'm bored too!

But eventually the speeches were over and people began to circulate around the room.

'Hi, Alix!' Chris Curtis of State Bank of Boston waved at her. 'How are you?'

'I'm great.'

'I've been meaning to call you,' said Chris. 'I haven't seen you in ages.'

'Busy lives,' Alix said.

'Don't talk to me about busy,' Chris sighed. 'We're up to our necks at the moment. How are things in Europa?'

'OK,' said Alix.

'Any fallout from that Paris loss?' he asked casually.

She smiled. Competitors always loved to hear about losses. 'Nope,' she said. 'Except that the Paris guys are frantically running around making sure that it can't happen again.'

'It always can,' said Chris gloomily. 'I remember when I was at – well, it doesn't matter. You're not in the market, are you?'

She looked at him in surprise. 'Me personally?'

'We're looking for people,' he explained.

'For what?'

'Couple of new jobs.'

'Reporting to?'

'Me,' said Chris.

She smiled at him. 'I'm happy where I am,' she said. 'But if I hear of anyone, I'll let you know.'

Paul walked over to them, carrying a couple of drinks.

'Do you know Paul Hunter?' she asked Chris.

'Of course.' Chris held out his hand. 'We met at some Christmas do. Last year or the year before. How are you, Paul?'

'Fine, thanks.'

'You worked in, um . . .'

'Journalism,' supplied Paul helpfully.

'Yes, that's it!' Chris grinned. 'Better not say too much in front of you. Don't want it all spread across page one.'

'Oh, I don't think there's anything you could tell me to fill page one,' said Paul.

'You'd be surprised.' Chris tapped the side of his nose with his finger. 'But say nothing, that's my motto.' He smiled at Paul and Alix and then returned to his table.

'What a shithead,' remarked Paul.

'Oh, he's OK,' said Alix defensively.

'He's a tosser,' Paul said.

'You're so charming,' she told him.

'That's your job,' said Paul, 'Aren't you supposed to be mingling?'

It was easier when he wasn't beside her. She could chat more freely with her colleagues and rivals, secure in the knowledge that he wasn't listening and wasn't about to make some smart remark about how mercenary they all were. And yet, she thought, it's so nice to know that he is here. She sighed, then smiled as Laurence Coleman walked over to say hello.

Paul had gone to the gents when Dave Bryant collared her.

'What on earth is he doing here with you?' he demanded. 'I thought you two had split up.'

'We had,' said Alix. 'We're good friends. It can be like that, Dave.'

He regarded her sceptically. 'No it can't.'

'Of course it can. When you're mature about it.'

'Bollocks,' he said rudely. 'Are you taking him back? Has he finished shagging the French piece?'

'Dave Bryant, don't be so utterly disgusting!' She was annoyed with him.

'Oh, come on, Alix. You can't go back. You know that.'

'I'm not going back,' she said. 'I don't know what gave you that idea.'

'Seeing you with him,' said Dave. 'I mean, Alix, he's living with somebody else!'

'Not right now,' she told him. 'Right now he's on his own.'

'And you think?'

She shrugged. 'I don't think anything. I wanted to bring someone along tonight – Des was so bloody insistent about it – so I brought Paul. It's perfectly simple.'

'There isn't a hope in hell that I'd bring one of my ex-girlfriends to a boring old fart evening like this evening,' said Dave.

'But you drag your new one along?' asked Alix.

'I don't know her too well,' admitted Dave. 'But we get on. And she was a sport about coming along tonight.'

'So was Paul,' said Alix sweetly.

'So was I what?' asked Paul.

'A sport about coming along tonight,' Alix told him.

'That's me.' Paul grinned. 'Sporty till the end.'

Alix went to talk about swap rates with Dermot Power of Citibank.

'I can't see them tightening,' said Dermot. 'Not in the current environment, Alix.'

'Neither can I,' she sighed. 'But it's been so one-way lately. Makes it very difficult to trade.'

'Or easy,' said Dermot, 'depending on your point of view.'

'Difficult,' she disagreed. 'There's no liquidity in the market. People just get caught up in positions they can't unwind.'

'Any position you get caught up in, Alix, I'll be only too pleased to unwind for you.' He smiled knowingly at her.

'I'll let you know,' she said and got up from the table.

She rejoined Paul. 'Sorry about that.' She sat down beside him. 'I got stuck talking to him. Couldn't get away.'

'That's OK,' said Paul.

She glanced at her watch. It was almost midnight. 'We can go soon if you like.'

'Whatever,' he said, 'it's up to you.'

'I'll just say a quick hello to Joan Farrell from Nedbank.' Alix got up again. 'I haven't had a chance to talk to her yet.'

Joan yawned then smiled at Alix. 'Sometimes I just want to pack it all in. Nights like tonight for example.'

'I know,' said Alix. 'I'd much rather be at home with a book.'

'Well, I was thinking of something more exciting myself,' said Joan. 'But this crowd wasn't it.'

'It's not the worst of them,' said Alix.

502

'Close,' Joan told her. 'All this crap about bringing partners along too. Ridiculous. They don't care about what we do and you spend the whole night feeling guilty because you're talking to people.'

'Where's Bill?' Alix looked around for Joan's husband.

'At the bar. With John, Peter, Trevor and Garrett. They're talking golf. At least that's a topic they can all share. What about Paul?'

'Oh, you know Paul!' Alix laughed shortly. 'He's sitting at the table making notes about us all.'

'At least he's never said anything.'

'He's with RTÉ now,' said Alix. 'He forced me – sort of – to do this interview with them.'

'Really!' cried Joan. 'How exciting.'

Alix made a face. 'Not really. I'm just terrified I've said the wrong thing and will make a complete fool of myself.'

'Oh, you'd never do that,' said Joan. 'You're competent, Alix.'

'You say the nicest things.' Alix smiled at her.

'It's true.'

∽

'I'm ready to go now.' Alix stood beside Paul. 'If that's OK with you.'

'Sure,' he said easily.

'I hope you didn't find it too boring,' she said.

'As boring as all the others,' said Paul.

'Oh, really?' She looked at him anxiously. 'I'm sorry.'

'It's not your fault,' he said. 'Even you couldn't make an evening like this exciting.'

'We need a few film stars,' said Alix. 'Make it more like the Oscars or the Emmys or whatever you want to call them.'

'Michael Douglas giving the keynote speech?' Paul smiled. 'I could think of worse.'

'You'd have to write the speech for him,' Paul laughed.

'No problem,' said Alix decisively. 'I could do it.'

'I bet you could.'

They stood at the top of the steps. It was raining. Not very heavy rain but enough to make sure that they'd be wet by the time they got back to the car.

'I'll run down and get it,' said Paul. 'Save you getting soaked.'

'Are you sure?' asked Alix. 'I don't mind, really.'

'Why should both of us get wet?' asked Paul. 'And it's no problem.'

'All right,' she said gratefully. 'Off you go.'

He was being really, really nice tonight, she thought. In this Paul she could capture the feelings she had with the old Paul. With the Paul who left you for Sabine, she reminded herself. But he had a reason for that. The reason was a house and a garden and children and a wife who was happy to stay at home all day. That was why he had gone. She had to force herself to remember why she hadn't stopped him.

The Rover pulled up outside the hotel. She ran down the steps and got in quickly.

'It's getting heavier,' she said as she wiped the rain from her face. 'I hope you didn't get too wet.'

Paul shook his head. 'I ran.'

He indicated and moved into the traffic.

'I stepped in a puddle.' Alix slid off her high-heeled shoes and wriggled her toes.

'Will I give them a blast of warm air?' asked Paul.

'That'd be nice.'

He switched on the fan and Alix held her feet under the vents. But they weren't dry by the time they arrived at her apartment five minutes later.

'Want to come in?' she asked casually.

'Why not?'

She was surprised. She'd been expecting him to say that he couldn't come in, that he had things to do. She'd expected an excuse from him.

'Hasn't changed a bit,' he said as he followed her in the door.

'Did you think it would?' she asked.

He considered the question for a moment. 'I suppose I did, although I don't know why. After all, you picked the décor, didn't you?'

'You never liked the white walls,' she said.

'It just seemed sterile to me,' Paul told her. 'I still think terracotta would be warmer.'

'I like white,' she said firmly. 'Would you like some coffee?'

'Sure,' he said.

He sat down in the armchair near the TV. Alix watched him covertly as she spooned Java into the percolator. He was sitting in his old chair, legs spread out in front of him, as he always had.

'I'm just going to take off my wet stockings,' she told him.

She closed the bedroom door behind her and peeled off the stockings. It was difficult having him in the apartment. She'd thought that seeing him here might convince her that he meant nothing to her any more, but it hadn't. It had made her feel more confused than ever. She slipped out of the grey dress and pulled on a sweatshirt and jogging pants. She didn't want to appear as though she was trying to seduce him now that he was back in the apartment.

She walked into the living room.

'Was the interview really OK?' she asked as she sat down on the sofa opposite him.

'Of course it was,' he said. 'I told you that.'

She shrugged. 'I wasn't sure.'

'That's not like you,' he said.

'What?'

'Uncertainty.'

'I've been less certain about things lately,' she told him wryly.

'About what?' he asked.

'Things.'

'Alix, if there was ever a word needed to describe you, uncertain is not that word. You've never been uncertain. You've always known exactly what you want and exactly how you intend to get it. Uncertainty was for other people, not Alix Callaghan.'

'You have a warped view of me.' She tucked her legs underneath her.

'No,' he said. 'I know you so well.'

'What am I thinking, then?' she asked.

'You're wondering if I still find you attractive,' said Paul.

Alix flushed.

'That's not difficult,' Paul said. 'After all, I'm wondering if you still find me attractive.'

'Are you?'

'Of course,' he said. 'Look, Alix, I know it's over between us but that doesn't mean I stopped caring about you. You still matter to me.'

'And Sabine?'

'She's different,' said Paul. 'She'll give me all the things I want.'

'A wife and family,' said Alix.

'Yes,' said Paul simply.

'Why does it matter so much?' asked Alix. 'Why couldn't you have been happy with me, Paul?'

'I was happy with you,' he said. 'But you wanted different things from me, Alix. You wanted support for your career and someone who agreed with you all the time. And that wasn't what I wanted.'

'What did you want?'

'Someone to support *my* career,' he said. 'And someone who believed my opinion was as good as theirs.'

'I believed that!' Alix stared at him. 'I believed in your opinion. And I did my best for your career. I got you that interview with the managing director of Carlow China when that scandal broke and he wouldn't talk to anyone! How can you say I didn't support your career?'

'I'm sorry.' Paul got up and sat beside her on the sofa. 'I know you did your best for me. It was just that I felt you did it because you felt obliged to, not because you wanted to.'

'That's so wrong,' whispered Alix. 'So wrong.'

They sat in silence for a moment.

'But you're not sure about Sabine,' Alix said finally. 'She's gone home for a while.'

'We want to be absolutely sure,' said Paul. 'I love her, Alix. She's everything I wanted in a woman.'

'She's very pretty,' said Alix.

'How do you know?' asked Paul. 'You hardly remember her, do you?'

'There was a picture,' said Alix hastily, 'of us at the Europa Bank reception. She was in it. She's blonde and small, isn't she?'

Paul smiled. 'Yes.'

'Complete opposite of me, in fact.'

He made a face. 'Yes.'

'And ready to have lots and lots of babies.'

'Yes,' he said again.

'But what about her career as a decorator?'

'Interior design,' said Paul.

'Whatever.'

'It's not the same as being a dealer. She can be home when she chooses.'

'But she'll still be the one painting the house in whatever colour she wants.' Alix forced a smile. 'You won't be able to voice your opinion on that one with her either.'

He laughed. 'I suppose not.'

Alix yawned. 'Sorry.'

'Tired now?' asked Paul sympathetically.

'You know how it is.' She closed her eyes and leaned back. 'With the possible changes in Europa, I'm trying to keep on top of everything and it isn't always easy.'

'Why do you do it?' asked Paul. 'Why do you push yourself all the time?'

Alix opened her eyes again. 'I don't.'

'You do,' Paul insisted. 'Over and over again, Alix. Why don't you just do something easier with your life?'

'Why should I?' she demanded. 'I like what I do, Paul. That's what you've never really understood, isn't it? I enjoy it. Yes, it makes me tired. Yes, it can be stressful. But I like it.'

'It won't always be there,' said Paul.

'What do you mean?'

'You know, Alix. When you get older and burnt out. It won't be there for you then. And you won't have anything else.'

'That's bullshit,' she told him. 'I won't be in dealing all my life, but I'll move on. There are other aspects to financial services, you know.'

'I love your passion,' he told her. 'I just wish you could have been like that about us. And about a family.'

Alix said nothing.

'You're so – so – exhilarating to be with,' said Paul.

'Not exhilarating enough,' said Alix. 'You left me.'

He leaned towards her and touched her cheek. She didn't move.

'I had to leave you,' he said. 'You know that.'

She held his hand against her cheek. 'Do I?'

'Alix—'

'*Do* you still find me attractive?' She smiled at him.

'Oh, Alix.'

'I still find *you* attractive,' she told him. She turned her head and kissed him on the hand.

'Alix, I—'

'But it's so hard to know what's just physical and what's more than that.'

'Physically, Alix, you're very, very attractive.'

'So are you.' She moved closer to him, still keeping his hand in hers.

'Thanks,' he said.

She leaned her head on his shoulder. 'I meant to thank

you more,' she said conversationally, 'for coming to the dinner.'

'I didn't mind.'

She stretched out on the sofa until her head was lying in his lap. She let go of his hand, put both of hers beneath her head and closed her eyes again.

'Alix, I should—'

'I get lonely,' she said. 'I know it's stupid but I get lonely at night.' She opened her eyes and looked at him.

'I can understand that,' he said.

She moved her head very slightly and felt him move beneath her. 'Paul!'

'Well, Alix, it's not easy when you—'

She giggled and sat up facing him. Her eyes glinted green as she looked at him. She reached into her hair and undid the diamanté clip that had held it in place. It fell around her shoulders in a cloud of newly coloured auburn.

'God, Alix, you're so lovely when you do that!'

'Paul, I deliberately changed into my ancient sweatshirt and pants so that you wouldn't think I was trying to come on to you or anything.'

'Alix, you'd look lovely in a sack!'

'No, Paul.' She grinned at him. 'I look lovely in the sack!'

He laughed and so did she. She put her arms round his neck and drew him closer to her. He smelled of Dune for men. She smiled. She'd introduced him to Dune for men.

'Alix, this probably isn't a very good idea.'

'I know.' She kissed him gently on the lips.

'It's probably a very bad idea.'

'I know.' She kissed him on his forehead.

'But it's a very pleasurable idea.'

'I know.' She lifted her sweatshirt over her head and dropped it on the floor. She wasn't wearing anything underneath.

'Oh, God, Alix.' He buried his head between her breasts and she held him fiercely to her as he moaned her name over and over again.

⤚

They lay side by side on the sofa. Alix could hear the thud of the rain against the window and the gentle gurgle of the percolator. The aroma of Java was enticing.

'Would you like some coffee?' she asked.

'What?' He opened his eyes.

'Coffee? Remember, I was making coffee.'

'Oh, yes. Coffee.'

'Would you like some?'

'Yes.' He struggled into a seated position.

'I'll get some for you in a moment,' she said. 'I just need to use the bathroom first.'

She slid away from him and picked up her sweatshirt and pants. She carried them into the bathroom with her. She stood naked in front of the full-length mirror. It was a good body, she thought. Firm in the right places. Round in the right places. She smiled at herself through her half-open eyes. She felt warm and languid and good about herself.

She stepped under the shower for a moment, then dried off briskly and pulled on her clothes.

Paul was still sitting on the sofa, although he'd fastened his shirt and trousers.

She poured out some coffee and carried it over to him.

'It'll have to be black,' she told him. 'I forgot to get milk earlier.'

Chapter 36

Paul sat behind the steering wheel and waited for the lights to change. It was 3 a.m. He'd wanted to leave after the coffee but Alix had talked to him about Europa Bank and her job and the possible move to Paris and he hadn't been able to shut her up. He felt sick every time he thought about making love to Alix. In his heart he hadn't wanted to, in his mind he'd wanted to be stronger but his body had let him down. Or not, he thought with a wry smile, as he remembered the pleasure of being with her. The very physical pleasure. She was a more inventive lover than Sabine. She was more exuberant, more joyful and certainly more acrobatic. Sabine liked him to lie side by side with her, before flipping her onto her back and entering her. Alix had twisted and turned on him, kissing every inch of his body, allowing her long hair to drift over him, sometimes beneath him, sometimes beside him and then, finally, on top of him. And it had been bloody wonderful. But with Sabine – with Sabine it was more meaningful.

The lights changed and he moved forward. Would Alix be able to see it as a one-night stand? He felt himself break into a sweat as he remembered her telling him, very soon after they first met, that she didn't go in for one-night stands. But this was different, wasn't it? She couldn't really believe

513

that he would go back to her, could she? Because no matter how truly fantastic she was in bed, Alix Callaghan wasn't the woman he wanted to spend the rest of his life with. He loved Sabine Brassaert and he wanted to marry her. He only hoped that tonight hadn't ruined everything.

◃~

Alix rinsed the coffee cups and left them on the drainer. She was trying to decide whether she'd always meant to make love to Paul tonight. Whether the idea had been there in the back of her mind from the moment she'd asked him to accompany her to the dinner. Probably, she admitted to herself. She'd wanted to see if she could do it. Prove to herself that he was still attracted to her despite the so-called charms of the Parisienne. She wondered exactly how guilty Paul was feeling right now. She'd phone him tomorrow, she thought, as she climbed into bed and, almost immediately, fell asleep.

She didn't wake up until almost noon. It was the longest she'd slept in ages and she felt full of energy as soon as she got up. She thought about ringing Paul but decided against. If she called now, she'd appear needy.

She dressed in her sports clothes and drove to the gym where she ran on the treadmill for half an hour before doing a circuit of weights.

'You look very chirpy today,' remarked Patty McCullogh as she encountered a perspiring Alix on the way to the changing rooms.

'I'm in a good mood.' Alix grinned at her. 'I've had a good night's sleep for the first time in ages.'

'Looks more like you've had a good night's sex,' said Patty.

'Patty!' Alix blushed.

Patty laughed. 'It's a much better workout than this will ever be!' She waved at Alix and ran upstairs to the aerobics class.

She's probably right, thought Alix, as she stood under the shower. Sex certainly gets your heartbeat up. And in a much nicer way than a workout in the gym.

That evening, she dropped in to see Carrie.

'I wasn't expecting you,' said her mother as she opened the door. 'You didn't phone.'

'Do I have to?' asked Alix, although normally she rang before visiting her mother.

'Of course not.'

Alix followed her into the living room and sat down in the armchair near the bay window.

'Would you like a drink?' asked Carrie.

'A glass of wine would be nice,' said Alix.

Carrie went to the kitchen to get the wine and Alix sat back in the armchair. *He* might have sat here, she thought. Talking to Carrie, looking around the room critically, thinking that Imogen would have done it differently. She clenched her fist.

'To what do I owe the pleasure?' Carrie returned with a bottle of Pinot Grigio and a couple of glasses.

'I hadn't seen you in a while,' said Alix. 'I thought I should call in.'

'I'm sorry it's such a chore.' Carrie handed her a glass.

'It's not a chore, you know it's not.'

Carrie settled into the chair opposite. She looked tired, thought Alix, and older. She was wearing a loose jumper and a pair of trousers, both of which had seen better days. Alix was suddenly aware that she hardly ever saw Carrie looking anything but elegant. But that was because Carrie always had a warning of her impending arrival.

'What?' asked Carrie.

'Sorry?'

'You're staring at me. What's the matter?'

'I'm not staring,' lied Alix. 'I was just thinking.'

'And?'

'You look tired.'

'I've had a busy day.' Carrie sipped the wine. 'Lots of people came in without appointments and we were on the go until six.'

'You shouldn't work so hard,' said Alix.

Carrie laughed. 'That's rich, coming from you.'

'I'm younger,' said Alix.

Carrie lifted her eyebrow. 'Thank you. That makes me feel good.'

'What I mean is,' Alix struggled to find the words, 'I'm still at an age where I need to work. Surely you could sell the salon now and retire?'

'And do what?' asked Carrie.

Alix shrugged. 'I don't know. Gardening, reading, travelling?'

'Really, Alix.' Carrie made a face at her. 'Can you see me gardening?'

The house in Ranelagh had a tiny front garden with a small lawn and a couple of bushes. At the back of the house was a paved patio area with a few tubs.

'Maybe not,' admitted Alix. 'But I sometimes think you work too hard.'

'I like it,' said Carrie. 'I need to have something to do.'

They sat in silence for a moment.

'I was disappointed you didn't come to dinner with Wyn and John,' said Carrie eventually.

'I told you,' Alix said, 'I had a work commitment that night.'

'And if you hadn't?' asked Carrie. 'Would you have come then?'

'Probably not,' admitted Alix.

'It's not such a big deal,' Carrie said.

'Yes it is,' said Alix. 'To come back after all this time and then lay on all this stuff about his daughter and a baby – it's a big deal. It wouldn't have been a big deal if he'd stayed away.'

'Alix, life is too short to bear grudges,' said Carrie. 'I hated him for ten years. But I got tired of hating him.'

'I don't hate him,' said Alix. 'I don't care about him one way or the other.'

'Most people like to know their parents,' said Carrie. 'They like to know their roots. I think it would have done you good to meet him.'

'I don't want to be forced,' Alix told her. 'I don't want someone coming into my life and making me like them.'

'Who says you'd like him?' Carrie grinned. 'You might hate him. But at least it'd be a choice.'

'Well, right now I choose to have nothing to do with him,' said Alix dismissively. 'Anyway, he's gone back to the States, hasn't he?'

Carrie nodded. 'Kate's baby is due very soon. He wanted to be back with her.'

'Have you met her?' asked Alix.

'No.' Carrie shook her head.

'But you've seen a photograph?'

'Yes.'

'And does she look like us?'

'A little.' Carrie stood up and opened a drawer in the little desk in the corner. 'Here.' She held out a photograph.

Alix took it from her but didn't look.

'It was a long time ago, Alix,' said Carrie gently. 'Things change.'

Alix glanced at the photograph. The girl in it was sitting on the bonnet of a car, smiling at the photographer. Her long, dark hair was being blown by the wind and she squinted in the light of the sun. But Alix could see the resemblance straightaway. Kate, her half-sister, looked like her. And like Wyn, too.

She glanced up at Carrie. 'Family resemblance,' she said.

Carrie smiled. 'Your father's genes, all right.'

'I don't have to like him.' Alix handed the photograph back to Carrie. 'I don't have to like her either.'

'Nobody says that you do. But Alix, even though he walked out and even though I wanted nothing more to do with him, he didn't forget you completely. He bought you birthday cards.'

'I know,' said Alix. 'Wyn told me.'

'Would you like them?'

Alix shook her head. 'No.'

'Fine,' said Carrie.

'Wyn says that he's president of some corporation,' said Alix.

Carrie nodded. 'He's worth a lot of money.'

'I don't care about that.'

'Of course not. But it's nice to know all the same, isn't it?' Her eyes twinkled.

'He can't come back and buy us with money.'

'He's not trying to,' said Carrie. 'He hasn't actually offered you any money!'

Alix laughed then bit her lip. 'It's just hard,' she said. 'I've always hated him for leaving us. And now I think I hate him more for choosing them over us.'

'I understand,' Carrie said. 'I really do.'

Alix drained her glass. 'Actually, the reason I stopped by was to tell you about Paris,' she said in a firm voice.

'Paris?'

'I've been offered a job there.'

'Really? And do you want to take it?'

'I don't know yet.' Alix outlined the changes in Europa Bank. 'It'd be an interesting opportunity,' she told Carrie.

'I'll miss you if you go,' said Carrie.

Alix smiled at her. 'Thanks.'

'You don't think you could get another job here?'

'I probably could,' Alix told her. 'In fact, at the Institute dinner last night I was chatting to a guy from State Bank of Boston who sounded like he might be interested in offering me something. But I don't think it would be as interesting as the job I have now. I might be better off in Paris.'

'Financially or socially?' asked Carrie.

'Both,' said Alix.

'Do you have friends in Paris?'

Alix shrugged. 'Not close friends.'

'Alix, don't you think it would be really hard to go somewhere new, without anyone?'

'No,' said Alix. 'People do it all the time.'

'Maybe they do,' said Carrie. 'But are they happy?'

'Well, I'm not exactly rolling around in social activity here right now,' said Alix.

'What about Paul?' asked Carrie.

Alix drained her glass. 'Paul wants to get married and have children, but not with me.'

'Have you seen him lately?'

Alix blushed as she remembered last night. 'Yes,' she said. 'I met him yesterday.' She looked at Carrie. 'I've been stupid about Paul.'

'Why?'

'I kept thinking of him as someone who got away from me. And I wanted him back because my pride was hurt. But he loves someone else. I know he does.'

'So you've put him behind you now?'

Alix sighed. 'I still can't help feeling resentful. That he wanted something I couldn't give him.'

'Life is like that,' Carrie told her. 'It'd be boring if it worked out the way you wanted all the time.'

'I guess so.'

Carrie smiled at Alix. 'You don't like it when things don't go according to your plans, do you?'

'No,' said Alix. 'But Paul left for a reason. And that reason is still the same. So, although there's a part of me that would like to have him back, it wouldn't work.'

'He wants kids and you don't.'

Alix nodded. 'Maybe one day I'll meet the person I want to have them with. Maybe one day someone will make me change my mind about marriage and families. But I don't think so. I would have lived with Paul forever. Or for a long time anyway. But the whole settling down thing? That's not me, Carrie.'

'Why?'

Alix shrugged. 'I don't know. It just doesn't appeal to me.'

'It didn't especially appeal to me either,' said Carrie. 'But when I look at all the things I've done, what I'm most proud of is you and Wyn.'

'Gushy sentimentality doesn't suit you,' Alix told her.

'It might be sentimental, but it's true.'

'The bottom line is that I'm not ready for it,' said Alix. 'And I don't know if I ever will be.'

'You've got to let people matter to you,' said Carrie. 'You can't spend your whole life only letting them know a part of you.'

'Don't talk rubbish,' said Alix.

'Alix, you know that saying, don't you? That on your deathbed you'll never say you wish you'd spent more time at the office.'

Alix laughed. 'I doubt very much that people say they wished they'd spent more time slaving over a hot cooker either.'

'You're impossible,' said Carrie. 'But I do love you. And if you want to go to Paris, that's fine by me. Just be happy, Alix, that's all.'

'I will.' Alix smiled at her. 'I promise.'

∽

It was dark and it was raining. She got into the car and drove towards the apartment. But she didn't stop. She drove across the toll bridge and out along the Malahide Road. She wished she didn't feel so uncertain. She wished she knew what was

521

right for her. She wished she knew what sort of person she really was.

Paul's house was in darkness. She sat outside and thought about ringing the bell and waking him up. But she didn't. She drove home instead. She told herself that she'd made the right decision.

Chapter 37

It was a busy day in Europa Bank, Paris. Alix walked around the dealing room with Guy, stopping every so often to check a news headline or an exchange rate. The dollar had started the day looking strong but had begun to slide and was now at its lowest level in weeks. The markets were jittery, the dealers losing money.

'I need to phone Dublin,' she told Guy. 'See how they're getting on.'

'Sure.'

She picked up a phone.

'Europa Bank, dealers.' Jenny sounded under pressure.

'Hi, Jen. It's me.'

'Oh, hi, Alix.'

'How are things?'

'Busy,' said Jenny. 'We've had a lot of customers on asking about the dollar. It's very jumpy.'

'I know. I think there's something going on, Jenny, but I don't know what. I get the feeling it's a Latin American problem. How are our positions?'

'OK,' said Jenny tersely.

'Don't get stuck with anything,' warned Alix. 'We don't need any hassle right now. Can I have a word with Dave?'

'Yes. Hang on.'

'Hi, Alix.'

'Dave, is everything OK?'

'More or less,' said Dave.

'Which?'

'Well, I sold some of our bonds earlier which was a bit of a mistake. But we'd got a really good bid for them at the time and I thought – well, you know.'

'It doesn't matter about the bonds,' said Alix although she was annoyed at the sale. 'Just keep things pretty flat, will you? There's a lot of business going on here and the volume is high. People are very nervous and there are too many different attempts at explaining it. Nothing substantive yet, Dave, but I'll let you know if I hear anything. Keep it safe. It's so near the end of the year now we don't need to take any shit.'

'OK,' he said.

'Dave?' A sudden tremor of nervousness went through her. 'Everything is all right, isn't it?'

'We've got it under control,' he told her. 'Don't worry.'

'Fine,' she said.

'Everything is all right, yes?' asked Guy.

'Yes,' she said, although she felt uneasy for a reason she couldn't fathom.

'Come into my office,' said Guy.

She sat opposite him.

'We are making you a very fair offer to come here,' he said. 'And it is easy for you. You don't have to worry about a family.'

'I know,' she said.

'So, what will your answer be?'

She glanced out of the glass wall at the frantic, busy dealing room. It would be fun, she thought. And she could do well here.

'I'll be happy to join you,' she said.

'Excellent!' Guy leaned forward and kissed her on each cheek. 'I am very, very happy. We want you to start as soon as possible. Two or three weeks.'

'I need to sort out some things in Dublin first,' said Alix. 'I'll let you know the earliest date I can come.'

'That's fine,' said Guy. 'Perhaps we should go to dinner tonight, Alix? Have a celebration?'

'Perhaps,' she said.

'You are staying at the Georges V?'

She nodded.

'We can eat there. Eight o'clock?'

'OK, Guy. Eight o'clock.' She glanced at her watch. It was nearly four o'clock now. 'I'll see you then, Guy. I'll get back to the hotel now.'

'How boring,' said Guy.

'Well,' she confessed, 'I thought about taking a little detour through the Galleries Lafayette on the way.'

She was standing in the lingerie department of the store when her mobile phone rang.

'Hello?'

'Alix?'

'Yes, who's that?'

'Alix, it's me, Richard. Richard Comiskey.'

Sophia's husband. Alix hadn't quite got used to thinking of him like that.

'Alix, Sophia wanted me to call you. She's in hospital. She had a fall.'

'What!' Alix grasped the phone more tightly.

'She's OK, Alix. But we don't know about the baby. She was knocked out and – Alix, she wants a female friend.'

'Of course, Richard. I'll be there.'

'I'm sorry to spring this on you, Alix. I rang your office but they said you were at a meeting. So I called your mobile because Sophia is so upset. I thought she'd want me with her. But she keeps asking for you.'

'It's no problem, Richard. I'll get to her. I'll be there this evening. Which hospital?'

He gave her the name and the phone number and rang off. Alix stood amid the thongs and the bustiers and the camisoles and prayed that her friend would be OK. And that the baby would be OK. It didn't seem possible that she might lose the baby. Sophia had been so happy about this pregnancy. It meant so much to her. Life's a bitch, thought Alix despairingly. A real bitch.

She hurried back to the hotel, rang the airport and reserved a seat on the next flight to London. Then she rang Guy Decourcelle to tell him that she had to go back and couldn't meet him after all.

Guy sounded peeved rather than concerned, but Alix didn't care.

The airport was crowded and she almost missed the flight. She didn't have time to check in her luggage and was looked at disapprovingly by the stewardess who took her case – slightly too big to be cabin luggage – at the aircraft door.

Alix was hot, worried and bad-tempered when she sat down. Her mood wasn't improved by the fact that the man beside her was so big he almost took up half her seat too. She'd asked if there were any business class seats available, but the flight was full.

'Excuse me.' The voice came from behind her. She looked round. 'I thought it was you,' said Matt Connery.

'What on earth are you doing here?' She turned in her seat.

'Same as you,' he grinned at her. 'Flying to London.'

'I'm sorry, that was a ridiculous question. But I thought you were away. You said that you were away until next week.'

'I am.' He laughed. 'We're in Paris, in case you hadn't noticed! I've been in Japan and had to do a stop-off here. I didn't expect to bump into you, though.'

'I told you I'd be in Paris.'

'Well, I promise you, I didn't detour especially to accost you.'

'I'm sure you didn't,' she said dryly.

'Why don't you sit beside me?' he asked.

'Because the flight is full,' she said softly, 'and I don't think anyone would want to swap seats.'

'Ah, but there's a spare seat here,' said Matt. 'I booked two. I was going to do some work on the way and business class was booked up. So this was my solution.'

'But you can't work if I'm sitting beside you,' objected Alix.

'I could,' he said, 'although maybe I wouldn't want to.' He grinned again. 'It'd be more comfortable.'

Alix shot a glance at her travelling companion again. Matt was right. It would be a damn sight more comfortable. She excused herself and changed seats.

'Better?' asked Matt as she fastened her seat belt.

'Much,' she agreed. 'But don't let me stop you doing whatever you want to do.'

'I've a meeting in the City tomorrow,' said Matt. 'I'm putting the final touches to our presentation. But it can wait.'

'Honestly, Matt, I don't want to—'

'You're not,' he said. 'Were you at Europa Bank in Paris today?'

She nodded.

'And what's in store for you in London?'

For a moment she'd forgotten about Sophia but now she remembered. 'I'm visiting a friend,' she said. 'She's in hospital.'

'Oh, I'm sorry,' said Matt.

'She's pregnant,' said Alix.

'And is everything OK?'

Alix shook her head. 'I don't know. She had a fall. I don't know how serious.'

'I'm sorry,' said Matt again.

'She wants to see me.' Alix looked at him. 'Though goodness knows why. I can't be of any practical use to her. I think her husband's a bit put out about it.'

'Maybe it's just a woman thing,' said Matt.

'Maybe,' said Alix. She bit her lip as she visualised Sophia lying in a hospital bed, frightened and ill.

The engines of the plane roared as it sped down the runway and lifted into the air.

'I never like that bit,' said Matt.

'Don't you?' Alix looked at him in surprise. 'I do.'

'Don't you ever think that it might not manage to make it?'

'No,' she said. 'Do you?'

'All the time,' he confessed. 'I fly a lot but I absolutely hate it. That's why I'm more than happy to have someone to talk to.'

'OK,' said Alix. 'What would you like to talk about?'

'Anything,' said Matt.

'Currency markets were very volatile today,' she said.

'Were they?'

'Yes. And it was very exciting being in a big room where there was a lot of tension, but I was worried about things in Dublin.'

'Don't you trust them?'

'I do,' she said. 'It's just – oh, I feel better being in control of it myself.'

He looked at her thoughtfully. 'Do you feel like that about everything?'

'Like what?'

'Being in control?'

'Don't be stupid,' she said shortly.

'Sorry,' said Matt.

The silence was uncomfortable. Alix stared straight ahead of her and thought about Sophia.

'I was talking to someone who knows you yesterday,' said Matt.

'Oh?' She turned towards him again.

'A guy named Ossie Livsey. I met him in Tokyo. He said that he knew you when you worked in London.'

She smiled slightly. 'Yes. He was a good client. What's he doing now?'

'Working for Sony,' said Matt. 'We're hoping to link up with Sony for one of our products.'

'Hope it works out for you.'

'Thanks.'

Alix turned away again and took her notebook out of her briefcase. There was no reason for her to look in her notebook but she made a show of turning the pages and stopping from time to time as though she was absorbing important information.

Matt was trying desperately to think of something to say to her. He sensed that she was upset and he wanted to be able to comfort her. But he didn't think that being nice would work. The kinder he was, he decided, the more Alix would retreat into herself.

Was it really worth the effort? he wondered. There were a number of women in his life and he'd always had easy relationships with them. Mostly, he knew, because he travelled around so much. So he didn't have to form any deep commitment to any of them. And it was good for his ego that they all hugged him when he was going away and phoned him and wanted him to come back.

But Alix didn't care. It was, he thought, stupid to think of her in terms of someone he could have a relationship with, when so far he'd only managed to suggest a dinner that might or might not actually happen. Yet the more he talked to her and the more he saw of her, the more drawn to her he became.

'Is it true that Europa Bank is interested in merging with Credit Agricole?' asked Matt. There was absolutely no truth in it, he'd just made it up to have something to say.

'Pardon?' She looked at him in surprise.

'Maybe it wasn't Europa Bank, maybe it was someone else,' he said.

'You never know.' Alix closed her notebook. 'Banks are always merging. Economies of scale and all that. But I don't think Europa Bank is thinking on those lines at the moment.'

'I know they're not.' Matt had no idea why he was going to tell her the truth. 'I made it up.'

'What?' She looked at him in astonishment.

'I wanted to talk to you and I thought that mentioning Europa was the best way of getting your attention.'

She laughed and he was pleased to see that it was a genuine laugh. 'You don't have to talk about the bank to get my attention.'

'But you like talking about it.'

'I must be very boring,' she said wryly.

'No.'

'So what do you and the boyfriend talk about?' asked Matt.

'Sorry?'

'Mr Hunter. You said that there is – sometimes – a Mr Hunter.'

'Sometimes,' she told him. She thought of Paul who had loved her and left her and gone to bed with her again anyway.

'Alix?'

'You want to know about Paul?' she asked. 'I'll tell you. I was crazy about him. I lived with him for three years. We split up during the summer but we still see each other from time to time. I did an interview with RTÉ for him a while ago and, in return, he came to the Institute dinner with me last week.'

'So it's one of those adult, civilised kind of things,' said Matt.

'Absolutely.' Except, thought Alix, for the slight matter of him living with Sabine. Which I'm not going to tell Matt Connery about. And for the slightly more serious matter of making love to him after the dinner. Which I'm definitely not going to tell Matt Connery about!

'And you see other people?'

'Yes,' said Alix.

'So my dinner invitation isn't a problem?'

'I presumed it was a thank-you dinner for the advice we've given you,' said Alix. 'I know you said you wanted it to be a friendly kind of dinner but you're hardly likely to make a grab for me, are you?'

'Of course not,' said Matt, although he wasn't so certain.

'You see.' She smiled.

'It's just that . . .'

'Yes?'

'I kind of thought of this dinner in a different sort of way.'

'What kind of way?'

'Well – as a – a date.'

'A date?' She stared at him.

'Yes,' he said. 'A date.'

'Oh.' Alix was flattered he'd asked her but uncertain of how she felt. Or how he felt. What he really wanted from this – date.

'Look, it doesn't matter,' said Matt. 'I'm sorry. I've obviously overstepped some mark or other. Forget it!' He opened his laptop computer and started to work.

'*I'm* sorry,' said Alix. 'I didn't handle that very well.'

He looked up from the computer. 'Look, I like you and I wanted to take you to dinner. You don't want to. It's not a big deal. I'm sorry. I thought, perhaps, there might be something between us. But I was wrong. Forget it.'

'What did you think was between us?' asked Alix.

'I don't know,' said Matt. 'I simply felt as though we clicked.'

'On a business level,' she told him. 'But personally – how can you know?' And yet, she thought, as a shiver ran through her, he was right. There was something else. Only she didn't have time for it now. Not since she was going to Paris. And Paris was important to her.

'I can't,' he said. 'You're right, of course.' He turned back to his computer and began working again.

He didn't stop until the stewardess announced that they had begun their approach to Heathrow and asked passengers to switch off all electronic equipment.

The cabin lights were dimmed. The plane circled the airport. Alix looked at her watch. It was nearly seven. It would take an hour to get to the hospital. She hoped they'd let her in to see Sophia.

The plane continued to circle the airport. Alix hated the amount of time wasted in circling over Heathrow. She glanced at her watch again.

'We seem to be doing this for a long time,' said Matt suddenly.

She nodded. 'Probably in some huge stack,' she said.

'I hate this part too,' he told her. 'I'm always afraid that a plane taking off will fly straight into us.'

'You won't know anything about it if it does,' she said prosaically.

'Thanks for the words of comfort!'

An air of concern was building up inside the cabin. They'd been circling for nearly twenty-five minutes. According to the stewardess, they'd been due to land at seven.

'Do you think there's something really wrong?' asked Matt. 'Are we flying around dumping fuel?'

'I wouldn't say we've much to dump,' replied Alix. 'It's a short flight, after all.'

Quite suddenly the tone of the engines changed and the plane made a rapid descent, bumping its way through the low cloud cover and thudding onto the runway.

'Good God,' said Alix. 'That was a bit rough.'

They came to an abrupt halt.

'Welcome to London,' said the stewardess.

They didn't move for another five minutes, then the captain announced that there'd been a slight problem with the undercarriage but it had just been a faulty light. 'We wanted to be sure the wheels were down properly!' he joked.

Alix shot a look at Matt who was pale in the cabin lights.

'There you are,' she said. 'You've lived to tell the tale.'

'I was scared,' he told her.

'Oh, come on, I bet you weren't really.'

'I was really,' he said. 'I told you, I don't like flying.'

'You're the second man I know that doesn't like it. Remember the clay pigeon shoot? One of the other guys was shitting himself in the helicopter. Although you didn't look worried then.'

'I had to put a brave face on it then,' said Matt. 'Weren't you a bit worried?'

'Not in the helicopter,' she said.

'Just now, I meant.'

She shrugged. 'I was concerned. More because I guessed there was something wrong and didn't know what it was.'

'Alix?'

'Yes?'

'Have you ever cried?'

She laughed. 'Big girls don't cry.'

They shared a taxi to the city. Matt let her out at the hospital.

'I hope your friend is OK,' he said.

'So do I.' She held out her hand. 'Thanks for the lift. And thanks for giving me the seat on the plane too.'

'Any time.' He took her hand. His grasp was firm. They

looked at each other for a moment, then Alix pulled her hand away and scrambled out of the cab.

~

Sophia was terribly pale. Alix tiptoed into the room where Richard sat beside his wife. Sophia's eyes were closed.

'Hi,' Alix whispered.

'Hi,' said Richard. 'She's been asleep for the last couple of hours. They think everything is going to be OK.'

'Oh, Richard!' Alix pulled up a chair. 'I'm so glad.'

'So am I,' he said. 'I was so worried about her. And she was really agitated. She kept asking if I was OK and then asking for you, Alix.'

'Why me?'

Richard shook his head. 'I don't know. But she was so insistent. They gave her something to calm her down, I think, but she still kept asking for you.'

'I'll stay with her for a while,' said Alix. 'Do you want to grab yourself a coffee or something?'

'That'd be great,' said Richard. 'I'll be back in ten minutes.'

He left the room. Alix sat in the dim light and looked at her friend. Suddenly, Sophia opened her eyes.

'Alix,' she said.

'I'm here, Soph.'

'Thanks. Thanks for coming.'

'Of course I came. Richard phoned me.'

'Oh, Alix, it was all my own fault!' Sophia looked at her in anguish. 'I did it. If we lose the baby it'll be my fault.'

'You're not going to lose the baby,' said Alix.

'They don't know that.'

'Richard says they think everything is OK,' Alix told her. 'Don't worry, Sophia.'

Sophia sighed. 'I hope you're right.'

'They wouldn't lie to him, Sophia. Really they wouldn't.'

Sophia bit her lip.

'What happened?' asked Alix.

'I was going to a meeting,' said Sophia. 'The doctor told me to take it easy because my blood pressure was a bit high, and I've been trying, honestly I have. But we're bringing a new issue next month and I needed to get a few things tied up. Ramon had left a bundle of the legal stuff with me. I'd been reading it and I got really tired.' She rubbed her eyes. 'I nodded off, Alix. Imagine that! In my office. The meeting was on the floor below and the phone rang five minutes after I should've been there. I got an awful fright. So I picked up the legal papers – and you know how much it can be sometimes, there was a big bundle and it was heavy – and I waddled as fast as I could to the lift. But it was stuck on the ground floor so I decided to go down the stairs. Between carrying the papers and trying to hurry, I lost my balance and I fell.'

'Oh, Sophia!'

'I blacked out. I don't remember anything! Obviously someone came looking for me and they found me. But I'd been there for a while, Alix. You know how it is in those buildings, nobody ever uses the stairs.'

'You poor thing.'

'So it was my fault,' said Sophia again. 'Alix, you know I want this baby. I told you how important it was to me. Ramon could have done everything to do with this issue, but no, I had to be in charge, I had to do everything. Despite the doctor's advice. And because of that, I nearly lost my child, Alix.' Tears formed in her eyes. 'And I would have lost it because I'm selfish and shallow and stupid.'

'You certainly are not,' said Alix. 'You're kind and caring and you've worked very hard to get where you are. So you wanted to prove you could still do it. So what? You made a mistake, that's all.'

'But it was nearly a fatal mistake,' said Sophia miserably. 'I didn't want people to think that I was giving less than a hundred per cent just because I was pregnant. But that *was* stupid and selfish. Because you can't do everything, you really can't.'

'Hundreds of people before you and after you will probably want the same,' said Alix. 'And it's not fair, Sophia. I know how hard you've worked. I know that you don't want to give it all up. I know how you feel.'

'But not about the baby,' said Sophia. 'You don't know about that, Alix, because you don't feel this way.'

'Maybe not,' admitted Alix. 'But maybe one day I will. And then I'll be asking you for advice, Sophia. You've given me lots of good advice in your day!'

Sophia smiled wanly. 'And have you been taking any of it?'

'Well,' Alix said. 'If you want to hear about a real humdinger of a mistake, let me tell you about the night of the Institute dinner.'

Chapter 38

She'd intended to catch the early morning flight back to Dublin but it was booked out. And then she decided to spend more time in London. There really wasn't any great rush to go back. She was going to leave at the end of the year. Dave could cope on his own. Richard suggested she spend the night in their house in Chelsea and she agreed. But she called the office from Richard's on Friday morning to check on how things were and to let Dave know that she wouldn't be back until Monday.

'Everything OK?' she asked.

'Sure, fine.' Dave sounded casual.

'How about the dollar?'

'It's still strong but it'll probably start to drift down again.'

'All the same, Dave, keep it simple.'

'Sure.'

'No trades about to blow up in our faces?'

'No,' he said cautiously. 'How was Paris?'

'Fine,' she said. She thought Dave sounded tense. She was tempted to hop on the next flight back, just to be sure everything was OK. But she knew that she was being paranoid.

'Have you decided to desert us?' Dave broke in on her thoughts.

She laughed. 'I'll talk about it when I get back. In the meantime, please don't rock the boat, Dave.'

'So you will desert us,' he said flatly.

'I'll see you Monday,' she told him.

'OK, Alix. Have fun.'

It was nice to have an unexpected day off. She had a leisurely breakfast and then went to the hospital to see Sophia. She looked much better this morning, Alix thought. The colour had come back into her cheeks and she'd lost the terrified look of the previous night.

'The baby's OK,' she said when Alix sat down beside her. 'Oh, Alix, it's been a nightmare!'

'I know.' Alix took Sophia's hand and squeezed it. 'But now you can stop blaming yourself and get better.'

'It *was* my fault,' said Sophia. 'I should have known better, Alix. Really I should.'

'Lots of us do things when we should know better!' Alix smiled at her.

'Like the night of the Institute dinner?' asked Sophia.

Alix sighed. 'That was incredibly stupid of me,' she said. 'I had some wild idea that I could get him back because he'd find sex with me so irresistible. I even told myself he might phone although, to be honest, Soph, I knew he wouldn't.'

'So it's definitely over?'

'Sophia, he left me because he didn't think I was the woman he wanted to spend the rest of his life with. I've spent ages thinking about that. If I told him I'd change, would it really make a difference?' She made a face. 'I don't think so. I know he felt guilty about having sex with me. He loves Sabine. And she doesn't even have to think about the baby thing!'

'And do you think you'll start to think about the baby thing?' asked Sophia.

'I wish I knew.' Alix grimaced. 'I don't have any maternal urge, Soph. But what if I suddenly do? What if my hormones kick in and I'm too late to do anything about it? What then?'

'I don't know,' said Sophia. 'I wish I could advise you.'

'I like my job.' Alix stared into the distance. 'I really don't feel ready to chuck it all in yet. I thought I'd spend a few more years in Europa Dublin. I wasn't bored with it or anything. But there *will* be changes because they've had a huge trading loss in Paris. Derivatives.'

'You serious?'

Alix nodded. 'So they've fired two people and, according to Guy, they'll be letting more go. They'll also be taking greater control over some of the branches, which would limit my autonomy in Dublin. But they've offered me a job in Paris. A good job, Sophia.'

'And do you want to take it?'

'I've already said yes.' Alix bit her lip. 'It's a great career move and I'd be mad not to.'

'But?'

'But I'm questioning whether or not I really want to. I'm scared, Sophia.'

'Of what?'

'Of this bloody biological clock thing. It's a ticking bomb and I'm scared that one day it'll go off and I won't know what to do about it! Or, even worse, it never goes off and one day I'm full of regrets.'

'You'll know if it goes off,' said Sophia.

'You didn't. You had to wait until someone primed it.'

Sophia sighed. 'Alix, I don't have the answers for you.'

'I know. I didn't expect you to have.'

'So what now?'

'I go home. And I tell them that I'm taking the job in Paris.'

'Maybe you'll meet someone there,' said Sophia.

'I wouldn't count on it,' said Alix.

∽

There was a woman with a baby sitting beside her on the plane. The woman wasn't much younger than she was. She held the baby on her lap and spoke to the child all through the flight. From time to time she smiled at Alix and Alix smiled tentatively back. At Dublin airport they were met by a man who gathered them into his arms and kissed them. Alix watched them for a moment, then walked away.

∽

She watched CNN that night. The dollar had soared during the day. There was a rumour of a potential Latin American debt default. Alix shuddered. She was glad that she'd told Dave to keep things tight.

There was no point in taking undue risks so close to the year end. And, she mused selfishly, she wanted to leave Europa Bank Dublin in the knowledge that her last couple of months had been profitable. She logged on to the computer and tried to connect to the bank. But there was a problem with the modem and she couldn't gain access.

It doesn't matter, she thought as she climbed into bed. She didn't need to know. Dave would have told her if there were any problems.

～

She went shooting on Saturday and racked up a very respectable score. Niall asked her if she'd like to go on a trip they were arranging for the following March. 'To Italy,' he told her. 'We'll be guests of a club there and then we'll go on a tour of the Perazzi factory. It'll be great fun, Alix.'

'I'm sorry, Niall.' She put her gun into its case. 'I won't be here next March. I've been offered a job in Paris and I've decided to take it.'

'You lucky thing!' Niall looked at her with envy. 'I'd love to work in Paris.'

'Would you?'

'You bet! All those gorgeous women!'

She laughed. 'It's as good a reason as any. I'll try and come here as often as I can before I go.'

'Sure,' said Niall. 'We'll miss you, Alix.'

'Thanks.'

She got into her car and drove home. Halfway there, she detoured and called to see Wyn. She handed the obligatory earplugs to Aoife and Nessa and followed her sister into the kitchen. Wyn filled the kettle and switched it on.

'I have news for you,' said Wyn.

'Oh.' Alix took a shortbread biscuit from the tin her sister had placed in front of her.

'Kate had a baby boy yesterday.'

Alix broke the biscuit in half. 'Really.'

'Yes. They're calling him Aaron.'

'Stupid name,' said Alix.

'He weighed nine pounds.'

542

'Bit of a hip cracker.'

'She's fine. John and Imogen are delighted. So's Jack. Kate's husband's name is Jack, I don't think I told you that before.'

'And Carrie?'

'Carrie is delighted too.'

'I'm glad everyone is so delighted.'

'Alix—'

'I've taken the job in Paris,' said Alix. 'I'll probably start in January.'

Wyn stared at her. 'I wish you hadn't.'

'Why?'

'I'd prefer if you were here.'

'You won't notice I'm not. You'll have lots of other things to occupy you. Like John and Imogen and Kate and Jack and the nine-pound baby.'

'Aaron,' said Wyn.

'Whatever.'

'Alix, maybe you should see Paul. Talk to him. Get back with him.'

'As you so kindly reminded me once before, Wyn, he's living with someone else. He has no interest in getting back with me.'

'How do you know?' asked Wyn. 'Maybe it's all gone wrong with the French tart.'

Alix smiled at her. 'He sent Sabine back to Paris last weekend. She was homesick. He came with me to the Institute dinner.'

'Alix! You never told me.'

'I slept with him.'

'Alix!' Wyn was stunned.

'If he was going to come back to me I think I would have heard from him before now.'

'Oh, Alix.'

'Wyn, could you stop saying my name like that?'

'But, Al—, but why did you sleep with him?'

'To see if he wanted me.'

'And he obviously did.'

'He wanted sex with me, Wyn. It wasn't quite the same thing.'

'And he didn't even call you?' asked Wyn. 'He slept with you and he didn't even call?'

Alix smiled wanly. 'I think he was embarrassed.'

'I think he's a shit.'

Quite suddenly, Alix wanted to cry.

'You're better off without him,' said Wyn.

'And I'll be even better in Paris,' said Alix as she broke the biscuit again.

∽

When she got home she tried to log on to the bank's computer again. But there was still a problem with the modem.

On Sunday she went to the gym. She felt as though her life was getting back into some kind of order. The shooting club and the gym had always been part of her weekends before Paul had walked out.

She wished he'd called. She understood why he hadn't but she didn't want to be understanding. She wanted him to ring and say that he really loved her and that, even if he did decide to marry Sabine, he'd always love her. She knew that she was being completely stupid but she couldn't help wanting him to say it all the same.

When she got back from the gym the green light was winking

on her machine to tell her that she had a message. He'd called after all, she thought as she pressed playback.

'Hi, Alix, this is Matt Connery.' He cleared his throat. 'I just rang to say that I hope your friend is feeling better and that my invitation to dinner still stands. It's become a matter of principle with me now – it was easier to conclude the Tokyo deal than get you out for something to eat! I'll call again. Take care.'

Take care. It was used so impersonally these days and yet, the way Matt had said it, it sounded like he meant it.

Take care. But what was the point in beginning a relationship with him when she'd be in France in a few weeks' time? And he seemed to spend half his life globetrotting. They'd be a couple trying to schedule a night's sex between important business meetings and working on month-end figures. That wasn't what she wanted.

But sex with Matt Connery. She exhaled slowly as she thought about it. He was an attractive man. She'd found him attractive from the moment she set eyes on him as she sat on the steps of Europa Bank and smoked her last cigarette. Almost her last cigarette anyway! Even though she'd been annoyed at him for baiting her. There was something about him that she liked. But liking wasn't enough. Finding someone sexually attractive wasn't enough. God, she thought, what the hell did anyone get out of a relationship these days?

Work was simpler. At work you knew where you stood, where the boundaries lay, what people expected of you. And you knew what to expect of them too.

∽

She arrived at the bank at five to seven on Monday morning.

She was surprised to find Dave, Gavin and Jenny already at their desks.

'Good morning,' she said as she hung her coat on the coat stand. 'You're all very bright and breezy this morning.'

'Under the circumstances I thought we should be here early,' said Dave.

'I don't think Des is really going to notice how early you get in.' Alix sat down and switched on her monitors. 'And if all three of you arrive at the same time it isn't going to help anyone's chances!'

'Not those circumstances.' Dave looked at her in astonishment. 'The position, Alix. That's why we're early.'

It was her turn to look at him in astonishment. 'What position?'

'Didn't you check?' he asked. 'I thought you'd check. I expected you to call me last night.'

'What are you talking about?' She stared at him. 'What the hell is going on, Dave?'

'Why didn't you log in when you got home?' he asked. 'You always do.'

'My modem was down,' she replied slowly. 'Dave, what the fuck has happened?'

'We're short dollars,' he said.

'How many?'

'Five million.'

'Five million! What the hell are we doing short five bar? I thought I said that we didn't want to run anything. What kind of level, Dave?'

'Thirty-six,' he said.

She glanced at the screen in front of her. 'That's not so bad,' she said, relief in her voice. 'They're offered at forty.'

'They're offered at 1.2140,' said Dave. 'We're short at 1.2346.'

Alix looked at him in horror. What Dave had just told her meant that they were currently showing a loss of over eighty thousand dollars. Europa Bank had a policy of cutting any single position that showed a loss of over fifteen thousand.

'You're joking,' she said finally. 'How could we be? And how come we're still running it? Does Des know about it? Have you told him?'

'Jim Carroll of Harris rang late on Thursday evening,' said Dave. 'He wanted to buy dollars. The rate was fair at the time, we thought we could make a little out of it. The dollar was looking pretty shaky then and there seemed to be a few sellers around. So we decided to run it overnight. We left a stop-loss order with New York in case it spiked up. But it didn't. When we came in on Friday morning everything was fine although it was still around the same level. We were just talking about what we should do when it went ballistic. One minute it was trading at 1.2350, next minute it was 1.2250. The Latin American rumour had hit the market. Apparently there'd been some talk of it in Tokyo overnight but the euro hadn't really weakened off. Then the yen started to go. There were big flows back into the dollar and so when Europe opened everyone was a buyer.'

'And why didn't you cut it at 1.2250?' demanded Alix. 'At least that would have been only forty thousand down the toilet.'

Gavin looked uncomfortable. 'The charts looked so overbought,' he said. 'After all, Alix, it moved on a rumour. The dollar has been getting weaker for ages. There isn't any fundamental reason for it to be stronger now. The Fed will almost certainly cut rates again and . . .' He broke off as her eyes glinted green at him.

'What about our loss limits?' she asked.

'But it was wobbling at that level,' Gavin said. 'It really and truly looked as though sellers would come in again. You know how that can happen, Alix. So we waited. It began to move in our direction so we reckoned we could get the loss down to about twenty thousand. And then there was some talk about debt rescheduling in Latin America. Well, you know that can sometimes have a negative effect for the dollar. But it didn't this time. Everyone started buying it again.'

'And were you running this position when I called you on Friday?' She looked at Dave whose expression was anxious.

'Yes,' he said.

'And you didn't tell me about it?'

'What would have been the point?' he asked. 'There was nothing you could do, Alix. You could debate whether to run it or not. But you weren't going to be able to conjure a new rate out of nothing.'

'Dave, I am still responsible for everything that happens in this room. How dare you decide not to tell me about this! And how on earth do you expect me to explain away the fact that you've busted through our limits on a commercial trade? I'm surprised that Des and Pat haven't been stuck to the dealing room door like glue!'

'Des was away on Friday,' said Dave uncomfortably. 'And Pat left early. So they haven't seen the loss yet.'

She shook her head. 'I don't believe it,' she said. 'Look, guys, if this is some kind of wind-up tell me now. I can't hack the idea of this sort of loss. It's so fucking senseless.'

'It's not a wind-up,' said Gavin. 'Alix, I'll take responsibility. It was my fault. Dave wanted to cut it but I said no.'

'You said no!' She froze him with her glare. 'You! Who are you to tell him whether or not to cut a position? What kind of fantasy world do you think you're inhabiting? What books have you been reading, Gavin? *Rogue Trader? Bonfire of the Vanities?* You fucking idiot! And as for you,' she turned to Dave, 'what were you at? You're supposed to keep people within limits, not let them trash through them. You're supposed to monitor the risk we're running. I can't believe this, Dave. I really can't.'

'It's true all right,' said Jenny miserably. 'But it was one of those things that just happened, Alix. Even if you'd been here it would have happened.'

She switched her glare to Jenny. 'I don't think so.'

The three dealers exchanged uncomfortable glances while Alix stared at the monitor. At the European opening, the dollar was doing them some favours, drifting slightly against the euro. But would it continue to move that way? Alix bit her lip as she looked at the screen. If the Latin American story was nothing more than a rumour then it probably would. The market had a habit of getting into a frenzy about something for a couple of days and then forgetting all about it. Yet Alix was uncertain. She'd picked up a very strong vibe in Paris that there were some large buyers of dollars in the market. Maybe they had more information by now. She picked up the phone.

'Jean-Louis. *Bonjour*,' she said as the French dealer answered her.

'Hi, Alix. How are you this morning?'

'I'm OK,' she said. 'I wanted to ask you a question, Jean-Louis.'

'Sure.'

'Remember I talked to you on Thursday about the Latin American stories? About a possible default?'

'Of course.'

'What do you think of those rumours now?'

'I am not certain,' said Jean-Louis. 'I think there is something to them, Alix, because I was talking to our correspondent in Brazil and he said that a number of banks were quite worried. But there is nothing concrete and it could simply be that the country concerned will make a late interest payment.'

'Even that would have a knock-on effect on the markets,' said Alix.

'Oh, yes. But I do not think it is something on which I wish to wager the family jewels.' Jean-Louis laughed.

'I understand,' said Alix. 'Why do you think the dollar is weaker this morning? Is it because of American exposure to the region?'

'Just profit-taking,' he said. 'I think it will pick up again later. For sure, long term it will come down though.'

'OK, Jean-Louis. Thanks.' She hung up.

'What do you want to do?' asked Dave.

She sat back and stared at the ceiling. She could cut the position and book the biggest loss she'd ever made in her life. Des Coyle and Pat Enright would have seizures and would probably fire everyone in the dealing room. But she could argue that the loss was quantifiable and, set against the profits of the department over the whole year, not as bad as it first looked. She could run the position and hope that the dollar collapsed. It had already pulled back this morning and it could do more. If the rumours of a default were completely scotched, then it could get back to the level it was on Thursday. They might not have to book the loss at all – although it was already showing on their Friday night profit and loss account. Every currency position showed the rate at which the position had been taken and the rate at which the position could be immediately cut. When Des and Pat saw the P&L, they'd have hysterics.

She could add to the short position by selling even more dollars. That would alter the average rate at which they were short and, if the dollar did maintain its downward momentum, they could hit break-even more quickly. But would it continue to weaken? Would people want to buy euros instead of dollars? How comfortable would she feel about being even shorter and compounding the break in their limits? She would have to cut the position by the end of the day anyway. If not sooner.

She looked at the monitors again.

'Technically, it's really overbought,' said Gavin.

'You thought that on Thursday,' she said.

'I know. But it is.'

'Maybe the trend has changed.'

'Why?' asked Gavin. 'Things are exactly the same in the US as they were last week.'

But if there was a default there could be a so-called 'flight to quality'. Traders, especially in the US, would buy dollars and dollar assets instead of overseas assets. How worried would the New York guys be when they came in to work this week? She stared at the screens while she considered her options.

'Dave, I want you to buy back the fiver,' she said finally. 'And I want you to buy another five.'

'What?'

'You heard me.'

'You're going long?' he asked.

'Yes,' said Alix. 'And Jenny, buy five million of the US thirty-year bond too.'

Dave stared at her. 'You're taking the complete opposite view.'

'Yes,' she said.

'Alix, that's fucking ridiculous. Just because you think we were stupid doesn't mean you should be even more stupid!'

'I know,' she said.

'Don't you think we're putting all our eggs into one basket?' asked Jenny. 'After all, this could go horribly wrong.'

'I'll cut it if it's going horribly wrong,' said Alix. 'I won't let our losses go above a hundred and forty.'

Gavin winced. The amount of the loss, for a small bank like Europa, was horrendous.

'Do it,' said Alix.

They bought the dollars at 1.2150. Now, instead of wanting the dollar to weaken further, they needed it to go up in value. Because the rate was quoted in dollars per euro, they needed to see the price go down.

This meant that – when they eventually sold the dollars – they would get more euros in return. Jenny bought the bonds at a price of 106.25. They needed the bonds to go up in value too, though in this case they wanted to see the price go up. Alix was betting that the gains she would make on the bonds, plus the profit she hoped to make on the new dollar position would wipe out Friday's loss. It was a dangerous bet.

Alix glanced at her watch although there were clocks all around the dealing room. It was eight o'clock.

At a quarter past eight, Pat Enright phoned.

'What the hell is wrong with the P&L?' he asked. 'It's showing a loss of nearly a hundred and thirty thousand on the foreign exchange book, Alix.'

'I know,' she said.

'It's not a real loss, is it?' asked Pat disbelievingly.

'Not for long,' she said.

'But what happened?'

'Can I get back to you?'

'Alix, I need to know.'

'I'll call you back. I promise.'

Dave looked at her. 'Pat or Des?'

'Pat,' she said. 'Des would be in here by now.'

'Alix, I'm sorry,' he said.

She watched the numbers. The rate hovered between 1.2130 and 1.2160. The price on the bond was unchanged.

She rang Eileen Walsh. 'What time is Des due in?'

'Not until twelve,' said Eileen. 'He's at meetings until then. Do you need to contact him, Alix?'

'No. I'll catch him at twelve,' she said.

That was her cut-off, she decided. It had to come right by then otherwise she'd have to sell the extra five million dollars she'd just bought, sell the bonds and take the loss.

They'd pull the offer of the Paris job, she thought bleakly. Even if she made money out of this trade they'd decide that she couldn't keep control of people. It'd be like the head of derivatives in Paris who'd had to go because of the actions of his junior trader. She felt sick. Losses always made her feel sick. And this gamble that she was taking made her feel even sicker. Because it was a gamble. She was betting money on the fact that the tension she'd felt in the Paris dealing room when they'd been talking about Latin America was real, that the rumours were based on fact, that people would, as she hoped, flock to the dollar as a safe haven. And she could be completely and utterly wrong. It was different when she took a position because she really and truly believed in it. Those times, she felt in control of the situation, she felt that she'd covered all the bases. This was more like a smash-and-grab raid, hoping that she'd get lucky.

Better to be born lucky than smart, she reminded herself.

The phones were ringing now as their customers called to do trades. No new positions, she told the others, cut everything. We have to keep our eye on the ball.

The rate still hadn't moved very much by the time Matt Connery phoned.

'Europa Bank dealers,' said Gavin.

'Hi, Gavin, it's Matt.'

'How are things, Matt?'

Alix glanced up but Gavin wasn't looking at her mockingly as he usually did when Matt called.

'Sure, I can buy some dollars from you,' said Gavin. 'How many? Hold on a second.'

'Connery wants to sell us a million dollars,' he said.

'Quote him and if he deals cut it straightaway,' said Alix.

'I can do that for you at 1.2155,' said Gavin.

'Fine,' said Matt.

'OK.' Gavin gestured to the others that the trade had been completed. Jenny immediately got on the phone and sold the dollars at a profit of two hundred dollars.

'Another four hundred trades like that and we're out of the woods,' said Alix dryly.

'Alix, he wants a word with you,' said Gavin.

She clicked into the line. 'Hi.'

'I phoned at the weekend,' said Matt.

'I know,' she said. 'I got your message. And Sophia is fine, thank you.'

'I'm glad.'

'So am I. She's a good friend.'

'I was wondering about that dinner,' said Matt. 'I know we never seem to manage it but—'

'Any day this week,' said Alix.

'What?'

'Any day this week.'

'You've completely thrown me.' Matt laughed. 'I expected any day next month.'

'I'll be busy next month,' she said.

'Are you OK?' asked Matt. 'Only you sound odd today.'

'I'm fine,' she said, 'just a bit busy, that's all.'

'How about Friday?' suggested Matt.

'OK,' said Alix. 'Where?'

'I hadn't really thought about it. Anywhere you like.'

'The Tea Rooms at the Clarence,' she said. 'Eight o'clock.'

'When you decide to do something you don't hang around,' he said admiringly. 'The Tea Rooms at eight it is.'

'I'll see you then.'

'OK, Alix. Are you certain everything's all right?'

'Absolutely,' she said. 'Goodbye, Matt.' And she clicked out of the line.

'What's the story between you and him?' asked Gavin.

'Pardon?' Her tone was chilly.

'It's just that when he asks for you it's more of a personal thing.'

'It's not a personal thing,' said Alix.

'I thought . . .' But Gavin didn't finish the sentence.

∽

Pat Enright came into the dealing room at ten o'clock.

'Alix, what the fuck is the story about this loss?' he demanded.

'It's a loss,' she said. 'We're doing our best to turn it into a profit. If we haven't done it by today, we can't.'

'For Christ's sake, Alix! Why didn't you tell me about it? What happened? Do you know that you closed the positions over limit at the weekend? I'll have to report it to Des.'

'I know,' she said.

'What the hell was going on?' he asked.

'A misjudgement,' said Alix.

'Well, I don't think Des will be misjudging much when he sees this,' said Pat furiously. 'What are you trying to do, Alix? Close the place down?'

'Pat, if that's the most constructive thing you have to add to the day can you kindly fuck off out of here? We're busy.'

He stared at her for a moment then left the room, banging the door behind him.

She had a stitch in her side. Every time she took a breath it hurt.

At a quarter to twelve the exchange rate slithered in their direction. The dealers exchanged glances as they saw it move from 1.2135 to 1.2100. Alix flicked through the news screens to see if there was anything new about Latin America. There was nothing.

'Maybe we should just book the profit on this morning's fiver,' said Jenny.

'No point.' Alix wished she could breathe properly.

It edged their way a fraction more.

'Cut it,' said Gavin. 'At least this way we're getting the loss down.'

'Didn't I tell you before to run with your profits and cut

your losses?' said Alix. 'Something that you could have borne in mind last week.'

'I know,' he said.

'We'll wait,' said Alix.

She was doodling on the edge of the *Financial Times* when the headline flashed up. The only word she saw was default.

'Alix!' Dave's voice held suppressed excitement. 'It's happened. They've missed a payment. It's been confirmed.'

She looked at the clock. It was five to twelve. She looked at the screens. The dollar was now trading at 1.2050. Someone from the States was bound to come out with a comment about selling dollars to help the Latin Americans. But not yet, thought Alix. Not yet.

'Cut it now,' pleaded Gavin. 'We've clawed back half of it.'

'Where's the bond trading?' she asked Jenny.

'It's up,' Jenny replied. 'Screens are showing 106.75.'

Between the strength of the dollar and the profit on the bond they were now making over sixty-five thousand dollars. Not enough to wipe out Friday's losses, but they were back inside their limits. She could explain it away as some kind of a strategic bond/foreign exchange position. She could make them believe her. It would be the sensible thing to do.

The phone rang.

'Alix, get down here right away,' said Des Coyle.

'Shortly,' she said.

'Now,' said Des.

'I'm trying very hard to cut something here, Des. I can't.'

'Yes you can,' said Des.

'If you want to talk to me, come up here. But leave it for another fifteen minutes,' Alix told him. 'We're busy.'

'You could have gone down,' said Dave. 'We would have looked after it for you.'

She laughed shortly. 'Oh, yeah?'

'Alix, you know Des. He doesn't like that kind of treatment.'

'Tough,' said Alix.

The dollar was now trading at 1.2000.

She phoned Jean-Louis in Paris.

'It's crazy here,' he yelled. 'I can't talk to you, Alix.'

'Are there still buyers of dollars?' she asked.

'Yes,' cried Jean-Louis. 'It will stop. It will turn around. But I don't know when.'

She rubbed her forehead. Neither did she. And she knew it would stop. But not yet, she thought. Not yet.

Des pushed open the dealing-room door and stalked in. 'I want to talk to you, and I want to talk to you now,' he said.

'Des, I'll happily talk to you,' said Alix. 'But not now. I know there was an unauthorised breach of our limits. I know there is over a hundred-thousand-dollar loss sitting on the P&L account. I'm trying to get that back, and right now, I'm succeeding. So don't bug me, Des. Not now.'

He stared at her. Her jaw was set and determined, her eyes were flashing green and she had an intense look on her face that brooked no argument.

'When you've cut it,' said Des. 'In my office. As soon as.'

'Fine,' she said.

She cut the dollar position at 1.1890. At the current rate it left them with a foreign exchange profit of almost one hundred and seven thousand dollars on that day's deal, which she could offset against the previous loss. She cut the bond position at 106.90. Her gamble had paid off. They had made thirty-five thousand dollars on the bond. They had wiped out their losses and booked a net profit of over sixty thousand dollars. It was one of the best trades she'd ever done.

When the trades were booked she got up and walked out of the room. She went into the ladies' where she threw up. Then she went down to Des's office to explain.

Chapter 39

Her TV interview was shown that night. She'd completely forgotten about it until she picked up the paper and saw the programme listings. She sat in the apartment and watched herself talking about what it was like to be a successful woman and wondered if anybody watching would ever guess that Alix Callaghan had been sick that afternoon because a trade had gone right.

She'd gone down to Des and given him a highly edited version of events.

'They couldn't cut it,' she told him. 'The market moved so quickly they were just left completely exposed. It happens sometimes, Des, but not very often.'

'It never happens when you're there,' he said.

'One day it probably will.'

He'd ranted and raved at her. He was going to fire Dave. Fire Gavin. Probably fire Jenny. He wasn't letting her go to Paris, she was far too valuable where she was. He was cutting all their limits. There was to be no trading in future.

'Des, take some time out and think about it all,' said Alix. 'We'll sit down with Pat and talk about it later in the week.'

'I'll never understand dealers,' Des said. 'Never.'

They'd looked anxiously at her when she came back into the room.

'It's OK,' she told them. 'It's sorted.'

It wasn't completely sorted, of course. She knew that there'd be more questions, that procedures would change, that limits probably would be cut back. But Des wasn't going to fire anybody. Des still wasn't exactly sure who was to blame.

'Doesn't he want to talk to me?' asked Dave.

'Or me?' asked Gavin.

'Don't flatter yourselves.' Her smile was tired. 'He barely managed to talk to me!'

'Who does he blame?' asked Jenny.

'Nobody is being blamed,' said Alix. 'It was a dealing-room position. That's the end of it.'

'Alix, thanks.' Dave had looked at her in disbelief. 'Why didn't you just shaft us?'

'Why would I do that?' she'd asked dryly. 'I'm sure you'd never shaft me.'

They had looked at each other in silence and then the phones had begun to ring again.

∽

Wyn phoned her after the interview. 'Hey, Alix, you were great on TV. You looked fantastic. Very ballsy.'

'Wyn! I looked sophisticated,' she said.

'That too. Has Paul phoned?'

'No,' said Alix. 'He's not going to phone. Don't be silly.'

'He's a bastard not to call you,' said Wyn. 'The least he could do would be to ring on the pretext of saying you looked good tonight.'

561

'He's seen the interview already,' said Alix. 'And he already told me I looked good.'

'Do you know, I hardly recognised you as my sister,' Wyn mused. 'I look at this person and I think, I knew her when she had runny egg on her face.'

Alix laughed.

'Or, I knew her the day she was so scared about the school test that she wet her knickers!'

'Wyn!'

'Well, you did.'

'I had a kidney infection,' said Alix.

'Right,' said Wyn. 'I believe you.'

'I'm going now,' Alix told her. 'I can only take so many compliments in one night.'

'It was great,' said Wyn again. 'Oh, by the way, are you free to baby-sit on Friday night?'

'I'm sorry,' said Alix, 'but I can't, Wyn. I'll be out.'

'Some other work function,' said Wyn in disgust. 'Another Bankers' dinner?'

'No.' Alix smiled. 'Although I suppose it's kind of work. I'm going out with a client. But he wants to be my friend.'

'What?'

'That's what he's been telling me.'

'Alix, are you going out on a date?'

'I'm not sure,' said Alix. 'I'll tell you afterwards.'

'Oh, Alix.' Wyn sounded delighted. 'Can I ring Carrie and tell her?'

～

Alix left the office at half four on Friday. She went to the hairdresser's where she had her hair coloured and cut.

'Will you put it up for me?' she asked Tina.

'Oh, Alix, why don't you leave it down?' said the stylist. 'It's so nice that way.'

'I prefer it up,' said Alix.

'You're the customer.' Tina sighed and complied with Alix's request. 'But it makes you look so bloody severe!'

When Alix went home she took the Lancôme nail varnish from the bathroom shelf and painted her nails. She was surprised to find that her hand was shaking a little. She couldn't be nervous, could she? Not about dinner with a client. Even if he did want to be her friend.

She inspected the contents of her wardrobe and chose Jasper Conran again, but this time a bright fuschia-coloured dress that made her skin look darker and her eyes greener. She wore her plain gold earrings and gold chain. She sprayed herself with Dune.

She was ready almost an hour before she was due to meet him.

She arrived at the fashionable Clarence Hotel at exactly eight o'clock. Alix was incapable of being unpunctual even though she'd told herself that Matt would expect her to be at least five minutes late. But the taxi had arrived on time and even heavy traffic on Pearse Street hadn't delayed her.

He was already at the table. He was looking straight ahead of him, across the room. He didn't see her.

She walked over to the table. 'Hi,' she said.

He stood up. 'Hello, Alix.'

She shook his extended hand. It might be a date, she thought, but we're observing the niceties of our business relationship.

'You're on time,' said Matt.

She smiled. 'Of course.'

'I thought you would be,' he said. 'You look like the kind of person who'd be on time.'

They sat down opposite each other.

'I hope you haven't been waiting long,' said Alix.

'No.' Matt shook his head. 'I had a drink in the bar before I came in here. Regretfully there were no beautiful people or celebrities lounging around.'

'I wouldn't have taken you for a celebrity kind of guy.'

'Oh, I don't know.' He grinned at her. 'The last time I was here I almost bumped into Eva Herzogova. Or Helena Christiansen. One of them anyway.'

'You didn't get her number?'

'Nope.' He grinned again. 'But I told myself I'd have better luck next time.' He opened the menu in front of him. 'Do you want to get the ordering out of the way? Then we can chat.'

'Sure,' she said. Chat about what? The way he said it made it sound like an interview.

She skimmed through the menu. 'Goat's cheese and risotto,' she said.

'Wine?' he asked.

'Whatever you like.'

He ordered a Soave. 'Since you're having risotto,' he said. 'Besides, I like Italian white.'

'So do I,' said Alix.

'You know, I can't believe we're actually here having dinner. It seems like months since I asked you.'

'I'm so much in demand!' She laughed.

'I'm not surprised,' said Matt.

She smiled slightly and fiddled with her napkin.

'How was business this week?' he asked.

She groaned. 'Hectic.'

'The Latin America debt problem certainly gave the dollar a boost. Great for me because we were long from a Californian deal we'd just completed. Although I did sell some to you guys a bit too early. I hope you made money out of it!'

She wasn't going to tell him about Europa Bank's dollar trade. Or about getting sick afterwards. 'It was a crazy day,' she said. 'We made money overall. But it wasn't easy.' She felt her stomach churn at the memory of sitting in Des Coyle's office and trying to explain it to him without giving him too much information.

'I'd expect nothing less than that you made money,' said Matt.

'It's my job.'

'You love it, don't you?'

She shrugged. 'I suppose I do. It's all I ever wanted.'

He looked at her thoughtfully. 'I watched you on TV,' he said. 'That was the impression you gave.'

'It must be right.'

'What about your boyfriend?' asked Matt. 'What did he think?'

The waiter appeared with their starters before she could answer. Matt cursed the other man for his sense of timing. Now Alix could change the subject. And he really wanted to know about her occasional boyfriend.

But, to his surprise, she answered him.

'Paul set up the interview,' she said. 'He works in RTÉ. I don't see him any more.'

'I'm sorry,' said Matt.

'Are you?' She looked at him questioningly. 'Given that you're taking me out to a "let's be friends" dinner, I thought you'd be pissed at me if you thought I was still seeing some-one else.'

He laughed. 'I was trying to appear caring and thought-ful.'

'Don't,' said Alix. 'It's not necessary.'

'But I am caring and thoughtful,' protested Matt. 'I like to think so anyway!'

'What about you?' asked Alix. 'What about the women in your life?'

'Oh, not that many,' he said dismissively. 'I don't have time, to tell you the truth. I have a lot of female friends, but that's all.'

She felt a frisson of disappointment. She was obviously to be another in a line of women friends that he could take out whenever he needed someone. Sitting here opposite him she'd wondered if there could be something more. He was attractive, there was no doubt about that. She liked the way his blue eyes twinkled at her. She liked his broad shoulders, his apparently well-built body and the way he seemed to glow with health and vitality. She'd let her mind imagine later in the evening, when he'd try to kiss her, and it hadn't been an altogether unpleasant thought. But now he was implying that he wanted a platonic kind of relationship. She sighed. She didn't even have time for a platonic relationship with him. Soon she'd be in Paris with a whole new circle of people to get to know. Despite Des's misgivings about letting her go in the wake of the dollar debacle, he'd managed to get over things enough to agree that she should go to Paris as planned and that Dave would take over her job.

'You OK?' he asked.

'Sure. Why?'

'You were thinking of something and it didn't seem to be very pleasant.'

'Work,' she said.

He sighed. 'I was hoping that, after our initial obligatory conversation about the markets, we could forget about work!'

'OK.' She smiled. 'No work talk.'

They looked at each other in silence for almost a minute and then both of them began to laugh.

'Are we that boring that we don't have anything else to talk about?' she asked.

'Tell me about that interview,' said Matt. 'What was it like? You seemed so self-confident but it must have been quite nerve-wracking.'

She shrugged. 'Not really. You just talk to the person in front of you. You don't think about anything else.'

'You gave him a run for his money.' Matt laughed. 'I could hear the fear in his voice when he was asking some of those questions.'

'That wasn't fear.' Alix made a face. 'He was trying to taunt me. You didn't see his face! He wanted something controversial about working women and kids and all that sort of thing.'

'But you must think about it,' said Matt. 'Having a family.'

Alix smoothed her hair. 'Sometimes.'

'And?'

'And what?'

'Do you think there'll come a time when you want to chuck it all in and stay at home?'

'Perhaps,' she said, 'but it hasn't happened yet.'

'You obviously didn't want to do that with the RTÉ man.'

'No.'

'Was that what went wrong?'

'It was more than that,' said Alix slowly. 'I cared about him a lot, but not enough, it seemed.'

Their main courses arrived and Alix busied herself with black pepper and Parmesan cheese.

'So what's your favourite city?' Matt watched her as she laced her dinner with pepper. He could see that she didn't want to talk about Paul Hunter. 'After all, you must have travelled a lot.'

'Not as much as you,' she told him. 'I don't have a favourite.'

'What about Paris?' he asked. 'You must spend a lot of time there.'

'I never get to see much of it,' she said ruefully. 'I always seem to be rushing from hotel to bank and back again. Do you know,' she looked at him guiltily, 'I've never even been in the Louvre?'

'Oh dear,' he said. 'What about the Arc de Triomphe?'

'Can you get inside that?' she asked in surprise.

'What cultural things have you done there?' he asked.

'Bought lots of clothes,' she said positively. 'Very, very essential when you're in Paris!'

They laughed and this time the laughter was easier, more natural. Matt topped up her glass with wine.

'I like the way you dress,' he said. 'You always look very chic.'

'Thank you. But you haven't seen me outside working hours.'

'This is outside working hours.'

'You know what I mean. Flopping around in jeans and a T-shirt.'

'They're probably designer jeans,' he said.

She grinned. 'You might be right.'

She was enjoying herself. He was easy to talk to. Whenever he sensed that she was uncomfortable with a topic he immediately began to talk about something else. He told her about Malaysia and California and his trips to Tokyo. He related stories about long-distance flights where he was terrified to get out of the seat in case something awful happened while he wasn't strapped in. He told her how he'd been poached from another company by Anatronics and how it had been the best move of his career.

'But I don't like the travelling,' he said. 'I'd prefer to stay in one place for more than a couple of weeks. And that's not only because of the flying paranoia.'

'I like travelling,' said Alix. She finished her coffee and glanced at her watch. It was almost eleven. She couldn't believe that they'd been here for three hours! The time had raced by.

'Shall we go?' Matt signalled for the bill.

'That was really nice,' said Alix. 'Thank you.'

'My pleasure,' said Matt.

They walked outside. A cold wind blew along the street and Alix shivered. The jacket she was wearing was far too light for the time of year.

'Would you like a nightcap?' asked Matt.

She meant to say no but she said yes.

They pushed their way through the throng in Thomas Read's.

'This is crazy!' Matt had to shout above the music and the buzz of conversation.

'But lively,' she mouthed back at him.

He nodded. They were squashed against the wall, almost unable to move because the pub was so full.

'Do you come here often?' cried Matt.

'What?'

'Is this one of your haunts?'

'Are you mad?' she asked. 'This is far too trendy for me.'

'Would you like to go?'

She shrugged.

'Come on.' He drained his glass. 'It's impossible to talk here.'

She followed him outside again.

'I guess I'd better head home,' she said.

'OK,' said Matt. 'Do you want me to come with you? See you safely inside? Or would you prefer if I left you now?'

'You don't have to come back with me,' she said. She looked at him carefully. 'But you're welcome to come. Perhaps have coffee. Or a drink.'

'OK,' said Matt.

They sat in the taxi in silence. She wanted him to come to the apartment with her but she didn't know what she wanted when they got there. She still only had vague memories of the night he'd brought her home before. She knew that he'd left almost as soon as he'd drunk his coffee. She wondered if he'd do the same this time. If she wanted him to do the same this time.

'Come in,' she said as she unlocked the door.

He followed her inside and took off his leather jacket which he hung over the back of a chair.

'There's a coat stand over there,' said Alix.

He said nothing but hung the jacket up.

'I'm sorry,' she said.

'Sorry?'

'It's just that living on my own now I've got fussy. I don't hang things over chairs and I put things away – it's stupid.'

'It's OK,' said Matt. 'I'm a tidy person myself. I didn't see the coat stand.'

'Thank you,' she said.

'I'm telling you the truth,' said Matt. 'Not just trying to make you feel good.'

She smiled. 'Would you like coffee? Or a drink?'

'Whatever.'

'I'm going to have a drink,' she said. 'I try not to drink coffee too late because I don't sleep.' She walked over to one of the pale units and took out a bottle of Bacardi Spice. 'What will you have?'

'Beer?' he asked.

'In the fridge,' she said. 'I'll get it in a second. Or you can help yourself if you like.'

'I'll do it.' He went into the tiny kitchen and opened the fridge. She liked yoghurt and cheese and tomatoes, he decided, as he looked at the contents. And lots of juices. And chocolate – there was a huge bar of Cadbury's on the top shelf. But she seemed to like beer more than anything else – there were a dozen bottles of Miller in the fridge. And a mixture of Californian Chardonnay and Italian white wines.

'Expecting to be snowed in?' he asked as he walked back to the living room.

'Pardon?' She was sitting on the sofa, her legs tucked beneath her.

'Lots of beer. And wine.' He sat down beside her.

She laughed. 'I know. My sister goes mad when she comes to see me. I'm a terrible shopper. I buy all the wrong things but I always seem to have loads of beer and wine. And I don't drink all that much. Honestly.'

'Is she your younger or your older sister?' asked Matt.

'Wyn's nearly five years older than me,' said Alix. 'She tries to mother me sometimes. That's why she lectures me about the contents of my fridge.'

'Do you have any other brothers or sisters?'

Alix paused with the glass halfway to her lips. She could see the picture of Kate, hair blowing in the wind, sitting on the car. She felt as though someone had hit her in the stomach. She shivered.

'Alix?' He looked at her in surprise. The expression on her face was unreadable. 'Are you all right?' She looked frozen, he thought. Terrified.

'Excuse me!' She put the glass on the table and almost ran into the bathroom.

Matt stared after her in amazement. What had he said to upset her? Asking about her family? Surely not. Unless there'd been some terrible tragedy. Oh shit, he thought helplessly, I've ruined it now. Maybe she had a brother or a sister who got killed or something and I've reminded her about it. You idiot, Connery. It was going so well!

Alix sat on the edge of the bath and tried to breathe evenly. She'd been about to say no, only one sister, when she'd thought of Kate. And suddenly she hadn't been able to say it. She hadn't been able to ignore the fact that Kate was a real, living person. With a baby. And a husband. And a father who was her father too.

This is crazy, she thought, as her eyes filled with tears. I'm sitting here crying! What's there to cry over?

'Alix?' Matt tapped at the bathroom door. 'Are you OK?'

'Yes,' she said shakily. 'I'm fine.'

'Are you sure?'

'I'll be out in a second.' She checked her face in the mirror and thanked God for waterproof mascara.

'Sorry about that.' She smiled wanly at him as she sat down again.

'Did I say something?' he asked.

Oh God, she thought, I want to cry again. I'm fine. She pressed her fingers against the bridge of her nose.

'Alix, if there's something wrong, please tell me.' Matt moved closer to her. 'I know I'm almost a complete stranger but if I can help at all . . .' His voice trailed off.

She shook her head wordlessly. Why was she behaving like this? She never behaved like this in front of other people. Never. She was a strong person. She didn't need blokes offering to be helpful. She didn't need to talk things through with anybody. Least of all someone she hardly even knew.

'I have a sister,' said Matt. 'Her name is Kathryn. We call her Kats.'

'I thought I had only one sister,' said Alix. 'I thought there was only Wyn. But – I have another sister. A half-sister. I didn't know about her until recently.'

'Alix.' He reached out and took her hands. 'How did you find out?'

'She's my father's child,' said Alix. 'Well, not a child now, she's twenty-nine.'

'And you never knew? You'd no idea?'

She shook her head.

'Your father kept it a secret?'

'He left us,' said Alix tightly. 'When I was three.'

Matt kept her hands enclosed in his. Don't say anything, he told himself. Keep quiet. Let her talk if she wants to.

'He went to the States,' Alix continued. 'He had a girlfriend

573

and she got pregnant and he left Carrie and Wyn and me and he went to the States with her.'

Matt put his arm round her.

'I only found out a couple of months ago. We didn't hear from him. Apparently he'd tried to keep in touch but Carrie – that's my mother – she didn't want him to. And so he stopped trying.'

He held her closely.

'Then he came back.' She was silent.

'And what was it like,' asked Matt finally, 'when you met him?'

'I didn't meet him,' she said fiercely. 'I couldn't meet him. He'd left us. For her. And now he wants Carrie to divorce him so that he can marry her. Because Kate has had a baby.'

'Did he want to meet you?'

'He said so. He came to the office one day. But I couldn't see him. I really couldn't.' She pushed her fingers through her hair and it sprang loose from its clip and tumbled around her face.

'And do you wish you had?' asked Matt.

She looked up at him and smiled slightly. 'I don't know. Part of me. And another part of me doesn't care.'

He pushed her hair out of her eyes. He knew that it wasn't a great time to feel incredibly turned on but he couldn't help it. She was so beautiful and so strong and now, suddenly, so vulnerable. And he desperately wanted to take her to bed.

'I'm sorry.' She pulled away from him. 'I don't know why all this just came spilling out. I don't usually behave like this. I'm an idiot.'

'It's OK,' he said.

'Just forget about it. It's probably the wine and the Bacardi.'

'I don't want to forget about it,' said Matt. 'I'm glad you felt you could tell me.'

Why had she told him? She wished she knew. She'd had no intention of telling anyone about John or Kate or Imogen. She hardly believed in them herself! But now, by spilling out her guts to Matt Connery, she'd made them real. She could imagine Kate sliding off the bonnet of the car and kissing the man who'd taken the photograph. John Callaghan. And maybe linking her arm with his and walking into the house where Imogen was making tea. The pictures flooded into her mind. They were real people. With real lives. And now they were part of her life.

'You were so nice to me tonight,' she told Matt. 'It was a lovely evening. I'm sorry for messing it up.'

'You didn't,' he said.

'You'll never want to deal with us again,' said Alix. 'Knowing that there's a complete flake in the dealing room.'

'Don't be ridiculous,' said Matt.

She sighed and began to twist her hair into a knot at the back of her head.

'Do you want me to go?' asked Matt as he watched her.

'Do you want to go?'

'Alix, I know you're upset and maybe not thinking straight right now. It's not a fair question to ask.'

She looked at him questioningly.

'Of course I don't want to go,' he told her. 'I want to stay. I want to put my arms round you and hold on to you and comfort you and I really, really want to stay.'

'Do you?'

'Don't make me say it again.'

She reached out for him. 'Is this a needy, take-advantage-of kind of situation?'

'Well, yes,' he said. 'That's why I probably should go.'

'I want you to stay,' she told him. 'I want you to take advantage of me.'

'Which is worse?' She was in his arms now, her head on his shoulders, her hair falling loose again. 'Doing something I'd regret or not doing something I'd regret?'

'Matt.' She looked at him. 'No regrets. Just something we both want to do.'

'Oh, God,' he said as she undid the buttons of his shirt. 'OK, Alix. No regrets.'

Chapter 40

S he sat and stared across the room. The words painted on the wall were directly opposite her desk. *'De l'audace, encore de l'audace, et toujours de l'audace!'* During the day, when she was busy, she never noticed them. But now, when almost everyone had gone home, she couldn't help but be aware of them. And be reminded of Sabine. If it hadn't been for Sabine, thought Alix, she might be in Dublin tonight, curled up beside Paul as she had been last Christmas when everything had seemed so settled and so secure.

She had finally rung Paul. It had taken three phone calls before he eventually spoke to her.

'I've been busy,' he said defensively. 'I meant to call you, Alix. Really I did.'

'No you didn't,' she said. 'What would you say if I told you that I was pregnant?'

'What!'

'That's what you'd say?'

'Alix, you can't be,' he said urgently. 'I mean, I thought, I assumed—'

'Keep your cool,' she said. 'I'm not. I just wondered what your reaction would have been.'

'If that was a joke it wasn't very funny,' snapped Paul.

'It wasn't meant to be,' said Alix. 'You could've rung me. Let me know that our night of passion was a horrible mistake.'

'It was a mistake,' admitted Paul. 'It wasn't horrible, though, Alix. It was great. But it was wrong. And I'm sorry.'

'So am I,' said Alix. 'I could have stopped you and I didn't. And the reason I'm ringing, Paul, is to wish you luck with Sabine and tell you that I'll be starting my job in Paris next week.'

'I hope it works out for you,' he told her. 'I really do, Alix. I care about you a lot.'

'Thanks,' she said. 'And I care about you too, Paul. I hope you have lots of lovely babies.'

It had been easier than she thought to finally get him out of her head, out of her heart and out of her life. Even though the quotations still got to her.

Matt Connery had been a different story. Making love to Matt Connery had been almost perfect. He'd been a considerate lover, finding out what she liked and what she didn't, kissing her gently and then more urgently, being both aggressive and tender and making her body tingle with desire. And then, the next morning, he'd brought her a cup of coffee while she lay between waking and sleeping, still languid with satisfaction.

'There wasn't much milk,' he told her as he handed her the cup.

'There never is.' She sipped it cautiously.

'You did say you were a terrible shopper.'

'Especially milk.' She smiled at him.

'Alix?'

'Yes?'

'Last night.'

She looked at him warily.

'It was wonderful.'

She nodded. He was right. It had been fantastic.

'We seemed to – it worked, didn't it?'

'I'm glad you thought so.'

'You didn't?' He looked at her anxiously.

'It's not that.' She placed the cup on the bedside locker and sat up properly.

'What then?'

'It's simply – I was offered a job in Europa Bank, Paris. I accepted. I start in a few weeks' time.'

He stared at her. 'So what was last night all about?'

'No regrets,' she told him. 'That's what we agreed, wasn't it?'

'Yes,' he said. 'Of course. No regrets.' He walked over to the bedroom window and looked out.

'It was great,' said Alix. 'Really it was, Matt. And I like you a lot. It's just that – what would be the point? You're committed to your career. So am I. When you do meet someone that you're interested in you'll want a woman that supports you and looks after you and has babies for you. And I don't think I'll ever be that sort of person.'

'How do you know what sort of person I want?' he asked.

'Because, in the end, that's what you all want,' she told her. 'It's what Paul wanted despite the fact that he used to say kids were messy little beggars and he couldn't stand them. Despite the fact that he used to tell me he'd always be there for me. It's even what my father wanted. He walked out on a family, but he walked right back into another one! It wouldn't be any different with you, Matt. I know it wouldn't. I thought about it last night while you were asleep.' She'd thought about it as she'd looked at him and wished that she was a different kind of person or he was a different kind of person and she knew that it would never work.

'You made all these decisions without talking to me,' said Matt.

'We could go out some more and then it'd be harder because I'd care about you more,' said Alix. 'But I've got to take this job and you've got to get on with traipsing between Tokyo and the States and Ireland.' She shrugged. 'We'd tell ourselves everything would be fine but it wouldn't be.'

'I see.' Matt turned towards her and she'd never seen his eyes look so hard. 'I'm glad we had last night. I don't have any regrets.' He smiled slightly then kissed her on the forehead. 'Thanks, Alix. I'm sure I'll be talking to you before you go to Paris.'

And he left.

But he didn't talk to her before she went. Gavin had talked to him. Gavin had done three profitable trades with Anatronics and had made money out of a five-year swap for them too.

'I really feel as though I'm getting to grips with that account,' he told Alix on her last day. 'It took a while – I thought that you were going to mess me up with it, Alix. Sorry.'

'I told you, I wouldn't knowingly mess any of you up.'

'You got us out of a few in our time,' said Dave. 'Especially the dollar trade. I only wish I could tell people about it.'

'For God's sake don't!' she exclaimed. 'You'd have us in all sorts of trouble.'

'I think Des has forgiven us,' Dave said.

'He might have got over it,' warned Alix, 'but he'll never forget, Dave. So take it easy.'

'I will,' said Dave. 'I promise.'

'I'll miss you,' said Jenny as they had a drink in O'Reilly's together. 'You were great to work for.'

'I'm sorry I didn't do more for you,' said Alix. 'I've often wondered how right you were when you accused me of not giving you enough respect, Jenny. Maybe it was more true than I wanted to believe.'

'I don't care,' Jenny told her. 'You came through for us when you had to and that's good enough for me. Besides,' she grinned, 'Dave told me that I'll be the senior dealer, not Donnelly.'

'I'm glad,' Alix said. 'It's the right decision.'

It had seemed strange to walk down the steps for the last time. Not the last time, she'd told herself as she clamped down on the sentimentality. She'd be back. She'd be back when she was head of European trading. Which was Guy's job. She was pretty sure that one day she'd get Guy's job.

'Alix!' Guy's voice broke through her memories. 'I thought you were going home today? For Christmas?'

'Yes.' She stood up. 'I was daydreaming.'

He grinned. 'Thinking of how good it's been since you came?'

She grimaced. There had been a number of good days and one truly awful one when swaps had traded in the complete opposite direction to her expectations. She'd booked a loss and had been annoyed with herself.

'I think it's working out well,' said Guy. 'You get on with everyone. You're cut out for this job, Alix.'

'*Merci beaucoup*,' she said.

'Have a good time in Dublin,' he told her. 'We'll see you on the thirtieth. But Alix, if you want to take an extra day off, it's OK. For you we can wait until the New Year if you prefer.'

'Not at all,' she said briskly. 'I'll be back, Guy. I hate the end of the year anyway. I'd much prefer to be working.'

She picked up her bag and her case and took the lift to the ground floor. It seemed slightly crazy to be going home so soon after she'd arrived but Carrie had been insistent that she come back for Christmas and she had agreed. Besides, she thought, Christmas on her own in Paris was taking self-sufficiency a little too far.

~

The apartment was warm. Wyn had been in earlier in the day and had turned on the central heating. She'd also left some milk in the fridge and bread in the bread bin. Alix smiled as she read her sister's note: 'Make yourself some coffee with milk! See you on Christmas Day. Hope you have lots of paracetamol – the kids go manic at this time of year. Give Carrie a ring when you get in. Love, Wyn.'

She looked at her watch. It was nearly eight o'clock. She'd call Carrie soon but now she wanted to sit in the silence of her own apartment and appreciate her own things around her.

The apartment in Paris was fine. Small, but with everything she needed, and in a nice location near Montmartre. It wasn't home yet though, and she had missed this place. She'd rent it out next year, she thought as she poured herself a drink. Make it pay its way.

She woke up early the next morning, wide-awake and with a feeling of anticipation. As a child she'd always loved Christmas Eve. She'd loved the thrill of the preparations, the hope of getting the things she'd asked for and the pervading smell of Carrie's attempts at home cooking that wafted around the house. It was the same every year and Alix had liked the sameness of it all.

Carrie had booked the Peacock Alley for dinner. Since they'd all be at Wyn and Terry's for Christmas Day, Carrie had yearned for some quiet sophistication on Christmas Eve and Alix had been only too pleased to fall in with her mother's plans. Last year she'd gone to the pub with the other dealers and had been collected by Paul at nine o'clock. He'd been out with friends too and it hadn't bothered him that she'd been drunk. They'd bought Chinese takeaway and had spent the evening at home eating prawn crackers and (in Alix's case) drinking the bottle of port that one of her clients had given her.

She met her mother at the restaurant. Carrie looked wonderful, thought Alix. She was dressed in a green velvet dress and wore emerald jewellery and looked anything but a mother of two grown-up girls.

'Hi, Carrie!' She kissed her mother and sat at the table. 'Sorry I'm late. Traffic was terrible.'

'You're on time.' Carrie looked at her watch.

'It's twenty-five to nine,' Alix objected. 'You said half eight.'

Carrie laughed. 'Five minutes give or take is on time.' She looked at her daughter critically. 'You're looking well, Alix. How's the job?'

'It's fine.' Alix unfolded her napkin. 'It takes a bit of getting used to, of course. And the dealing room is so big compared with Europa Dublin. But I think I'm settling in OK.'

'Homesick?' asked Carrie.

'A little,' Alix admitted. 'But I'll get out a bit more in the New Year and organise a social life for myself. Until now it's all been settling in, that sort of thing.'

'And your new boss – Guy. Is he OK to work for?'

'Actually, that's the best part,' said Alix. 'When I was in Dublin he was always needling me. But he's a lot more professional in Paris. I'm getting on much better with him than I expected.'

'Is he married?' asked Carrie.

'Really, Carrie!' Alix looked at her in annoyance. 'Why do you want to know that?'

'I wondered if there would be a new man for you,' said Carrie. 'It's a romantic city, after all, isn't it?'

'It might be,' said Alix, 'but Guy Decourcelle *is* married with a couple of kids and although he tried to haul me off to bed with him a few times in the past, I have no intention of getting involved with him.'

'I see,' said Carrie.

There was an awkward silence and they were rescued by the waiter taking their order.

'Are you looking forward to tomorrow?' asked Carrie.

Alix made a face at her. 'Christmas *chez* Terry and Wyn and two hyperactive children? Only if they have a large bottle of vodka stored somewhere.'

Carrie laughed. 'It's only once a year.'

'Thank God,' said Alix. 'But those kids are a handful all year round. I don't know how she copes.'

'You do,' said Carrie. 'When you have children, you just do.'

'Not something that'll ever bother me.'

'Alix, there's something we have to discuss,' said Carrie.

Alix looked at her mother warily. 'Not more skeletons tumbling out of the family closet?'

'Don't be ridiculous,' said Carrie.

Alix shrugged. 'How am I to know? You kept enough stuff from us before.'

'I thought I was doing things for the best.' Carrie bit her lip. 'It's not easy to get it right, Alix. You think you've made the right decision and then, years later, you question it.'

'No point,' said Alix. 'What's done is done.'

'Alix, John and Imogen are in Dublin again.'

'Oh, for heaven's sake!' Alix stared at her. 'What's wrong with their bright, exciting, full-of-richness life in the States? What the hell are they doing here?'

'Kate and Jack wanted to come over for Christmas. John managed to fire them with enthusiasm and, of course, Imogen has kept in touch with her own family. So they're here.'

'Where?' Alix looked around as though they would walk by at any moment.

'They're staying here, in the Fitzwilliam Hotel. Kate and Jack and Imogen are having dinner with Imogen's brother tonight.'

'How nice,' said Alix.

'John didn't go.'

'Why? Don't they approve of him?'

'He knew that we were having dinner together, Alix. He wanted to meet you.'

Alix stared out of the window at the hustle and bustle of Christmas Eve in the city. She was angry with Carrie for telling her this, for meeting her under false pretences.

The waiter put bowls of pumpkin soup in front of them.

'Alix, I really think you should meet him. Bury the past.'

'I suppose you're going to say that it's Christmas and I should be in a loving and family-oriented mood,' said Alix sourly.

'I just think that you're carrying a heap of bitterness inside,' said Carrie. 'And meeting him would help.'

'I have nothing inside,' said Alix. 'I don't give a fuck about him one way or the other, Carrie. I know you think that I should, but I don't. I don't feel bitter. I don't feel anything.'

'What makes you feel, Alix? What gets through to you?'

Alix stared at Carrie. 'Lots of things.'

'But John doesn't make you feel anything?'

'Only pissed off,' said Alix. 'Who does he think that he is, coming over here, trying to worm his way back into our lives?'

'He loves you,' said Carrie.

'Oh, don't be absolutely ridiculous.' Alix stirred her soup angrily. 'He loves himself. He just wants to make everything OK for himself.'

'It's not like that,' said Carrie.

'Yes it is,' snapped Alix.

Carrie sighed. She was hopeless at this kind of thing, she thought. Wyn had encouraged her to meet Alix and try and persuade her once again to see John. Wyn had suggested that in the more impersonal atmosphere of the restaurant in the same building where John was staying, Alix might be more inclined to meet him and less defensive about it. But, Carrie realised, they'd underestimated Alix.

Alix stared at the bowl of soup and raged inside. She was fed up with this war of attrition, of all of them trying to make her do things she didn't want to do. They kept going on about forgiveness as though it would make any difference to her life. They watched too much Oprah and read too many self-help books.

Carrie couldn't think of anything to say. She should have waited until after the meal, she realised. Now, Alix would sit in quiet fury and push her food around her plate without eating it.

Alix felt a little sorry for her mother. It hadn't been easy for Carrie, she knew that. And tonight had probably been the product of some ridiculous conversation with Wyn who had probably decided that she might feel differently simply because it was Christmas.

She put down her spoon. She wasn't hungry.

'All right,' she said.

'All right what?' Carrie looked up at her.

'If it'll make you feel better, Carrie, I'll meet him.'

'You will?' Carrie pushed her bowl away. 'When?'

'Now,' said Alix. She stood up. 'I'm not hungry. He's here, isn't he? Let's get the whole thing over and done with.'

'Are you sure?' Carrie stared at her in amazement.

'Look, I don't want to spend every time I meet you skirting around this subject,' said Alix. 'I'll meet him, say hello and goodbye and that'll be the end of it. OK?'

'Yes,' said Carrie. 'OK.' She signalled for the waiter who nearly had a fit when he realised that they were leaving. Carrie signed a Visa chit for the uneaten meal and they walked down to the hotel foyer.

I'm out of my mind, thought Alix as she stood by the wall. I've let them manipulate me.

'He'll be here soon,' said Carrie. 'I'll wait for you in the bar.'

'Fine.'

Alix hoped that she looked OK. She was wearing a red woollen dress by Joseph and black shoes with a low heel because she hadn't wanted to tower over her mother. She wished that she was wearing a suit. She always felt confident in a suit.

'Hello, Alix.'

They stared at each other for a moment. He was taller than she'd expected and looked younger. His grey hair was brushed back from his forehead and his eyes, grey-green, looked anxiously at her. He reminded her of Wyn whenever her sister wanted to tell her something that she might not want to hear.

'Hello,' she said.

'I'm glad you decided to meet me.' He smiled at her.

'It's for Carrie's sake, not mine,' said Alix.

'I don't care whose sake it's for,' said John Callaghan. 'I've missed you. I'm sorry.'

She wasn't going to give in, she thought. She wasn't going to feel emotional about this. She wasn't going to let him think that she cared one way or the other.

But when he held out his hand to her, she grasped it and, quite suddenly, his arms were round her, hugging her fiercely while he said 'I'm sorry' over and over again. And she was whispering 'It's OK, it's OK' while the tears slid down her cheeks.

Chapter 41

'When will you be back again?' asked Wyn as she sat in Alix's apartment and watched her pack.

'I'm not sure.' Alix tugged at the zip of her case. 'Depends on how busy we are. You never know, though. I might get a business trip back soon.' She hauled the case off her bed. 'You should come over and visit me, Wyn. I'm sure you'd love it. Only the apartment is so tiny there wouldn't be room for all your shopping!'

Wyn laughed. 'Will you move?'

'Oh, yes,' said Alix. 'It's just temporary. But Wyn, please get me some nice tenants for this place. I don't like to think that it'll fall into the wrong hands.'

'Don't worry,' said Wyn. 'I'll look after things for you.'

The buzzer sounded.

'That's my cab,' said Alix. She kissed her sister on the cheek. 'Thanks for everything.'

'Alix?'

'Yes?'

'Are you glad you met him?'

Alix was silent for a moment. She wasn't sure that glad was the right word. When John had hugged her it had been the strangest feeling of her life. She'd often heard people talking about a weight being lifted from them, and that was exactly how she had felt. Of course, afterwards, their conversation had been stilted and awkward, with neither of them sure of what they wanted to say; yet Alix had felt more at ease with herself than she ever had before. She still hadn't got used to the feeling.

'I suppose I am,' she said. 'But I don't think I'll ever feel close to him.'

'That doesn't matter.' Wyn picked up the case. 'You've taken the first step. I'll lock up afterwards. You go ahead.'

'OK,' said Alix. 'I'll give you a call on New Year's Eve. I'm sorry I can't be here, but I promised to be back in Paris. Guy has invited me to a party so I won't be sitting at home moping. You don't have to worry, Wyn.'

'I'm your older sister. It's my job to worry,' said Wyn.

Alix hugged her and they went out to the cab.

Wyn waved to her until the taxi was out of sight then she went back up to the apartment. It was a lovely apartment, she thought. She could understand why Alix liked it so much. She tried to imagine Nessa and Aoife running around in it but failed miserably. It was very peaceful, she thought. She made herself a cup of coffee and sat down. Ten minutes, she told herself, and then she'd go back to the madhouse. But she didn't get as far as drinking the coffee. In the silence and the peace of the apartment she closed her eyes and fell asleep.

⮂

The phone rang and Wyn jumped into wakefulness.

'Hello?'

'Alix?'

'No, this is Wyn.'

'Oh, Wyn. Her sister.'

'Yes. Can I help?'

'I was looking for Alix.'

'You've missed her,' said Wyn. 'Sorry.'

'Oh. Will she be back soon?'

'No,' Wyn said. 'She's gone back to Paris.'

'Bloody hell! Already?'

'Can I take a message or anything? Who's calling?'

'I'm a – friend, I suppose.'

'Which friend?'

'My name is Matt.'

'Are you the date?' asked Wyn.

'Pardon?'

'The date? Alix told me that she was meeting a client a while ago and it was a date.'

'Did she?'

'Well, I'm not sure how certain she was about it being a date. She said you wanted to be friends. Was that you?'

Matt sighed. 'Yes. That was me.'

'But it didn't work out?'

'Not the way I'd hoped,' said Matt. 'But I want to change all that. I tried to meet her in Paris.'

'Oh.' Wyn clutched the phone more tightly. 'Where are you now?'

'I'm in Dublin,' said Matt. 'They told me she was in Dublin for Christmas. I rang a few times but she was never at home and she didn't leave her damn machine on.'

'I don't suppose she was expecting people to phone,' said Wyn.

'I called round on Christmas Eve but she wasn't there.'

'She was with our parents,' said Wyn.

'Parents?' said Matt. 'Both of them?'

'Yes.'

'You mean, she's met her father?'

'What do you know about it?' asked Wyn. She couldn't believe that Alix had told anyone about Carrie and John. Even if they'd been on a date! It wasn't her sister's style. Besides, she'd been in denial about John until a couple of days ago.

'Everything,' said Matt.

'You're joking!'

'She told me about him before she went to Paris.'

'Alix *told* you?'

'Shouldn't she have?'

Wyn was amazed. 'I just wouldn't have expected her to. She's not the sort of person who—'

'She probably didn't mean to. But – she did.'

'Are you and Alix – is she . . . ?'

'Good question,' said Matt. 'We've been out together once. Only once! But it was wonderful. Then she dumped me to go to Paris! She has some weird notions, your sister.'

Wyn exhaled slowly. 'That's Alix.'

'She's so practical,' said Matt. 'She told me that it wouldn't work because I'd only want her to settle down and have babies and I'd be hopelessly unsupportive of her work.'

'That sounds like my sister,' said Wyn grimly.

'And I let her say all those things and I let her go. But I made a mistake. I want to talk to her again. I've thought of nothing else but her since she went.'

'Oh, my God.' Wyn was enthralled. She was in the middle of Alix's relationship – a relationship that she hadn't even known existed. So typical of Alix not to tell her. To pretend that her life was caught up in Paris and in her job. While all the time she was part of a real-life romance. The things that Matt Connery was saying certainly sounded romantic enough to her.

'She didn't tell me much about you,' she said to Matt.

'She doesn't seem to tell people much about anything.'

'So what do you want to do?' asked Wyn.

'What time is her flight?' asked Matt.

'Two o'clock,' replied Wyn.

'I'm going to the airport.' And Matt hung up.

Wyn stood in her sister's living room in complete shock. Then she picked up the phone and dialled Carrie's number.

~

Dublin airport was crowded. Alix checked in her luggage and went straight through to the departure area where the crowds were a little thinner. She bought a coffee and sat down at one of the tables. She took a copy of *Marie-Claire* out of her bag and skimmed through it. But she kept thinking of the last few days, of Carrie and of John and of meeting her half-sister Kate and Kate's adorable baby son. She hadn't expected to meet Kate, but when John suggested it she'd agreed. And Alix had liked her. She wasn't a dreamy, fragile person at all, but a strong-willed woman who worked in a call centre and had fifty staff working for her. Alix had been very wrong about Kate. They'd agreed to keep in touch. And Alix felt that they probably would.

Her flight was called and she joined the queue to board. As the plane hurtled down the runway, Alix turned over a page in the magazine. Then she stopped reading and looked out of the window. This time, it seemed more real. This time it actually hurt to go away.

❧

Matt watched the plane take off. He thrust his hands in his pockets and cursed under his breath. He'd imagined calling to her as she walked through the gates. He'd imagined her turning round and seeing him and running towards him. He'd imagined her falling into his arms and telling him how much she loved him. He hadn't imagined spending twenty minutes trying to find a parking space. He hadn't imagined pushing his way through the crowded terminal only to discover that the flight had already closed. He hadn't imagined going home without her.

❧

She wasn't looking forward to work the next day. There still seemed to be too much stuff going on in her head to care about work. For the first time in her life it seemed unimportant in relation to everything else. But she'd be OK when she got in, she decided. When she sat down in front of the screens and looked at the numbers, a different part of her brain seemed to take over and she slotted back into the rhythm as though she'd never been away. That was the way it always worked.

She unpacked her bags and curled up on the sofa. She switched on CNN and watched the market news from the States.

She was restless. She couldn't stay sitting in front of the TV. She pulled on her heavy quilted jacket and her fur-lined boots and crossed the Place du Tetre towards the Sacré Coeur. She walked up the steps to the cathedral and stopped to look over the lights of the city. It was beautiful here, she thought. People were right when they called Paris romantic. It seemed such a shame to be here on her own. She thought of Paul but without the anger that she'd felt before. She thought of Matt Connery and she bit her lip. She remembered the way he'd kissed her. The way he'd held her. She remembered how very secure she'd felt with him beside her.

She hadn't expected to see many people around tonight but there were. A young couple sat on the steps near her. They huddled together for warmth and kissed each other. Alix watched them for a moment, then, embarrassed with herself, she turned away. She stopped at the little shop at the bottom of the steps and bought herself a paper-thin crêpe dredged in lemon and sugar. She ate it as she walked back towards her apartment, shivering slightly in the cool easterly breeze.

'Alix!'

She was so surprised that she stopped with the crêpe between her teeth. She turned round.

'Alix!'

She blinked in astonishment. It couldn't really be Matt Connery walking along the street towards her. She had to be imagining it. But it wasn't her imagination, it was definitely him – she recognised his voice and his build and even the way he walked. Her heart began to beat faster. She bit into the crêpe and swallowed the chunk without chewing it. She wiped the lemon and sugar from her lips.

'Matt! What on earth are you doing here?' she asked as he caught up with her.

He looked at her in silence. He'd never seen her looking like this. Casual and relaxed, her long hair flowing loose and blowing across her face. She looked younger, less commanding and very, very shocked to see him.

'Look,' he said, searching for the right words, 'I know this seems crazy to you. I'm sorry if I surprised you.'

'You've surprised me but it's OK.' She looked around for a bin to dispose of the remains of her pancake. 'Are you here on business?'

'No,' said Matt.

She looked at him inquiringly. She wanted to reach out and touch him, to make sure that he was real.

'I think I've made a horrible mistake,' he said.

'Do you want to walk back to my apartment with me?' she asked. 'It's not far – about five minutes. You can tell me about your horrible mistake if you like. Or not.'

He fell into step beside her. It had seemed such a great gesture to make, to follow her here. He'd phoned Wyn when he missed the flight and she'd given him Alix's address and encouraged him to come. But, he realised, it was a crazy, stupid thing to have done and Alix – even this different Alix – would treat him with cool politeness while hiding her embarrassment at his actions. Maybe he would be better off pretending that he was here on business. That it hadn't been some kind of mad desire on his part to pull her into his arms and tell her over and over again that she was the only woman in the world for him.

'Here we are.' Alix stopped in front of an old, green-painted door. 'It looks worse than it is.'

He followed her up a narrow, dimly lit stairway and into the tiny apartment.

'Coffee?' she asked. 'Or something stronger?'

'Stronger,' said Matt. 'Cognac if you have it.'

'*Bien sûr.*' She smiled at him. 'When in France . . .' She

poured a generous measure of the amber liquid and handed it to him.

'I heard you met your father,' said Matt. 'I'm glad.'

She stared at him. 'Who told you that?'

'Your sister. Wyn. I was talking to her today.'

'Today!' Her tone echoed her astonishment. 'You were talking to Wyn today?'

He nodded.

'Why?'

'Because I rang your apartment and she was there.'

Alix blinked. 'You rang my apartment? But you knew that I was in Paris.'

He shrugged. 'I knew that you were in Paris last week,' he said. 'But the day that I was in Paris, you'd left for Dublin.'

'What were you doing here?' she asked.

'I was visiting another company,' he said. 'I rang to see if you'd meet me. But you'd left to go home.'

'That was a pity,' said Alix carefully.

'I was coming to Dublin the next day myself,' said Matt. 'So I thought I'd manage to catch up with you. But whenever I rang you didn't answer and the day I called to your apartment, you were out.'

'I'm sorry,' she said. 'You seem to have gone to a lot of trouble to see me.'

'Of course I did,' he said. 'You don't think I was simply going to leave things the way they were?'

'What do you mean?' she asked.

'Oh, Alix, don't make me humiliate myself by telling you how much you mean to me,' said Matt. 'I already feel like a complete idiot for coming here in the first place.'

She stared at him. 'I thought you agreed with me,' she said.

'I thought that you knew that our careers were really important and that I wouldn't be able to support you the way you'd probably want . . .' Her voice trailed off.

'You said all those things,' Matt reminded her. 'I didn't agree or disagree on anything.'

She got up and hugged her arms across her chest. 'I didn't want to get involved,' she told him. 'I care about you, Matt. But it'll be like Paul and me. One day you'll want more than I can give you and it'll be me that ends up feeling hurt.'

'Alix, I'll never want more than you can give me.'

She wanted to believe him. Since she'd come to Paris she'd thought about him more than anyone else. More than Carrie or Wyn or Paul. A day hadn't gone by when she hadn't thought about him. And how wonderful it had been with him. And how much she missed him. But she didn't want to admit to herself that she missed him. She wanted to know that she could cope without him. She didn't need anyone to help her live her life.

'My career is important to me,' she told him. 'I've worked so hard to get where I am.'

'I'm not trying to take it away,' said Matt. 'I'm just suggesting that there might be room for something else too.'

'I don't want to get it all wrong,' she said slowly. 'I seem to get it wrong quite a lot when it comes to relationships and I'm getting too old to keep making the same mistakes over and over again.'

'Alix, you're only thirty-three!'

'I've got grey hairs,' she told him.

He laughed. 'So have I. They're a mark of experience!'

'I'm sorry about the things I said to you that morning,' said Alix. 'But I was afraid that if I went out with you again I'd suddenly decide I didn't want to take this job and I'd be turning down a great opportunity. Matt, let's face it, you're working in Dublin, I'm here. It doesn't make a lot of sense.'

'Who says it has to make sense?' asked Matt. 'We can commute until I get a job here.'

She laughed. 'You – work here?'

'Why not?' he asked. 'You said yourself that I spend a lot of time travelling. I do. It doesn't much matter to me whether I work in Ireland or on the Continent. I speak French. I also speak Italian, German and a little Spanish.'

'Matt, I can't ask you to throw away *your* career for me,' she said. 'You'd always resent it and I'd always feel guilty.'

'Alix, I wouldn't be throwing away anything. I love what I do but there are more important things in life. Anatronics is about to be bought out by a US animation company. I'll make a good sum from my shareholding. I have time to choose what I want to do.' He got up and stood beside her. 'If you want me to go, I will, Alix. But I had to talk to you. The last time you were the one who did all the talking.'

She looked into his eyes. His deep blue eyes which returned her gaze with concern and affection.

'How much money?' she asked.

'Sorry?'

'From the shareholding?'

He pulled her towards him. 'Alix, you're not the only one who can make money. Are you afraid you'll have to support me?'

'It was a big problem with Paul.' She leaned her head on his chest. 'He resented the fact that I earned more than him. I think that was partly why he left me.'

'You won't earn more than me,' said Matt.

'Really?' She lifted her head to look at him. 'The deal is that good?'

'Alix, my shareholding is worth a lot. Money is not the immediate problem. Whether you think you can bear to go out to dinner with me ever again is of more concern.'

'Oh!' She leaned her head on his chest again. 'What about the baby thing?'

He smiled. 'What about it?'

'It's just that I don't know if I'll ever want children. Maybe I will. But maybe I won't, Matt, and then you might want—'

'Alix, I love you. You. Not what you can give me. Not money. Not children. Not anything. Just you.'

They stood immobile in the centre of the room. She could feel the beat of his heart beneath his cotton shirt.

'I can't say that,' she whispered. 'I'm not good on words.'

'You don't have to,' he told her. 'Just give it a chance.'

She pulled his face towards her. He kissed her on the lips. She held him more tightly. She could feel his arms round her, drawing her closer and closer to him, and it felt good.

'The bedroom is over there,' she mumbled.

He lifted her up and carried her across the room.

'That was brave,' she said as he dropped her onto the bed. 'Not many people can carry a five-feet-eight-inch woman into her bedroom and live to tell the tale.'

'Shut up, Alix,' said Matt and kissed her again.

∽

She took her extra day off work the following morning. Markets were volatile ahead of the year end. Swaps were dealing frantically as traders tried to close out their books. But there was nothing that she could do about it. There'd be other deals, other trades. But for today, she was far too preoccupied to care.

Isobel's Wedding

Thanks to:

My agent and friend Carole Blake who introduced me to
a great group of people at Headline and changed my life
for ever.

My extended family, the best PR people I know.

Colm, who'd rather be in Spain.

And, of course, to those of you who buy my books – I hope
you enjoy reading them as much as I enjoy writing them.

Chapter 1

The Wedding (Francisco Goya, 1791)

I was trying on the wedding dress when Tim phoned. Actually I was twirling around in front of the full-length wall mirror, admiring the way the skirt billowed around me in a carefree puff of white chiffon, when I heard the phone ring. It had taken me longer to make this wedding dress than any other I'd ever done, but this was *my* dress. This was the dress I'd wear when I married Tim in two weeks' time and it had deserved all of my time and all of my attention. I smoothed the skirt and fingered the tiny white pearls neatly hand-sewn onto the bodice. There were four hundred and twenty of them. I'd never sew a pearl onto a dress again.

'Isobel! It's for you!' Alison stood at the bottom of the stairs and yelled at me. 'It's your fiancé.' She broke into a guffaw at the word 'fiancé'. She always did. Alison, who was twenty-one, thought I was out of my mind to be getting married. Alison didn't approve of marriage; she believed that husbands only tied you down, limited your potential, trapped you for the rest of your life. She thought I was too young to tie myself down to one person. But I wasn't. I was exactly the right age. Twenty-seven. Long enough on my own to

1

have had some fun and make a few elementary mistakes. But mature enough, now, to know exactly what I was doing. To be ready to become Isobel Malone instead of Isobel Kavanagh.

I stared at my twenty-seven-year-old reflection. Brown eyes, red-rimmed from spending too much time at my sewing machine, a pale face that was looking forward to our honeymoon in Rhodes, and soft brown hair which was halfway between lengths because I wanted to be able to put it up for the wedding. It was a pity I wasn't taller because the dress would have looked truly gorgeous if I'd been a tall, willowy, Stella Tennant sort of person. But I'd stopped growing around the five-foot-one mark and remained the short one in our family. At least I was slim, although that was probably because I'd almost stopped eating in the last two weeks. There simply hadn't been time.

Alison (unlike me in almost every respect – taller, tousle-haired and bigger-boned) thumped her way up the stairs and pushed open the bedroom door. 'Are you deaf?' she demanded. 'It's Tim—' She broke off and stared at me. She hadn't seen the finished dress before. 'Oh, Isobel.' Suddenly her face was softer, gentler. 'It's beautiful!'

I grinned at her. 'Thank you.'

'I mean it,' she said. 'It's lovely. *You* look lovely.'

'I'll look more lovely when my hair is done properly and I'm wearing all the right bits and pieces.'

'You're like Cinderella going to the ball,' she breathed as she fingered the gossamer-light material. 'I never thought it would look like this.'

'Oh, for heaven's sake!' I laughed at her. 'Come down to earth, Ali. You're the one who thinks I'm off my head to be getting married in the first place.'

She shrugged. 'I just don't think that women can be

themselves if they're chained to some man,' she said. 'As soon as a girl gets married she puts her husband's needs ahead of her own. It's this nurturing thing. We can't help ourselves. That's why you shouldn't get married in the first place.'

'And what if you're truly in love?' I asked her as I slipped out of the dress and placed it carefully on the padded hanger. 'What then?'

She shook her head. 'Love is delusion,' she said. 'People only think they're in love.'

'Wait until you've fallen for someone yourself before making that judgement,' I told her briskly. 'I'll remind you of this conversation when you're mooning about over some bloke who doesn't take a blind bit of notice of you.'

I pulled my dressing-gown over my white slip and hurried downstairs, leaving her still gazing at the dress.

I picked up the receiver. 'Hi there.'

'What on earth were you doing?' asked Tim. 'I've been hanging on for ages.'

'Discussing the meaning of love with Alison,' I told him. 'She doesn't believe in it.'

Tim broke into a fit of coughing.

'I hope you're not getting a cold,' I said. 'It'd be terrible if you were too sick to say "I do".'

'I wanted to meet you,' said Tim.

'We're going out tomorrow,' I told him. 'And I was going to finish off the bridesmaids' dresses tonight.'

'I need to see you tonight,' said Tim. 'Really I do, Isobel.'

I sighed. 'It's not that I don't want to see you. It's just that I've so much to do!'

'Please, Isobel.'

'But there's only two weeks and—'

'Isobel, please.'

'Oh, OK.' I ran my fingers through my hair. 'I suppose I can practise with the headdress another evening.'

'Meet you in Kiely's?' he said.

'Tim!' Kiely's, in Donnybrook, was close to Tim's red-bricked, bay-windowed townhouse. I lived in Sutton, at least a twenty-minute drive over the toll-bridge.

'I left the car in for a service today,' he said apologetically. 'I thought I'd have it back this evening but it wasn't ready. So I'm without wheels.'

'Oh, OK,' I said again. I always gave in to Tim, I couldn't help it. Maybe that was what Alison was talking about.

'Half an hour?' he said.

'An hour,' I told him. 'I need to get dressed. I was trying on my wedding dress when you called.' I laughed suddenly. 'I hope it's not bad luck to be trying on the dress when your fiancé phones – like him seeing you in it!'

Tim laughed too but he didn't sound convincing. It was all getting a bit much for him, I thought. Endless discussion about who to invite and what sort of menu to have, and which band to choose. All sorts of things that seemed so important at the time but probably weren't important at all really. In the end, the only important thing was that Tim loved me and that I loved him. The rest was incidental. But the incidental things took up most of our time these days.

∽

I reversed my white Peugeot 205 out of the driveway and turned onto the coast road.

It was a grey, depressing evening. A thin layer of cloud blocked out any trace of blue sky and a cool easterly breeze whipped across the bay taking the struggling

4

warmth out of the sun. I hoped it would be fine for my wedding day. I dreamed of blue skies with cotton-wool wisps of cloud and still, warm air. I could be lucky, I thought, as I sped along the road. It would be May by then and the weather might have turned.

It took me half an hour to get to Kiely's. Cars littered the surrounding streets and I abandoned mine on a double yellow line. I hoped I wouldn't get a ticket but, if I did, I'd make Tim pay for it. Friday night was a bad night to arrive late to a pub.

I pushed open the door. A haze of blue-grey smoke wafted towards me and my eyes began to water. I looked around the heaving throng of people for Tim. Why on earth did he insist on meeting in crowded places?

Finally I saw him, leaning against the wall, pint of Guinness in his hand. He was incredibly handsome, I thought smugly. His hair was jet-black and fell in an endearing fringe over his navy-blue eyes. His face was tanned and healthy, with high cheekbones, the sort I'd die for myself. He wore an oversized maroon Aran jumper and ragged Levis.

My heart skipped a beat when I saw him – sometimes I found it hard to believe that he was mine.

I wormed my way through the crowd and tapped him on the shoulder.

'Oh, hello.' He looked startled. 'I didn't see you come in.'

'You can't see anyone in here,' I said. 'It's just one pulsating blob of people. Why didn't you pick somewhere quieter?'

'It was quieter when I came in,' he told me. 'It seems to have filled up in the last half-hour.'

'Do you want to stay here?' I asked. 'Would you like to go somewhere else?'

'No, here is OK. Do you want a drink?'

'Orange juice is fine,' I said.

He nodded, handed me his pint, and made his way to the bar. He wasn't in a good mood, I thought, as I watched him. There was something wrong. I hoped it wasn't his mother again. She'd kicked up blue murder because we'd limited the family invitations to twenty-five from each side and Tim had refused to allow her to add on some distant cousin he couldn't even remember.

'It's all right for Isobel,' Denise Malone had told him. 'She has a small family. There probably aren't twenty-five people on her side anyway.'

'Of course there's twenty-five on my side,' I'd retorted angrily when he told me. 'I'm not squeezing my family out just so that she can invite a crowd of freeloaders!'

It had all been very silly, got very heated, for no real reason. In the end, Denise's sister rang from the States to say that she'd love to come but that she really couldn't afford the trip over in May, since she'd already booked her holidays for July. So there was space for Cousin Maddy or Dotty or Biddy after all and no need to rearrange anything.

'Here you are.' Tim handed me the glass of orange juice and retrieved his pint.

'Cheers.' I raised my glass but he was already taking a deep mouthful of Guinness.

'I needed to talk to you,' he said. He wiped the thin cream line from his upper lip. 'I'm sorry I dragged you out tonight.'

'I don't mind.' I put my head on his chest. 'I know I said I was busy, but I'm never too busy to see you. Darling,' I added teasingly.

'It was important to talk to you,' he said.

I looked up at him. Something was wrong, and from the tone of his voice it was a bit more serious than trouble on the Dotty, Maddy and Biddy front. 'What's the matter?' I asked.

He wiped at the condensation on the outside of his glass.

'What's the matter?' I asked again.

He looked up at me. 'I can't go through with it,' he said abruptly.

I heard the words but they didn't mean anything to me. 'What?'

'I can't go through with it,' he said again, a touch of desperation in his voice. 'I can't, Isobel. I need some time. I want to postpone it.'

'The wedding?' I stared at him. 'You want to postpone the wedding?' I clutched at my glass of orange juice.

'Yes.' He nodded and took another mouthful of Guinness.

I could still hear the buzz of the people around us, but their voices were muted, distant. I felt as though I was wrapped in a cocoon, separated from the world outside. My voice was paralysed. I opened my mouth and closed it again. I blinked a couple of times. 'You're joking,' I croaked finally.

'I'm not joking, Isobel.' His look was anguished. 'I need more time.'

'More time for what?' I demanded, the words tumbling out now. 'What could you possibly need time for? We've known each other for nearly two years. We've been engaged for six months! If you had a problem with it, why didn't you say so before now?'

'I didn't feel this way before now.'

'Feel what way?' I asked.

'Trapped,' he said.

I rummaged in my bag and found my asthma inhaler. I shook the canister a couple of times and then squirted the fine spray into my tightening lungs. Tim watched me.

'Are you all right?' he asked.

My breath was coming more easily again. 'No,' I said. I clutched the inhaler in my hand.

'Put it back in your bag,' he said. 'You don't really need it.'

'It's smoky in here,' I told him. 'You know I wheeze when it's smoky.'

'I thought it was me,' said Tim. 'I didn't mean to upset you.'

'And what did you think telling me you wanted to postpone the wedding would do?' I demanded. 'Make me dance around the pub with delight? I can't believe this, Tim. I really can't. Tell me you're joking. Tell me you don't really mean it. Why do you feel trapped? Is it just nerves? Is it—' I broke off. I couldn't talk any more. The tears were streaming down my face.

He watched me uncomfortably. He pulled a cotton hanky from his jeans pocket and handed it to me. I was crying far too much for it to be of any use. I knew that people were looking at me, but I didn't care. I could cry if I felt like it. I could have an asthma attack if I felt like it. I could die if I felt like it. I gulped and started to cough. I couldn't breathe properly. I thought, frantically, that maybe I *would* die.

'Isobel!' Tim's voice was harsh. 'Stop crying like that. You'll make yourself sick.'

'*You're* making me sick,' I said, gulping the smoke-laden air through my sobs. 'You're the one that's doing this to me.' I shook the inhaler again and took another dose.

'Isobel!' Tim grabbed me by the arm. 'Stop it. Stop it now.'

He steered me out of the pub and into the darkening street. I rubbed my eyes with his hanky.

'How could you do this to me?' I asked. 'Why? Why

8

now? If you don't love me, why have you let it go this far?'

'I'm not saying I don't love you.' Tim pushed a lock of hair out of his eyes. 'I *do* love you, Isobel. I just don't feel that I can marry you. Not yet.'

I stared at him as I twisted the hanky around and around in my hands. I really couldn't believe I was hearing this. Part of me expected him to tell me it was all a joke, but I knew it wasn't. He looked too uncomfortable, too miserable, too serious for it to be a joke.

'We've been practically living together since we got engaged,' I said, trying to breathe calmly and evenly. 'Surely that must have helped you to think we could live together for ever.'

He sighed. 'That's just it, Isobel. Right now, everything is perfect. You stay with me most weekends, you go home during the week. You stay with me if we go out somewhere. But you're not there all the time. I know sometimes I'd like you to be there all the time – that's why I thought we should get married – but now I'm afraid. I like being on my own too. I'm not comfortable with the idea of having someone wanting to know where I am every minute of the day.'

'But I don't want to know where you are every minute of the day,' I said despairingly. 'I only want to know that you'll be with me every night.' I blew my nose and shoved the hanky into the pocket of my jeans.

Tim leaned against the wall and stared ahead of him. I remembered the day we'd met, at a twenty-first birthday party in the St Lawrence Hotel, in Howth. It had been a noisy, crowded party and I'd gone outside for a breath of fresh air. Tim was outside too, busily typing something into a personal organiser.

'What on earth are you doing?' I asked. I'd had a few

drinks – normally I wouldn't have butted into someone's private business.

'Making a memo of something I have to do tomorrow,' he said.

'You don't look like the business type.' I hiccoughed gently.

He laughed. 'I'm the computer type,' he said. 'I design computer software. I've been stuck on something for days and it suddenly came to me. So I thought I'd better get it down because sure as hell I'll never remember it in the morning!'

I grinned at him. 'Sounds reasonable.'

'Are you at the party?' he asked.

I nodded. 'But it was so hot and crowded I thought I'd come outside for a while. It's lovely out here, isn't it?'

'Want to go for a walk?' he asked.

'Why not?'

We walked along the pier together. The water lapped gently in against the wall and the wires from the boat-sails jingled against the masts. The moon sent a shaft of silver light across the harbour. We chatted as though we'd known each other for ages. Tim was unlike anybody else I'd ever met. I worked in a print and packaging company as the personal assistant to the managing director. I was used to people in suits, to graduate trainees wanting to get on, to the factory floor and the commercial work ethic. Tim was a creative sort of person. I'd always thought that computer people were boring and obsessed. I thought that they had to think in logical progression, like machines. I was way out of date. Tim said that he saw the results of his programmes before he'd ever written them; he thought in broad pictures as though he were making a film or writing a book.

'Wow,' I said. 'That's a sort of computer-nerd thing to say, isn't it? "Wow"?'

10

He laughed and put his arm around me. 'Wow,' he whispered as he drew me closer to him.

It was love at first sight. It was always like that for me, though; I fell fast and hard and then fell out of love as quickly. But it was different with Tim. With Tim, I knew that it would last for ever.

How could it all have gone wrong? I thought bleakly. We were so right together. Not opposites, exactly, but complementary. When he was working on a project, he was lost to me. When he'd finished, he was devoted. And I was always there, content to be with him, secure in the knowledge that no one else could love him as much as me, and that there was no one else in his life to usurp me.

He earned a lot of money as a software designer. The day I met him, he'd bought his townhouse in Donnybrook. He had a company car. He took two holidays a year: one to the sun any time between May and September, and a skiing holiday in February. I didn't weigh him up in monetary terms and decide that he was a good catch, but he was. I loved him and I thought he loved me.

I thought we worked as a couple. I thought that everything between us was perfect. I thought that I understood him. How could I have understood him when he was going through such agonies?

'I'm sorry.' I slipped my arm into his. 'I didn't realise it was getting to you so much.'

'I'm sorry too.' He hugged my arm to his side. 'I thought I was ready for this. Truly I did, Isobel. But I can't do it. I can't stand in the church with our friends and family and make such a big issue out of it all.'

I looked at him hopefully. 'Would you go through with a quick wedding in a register office?'

He disentangled my hold on him. 'Not yet. I can't do anything yet.'

We stood silently beside each other. Part of me felt sorry

11

for him. Part of me wanted to kill him. Part of me wanted to kill myself.

How could I walk into the office on Monday and tell them all that my wedding was off? The wedding that had been practically the sole topic of conversation in the company for the past month? How could I tell them that the Conrad was cancelled, that the gifts were being returned, that the honeymoon to the Greek islands wasn't going to happen? It would be awful. They'd be sorry for me. They'd put their arms around me and tell me that it wasn't the end of the world and then, when I wasn't there, they'd discuss it in breathless whispers and say that they knew it wouldn't have worked and that I'd made such a fool of myself over Tim Malone.

'I just need some time,' he said. 'That's all.'

I said nothing. There was nothing I could say. I stared across the road without seeing anything.

'I thought perhaps you might like to go on the honeymoon,' said Tim suddenly.

'What?'

'The honeymoon. It's paid for. I feel terrible about this, Isobel. I thought you might like to go on the holiday.'

'With you?' I stared at him incredulously.

'Of course not,' he said. 'With a friend.'

'Oh, Tim.' I burst into a fresh paroxysm of tears. '*You're* my best friend. I don't want to do anything without you.'

He held me to him and allowed me to sob all over his jumper. He patted me gently on the back and whispered that he still loved me.

'So why won't you go through with the wedding?' I cried. 'Why?'

'I've told you,' he said helplessly. 'I just can't. I still want to see you, Isobel. I don't want us to break up. I just want to postpone things for a while, that's all.'

'How can we go on seeing each other?' I sniffed. 'People will think we're insane.'

'When did we ever care what people thought?' he murmured into my ear. 'When?'

I leaned against his chest, the rough wool of the jumper coarse against my face. My eyes were closed. I still couldn't take it in. I couldn't believe that Tim felt the way he did. He hadn't shown it before now. I sighed deeply and he held me closer.

'How can you hug me like this?' I asked as I lifted my head to look at him. 'How can you hold me tight and not want to marry me?'

'It's not that I don't want to marry you, Isobel. I do. I just don't want to do it now. It would be a mistake to do it now. Really it would.'

'Is there someone else?' I hadn't wanted to ask, was afraid of his reply.

'Of course not,' he said sharply. 'How could there be? I haven't had eyes for anyone but you.' He kissed me on the forehead. 'It's such a big step, that's all.'

I leaned against his chest again. 'But I thought we were ready for it.'

'I'm so busy in work at the moment,' he continued. 'I'm working a twelve-hour day. I don't have time to be with you. I don't want to feel guilty that you're at home without me.'

I was silent.

'When I get myself sorted out,' he said. 'Later in the year.'

I moved away from him. 'What makes you think you'll be more likely to marry me later in the year? What if there's another project, something else to keep you working so hard? I know that you're busy. I understand that, Tim.'

'It's different now,' he told me. 'I know that if we were

13

married I'd be rushing a job just to get home. And I know that you'd be pissed off with me for not being there when you wanted. It's the wrong time, Isobel. That's all.'

'And you still love me?' I looked at him doubtfully.

'More than anything,' he assured me, and drew me towards him again.

~

There was a ticket on my car. I ripped it from behind the wiper, crumpled it into a tiny ball and flung it into the oily puddle in front of the Peugeot. Tim had half-heartedly asked me to go back to the house with him, so that we could talk things over. But I didn't want to talk things over with Tim. I needed to be on my own for a while. I needed to get my thoughts together, to make sense of what he had told me.

I still couldn't understand why. It was easy for him to say that he needed time, or that he felt pressurised, or that he was too busy at work. But it was hard for me to believe that they were insurmountable obstacles to true love. And I'd thought that what Tim felt for me and what I felt for him was true love. I'd never been this close to another person before. I'd never shared their dreams or desires or the trivial details of anyone's life the way I had with Tim. I knew the kind of toothpaste he preferred. I knew that biological washing-powders brought him out in a rash. I knew that he liked jazz music, mountain walking and Chinese food. I knew that he was cranky in the mornings, at his best late at night. I knew that when he was taken over by a problem he couldn't leave it alone until he'd worked it out. I knew so much about him, I thought, as I unlocked the car door, but suddenly it wasn't enough. I hadn't known that the thought of marrying me had been so truly terrible to him.

⁓

My parents were watching TV when I arrived home. Alison had gone out with some girlfriends, but – unusually – Ian, my loose-limbed, nineteen-year-old brother, was sprawled across the sofa, his legs dangling over the armrest.

'Susan Purcell rang a few minutes ago,' said Mum as I walked into the living room. 'She's dropping around tomorrow night with your wedding present. She told me that she's bought a Paul Costello suit for the wedding!'

'She should have saved her money.' I'd taken another puff of my inhaler before coming into the house but my breathing was still uneven.

'Oh, Isobel, a suit like that will last her for years,' said Mum. 'It's the kind of thing you can wear over and over again.'

'I meant, she should have saved her money on the wedding present,' I said. It was an effort not to cry again. 'I won't be needing her sheets or toaster or waffle-maker or whatever she's bought.'

Mum pointed the remote control at the TV and silenced Pat Kenny. 'What happened?' she asked.

'The wedding's off.' I flopped onto the sofa beside Ian, who sat upright and stared at me in amazement.

'Off!' Mum, Dad and Ian echoed my words together.

'Off,' I repeated.

They exchanged glances. 'Why is it off?' asked Dad finally.

'We've postponed it,' I said.

They were silent for a moment.

'Why?' asked Ian.

I twirled my glittering diamond engagement ring around on my finger. It had never occurred to me to give it back to Tim – to make some kind of gesture by flinging it at him in temper.

'Tim feels that he's not quite ready for the commitment.'

'The bastard!' Ian stood up, his six-foot-one frame towering over me. 'I'll tear him apart. Who does he think he is? Not ready! Hasn't he been sleeping with you for the past year and a half!'

'Ian!' I looked at him in horror. It wasn't that my parents didn't know that Tim and I had slept together – given that I spent so many nights in Donnybrook it would have been pretty strange not to – but we never spoke about it, as though by ignoring it they could pretend that I was still an innocent virgin.

'He's got a bloody nerve.' Dad was angry. The tip of his nose was red, which was a sure sign.

'Oh, Isobel.' Mum put her arms around me. 'I'm so sorry.'

I felt the lump in my throat and swallowed hard, blinking furiously to get rid of the tears that threatened to spill down my cheeks. I was tired of crying. I didn't want to cry in front of my family.

'It's for the best,' I said shakily. 'It'd be terrible to get married and then decide it had all been a mistake. Anyway,' I cleared my throat, 'we haven't broken off our engagement. We've just postponed things until later in the year.'

'But you won't be able to book the Conrad for later in the year,' said Mum. 'It was a struggle getting it for Saturday week! Don't you remember? You won't get any decent hotel at such short notice. How much is it going to cost to cancel it now?' She put her hand over her mouth in dismay. 'Not that the money is important, of course, darling. Your happiness is. But all the same—'

'I don't want to talk about it now,' I said. 'I'm tired. I'm going to bed.'

'I'll bring you up some hot milk,' said Mum. 'Help you sleep.'

'I don't need hot milk,' I told her. 'I'm perfectly well able to sleep, thanks. I'm exhausted.'

I opened the door of the front room. The presents were there, neatly piled to one side. The Egyptian cotton bed-linen. The set of Newbridge cutlery. The Waterford glass decanter. I wanted to pick up the Waterford glass decanter and hurl it across the room. But I didn't. There wouldn't have been any point. Besides, it wasn't my decanter to throw anywhere. Half of it belonged to Tim.

∽

I couldn't sleep, of course. I lay in the bed and stared at the ceiling, wondering how my life could crumble around me like this. My wedding dress hung on the outside of the wardrobe, mocking me. I hadn't the heart to put it away. I couldn't bring myself to touch it.

I heard Alison come in around one o'clock and the muted tones of her conversation with Ian. I pulled the covers around me and tried to make myself fall asleep. I didn't want to talk to Alison.

She pushed open my bedroom door and tiptoed to the bed.

'Are you awake?' she whispered.

I kept my eyes tightly closed and tried to breathe deeply and evenly.

'You can't possibly be asleep.' Her voice was louder.

I didn't move.

'OK,' she said. 'Don't talk to me now. I understand. But you're well rid of him, Issy, and you know it. He's a shit. He always was a shit. I never liked him.'

17

You liar, I thought, as I kept my eyes closed. I've seen you looking at him. You know as well as I do that he's an attractive, sensitive bloke and you probably fancy him yourself.

'I'll talk to you tomorrow,' she said finally. 'It's probably for the best.'

I supposed everyone would tell me that. It's for the best. People always say it when something rotten happens, as though rotten things can actually make your life any better. I couldn't see how calling off the wedding I'd dreamed about since I was a child was for the best. I wanted to believe that it was simply postponed for a few months, but there was a band of ice around my heart that told me it could be postponed for ever.

I don't know when I eventually fell asleep. When I did, I dreamed of my wedding. It was taking place as though nothing had happened. Tim stood at the altar and smiled at me as he took my hands in his and promised to love me. I promised to love him too. It was only when we posed outside the church for the photographs that I realised I wasn't wearing my beautiful wedding dress but some old net curtains which had been in the hot-press for years.

'It isn't a valid wedding,' Father O'Brien told me mournfully. 'You have to wear a dress to make it a valid wedding. I'm very sorry, Isobel, but it's all been a dreadful mistake.'

Chapter 2

The Lovers' Complaint (Joan Miró, 1953)

Mum was waiting for me when I got up on Saturday morning. I stumbled downstairs and took some Hedex from the box in the cupboard while she hovered around me, teapot in hand, an anxious expression on her face.

'Do you have a headache?' she asked.

'No,' I snapped. 'I'm overdosing on paracetamol.'

She looked hurt. 'I only asked.'

'Thanks,' I said. 'But I'm fine. It's just from tiredness.'

'I couldn't sleep either.' She poured a cup of tea and handed it to me. 'I kept thinking of what I'd like to do to him. How dare he treat my daughter like that!'

'Oh, Mum, please.' I sat down at the table and listlessly buttered a slice of overdone toast.

'But, honestly, Isobel! How can he just change his mind like that? Didn't he talk to you about it? Hasn't he said something before now?'

I shook my head. I didn't want this conversation.

'But if he felt that strongly it can't have taken him until now to decide. You've been engaged for six months.'

'I know,' I said.

'What does his mother think?'

'I don't know. I haven't spoken to her.'

'I hope she's proud of him.' Mum refilled the kettle. Water splashed angrily from the tap.

'It's not her fault,' I said.

'It's her fault the way she's brought up her son,' said Mum. 'And that's what I'll tell her.'

I stared at her in horror. 'Tell her?'

'You don't think I'm going to sit around while her precious son throws my daughter over, do you? I'm going to tell her exactly what I think of him!'

'Mum!' The thought was terrifying. 'Please don't. It'll only make things worse. Besides, we haven't called off our engagement. We've just postponed the wedding.'

'Huh!' Mum snorted.

She went on and on at me. I stopped listening and played with my toast. I wasn't hungry. A great way to diet, I thought bleakly. I wasn't even thirsty.

In the afternoon I borrowed Ian's mountain bike and went for a cycle along the seafront. It was still windy and I was buffeted from side to side as I tried to keep the bike upright. I hadn't cycled since my schooldays. I was out of practice. But at least it kept me out of the house and away from Mum. I didn't know which was harder to bear, her rage or her comfort.

She was on the phone when I got home.

'Of course I see your point of view,' she was saying. 'But I can't believe that he's just dumped her like this.'

Thanks, Mum, I thought. Dumped her. A very sensitive way of putting it.

'Well, my daughter is worth ten of your son!'

Oh, God. My worst nightmare. She was on the phone to Denise Malone. For some reason, despite their similar backgrounds, Mum and Mrs Malone had never hit it off. Neither of them thought that their offspring's choice

20

of partner was the one they'd have chosen themselves. Mum didn't like Tim's studied scruffiness. Mrs Malone wouldn't have liked any girl Tim brought home.

'Get off the phone,' I hissed as I took off my sweatshirt. I was sweating from the exertion of cycling against the wind.

Mum made faces at me and continued the conversation.

'I think it's ridiculous. Two weeks! Of course it's better now than later – but even still. No, I don't think he's being fair.' I could see her cheeks redden and her grip on the receiver tighten. 'You might think so.' Silence. A sigh. Gritted teeth. 'Yes. No. Goodbye.' She turned to me. 'Stupid woman,' she said and put her arms around me.

∽

I half-thought that Tim might ring me even though I'd asked him not to. Every time the phone rang my heart jumped and, even when I found out that the call wasn't for me, my whole body trembled for ages afterwards. I wondered what he was doing. Working, I supposed, that great panacea for all men. 'I'm too busy, I'm working.' Tim had used it a lot as an excuse in the past, but I always thought it was genuine. Now, for the first time, I was unsure. I felt insecure and frightened. The family didn't help – they went on and on at me.

Alison was the only one who was pleased.

'It's not that I want you to be miserable, or anything,' she said. 'But you don't need Tim Malone to make you happy.'

'Oh, sod off,' I replied and banged the bedroom door shut.

Mum wanted to know about cancelling things. 'Because you'll have to inform the hotel, you know, Isobel. God

21

knows how they'll react. And there's the band, and the photographer. I don't know what you should do about the cake. I'm sure it's baked already, but maybe it's not iced. That way we'll be able to use it as a Christmas cake—'

'Oh, for God's sake!' I stared at her in exasperation and walked out of the kitchen and into the back garden.

The tulips splashed vibrant red in the flowerbeds, surrounded by yellow, purple and white pansies. The lawn was emerald green, with neat stripes. Dad loved the garden and spent hours working in it. Usually I felt it was an oasis of peace and serenity, but today its structured elegance made me want to pull up the flowers and trample on them.

'D'you want me to go around and talk to him?' Ian was sitting on the garden bench. I hadn't noticed him at first.

'And say what?' I asked.

'Dunno.' Ian motioned to me to sit beside him. 'Tell him that he's a fool and that he's missing out on a really great woman.'

My brother never normally spoke to me like this. I laughed sourly. 'We've just postponed it,' I said. 'There's no need to tell him anything.'

'You look far too upset for someone who's happy about postponing things,' said Ian. 'You're too pale and you look sick.'

'Thank you for the vote of confidence,' I said. 'You can rush around and tell him I'm wasting away.'

'I'm only trying to help,' said Ian glumly.

'I know.' I leaned my head on his shoulder. 'I'm sorry.'

Thankfully, Dad didn't try to talk to me. He just squeezed my arm every time I walked by him, and allowed me to read the newspapers before him.

22

It was a long weekend. I couldn't get Tim out of my mind. Everything I did, I imagined doing as Tim's wife. My soon-to-be-married state had become so much a part of me, I couldn't adjust to it not happening. I still couldn't understand why Tim felt trapped. I'd never pressurised him. I didn't force him into asking me to marry him. It didn't make sense. None of it made sense. I wished I could stop thinking about it for even a couple of minutes but I couldn't. I didn't sleep on Sunday night either.

I toyed with the idea of staying out of work on Monday, but that would have only made things more difficult. I went in early instead. I wanted to be at my desk, outside Barry Cleary's office, before any of the other staff arrived. I didn't want to walk the length of the open-plan floor while someone called out '*Only two weeks to go!*' and made me burst into tears again. I'd tell them, of course, but in my own time.

I switched on my computer and called up the memo files. The folder marked 'personal' contained the list of people we'd invited to the wedding and the presents that they'd given us. I'd need that list to return the presents. Or should I return the presents, I wondered, if Tim and I decided to get married in the autumn? What were the chances? I asked myself savagely. Did he really mean 'postpone' or did he mean 'call off'? How could I know? I'd been too shocked to talk to him properly on Friday night. I should have gone back to his house as he'd suggested and made him tell me exactly what the problem was and exactly when he intended to go through with things. I should have phoned him yesterday, despite telling myself I didn't want to. Now I was in limbo. I leaned my head on the monitor and sighed deeply.

'Are you all right, Isobel?' Lesley Morrissey stopped at my desk. 'Have you got a headache or something? I've got Panadol in my bag if you want.'

I looked up at her. 'No thanks, I'm fine.'

'You don't look fine,' she said, putting a green folder bulging with invoices on the edge of my desk. 'You're white as a sheet and you've got black circles under your eyes. All this wedding stuff is getting you down.'

I took a deep breath. Might as well start with Lesley, I thought. Let her be the one to break the news to the rest of the people in the office. 'There isn't going to be a wedding,' I told her. 'Not in two weeks anyway.'

'Isobel!' She looked at me in shock. 'Why?'

I wanted to say that I'd got cold feet, that I was the one to call it off, but I was afraid that she'd find out the truth. I didn't want her to feel sorry for me. I didn't want sympathetic looks following me around the office.

'We've been talking about it,' I said. 'We decided it was getting out of hand. The preparations, the fuss. There were arguments about the guests.' I shrugged. 'It didn't seem like an enjoyable thing any more. So we've decided to postpone it.'

'Until when?' Her grey eyes were wide in surprise.

'I'm not sure. October maybe. Or November. Or next year.'

'But, Isobel—' Her expression was a mixture of sympathy and amazement. 'I thought you were really happy about getting married. I thought that you couldn't wait to be with Tim.'

'There's a difference between being married and the wedding itself,' I said, although I was saying the first words that came into my head and I hadn't a clue if they made sense. 'I'm not sure we were ready for the wedding, even if we did want to be with each other.'

'Why don't you call off the big do, and get married quietly instead?' she asked. 'If it means that much to you.'

'Maybe we'll do that,' I said. 'But not on Saturday week.'

Then Barry Cleary, the managing director, walked into his office and Lesley scurried back to her desk. I could see her telling the other girls, Niamh and Anna, who tried hard not to look in my direction, but who shot surreptitious glances at me when they thought I didn't notice. I didn't care. I wasn't sure whether or not Lesley would give my version of the events, or whether she'd end the conversation with 'she's putting a brave face on it, but he's obviously dumped her'. What were they to think, after all? People don't call off their weddings just because the fuss is getting a bit much. I wondered, suddenly, if they'd already had a collection for me. A brown-paper envelope passed surreptitiously around the office with much giggling. For Isobel's wedding present. I felt sick.

I brought Barry his cup of coffee. He was reading the *Irish Times* business page. 'Interest rates down again,' he commented as I put the cup in front of him. 'Good news for mortgage holders.' He stirred the coffee. 'I suppose that's the sort of thing that'll occupy you now, Isobel. Things like the cost of your mortgage and carpets and furniture.'

'Possibly,' I said. 'But not in the immediate future.'

'You'll have to take responsibility for your own financial affairs.' He took off his gold-rimmed glasses and placed them on the desk. 'Don't be kept in the dark by that husband of yours.'

Why were they all talking about him today? Barry had hardly mentioned the wedding since the day I'd got engaged.

'Actually, Barry, I'm not getting married as soon as I thought after all.' I tried to sound nonchalant, but the words came out as a croak.

'Pardon?' He looked at me quizzically.

'The wedding,' I said succinctly. 'It's off.'

'Isobel!'

Couldn't anyone come up with a different reaction? Couldn't somebody, for once, just look surprised? Couldn't they say 'that's a shame' without saying 'Isobel!' and looking at me as though I'd contracted a fatal disease?

'We've changed our minds,' I said. 'We've postponed it.'

He stared at me. 'Sharon will be disappointed,' he said finally. 'She was looking forward to it.'

'Maybe later in the year,' I said.

'Really?'

'I'm not sure.'

I couldn't stay in his office. The shreds of my self-control were beginning to disappear. I picked up my notebook and fled to the ladies'.

I didn't want to stay in there too long. If I did, someone would be dispatched to find out if I was OK. There seemed to be a kind of antenna around the office, something that let the other girls know if one of us was upset. They knew the difference between going to the loo to answer the call of nature and going to the ladies' to cry your eyes out.

So I wouldn't cry my eyes out. I would get myself under control and I'd go back to my desk to get on with my work. I looked at myself in the mirror. Lesley was right. My face was ashen and my eyes were smudged with black shadows. I pinched my cheeks to bring the colour back. It didn't really work. I should have come into the office layered with make-up so that I didn't look so awful. But I hadn't the heart to put it on before I left the house. Now I wished I had.

'Would you like to come to the pub for lunch today?' asked Niamh as I passed by her desk.

'Thanks, but I'm actually busy,' I lied.

'Feeling OK?' she asked.

'Fine.'

My phone was ringing when I reached my desk.

'What's this I hear?' Marion, the receptionist, was at the other end.

'Hi, Marion. Can you call me back? I'm kind of busy at the moment.'

'Don't play games with me,' said Marion. She was the oldest of us, in her late thirties, married with three children. 'Is it true?'

'If you're asking about the wedding, yes, it's true.'

'But why?'

'Marion, please.' I clutched the receiver. 'I'll talk to you about it later, not now.'

'All right,' she conceded. 'You don't sound great, Isobel. Take care of yourself.'

'Thanks,' I said.

I got through the day. I kept myself to myself and ignored the glances of the other girls. The men knew something was up but they weren't as clued in as the girls. None of them made any comments to me.

By half-past five I was exhausted. I saved my work, switched off the computer and locked my desk. Lesley, Niamh and Anna had all left around five. I called to Barry that I was going home, and then I hurried out of the building and into my car.

I felt as though people were looking at me, although I knew that they couldn't be. I thought that they were noticing my engagement ring and nudging each other to share the knowledge that it was all a sham. Tim Malone had never intended to marry Isobel Kavanagh. How dare I strut around the streets flashing that diamond as though it was a symbol of something? It was only jewellery. Jewellery I wasn't entitled to wear.

I ripped the ring from my finger and threw it into the glove compartment. My hand felt naked without it.

The traffic was heavy and it took over an hour to get home. The family were sitting in front of the TV when I got in. My mother told me that there was some bolognese in the pot and she'd re-heat it for me if I wanted. She'd put on some spaghetti, too, if I liked. I was getting tired of her fussing around me all the time. I knew that she was trying to be supportive but she was killing me with kindness. I wanted her to stay watching *999* and shout to me that I was late and I'd have to make my own dinner.

'I'm not hungry,' I said as I curled up in an armchair with a well-thumbed copy of *Rebecca*.

'You've got to eat,' she said. 'You can't sit around pining.'

'I'm not pining,' I told her. 'I had lunch with the girls in the office. I'm fine.'

'Where's your engagement ring?' asked Alison suspiciously. 'Have you sent it back to him?'

'Shit!' I exclaimed, jumping up from the armchair. 'It's in the car.'

'What's it doing there?' asked Dad.

I didn't reply.

I retrieved the ring and slid it onto my finger again. It sparkled in the evening sunlight. I felt the ice around my heart again and took a puff of my inhaler.

'So is Shitface going to call you?' Alison looked up at me as I came in.

'Don't talk about him like that,' I snapped. 'I'm still engaged to him, we're still going to be married.'

'Leave your sister alone,' said my mother to Alison.

'Why don't you all leave me alone?' I snarled and went upstairs to my room.

I wished I'd moved out of the family home before now. I'd thought about it a couple of times, but I liked living with my family and I had expensive tastes when it came to property. Nothing I liked was ever remotely within my reach. In an apartment, I wanted somewhere bright and airy, with views over the city. In a house, I wanted a period home with a huge sunlit garden. Even Tim's townhouse wasn't really my cup of tea. But I'd have happily lived there if I was married to him.

I looked at my watch and wondered whether my friend Julie was back from her weekend away in Kerry with the girls from her tennis club. I needed to talk to Julie. She'd understand how I felt.

'I've just got in,' she said breathlessly, when I phoned. 'We had a wonderful time and I'm glad I took today off so that we could stay a little longer. It's amazing how refreshed you feel after a couple of days away.'

'Would you like to go for a drink?' I asked.

'Oh, Isobel, I'd love to, but I'm exhausted. I drove home and it's such a long drive from Killarney. The back of my neck aches.'

'I'd like to talk to you,' I said.

'I could meet you for lunch tomorrow,' she suggested.

'I'd really like it if you could meet me tonight.'

'Is there something wrong?' she asked. 'You sound funny.'

'Meet me,' I said.

'OK.' She knew that there was something wrong now. 'The usual?'

'Fine.'

'See you in half an hour?'

'Perfect.'

I changed into jeans and a sweatshirt and brushed some bronze onto my pale face. 'I'm going out,' I called to my parents. 'See you later.'

The pub was half-empty, quiet enough on a Monday night for us to be able to talk. Julie arrived a couple of minutes after me and strode over to the corner table where I sat.

I'd known Julie Donegan since we'd done a business course together eight years before. She was tall and slim with flawless skin and grey-green eyes. Her hair was naturally brown but she changed its colour every few weeks; today it was shining copper and fell around her shoulders in ordered disarray. She wore black jeans pulled tight at the waist, teamed with a crisp white blouse. I wished that I could look as graceful and elegant as Julie, but I was born too much of a tomboy for that. My hair was a mess, my sweatshirt had an old chocolate stain on the cuff and my jeans were the ones I'd worn doing the garden the previous week, so that there were grass stains on the knees.

'You look great,' I said as she sat beside me.

'You look like shit,' she told me. 'What's the matter?'

I fiddled with my engagement ring. 'The wedding's off,' I told her.

'Isobel!'

Even Julie, I thought wryly. Even my best friend could only exclaim my name and look at me in horror.

'Postponed indefinitely,' I added.

She waved at a lounge-girl. 'A couple of Southern Comforts, please.' She looked at me. 'Why?'

It was easier to tell Julie. I didn't feel that I had to pretend with her. 'He felt trapped.'

'Bullshit,' she said. 'He got cold feet.'

'I don't know what he got,' I said unhappily. 'But he got enough of it to decide that he couldn't marry me.'

'But, Isobel.' She grabbed me by the hand. 'It doesn't make any sense. Why didn't he get cold feet before now?'

'I don't know.' I took back my hand so that I could rummage in my bag for a tissue. I knew that the tears were going to fall again.

'Here.' She handed me one.

I blew my nose.

'So you're still engaged?' She looked doubtful.

'I think so.' I knew I looked doubtful too. 'He says he still loves me. He just feels that everything has got out of control.'

Julie paid for the drinks. 'What do you think?'

'Right now, I don't think anything. I feel terrible. My family keep looking at me as though I've got only weeks to live. Ian wants to beat the crap out of Tim. Alison keeps telling me that it's definitely the best thing that could have happened. Mum doesn't know what to say to all the people we've invited, and Dad sits there saying nothing but looking mournful.'

Julie laughed, and the sound of her laughter made me feel a little better.

'I told them in work,' I said. 'You know the way they are in my office – the wedding was the only topic of conversation. They kept looking at me when they thought I was preoccupied. Half-sympathetic, half-ghoulish looks. I'm sure they'd just bought me a present too. All last week Lesley kept asking me about the colour of things in the kitchen.'

'I bought you a present,' said Julie blankly. 'A set of crockery.'

'Oh, Julie!'

'Never mind.' She laughed again. 'Mum'll be pleased to have more dishes. Since she got the dishwasher she doesn't care how many odd cups of coffee or snacks we have.'

I swirled the golden drink around in my glass. 'I thought I had it all,' I said. 'I thought I was so lucky. I thought I was marrying someone who loved me. Even better that he was successful and happy in his own right. I felt part of him, Julie. I don't understand.'

'Men are impossible to understand,' she said briskly.

31

'Not Tim,' I said. 'Tim was always straightforward.'

She raised an eyebrow enquiringly at me.

'Until now,' I said.

'D'you think there's someone else?'

I picked up a beermat and broke it in half. 'No.'

'Are you sure?'

'I can't be certain.' I broke the two halves into halves again and dropped the pieces into an ashtray. 'But I truly don't think so. Why would he want to stay engaged if he had another girlfriend? It would be easier just to tell me and get it over with.'

She shook her head. 'You never know what people will say or do if they think they're making life easier for themselves. Even Tim.'

I drained my glass. 'I want to kill him.'

'I'm glad,' she said.

'Glad?'

'At least you're angry. It's better than being miserable.'

'I'm miserable too,' I said. 'I still love him.'

We had another couple of drinks. The pub filled up some more. I looked around at all the couples sitting close to each other, sharing secrets, whispering into each other's ears, occasionally kissing each other. It wasn't fair, I thought. I'd been part of all that and now he'd changed everything.

'Come on,' said Julie. 'Let's have one for the road and then go home.'

We had one for the road, then another for the road, then one for the bumps on the road and finally one for the holes in the road. My head was spinning by the time we left the pub and I almost fell as I stepped off the pavement.

'Be careful,' giggled Julie. 'Don't break a leg or anything.'

'I am careful,' I said as I clutched at her for support. 'I'm very careful. Very careful, very drunk.'

'You probably haven't been drunk in ages.' She put her arm around me. '*I* haven't been drunk in ages.'

'It's not a solution,' I said sanctimoniously.

'Nobody said it was.' She burped gently and looked surprised. 'But it can be a comfort.'

'You're my best friend,' I told her. 'And I love you.'

'And I love you.' Her words were slurred. 'You're my best friend too, Isobel. And you're more important to me than any – man.' She spat the last word.

'But you have Declan,' I protested, surprised at myself for remembering the name of her latest boyfriend. Julie wasn't exactly a one-man kind of woman. 'He's nice.'

'He's OK. But I don't love him.'

'I love Tim,' I moaned. 'I can't stop loving him, Julie. He's part of my life.'

'He's a bastard,' she said.

'He said that we might get married at the end of the year.' I almost walked into a lamp-post. 'He just needs some time.'

'He just needs a boot in the arse,' said Julie.

I laughed. 'A boot in the arse. Good idea.' I kicked out at an imaginary Tim. 'Gotcha!'

We reached the turning for Julie's house.

'I'm going to have a hangover in the morning,' I said.

'Me too.' She tried to focus her eyes. 'But it was worth it. Don't let him get to you, Isobel. Keep your chin up.'

'Sure,' I said. 'Absolutely.'

But it was hard not to let him get to me. It was hard when I felt that my whole life had been ripped apart.

～

DeltaPrint, the company I worked for, had its main offices in Stillorgan and two factories, one in Leopardstown and the other in Tallaght. I sat in the morning traffic, my hangover headache nailed behind my right eye, and wished that I worked somewhere nearer to home. The cars crawled towards the booths on the toll-bridge. One of the things I'd looked forward to when I'd married Tim was not having to cross the river every day. The journey would have been against the traffic every morning. I'd have had to put up with this nightmare for only another fortnight. I leaned my head against the side window. I felt rotten.

Alison had left a note for me on the kitchen table. '*Shitface rang*' was all it said. I wondered when Tim had called. If, perhaps, he'd changed his mind, realised that he was suffering from nerves. I laughed bitterly. Changing his mind again would cause even more chaos. I'd cancelled the hotel, the band and the photographer yesterday, trying to ignore the compassion in their voices as I told them that we were delaying the wedding.

I wondered if I should sell my dress. My wonderful Cinderella dress would end up as a small ad that said '*Wedding dress, size 12, never worn*'. People would look at it and cluck with sympathy, but they wouldn't want to buy it because it might be unlucky. I couldn't bear to think of that beautiful dress never being worn.

Dressmaking was my hobby. I'd thought, once, that I might make clothes for a living, but I didn't want to go to college and study design. I preferred doing my own thing, once-offs for friends and family. People around home knew that I made clothes. I'd done heaps of wedding dresses before I'd done my own. I thought of all the other girls wearing Isobel Kavanagh originals as they floated happily down the aisle, and I ached to be one of them.

Barry was in the office before me. I popped in to see if there was anything he wanted.

'Are you taking your holidays?' he asked bluntly. 'You're down for two weeks in May and you've arranged for someone from the agency to temp for you. Do you want to cancel that?'

I liked the way Barry was being matter-of-fact about it. There was no sympathy in his voice, only practicality.

'No,' I said. I needed the time off. I was drained from the preparations anyway, even if they hadn't come to anything.

'That's fine,' said my boss. 'Can you run me a report on the orders from DeltaPac?'

'Sure,' I said, and went back to my desk.

I'd worked with Delta for five years. I liked the company, I got on with Barry and I received regular salary increases and a bonus every Christmas. I'd have happily stayed with Delta after my marriage, although I'd told Tim that I wanted to have a baby before I was thirty and maybe give up work then. I'd always thought he was happy about the idea but perhaps that was what had spooked him. From being a carefree single man to someone whose wife wanted to be surrounded by nappies in a couple of years. Maybe I'd seemed too clinical about it. I clenched my fists under the desk. I wished I knew what I'd done. That was the worst part. I felt as though it must be my fault, but I didn't know how.

The phone rang, my private direct line.

'Good morning,' said Tim.

'Hi.' I felt my face flush.

'How are you feeling?'

'OK.'

'I'm glad. I feel terrible.'

'Really?'

'Of course. You don't think I'm pleased with myself,

do you? I've handled everything so badly. I didn't mean to do it the way I did. I upset you and I never wanted to upset you. I need to talk to you. Can we meet for lunch?'

I needed to see him. 'I suppose so.'

'Thanks. I'll pick you up around twelve-thirty.'

'I'll be outside,' I said.

I stood outside the yellow-bricked office building and watched the cars whiz by, scanning them for sight of Tim's sporty red Alfa. He was five minutes late. I tapped my foot impatiently on the pavement and tried not to think about the girls in the office who'd walked by me on their way to the village for lunch.

Eventually the car pulled up beside me.

'Sorry I'm late,' he said as I climbed in. 'Some idiot had blocked me into the car park. D'you want to go to Gleeson's?'

'OK,' I said.

Tim executed a horrendous U-turn and headed back towards Booterstown.

'How are you feeling?' he asked.

'You asked me that on the phone,' I said. 'I'm fine.'

'Good.' He changed down a gear and screamed past a builder's truck.

'Could you drive a bit slower?' I asked.

He glanced at me. I never asked him to drive slower.

He pulled into the car park of the pub and switched off the engine. 'I'm starving,' he said. 'I could eat a horse.'

He ordered steak and chips with mushrooms and potatoes. I ordered an omelette.

'You should eat a bit more than that,' he protested.

'It's all I want.' I fiddled with the silver chain on my wrist. 'I'm just not hungry, that's all.'

He was silent. He picked up a sachet of sugar and shook it, then replaced it in the little chrome dish.

'I didn't mean to be so abrupt on Friday,' he said eventually. 'I know that I should have talked to you properly. Told you how I felt, but I couldn't. Everything seemed to be so out of control. I didn't know what to do. Whenever I wanted to talk about it, you'd tell me something about the bridesmaids' dresses or the menu or the cars or a million other things. There never seemed to be the right moment to say I was getting overwhelmed by the whole thing.'

'I thought you wanted to get married,' I said. 'If you wanted to get married then all the stuff about the wedding day shouldn't matter. It's only one day in your whole life.'

'I know.' He picked up the sachet of sugar again. 'I don't know why I got cold feet.'

'Have you changed your mind again?' I looked at him, half-hopeful, half-horrified.

'No.' His response was definite and my heart sank. 'I can't do it yet, Isobel.'

'Do you think you ever can?' I asked.

'I don't know.'

'So we're not really talking about postponement here, are we? We're talking about it being over.'

He looked anguished. 'I don't want it to be over.'

'Well, it has to be, doesn't it?' I was impatient now. 'If you don't want to marry me, then it's going nowhere.'

'Why do we have to get married?' he asked. 'Why don't you come and live with me for a while?'

I was silent. Was this what he really wanted? Me without the marriage? I'd thought about living with him, we'd discussed it before, but then we'd decided that we wanted to show our commitment to each other by getting married.

'It would work,' he said. 'And we could both get used to being with each other all the time.'

The waitress put our food in front of us. Tim rubbed his hands and sprinkled salt onto his steak. The steam rose from my omelette and the smell of eggs made me feel sick.

'It's not that I don't want to be with you,' he went on through a mouthful of chips. 'It's just that marriage is such a big step.'

'So why did you want to get married in the first place?' I demanded. 'You were the one that asked me, Tim. I never made you do it.'

'Well—' He made a face. 'You were always talking about friends who were engaged. We seemed to spend a lot of time with married people. It got to me, I suppose.'

'Did I force you into it?' I was perplexed. I honestly hadn't thought that I was making him feel like that.

'Not forced,' he said. 'I don't know, Isobel. I just felt I had to ask you, and then it seemed to have a life of its own.'

I knew what he meant. There was so much paraphernalia attached to getting married that you tended to lose sight of what it was all about.

'I'm sorry you felt like that.' I poked dispiritedly at my chips.

'There's so much about you that I love,' he said. 'It's the marriage thing I'm uncomfortable with.' He grinned. 'So, if you want to move in with me for a while, help me get my head together—' He looked like a little boy when he put his head to one side like that and peered through his fringe. It was hard to resist him. But I was supposed to marry him, not just live with him. Maybe a year ago, if he'd suggested it then, I would have happily moved in. But he hadn't asked; he'd asked me to marry him and I knew that now I couldn't settle for less, stupid and all though it seemed.

'It wouldn't work,' I said.

'Oh, come on, Isobel, you haven't even thought about it properly.'

'But it's not what I expected.'

'Sometimes people have to settle for what they didn't expect.'

I moved the chips around on my plate. This wasn't what I wanted. But was he right? Did I want too much?

'I don't know,' I said finally.

His mobile phone rang. I almost jumped out of my skin.

'I'll be there soon,' he told the caller. 'I'm entitled to a break. I need some time. Of course it'll be done by four. Give me a rest, Greg! No. Yes. Talk to you later.' He shrugged. 'Never a dull moment. Told you I was busy. I can hardly get out of the office these days.'

'Poor you,' I said.

'Look.' He wiped his mouth with the paper napkin. 'I know that this has been a shock to you, Isobel, and I know that I've been a shit about it. But I also know that I love you. Why don't you do as I suggested on Friday, go on the honeymoon with one of your friends, and we'll talk about it again when you come back. It'll give us both time to think things over, and at least you'll have a break.'

A break would be nice, I thought wistfully. And I needed to get away from the solicitous glances, the well-meaning sympathy.

'OK,' I said.

'Great,' said Tim. He kissed me on the cheek. 'I'm glad you understand.'

Chapter 3

Women Running on a Beach (Pablo Picasso, 1922)

It had seemed ideal when Tim and I first discovered that the flight to Rhodes departed at one o'clock in the morning. Our plan was to go straight from the reception to the airport and hop on the flight to our honeymoon destination. No messing about with an overnight stay in Dublin where Tim's friends could have arranged practical jokes on us – just a night-time flight to the sparkling Aegean and two weeks of sun-soaked bliss.

Sitting in the departure lounge with Julie, waiting for the delayed flight to be called, didn't have quite the same appeal. She kept looking anxiously at me as though I'd suddenly disintegrate into a sobbing wretch, and kept up an inane conversation which I supposed was meant to distract me from the fact that, by now, I should have been a married woman.

I closed my eyes and leaned back in the seat. It had been a truly awful day.

I'd woken up at seven, to the birds singing joyfully in the apple-tree outside my bedroom window and the sun streaming through the light cotton curtains. It was a beautiful morning. I gazed out into the flower-filled back garden, where I'd intended to have some pre-wedding photos taken, and tears of misery and disappointment flooded down my cheeks. I tried to tell myself that it was very insecure to feel like this, that no girl in this day and age needed a husband to feel complete, that I shouldn't be crying for something that might never have worked in the first place. I tried to reason that, if Tim felt so unsure about things, it was better to wait until he was more certain. But it didn't stop me from crying. I did my best to sob silently because the thought of my mother rushing into my bedroom to comfort me was too much to bear.

Each time I looked at my watch I thought of where I should have been – at the hairdresser's, getting my make-up done, arriving at the church, walking down the aisle, saying 'I do' to Tim. I wondered what he was doing, half-expected him to call. But he didn't.

I went into town. It was the easiest way of avoiding Mum's stricken face and Alison's triumphant one. Dad and Ian had gone to a football match and had left the house without saying anything. I think Dad wanted to pretend it was just another Saturday.

Grafton Street was hot, crowded and dirty. I spent a fortune on clothes that I didn't need. I bought two linen suits in Monsoon, a beautiful silk jacket in AirWave, two pairs of Bally shoes, half-a-dozen T-shirts, a wraparound skirt and three one-piece swimsuits in M&S.

I arrived home with dozens of carrier bags and a hole in my bank balance and I didn't care.

'My God,' said Alison when she came into my bedroom. 'Did you go completely mad?'

'Why not?' I asked. 'I don't need the money for anything else.'

'Are you bringing that lot on holiday with you?'

'The T-shirts, I suppose.' I folded them neatly and put them into the suitcase. 'And the swimsuits.'

41

'You'll have a great time in the sun,' she promised. 'It'll be lovely to get away and you'll feel miles better when you come back.'

'Yes.' I tried to sound enthusiastic but it was very hard.

'What time's Julie calling around?'

'About eleven,' I said. At eleven, Tim and I should have been dancing together in the ballroom. At eleven, I should have been married for nearly eight hours. I snapped the suitcase closed.

'I'll be thinking about you tomorrow, lying on the beach having a great time,' said Alison.

'Shut up, will you,' I said, and went downstairs.

~

Julie slept all through the flight but I couldn't. So I was relieved when we finally touched down in Rhodes. It took over an hour to retrieve our luggage and nearly another hour before the bus trundled into the town of Rhodes. I'd been tired and cranky until then but I gasped with sudden delight when we turned onto the quayside and saw the hundreds of boats and ferries bobbing up and down in the water. The sunlight was dazzling off the white flagstones, the walled city made me feel as though we'd stepped back in time and the fishermen selling sponges, even at this early hour, looked like they'd been there for ever.

'Isobel!' gasped Julie. 'It's wonderful.'

'Gorgeous,' I breathed.

When I'd thought of Rhodes, I'd pictured tourists and restaurants, sunbathing and late-night bars. I hadn't imagined anything quite so timeless.

The Hotel Kos was a five-minute walk from the beach. It was very modern – smoked-glass, pink marble and very cool. I was glad to be out of the scorching sun for a while

– I wondered what on earth it would be like at midday if it was this hot already.

We were on the second floor. We threw our suitcases on the bed, pulled open the heavy curtains and stepped out onto the balcony.

There were people lying around the pool already, smearing themselves with lotions as they settled down for the morning. The pool was big – kidney-shaped with a small bridge running across the narrow part. Children jumped from the bridge into the deep end despite the notice that told them not to. I wished I had the nerve to jump into the water like that but swimming was never one of my strong points. Maybe it was because of my asthma, but whenever I swallowed water I was never able to cough it out properly and always ended up gasping for breath and clinging helplessly to the side of the pool while people clustered anxiously around me.

There was a small bar at the far end where a few people had gathered for poolside drinks.

'Tell me you're glad you came.' Julie wriggled her shoulders with pleasure at the warmth of the sun.

'Of course I'm glad I came,' I said. I was glad I had come, but I wished it wasn't Julie beside me. I should have been here with Tim. I tried not to think about him, tried to push him to the furthest recesses of my mind, but it was impossible. I felt the easy tears welling up again and I turned into the room so that Julie wouldn't see them.

'D'you want to unpack now, or go out straight away?' she asked.

I shrugged. It didn't matter. Nothing mattered.

We unpacked. When we'd put everything away, we wandered around the hotel and out to the pool. We draped our towels over a couple of sunbeds and turned them so that they faced into the sun.

'This is the life,' sighed Julie happily. 'I think I'll

lie on my stomach. Will you rub some cream onto my back?'

'Sure.'

She yelped as the cold cream hit her shoulders and I laughed as I rubbed it in.

'Are you OK, or do you want me to rub some on you?' she asked.

'I'm fine,' I said. 'I'll sit up and read for a while.'

I covered myself with Factor 10, perched my sunglasses on my nose and opened my book. But after five minutes the words jumbled in front of my eyes and I felt myself getting sleepy. I lay down on the sunbed and stared up at the cloudless blue sky. It wasn't fair, I thought miserably, it truly wasn't fair.

My eyelids fluttered closed. I fell asleep. I woke up when somebody jumped into the pool and sent a tidal wave of water over my feet. I turned to the sunbed beside me to see if Julie was awake too. It was empty. I looked around for her and finally spotted her at the far end of the swimming-pool. She was treading water and talking to two men. Quick work, even for Julie. I stood up and stretched.

'Isobel!' She waved at me. 'Come in! It's lovely.'

Julie would have walked to the side of the pool and dived in beautifully, but I lowered myself gingerly into the cold water. I gasped as I launched myself into my inelegant breast-stroke and lumbered down the pool to Julie.

'So you finally woke up,' she giggled as she held on to the rail. 'I thought you were going to sleep for ever.'

'I was exhausted,' I said.

'I was going to wake you up just to turn you over.' She disappeared underwater for a moment, then emerged again. 'I thought you might burn to a crisp.'

I glanced down at my chest. It was turning red.

'I'm OK,' I said.

'I want you to meet my two friends.' She gestured at the men she'd been talking to, who'd swum across the pool and back while I swam to her. 'This is Ari and Andreas – Andy for short.'

'Hi,' they said in unison.

'Ari and Andreas?' I looked at them quizzically. 'Are you Greek?'

They laughed. 'No,' said one. 'We're American.'

'American!' I said. 'I always thought when Americans did Europe, they just did capital cities.'

'We're Greek-American,' the nearest of the two explained. 'Ari and Andy Jordan in the States, but Ari and Andreas Iordanopoulos in Greece. We were at a family wedding in Piraeus, now we're here for a holiday.'

'They've been here a couple of days already,' explained Julie. 'They've offered to take us to dinner tonight.'

I looked from them to her.

'We're full board in the hotel,' I said blankly.

'That doesn't matter,' she said. 'Nobody says we have to eat here every night.'

'I suppose not.'

'Hey, if you don't want to eat with us it's no problem.' The Greek-American didn't look at all put out. 'We thought it'd be kinda nice to go out with you guys, but don't feel obligated.'

I felt dreadful. They were so polite and I was so rude. 'I'm sorry,' I said. 'I didn't mean that I didn't want to eat with you. I'm a bit sleepy still – my brain isn't functioning all that well.'

He laughed. 'Don't worry. We're going to the beach this afternoon. We'll see you back here – maybe around eight?'

'Sounds great,' said Julie.

'Fine,' I said.

I climbed out of the pool and went back to my sunbed. The paving stones were scorching underfoot.

'You didn't have to sound so enthusiastic!' said Julie sourly as she joined me.

'I'm sorry,' I said. 'I didn't mean—'

'It doesn't matter.' She wriggled her toes. 'But I want to have fun, Isobel, and I want you to have fun too.'

I smiled at her. I'd do my best.

～

My nose was burned. It glowed in the evening sunlight and sent Julie into a fit of giggles every time she saw it.

'Leave me alone,' I said good-naturedly. 'A different bit of you could be glowing – we just can't see it.'

'Too right,' she laughed. 'Here, put some powder on your nose, bring it down a little.'

I dabbed at my nose with *Lancôme*. 'What d'you think?'

'Better.' She nodded. 'What are you going to wear?'

'Denim skirt, white T-shirt.'

'Oh, Isobel, that's too boring. Why don't you wear that lovely printed sun-dress?'

I stared at her. 'I'm not dressing up,' I said. 'Just wearing something comfortable.'

'But you should make an effort,' she said.

'I'm on holiday. I don't need to make an effort.'

Julie ignored me as she did her face, draped herself with jewellery and slipped on a bright yellow Lycra dress.

'Are you planning on seducing one of those blokes?' I asked her. 'Because if you are, the other one will be very disappointed if he doesn't get me.'

'Fancy your chances, do you?'

'Don't be stupid. But I don't want them to think that there are two of us on offer.'

'I'm not on offer, as you so delicately put it.' She sprayed herself liberally with *Trésor*. 'I'm just dressing for dinner.'

I sighed and put on some lipstick.

Ari and Andreas were waiting for us in reception. They were both tall and dark and, I guessed, in their mid-twenties. They both wore faded Levis and cotton shirts.

'I'd better re-introduce us, since we're wearing clothes,' said the taller of the two. 'I'm Ari Jordan and this is my brother, Andy.'

'Pleased to meet you,' I said. 'I'm Isobel Kavanagh.'

'Don't tell me you don't remember my name?' Julie pouted.

'You're Julie,' said Andreas, linking his arm with hers. 'Do you want to go tourist or local?'

'I know that it's naff to want to be touristy,' said Julie. 'But could we leave the tiny little ethnic doesn't-look-much-but-the-food-is-wonderful until another night? I'd like to go to somewhere brash and bright where I can see what's going on.'

Andy laughed. 'Let's go into the old town.'

The restaurant they brought us to was perched high in the walls of the old town. From it, we had a wonderful view of the renovated market square with its fountain, its brightly lit cafés and restaurants and hundreds of small shops. The pedestrian streets were thronged with carefree people strolling around in the balmy warmth of the evening.

Julie, Andy and Ari talked about holidays. I heard the conversation but couldn't bring myself to take part. I ached with loneliness inside. I wanted to go home.

I listened as the talk covered a range of topics. Andy worked as an analyst in a petro-chemical company while Ari was a chiropractor. They lived in Florida. They came to Greece every year. I liked them but I still wanted to go home.

After the meal they walked back to the hotel with us.

'Fancy a nightcap?' asked Julie.

'I'm practically asleep on my feet as it is,' I told her. 'You go ahead if you like.'

She looked at the Jordans enquiringly.

'Why not?' said Andy.

I said goodnight and went up to the room, leaving it unlocked so that Julie wouldn't disturb me when she came up later. I pushed open the balcony doors and sat on the wrought-iron chair. Sounds of music and laughter floated up from the bar. I leaned my head against the whitewashed wall and tried not to think that, if Tim had been with me, we would have been in the bar together, laughing and joking, listening to the music. And then we'd have come back to this room and made love. I definitely didn't want to think about that. I wrapped my arms around myself and rocked back and forward in the chair. It was all wrong being here without him. It had been a mistake to come with Julie.

I sat on the balcony for about half an hour and then decided to go to bed. I'd no idea when Julie might come up and I'd no intention of sitting waiting for her as though I were her guardian.

But as soon as I'd slid under the single sheet I was wide awake again. The demon thoughts chased around and around in my head. Thoughts of Tim. What was he doing now? Was he missing me as much as I was missing him? Did he regret what had happened? Was he pacing up and down in the Donnybrook house, wishing that he'd kept his mouth shut because he'd made a dreadful mistake?

Probably not, I thought bitterly, as I twisted and turned, unable to get comfortable. He's probably out with his mates, having a few pints, perfectly happy. I groaned and punched the pillow a few times. I wanted to be asleep. I didn't want to think about Tim.

It was about an hour or so later when Julie came up. She tiptoed around the room, then clattered into the edge of my bed. She gave a muffled curse but I lay still and I heard her sigh with relief that she hadn't woken me.

She got into bed and was asleep almost instantly, snoring very gently.

I tossed and turned some more, before finally falling into a fitful sleep. But I woke early the next morning, early enough to be sitting on the balcony again when the sun rose to spill pink-gold light across the sky and begin another scorching day.

⌒

We slipped into a lazy routine of sunbathing, swimming and meeting the Jordans in the evening. I didn't mind going out in a foursome, but I felt uncomfortable when Julie sidled up to Andy and he put his arms around her while Ari and I sat beside each other like brother and sister.

There was a reason for that, and it wasn't all because I had no interest in meeting another man. Ari Jordan had no interest in meeting a woman either. I'd prepared my speech the second day, to tell him that I liked him, he was a decent bloke, and I didn't want to appear pushy or anything, but I was trying to get a relationship into perspective and I didn't think it would be a good idea to get involved with anyone else. It was a pretty good speech and I rehearsed it a couple of times to get the tone right. But Ari pre-empted me.

'I don't want you to get the wrong idea about me and my brother,' he said as we sat beside each other while

Julie and Andy smooched on the dance floor. 'He's obviously very keen on your friend. It's just that I—' he looked at me anxiously. 'I'm not actually interested in girls.'

I didn't catch on straight away. 'I'm not interested in men at the moment either.'

'No.' Ari shook his head. 'You don't understand. I am not interested in girls. At all.'

I stared at him. 'At all?'

'At all,' he said firmly.

I looked at his tanned face, amber-flecked eyes and sun-bleached hair. He was very attractive. 'But you're interested in – um, men?'

He grinned nervously. 'Well, yes.'

'Oh.' I didn't know what to say. I'd never met a guy who'd said he was gay before. I knew *of* gay people, I'd met a few blokes who were *supposed* to be gay, but I'd never sat face to face with a guy who told me that he was interested in other men.

'Does your brother know?' I asked curiously. I couldn't understand why Andy Jordan would try to double date with a couple of women when his brother would prefer to be somewhere else.

Ari sighed. 'He knows. He's OK about it. But I don't think he entirely believes it.'

'You don't look gay,' I said.

'And what does that mean?' asked Ari. 'That I haven't got a tattoo across my face saying *Gay Pride*?'

'No.' I blushed. 'I'm sorry. Of course not. I just meant that, well, you know, some gay men look very pretty and you're not pretty, you're good-looking.'

Fortunately Ari laughed. 'I'll take that as a sort of compliment.'

'Thanks.' I smiled at him. 'And your brother is interested in girls?'

'He seems very interested in your friend,' said Ari. 'Although sometimes I think Andy goes out with hundreds of girls to prove himself. You know, his older brother is gay but he wants everyone to know that he's one hundred per cent hetero. So he lines up as many women as he can.'

I nodded in understanding. 'But I hope he doesn't break Julie's heart. Although her heart is pretty OK. She usually does the breaking, I think. Not like me.'

'Tell me about your boyfriend,' said Ari. 'What's he like?'

'Want his phone number?' I asked glumly.

'No,' said Ari.

'I'm sorry.' I sighed. 'We'd been going out for a couple of years. We decided to get married. Then he decided that he'd been pressurised into it and he called it off. Julie and I are on my honeymoon at the moment.'

'The shit!' Ari smiled sympathetically. 'The least you can do is have a fun time while you're here.'

'That's what I keep telling myself,' I muttered. 'But I don't know whether I can or not.'

'You've got to,' said Ari. 'No guy is worth it. Take it from me.'

He grinned and squeezed my shoulder. I squeezed him back.

⌒

'Why don't you loosen up a bit,' said Julie as we got ready to go out the next night. 'Ari's a nice guy.'

'I know,' I said. 'He's very nice. He just happens to be gay.'

'Isobel!' She stared at me in shock. 'He can't be.'

'He is.'

'But—' She looked bemused. 'He doesn't *look* gay.'

51

'How did you expect him to look?' I demanded. 'Have *Gay Pride* tattooed across his forehead?'

She looked as abashed as I had done. 'I suppose not.' Then she glanced anxiously at me. 'But Andy isn't gay.'

'No,' I said. 'As I'm sure you've already verified.'

'Not yet,' she said. 'But maybe he's one of those blokes who's unsure about his sexuality.'

I grinned. 'He seems pretty sure about it to me.'

'Well, me too,' she conceded. 'But who knows?'

'Ari does,' I said. 'And he says that Andy is one hundred per cent.'

'I hope so. I wouldn't have believed it about Ari.'

'Neither did I until he told me,' I admitted.

'Bit of a waste,' said Julie pensively.

'For womankind generally, I suppose.' I fastened my Majorcan pearls around my neck. 'But not as far as I'm concerned. He's a nice guy and he's good company. That's all. Besides, even if he was interested in women, I'm still engaged to Tim.'

'You can't sit around and mope,' she said briskly. 'Is Tim sitting around moping?' She dabbed perfume behind her ears.

'He might be,' I said.

'Grow up, Isobel.' Julie looked at herself in the mirror and adjusted her earrings. 'Men don't sit at home and mope.'

'Even if he's out having the time of his life, it doesn't mean that I want to.'

'You can't spend all your life waiting for him,' she said.

'I'm not going to.'

She flicked a brush through her hair and turned to me. 'And what are you doing now?' she asked. 'You're on holiday. You should be having a good time. But you're miserable because he's let you down and he didn't even have the guts to tell you that it's for good.'

I stared at her. 'We've only postponed the wedding.'

'Oh, Isobel.' She sighed deeply. 'You haven't rescheduled it, have you? When exactly is it meant to take place?'

'I don't know. We haven't decided yet.'

'You mean *he* hasn't decided,' she retorted. 'Hasn't decided whether he wants to keep you hanging on a string or whether he does need someone to wash his socks and cook for him every night.'

'That's not fair.' I got up and went into the bathroom. 'He's just unsure of himself, that's all.' I stared at my reflection in the mirror. My face was tanned and healthy, but I still had shadows under my eyes.

'Isobel, maybe he really was overwhelmed by everything.' Julie stood in the doorway. 'But was it really fair of him to decide that, a couple of weeks before you got married? And he hasn't given you any decent commitment for the future.' She bit her lip. 'I don't want to preach at you, honestly I don't. But I can't see how you can trust him. What happens when you get near the next date? Does he get cold feet all over again?'

'I don't know.' I washed my hands. I hadn't needed to wash my hands, but I wanted something to do. The water cascaded over my engagement ring. I didn't wear it during the day so that there was no fine white line on my finger. But I needed to wear it at night.

'I'm sorry,' she said. 'I shouldn't have said any of those things.'

'It doesn't matter.' I patted my hands dry. 'You're probably right. I don't know any more, Julie. I don't know whether I love him or I hate him.'

'I'd hate him, personally.' She hugged me. 'But I won't preach any more – no matter what you decide to do.'

'Do you think I should break it off with him completely?' I asked.

She leaned her head against the door frame. 'Yes.'

'Why?'

'Like I said – you'll never be sure of him.'

'But maybe I can be.'

'Maybe.' She stretched her arms over her head. 'It's just that I wouldn't feel comfortable with someone who did what Tim did.'

'You've never loved someone like I love Tim,' I said.

'No.' She bit her lip. 'I don't want you to be hurt. Not by someone who isn't worth your tears.'

I smiled lopsidedly at her. 'Thanks.'

'Come on,' she said. 'We'll be late for dinner.'

❧

The Jordans brought us to a restaurant near the port. I watched a huge cruise ship, decked from bow to stern in coloured lights, gently glide into the deep-water dock. That would have been a nice honeymoon, I thought. Drifting through the Mediterranean, stopping at different ports. I wondered whether I ever would go on honeymoon with Tim. Whether Julie was right. Whether I would ever truly trust him again.

❧

It was as though we'd known the Jordans all our lives. Later in the week we went back to Andy and Ari's villa after the meal. It was a small, two-bedroomed house, with tiled floors and whitewashed walls. Andy went to get some beer from the fridge, while Ari disappeared somewhere.

'Would you mind if I stayed here tonight?' whispered Julie.

I'd expected this to happen. I shook my head.

'He might not ask me,' she murmured. 'But I'd like to if he does.'

'Whatever you want,' I said. 'Be careful, that's all.'

'Don't worry.' She grinned at me. 'Be prepared, that's my motto.' She patted her bag and winked.

I drank a beer and then told them I was going back to the hotel. 'But you stay a little longer if you like,' I told Julie. 'I'll fall asleep straight away. Don't worry about what time you come in.'

'I'll walk with you.' Ari got up before I could stop him.

It was a sixty-second walk from the villa to the hotel. 'Not much of a walk,' I said.

'Do you want a nightcap?' he asked.

'I'm tired,' I told him. 'I want to go to bed.'

'I'm sure that's where my brother and your friend are right now,' he laughed. 'That's why I suggested the nightcap.'

We sat together in the bar. To anybody watching us, we probably appeared to be a perfectly happy couple. They'd think that we were a perfectly happy engaged couple, I thought, as I glanced involuntarily at my ring. How wrong they'd be. I laughed suddenly.

'Nice to hear that.' Ari smiled.

'Just thinking.'

'About?'

'Us.' I grinned at him. 'People think that we're going out together. That we're a normal couple.'

'What's normal?' he asked.

I flushed. 'I meant—'

'I know what you meant.' He looked tired. 'It's OK.'

'Is it difficult for you?' I asked.

'Yes,' he answered. 'Some guys cope very well. Some don't cope at all. I'm somewhere between the two.'

'Do you have a boyfriend?' I hadn't wanted to ask before now, felt the question was too personal.

'I had,' said Ari. 'We were together for a year. He left me.'

'For another man?' I asked.

'At least it wasn't for a woman,' said Ari wryly.

'So you're miserable too,' I said. 'And every night you sit and listen to me wallowing in self-pity.'

He shrugged. 'I like you, Isobel. And you need to talk about it.'

'That's very American,' I told him. 'Talking about everything. I need to think about it. That's all.'

'Have another drink,' he said. 'We could get bombed tonight.'

I shook my head. 'Better not. We'll feel awful in the morning.'

'Have one more anyway.' Ari glanced at his watch. 'Give your friend and my brother time to—'

'Oh, God, yes.' I ran my fingers through my hair. 'I'd forgotten about them.'

He got the drinks and we sat in companionable silence for a while.

'What are you going to do about your boyfriend when you go home?' Ari asked.

'I don't know.' I swirled the drink around in my glass. 'I couldn't believe he'd do what he did to me.' My voice shook. 'He humiliated me.'

And that was the whole thing. Leaving aside the shock, the hurt and the betrayal, it was the feeling of humiliation that had bitten so deep. Knowing that people would look at me and say, 'There's Isobel Kavanagh – she was practically left at the altar.'

'You'll get over it,' said Ari.

'How do you know? I might be deeply scarred for life.'

'You might be, but I doubt it.' Ari smiled gently at me. 'You're a tough person.'

'No, I'm not.'

'You are,' he said. 'You're here, holidaying with your friend. Going out with Andy and me.'

'I feel safe with you,' I said dryly. 'I know that's very unfair.'

'No.' Ari shook his head. 'I'm glad you feel that way.'

'I don't like dumping my life in your lap. Especially when you've got your own problems.'

'Don't mind me,' said Ari. 'Your fiancé is a shit. When you go home you should fling that ring in his face.'

'I couldn't do that.'

'Well, keep the ring, but break it off with him anyway.'

'Did Julie put you up to this?' I asked curiously. 'Because I had a very similar conversation with her earlier tonight.'

He shook his head. 'But the two of us have independently come to the same conclusion. Don't waste your life on him, Isobel.'

'Thanks for the advice.' I finished my drink and stood up. 'If you don't mind, Ari, I'm going to bed now. Julie and Andy can take their chances.'

'Goodnight.' He took me by the hand and squeezed it gently. His touch was warm and dry.

I held his hand for a moment. 'Goodnight,' I said, and went upstairs.

Chapter 4

Woman Lying Down (Salvador Dalí, 1926)

I was nervous about going home. I didn't know what to expect from Tim and I didn't know exactly how to behave with him. Julie continued to tell me that I should make a clean break, start all over again. Ari Jordan thought the same. But that didn't make them right, I told myself. They didn't know Tim. If the same thing had happened to somebody I knew, then probably I would have offered similar advice – he's not worth it, forget him. But you can't just forget people and you can't just throw away two years of a wonderful relationship.

❦

Alison told me that I looked great. 'Healthier,' she said critically, 'although you still have a pained look about you.'

'That's because the flight is so long,' I told her. 'And I dozed off at a funny angle. I've got a crick in my neck.'

'He didn't ring while you were away,' she said.

'Who?'

'Shitface.'

'Why should he?' I asked. 'He knew I wasn't here.'

'Ha!' she exclaimed triumphantly. 'You knew who I meant.'

'Of course I knew who you meant.'

'Have you decided to give him the order of the boot?' she asked. 'Have you come to your senses at last?'

'Give me a break, Ali,' I sighed. 'I'm not making any major decisions at the moment.'

～

The girls in work told me I looked great too.

'And your hair is lovely like that,' said Niamh.

I smiled. My hair had grown enough to be tamed into a single plait. I liked it that way too, although I knew I'd probably get it cut again. I wasn't really a long-haired person.

I sat at my desk and took out my diary. Barry was at a meeting in Naas all day which suited me. It meant time to catch up on some paperwork. It also meant that I'd be able to phone Tim.

I'd called the previous night but his answerphone cut in with its jokey '*Tough, you've missed me*' message. I didn't want to leave a message on the machine, I needed to talk to him myself. I still didn't know what to do about him.

I phoned his office at noon which was usually a good time to catch him. 'He's not here this week,' said Shauna, the receptionist. 'I think he's gone to the States.'

He did that from time to time. The software company was owned by an American parent, which in turn was owned by some company in the Far East. Tim had been to California a few times, and to Tokyo twice. I often wondered if anyone knew exactly who owned what in the corporate world. Whether there was one single company that owned everything, only nobody quite realised it yet.

'Do you know when he's due back?' I asked.

'At the weekend, I think,' replied Shauna. 'If you hold on a moment, I'll check.'

Classical music played while I waited. I preferred silence.

'He'll be back on Friday night,' she said. 'Isobel?' Shauna clicked back into the line.

'Yes.'

'We're all really sorry about what happened.'

'Thanks,' I said.

'But if both of you were unsure then it was a wise decision.'

Was that what he'd told them? Better, I supposed, than saying it was his idea.

'Thanks,' I said again.

'I hope you *do* get married. I always thought you were perfect together.'

'We'll see,' I said, although I hoped so too.

I couldn't give up on Tim although I was disappointed that he hadn't left a message for me to say that he'd be away. But he was a laid-back person, the sort who doesn't think about leaving messages, or washing last night's dishes or filling the car with petrol before going on a long journey. I put it down to his brilliance at computers. Maybe even genius. You don't expect a genius to be the same as a normal person.

I went to the townhouse while he was away. I'd left a pair of shoes there which I needed, and some lipstick which I didn't really need but wanted to retrieve anyway.

His car was in the driveway. I parked behind it and slid the key into the hall door. The alarm beeped at me and I tapped in the code numbers to silence it.

The house was still and quiet. I pushed open the door to the living room. A foil tin sat on the coffee-table, the remnants of a curry congealed inside it. I wrinkled my nose at the smell. A number of computer magazines were strewn across the floor and one of Tim's workpads lay open, the writing and squiggles on it proof of his industry over the past few weeks.

I picked up the remains of the curry and deposited them in the bin. I tidied up the magazines and left the workpad, still open, on the table. I put away the dishes that were on the draining-board and wiped breadcrumbs from the kitchen table. I filled the vase of flowers with fresh water. Not like Tim to have flowers, I thought. They were gladioli, my favourites. I wondered if he'd bought them because of me.

His bed was unmade, the duvet piled into a heap in the centre. The bedroom smelled, unmistakably, of Tim. A combination of *Badedas* shower-gel and *Ralph Lauren* aftershave. I sat on the bed and buried my face in the duvet. I missed him so much it really, truly hurt.

My shoes were in the wardrobe. I put them into a plastic bag along with the lipstick which had been on the chest of drawers. I straightened the duvet and plumped up the pillows. I should have been doing this anyway, I thought, suddenly. If things had gone according to plan I would be Isobel Malone and I would be plumping up the pillows and making the bed because Tim would expect me to. And because I'd be happy to do it. I would be living in this house instead of simply visiting it.

'How could you do this to me?' I said the words out loud. 'How could you!' I threw the plastic bag containing my shoes and my lipstick across the bedroom. 'Why did you do this to me?' Then I collapsed, sobbing, onto the bed.

The phone rang and startled me. I heard the answering machine whir into life and Tim's voice echoed around the house.

'It's me.' The caller was female. 'I thought I might catch you before you left. I wanted your first set of notes on the Saracen project. It doesn't matter. Catch you later on.' I heaved a sigh of relief. It was work. For one horrible, heart-stopping moment, I thought that the strange female voice might have had something to do with Tim calling off our wedding. But that was silly. I was creating monsters for myself.

I gathered up my shoes and lipstick and let myself out of the house.

~

I rang him again on Friday night, but the answering machine was still on. This time, though, I left a message for him to call me when he got home.

He phoned on Sunday afternoon.

'How did you enjoy your holiday?' he asked.

'It was lovely,' I answered steadily. 'The hotel was nice, the weather was gorgeous and I had a wonderful rest.'

'That's good,' he said. 'Isobel, were you in the house while I was away?'

He sounded aggrieved.

'Well, yes,' I replied. 'I wanted to get a pair of shoes that were there. I phoned your office and they said you'd be away until this weekend and I needed the shoes before then.'

'So you're responsible for tidying everything up.'

'I didn't throw anything away,' I said. I knew that sometimes the most awful rubbish was very important to Tim. 'I just threw out your disgusting curry left-overs.'

'Thanks,' he said. 'But you really shouldn't have cleaned up after me. I can do it myself.'

'I couldn't help it,' I told him. 'It was so horrible and I couldn't imagine what it might be like by now.'

'It was very good of you,' he said.

'That's me.'

'D'you want to meet for a drink?'

'Tonight?'

'I suppose so.'

'OK,' I said. 'I'd like a drink.'

We met in Clontarf Castle. Alison made a face at me when I said I was meeting him, Mum looked worried and Dad rustled his newspaper.

'I need to talk to him,' I told nobody in particular as I grabbed my keys from the mantelpiece.

The castle was bathed in evening sunshine and it seemed a shame to go inside. But I found a couple of seats beside the window, ordered myself a beer and waited for Tim. I was early. I was annoyed at myself for being early – I should have been late and left him waiting for me. That's the least that Julie would have advised. But the traffic-lights had been green all along the coast and I'd got here much quicker than I'd intended. I took my diary out of my bag and made a show of studying it so that people wouldn't think I was waiting for someone.

I'd almost finished my beer when he arrived. I sensed his presence before I saw him. He hadn't seen me yet. I waved in his direction and he nodded at me.

'Sorry I'm late,' he said as he sat down. 'There was an accident on Morehampton Road. Delayed me a bit.'

'That's OK.' I signalled to a lounge-boy and ordered drinks.

'You look wonderful,' he said. 'The holiday seems to have done you the world of good.'

'I feel a lot better,' I admitted. 'I was pretty shattered, you know.'

He took my hand. His touch was soft and familiar. I felt myself dissolve inside.

'I'm really sorry, Isobel.' He squeezed my hand even

tighter. 'I wouldn't have hurt you for anything. You know that.'

I nodded.

'Afterwards I thought that I was an idiot. That I should have gone through with it anyway. That we would have worked it out. But I couldn't be certain.' He pushed his fringe out of his eyes but it flopped back again almost immediately. 'You're very special to me, Isobel.'

'I should hope so,' I said. 'Allegedly, we're still engaged.'

'Of course we are,' said Tim.

I sighed with relief. 'And do you have an idea of when we should get married?'

'Not yet.' He tapped the edge of the table. 'I'm sorry, Isobel, I really am. I need a bit more time to think.'

Alison and Julie's warnings flashed through my head.

'I need to know,' I told him. 'I need to be sure about things.'

'I'm sure that I want to marry you,' said Tim. 'I'm just not sure when.'

I bit my lip. This wasn't really what I wanted to hear.

'I'd still like it if you lived with me,' he added. 'I was put out when you came and collected your shoes. It seemed like you were trying to move away from me.'

'It wasn't that,' I told him. 'They were my flat shoes. I needed them to wear with jeans.'

'When I see you sitting in front of me, I know that I was mad,' said Tim. He shook his head. 'Everybody told me that I was mad.'

'It was a horrible thing to do.' All at once my anger returned. 'You made a fool out of me, Tim. Everyone looks at me and thinks "There's that poor girl who was dumped at the altar". I had to go and face everyone in work. I had to cancel the hotel and the band and the photographer and everything. Mum and Dad are

64

devastated. Ian wants to kill you. Only Alison thinks I've had a merciful release.'

He smiled. 'She would.'

'She might be right,' I said tartly. 'It was cruel, Tim. Really cruel.'

'I know.' He took my hands again and enveloped them in his. 'I hated myself for doing it. But it seemed right to me at the time. Maybe it was all wrong, I don't know. But it would have been awful to get married when there was a nagging doubt there. You do see that, don't you?'

'Oh, I see it all right,' I said. 'Julie thinks I'm far too understanding.'

'We've had a good relationship,' said Tim. 'It can withstand this, can't it?'

He looked so vulnerable sitting in front of me. My anger melted away. 'Of course it can,' I said.

~

The family was gathered around the TV. I sat down in my favourite armchair and picked up the paper.

'Well?' said Mum.

'Well what?' I turned over a page.

'Well what has he got to say for himself?'

'Nothing new,' I told her. 'He's sorry, of course.'

'Huh!' She snorted. 'I don't want you wasting your time with him, Isobel. There's other fish in the sea.'

'Mum,' I sighed. 'I'm sure there are plenty of other fish in the sea. You've told me that often enough. Remember when I split up with Alan Davenport? That's exactly what you said then. And the Niall Dillon episode? There's no need to trot out all the old lines.'

'I'm only trying to help,' she said.

'I know,' I said. 'But this is something I can work out for myself.'

'I wish I could believe that,' she said moodily, and turned back to the feature film.

~

Tim asked me to go to the launch of one of the company's new software packages the following Friday. There was to be a corporate presentation in the afternoon and a dinner that evening. I wasn't going to the corporate presentation, but I was looking forward to the dinner. I rushed home from work to get ready and locked myself in the bathroom, much to the annoyance of Ian who was going out too.

'It'll only take you a couple of minutes to shower!' I yelled through the locked door.

'I need to shave as well,' he protested. 'Hurry up, Issy, you're not the only member of this family who goes out, you know.'

I was wearing a midnight-blue dress with a low-cut back to show off my tan. I pulled my hair into the plait again and tied it with some dark blue velvet ribbon. I was pleased with the effect. I made sure that my make-up looked very natural and doused myself in *Allure*, which was Tim's favourite perfume.

'You look fantastic,' said Alison as I came downstairs. 'Far too good for Shitface.'

'Stop calling him that.' I tightened the butterflies at the back of the diamond and sapphire earrings Tim had given me for my last birthday.

'I'm just concerned about you,' she said.

'Give it a rest.' I looked out of the window. Tim was picking me up but he'd balked at coming into the house. I wasn't too keen on him running the gauntlet of my family either, so I said that I'd watch out for him if he just parked outside. I heard the distinctive roar of his car coming down the road, picked up my bag and hurried out.

'God, you look beautiful,' he said as I got into the car.

I knew I did. I'd spent a lot of time working on looking beautiful.

'Thanks.'

'I won't be able to keep my hands off you, looking like that.'

'You'd better,' I told him. 'Unless you want to scandalise the board of Softsys.'

'It'd take a lot to scandalise them,' Tim laughed as he sped down the coast road.

'Well, don't try anyway,' I said.

The dinner was in Jurys. I'd expected Tim to moan about picking me up, because he could have walked to the hotel, but he didn't seem to mind. Guilt was working wonders on him.

We walked into the hotel together and I knew that we looked good as a couple. Tim, as I often told him, cleaned up well. When he was prised out of his T-shirt and jeans and forced into a suit, he looked handsome and desirable.

Tonight's dinner was black-tie – not very usual with the software crowd – but Tim said that they all liked to dress up occasionally. He looked fantastic in his tux and he wore it with a confidence he said he didn't feel.

'It's great on you.' I adjusted his bow-tie for him. 'You look like a grown-up.'

'I don't want to be grown-up,' he said. 'I want to be young for ever.'

'Come on, my little Peter Pan,' I said. 'Let's join the throng.'

I knew most of the Softsys people. Shauna, the receptionist, was standing just inside the door, a glass of wine in her hand.

'Isobel!' she cried when she saw me. 'It's great to see you!'

'Thanks.'

'You look wonderful. Have you been away?'

'I went to Rhodes,' I said and the penny dropped. Shauna blushed furiously.

'I'm sorry,' she said. 'I've put my foot in it.'

'It's OK.' I grabbed a glass of wine from a passing waiter. 'There's a lot of people here tonight.'

'This is one of our biggest products this year,' she told me. 'Some of the US guys are over.'

'Great,' I said. I watched Tim as he walked over to a tall, fair-haired man and shook his hand.

'Tim's been very quiet these last few weeks,' said Shauna. 'Of course he had his US trip, but I think he really missed you, Isobel.'

'It's his own fault,' I told her.

'Isobel!' Dave Brennan, one of the other designers put his arm around me. 'How are you?'

'Great, Dave, thanks.'

'You're very good to come along,' he said. 'We weren't sure you would.'

'Why shouldn't I?' I asked.

'Oh, well.' He looked embarrassed. 'We thought you mightn't like to.'

'Don't worry about me, Dave,' I said. 'I'm fine.'

People began to take their seats at the tables. Tim and I were near the top table. 'High in the pecking order,' he told me. 'Not that I really want to worry about that sort of thing.'

Maurice Fitzgerald, the company MD, made a speech about the new product, telling us how it would make other, similar systems, obsolete. Industry standard, he said a few times. I didn't listen to Maurice but glanced through the menu. The different courses had been given computer-speak names – '*Melon bytes*' for starters, followed by '*Megabytes of beef with a lyonnaise potato interface*'. Maurice finished his speech and the food was brought around.

I sipped my wine then spluttered as I felt Tim's hand on the top of my leg. The midnight-blue dress had a slit along the side which Tim had noted approvingly in the car. Now I could feel his fingers moving gently across my thigh. I looked at him, but he was turned away from me, talking to the man on the other side of him. I squeezed my legs tightly together and Tim slapped me softly with his fingers. I opened my legs slightly and, when he moved his hand between them, squeezed them closed again and trapped him. I could feel him flex his hand between my legs but he couldn't move it. I continued to eat the starter and began to talk to Dave who was sitting on the other side of me.

Finally, Tim leaned towards me and whispered into my ear, 'Let go.'

'Why?' I whispered back.

'Because I want to butter my bread-roll.'

'You should have thought of that earlier.'

'I know.'

'Keep your hands to yourself until later.'

'Spoilsport,' he said as I loosened my grip.

⁓

Tim didn't like dancing. I adored it. But there was no chance of getting him to dance with me.

So I danced with Dave and Maurice, with two other software developers, Keith and Greg, and with the bloke from the Californian office, Duane. It was fun dancing with Duane because he was well over six feet tall and was the thinnest man I'd ever met. He was, he told me, African-American. I told him that I'd recently met Greek-Americans. I wondered were there any people who were simply Americans.

'Native Americans,' he said politically correctly and very seriously and I dissolved into a fit of giggles which he didn't understand.

It was nearly one-thirty when Tim finally decided to suffer the obligatory dance with me. The band was playing smoochy love songs and he held me close to him while the music washed over us.

'I've had too much to drink,' he murmured sleepily. 'I didn't mean to.'

'It's OK,' I said.

'Not really. I wanted to be awake.'

'You'll wake up when you go outside,' I told him. 'The fresh air will do it for you.'

'Come home with me tonight,' he said as he pressed closer to me. 'Stay with me tonight.'

I wanted to stay with him more than anything. I'd thought about it before I'd even left my house earlier that night. I'd wondered would he ask.

'But will you still love me tomorrow?' I breathed the words of the song into his ear.

'I love you right now,' he said.

The night air was cool. I shivered as the breeze hit my bare back.

'Here.' Tim took off his black jacket and hung it around my shoulders.

'I don't need your jacket,' I protested.

'I've a long-sleeved shirt on,' he said. 'You'll freeze to death. Much good you'd be to me if you froze, Isobel, don't you think?'

'But imagine the fun you'd have warming me up.'

He took me by the hand and we walked up Pembroke Road. The leaves of the trees rustled in the breeze. The road, normally so crowded with traffic, was quiet, the tall houses in darkness.

Tim whistled softly as we walked and I cuddled up to him. They would be so annoyed with me, I thought as I smiled slightly to myself, Alison and Julie, Mum and Dad, Ian – and Ari Jordan. All those people who thought I shouldn't give Tim a second chance. All those people who were ready for me never to forgive him. And they were all so wrong.

We turned into his narrow driveway. The yellow porch light glowed dimly. Tim fumbled for his keys and dropped them. I picked them up and handed them to him. He opened the door. I switched off the alarm.

We stood facing each other in the hallway. I let Tim's jacket fall from my shoulders. He loosened the straps of the midnight-blue dress. It slid from me into a circle of blue velvet. I was wearing a navy body underneath, no stockings. Tim looked at me wordlessly. I looked back at him.

He picked me up and carried me up the stairs. He put me onto the bed. He stood at the end of the bed while he fumbled at his bow-tie, took off his shirt. I liked Tim's chest. Not a hugely muscled chest, but firm with a springy covering of curly black hair. Sometimes I would run my fingers through the curls and he would gasp in pain and in pleasure.

I lay immobile on the bed. He positioned himself over me and undid the silk body. His expression was serious as he made love to me. Sometimes he moved very slowly, so that he was hardly moving at all. Then he would pick up his rhythm until he seemed to be possessed, before suddenly slowing down again. He was wonderful to me that night. He touched me in all the places I liked most to be touched. He left gentle kisses all over my body. And when I told him that I could stand no more, he entered me again, more fiercely, with more determination and I shuddered and cried with pleasure.

We crawled under the duvet together. He fell asleep straight away, his eyelashes forming straight black lines on his cheeks. I looked at him in the shadow of the darkness and I wanted to cry with love for him.

I knew that he was the only man I would ever love. I knew that one day I would marry him. And be happy.

Chapter 5

La Vie (Pablo Picasso, 1903)

It was warm, but the rain hissed against the window and formed tiny pools of water in the cracks between the paving slabs of the patio. I pressed my nose against the glass and looked up at the sky. The grey clouds were skimming the top of the trees and it seemed impossible that somewhere up there was a blue sky and a fiercely burning sun.

I searched the utility room for my rain jacket but I couldn't find it. It was probably in Tim's house.

The front door slammed as Ian went out. A few moments later, Alison was gone. I wondered how my parents felt about their children growing up. Would they be sorry or relieved when we all finally left home?

The jacket might be bundled onto the top shelf of my wardrobe, I thought suddenly. That was where I usually threw clothes that weren't in daily use. I ran upstairs to check, but it wasn't there. I was on my way downstairs again when the phone rang.

'I'll get it,' I called as I picked up the receiver.

'Isobel! Glad I caught you.'

'Hi, Tim.' I glanced at my reflection in the hall mirror, smoothed my eyeshadow a little with my middle finger.

'Isobel, I'm really sorry but I can't see you tonight.'

'Why not?' I hadn't seen Tim in almost a fortnight – he was working very hard on the new software application.

'Because I'm up to my tonsils in work,' he said. 'I'm ringing from the office – haven't had time to get home yet.'

'How long will you be there?' I asked.

'I'm not sure. It depends on how this thing looks after I fiddle about with it a bit. Could be an hour, could be twelve hours.'

'Oh, Tim. I was looking forward to seeing you.'

'I was looking forward to a night out too,' he said. 'I need to come up for air! But I absolutely can't leave this at the moment.'

'Why don't I come over to your house and cook you dinner?' I suggested. 'I could have it ready for you when you come in, and you could flop in front of the TV.'

'Nice thought.' I could almost see Tim smile. 'But I really don't know how long I'll be, and I'd hate you to go to all that trouble.'

'It wouldn't be any trouble,' I said.

'All the same.' Tim was firm. 'It wouldn't be fair. Why don't you go out and have a good time and I'll give you a buzz tomorrow?'

'Oh, OK then.' I knew I sounded mulish but I couldn't help it.

'I'll be finished by tomorrow,' promised Tim.

'I said it's OK.'

'All right. I'd better go. Sooner I start again, sooner I finish.'

'OK. Take care.' I replaced the receiver and sighed.

Not for the first time I wished that Tim's job didn't seem to mean so much to him, that he didn't commit himself so completely to every project he was involved in.

I wandered back into the living room and sat down.

Mum looked up from the TV. 'I thought you were going out.'

'I was. Tim's working late. That was him on the phone.'

She made an indeterminate clucking sound.

'Don't,' I said.

'Don't what?'

'Make that noise.'

'What noise?' She looked the picture of innocence.

'You know quite well,' I said as I picked up the *Evening Herald*.

Saturday night, I thought glumly, and I'm stuck here watching boring TV with my parents. What a frumpish thing to do. I flicked through the newspaper without reading it and came to the cinema pages. Maybe I'd go to the pictures, I thought. There was a new James Bond movie showing. Tim hated James Bond. I wouldn't care if I was on my own. Maybe Julie was home. She liked Pierce Brosnan. I threw the paper to one side and phoned her.

'I'd love to go,' she said.

'Great. I'll phone and book seats on my credit card. D'you want me to pick you up?'

'Fine,' she said. 'What time's the film?'

'Eight forty-five,' I told her. 'I'll call around for you in fifteen minutes.'

Mum clucked again when I said I was going out with Julie. Dad was immersed in the newspaper.

The rain was heavier now. It hammered against the pavement and beat against the windscreen of the car. I turned the wipers on fast, so that they flapped over and back in their own demented dance.

'What a foul night,' gasped Julie as she climbed into the car. 'Maybe I should have stayed in and watched TV after all!'

'Nonsense,' I told her. 'You know you wanted nothing more than to come out with me.'

'I thought you'd be out with Tim tonight,' she said, brushing rain from her jumper.

'I should have been,' I admitted. 'But he's working.'

Julie didn't mind being second choice. 'I suppose if I was in love with someone I'd want to be with him rather than a girlfriend,' she said jauntily. 'Even if the man is Tim Malone.'

'Oh, shut up.' I turned onto the main road.

We ran from the car to the cinema but we still got soaked. I'd thought I had an umbrella in the car but it had unaccountably disappeared.

'It doesn't matter.' Julie looked around the heaving throng in the foyer. 'Let's get some popcorn and ice cream.'

We loaded up with supplies and made our way into the darkness.

Afterwards, Julie suggested we go for something to eat.

'After popcorn and ice cream!' I exclaimed.

'I didn't have any dinner,' she told me. 'And popcorn doesn't exactly fill you up.'

So I drove to a small restaurant in Malahide, where the food was inexpensive but very good. It was full of couples gazing into each other's eyes over the flickering candles on the wooden tables.

'God,' murmured Julie. 'I feel like a complete gooseberry.'

I laughed. 'Who cares?'

We ordered blackened chicken and garlic potatoes. When the food came, I realised that I was hungry.

'Have you heard from Andreas the Greek lately?' I asked Julie casually as I blew on a portion of chicken.

Even in the candlelight, I could see her blush.

'Oh?' I grinned at her.

'He phoned tonight,' she said. 'Just before you, in fact.'

'Well, well, well.' I bit into a piece of chicken and the spices nearly blew my head off. I gulped at my glass of water.

'Serves you right,' laughed Julie as I dabbed at my watering eyes. He'd rung her a couple of days after we'd got home from Rhodes but she hadn't mentioned him since.

'He's phoned a few times,' she said.

'Julie!'

'I really like him,' she said defensively.

'He must really like you,' I said, 'if he's the one doing all the phoning!'

'He might,' she said non-committally.

'Julie Donegan! Are you conducting a long-distance affair with this bloke?'

'I'd like to,' she said. 'But it's very difficult when you're at the other end of the phone and you know the person you're talking to is hundreds of miles away.'

'I guess so.' I ate another piece of chicken, more cautiously this time.

'There was something about him,' she said dreamily. 'I haven't felt this way about anyone before.'

'Really?'

'Really. And I know you'll say it's because we were on holidays and everything was idyllic, but it isn't like that, Isobel.'

I scratched my cheek. 'I'm delighted.'

'It's all very well being delighted,' she told me waspishly, 'but he's in Florida and I'm in Dublin. It's not exactly an easy relationship.'

'I can see that.' I filled our glasses with more water. 'Are you going to go and see him or anything?'

'He's asked me to,' she said. 'In September.'

I whistled under my breath.

'Don't look so surprised,' she said. 'I might go.'

'*Do* go,' I said, surprised at my own insistence. 'Go and decide whether you love him or not.'

'Goodness, Isobel.' She laughed at me. 'That sounds very intense.'

'I know.' I smiled ruefully. 'I just want you to be happy, Julie.'

'And what about you?' she asked. 'Are you happy?'

I sipped my water. 'Of course.'

'Resolved your differences with Tim?'

'Yes.'

'When are you getting married?'

I sipped my water again. 'I'm not sure.'

'Haven't you set a date yet?'

'No,' I said. 'But that doesn't mean anything, Julie. We're still going to do it. It's just that he's really busy at the moment, finishing some project. When it's wrapped up, then we'll discuss the wedding.'

'I'm glad you're happy,' she said seriously. 'But don't let him hurt you again.'

'I won't,' I said, and applied myself to the serious business of eating.

⌒

Alison was making toast when I came downstairs the following morning. The rain of the previous day had disappeared and the sun was brilliant in the washed blue sky. I poured some cereal into a bowl and sat in the cane chair near the kitchen door.

Alison leaned against the wall and yawned widely. Her hair fell into her eyes and she pushed it back lethargically.

'Where were you last night?' I asked. 'You look wrecked.'

'I feel wrecked,' she admitted, yawning again. 'Suzy had her going-away drinks last night. I didn't get in until half-four this morning, but I couldn't sleep.'

'When does she leave?' Suzy, an old friend of Alison's, was going to Australia for six months.

'Tonight,' said Alison. 'If she wakes up.'

'Will she enjoy it?'

'Australia?' Alison poured some milk into a glass and drank it in a single gulp. She wiped the white moustache from her lip. 'I'd say so. She says she'll do a lot of travelling. She has an aunt or cousin or something in Perth so she'll go there for a while, then get around.'

'It'd be nice to work abroad,' I mused.

Alison nodded, then winced. 'Bloody head,' she muttered.

'Your toast is burning,' I said.

'Shit!' She fiddled with the toaster and held the two blackened pieces of bread between her fingers. 'I hate burnt toast.'

'Put on some more,' I said.

She sighed and threw the toast into the garden. 'Doesn't matter. The smell of it burning has put me off.'

She filled the kettle and plugged it in. I watched her while she leaned against the wall again. Most people never thought of Alison and me as sisters because we were so unalike. But despite the fact that we disagreed on hundreds of little things we managed to get on well together.

The kettle boiled and she made coffee for both of us.

'I begin to feel more human,' she said as she sipped hers. 'I can feel my red corpuscles getting up and wandering around in my bloodstream again.'

I laughed. 'Mine are marching around already. I feel

very energetic today. Maybe I can persuade Tim to play tennis with me.'

'Oh!' Alison put her cup on the table and stared at me. Then she blushed. The colour started at her neck and very slowly flooded her face. She put her hands to her cheeks as though to hide it.

'What's wrong?' I asked in surprise.

'Nothing.' She picked up the cup and sipped her coffee again.

'Alison!'

She looked uncomfortable.

'Come on,' I said. 'Whatever it is, you might as well tell me.'

A wasp came in through the open kitchen door and buzzed around the kitchen. Alison flapped a towel ineffectually at it as she tried to persuade it out of the door again. It careered into the window and buzzed frantically. Alison threw the towel at it and scored a direct hit. The wasp fell onto the draining-board and spun around.

'I think I've killed it,' she wailed.

'Maybe not,' I said. 'Put it outside, it might recover.'

She scooped it onto some kitchen paper and threw it out onto the grass. 'That way I won't know whether it dies or not,' she said as she emptied the remains of her coffee down the sink and rinsed her cup. 'I'd better go and get dressed.'

'Not until you tell me what you were so put out about,' I told her.

'It was nothing.'

'Don't give me that crap,' I said with sisterly feeling. 'Tell me.'

I could always make her tell me things.

'It's just – I thought you were going out with Tim last night,' she said.

I looked at her in surprise. 'I was. But he couldn't

80

meet me so I went out with Julie instead. There's nothing wrong with that, is there?'

'No,' she said.

'So, what's the problem?'

'I met Tim last night.'

'Oh?'

'Well, not met, exactly. I saw him. And I thought he was meant to be with you.'

'Where did you see him?' I asked.

'In Donnybrook,' said Alison.

'Probably went out for a drink after he finished his work,' I told her. 'I know that if I ever work late all I want to do is flop in front of the telly, but Tim likes going for a drink to unwind. He says that some of his best ideas come to him in a haze of alcohol, only he can never remember them afterwards.'

Alison still looked uncomfortable.

'So did you talk to him?' I asked. I could imagine what their conversation would be like. Alison held a grudge. That was another difference between us. I can never stay angry with someone, but Alison can store up rage to use months later on her unsuspecting victim.

'No,' she said. 'I was going to, but I didn't.'

'I still don't see what the fuss is about.' I drained my cup. 'Just because you don't like him any more.'

'I don't want to cause you any hassle,' she said defensively. 'Really I don't. And I don't want you to get mad at me.'

'What have you done?' I asked, suddenly alarmed. 'Don't tell me you did something awful?'

'Of course I didn't.' She sounded indignant. 'What d'you take me for.' She sighed deeply. 'It's only – well – there was someone with him.'

'What do you mean?'

'I didn't meet him in a pub,' she said. 'We went for

something to eat. And he was there, in the restaurant. I thought you were with him because the girl who was there looked very like you. Only her hair was longer. And I think she had blue eyes. Maybe it was just blue eyeshadow. I can't remember properly. We'd had a few drinks by then. And I was going to go up to him and say hello – maybe say that he was a shit or something – I don't know—' she looked at me unhappily. 'But this girl was with him.'

'So what?' I tried to ignore the painful pounding of my heart in my ribcage. 'He was probably working late and decided to go and have something to eat.'

'I know,' she said miserably.

'So why are you getting so upset?'

'I don't know.' She rubbed at her eyes. 'I suppose – I saw him with this girl – I don't know what I thought.'

'The worst obviously,' I said angrily. 'Just because you didn't want me to get married in the first place! And he let me down! And you think he's going to let me down over and over again! Well, that's not going to happen, Alison Kavanagh. OK, so things went wrong a couple of months ago. That doesn't mean that Tim and I haven't sorted out our differences and made decisions about our lives. And I'm not going to get upset because he has dinner on Saturday night with a work colleague.'

'I know. I'm sorry,' she said.

'Fine,' I told her.

I pulled my dressing-gown tighter around me and went upstairs. I locked myself into the bathroom and turned on the shower. The room filled up with steam. I hung my dressing-gown on the bathroom door, and slipped out of my pale pink pyjamas.

I wished Alison hadn't told me. It wasn't that I didn't believe that Tim had been working. I was sure he had. I knew how involved he became in every project and

I knew, too, that he often had someone working with him. But I was unhappy that he'd gone to dinner with this unknown girl instead of phoning me and asking me if I'd like to see him.

Silly, I told myself, as I stepped under the spray. Why should he ring? Would I, if it had been the other way around? If I'd been in the office and wanted something to eat, would I have tried to call Tim or would I have suggested to one of the girls that we'd go out together? I wasn't sure. It had never happened.

He might have phoned, of course. He could have called and found out that I was at the cinema with Julie and so decided to go and eat with this girl. Sensible thing to do, really.

I turned off the shower and wrapped a towel around me. I'd phone him myself and sort things out. That was the best thing to do.

Condensation dripped from the wall mirror. I drew a heart on the steamy surface and wrote Tim's name in the middle. It was a stupid thing we used to do in school. Write some guy's name in the steam and he'd fall for you. I shook my head and rubbed the mirror with some toilet roll. I was engaged to Tim, for God's sake! I shouldn't feel the need to write his name on the mirror.

'Isobel?' Alison rapped at the door.

'I'll be out in a minute.'

'Isobel, I'm sorry.'

'For what?' I asked as I towelled myself briskly.

'For telling you. I shouldn't have said anything.'

'Don't be daft.' I ran a wide comb through my hair and winced every time I reached a tangle.

'But it was silly of me. I mean, you're right, she was probably just from work and everything.'

'It's OK,' I told her.

'All the same—'

'Forget it, will you!' I shouted. 'It doesn't bloody matter.'

But of course it mattered, I thought, as I sat on my bed and blowdried my hair. No matter how innocent it was, I hated to think of him sitting in a restaurant on a Saturday night with another woman. Especially as he'd broken off a date with me – just minutes before I'd set out to meet him! There couldn't be anything in it, could there?

'You'll never be able to trust him again,' Julie had said, and although I'd dismissed her dire warnings, her words came back to echo around my mind. Now the seeds of doubt were growing into a wilderness of mistrust, much as I tried to stop them. I flung my brush on the bed. I wished that Alison had kept her mouth shut. Then I wouldn't know about Tim. It wouldn't make any difference.

I sat on my bed and curled my knees up under my chin. But why should it make any difference? It wasn't as though he was having a relationship with this woman. Was it?

The chill band of insecurity wrapped itself around me. Maybe he was. Maybe she was the reason he'd called off the wedding. Perhaps he was in love with her.

But if he was in love with her, my distracted mind tried to reason, why would he say that he wanted to stay engaged? Why didn't he just break off the engagement, tell me it was a dreadful mistake and that he was crazy about someone else? Why would he have sent me on holiday with Julie and then made love to me so wonderfully when I came home? It didn't make any sense.

I would ring him now, I decided, and find out. There was no point in sitting here allowing my fevered imagination to get the better of me.

Alison was in the kitchen again when I went downstairs.

'Don't worry,' I told her. 'Everything's fine. I'm going to phone him.'

She looked anxiously at me.

'Why don't you go out?' I said. 'Stop hanging around looking like a sad spaniel.'

'Maybe I will,' she said. 'Clear my head.'

'It'll do you good,' I told her.

I waited until she'd gone before I rang Tim's number. The answerphone responded. I hung up.

Maybe he was still in bed. He did that sometimes, stayed in bed really late on Sundays. Often, when I met him on Sunday afternoons, he was only just up and we'd go into town and have brunch. He always left the answerphone on when he was in bed.

I tried again half an hour later. The answerphone clicked in again.

He couldn't be in bed with her, could he? I hadn't wanted to formulate the thought, had firmly resisted the picture of him lying beside a lovelier model of me. He wouldn't be in bed with her. It was disloyal of me even to think it.

Alison came back from her walk. Mum and Dad came back from theirs. Ian was out with friends.

I rang again. Still the answerphone.

I couldn't take it any more. I had to go and see him. If he was in bed and asleep, I would tell him I was sorry and then get into bed beside him. Of course, he might be working. He left the machine on when he worked too. And I hadn't left any messages, had been too nervous to leave any messages.

I was acting like a teenager. He was my fiancé, after all. He loved me. He'd said so.

But he hadn't proved it, said the demon in my head. When it came to the crunch, he couldn't prove it.

I took my car keys from the hall table and went to see Tim.

Chapter 6

Dismal Sport (Salvador Dalí, 1929)

A wall of warm air hit me when I opened the car door. The smell of hot vinyl was overpowering. I wound down both driver and passenger windows and wished I had a sunroof. The steering wheel was almost too hot to touch. It was amazing that today was so hot, given the almost torrential rain of yesterday.

The sun dazzled me as I drove. It reflected off the sea in brilliant sparkles of light. I felt around in the glove compartment for my sunglasses – I hadn't needed them since I'd come back from Rhodes. I shoved my Tina Turner tape into the cassette and turned the volume up.

I couldn't make up my mind whether to drive quickly or slowly. Part of me wanted to be beside Tim now, this very second; another part of me was scared that my worst fears – the ones I didn't even allow to come into my head – would be realised. I hated him for putting me through this.

The Alfa was in its place. He was at home, although I wasn't sure whether that made things better or worse. I sat outside the house for a moment, the engine idling, afraid to confront him.

This is silly, I told myself finally, and switched off the engine. I left the windows open and the door unlocked.

It was ages before Tim answered the doorbell. He was wearing a blue T-shirt and grey shorts and his feet were bare. He looked at me in surprise.

'I didn't think you were coming over this afternoon.'

I stared at him. 'You were supposed to ring me.'

'Not until tonight.'

'Can I come in?' I felt like a stranger standing on his doorstep.

'Of course.' He opened the door wider and I stepped inside. 'I'm sorry,' he said. 'I was busy. And I didn't think you'd come all the way over here.'

The back door was open. Tim walked through the house and into his small patio garden. 'We were working,' he said as I followed him outside.

The girl was sitting on Tim's swing chair, her feet curled underneath her. She wore a long, shocking pink T-shirt that almost covered her figure-hugging Lycra shorts. Her hair was pulled back from her face but I knew immediately what Alison had meant. She was very like me.

'This is Laura,' said Tim. 'She's my partner on the Saracen project.'

Laura took off her huge, wrap-around sunglasses. Her eyes were brilliant blue. 'Hi,' she said lazily. 'You must be Isobel.'

I nodded, not trusting myself to speak.

'Tim was right,' she giggled. 'We could almost be sisters.'

'You've the wrong colour eyes,' I said, looking directly into them.

'Otherwise she's just like you, isn't she?' said Tim. 'I thought I was seeing things when she walked into the office.'

She got up from the seat. She was also much, much

taller than me. A better height for him, I thought. Her head would nestle comfortably on his shoulder, not somewhere halfway between his stomach and his armpit like mine.

'Maybe I'd better go,' she said. 'We've got most of the work done anyway.'

'But we still have to figure out that program-freezing problem,' protested Tim.

'I've got a theory about that.' Laura launched into some explanation which made no sense to me whatsoever. I sat on an upturned terracotta pot and listened to my fiancé and his colleague argue about it while I pulled at the leaves of his escallonia bush.

He couldn't really be having an affair (can you call it an affair when you're not actually married?) with this girl. Surely if he wanted someone else, he wouldn't have picked a clone of me – even a taller, more intelligent, blue-eyed version? Tim's fantasy girls were always blondes with gravity-defying busts, tiny waists and voracious sexual appetites. I wished she'd go away. I wanted to talk to him.

Eventually they finished their discussion. She would work on the freezing problem. He'd put the final package together. It would only be a week behind schedule.

She waved at me as she left. I smiled at her, although I don't think I'd have liked it very much if someone had given me that kind of smile. It didn't reach my eyes. It hardly reached my mouth.

They spent ages at the front door but they were still only talking. I could see them from where I sat.

Tim came back into the garden carrying a couple of cans of Carlsberg. He opened one and handed it to me. He always opened cans of beer for me because I could never seem to manage it without breaking a nail.

'Thanks,' I said.

'Lucky you didn't arrive earlier.' He took a deep draught of beer.

'Why?'

'We were really busy.'

'Is that why you didn't answer the phone?'

'Did you phone?' He looked surprised. 'I didn't hear it. The machine is on anyhow.'

'I know. I didn't bother leaving a message.'

'You should have. I've been in and out. I would have seen the light blinking.'

'I didn't know what to say.'

'You could have done what you're supposed to do.' He laughed. 'Left your name and number and the time of your call and I'd have called you back!'

'Yeah, right.'

'Oh, for God's sake, Isobel. What's the matter with you?'

Now that the time had come to confront him, I was afraid. I'd rehearsed it in the car on the way over, as the music had soothed me, and I thought that I could sound reasonable and fair. But now, with Tim sitting opposite me, I knew that I'd sound shrewish and whining. The sort of girlfriend I detested. Clinging. Suspicious. Untrusting. But it was his fault that I was untrusting, I thought miserably. He shouldn't have treated me the way he did.

'Ali saw you last night,' I said casually. 'In Furama.'

'Did she?' He looked surprised, but not guilty. 'I didn't see her.'

'You were with someone. Laura, I suppose.'

'Is that what this is about?' he demanded, his voice suddenly harsh. 'An inquisition into my movements last night?'

'It's not an inquisition,' I protested. 'I just wanted to know, that's all. You were supposed to be going out with me. Ali saw you. She thought it was me with you and then she realised it wasn't.'

'So she rushed home to tell tales.'

'That's not fair,' I said. 'She told me this morning, but only after I'd wormed it out of her.'

'I'll bet that was hard,' he muttered. 'Your sister never liked me.'

'Your mother never liked *me*,' I said with false brightness.

He swallowed the rest of his beer and kicked the can to the end of the garden. It echoed noisily off the flagstones.

'Laura and I were working late. I took her to dinner when we'd finished. That's not a crime and I don't like you acting as though it was.'

'I'm not,' I said.

'Yes, you are.'

We stared at each other for a moment and I thought there was more than anger in his eyes. I didn't like it.

'I'm sorry,' I said.

'We were working here this afternoon, too. We'd almost finished. Would have finished if we hadn't been interrupted.'

'I didn't mean to interrupt you.'

'I said I'd ring you tonight, and I would have.'

'It's just that I haven't seen you in ages,' I said.

'You don't own me,' said Tim.

A bird flew into the garden and hopped around. Its body was brown with a greenish tinge. Its beak was yellow. I didn't want to speak because I might disturb it. I couldn't speak anyway because I knew that if I did, I would cry.

There was too much resentment in Tim's voice. Too much hostility. At that moment I knew that Tim didn't love me any more.

I shivered in the warmth and bit my lip. I stood up. The bird flew out of the garden with a noisy flutter of its wings.

I cleared my throat. 'It isn't going to work, is it?'

'What?' Tim looked up from the weeds he'd been pulling.

'Us.'

'Don't be stupid, Isobel.'

'I'm not being stupid,' I said. 'I'm being realistic. I should have been realistic before. I was stupid before. How could you possibly decide not to marry me in May but still want to go out with me? Why did I think that it was a reasonable idea? What pathetic sort of creature did you think I was?'

'I never thought you were pathetic,' said Tim.

'But you don't want to marry me.'

'It's not that.' Tim looked uncomfortable. 'I'm just not ready to get married. I explained all that to you, Isobel.'

'I know you explained it to me,' I said. 'But I didn't listen to you. I didn't want to listen to you. I wanted to pretend that everything was all right. But it isn't all right – it can't be all right.'

'I needed some time.'

'You did. I didn't. But I was going to give you time because I thought I should.' I shook my head. 'No wonder everyone kept looking at me so anxiously. They thought I was cracked. You did the closest thing to ruining my life and I still ran after you like a lovesick teenager!'

'Stop being dramatic.' Tim looked angry. 'I didn't ruin your life or anything like it. I would have ruined it a lot more if I'd married you and then decided that I should have waited. I did you a favour, Isobel.'

'Oh, right.' I laughed bitterly. 'It was a great favour

letting me cancel everything. Knowing that I had to face everyone and tell them that you didn't want to get married. It's a great favour to be humiliated like that, Tim.'

'I thought you understood.'

'I understood that my heart was broken,' I said. 'I understood that all right.'

'But you seemed to be OK.'

'I'm good at that,' I told him. 'I'm a PA. I'm good in a crisis. I could work my way out of the crisis. Rearrange things. Cancel things. I could do all that without bursting into tears but I cried every single night of my so-called holiday in Rhodes.'

He looked uncomfortable. 'I'm sorry,' he said again.

I didn't want it to be like this, but I didn't have any choice. I'd been living in some kind of dream world myself lately. Trying to pretend that the wedding wasn't due to happen until next year. Trying to pretend that it could be exactly as it was before.

I eased the engagement ring from my finger and handed it to him.

'I should have done this before,' I said. 'I was a fool.'

He turned it over and over in his hand. For a second, I thought he might give it back to me, but he clenched his fist around it.

'I'll keep it.' He looked up at me. 'Maybe we'll use it again.'

I shook my head, bit my lip and walked out of the house.

∼

I drove as far as the canal, then pulled over to the side of the road. I fumbled in my bag for my inhaler and squirted a dose of the fine mist deep into my lungs. I held my breath for ten seconds, then released it slowly. The rattle in my chest had subsided. I felt a little calmer.

They had been right and I was wrong. Even if Tim's relationship with Laura was purely professional – and it could easily be, I'd seen no real signs to prove otherwise – I couldn't accept his word. It was no way to plan a marriage and no way to live my life. I would have to forget Tim and find someone else. Or not. I shivered in the warmth of the sun. There was no need to find someone else. I was perfectly capable of living life on my own. I could get an apartment after all. Perhaps I could afford something near work. I'd be getting away from home then, and from the places I knew since childhood. There was, after all, something ridiculous about the idea of a twenty-seven-year-old woman living in the parental home.

I shuddered at the thought of arriving home without my ring. I didn't want to go through it all again.

~

I drove past our house and around the corner to Julie's. She was sitting in the back garden, topping up her tan. Her parents had gone for a walk, she told me, and would probably be out for ages. I sat on the neatly mown grass and extended my hand to her.

'What happened?' she asked calmly.

I'd thought I'd be able to tell Julie without bursting into tears, use her as practice before I went home, but the tears flowed anyway. She said nothing while I scrubbed at my eyes with a crumpled tissue. She went into the house and came back with a box of Kleenex man-size.

'So?' She handed the box to me and I took another tissue.

I blew my nose. 'I've broken it off with him.'

'I thought you'd sorted everything out?'

'I wanted to think that we had.'

'But what went wrong?'

I pulled at a blade of grass and tore it into tiny pieces.

'Was it last night?' she asked. 'When you didn't go out?'

Only last night, I thought. It seemed like years ago.

'Ali saw him,' I told her. 'He was with another girl.'

'The shit!' Julie's eyes blazed with fury. 'The absolute shit! How dare he? After all he's said. I'd like to strangle him.'

'It wasn't like that,' I protested, wondering why I was defending him. 'She was from work. They were doing a project together.'

'Oh, really.' Julie's voice was full of disbelief.

'I believe him,' I said. 'He told me that they worked late and went for something to eat. It's not exactly a crime, Julie.'

'Huh,' she said.

'But I couldn't help wondering.' I pulled another blade of grass. 'And I thought about what you said – that I'd never be able to trust him again. And I knew that I was suspicious of him and that I didn't trust him.'

'I'm sorry if I made you feel—'

I shook my head vigorously. 'It's not your fault. I kept wondering, that's all. He said he'd ring today but I rang him instead. There was no answer. So I just thought the worst and hurtled over to see him.'

Julie's eyes opened wide. 'And?'

'She was there,' I said. 'But there wasn't anything going on, really there wasn't. They were working in the garden. They had books and papers with them and I believe him when he said that was all they were doing.'

'So, why have you broken it off?'

'Because I'll never be certain,' I wailed. 'I'll never feel

one hundred per cent convinced that he married me because he loved me and that he really wanted to. He got really pissed off because I wanted to know about her and I don't blame him. We were never like that before, Julie. You know that. He went out with his friends, I went out with mine. We never questioned each other.'

'Maybe you should have,' she said darkly.

'I don't think so.' I leaned my head on my knees and closed my eyes. My finger felt strange without the ring, knowing that I'd never wear it again. I couldn't quite believe that I was the one who'd actually done it, who'd decided that we wouldn't be getting married in the future. I still felt that it was Tim's decision, not mine.

'So what are you going to do now?' asked Julie.

I sighed. 'I don't know. I thought maybe about getting a flat, something near work.'

'Buying one?'

I shrugged. 'I could probably afford it. I was thinking about it on the way home. I don't want to live at home any more, Julie. It's too constricting. And they'll be following me around, oozing sympathy. Mum'll be trying to get me out and about meeting other men – you know her, it's a husband or nothing as far as she's concerned.' I wiped my eyes with the back of my hand. 'Maybe that's why I felt so strongly about marrying Tim. She was always going on at me about getting married before I was thirty. The last time we talked about it she said that I was leaving it a bit late to have a family! I told her that I was young enough but she handed me an article about infertility in women over thirty and how having a career and putting off babies until you're older can be a drastic mistake. I tried to tell her that I haven't actually got a career, I just have a job, but it didn't cut any ice with her.'

Julie laughed. 'Your mum was always the homebird type.'

'You'd think that she'd want us to go out and have a good time,' I said. 'After all, she was married when she was twenty and I was born a year later. You'd imagine she'd like me to have fun.'

Julie sighed. 'You know parents. They always want the opposite of what you'd expect. Remember when I was going out with Will? My mother did everything she could to split us up, even though she'd been nagging at me for ages to find myself a boyfriend.'

I laughed unconvincingly. 'Well, yes, Julie – but *Will*?'

'OK.' She grinned at me. 'So he looked like a Hell's Angel, but he was a decent bloke all the same.'

'Julie, he used to scare the living daylights out of me,' I told her. 'I was always terrified I'd meet him with a gang of his mates and they'd do unspeakable things to me.'

'Isobel!' She looked offended. 'He wasn't like that.'

'I know that,' I said. 'It was the way he made me feel.'

'He didn't last long anyway,' she sighed. 'He was just my rebellious phase.' She waved her hand at the freshly painted house, the immaculately tended garden and frowned. 'I needed to have something different to this.'

I nodded. Julie's house was similar to mine. Both four-bedroomed, semi-detached, built in the nineteen-fifties. Big rooms, big gardens and all rewired, double-glazed and owned by people of my parents' age. People who'd gone through the lean, early, married years, had accumulated a little money, who'd spent it on a yearly holiday and fitted kitchens, new bathrooms and sunny conservatories.

I hadn't gone through a rebellious phase. I wanted to be one of those people. Only Tim and I wouldn't have had lean times, we would have been a successful, happy, married couple.

Oh God, I thought despairingly, I'd had it all planned

so neatly. And it had nearly happened. Why hadn't I seen that Tim was getting cold feet? Why hadn't I anticipated his doubts? Why hadn't I stayed the sort of girl he wanted to marry? Why me, I cried silently. Why me?

Julie was silent beside me. She stared into the distance and allowed me to regain my composure.

'It feels awful now,' she said after a few minutes. 'But you *will* get over it.'

I gave a wry smile. 'I know I'll get over it. People get over things. But I'll never feel the same about anyone again.'

'You'll find someone else someday and you'll feel even better,' she told me.

'Let me wallow in my misery,' I said wanly. 'I'll tell you when it gets better.'

'OK.' She hugged me. 'D'you want to come inside and see the new suit I bought?'

I nodded and we went inside to talk about things that really matter.

⁓

Strangely, it was Ian who noticed that my engagement ring was missing.

They were having dinner when I arrived home. I could smell the roast beef as soon as I walked into the house and I wondered why Mum would want to cook a Sunday roast in weather like this.

'It was wet and cold yesterday,' she pointed out when I told her that she shouldn't have bothered cooking.

'Besides—' Ian helped himself to more potatoes, 'I'm a growing lad. I need my food. You girls might want to wander around like half-fed waifs, but I need to build muscle.'

'Muscle!' I jeered, pinching his waistline.

He caught me by the wrist and held up my hand. 'Where's your ring?'

There was silence at the table. Dad put his knife and fork in the centre of his plate and looked at me expectantly.

'I gave it back,' I said. 'I changed my mind.'

'Oh, shit,' said Alison.

'Alison Kavanagh!' Dad looked angrily at her. 'You know I don't like that sort of language.'

'Sorry,' she muttered as she looked at me from beneath her long lashes. 'Is it definitely off, Isobel?'

I nodded.

'But I thought you'd sorted it out,' cried my mother. 'I thought you said that you'd get married in the autumn. I thought you were going to go through with it.'

'I thought you'd be pleased,' I said shortly.

There was silence again.

'I'm pleased,' said Dad.

'Me too,' said Alison.

'Whatever you want,' said Ian.

'Well, of course I'm pleased.' Mum sounded unconvinced. 'I told you he wasn't worth it, after all! But you don't seem to know your own mind, Isobel. I just don't want you to do something you'll absolutely regret. I don't want you breaking it off out of pique.'

'I didn't break it off out of pique.'

'Why did you?' asked Alison quietly.

I clenched my fists under the table. 'Because I didn't think I could be sure about him. Because I felt that it would take him a long time to be sure about me. Because I didn't want to take the chance.'

I'd ruined dinner for them. Possibly Ian would keep eating, but I could see from everybody else's expression that my news was almost as great a blow as the postponement of the wedding.

'I'm going up to my room,' I said. 'Don't all come charging up to make sure I haven't slit my wrists or anything. I'm fine.'

I lay on the bed and stared at the ceiling. I wanted to make plans for the rest of my life. There was no point in thinking about Tim Malone any more. He had to be consigned to the past, with the other boyfriends whom I'd once thought I loved. I remembered Alan Davenport, the first guy I'd ever been truly crazy about. Our romance had only lasted a few months – it had been based more on physical attraction than anything else – but I was shattered when we split up. It was the same sort of feeling now, I told myself. As though part of you has been suddenly ripped away. But you get used to it after a while. Then one day you wake up and it doesn't hurt any more. You try to remember what he was like and you can't. You forget what your favourite song was, or his favourite colour. You stop wearing the perfume that made you sneeze but that he liked. You go back to wearing cotton knickers and bras instead of wispy bits of voile. You turn into a normal person again.

But while you're waiting for the pain to go away, for time to kick in with its healing powers, it's hell. And for me, right then, it was the worst hell I'd ever been in.

∽

Alison knocked at the door a few hours later. I hastily scooped the photographs of Tim and me into a shoebox and shoved them back underneath the bed. I opened the biography of Jackie Kennedy Onassis that was on my bedside locker.

'Are you OK?' she asked as she came into the room.

'Of course.'

'What happened?'

'Nothing.'

'Oh, come on, Isobel. Something must have. Why did you decide to break it off?'

'I didn't exactly decide to break it off,' I said. 'He was the one that started it.'

'I know. But you said – I thought—' She looked miserable.

'It's nothing to do with you,' I told her. 'I mean, nothing to do with what you told me.'

'But, Isobel—'

'Really it isn't. I went over to him and we talked. While we were talking I realised that I can't wait for ever for him. And he wasn't certain about anything. So I thought that it was better to make a clean break of it there and then. Get it over with.'

'Oh, Isobel!' She put her arms around me and hugged me. 'I'm so sorry!'

'What have you got to be sorry about?' I asked as I disentangled her arms. 'You've probably done me a favour.'

'I may be stupid, but I'm not that stupid.'

'Really, Alison. It could have been a dreadful mistake to marry him.'

'But you seemed to have worked it out. If it wasn't for me—'

'—it would have been something else,' I finished for her. 'Don't feel guilty.'

'I feel guilty because I'm glad you broke it off with him,' she admitted. 'I just didn't think you should get married to him. He was always such a super-confident person. I thought he didn't give you enough credit.'

'I thought you just didn't believe in marriage.' I smiled at her.

'That too,' said Alison. 'But – he was so sure that he had a great job and you were just a secretary.'

'I'm not just a secretary,' I told her. 'I'm a PA. It's much more than typing and making coffee!'

'I know.' She hung her head. 'I'm sorry. I'm saying all the wrong things.'

'It doesn't matter.' I kissed the top of her head. 'Leave me alone now, Alison. I'll be fine.'

∽

Easy to say, I thought, when she'd closed the door behind her. Easy to say, easy to pretend. I'll be fine. I was still telling myself that when I finally fell asleep.

Chapter 7

Inverted Personages (Joan Miró, 1949)

B ut, of course, I wasn't fine. I went into the office
every day, came home again every evening, even
went out occasionally with Julie – but I wasn't fine. I
tried to behave as though everything was OK. I didn't
sob over my computer terminal. I answered the phone
briskly and efficiently. I did the shopping for Mum at
the weekends. I tried not to talk about Tim when I was
with Julie. But nothing could take away the empty feeling
inside and nothing could make me believe that I would
ever be happy again.

I told myself that time was all I needed. A great healer.
I reminded myself of all those clichés over and over again
as I peered at folders full of invoices through eyes that
were blurred with unshed tears.

'Isobel.' Barry stood at the door to his office. I blinked
a couple of times to clear my eyes. 'Can you come in for
a moment?' he asked.

I followed him into the office and sat in the chair in
front of his desk. He took a pen from the black leather
container on the desk and rolled it around in his hands
a couple of times. I watched him silently.

He cleared his throat. 'How are you feeling?' he asked abruptly.

I was surprised at the question. I looked at him in astonishment. 'How am I feeling?'

'Yes,' he said. 'Generally.'

I swallowed. Whenever people asked me how I felt, the urge to cry washed over me and it was all I could do not to burst into tears again. 'I'm fine.'

'Are you?'

I nodded. 'Absolutely.'

He said nothing.

'Well, almost absolutely.' I shrugged. 'Sometimes I feel a bit down, to be perfectly honest, but most of the time I'm OK.'

'You've got over the thing with Tim?'

'It's hard to be sure you're completely over something,' I told him. 'But, yes, I am.'

'I'm glad to hear it.' He smiled slightly. 'But I'm not sure that I'm as confident as you are about that.'

'Why not?'

He took a file from his desk. 'These invoices. You sent DeltaPac ones to DeltaCon and vice versa.' He took out another file. 'Staff payroll. You left it in the top drawer of your desk last night. You didn't lock it away as you're supposed to.'

My lips were dry. 'I'm sorry, Barry. It was an oversight.'

'Finally—' He opened his diary. 'Can you tell me why you booked me on a flight to Manchester for tomorrow when I'm supposed to be going to London?'

Oh God, I thought. How could I have done all these things wrong?

'I'm sorry,' I said again. 'I don't know what happened. I wasn't concentrating properly. I'll sort it out.'

He looked at me thoughtfully. 'You've been with me a long time, Isobel. We work well together, I think.

You've made a positive contribution to the company. Up until now.'

I felt a stab of fear. Was he going to fire me? He could, because of the payroll. I couldn't believe I'd left the payroll in an unlocked desk drawer.

'I've never had to talk to you like this before,' he continued, 'and I don't much like doing it. But it can't go on like this.'

'I know that these are bad mistakes,' I said. 'I do. Really. And I'm truly sorry. I didn't realise how much I'd let my concentration slip.'

'It's not only major things like this,' said Barry. 'It's not passing on messages. Being abrupt with callers. Not being part of the team.'

I bit my lip. So much for thinking that I answered the phone in an efficient manner. I was going to lose my job. Not content with losing a fiancé, now I was about to become unemployed. Careless, as Oscar Wilde might have put it.

Barry got up from behind the desk and sat on the edge of it. 'I'm sorry about your wedding,' he said, his tone marginally warmer. 'I know it must have been a terrible blow to you. But life goes on, Isobel, and you can't spend your whole life pining away.'

'I'm not pining,' I told him.

'You're not working either,' he said.

I fiddled with the belt of my skirt. I couldn't meet his eyes.

'This is a warning, Isobel.' He sounded tired. 'I don't want to lose you. As I said, you're a good worker. Usually. But you have to get back into gear. Stop wearing dreary clothes to the office. Perk up a bit. It's not as though you've been bereaved.'

But, for me, it was. I couldn't see how anyone who'd lost a partner could be less gutted than I was.

'Thanks, Barry.' I glanced at him. 'I appreciate what you've said.'

'That's OK,' he told me. 'I'm sorry I had to say it, but—' He grimaced. 'Everyone has something happen to them at some time in their lives that is as heart-rending and miserable as what happened to you. It takes different forms for different people. But there's always something. That's the way life is.'

I wondered what heart-rending and miserable thing could have happened to Barry Cleary. I couldn't think of anything offhand.

But Barry was right. I had allowed myself to be consumed by my own unhappiness. I had to snap out of it. Let myself live again. Take control of my own destiny.

I stood up. 'I promise you won't have to talk to me about it again,' I said.

'Good.' He smiled at me. 'It's important that we all pull together.'

I went back to my desk and tried to clear my thoughts. A trickle of sweat slid down my back. My job had been on the line. I knew that Barry liked me, but it wouldn't have stopped him firing me if he believed that I couldn't work as I had before. I bent my head over the invoices and checked them more thoroughly than ever.

∽

I bought a new suit in red wool and wore it into the office the following week. Red suited me and I knew that it brought the colour back to my cheeks. I wore more make-up, some nice jewellery and made an effort. I went to lunch with Niamh and Anna. I was bright and cheery every time I went into Barry's office and I cultivated an air of super-efficiency that surprised even me.

∽

I was sitting at my desk, correcting a draft of a speech that Barry intended to give at a management conference in Killarney. It was the first time he'd been asked to speak at something like this and he wanted it to be perfect. It nearly was, I thought, as I read through it. It hit the right note. Not too boring, not too light-hearted. Competent, I decided.

'Isobel?' John Ferguson, from the marketing department, stood in front of me.

'Hi.' I put the text of Barry's speech to one side and looked up at him.

He smiled nervously. 'How are you?'

'Fine,' I replied. 'You?'

I didn't know John very well. He'd joined DeltaPrint the previous year and, although I'd worked with him a couple of times, he kept himself very much to himself. I didn't think he particularly liked me – thought, perhaps, that I was too fun-loving, too flighty.

'I was wondering,' he said, 'if you were doing anything on Friday night?'

I stared at him. 'Friday night?'

'Yes.' He made a face. 'I've got tickets, you see. For the Mary Black concert. I thought you might like to come.'

'Oh.' I didn't know what to say. I'd no idea he'd intended to ask me out. Ask me out! A date! Was this time, I wondered sardonically, trying to help the healing process along?

'Of course if you're busy—' he said hastily.

'No,' I told him. 'I'm not busy.' I was silent for a moment. 'It's very nice of you to ask me, John. Truly it is.'

'But?' he said.

I smiled crookedly. 'But I can't go out with you. Not yet.'

'Why not?' he asked.

'I'm not quite ready to go out with someone yet,' I told him. 'I'm sorry.'

'Don't worry about it.' His tone was even. 'It doesn't matter.'

'Maybe some other time,' I said.

'Sure.' He forced a grin. 'Let me know.'

'Yes,' I said. 'I will.'

He walked back through the office and I pinched my nose between my fingers. I should have said yes. It wouldn't have hurt to go out with him. He'd obviously gone to the trouble of getting the tickets. Now I'd hurt his feelings and I didn't want to hurt anyone's feelings. I was too much of an expert on hurt feelings myself.

Damn, I said, drawing a black line through a repeated word in Barry's speech. Damn, damn, damn.

❦

The speech was a great success. *Business & Finance* did a report on the company which caused a flurry of activity in the office. We landed an important contract, I worked late three nights a week and Barry didn't have to talk to me again about efficiency and commitment. But time, even as it marched inexorably onwards, still wasn't doing much healing for me. One day in early September I went to Mum's wardrobe to look for a jacket and I saw my wedding dress. It was still swathed in tissue paper and covered in plastic. It hung there, white, immobile, haunting.

There was no one else in the house. I took out the wedding dress and laid it carefully on the bed. It was beautiful. Really beautiful. I slipped it from the hanger and held it in front of me. I was darker now than I'd been in April and my tanned skin accentuated the white of the dress. The four hundred and twenty tiny pearls glistened in the afternoon sunshine.

I took off my jeans and top and slid the dress over my head. My heart was thumping in my chest as though I were committing a criminal act. I pulled up the zip, ran my fingers through my hair and stood in front of the mirror.

I'd lost weight. The dress had been a perfect fit, now it was slightly looser around my waist. I turned around slowly. The material rustled. I stared at myself. Face, paler than usual under the dusting of my tan, eyes dark and miserable, hair long and lank. Had I looked like this before? I didn't know. I felt as though the person in the mirror was a stranger. A woman in her wedding dress. I watched my eyes fill up with tears and refused to blink to stop them from falling.

I took off the wedding dress and brought it into my own room. I laid it out on the bed. It was like a ghostly shroud. I took my dressmaking scissors from the cupboard and sliced it neatly up the centre. My tears fell as I cut it again and again, lengthways, sideways, across the bodice, through the skirt, until it was reduced to a rubble of white ribbon and pearls. Then I bundled it into a plastic bag and shoved it under the bed.

$\backsim$

Julie and I went for a walk around Howth Head the following day. It was hot when we started, but one of those days when grey clouds can appear out of nowhere and send a torrent of rain onto the unwary. For most of our walk, though, the sun glittered on the deep blue water of the open sea and the gorse lit up the hill in a blaze of yellow.

'I'm going to Florida next week,' said Julie while we sat on a boulder and gazed at the horizon.

'Really?' I turned to look at her. 'To stay with Andy?'

'Of course to stay with Andy.' She laughed. 'There's no other reason to go to Florida!'

'I know.' I picked at the corner of my nail. 'I hope you have a great time.'

'I hope so, too,' said Julie. 'I was wondering if you'd mind giving me a lift to the airport?'

'Of course not.' I stretched my legs in front of me. 'You lucky thing.'

'Well, even if Andy and I decide we hate each other, I'll still have a good time,' said Julie. 'And another holiday would be nice.' She looked critically at me. 'You could do with one yourself, Isobel. You look wretched.'

'Gee, thanks.' I punched her gently on the shoulder. 'You make me feel so good.'

'These last few days,' said my friend, 'you're paler and listless and – oh, not yourself.'

'I don't know what's myself any more.' I sighed and rested my head in my hands.

Julie was silent. A gull screeched overhead.

'I thought everything was going well for you,' she said eventually. 'You were busy in work and you seemed OK.'

'I know.' I didn't look up and my voice was muffled. 'But sometimes I feel as if I want to forget everything, Julie. Just sit down somewhere and fall asleep and not bother waking up.'

'Isobel!' She sounded horrified. 'You don't mean that.'

'I don't know what I mean,' I said miserably. 'I don't care any more.'

'Oh, Isobel.' She put her arm around me. 'Don't feel

like that! Of course you care about things. You just need something to keep you interested.'

'Like what?' I looked at her. 'Like what? My whole life is pretty useless. What have I ever done, ever achieved? I've got a crummy job in a boring paper factory; despite all my talk I haven't managed to move out of the family home; I've lost my fiancé and I can't get over it. I'm hopeless.'

'No, you're not,' said Julie firmly. 'You're depressed and feeling sorry for yourself, but you're not hopeless. And you'll get over Tim, you know you will.'

'But I don't want to get over him,' I cried. 'I want to love him!'

Julie sighed. 'There's no point in wanting that.'

'I can't switch it off,' I said. 'I thought I could. But he's in my mind, in my heart, in my dreams. All the time. I can't see anything or do anything without thinking of what it would be like with him. I thought it would get easier with time, Julie, but it's not. It's worse.'

'Oh, God,' said Julie as she put her arm around me again. 'I wish I could help. Truly I do.'

∽

There was no one who could help me. I thought that maybe I was really ill. A girl I'd gone to school with, Eilish Murphy, had been off for an entire term with depression. We'd laughed about it in the cloakrooms, wondering what on earth someone who had porcelain skin and sapphire-blue eyes had to be depressed about. Someone said it was because she'd split up with her boyfriend but I was convinced that there had to be more to it than that. Now, I wasn't so sure. And I hated the me that had mocked Eilish behind her back. I was sure people were mocking me.

One evening, when I was alone in the house, I took out the phone book and looked up Tim's name. It felt strange to see it there, in black and white, confirming that he still existed. I touched the print, feeling incredibly silly. *Malone, T. J., 8 Berkeley Mews, Donnybrook*. And his phone number. The phone number I knew off by heart.

I needed to talk to him, to hear his voice. Not to be with him, exactly, but to know that he was there. To share a couple of stories with him, perhaps. I picked up the phone and dialled, remembering to withold my number. It'd probably be the answering machine and I wouldn't leave a message. Didn't want him to think that I was a nutter.

'Hello.' His voice, well-remembered.

I opened my mouth but no sounds came out.

'Hello,' he said again.

I held the receiver away from me and looked at it.

'Hello.' Impatient this time.

I put the receiver back to my ear.

'Is there anyone there?' Angry now.

I said nothing, could say nothing.

He replaced the receiver at his end. I listened to the buzz of the line.

I hung up. My hands were trembling, my knees shaking. I swallowed a few times, then dialled again.

'Hello?'

I still couldn't speak.

'Look, is this the same person as before? I can't hear you.'

Of course you can't, I thought. I'm not speaking. But you should know it's me, Tim. You should sense it.

'If it's a real phone call, try later. If you're some crack-head, then piss off!'

I smiled bitterly. 'Piss off,' I mouthed silently.

He hung up.

I dialled again.

'Yes.'

I love you, Tim. I sent the message to him by thought. Surely he'd understand. Surely he knew it was me. Who else could ring him?

'If you don't stop this, I'm calling the police.'

But not for me, Tim. You can't call the police for me.

He hung up again. I dialled his number once more. But he'd left the phone off the hook. I supposed I would have done the same.

I wondered if I was going a little bit crazy. I didn't think so but I couldn't be sure. The last week or two had seemed so unreal. It was as though I was alive but not living. Watching everything rather than being part of it.

I'd ring him again later. I needed to hear his voice.

I brought Julie to the airport. She bubbled with excitement at the prospect of seeing Andreas the Greek.

'I know it'll probably be completely different,' she told me as we sat in the coffee shop together. 'But I have to know.'

'He was really nice,' I assured her. 'He probably won't want to let you come home.'

'I'll have to come home.' She grinned and broke a piece off her pastry. 'I don't have any more holidays left.'

'You're a lucky bitch going to the States like this,' I said.

'Andy was hoping that you and Ari—' Julie made a face.

'He's *gay*, Julie, for heaven's sake!' I shook my head. 'I certainly wouldn't try pursuing a gay man. Do irreparable damage to both our psyches! Besides, even if he wasn't gay, he wasn't my type.'

112

'Nobody's your type right now,' she told me.

'I know.' I spooned the froth from the top of my cappuccino. 'I'm beginning to think that Alison's right. I shouldn't get married.'

'I bet you anything she's hitched before she's twenty-five.' Julie grinned at me. 'And she'll have you hard at work making some fairy-tale wedding dress for her.'

I said nothing.

'You haven't done any dressmaking in ages,' Julie continued.

'Haven't felt like it,' I said shortly. How could I? When nearly everything I did was a wedding dress or a bridesmaid's dress? Where could I summon up the enthusiasm for that?

Julie looked at her watch. 'I suppose I'd better get going.'

I walked to the departure area with her.

'Have a good time,' I said. 'Don't do anything I wouldn't!'

'Gives me great scope,' she giggled. She hugged me. 'Thanks for the lift. See you in a week.'

'See you,' I said as she walked away.

～

The following Friday I went out with the girls from work. We went to the Orchard for a few drinks, then into town for something to eat.

I wasn't hungry. My head ached from the drink which was stupid because I should have been able to drink more than two beers without feeling weird. But I still felt detached from reality, still felt that there was someone else living my life.

Marion was in good humour. 'I don't get out enough by myself,' she said as she ordered Pavlova for dessert.

'The trouble about being married and having kids is that you always put them first.'

'Not always, surely,' said Niamh. 'After all, you have a life too.'

'I know,' Marion said. 'But my life is so tied up in their lives. You have kids, you want everything for them.' She shrugged. 'I like what I have but I like to get out.'

'I like getting out, too.' Niamh was the youngest in the office, she was twenty. 'I can't imagine what it'd be like to have children.'

'My sister is always tired,' said Lesley. 'She had her second during the summer. He's a lovely baby but he just cries and cries. Poor Simone is exhausted. Even though Stephen wants to help, Noel won't go to anyone but his mother. And Phoebe is so jealous! Simone is afraid that she'll try to poke Noel's eyes out or something.'

'That's terrible,' said Anna.

'They usually get over it.' Marion's eyes lit up as the Pavlova was put in front of her. 'Joyce hated Len when he was born, but it only lasted a few months. And she adored Betsy. Still does.'

I listened to the conversation but didn't participate. I'd no interest in talking about babies and children.

Everyone wanted to go to a nightclub but I was too tired. They didn't try too hard to persuade me – I knew that I'd been a drag all evening. I'd wanted to be bright and witty and cheerful, but I couldn't.

So I walked down Grafton Street, swarming with people at midnight, and stayed miserable.

Tim was standing outside River Island. He wore black jeans, a white shirt and a multi-coloured waistcoat. He needed a haircut. There were three other people with him. All male, I noted with some relief. They were talking animatedly.

I didn't know whether to go over to them or not. I

stood indecisively outside McDonald's among a chattering throng of teenagers and wondered where Tim and his friends were headed. Suddenly Tim nodded to them and began to walk towards College Green. I hurried after him. Tim always walked quickly. I was getting breathless as I tried to catch up with him.

He stopped at the pedestrian lights and I stood beside him.

'Hi,' I said casually.

He turned around in surprise. 'Isobel.'

'That's me.' I smiled at him. My smile was safe, friendly.

'How are you?' he asked.

'Great. You?'

'Not bad,' he said. 'I was out with some friends.'

'Me too.'

The lights changed and we both crossed the road.

'Where are you off to now?' I asked.

'Home.'

'You should have gone the other way to try for a taxi,' I said, nodding at the long queue. 'It takes for ever.'

'I have my car,' said Tim. 'I parked it in a sidestreet.'

'You'll have been clamped,' I told him. 'Or towed away.'

'Probably.' He grinned at me. 'But that's life.'

I wished he hadn't smiled. His face lit up when he smiled.

'Are you going home?' he asked.

I nodded.

'Do you want a lift?'

'It's the wrong way,' I said.

'I don't mind,' said Tim. 'I don't like to think of you hanging around here on your own.'

'If you're sure—?'

'Of course I'm sure. I wouldn't have said it otherwise.'

'Thanks.' I followed him through the streets until we came to his car. Still there, no ticket, not clamped.

'You see,' said Tim. 'You gotta take a chance.'

I fastened the seat belt as Tim started the car.

'So, how's everyone?' he asked.

'Fine.'

'Alison?'

'She's great.'

'Got a job yet?'

Alison had a degree in town planning, but she was working in a shoe shop at the moment.

'No,' I said. Alison didn't regard the shoe shop as a job.

'She'll get something eventually.' Tim went through amber lights on O'Connell Bridge and I winced.

'She hopes so.' I shifted in the seat. 'How is the Saracen project coming along?'

'Completed, thanks,' he said. 'It was one of those nightmare things. Seemed so simple but we kept running into stupid problems all the time.'

'How's Laura?' I asked casually.

'She's in California at the moment,' he replied. 'Lucky cow.'

'Very,' I said. 'Julie's in Florida.'

'Is she? Holidaying again?'

'Remember I told you that she'd met a bloke in Rhodes? A Greek American?'

He furrowed his brow.

'I did tell you,' I said. 'Anyway, she's gone to see him.'

Tim whistled. 'A holiday romance!'

'Maybe,' I said. 'I can't see it coming to much myself, but you never know.'

I clasped my hands together. I was suddenly conscious of my ringless engagement finger. I rubbed it gently and wondered what Tim had done with my ring.

He turned on the radio. They were playing sixties songs. Tim liked the sounds of the sixties. I always told him that he was just being pretentious.

We drew up outside my house. The windows were in darkness.

'Thanks for the lift,' I said. 'It was very good of you.'

'No problem,' said Tim.

'Drive safely home.'

He laughed. 'Isobel!'

'Sorry,' I said. 'I know, I sound like your mother.'

'Not quite,' he said. 'But almost.'

There was real amusement in his voice. I turned to him and smiled. 'And wear your vest when it's cold.'

He laughed again. 'Goodnight, Isobel.'

'Goodnight, Tim.'

I hadn't meant to kiss him and I hadn't meant to let him kiss me. But it was one of those things that just happened. One minute we were sitting in the car as polite friends, the next we were kissing as though we were lovers who hadn't seen each other in years. Which we almost were, I told myself as I kissed him. His kisses were long and searching. I let him hold me, revelling in the warmth of his body and the strength of his arms.

'Isobel,' he murmured as he came up for air.

'Oh, Tim,' I gasped. 'I've missed you so much.'

He broke away from me and regarded me with his huge, thoughtful eyes.

'I'm sorry,' he said. 'That was a mistake.'

I stared at him. 'A mistake?'

'I shouldn't have kissed you. It wasn't fair.'

'On who?'

'On you. On me.'

'Why wasn't it fair?' I tried to calm my racing heart.

'You know why,' said Tim. 'I'm sorry.'

117

I touched him on the cheek. He recoiled as though I'd slapped him.

'I'm not trying to hurt you,' I said.

'But I'll hurt you,' said Tim. 'I don't want to hurt you any more than I already have.'

I counted to ten. I had to be calm. 'It's OK. We're friends.'

'Are you sure?' Tim looked curiously at me.

'Of course. A kiss between friends.' I laughed lightly.

'I haven't been a very good friend to you.'

'You have tonight,' I said. 'You drove me all the way out here.'

'I'd have done that for anyone,' said Tim.

'But you did it for me.'

'I'd better go,' he said.

'Are you sure? Do you want to come in and have coffee?'

He shook his head. 'Really. I have to go.'

'OK.'

'Take care, Isobel,' he said as I got out of the car.

'Give me a call sometime.' I waved at him as he drove away.

I hugged his kiss to me as I got into bed. Of course he'd been shocked when he kissed me. Surprised, I guessed, at the depth of the passion that was still there. He still loved me, I thought. Must still love me. To drive out of his way like that. To kiss me in the way he did. He might not be ready to live with me but he hadn't got over me yet.

I fell asleep cuddling my pillow and dreamed of him again.

∽

I wasn't going to ring him but I did. Saturday afternoon, when Ian and Dad were watching *Grandstand* on TV,

Mum had gone shopping and Alison was working. I dithered around beside the phone for a while, then dialled Tim's number.

Sometimes I thought that the person who invented the answering-machine should be shot. Tim could be at home, working, but I wouldn't know because I hated leaving messages for him. Besides, there wasn't a message I could leave. I hadn't any real reason to ring him, I just wanted to talk. I listened to him telling me to leave my name and number after the tone and hung up without saying anything.

I wished Julie was here. I didn't want to be on my own. I wanted to talk to someone about Tim and, even though Julie would simply tell me that I was off my head to still care for him, I needed to talk about him.

In the light of day, and without a couple of drinks inside me, I knew that I was silly to think he might still care. So he drove me home. So what? He didn't take me up on my offer of coffee (couldn't I have thought of something more original?) and he didn't try to raise false hopes by saying anything remotely loving to me. But he'd kissed me and it had been the sort of kiss that you dream about. So maybe he did still love me. I shook my head. Why is life so complex? Why aren't things more cut and dried? Tim dumped me – it was over. That's how things should have been. I should hate him. Yet I couldn't do that and, no matter how much I tried, I couldn't prise him out of my heart.

I rang later that evening, too, but this time the machine was switched off and nobody answered the phone. I wondered where he'd gone, who he was with, what he was doing. When I woke up at four o'clock in the morning I had to fight the impulse to ring him then, to talk to him while he lay in bed, hair tousled, eyes dulled by sleep.

Grow up, I told myself as I thumped my pillow. You're twenty-seven, not seventeen.

∽

Barry wasn't in on Monday. He phoned the office to say that he was going to Cork to meet someone and that he'd be out for the day. I had things to do but I wasn't wildly busy. At eleven o'clock I rang Tim's office.

'He's away,' Shauna told me. 'He's in California.'

'California,' I repeated dully.

'Yes,' she said. 'There was a presentation on the Saracen project. Tim, Jack Benson and Laura Hart have gone.'

'Oh,' I said.

'He'll be back next week.' I could hear the curiosity in Shauna's voice. 'Was there anything urgent, Isobel?'

'No,' I said. 'Nothing at all.'

I stared blankly in front of me. He was in California. He was in California with Laura. Laura who looked like Isobel, only more beautiful. Laura who knew what he was talking about when he said things like 'Token Ring' and 'Ethernet' and 'Extension Folders', all of which used to send me into a fit of giggles. Tim was in California with Laura and I was a fool.

'We're going bowling after work.' Lesley stood in front of me. I hadn't even noticed her. 'D'you want to come?'

I blinked at her and shook my head. 'Things to do.'

'Like what?' demanded Lesley.

'Bits and pieces,' I said.

'Oh, come on, Isobel. You can't sit around doing nothing your whole life.'

'I'm not,' I told her. 'I'm making a dress for a friend. She's coming around for a fitting tonight.'

'Oh.' Lesley looked abashed and I thought how easy it was to lie to people. 'OK.'

'Have a good time, though,' I said as I rummaged around in my desk drawer for something to do.

'Sure,' said Lesley. 'Next time, maybe.'

'Next time,' I said.

My fingers closed around a set of keys. I'd forgotten that they were there. Keys to Tim's house. The spare set. I'd given him back my keys but I'd forgotten about the spare set. I supposed he'd forgotten too.

I stared at them in my hand. I should post them through his letterbox. There was no need to leave a note or anything, he'd know they were from me.

I left work early and drove to his house. His car wasn't there. I stood at the front door and opened the letterbox while I clutched the keys in my hand. It seemed such a final thing to do. I debated with myself for a moment, then unlocked the door.

As the alarm beeped at me I hoped that Tim hadn't changed the code. I couldn't quite see how I could explain myself to the guards if they arrived. He was my fiancé, officer, and I was returning a set of keys. It sounded lame.

But the numbers were still the same. The silence of the empty house wrapped itself around me and I felt light-headed from simply being there. The last time I'd done this, there had been a reason and Tim and I were still engaged – however tenuously. This time I had no right to be there whatsoever. I was probably committing some sort of crime although it couldn't really be breaking and entering when I hadn't actually broken anything. I closed the hall door gently behind me.

It was unnaturally tidy. Cups and saucers were washed and stacked neatly on the drainer. There were no foil containers half-filled with curry, no magazines and workpads strewn across the living-room floor. Even the desk where his computer sat, silent and dark, was tidy. Well, that was going too far, tidier than usual anyway. It didn't look like Tim's house any more. I didn't feel part of it any more.

I tiptoed upstairs. My heart was pounding. I kept telling myself that I'd no right to be here and that I should go home straight away but I couldn't stop myself. God, I thought suddenly, what if he's still here after all? What if he only pretended to go to California and he's here, in bed, with the lovely Laura? I nearly vomited onto the stairs at the thought.

The bedroom was empty, but the bed was neatly made. I stood in the doorway and looked around. A gleam of light caught my eye and I walked over to the dresser.

My engagement ring lay there and it was the diamonds that had sparkled. I picked it up and slipped it back onto my finger again, but it seemed to burn against my flesh and I knew that I shouldn't have done it. I replaced it carefully on the dresser and looked at the other jewellery that was there – a signet ring that I'd given Tim when we got engaged and a pair of earrings that didn't belong to me. The stones shone blood-red in the gold setting.

I stood there for a moment feeling dizzy. Then I took the earrings and flushed them down the toilet.

I don't know how long I stood in the bathroom. Time didn't have any meaning for me and my legs were frozen. I couldn't move, couldn't think.

The sound of a car pulling up outside finally galvanised me into action. I ran back into the bedroom and peeped out through the net curtains. Tim's next-door neighbours were arriving home. I heaved a sigh of relief and went downstairs again. I'd have to wait until they were safely indoors – I didn't want to meet them and risk them telling Tim that they'd seen me.

I stood beside the silent computer and couldn't resist the urge to switch it on. It whirred and gurgled into life as the icons popped onto the screen. I dragged the file entitled 'Saracen 2' into the trash. I knew that Tim, like all good programmers, would have backed up his files. And that he probably had files at work as well as at home. So I wouldn't be doing anything more than inconveniencing him by my actions. I slid the disk that he'd so carefully labelled into the zip drive and dragged its contents into the trash too. Then I selected the *Empty Trash* command.

'*The trash contains 4 items which use 30mb of disk space. Are you sure you want to permanently remove these items?*' asked the computer. I clicked on the OK icon and watched the files disappear.

Then I replaced the disk in its box and switched off the computer. I put the second set of keys to the back of Tim's desk drawer where he wouldn't find them for ages, set the alarm and drove home.

Chapter 8

Mother and Child (Pablo Picasso, 1971)

Tim didn't ring to find out whether it was me who'd erased the data on his machine. I didn't know whether he'd even noticed – whether, perhaps, he thought that he'd managed to erase it himself. He never rang looking for the second set of keys either, so I presumed that he'd forgotten about them or that he'd found them in the desk and imagined that he'd put them there himself.

I waited for him to call, of course. Each time the phone rang my heart started to thump in my chest and I was sure that everyone could hear it. But they continued to take their phone calls – Mum's friends at the bowling club, Ian's pals, Dad's workmates, Alison's eclectic gathering of friends. Julie was the only one who telephoned me. I hadn't realised that my circle of friends had dwindled so much over the past few years. But I'd lost touch with a lot of people when I'd started going out with Tim. The only other phone calls for me were from people asking me to do dresses, but I hadn't the heart to accept any orders. I didn't feel able to do a wedding dress again, and all of the calls were for wedding dresses.

I still lived each day in a world of my own. I knew that

I was going through the motions – that I was getting my work done, sitting around at home, occasionally going out – but all of those things seemed to be happening to someone else, not to me. Sometimes – despite my desperate efforts to be always efficient – Barry had to buzz the intercom on my desk a couple of times before I even realised that he'd called me; sometimes I read whole chapters of books before I noticed that I'd read them before; sometimes I sat through entire TV programmes without remembering a single thing that had happened on them.

I still thought about moving out of the house but I couldn't summon up the enthusiasm to go apartment-hunting. That was my trouble – I couldn't summon up the enthusiasm to do anything very much.

The days grew shorter, the weather more atrocious, the thought of dragging myself out of bed every morning more and more difficult.

Every now and then I sat at my desk and typed Tim's name onto my computer screen over and over again in one big word – *TimTimTimTim* – until someone approached and I deleted it with a single keystroke. Sometimes I still practised how my signature should have looked, writing Isobel Malone in my big, loopy handwriting before shredding the paper I'd written on into tiny pieces. Sometimes I told myself that I was better off without him; that, when I got over things properly, I'd be thanking God it was over between us.

And sometimes I disappeared into the loo and bawled my eyes out as quietly as I could.

Andy Jordan was visiting Ireland for Christmas. Julie had invited him when she was in Florida and he'd accepted straight away. Julie was crazy about Andy and I was pleased for her but envied her too.

'He makes me feel all fizzy inside,' she confided one

evening when we'd gone for a drink together. 'Even when he talks utter rubbish, I enjoy listening to him speak!'

I laughed. 'That's because he sounds different. Makes him more attractive.'

'He is attractive, isn't he?' She beamed at me. 'You've only seen him in casual clothes, Isobel, but we went out to dinner one night when I was over there and he wore this fabulous suit. Navy-blue silk jacket and trousers! God, you'd never get an Irish man into navy-blue silk.'

She was probably right.

'I hope he won't freeze to death here,' she continued anxiously. 'He's never been anywhere really cold in his life.'

'I thought you said he went skiing in Colorado?'

She made another face. 'That's different. That's crisp cold. Not the dark, miserable sort of damp wetness that we get here.'

'I hope you didn't tell him that it'd be dark, miserable and damp,' I said.

'I told him to pack lots of jumpers and a raincoat. He said he didn't have a raincoat.'

'I bet he does,' I told her. 'He's only having you on, Julie.'

'D'you think so?' She shook her head, since last week a cascading tumble of auburn curls.

'Probably,' I said.

'I can't wait for him to get here. I bought him an Aran jumper for Christmas. Although he'll probably never get to wear it when he goes home!'

'There's probably not a great call for them in Florida,' I agreed.

I could see Tim in the maroon Aran jumper the night he'd told me that the wedding was off. I could see the pull in one of the diamond patterns where he'd caught the jumper on a nail in his garden shed. It was crystal clear, as though he was standing in front of me.

'Isobel?' Julie looked at me curiously. 'Are you OK?'

'Sure.' I let the image of Tim dissolve. There were only strangers surrounding us and none of them wore maroon Aran jumpers.

'You looked miles away.'

'Just thinking,' I said. 'What colour is the Aran?'

She stared at me as though I'd gone off my head. 'Cream, of course. Are you sure you're OK?'

'Of course I am,' I said impatiently. 'D'you want another drink?'

She shook her head. 'I'd better get home. I promised Mum I'd ice the cake for her tonight. Honestly, Isobel, you'd think she'd just go out and buy a cake like most people do these days, but no, it has to be home-made.'

'Mine's the same,' I said as I pulled on my soft red coat. 'Puddings, cakes, mince-pies – she does the lot! I wouldn't mind but she says she hates it.'

'Why does she bother?'

'I don't know. It's probably some primeval nurturing thing. Of course Ali goes mad and tells her not to bother – but my darling sister doesn't say no when a plate of mince-pies and cream is put in front of her!'

Julie laughed. 'I hope Andy has a good appetite when he comes over. Mum'll be very disappointed if he doesn't.'

'I'm sure he'll have a ravenous appetite,' I told her, 'and I bet it won't be for food.'

She made another face but she didn't tell me I was wrong.

⤙

Mum's sister, Rachel, her husband Dennis and their

fourteen-month-old baby daughter, Sorcha, were spending Christmas with us. Rachel and Dennis had moved to London when they married five years ago, but they wanted to come home for Christmas. They were going to spend three days with us and three days with my grandmother before going home. Rachel and Dennis were the only family we had. Mum and Rachel were Granny Behan's only children and Dad was an only child himself. There was a twelve-year age gap between my mother and her younger sister and Rachel sometimes seemed more like an older sister to me. I'd certainly never called her Aunt Rachel and it would have sent her into a fit of giggles if I had.

Rachel worked in an insurance company. I wasn't sure exactly what she did but she had an office of her own with her name on a chrome plate on the door, a company car and she earned a good salary. Dennis was a recruitment consultant in the City. Between them, they earned a lot of money.

I was taking sausage rolls out of the oven when Dad arrived home with them.

'Hello, Issy!' Rachel swept into the kitchen and threw her arms around me.

'Hi, Rachel, don't touch any of those, they're hot.' I pecked her on the cheek.

'Hello, Rachel,' said Mum.

'Helen! You look great!' Rachel hugged my mother and kissed her on both cheeks.

'Steady up,' warned Mum. 'You're not in London now. Although I didn't think they went in for all this kissing business in England.'

'Not usually,' admitted Rachel as she unwound a knitted scarf from her neck. 'I always wanted to come home like a prodigal emigrant and cause a fuss in the family.'

I laughed and Dennis walked into the room. Dennis was one of life's wonderful people. He wasn't hugely attractive – not the sort of man who'd draw gasps of admiration for his looks – but he was always kind and attentive and easy to get on with. Mum said he suited her flighty sister down to the ground because Dennis was a stabilising influence on her. For once I think my mum was right.

Dad followed them, carrying Sorcha.

'Good God,' I exclaimed as he came into the room. 'She's grown!'

The last time I'd seen the baby had been at her christening, when she'd behaved very demurely and had slept through the entire ceremony, only opening her dark-blue eyes when the priest splashed water on her forehead but never uttering a sound.

'She weighs a ton,' moaned Dad as he set her down on the floor and she tottered unsteadily towards a chair.

'She's lovely.' Mum wore the particular besotted look that most women use when they're looking at babies. 'Isn't she a pet?'

'I hope you think so when she wakes up screaming in the middle of the night,' said Rachel darkly. 'She's teething at the moment. See how red her cheeks are? They're driving her mad.'

'Poor little thing.' Mum picked her up and cuddled her. 'Don't you worry, honey, we'll look after you.'

Sorcha beamed at Mum, nestled up to her, then bit her on the ear.

'Sorcha!' Rachel looked horrified but Mum pretended she wasn't hurt.

I chuckled to myself as I put the sausage rolls on a wire cooling tray.

'So, how's business, Dennis?' The men disappeared into the living room while we stood around the kitchen.

Mum was still rubbing her earlobe while Sorcha had buried her face in her mother's chest.

'She's tired,' said Rachel apologetically. 'She does things like that when she's tired.'

'Do you want to put her to bed?' asked Mum. 'Or would you like some tea or coffee first?'

'Tea would be great,' said Rachel. 'I'll give her some milk and a biscuit. The gnawing should help.'

It was after midnight when we finally got to bed but I didn't care that it was late because I didn't have to go to work on Christmas Eve and I knew I could lie in bed in the morning.

⌒

I didn't get much sleep on Christmas Eve morning, or on Christmas Day either. Sorcha was awake at six and insisted on going on a tour of the house both mornings.

By Christmas night, Rachel confessed that Sorcha's insatiable curiosity and boundless energy were sometimes exhausting.

'You were like that too,' said Mum.

'As a child, perhaps,' Rachel said. 'Not now.'

'You should have had her sooner,' Mum told her. 'Then you wouldn't be so tired. It's much harder when you're an older mother.'

There was a taut little silence and Rachel raised an eyebrow. 'I hope you don't mean that the way it sounded, Helen.'

Mum looked uncomfortable. 'Probably not. It's just so tiring looking after children. I was tired when Isobel was born. I can't imagine what it must be like for you, at work all the time, rushing around the place. And that little bit older.'

'I'm fourteen years older than you were when you had Isobel,' grinned Rachel. 'And I know that it's exhausting. But I'm in good shape, good health and I have a wonderful husband who looks after both of us.' She squeezed Dennis's arm affectionately.

'I don't think it's a good idea to work and have a child. Particularly late in life.' Mum persisted with the conversation and I could have shot her.

'Don't be so old-fashioned.' Rachel bounced Sorcha on her knee. 'I couldn't look after myself when I was in my twenties, let alone another person.' She smiled at Mum. 'Look at her, Helen! She's completely dependent on me. Can you imagine her being completely dependent on me when I was in my early twenties?'

Mum looked abashed. 'No.'

'You see?' Rachel tickled Sorcha under the chin and the baby squealed in delight. 'You see? My big sister is just a nag, Sorcha. Just – a – nag!' She held the baby over her head and both of them laughed uproariously.

Mum sighed and opened a box of Dairy Milk. We sat back and watched the movie.

∽

I offered to baby-sit on St Stephen's Day while Mum, Dad, Rachel and Dennis went out together.

'You're sure you can manage?' Rachel looked unusually worried.

'Rachel! I have a younger brother and a younger sister. It comes back to you, you know.'

'She should be OK but she might fret because she's in a strange house.'

'We'll be fine,' I promised. 'Honestly.' It was strange to see Rachel looking so worried. I guessed that motherhood did that to even the most laid-back of people. 'Honestly,'

131

I repeated, 'once you've put her to bed there isn't exactly a lot to do.'

Eventually they went out, followed shortly by Ian (meeting his mates) and Alison, who refused to say where she was going.

'You're not my guardian,' she snapped when I asked.

'OK, OK.' I made a face at her. 'Do whatever you like. I don't care.'

It was odd to be in the house on my own with a baby. Rachel had set up the baby monitor so I curled up in the armchair with *Wuthering Heights*. My reading material was still bleak. I couldn't take sugary sentiment, especially at Christmas.

I peeked in on Sorcha an hour later. She lay stretched out in the cot that Mum had borrowed from a neighbour, one hand gently resting on her cheek. She was so pretty, so small, so vulnerable. I knew that I was looking at her in the exact same gooey way as Mum looked at her. But it was hard not to. God, I thought, wouldn't it be great to be a baby again. Nothing to worry you, just lie there and wait for people to pander to your every whim.

I leaned over and touched her. Her skin was soft and warm. It must be incredible to have a baby of your very own, I thought. Someone that was part of you. What must it be like to touch a person that you had created yourself? I resolutely put images of Tim out of my mind. I didn't want to think of the baby I could have created with Tim.

She woke up around midnight. I shot out of the chair as her thin wail came from the baby monitor and ran upstairs two at a time. She was sitting up in the cot, eyes laden with tears, cheeks wet.

'What's the matter?' I asked. 'What's wrong?'

She wailed again.

I picked her up and she stopped crying. I held her

close to me and breathed in her baby smell. 'Are you all right?'

Her cry was more half-hearted this time. I walked around the bedroom with her, rocking her gently in my arms. 'Who's a good baby?' I asked, then laughed at the absurdity of the question.

She stared at me, her eyes huge in her round face. 'You're so lovely,' I whispered and held her close to me.

I sat down in the high-backed wicker chair in the corner of the room. It was peaceful holding her like this. It was nice to feel that someone needed me. I felt more relaxed than I had in ages. Sorcha opened her eyes and looked straight at me. I leaned down to her and kissed her. Her eyes flickered, then closed.

I woke up when Rachel pushed the bedroom door open and tiptoed inside. Even when I woke I didn't move so that the sleeping baby was undisturbed. I was amazed that I'd slept holding her in my arms.

Rachel smiled at us. 'Was she a lot of trouble?'

I shook my head. 'She woke up and whimpered for a few minutes, then fell asleep again.' I shifted in the chair and pins and needles ran through my arm. I grimaced and Rachel laughed under her breath.

'She's heavy,' I said.

'I know.' Rachel gathered her from me and put her back in the cot. Sorcha sighed deeply but stayed sleeping. We stood and looked in at her.

'They're so innocent,' said Rachel wistfully.

'It's hard to imagine that either of us was once that small,' I said.

'Everybody says that they grow so fast, too.' Rachel rearranged the pink and yellow blanket over her daughter.

'Will you have any more?' I asked.

'I don't know,' replied Rachel. 'I'd like to, I think. It's hard work, though.'

'Give up your job,' I said blithely. 'Follow Mum's advice. Then you'll have plenty of time and you won't be so tired.'

'I think you get tired anyway.' Rachel smiled at me. 'And I wouldn't dream of giving up my job. I've worked too hard to get where I am.'

'I think I'd give up mine,' I said dreamily. 'It would be wonderful not to have to clock in every morning.'

Rachel was silent for a moment. 'So how are you doing?' she asked finally. 'Since you broke up with Tim?'

I'd wondered when she was going to ask me, how she'd work it into the conversation. I knew that eventually she'd have to ask. I'd want to ask if I were her.

'Fine,' I said.

'You sure?'

'Of course.' I was *not* going to cry, I told myself. There was no need to cry. It was eight months later, for God's sake!

'Must have been pretty horrible for you.'

'Mmm.'

'And I guess Helen wasn't a lot of help.'

'She was a bit cut up about it,' I admitted.

'Gone out with anyone else?' asked Rachel casually.

'You must be joking!' I laughed bitterly.

'Oh, come on. You'll want to go out with someone else,' Rachel said. 'You know you will. Have you got over him?'

'I don't know,' I said, and started to cry again.

Rachel said nothing but handed me a tissue from the box beside the cot. I wiped my eyes, blew my nose and took a puff of my inhaler.

'You haven't got over him?'

'I keep thinking I have,' I said. 'And then something happens and I start to cry like this all over again. It's not fair, Rachel. I've tried, really I have. But he won't

134

go away. I imagine him all the time. Everywhere I go, everything I do, he's there in the background. When I go out with the girls – admittedly not very often – I think of how I should be a married woman. When I go out with my pal, Julie, she talks about her boyfriend and I feel a total failure. When I drive around town I see places we've been, pubs we've been in, cinemas, restaurants, everything! And I can't look anywhere without seeing him there!'

'Oh, Isobel.' She put her arms around me and hugged me to her. 'It'll get easier, truly it will.'

'Everybody says that,' I sniffled. 'But nobody knows. They're just assuming.'

She reached out for another tissue and I took it from her.

'Why don't you come to London for a while?' she asked. 'Get a job there, give yourself a bit of a break.'

'I don't think so,' I said. 'I've never wanted to work in London.'

'But it would break the cycle for you,' said Rachel. 'You wouldn't picture Tim everywhere you went. You'd be with a whole new set of people. It'd be good for you, Isobel.'

I sighed. 'Maybe.'

'Definitely,' she said. 'Why don't you give a few of the agencies a ring? They're crying out for good secretarial and admin staff. I bet you your first week's salary that you'll get a job straight away.'

I smiled weakly. 'I'll think about it.'

'Promise me,' said Rachel. 'Don't just say it.'

'I promise,' I said. 'I really promise.'

⌐

I went to a New Year's Eve Ball with Julie and Andy.

I didn't want to go because I thought that I'd be a wallflower and a gooseberry all at the same time, but both of them insisted. It was for a good cause, Julie told me, as she handed me the ticket and asked for a cheque. The more people that came along the better.

I took my midnight-blue cocktail dress from the wardrobe. I hadn't worn that since the night of Tim's software dinner. I was certain I could smell the lingering traces of *Ralph Lauren* but I'd had the dress cleaned since then so it wasn't possible.

'You look wonderful,' said Andy as I got into the taxi with them.

'Thank you.'

'Fabulous dress,' said Julie. 'Did you make it yourself?'

I nodded. 'Ages ago. It's nearly two years old.'

'It's ageless,' said Julie. She wore a black sheath dress with a tiny diamond brooch on the shoulder. With her auburn curls piled on top of her head she was about six feet tall and looked extremely elegant. She'd had her nails done, I noticed. Julie was an occasional nail-biter, but tonight they were long, even and polished a vibrant red. 'Sculptured,' she whispered when I nodded at them.

'Look great,' I whispered back.

'I'm getting left out of things,' Andy complained and Julie laughed and told him we were having a girly conversation and he should just butt out.

The hotel was crowded with people in party dress, crushing their way to the bar. A silver banner wished us all a Happy New Year and a band mangled some well-known melodies. I sighed. I wished I hadn't come. It was all very well to say that I'd done it because it was for a good cause, but if I wanted to support a good cause I should have just given Julie the money.

I hated New Year at the best of times. Everyone being nice to everyone else, singing stupid songs, making stupid resolutions, grimly determined to have a good time.

'Southern Comfort on the rocks.' Andy handed me a drink.

'Thanks.' He stood there with Julie's gin and tonic in his hand. 'She'll be back in a minute,' I told him.

He put the drink on a nearby table. 'So how are you doing?' he asked. 'Gotten over your ex-boyfriend yet?'

'Sort of,' I replied. I took a gulp of Southern Comfort and enjoyed the warm glow of the alcohol as it went down.

'You're far too nice to worry about a shit like that,' said Andy.

'He wasn't a shit,' I said.

'Of course he was.' Andy looked angry. 'You don't leave a lady at the altar.'

'He didn't quite leave me at the altar.' I laughed and was surprised that it came out as a genuine laugh and not somewhere between a laugh and a sob. 'There were two weeks to go, you know.'

'Even so.' Andy still looked angry. 'It wasn't a very nice thing to do.'

'No, it wasn't,' I agreed. 'But it was better than getting married and then deciding that it was all a horrible mistake.'

'Julie told me that you went out with him for a while afterwards,' he said. 'Why on earth would you want to?'

'Because I thought that we might get back together. I still cared about him.'

Andy shook his head. 'I don't understand women. I never will.'

'You're not meant to understand us,' I teased.

'Not meant to understand what?' asked Julie.

'Women,' I told her.

'Exactly,' she said. 'You just have to love us.'

'Oh, I sure do that.' Andy smiled at her. 'Do you want to dance with me?'

She looked at me enquiringly.

'I don't mind,' I said. 'Go ahead.'

They walked onto the dance floor and he put his arms around her. He really was very attractive, I realised. I wondered if Ari had been as attractive. They'd looked alike, I remembered, but I wasn't sure how alike they'd been. I couldn't recall Ari very much – I couldn't conjure up his face.

I finished my drink and went to the bar. I wondered if I'd get blind drunk tonight. Maybe I should. Maybe my New Year's resolution should be to spend the next year in a haze of alcohol which would numb me completely so I wouldn't think about Tim or feel devastated whenever I realised that he wasn't part of my life any more.

I knew that I wouldn't. I didn't get drunk very often because, if I did, I usually had a raging hangover the next day. Besides, I didn't really like being drunk. I didn't like the loss of control, the muzzy, floating feeling. I drank another Southern Comfort and reflected that I could always just get drunk tonight.

Julie and Andy didn't mean to leave me alone for huge chunks of the evening but they spent ages wrapped around each other, swaying to the music and oblivious to everybody else.

At midnight we formed a circle and counted down to the New Year, the band played Auld Lang Syne and everybody kissed and hugged each other. Julie told me that this year would be the best year ever for me and I smiled and said that I hoped so. Andy hugged me and told me that Ari had said hello and that his brother thought I was one of the nicest girls he'd ever met and if I wanted to come to the States later in the year he was sure that Ari would be delighted to see me. I put my arms around them both and said that they were wonderful friends.

Andy ordered champagne and popped the cork very expertly so that none of the drink was wasted. I decided that if I was going to have a hangover, a champagne hangover was more exclusive than any other sort and I might as well drink it.

I suppose I had a good time. I wasn't really sure. I wondered would the time come when I could feel properly again, when I would know that I was happy or when I knew that I was sad. I watched Julie and Andy share a private joke and I cried inside.

I had a really rotten hangover the next day.

Chapter 9

Spain (Salvador Dalí, 1938)

The apartment was dark. The heavy, lined curtains effectively blocked out the light and the gentle heat of the afternoon sun. I supposed that in the summer months I'd be grateful for that but right now I wanted light and I wanted warmth. I pulled the curtains apart and stepped out onto the balcony.

It wasn't much of a view. I stared across the city at the jumble of apartment buildings and office blocks so different from the Dublin skyline I was used to. There were no landmarks for me, each building was new and unfamiliar. I felt my breath catch in my throat as I suddenly realised how very alone I was.

I hadn't chosen Spain. It had never been a lifetime's ambition to come and work here, but when the opportunity arose I knew that I'd be mad not to take it. Coming to Spain meant getting away from Dublin and its incessant reminders of Tim and how bloody awful my life had been since we split up. For the second time, I reminded myself. And, after all, the second time I'd been the one to pull the plug.

But it still didn't feel like that. I might have been the person who said it wasn't working, but I still felt like the person who'd been let down. I knew plenty of women would think that I was a complete loser, some sort of pre-feminist sad case, but I couldn't help it. Despite trying to fool myself day after day, I knew that things weren't getting any better.

And landing the job in Spain avoided the possible unpleasantness of Barry deciding to sack me.

After he called me into his office to 'talk to me' I tried really hard to get back to my old self. But my old self was too bound up in what I used to be – Tim's fiancée. Sometimes I'd walk into the coffee room at DeltaPrint and the chatter would stop and I'd know without a shadow of a doubt that I was the topic of conversation. Of course I was – nothing this dramatic had happened in DeltaPrint before.

Occasionally, I'd take a half-hearted look through the papers to see if there was another job. I told myself that Rachel was right, I'd be better somewhere else, but I looked without enthusiasm and was never convinced that I'd find anything to suit me. Barry caught me reading the *Guardian* supplement one day. I tried to close it as he walked by the desk but I only succeeded in knocking a box of paper-clips onto the floor in front of him.

'Oh, God, Barry, I'm sorry!' I scrabbled under the desk to retrieve them.

'Come into my office, Isobel.' Not a request – a demand. Very unlike him.

I perched on the edge of the chair and looked nervously at him. I hadn't made any huge mistakes, I was certain of it. Jim Loughlin had gone to London earlier in the day and I knew that I'd booked the right flight for him. I'd made backups of all the previous months' accounts. I'd confirmed Barry's attendance at the print and pack-aging conference at the IMI. There wasn't anything left to do.

He went straight to the point. 'It isn't working, Isobel.'

I stared at him.

'What d'you mean?'

'You know exactly what I mean.'

'But I've tried, Barry, honestly I have. And I know my work's been OK.'

'OK, maybe,' he said. 'But efficient, no. And it's so difficult to work with you now, Isobel. I'm afraid of saying the wrong thing and upsetting you.'

'You've never upset me,' I told him.

'That's because I try so hard not to.'

I was hurt and I felt the familiar sting of tears behind my eyes, but I said nothing.

'You don't act on your own initiative any more,' said Barry. 'I have to tell you to do things. I have to be on your case all the time. I have to check things in case you make mistakes.'

'I don't make mistakes,' I said tonelessly.

He sighed. 'No, you don't. But there's no joy in you any more, Isobel. No fun. No laughter.'

'I'm at work,' I said. 'There's no fun here anyway.'

'You didn't always feel like that.'

I studied my nails.

'However,' Barry paused and I looked up again. 'This might be of interest to you.'

He handed me a newspaper and I frowned because it was in Spanish. It took a few minutes for my Spanish to kick in. 'The actress and singer Madonna visited Madrid today,' I translated into English.

'Not that,' Barry interrupted. 'The advertisement beside it.'

'*Administrative Assistant. Fluent English. Computer literate. Required for prestigious training company.*' I glanced up at him.

'That's it,' he said. 'What do you think?'

'What d'you mean – what do I think?'

'Doesn't it sound like you?'

I looked at the paper again. 'Well, I suppose so, but it could be anybody. My English is fluent because it's my mother tongue. What about my Spanish?'

'You put on your CV that you were fluent in French and Spanish,' said Barry.

'I was,' I said. 'But I haven't spoken either of them in years.'

'I thought you went to Spain the year before last,' he said. 'Malaga, you said.'

'Yes, but Malaga is a touristy sort of city,' I pointed out. 'I didn't exactly need to use a lot of Spanish.'

'It doesn't matter,' said Barry. 'You're still fluent.'

'So what's this about?' I asked.

'Sharon's friend put that ad in the paper,' he told me. 'And Sharon thinks you'd fit the bill.'

Sharon was Barry's wife.

'Why did she think of me?' I asked.

'Because we talk about you at home,' said Barry. 'I asked her for advice on how best to deal with you and she gave it.'

'Get rid of me was the advice?' I stared at him.

'Don't be ridiculous,' he said. 'She thinks you need a change of scenery. Get away from Dublin for a while. Get out and about and have a good time.'

I swallowed the lump in my throat. 'I don't feel like doing that.'

'Not here, maybe,' said Barry. 'But, Isobel, Madrid! Think about it. Warm and sunny and such a beautiful city.'

Yeah, I thought, and me out of your hair.

'And if I'm not interested?'

'Isobel.' He frowned. 'Why shouldn't you be interested? It's a new life for you. You should be having fun, not sitting around moping over someone who isn't worth it. You're still young.'

I sighed. 'It's a big change.'

'You need a big change,' said Barry, 'and, Isobel, to be perfectly honest, I need a change from you.'

～

I stepped back from the balcony into the apartment. It was small but perfectly adequate. There was a living area, a galley kitchen, a bedroom and a bathroom. My first apartment, I told myself. A place of my own. I said it out loud to make it seem more real.

Gabriela Suarez, Sharon's friend and the Managing Director of Advanta, had organised the rental of the apartment for me. The company was paying my first month's rent, which was helpful. I was very grateful to Sharon for saying good things about me to Gabriela, but at the back of my mind I couldn't help thinking that they were all doing this to get me out of Barry's way. He had wanted to fire me, I thought bleakly, but he was afraid that it would tip me over the edge.

～

My mother nearly had a fit when I told her. She couldn't understand why I would leave my family and my well-paid job.

'I need a break,' I said.

'But why Spain? Why not somewhere in Ireland? Or London? Somewhere you can get home easily?'

'It's only a two-hour flight to Madrid,' I told her impatiently. 'I can come home any time I like.'

'It'll be too expensive,' she said. 'You won't be able to afford it.'

'There are plenty of cheap flights.'

She sighed. 'I don't like it, Isobel.'

'Oh, for God's sake.' I stared at her. 'I should have done this a long time ago.' I ignored the hurt look in her eyes.

⌒

'I don't believe you.' Julie looked at me in astonishment. We'd gone to the Bloody Stream for a drink and were wedged into a corner of the crowded bar. 'Madrid!'

'Why not?'

'No reason,' she said. 'I think it's absolutely marvellous. I'd love to go abroad to work. I don't know why I didn't.'

'I'm not sure about it,' I confessed. 'I know that Barry basically got me the job and I'm sure he did it because he couldn't stand me in the office any more.'

'He wouldn't have recommended you if he didn't think you could do it.'

'Sharon, his wife, recommended me.' I sipped my drink. 'I think she decided that I was driving her husband around the twist and she had to do something about it.'

Julie laughed. 'So what! It's a great opportunity, Isobel.'

'I know. But I'm scared.'

'Scared?'

'That I won't like it. That I'll be useless. That this Gabriela woman will hate me when she meets me.'

'Oh, don't be stupid.' Julie looked at me without any sympathy. 'You spend too much time navel-gazing, Isobel. Of course you'll like it. You won't be useless. And there's no reason for Gabriela to hate you.'

'I know,' I said. 'I just—'

'That bastard Malone sapped all your confidence,' said

Julie angrily. 'You never used to worry about new things before.'

'It's not that,' I said.

'It bloody is,' said Julie.

∽

'I think it's great,' said Alison as we sat in the living room the night before I went. 'It means I'll have somewhere to stay if I want to get a break.'

'I'm glad that's all I mean to you.' I grinned at her.

'Don't be silly,' she said. 'It means I can have your bedroom too. More space for my stuff!'

∽

'I wish I was going.' It was the first time in years Ian had been up before midday on a Saturday. 'I bet you'll have a great time.'

'I hope so,' I said.

'Send me photographs of gorgeous Spanish women,' he said.

'Why?'

'So's I can see what I'm missing.'

'There are plenty of gorgeous women at home,' said Alison severely.

'Not the same as continental women,' said Ian seriously. 'They all look so classy. They dress so well.'

I looked down at my frayed jeans. Ian was right. Continental women always looked sophisticated, even in frayed jeans. Whereas I looked as if I'd grabbed these out of the bottom of my wardrobe. I'd lost the ability to be stylish. I hadn't made a dress since the wedding dress. I hadn't bought new clothes in ages. Maybe Madrid was a good idea after all.

⤳

I opened my suitcase and began to unpack. I couldn't quite believe that I was here and that I didn't know when I'd be going home. It wasn't a holiday. I said that over and over again on the plane as we flew over the Pyrenees and I looked down at the snow-capped mountains. 'I'm going to live in Spain.' But it didn't sink in, somehow, and it still hadn't sunk in.

The only sound in the apartment was the faint hum of the fridge. Otherwise it was uncomfortably quiet. I couldn't even hear sounds from the adjoining apartments, and I wondered if anyone lived in them or whether they were vacant. I felt the quiver of loneliness again and tried to ignore it.

I went into the living area and switched on the portable TV for company. TVE was showing a football match between Real Madrid and Juventus.

I listened to the commentary as I continued to unpack, letting my ear become accustomed to the words and the cadence of the language. I'd been worried in case my Spanish had declined more than I thought, but I'd conversed reasonably well with Gabriela and now I could follow the commentator's anguish at the referee's decision to allow Juventus a free kick on the edge of the penalty area. '*Gooooo-aaa-lll!!!!*' he cried a moment later and I understood him when he said that Real were behind due to a monumental travesty of footballing justice.

Finally, all of my clothes were put away. I walked back into the living area and surveyed my apartment with the eye of someone who felt, marginally, more proprietorial.

It was sparsely furnished, but that wasn't a bad thing considering its size. A heavy darkwood table with four high-backed Spanish-style chairs was pushed against the counter that separated the living and kitchen areas. There was also a two-seater sofa and a small armchair. The TV stood on a corner unit with space for a video, but there wasn't any video. Not that I cared. I was relieved it had TV. That was it as far as the living room was concerned.

There wasn't room for furniture in the galley kitchen. There was an assortment of plates, cups and glasses in one cupboard and some knives and forks in the floor unit beside the sink.

I thought of the complete set of Royal Doulton china that Tim's aunt had given us as a wedding present and wondered what he had done with it. I should have kept one of the token toasters, I thought, as I rummaged around a bit more. And the coffee-maker.

There was shopping to be done, but I wasn't in the mood to do it today. I had to get some food, but everything else could wait.

The apartment was on the fifth floor of the Edificio Gerona, on a side road near the Paseo de la Castellana, one of the city's main streets. I took the lift down to the ground floor and walked out into the bright afternoon sunshine, clutching my map and trying not to look too much like a tourist. Even this early in the year Madrid had its fair share of them.

I walked all the way down to the Plaza de Colon before I noticed how much my feet were hurting. I bought water, bread, milk and fruit in a small shop and a copy of the newspaper *El Pais*. Then, feeling almost part of the city at last, I ventured down into the metro and caught the Liñea I back to the apartment.

The lift shuddered its way to the fifth floor. There was still nobody around. I wondered was I the only person living in the Edificio Gerona. Maybe it was condemned or something and that was why Gabriela Suarez hadn't minded paying my first month's rent.

∽

By eight o'clock I was sick of my own company and sick of TVE. Juventus, I discovered on the evening news, had beaten Real two goals to one. José Maria Olazabal had won a golf tournament in the USA. King Juan Carlos and Queen Sofia were visiting Italy. The Prime Minister had called for greater productivity in the increasingly competitive global market place. And tomorrow would be cloudy with a possibility of rain.

I switched off the TV and pulled on a sweatshirt. I braved the shuddering lift and went outside again. This time I turned the opposite way at the end of the road and, almost immediately, found a row of shops which included a brightly lit, crowded bar-café. I found a seat inside. The TV behind the bar was showing the highlights of the Real versus Juventus game and a cluster of men groaned aloud at the free kick decision and the subsequent goal. I leaned back in my seat and ordered a San Miguel.

I opened *El Pais*. A man squeezed into the seat beside me. I folded the paper so as to give him more room.

'*Gracias*,' he said.

'*De nada*.' It came quite naturally.

Juventus scored their second goal and the collective groan was louder. The man beside me clucked in disapproval and caught my eye. 'Real are playing like headless chickens,' he said.

'It was a poor decision earlier,' I murmured.

'You are English?' Obviously my accent wasn't as good as I thought.

'No,' I said. 'Irish.'

'*Irlandesa!*' He smiled at me and switched to English. 'I worked in Dublin for six months.'

'Really?' I said politely.

'Yes. In a restaurant in Temple Bar. It was called La Cocina.'

I nodded. 'I know it.'

'I never saw you there.'

'You wouldn't remember.'

'Of course I would,' he said gallantly. 'Nobody could forget such a beautiful face.'

I smiled. I knew it was a chat-up line but he did it so well.

'What is your name?' he asked.

'Isobel.'

'A lovely name,' he said. 'I am Ignacio.'

'Pleased to meet you.'

'For how long are you visiting Madrid?'

'Oh, I'm not sure,' I told him. 'I've just started to work here.'

'Really. Where?'

'A training company,' I told him. 'Advanta. We run computer courses as well as seminars to help business people become more efficient.'

He shrugged. 'I am sorry. I do not know it. I work for the Banco de Bilbao myself.'

'Perhaps I will open my bank account there,' I said.

'Please do,' said Ignacio. 'Here is my card. I will be delighted to look after you personally.'

I took the card and slid it into my bag. 'Thank you.'

'Can I buy you a drink?'

I shook my head.

'A coffee perhaps?'

'No, thank you, Ignacio.'

'Perhaps you would like to have dinner with me some night?' He smiled at me. 'It is difficult when you start work in a new city. I know. I would be delighted to show you around.'

'It's very good of you,' I said. 'But—'

'You do not have to decide now,' said Ignacio. 'But I often come to this bar. I would be glad to see you again.'

I smiled at him. 'Thank you very much.'

The Juventus Real match was over and the station had switched to British football and was showing Liverpool and Chelsea.

'They are a good team,' said Ignacio when Chelsea scored. 'But they will never be as good as Real.'

'No team will ever be as good as Real,' I said, although I hadn't a clue really.

'Spoken like a true Madrileña,' said Ignacio and gave me the full force of his Latin good looks in his smile.

'Not bad,' I could hear Julie and Alison say in unison. 'Your first day and someone has tried to pick you up.'

⌒

I arrived at Advanta's office early on Monday morning. So early that only the security guard was behind the receptionist's desk in the lobby. I sat down and waited while he phoned Gabriela Suarez to tell her that I was here.

I was nervous about meeting her. I'd imagined all sorts of people – from plump and homely to tall and elegant – but I couldn't pin a picture to the lilting voice I'd spoken to on the phone. She must be in her early forties to be a friend of Sharon's, but I couldn't guess at anything else.

The woman who emerged from the lift and stepped confidently across the foyer was close to my tall and elegant picture. She had short black hair, wore a dark brown Donna Karan suit and her watch, which I noticed when she extended her hand to shake mine, was a Rolex.

'Welcome to Madrid, and to Advanta,' she said. 'I hope you had a good journey and the apartment is all right.' Her English was flawless.

151

'Thank you, yes.'

'Come this way.'

I followed her into the lift and she pressed the button for the eighth floor.

'We have two floors in this building,' said Gabriela. 'The eighth is where we have the offices and the administration, and the seventh is where we have the conference and training rooms.'

I nodded.

'We have a full-time staff of twenty people and contract staff of thirty,' she continued. 'Some of the contract staff just do a couple of sessions a year – they are not full-time lecturers. But some are. We pride ourselves on the quality of our lecturers and the standard of our courses. It is our aim to be the best training company in Spain.'

The doors of the lift sighed open and we went through some wooden doors into Advanta's offices. They were bright and modern. The desks were light wood, the walls panelled in what looked like walnut. The carpet was silver-grey. Gabriela opened the door of her private office. It was a medium-sized corner office. Barry Cleary had once told me that all managers wanted corner offices because it was a sign of authority.

Gabriela sat behind her desk and looked at me. 'Sharon speaks very highly of you,' she said.

I was embarrassed. I didn't know Sharon Cleary all that well.

'I hope I'll work well for you,' I said.

'I hope so too.' She smiled slightly. 'You are the answer to a prayer really. I lost three of my best staff in one week. Careless, no?' I was silent. 'One girl got a better job offer, one decided that she wanted to go back to college and the third got married and moved to Barcelona.'

'A bit unfortunate,' I said.

'Well, I knew that Berenice was going to Barcelona,'

said Gabriela. 'That was why I advertised. But when the others handed in their notice too, I was in big trouble. I don't like taking temporary staff because I want people to be committed to the company, but it's hard to get the experience you need quickly.'

'I know nothing about training,' I told her. 'I did say that to you on the phone.'

'But you do have organisational experience,' she said. 'You are an administrator.'

'That's what I do best,' I said, trying to forget some of Barry's comments over the past year.

'Excellent,' said Gabriela. 'So I will take you to your desk, introduce you to some of your colleagues and leave you to it.'

She was very businesslike. I'd never worked for a woman before and I didn't know what to expect.

I soon learned that Gabriela Suarez was almost frightening in her efficiency. And, according to the other people in the office, she expected the same level of efficiency from her staff. People that were loyal to the company and who worked well were rewarded with good salaries and bonuses. Anyone who didn't work out left very quickly. I hoped that I'd work out. I'd been rejected by Tim and, I thought, by Barry. I couldn't stand it if I was rejected by Advanta too.

Chapter 10

Standing Nude (Joan Miró, 1918)

The days were easier than the nights. I was busy during the day, but when I got back to the apartment each evening I felt cut off from everyone. And at night, when I lay in the creaky double bed, I wondered what would happen if I was suddenly taken ill and nobody knew about it. The people in Advanta might just think I'd had enough and had hared back home. My family wouldn't know that I was lying unconscious in Madrid. Sometimes I couldn't sleep and I lay there wondering what was happening at home, what Julie was doing. What Tim was doing.

It never seemed so bad in the mornings, but the fears were very real at night.

On Friday nights the administration staff hit Leon's Tapas Bar for a drink and tapas before going home. It was, literally, one drink, but at least it was a way to get to know them better.

Sometimes Gabriela came along too, which she did that first Friday. She ordered drinks for everyone and handed me a glass of San Miguel.

'So how was your first week?' she asked.

'Busy.' That was true. I'd had a lot of familiarising to do, as well as the normal work.

'Do you think you can cope?'

'Of course.' I smiled at her. 'I think I'll enjoy it here.'

'That's good news.' She returned the smile. 'Magdalena tells me that you have changed the filing system for the assessments.'

'Not changed exactly.' I looked at her anxiously. 'It was on computer but I think you were using a less efficient application. I shifted it to Grail.'

'I know very little about the different programs,' said Gabriela. 'Once it is working and it doesn't cause extra administration, I don't mind what you do.'

'You should find this will be much quicker,' I said. 'And you'll be able to transfer files more easily.'

'Sounds good to me.' Gabriela looked pleased. 'What do you think, Magdalena?'

Magdalena Moyet was Gabriela's personal assistant. 'It's good,' she said. 'Isobel showed me a shortcut for moving the data around. It's very efficient.'

'My goodness.' Gabriela laughed. 'Perhaps I have done us a great service by offering you this job.'

'I'm glad you did,' I said. 'Thank you.'

'Luis!' Magdalena waved at one of the men who worked in the administration department. 'Come and talk to us.'

I hadn't spoken to Luis before although I'd seen him in the office a few times and knew that he had a reputation of being a real ladies' man. Went through Advanta like a dose of salts, Magdalena had told me on the first day. Nothing much to look at but absolutely fantastic in bed apparently.

He wasn't particularly good-looking. He was medium height with unkempt hair, blue eyes and absolutely no dress sense. Which was unusual in Madrid because, if the women were chic, the men were just as fashionable. But

Luis wore ancient suits and even older ties to work, and his shirts were a riot of clashing colours. All the same, he had a certain charm and when he smiled he seemed to smile especially for you. Not that he'd actually smiled for me yet.

'Hi.' He manoeuvred himself into a space beside us. 'A good week, Magdalena.'

'Not bad.' She grinned. 'Keep Gabriela in a few new suits.'

I glanced at the Managing Director, but Gabriela had turned to talk to someone else and hadn't heard her PA's comment. Her suits were all designer and her home was in a very fashionable area of the city. I hadn't realised that training was so profitable.

'So, Isobel, how did you enjoy this week?' asked Luis.

'It was good,' I said. 'I think I'll like it.'

'Excellent.' He looked at me appraisingly. 'And I like you already.'

'Luis!' said Magdalena warningly.

'I only meant that Isobel is a wonderful addition to our company.' He shrugged expressively. 'I have an unfair reputation, dearest Isobel, and one which Magdalena thinks I absolutely deserve.'

I watched them warily. Magdalena hadn't said anything about a relationship with Luis herself, although she'd winked when she told me that he was fantastic in bed.

'Don't be silly.' She punched him gently on the arm. 'Just because I never gave in to your advances.'

'There are only two women in the office that never succumbed,' said Luis. 'And Isobel is the other one.'

'What about Gabriela?' I asked, and the two of them exploded into laughter.

'She doesn't count,' spluttered Luis. 'She's the boss.'

'So?' I looked at him archly. 'If the man is the boss,

it doesn't stop him from chasing the women who work for him. Or it doesn't stop the women from chasing him. Why should this be different?'

They weren't sure whether I was joking or not.

'Gabriela wouldn't,' said Luis finally. 'And, to be honest, I wouldn't have the nerve!'

'So tell us about yourself, Isobel.' Magdalena pushed her long black hair out of her eyes. 'Why did you come to Spain?'

Nobody knew me here, I reminded myself. I could reinvent myself. I didn't have to bare my soul to them.

'Oh, I needed a change,' I told her. 'I was bored in my old job, I'd dumped my pathetic boyfriend and I didn't know what I wanted to do with my life. So I thought it would be nice to work abroad.'

'I wish I'd thought of that when I broke up with Francisco,' said Magdalena. 'I could have got a more interesting job somewhere else. That would have made him stop in his tracks.'

'Were you going out with your boyfriend a long time?' asked Luis.

'We'd got into a rut,' I explained. 'I'd fallen into the habit of going out with him.'

'I know exactly what you mean,' said Magdalena. 'And it's a habit that's hard to get out of.'

I nodded and drained my glass. 'Anybody want another?'

They shook their heads. 'Got to get home,' said Luis. 'But I'm meeting a group of friends at the Hard Rock Café later. Would you like to join us?'

'I don't think I can,' I said.

'Whatever you like,' said Luis. 'It's an informal group. We'll be there at ten.'

'Perhaps,' I said.

'Hope you can make it.' He smiled at me. 'Surely there's nothing else you have to do on a Friday night?'

'Not really,' I said. 'Perhaps some tidying of the apartment.'

'Isobel!' He looked at me as though I had two heads. 'On Friday!' And we all laughed.

∽

I'd bought wine during the week and stashed it in the fridge along with some cans of lager, half a melon and some smelly cheese. I opened a bottle when I went home and debated whether or not I would turn up at the Hard Rock. In the end I didn't go. I wasn't ready to socialise yet, to try out the new Isobel. A drink on Friday was enough for now. And I didn't want to get to know them too well. I didn't want to get involved.

I poured wine into a wide tumbler. I hadn't bought any wine glasses, just the wine. Luis probably doesn't have the slightest interest in you, a little voice muttered in my ear. Still, it'd be nice to think he had. Good for the ego.

The phone rang and startled me so much I almost dropped my glass. This was my first phone call. I'd rung home, of course, but nobody had rung me.

'Isobel?'

'Julie! How are you?'

'Great,' she said. 'And you? I rang to see how you were getting on.'

'OK,' I said cautiously. 'The work isn't too bad, although there's a lot of it. I'm in charge of booking lecturers and keeping tabs on them, that sort of thing. The boss, Gabriela, is quite nice. She—'

'Isobel! Shut up about work. I was enquiring about your *social* life.'

'I haven't had much time to have a social life yet,' I said. 'It's still my first week.'

'But you must have done something in the evenings,'

she said. 'I mean, you don't just go home and sit in front of the TV, do you?'

'I went for a drink with the people after work tonight,' I told her. 'Although they don't seem to have the kind of sessions we have at home. But that was nice. And I've enrolled for advanced business language classes on Wednesday nights.'

'Anything else?' asked Julie. 'Any gorgeous Latin hunks inhabiting your apartment block?'

'Not that I've seen so far,' I said. 'But you never know. Actually, I haven't seen anyone else on this floor yet. There is someone in the apartment across the hall because I've heard their radio. And I've seen people in the lobby. But I haven't met any of the neighbours yet.'

'Bet there's somebody,' said Julie.

'I don't work as fast as you,' I told her. 'But – I did meet a guy in a bar around the corner last Saturday.'

'The day you arrived!' she cried. 'I knew it, Issy, I knew you could do it!'

'Hang on,' I said. 'I haven't done anything yet.'

'But you spoke to him, didn't you?'

'A few words.'

'You see!' She was triumphant. 'I knew once you'd left here you could get back on track. And the best thing of all, Isobel, is that none of them know you're recovering from a mauling by the shit Malone.'

'Julie!'

'Oh, come on, Isobel. He almost wrecked your life. Now you can have a little fun again. Get out there, girl. Live a little.'

I laughed. 'You know me, Julie. I'm not that sort of girl.'

'When I met you first, you were exactly that sort of girl,' she said seriously. 'Remember? You had loads of boy-friends. Your only trouble was choosing one at a time.'

'I was younger then.'

'So what? You think you're ready for a pension now?'

'No.'

'Then have a good time,' said Julie. 'Remember, if it all gets too horrible you can always come home.'

'You're dreadful, Julie Donegan, really dreadful.'

'But I give good advice,' she told me. 'Every time.'

～

It rained on Saturday. I couldn't believe it. I thought the rain in Spain should be falling somewhere else. I needed to go shopping, rain or no rain.

The nearest metro station was a five-minute walk away. I caught the metro to Sol, the lopsided square that didn't much look like its name as rain cascaded down the street. I hurried into the Corté Ingles, one of Spain's best-known department stores.

I wandered around the household department, stamping down the thought that if I'd married Tim I'd have been doing this in Arnotts or Roches instead. I bought towels and bed-linen, some really pretty cups and saucers, and a cutlery set with brightly coloured handles. Then I realised that even these few purchases would be a nightmare to get back to the apartment, so I called a halt and caught the metro home again.

It didn't quite feel like home. But it was beginning to look like somewhere with a piece of my personality in it. I arranged the cups and saucers on the hardwood table and nodded my approval.

I listened to the TV while I cleaned the apartment. If you can call scrubbing a sink and tiles and polishing woodwork fun, then I had fun. It wasn't bad actually. In a kind of way, I enjoyed myself.

At five o'clock I made myself some soup and cut wedges

from the crusty bread I'd bought earlier. Nothing to this living alone, I thought, and it's great not to have Ian or Alison barging in and changing channel just as I'm getting into the movie. I was watching a dubbed version of *Pretty Woman* – I'd seen the film about a dozen times before. More than that, probably, because it had been one of Tim's favourite films and he'd regularly hire it out from the video store no matter how many times I told him it was rubbish.

'But she's so lovely,' he'd say as he drooled over Julia Roberts.

'You should be so lucky to find a hooker like that,' I remembered telling him. 'It's a complete male fantasy movie.'

'So what?' And he rolled over and pulled me closer to him. 'I need my fantasies.'

And so do I, I thought as Julia Roberts insisted on the fairytale. So do I.

∽

The movie was over by half-eight. I had to make the effort. Julie was right. There was no point in hanging around. I'd come here to have a good time and forget about Tim and that was what I was going to do.

I am Isobel Kavanagh, I told myself as I left the apartment. I am a confident woman. I can do whatever I like.

I went into the bar-café and sat in the corner again. I recognised some of the faces from last week, but not everyone. Then Ignacio pushed open the door and looked around. He smiled when he saw me.

'Isobel! It's nice to see you again.'

'You too,' I replied.

'You haven't called into the bank yet.'

161

I smiled. 'I haven't had enough money to call into the bank yet.'

'You don't need a lot.' He unzipped his soft leather jacket. 'Can I get you a drink?'

'That would be nice,' I said. 'I'd like a beer.'

'One beer.' He ordered a couple from the bar and sat down beside me. 'So, how have you enjoyed your time in Madrid so far?'

'Very well,' I told him. 'I like the company I work for and the people are very nice.'

I didn't know whether it was because I was speaking a different language or whether it was because I was out of practice chatting with men that my conversation sounded so stilted.

'Watched any good football matches lately?'

I grinned. 'Afraid not.'

'You should come to a game sometime. When Madrid play Barca. That's always a good contest.'

'You think so?'

'Oh, absolutely.'

Were the men in Madrid like the men in the tourist resorts? When I was twenty-two I'd gone to Magalluf in Majorca with a crowd of girls. We'd behaved very badly, got drunk every night and practically thrown ourselves at any man who came along. There had been plenty of English or Irish men in the resort but I preferred the Spaniards even though I knew that they were only interested in unencumbered sex. I'd slept with one of them, a skinny dark-haired guy whose name I couldn't remember. I came home feeling ashamed of myself. Sleeping with – Raul, I think – had been the only one-night stand of my life. Even though I'd had lots of boyfriends, I only slept with the ones who meant something to me, the ones I thought might be for ever.

'You are dreaming, Isobel.'

'Oh, sorry.' I looked at Ignacio. 'Did you say something?'

'I asked if you would like to eat with me later? There are some nice restaurants here.'

'Well, thank you, Ignacio but I'm sure you had other plans for this evening. Last week you were here with some friends. Surely you must be meeting them tonight too?'

'They are only my sporting friends,' he said. 'We play football together. I certainly don't want to spend the evening with them.'

'I'm not hungry,' I told him. 'Truly, I'm not. But another beer would be nice.'

'OK,' said Ignacio and called out to the barman.

The bar was packed with people but it had a different feel to it than a bar at home. There wasn't the intense seriousness about drinking that I always felt in a Dublin pub. Maybe it was because of the group of men in the corner playing dominoes as though they were in a tiny rural bar. Maybe it was because the women at the next table were drinking frothy cappuccinos and eating sugared almonds. Maybe it was simply that I didn't really know anyone.

'You are doing it again,' said Ignacio.

'What?'

'Dreaming.'

'No.' I smiled at him. 'I'm just taking in the atmosphere, that's all.'

I bought the next drink and he bought the one after that.

∽

Isobel Kavanagh, independent woman. I lowered my fifth beer. I am free of the past. I have put it behind me. I can do what I want, when I want. I am not attached to Tim Malone any more. It's over. Completely.

∽

It was quiet in his apartment.

'You are the most beautiful girl I've ever known,' he whispered softly.

'Don't be silly.'

'It is true. Your skin is so smooth. Your hair is so soft. Your eyes are like lakes.'

That was laying it on a bit thick, I thought.

He brushed the side of my cheek with his index finger. 'You are *muy frágile. Muy guapa.*'

Fragile and pretty. Not bad.

He drew his finger over my lips and down my throat. I was lightheaded from the drink, wished it had been Southern Comfort instead of beer. I didn't want to think that I might taste of beer.

He did. A mixture of San Miguel and Camel cigarettes. Very, very different to Tim. I couldn't help thinking of Tim, even as I allowed Ignacio to unbutton my red silk blouse. I was outside myself now. I could see him standing beside me and I could see my head on his shoulder. None of this was actually happening to me. It was like a scene from someone else's life.

'Oh, Isobel.' He slid the blouse from my shoulders. 'How beautiful.'

He unhooked my Wonderbra and it joined the blouse on the floor of his bedroom.

I didn't know how I felt. I didn't know why I'd come here, to Ignacio's small apartment on the other side of the city. When we'd left the bar I simply got into the taxi with him, he'd put his arm around me and suddenly I felt so protected that I wanted to stay there for ever. I knew so little about him but it didn't matter. Except for my one-night stand I always talked with my boyfriends before I slept with them. I knew their surnames for a start! And their parents' names and the names of their brothers and sisters, and what they liked doing and their favourite food and a whole heap of other things which I thought essential to a loving and committed relationship.

But maybe this was better. It was physical and exciting and it made me feel good.

He felt different to Tim. He moved more slowly, more deliberately. He asked me if I was happy, if it was pleasurable for me.

'Oh, *sí*,' I murmured, as I held him close to me. '*Sí, sí, sí*.'

~

I woke up at three o'clock with a thumping headache and wheezing chest. I struggled out from beneath the crumpled sheets and scrabbled under the bed for my handbag, my breathing worsening all the while. Eventually I found the inhaler and took a deep puff.

Ignacio grunted and rolled over in the bed, pulling the sheets with him. I sat immobile in case I'd wake him, then exhaled slowly. The air rattled out of my lungs. That's the thing with asthma. You can breathe in easily enough, it's pushing the air out that can be the problem.

But the inhaler had worked. I always wheezed when I had too much to drink, especially if it was beer or red wine. Red wine had the added disadvantage of making me sneeze.

It was cold in Ignacio's bedroom. I slipped quietly out of the bed and got dressed. I tiptoed into the bathroom and pulled a brush through my dishevelled hair. My eyes were faintly bloodshot and my mascara had smudged.

I'd come to Spain and I'd reinvented myself and I'd gone to bed with someone whose surname I didn't know. It was an appalling case of callous recklessness. Julie would have been proud of me.

I felt guilty about slipping out of Ignacio's apartment. But I didn't want to see him in the morning. I didn't want to see him again. He was a nice guy and I'm sure I would have got on well with him. But I didn't want to find out what his surname was, or what his parents' names were or anything about his brothers or sisters.

I wanted to be Isobel Kavanagh, free and single and happy to be that way. I wanted to be Isobel Kavanagh, heart-breaker. Isobel Kavanagh, the girl who had fun.

⁓

I woke up at eleven o'clock and I didn't know where I was. I looked around the room in confusion, expecting to see the Vincent van Gogh *Sunflowers* print that was on my bedroom wall at home. But the bare white wall seemed to rush at me and I closed my eyes because my head spun. Too much drink, I remembered now, and – Ignacio. The memory of Ignacio flooded my mind, blotting out everything else. I couldn't believe I'd gone to bed with him.

My cheeks burned. What had I been thinking about? Where had I left my senses? Somewhere over the Pyrenees? Isobel Kavanagh didn't go around jumping into bed with people. I remembered telling myself that last night, even as Ignacio had cupped my breasts in his hands and told me that I was the most beautiful girl in Madrid. I grew hotter at the memory. It was all very well to reinvent myself at night, I thought, but in the cool light of day the reinvention was a bit much to take. Julie had told me to have fun, but she couldn't have meant hop into bed with someone new a mere week after coming here.

I clambered out of bed, pulled my dressing-gown around me and went into the bathroom. My face looked the same. There was nothing in my eyes to tell the world that I'd slept with someone for the first time since Tim Malone. I smiled very slightly at my reflection. At least I'd done it, I thought. When I thought about sex I could think of someone other than Tim. He wasn't the last person I'd been with.

It gave me a feeling of comfort. Maybe it had been worth it after all.

Chapter 11

Vines and Olive Trees, Montroig (Joan Miró, 1919)

The phone on my desk rang and startled me out of a daydream in which I met Tim Malone while I was in a sports car driven by a handsome Madrileño. 'Oh it's you – um, Tim,' I was saying, looking at him as though trying to place his face. 'Nice to see you again.'

I picked up the phone. '*Hola!*'

'Isobel, it's Luis.'

'Luis.' I peered around the pillar so that I could see his desk even though his face was hidden by a tall potted plant. 'What can I do for you?'

'Do you have the file on the autumn courses? I can't find it anywhere.'

'No.' I knew I didn't have it, even without looking.

'Have you any idea where it might be?'

'Why should I, Luis? I've nothing to do with that right now.'

'I just wondered.' He sighed. 'I have mislaid it, and I cannot think of where to find it.'

'You probably left it in the boardroom after this morning's meeting,' I said, irritably. 'You're forever leaving things there.'

The red light on my phone flickered, a sign I had to take

another call. 'I'll talk to you later,' I said as I switched to the other line. '*Hola!*'

'I'd prefer if you answered the phone by using your name,' said Gabriela and I almost dropped the receiver. 'It's much better than just *hola*.'

'Of course,' I said. 'I'll remember that.'

'Please do.' She was calling from her mobile phone and static crackled along the line. 'Magdalena is out of the office today, I know. There are a number of people I was meant to meet this afternoon but I've been delayed here. Can you phone around and reschedule my appointments, Isobel? My diary is on my desk so it shouldn't be difficult.'

'No problem,' I said, pleased that she'd phoned me rather than anyone else. 'Is there anything else I can do?'

'No,' said Gabriela. 'But be nice to those people. I hate having to cancel engagements and I think it's rude to do it at such short notice. But I'm in negotiations at the moment and I simply cannot break them off.'

I'd no idea where she was or what she was negotiating about. All I knew about Gabriela was that she seemed to thrive on combining a highly successful business with raising two children. She seemed to really care that people were happy working with her and she took time to make everyone feel as though she knew them personally. But I still didn't want to get on the wrong side of her. Apparently she had an unbelievable temper if things went wrong. It didn't last long, Magdalena had told me, but it was truly awful at the time.

I rang around Gabriela's clients, told them that she'd been unavoidably detained and rearranged all the appointments with the minimum of fuss. It was the first time I'd felt efficient in ages.

At four o'clock Luis sat on the edge of my desk.

I looked up and knocked over my tray of pens and pencils.

'Don't sneak up on me like that,' I snapped.

'I didn't.' Luis made a face. 'You were engrossed in staring at your computer screen. What are you working on?'

'Nothing.' I bit my lip.

He leaned around to look at the screen, but it only displayed one of Grail's Screensavers.

'You're looking at that?' he asked curiously.

'No,' I said shortly. 'I was thinking.'

I'd been thinking about Tim. It had come to me suddenly, and in an overwhelming rush. I'd been typing in some figures on course attendances and I'd suddenly been transported back to Tim's house and an evening when I'd been lying on the sofa while he played around with the computer. And I'd walked up behind him and kissed him on the neck.

He'd been working on Grail then, on the very screen I'd been using. Seeing it now, working on it myself, had brought all the feelings and all the pain and all the humiliation back. And I'd almost cried, sitting in front of my personal computer, two thousand miles away, looking at something from my past.

'Are you all right?' asked Luis.

'I'm fine,' I said.

'I found the file,' he told me. 'You were right, it was in the boardroom.'

'Good,' I said.

'Can I ask you a question?' Luis gazed at me with his big, brown eyes.

'Sure.' I double-clicked on the spell-check icon. My Spanish spelling wasn't brilliant.

'Do you prefer women or men?'

I stared at him.

'It's a fair question, no?'

'It's a bloody cheeky question,' I snapped. 'And it's absolutely none of your business.'

'It is my business,' he protested. 'I need to know.'

'You don't need to know,' I said.

'Oh, *mia* Isobel.' He looked pained. 'It was an honest question. After all, you do not join us very often after work. You only talk about female friends out here. I thought, perhaps—' He shrugged.

'Luis,' I said dangerously. 'Piss off.'

∽

He couldn't seriously have believed I was attracted to women. He'd heard me tell Magdalena that I'd broken it off with my boyfriend. He was just getting at me because I wasn't flirty and charming with him like everyone else in the office. Even if Luis had been my type I couldn't have had a relationship with him that would end in tears and me being unable to stay with Advanta. And any relationship with Luis *would* end in tears, I was pretty sure about that.

∽

I went to my evening class that night and afterwards a crowd of us went to the bar in the nearby Lux Hotel and got blitzed. I was flirty and charming with Stefan from Norway and he told me, drunkenly, that I was the sexiest woman he'd ever known.

He was incredibly attractive. Unfortunately, he told me he was going back to Norway in two weeks. 'Otherwise I would try to know you better, Isobel.'

'How much better?' I could hardly speak. We'd been drinking vodka and I never drank vodka.

'I would want to know every centimetre of you,' he said. 'You are so lovely, so beautiful.'

I snuggled up closer to him. 'So, why can't you?'

'Because I will soon be back in Oslo.'

'But you're not there yet.'

He gazed into my eyes. I blinked a couple of times to get him into focus.

'My apartment is a ten-minute journey by taxi,' he said.

'What are we waiting for?' I asked.

~

I stood in front of the delegates to our conference on managing human resources. My hands shook and a trickle of sweat ran down my back even though the room was air-conditioned. This was the first conference I'd arranged by myself. The total responsibility had been mine – booking the room in the hotel, making sure we had the right speakers, arranging the buffet afterwards, checking that all the presentational equipment was ready. And then making sure that we had the right number of attendees and that they'd all signed in and received their information packs.

It was very interesting and exciting but it was scary. I'd never done anything on this scale in Delta.

Gabriela had been offhand when she mentioned it to me. 'I'll leave the organisation up to you, Isobel,' she said. 'Just let me know if there look like being any mishaps.'

But there weren't. Everything had run smoothly and now I was standing in front of an expectant audience ready to give my opening speech and introduce the speakers to them. I was terrified that I'd forget what to say and that my Spanish would desert me so that I'd be left standing like a goldfish opening and closing my mouth.

I moistened my lips, clenched my fists so that no one could see the tremble in my hands and launched into my introduction.

Nobody noticed that I'd left out one of the speakers. I remembered Cristina halfway through my presentation and managed to slot her name in as though I'd always meant to mention her out of turn. Then I was finished, Sofia took her place at the front of the room and I slipped out of the side door to grab a *café solo*. My legs were shaking so much I thought I'd collapse but I was elated. I'd got through it all and I hadn't made a mess of it and Sofia (known for her granite-like demeanour) had actually smiled at me as I made way for her. I exhaled slowly and leaned against the wall.

It was a good day so far.

It stayed like that. The seminar was a great success. Afterwards, as I sipped a glass of wine, I checked through the comment forms and was delighted to see that the delegates had rated the day highly. I floated back to the office.

Most of the staff had gone home but Gabriela was still in her office.

'Isobel!' she called as I walked by. 'How did it go?'

I couldn't keep the grin off my face. 'Great.'

She smiled at me. 'Good. I am pleased.'

'So were they, Gabriela.' I opened my briefcase and took out some forms. 'Look. This guy says that the organisation was excellent and the speakers couldn't have been better!'

'That must be my father,' she said, her face straight. 'I told him to write something nice.'

It took me a second to realise she was joking. 'They're all like that,' I said. 'Only one guy thought that Mario could have answered more questions. But everyone else was really pleased.'

'That's good.' She closed the file in front of her. 'I'm proud of you, Isobel. Sharon told me that I'd get a good worker in you and she was right.'

I blushed. 'Really?'

'Really. And I'm glad you're working with us.'

'So am I,' I said.

She switched off the desk light. 'Would you like to have a quick beer before going home?'

'Oh, I—'

'You don't have to.'

'Thank you, Gabriela. I'd like to.'

'OK, then,' said my boss. 'Let's go.'

Leon's, the tapas bar, was crowded but we managed to get stools near the door. Tapas bars are meant more for standing than sitting, but neither of us had the energy to mill around in the crowd.

'What would you like?' asked Gabriela.

'*Jamón serrano*, please.' *Jamón serrano* is a naturally cured ham and was one of the few tapas dishes that I really liked. Lots of bars are into shellfish, or squid or olives, none of which I'd managed to develop a taste for.

'Is that all?' asked Gabriela. 'You sure?'

I nodded.

'*Jamón serrano*,' she called to the waiter, '*y una ración de gambas y aceitunas por favor. Y dos cervezas.*'

Prawn and olives weren't too bad, I thought. It was when people ordered snails and octopus that I felt ill.

The beers were wonderfully cold.

'Congratulations,' said Gabriela. 'Your first seminar.'

'Thanks.'

'I meant what I said. You are an excellent worker, Isobel.'

'I'm glad you think so.'

She nibbled an olive. 'I was doubtful. I hadn't met you. But Sharon was so sure you would be good.'

God, I thought, she must have been absolutely desperate to get me away from Barry. I must have been making his life hell. What on earth would she have done if Gabriela had said no – or, even worse, if I turned out to be completely useless?

'And you like it here in Madrid?'

'Oh, yes,' I told her. 'It's wonderful.'

'You are not lonely?'

'Why should I be lonely?'

She shrugged in the expressive way that all continentals have. 'You are away from home. From your family and friends. It would be strange if you were not even a little lonely.'

'I suppose I am sometimes.' I wouldn't admit to Gabriela the terror of waking up on my own, gasping for breath and unable to find my inhaler, convinced I was going to die. It didn't happen often, but when it did it was utterly terrifying.

'I would be.' She smiled at me and her brown eyes were warm. 'But I have always been a very home-loving person.'

'I suppose I was too, in a way,' I said.

'But you still decided to leave.'

I looked straight at her. 'What did Sharon tell you about me?'

She ate another olive. 'That you were a capable, nice, hardworking woman. That you had had a misfortune in your life and you wanted to get away for a while. That I would do well to employ you.'

'Really.' I made a face.

'That is all she said. I do not know what your misfortune was. Nor do I care. As an employer.' She smiled at me. 'But as a friend, yes, I care.'

I blinked a couple of times. 'It's silly really.'

'Nothing is silly,' said Gabriela.

I was silent for a moment. I didn't know whether it was a good idea to tell her about me. I was trying to change my history, after all, and what was the point in trying to change if I told everyone my life story? And it wasn't really a very interesting life story. My God, other people really suffered. All I'd been was self-indulgent.

'I was engaged to be married,' I told her finally. 'We called it off. I was very upset.'

'But of course you would be upset!' she exclaimed. 'Who wouldn't be?'

'I was silly,' I said. 'He wanted to be friends. I thought we could make it go back to the way it was.' I sighed. 'But you can't, can you?'

'No. But you can go forward.'

I laughed. 'That's what people said to me. But, Gabriela, I didn't want to go forward. I didn't want things to change.'

'I can understand that.'

'Can you?' I asked in surprise. 'Most people thought I was stupid, I think. My friends kept telling me to go out and have a good time. But I didn't want to.'

'So you came to Madrid to – get away from it all?'

'I suppose so.'

'And have you had a good time here?'

'It's different. I'm enjoying the work. And the language classes.'

'And do you go out?'

I flushed as I remembered Ignacio. I still couldn't believe what had happened with Ignacio. And I thought about Stefan from Norway who'd passed out before we'd got anywhere, which was just as well. I'd caught a taxi home again, half-relieved but half-disappointed. I'd kind of fancied Stefan.

'Sometimes.'

'You have made some friends?'

'I've gone for a drink once or twice with some people from the language classes. There's a hotel opposite the college and sometimes a few of us go into the bar after class.'

'Irish people?'

I shook my head. 'English mostly. Some French and Dutch. And a Norwegian.'

'And have any of them become special friends?'

I laughed. 'I'm not in the market for special friends right now.'

'And how about the people from the office?' she asked casually. 'Have you gone out with them?'

I looked up from my beer. 'Not really. Only to this tapas bar once or twice. But I haven't been here very long, Gabriela.'

'Luis would like to go out with you.'

I smiled faintly. 'Luis likes to go out with everybody. So I've heard.'

She smiled too. 'Yes. He is not a faithful person, that one. But I like him.'

'I like him too,' I admitted. 'But I don't want to go out with someone from the office.'

'You are right,' said Gabriela. 'It makes life complicated and it is complicated enough already.'

I ate some *jamón serrano*.

'I was thirty years old when I met Alfredo,' said Gabriela suddenly. 'I hadn't been going out with anyone for a long time. Then I met him and I knew, instantly.'

'Really?'

She nodded. 'It was strange. We were at a dinner party. He knew the hostess, I knew the host. Alfredo sat opposite me. We both looked up at the same time and that was it. I knew.'

'Straight away?'

She nodded again. 'But, yes, Isobel. Immediately.

177

There was chemistry. I don't know what causes it. But, yes, straight away.'

I sighed. 'In that case I'm quite safe. I haven't met anyone who's made me feel that way here yet.'

'I had been very much in love with my previous boyfriend,' said Gabriela. 'I was surprised that I could fall in love with someone else.'

I made a face at her. 'Are you trying to be some sort of counsellor?'

'Of course not,' she said. 'But it's true, Isobel. I was crazy about Marco. We broke up. Well, actually, he dumped me for a Catalan girl who was working here. I couldn't believe it. I was absolutely broken-hearted.'

Somehow I couldn't imagine the controlled and capable Gabriela Suarez ever being broken-hearted. I said so.

'But, yes,' she said. 'I cried into my pillow every night!'

I laughed. 'You sound so dramatic.'

'To me it was,' she said. 'I thought I would never get over it. But I did.'

'How did you get over it?' I asked.

'I left my job and set up Advanta,' said Gabriela simply. 'It was the best thing I've ever done.'

So that was it, I thought. Simple. Instead of haring off to Madrid I should have stayed at home and started my own hugely successful business. Then I could be as rich as Gabriela, marry someone as successful as me – Gabriela's husband was a vet and hugely busy all the time – and when Tim Malone came looking for a job I could tell him that sorry, he wasn't up to it. Pleasant thought.

'So.' Gabriela drained her glass. 'I must get home. It was nice to have a drink with you, Isobel.'

'Thanks for asking me.'

'You will get over it,' she said. 'Have a good time in Madrid. But remember I want efficiency around the office. So please, I would like you to be in time every morning, and to be fit for work.'

I wondered if she was getting at me because the morning after I'd gone off with Stefan I'd been late for work. And so hungover I could hardly speak.

'Don't worry,' I assured her. 'I like this job and I want to get on here.'

She smiled. 'Glad to hear it. *Buenas noches*, Isobel.'

'*Buenas noches*, Gabriela.'

❧

Tonight's movie was *Alien 2*. I was glad it wasn't some weepy romantic drama. Or a light romantic comedy. There was nothing funny about romance. I poured myself a glass of wine and cheered when Ripley said, '*Get away from her, you bitch!*' She was a good role model, I thought, as I sipped the wine. Vulnerable, but tough in a crisis. An excellent role model, in fact. I finished the bottle of wine and went to bed.

❧

In Advanta, you were only as good as your last seminar. There were more courses to be organised, more lecturers to contact, more brochures to proof, more updating to be done on the computer. By now, I had completely reorganised the way we kept our records and it was much easier to cross-reference things. Magdalena muttered that the best thing ever to happen to the company was for that stupid cow, Camille, to have left. I bathed in the glow of her appreciation and was glad to go to lunch with her sometimes to hear of Camille's eccentricities or to share the latest office gossip.

'Luis has a new girlfriend,' she told me one afternoon.

'Really?'

She nodded. 'Her name is Maria. She works in the Corté Ingles.'

'In a shop!' I laughed. 'How could Luis meet anyone in a shop? I don't think he's ever voluntarily bought anything.'

Magdalena laughed too. 'No, it's odd. But even Luis goes into shops occasionally. And he met her and asked her out.'

'Is there anyone Luis doesn't ask out?'

'Probably not,' said Magdalena. 'But he doesn't mean any harm.'

'How long will his affair with Maria last?'

She shrugged. 'Who knows? With Luis it can be all charm and romance for a few weeks and then bang, it's over.'

'How long did you go out with him for?'

'Long enough for him to realise he wouldn't get me into bed,' she chuckled. 'It was fun, really.'

'But don't you find it wrong?'

'Wrong?'

'That he behaves like that.'

'Some men are made that way.' She accepted it quite easily. 'Luis is one of them. But you can't be angry with him because he always looks so helpless.'

She was right about that. The uncoordinated clothes, the ruffled hair, the air of having better things to do than worry about his appearance—

'And he is sweet,' she said. 'When my mother was ill he sent her flowers every day.'

'Was he still trying to sleep with you?' I asked, a little sourly.

'Not by then. He was just being nice.'

'Luis Cardoso isn't my type,' I said. 'So I won't be hopping into bed with him. I've better things to do.

Anyway, from what you say, Luis likes to sleep with his conquests more than once. That's not my style.'

'Isobel!' She stared at me. 'Have you slept with lots of men?'

'Not lots,' I said. 'But I hope to change all that.'

'Isobel!'

'Why not?' I demanded. 'Why should Luis sleep with as many people as he likes and I can't?'

'I don't know.' She looked confused. 'But it is different for a woman, don't you think?'

'I don't know,' I said briskly.

'Do you think about your Irish boyfriend a lot?'

'What?'

'The boyfriend you said that you had left. The one that caused you to come to Madrid.'

'He didn't cause me to come to Madrid,' I said tautly. 'I wanted to come anyway. And I think about him sometimes, but I'm having far too much fun here to think about him often. He's probably got another girlfriend by now anyway.'

'Are you sure you do not miss him?' asked Magdalena.

'Why should I miss him?' I made a face at her. 'I'm much too busy here to miss anyone.'

'You're so calm, Isobel,' said Magdalena. 'I wish I could be like you.'

I nearly choked on my coffee when she said that.

$\backsim$

I walked down to the bar-café that evening. I didn't know whether I wanted Ignacio to be there or not. I ordered a glass of wine and sat in the corner watching Sky Sports. They were showing Manchester United and Spurs. Ian was a United fan. Went to a lot of their matches. Had posters of the team on his bedroom wall. Well, not now.

They'd been taken down on the last redecoration and eighteen-year-olds don't stick posters of football teams on their bedroom walls. But he probably would have liked to. I missed Ian.

I ordered another glass of wine. The bar was half-full but there was no sign of Ignacio.

It had been stupid to come and expect him to be here. Especially since I'd sneaked out of his apartment without saying goodbye. But I needed to be with someone tonight. Someone who would call me wonderful and beautiful and would touch me in all the places I wanted to be touched.

I went home and drank a bottle of wine. It was easier to be on my own when I'd had something to drink.

Chapter 12

The Invisible Man (Salvadore Dalí, 1929/33)

S ometimes I felt as though I was two different people. There was the Isobel who was really happy about being in Madrid. Who enjoyed her work, drank *café solos* with Magdalena after work and walked along the winding streets at the centre of the city absorbing its history. And there was the other Isobel, who hated being away from home, who was afraid to be on her own in the apartment, who drank too much and who despised herself.

It was on one of the bad days that Julie rang.

'Hi,' I said unenthusiastically. 'How's it going?'

'Goodness, Isobel, you sound dreadful. What's wrong?'

'Nothing,' I said as my eyes welled up with tears. 'Why should anything be wrong?'

'For God's sake, I know you. I know that miserable tone of voice.'

I sniffed. 'I'm fed up.'

'Of what?'

'Everything.'

'Why?'

'Oh, Julie, I don't know why I came here!' I rubbed my eyes. 'People are OK, I suppose, but I'm not truly friendly with any of them. I need someone to talk to.'

'You need to get out and about,' she said briskly. 'You're in a great city and you're sitting in watching TV.'

'How do you know what I'm doing?'

'Well, I kind of assumed that's what you were at,' she said. 'If you were living the hectic social life you should be living, you wouldn't have been there when I called.'

I sighed. 'My social life is useless.'

'Come on, Isobel. What about the bloke you told me about? The bloke you met the first night you were there and—'

'Julie.' I interrupted her. 'I haven't seen him since. I don't want to get involved.'

'Who says you have to be involved?'

'Oh, Julie, you know how it would be. He'd take me to dinner or the movies and he'd phone me in work and suddenly we'd be a couple. And I don't want to be a couple.'

'Nobody's asking you to have a long-term commitment to the guy. Surely you'd be better off out with him than sitting in moping.'

'I'm not moping.'

'Don't lie.'

'Oh, OK,' I sighed. 'I *was* moping. I'm just going through a bad patch, I suppose.'

'Isobel, your bad patch could cover half a lifetime! Now stop sitting around and get out there.'

'Why are you so keen to have me out there?' I demanded. 'When you're so obviously in yourself?'

'Yes, well,' she muttered, 'I'm waiting for Andy to call.'

'How is Andy?' I asked.

'How should I know?' She snorted. 'He said he'd ring on Monday but I haven't heard a word. And I'm damned if I'm going to call him!'

'Don't be silly,' I told her. 'Call him. Maybe he's busy.'

'Maybe he is,' she said. 'But I'll tell you something, Isobel, this long-distance relationship isn't much fun.'

'I guess not.'

She laughed suddenly. 'We're a hopeless pair. You sitting around in front of the TV pining for a lost boyfriend, and me pining for one that's thousands of miles away.'

'I'll invite you to my next wedding if you invite me to yours,' I said gloomily. 'The way things are going, it's a safe invitation.'

'Never mind,' said Julie. 'We're women. We're strong. We'll survive.'

Oh yeah, I thought, as I pulled the sheet around me that night. But just surviving isn't enough.

~

I did make other friends in Madrid. Two of them, Barbara and Bridget, who taught at the college where I studied Spanish – invited me to a party at their apartment.

The apartment was crammed full of people by the time I arrived. They sat on the floor, draped themselves over the sofas and squeezed onto the balcony. I didn't know many of the people there and I sat around for ages feeling totally out of things before I poured myself a treble measure of Southern Comfort and decided to get blitzed.

It wasn't a bad party, I thought, as I drained my glass. There was a buzz about it and all I had to do was get involved. I refilled my glass and squeezed myself past a group of girls dancing flamenco.

'Sorry,' I said as I bumped into a fair-haired guy who was leaning against the wall.

'It's OK.'

'You're Irish?' I opened my eyes a little wider.

'Sure am.'

'From Dublin?'

'Drumcondra,' he said.

'I'm from Sutton myself.'

'Another Northsider.'

'What are you doing here?'

'God knows.' He made a face. 'I came with a gang of people. But they've disappeared. And you?'

'I know the girls who live here.'

'Lucky you.'

He was good-looking, although not by my usual criteria. He had the lean look, all right, but the blond hair was against my rules, as was the silky-smooth skin and the pale blue eyes.

'Finished?' he asked.

'What?'

'Looking at me.'

I blushed. 'Sorry.'

'If I looked at you like that you'd call it leering.'

'I wasn't leering.'

'What do you call it then?'

'Gazing.'

'Let's gaze somewhere else,' he said as he slipped his arm around my waist and pulled me close to him.

He wanted to go to my apartment but I didn't want anyone in my home.

'I share with four other guys,' he told me. 'There won't be any privacy.'

'I'm sure you'll think of something.'

He thought of something. He had the keys to the building where he worked. It wasn't a big modern office block like Advanta's – just a small, converted building.

He wasn't as good as Ignacio but it was the first time I'd made love on an executive swivel-chair.

Afterwards I insisted on getting a taxi home alone.

186

∽

Barbara had seen me disappear with him. 'Where did you go?' she demanded the following week when I met her and Bridget for coffee in the college's small café.

'Nowhere.'

'Isobel!'

'I can't remember.' I didn't want to talk about it. It had been a mistake.

'Can't remember?'

'I brought the Southern Comfort with me. We walked for a while. We drank.' I shrugged. 'I can't remember what else.'

'Isobel!' She grinned at me. 'When I met you first I thought you were such a strait-laced person. You didn't want to come to the party. I told you to lighten up. But I was completely wrong.'

'Not completely.'

'Come on. You disappear with probably the only decent-looking single male of the night and you can't remember where you went or what you did.'

'Actually,' I said, 'I just don't want to remember.'

'Remember what?' asked Bridget as she sat down at the table. 'Hi, Isobel. Guess you and John had a good time on Friday night.'

'John?'

'Christ, Isobel, don't tell me you can't even remember his name.' Barbara looked stunned.

'It's not that I don't remember.' I stirred my coffee. 'I never asked.'

'You are incredible.' Bridget looked at me with a mixture of awe and disbelief. 'How could you possibly spend the night with someone and not even bother to ask him his name.'

'I didn't spend the night with him,' I said.

'So you don't know whether you're seeing him again or not?'

I shuddered. 'I doubt very much I'll be seeing him again.'

'Why not?'

'I don't want to.'

'But—'

'Look, Barbara,' I said harshly. 'Any chance we could drop this subject? I'm bored with it.'

'Sure. No problem.' She exchanged glances with Bridget. 'Do you want to nip across to the hotel? See Tomás.' Tomás Medina was Bridget's boyfriend.

Bridget nodded. 'Just for an hour.'

'Coming, Isobel?'

I was very tired. We'd been extremely busy in work. I should go home and get an early night.

'OK,' I said.

The bar in the Hotel Lux was tiny. Tomás stood behind the horseshoe-shaped counter and polished glasses until they sparkled.

Bridget sat on one of the high stools at the bar and cooed at him while Barbara and I brought our drinks into the foyer. The Lux was a mid-priced hotel, probably used by businessmen who had a strict limit on their expenses and tourists who were on package weekends. There was a night-show too – Spanish Culture – which mainly featured flamenco dancers who weren't half as good as the girls who'd danced at Barbara's party.

Life was pretty much the same everywhere, I thought. Sitting in the Lux was no different to sitting in Jurys or the Burlington or the Conrad. The same crowd of people milling about. Standing impatiently in front of the lift. Looking around for a porter. Celebrating a birthday or an anniversary or a wedding. And then the business conventions in places called the Seville Suite or the Granada Rooms.

I drained my glass of Southern Comfort. 'Want another?' I asked Barbara. Her own glass was still half-full but she nodded.

I am drinking too much, I thought, as I brought back the refills. I'd never really been the kind of person who got drunk on a regular basis. But it was nice to feel the alcohol warm me and to experience the sudden detachment from the world.

Barbara was talking about her job. I couldn't believe that anyone would enjoy teaching English but she did. From the snippets of conversation I overheard in college, she was rated very highly by the students.

'I must come into your class sometime,' I said. 'Rate your skills like I do for Advanta's lecturers.'

'Oh, God, don't do that,' she said. 'I'd freeze up if I thought anyone was grading me.'

'How long will you stay here?' I asked.

'Dunno.' She shrugged. 'As long as I like it.'

'Do you?'

'Right now – yes. Maybe I'll be fed up in a few months, but it'll be summer soon and I like being here even though you could fry your feet on the pavement and you're practically a prisoner indoors.'

'I'm looking forward to that.'

'It's an inferno,' she told me. 'Really.'

'What do you do in the summer?' I asked.

'The college stays open for various classes. I have enough to do.'

'You like it, don't you?'

She nodded. 'Most of the time.'

'Lucky you.' I got up. 'Want another drink?'

'No thanks, I've only just started this one.'

'I'm getting one for myself.'

'Fire ahead. But not for me. Honestly.'

Bridget and Tomás were the only ones in the bar. They were cheek to cheek across the narrow counter. I coughed.

'Another?' asked Tomás and I nodded. He gave me a double. Not a good idea, I thought, as I walked somewhat unsteadily back to the foyer. I'd have a hangover and I didn't want a hangover. My work definitely suffered when there was an army of demolition men working in my head.

'Oh, sorry.' I bumped into someone who had emerged from the Spanish Culture show.

'Isobel!' Gabriela looked surprised to see me. 'What are you doing here?'

'I'm with a friend,' I said, trying my best to keep my eyes focused on her.

'A male friend?'

I shook my head. 'Female. From the language classes.'

'Have you been here long?'

'Not very,' I told her.

She looked at me. 'You seem to have had rather a lot to drink.'

'That's OK, isn't it?' I asked. 'As long as my work is OK it doesn't matter what I do on my own time. Does it?'

'Of course not,' she said. 'As long as your work is OK.'

'And you've told me it is.' I knew I should just shut up but I couldn't. 'You've told me lots of times.'

'I know,' said Gabriela.

'So that's all right then.'

'Absolutely.'

'And what I do after work is up to me.'

'Sure.'

'Good.'

'I will see you in the morning,' said Gabriela.

'Bright and breezy,' I told her. 'No problem.'

Bloody hell, though, I wasn't very happy about bumping into her. I had a good image at work – Isobel the cool, the efficient, the competent. I didn't want it mixed up with Isobel the drunk. I shrugged my shoulders. So what if I was drunk? It wasn't as though I got drunk that often. As long as I didn't start coming in late or taking surreptitious nips from a bottle of vodka in a brown-paper bag at the desk, it shouldn't make any difference to Gabriela.

I still wished I hadn't met her.

⌒

She said nothing about it the next day. I'd drunk almost a litre of water when I got home that night and had woken before the alarm in the morning. My eyes were a little bloodshot but otherwise I was fine. I put on a little extra make-up and wore my favourite Conran suit – royal-blue silk which clung to my body and gave me a very sophisticated look.

She buzzed me at eight-thirty. 'I want to go through the schedules for next month,' she said.

'I'm printing them now,' I told her. 'Can you give me five minutes?'

'Certainly, Isobel.'

I finished the printing job and brought the sheaf of papers into her office with me. She was leaning back in her brown leather chair, gazing at the ceiling.

'Here you are,' I said. 'The schedules.'

She sat up straight and leafed through them. 'Thank you.'

'There are only a couple of things I'd like to draw to your attention.' I pointed out the non-confirmed booking in a hotel and the double booking of one of the lecturers.

'But I have someone to take Mario's place for that,' I told her. 'And José is looking after an alternative venue for the hotel.'

'Fine,' said Gabriela. 'You seem to have it all under control.'

'I told you I had.' I smiled brightly at her.

She tapped her long nails on the surface of the desk. 'And you are feeling all right today?'

I feigned surprise. 'All right? Of course I'm all right.'

'You look fine,' she said, 'but I was worried.'

'Worried?'

'About you, Isobel. I was worried about you.'

'Heavens, Gabriela, why?'

'Do not play games with me,' she said harshly. 'You know perfectly well why.'

I said nothing for a moment. 'If you're worried that I had a few drinks last night, then don't be. I don't drink that often. I simply felt like it last night. I'm sure you've drunk too much from time to time, Gabriela.'

'Yes,' she said. 'But I've always had someone to look after me if I have.'

'I can look after myself,' I told her. 'I've managed pretty well so far.'

She sighed. 'I feel responsible for you, Isobel. I told Sharon I'd keep an eye on you.'

'Oh, for God's sake!' I glared at her. 'What do you think I am? A child? I don't need you or anyone else to keep an eye on me! I'm a responsible adult. And I thought you were my employer, Gabriela, not my nanny!'

For a moment I thought she was going to shout at me – fire me perhaps. Then suddenly she smiled. 'You are right, of course. And I am sorry. What you do is absolutely none of my business.'

'I'm glad you see it like that.'

'Once your work is OK.'

'Absolutely,' I said.

We stared at each other for almost a minute and then she told me that I could leave.

⁓

I walked home from work that evening. The air was warm and balmy and there was a feeling that summer was around the corner. The tourists wandered about the streets in shorts and backpacks and sat in the squares drinking beer. I liked the fact that I wasn't a tourist. I liked belonging to the city.

I bought a bottle of wine in the supermarket to have with my pasta. My diet had become incredibly healthy if you ignored the alcohol. I was existing on salads, pasta and fruit. I hadn't eaten meat in ages and I only had chips on the rare occasion I was grabbed by hunger in Sol and dropped into McDonald's. I'd lost weight but I didn't look unhealthy. I thought of joining a gym so that I could tone up my muscles as well, but that seemed too much like hard work.

Señora Carrasco, my next-door neighbour, was standing beside the lift.

'*Hola, Isobel.*' She smiled broadly at me.

I liked Señora Carrasco. She was in her mid-forties and a heavier version of Sophia Loren.

'*Hola, Teresa. Cómo estás?*'

'*Muy bien. Y tú?*' We had progressed from the formal to the friendly.

'*Muy bien tambien.*'

She beamed at me. 'Did you know there will be an exhibition of Miró paintings at the Prado next month? You must go, *Isobel*, it will be a wonderful opportunity for you.'

'Perhaps I will.'

'Oh, you must,' she said again as the lift arrived and we stepped inside. 'He is the most wonderful painter.'

I wasn't sure myself. I'd always thought Barcelona's greatest painter produced things that looked like mine when I'd been at school. But they were hard to ignore.

'I will certainly go,' I promised.

'Good.' She looked pleased.

The lift shuddered to a halt on the fifth floor. Teresa Carrasco waved at me as she let herself into her apartment.

She was right, of course. I should make the effort to see the sights of the city. It was practically criminal to live within fifteen minutes of one of the world's most famous art galleries and never to have been inside. Better for me to engage in some cultural pursuits, perhaps, than spend my nights partying with Barbara Lane and Bridget Evans. Or in avoiding the bar where I'd met Ignacio. Or in wondering would I ever see the mysterious John again.

I ate my dinner on the balcony, overlooking the city. I liked the noise of city living now. I liked the sounds of the cars and the rumble of the metro and the sudden laughter of people spilling out on the street from one of the other buildings around me.

I poured myself another glass of wine. There was something very civilised, I told myself, in living like this. A sophisticated city girl sipping wine on the balcony of her apartment. It was a pity that the block had been built in the seventies. It had all the charm of Liberty Hall. If I stayed here long enough I might move apartment. Into one of the lovely old whitewashed buildings with green shutters and wrought-iron balconies. With roses tumbling from terracotta pots and lobelia bursting from hanging baskets. I couldn't afford to rent an apartment like that yet. But one day. Maybe. If I stayed.

I finished the bottle of wine and went to bed.

Chapter 13

Three Dancers (Pablo Picasso, 1925)

E aster was late that year, almost at the end of April. The weather in Madrid was now spectacular – unbroken blue skies and temperatures climbing steadily into the high twenties. The traffic snarled its way around the main streets and a haze of exhaust fumes hung in the air. Drivers honked impatiently at anyone who had the temerity to wander into the wrong lane, or wait for more than a millisecond when the lights changed to green. More than once a volley of Spanish oaths flew through open car windows into the air.

But when the Madrileños left the city for Easter and went out into the country for the break, the traffic abated and the air quality improved.

I hadn't made any special plans for the holiday. Barbara and Bridget were going home for a few days and most of the people from Advanta had made plans. But Easter had sneaked up on me and, quite suddenly, I realised that I would be alone for a very long weekend.

I felt myself wheeze at the thought. I was afraid. Afraid of having no one to talk to, no one who cared about me. I wondered if Gabriela would allow me into the office to do some administration. It would be a good time to get some back-up work done, without the constant interruptions of telephone calls.

'Don't be ridiculous,' she said, when I suggested it. 'You need some time off, Isobel. You've been working too hard. You've got circles under your eyes.'

The circles under my eyes were because I hadn't got home until four in the morning. I'd gone to a nightclub with Barbara, whose first class wasn't until ten-thirty. She was happily sleeping it off while I nursed my hangover through the morning. Monday nights were not good nights for clubbing – it took me all week, even a shortened week, to recover.

I didn't want to press Gabriela on the idea of working over the holiday and didn't say anything more about it. But I felt panicky on Thursday when everyone said goodbye and rushed home early to involve themselves in the festivities.

⁓

Easter is taken much more seriously in Madrid than in Dublin. There are parades every evening as statues of different saints are carried around the narrow streets of the old city while penitents follow behind. With nothing better to do I joined the crowd in the main square – the Plaza Mayor – where a truly spectacular parade was headed by soldiers in dress uniform on horseback. They were followed by members of different religious groups dressed in flowing tunics of vibrant purples, reds and greens. As well as the coloured tunics, they wore high pointed masks and most of them walked barefoot. Someone in the good-natured crowd told me that, in older days, penitents used to beat themselves with ropes as they walked. Some of them still wore ropes around their waists – but I didn't see anyone using them for other than decoration, which was a relief. Some carried candles and some banged slowly and deliberately on huge drums.

We followed them around the streets and I was suddenly moved by the atmosphere of religion and penitence myself. I thought, miserably, that I'd been wasting my life in Madrid. That I'd been given a wonderful opportunity to start afresh and that all I'd done was turn into a drunken wretch who slept around.

I shivered in the evening warmth. I'd come to Madrid to get more in control of my life. But it seemed to me now that it had slipped out of my control even more than before.

On Sunday I took the metro to the Retiro Park where the atmosphere was light and fun-loving and I couldn't be depressed.

I loved the park. It was a huge expanse of green within the city and it was always full of people. I strolled along the path to the lake and enjoyed the distant sound of classical guitar while, in front of me, three young girls glided along on rollerblades, making skilful turns and jumps so that they almost floated in the air as their shocking pink skirts whirled around them. The guitar music wafted gently through the park, along with the laughter of the children who were watching a magic show and the occasional cries from families who were boating on the lake.

I sat on the steps overlooking the lake and watched the creaky rowboats float across the water. Behind me, a group of African men played traditional drums, the ethnic beat quirky but somehow pleasing.

I thought about Tim. I couldn't help it. The image of his face just appeared in my head and it was there before I could stop it. I wondered what he was doing while I sat here in the Retiro Park. Was he at home with the capable Laura Hart? Working with her? Or sleeping with her? I shook my head to dislodge the image of them writhing about on his bed. But, when I thought of Tim, it was nearly always of him with Laura, or with some other, indistinct woman. And I still felt jealous and hurt.

I wondered whether or not I'd ever be able to go out with anyone again. I thought, very briefly, that maybe I needed to see a psychiatrist. I couldn't unscramble my mind, put things in perspective. Sometimes, when I'd drunk a few glasses of wine and some Southern Comfort, I felt content and thought everything was OK but the feeling usually disappeared by the morning.

∽

The phone was ringing when I got back to the apartment.

I flung my sweatshirt onto the sofa and picked up the receiver.

'Hello?'

'Hello, Isobel. Happy Easter.'

'Alison! How are you?'

'Great,' said my sister. 'I've probably put on about a stone today because I've been eating Easter eggs, but otherwise fine.'

I hadn't bought myself an Easter egg. That would have been pathetic.

'How's everyone at home?' I asked.

'Fine,' she said. 'Guess what! I've got good news.'

'Oh?'

'I've got a job.'

'Really? What sort of job?' I did my best to sound enthusiastic.

'In Dun Laoghaire,' she said proudly. 'I'll be working with the council. Environmental work.'

'Oh, Alison, that's great.' I was really pleased for her. She hated the shoe shop.

'Isn't it.'

'When do you start?'

'In two weeks.' She sighed. 'I can't believe I'm finally getting to do what I wanted to do.'

'Everything comes to she who waits,' I said sanctimoniously.

'Oh, shut up.'

But I knew that she was smiling.

'I was wondering,' she said slowly.

'Yes?'

'If I could come over and stay with you for a few days? Before I start work?'

'Of course you can,' I said. 'But I won't be able to take any time off myself. You might get fed up on your own.'

'You're on your own all the time, aren't you?' she said. 'Why shouldn't I be able to wander around by myself? Anyway I was only thinking of a short visit – maybe Thursday to Monday, something like that?'

'Fine by me.' I liked the idea of Alison coming to stay with me. I wanted to show someone around my home, walk confidently with them through now familiar streets, take them to see tourist sights while knowing that I wasn't a tourist.

'OK.' I paused. 'How's things?'

'The usual,' she said. 'Boring. But Ian has a girlfriend! A blonde. Absolutely stunning. Dad's mouth drops open every time she walks in the door.'

'A girlfriend!' Ian wasn't a girlfriend type of person. Occasionally, he admitted to going out with a girl but he'd never brought one home before.

'I'm sure he does it just to annoy them,' giggled Alison. 'Mum looks at her as though she's a creature from outer space. And Dad's just jealous.'

I laughed. 'So what does this beauty see in our brother?'

'Actually she's had quite an improving effect on him,' said Alison. 'He's had his hair cut and he's stopped spending all his time taking motorbikes apart. Whenever he meets her he spends ages making sure that there isn't any oil-sludge under his fingernails and dousing himself in aftershave and stuff.'

'Good God.'

'Her name's Honey,' said Alison. 'She's a beautician.'

That was too much to believe and I said so.

'Seriously,' Alison told me. 'Well, OK, she named the salon "Honey's" and kept the name for herself. Her real name is Helga.'

'Is she German?' I asked.

'No,' replied Alison. 'I think it's a family name or something. But she said that it sounds like some kind of concentration camp supervisor which isn't exactly ideal for someone who gives electro-therapy for dodgy skin, so she changed it.'

'And Ian and Honey are an item.' I grinned to myself.

'I'll get a photo and bring it with me,' my sister said. 'You'll love her!'

～

I went on a culture-fest the next day. So far, my trips around Madrid had centred mainly on the shopping areas or the Plaza Mayor. I'd made one visit to the royal palace, but neither Barbara nor Bridget was all that interested in sightseeing and I hadn't wanted to do things on my own. But today I took off to the Prado and to the Reine Sofia, Madrid's most famous art galleries. I got lost in the Prado which is a common enough event but I saw the Miró exhibition that Señora Carrasco had urged me to visit.

I wasn't much of an art critic, but Madrid is full of reproductions of Picasso, Dalí, Goya and Miró, so I felt as though I knew the paintings already. The Mirós were bright and colourful but I thought that Picasso's Blue Period captured how I felt.

I was hot and tired after my gallery trek, so I bought a bottle of Volvic and went to the Retiro again. I sat beneath the shade of a chestnut tree and began to read the book on Picasso that I'd bought. But it was highbrow and worthy and, quite soon, I slid the book behind my head, lay down and fell asleep.

The guitarist was playing 'Hey Jude'. It slid into my dreams . . .

I was standing in the living room of Tim's Donnybrook house, while he poured glasses of red wine and handed them to me, one after the other.

'Don't look so sad,' he said, as I drank the wine in huge gulps. 'You can start to make it better.'

I took another glass from him. 'Can I?'

'Yes. Just drink the wine. You'll be OK.'

'I don't think so, Tim. I don't think I'm OK.'

'Come to bed,' said Tim. 'Come to bed now.'

I woke up with a start and looked around in confusion. People were still strolling around the park; nobody was looking at me. But I flushed with embarrassment at the thought that I had been dreaming about going to bed with Tim, while crowds of people were clustered around a guitarist only yards away from me. I felt they could see my dreams written across my face.

I got up in a hurry, and walked quickly out of the park.

∽

Honey was seriously beautiful. I leafed through the photos that Alison had brought and wondered how on earth someone as lovely as Honey had fallen for Ian.

'Told you,' said Alison. 'Wouldn't it make you spit?'

'I can't believe she's going out with Ian.' I shook my head. 'Is she blind or something?'

'Isobel! That's not fair.' Alison shoved another photo in front of me. 'He looks good in this, doesn't he?'

She was right. He looked great. I blinked a couple of times. When do you suddenly realise that your kid brother – whom you'd only ever known as a fearless space invader or a secret agent, who came home covered in mud from soccer played in teeming rain, who knew more about motor engines than human beings – when do you suddenly realise that he's the sort of bloke that another girl could actually find attractive?

'When he's dressed up like that,' said Alison, answering my unspoken question.

'God,' I said. 'He looks very – mature. So do you,' I added.

'You bitch!' She threw one of the brightly patterned cushions at me. 'You don't tell girls that they look mature!'

'Sorry.' I was suitably contrite. 'And if you look mature, I must look positively ancient.'

'You don't,' said Alison. 'But you're awfully thin.'

'It's just the fruit and vegetables,' I said carelessly. 'I can't seem to put on weight.'

'You're positively bony,' Alison told me bluntly. 'You need to eat more chips or something.'

'Great,' I said. '*Carte blanche* to pig out at last.'

'I mean it,' she said.

'Oh, give it a rest, Alison.' I laughed to show I didn't take her seriously. 'Stop talking about me.'

'Do you like it here?' Alison got up from the sofa where we'd been sitting and strolled out onto the balcony. I joined her. It was dark but the yellow glow of street lights hung over the city and the apartment block opposite was a checkerboard of lights.

'Yes.' I leaned over the iron rail. 'It's big and it's bustling and there are lots of people around all the time.'

'D'you find it lonely?'

'Sometimes,' I admitted. 'When I came here first especially. I felt like a stranger all the time. But I've got used to it now.'

'Made any friends yet?' she asked.

'A few,' I said. 'There's a couple of girls from Liverpool I'm friendly with. They work in the college I go to. And I've gone out with a few of the people from the office occasionally. So I'm getting into the swing of things.'

'Any boyfriends?' she asked casually.

'I thought you didn't agree with the idea of boyfriends.'

'Of getting married,' she corrected me. 'I've nothing against boyfriends.'

'Neither have I,' I said.

'So?'

I shrugged. 'Sometimes.'

'Sometimes?'

I got up and uncorked a bottle of Rioja. 'Occasionally.'

'Isobel, I don't want any more wine,' Alison protested. 'We shared two bottles over dinner. I'll have a thumping headache if I drink more.'

'Oh, come on.' I poured the wine into a glass.

'Honestly, no.'

'You're supposed to be on holiday,' I told her.

'And you have to go to work in the morning.' She grinned at me. 'I'm trying to do you a favour.'

'I'll be all right,' I told her.

She twisted a strand of hair around her finger. 'You never used to drink so much.'

'What d'you mean?'

'Wine. You drink a lot of wine, don't you?'

'It's a continental thing,' I told her blithely. 'Everyone drinks a lot of wine here.'

'But it's not like you,' she said.

'You'd be surprised.'

'Is everything OK?' she asked. 'I mean, you're all right, aren't you?'

'Of course I'm all right,' I said impatiently. 'God, Alison, you're not Mum, you know.'

She flushed. 'I know. I'm sorry. It's just that – you seem – different, that's all.'

'Of course I'm different,' I said. 'I've changed my whole life.'

'I know.' But she still looked troubled. 'I know.'

'What about Shitface?' she asked the following night. 'Do you ever think about him?'

I wanted to lie and say that he never even entered my mind. But she would have known I wasn't telling the truth.

'Not much,' I said, after a pause. 'I try not to.'

'I haven't seen him since,' she told me.

'I'd be surprised if you had.'

'I've been around Donnybrook a lot. I thought I might bump into him. Literally,' she added darkly.

'There's no need,' I said. 'I'm getting over it.'

'I'd still like to kill him.' She put her arm around my shoulder.

'Don't be daft.' But I was glad she'd said it all the same.

I brought her sightseeing. I got us lost in the Prado

despite my earlier visit. I told Alison that she was the one in the family who'd gone orienteering, but when we'd passed the portrait of the seventeenth-century royal family for the third time, we headed for the exit.

'Too many tourists,' said Alison in disgust. 'You can't get to see the paintings properly at all.'

So we went shopping instead. I dragged her around the Corté Ingles, and then we did the more upmarket Calles de Serrano and Velazquez, where Alison bought a pair of soft navy leather shoes and a navy and white suit.

'Work clothes,' she said happily as she paid for her purchases and we went outside again. 'God, it's hot.'

'I'm getting used to it,' I told her. 'Although the temperatures in midsummer can go screamingly high. Still, I'll manage to hack it, I guess.'

'Poor dear.' Alison smiled at me.

⌣

On Sunday evening we sat in the Plaza Mayor and drank cold beers under the shade of a huge parasol.

'This is heaven,' said Alison as she leaned back in her chair. 'I could stay here for ever.'

So could I, I thought, as I, too, leaned back and listened to the sound of the guitars being played at the opposite end of the square. Children ran backwards and forwards, playing chasing over the cobblestones while their parents stood around and talked volubly, only occasionally crying 'Antonio!' or 'Cristobal!' as a child tried to run out of their watchful gaze.

The sunlight fell in slanted shafts across the square. Pigeons hopped around beneath the tables. It would be a nice place, I thought suddenly, to sit with someone you loved.

The guitarists were playing Beatles music – the ballads,

slowly and easily, and they made the music sound much more than simple tunes. There were three of them. They wore T-shirts emblazoned with paintings by Miró. They also wore the obligatory faded jeans and trainers. A throwback to flower power, I thought, except for the Reeboks.

'So why haven't you found yourself a boyfriend yet?' asked Alison suddenly.

'What?'

'Come on, Isobel. I know you. You've always got some bloke in tow.'

'Not at the moment,' I said.

'You can't pine after him for ever,' she told me.

'I'm not pining.'

'Yes, you are.'

'Don't be so bloody silly, Alison.'

'I'm stating a fact,' she said. 'Nothing more.'

'I'm not pining. I don't have a boyfriend. I do have some friends. I'm not socially destitute.'

'But it's not like you,' she said. 'And what about your weight?'

'Oh, don't you go on!' I glared at her.

'What?' She looked defensive. 'What did I say?'

'Telling me to put on weight. Barbara keeps telling me too.'

'You see!' Alison was triumphant. 'Pining.'

'Eating less,' I said. 'That's all.'

'And drinking more,' she added.

'For God's sake, Alison!' I looked angrily at her. 'Stop bloody criticising me. OK, I know I'm drinking more. But I'm not being carried home every night! I'm doing well in work. I just need something for myself, that's all.'

'But—'

'But nothing.'

'It's a few bottles of wine a day, Isobel.' She looked miserable.

'Only because you're here,' I snapped. 'I'm trying to be a good hostess.'

'No you're not.'

'Look, Alison.' My voice was dangerously low. 'Mind your own business. You're very welcome to stay with me anytime you like, but don't interfere.'

'I—' She sighed. 'OK, Isobel. I won't interfere.'

~

We didn't talk about me again. She had a good time in Madrid and said that she was sorry to be going home. I left her at the check-in desk of Barajas International Airport.

'Have a good flight,' I told her.

'I will.'

'And good luck with the new job.'

'Thanks.'

'And take care of yourself.'

'You too,' she said.

I hugged her. 'I'm glad you came.'

'Thanks for having me.'

'Come again.'

'I will.'

The apartment was quiet without her.

Chapter 14

Bathers of the Costa Brava (Salvador Dalí, 1923)

It got hotter and hotter. I knew now what the Madrileños meant when they called the city an inferno. The sun seemed to penetrate the stones of the buildings, the concrete of the roads and the paving slabs so that everything radiated an intense, dry heat. Although we worked an eight-to-five business day in the office, I got into the habit of snatching a siesta as soon as I got home and going out later at night when the heat wasn't as fierce.

Occasionally I went out with the people from the office, but more often it was with Barbara and Bridget. Those girls knew how to have a good time and, when I was with them, I had a good time too.

I met Ignacio again. I'd been in the bar once or twice but hadn't seen him there. I had reckoned he was just as pleased not to see me – why would he want to have a relationship with an Irish girl?

He was at the counter, sipping a San Miguel.

'*Hola*,' I said.

'Isobel!' He put the glass on the counter and stared at me. 'I didn't think I'd ever see you again. I thought, perhaps, you had gone home.'

I shook my head. 'No. But I've been very busy.'

'All the same.' His eyes were black. 'I thought I might have heard something from you. Why did you walk out on me?'

'I'm sorry,' I said. 'I know it was a horrible thing to do. I don't know why, Ignacio. I really don't.'

'Well.' He smiled. 'Would you like something to drink now?'

I ordered a Viña Sol.

'What have you been doing with yourself?' he asked. 'Having a good time?'

'Working hard,' I told him.

'Oh, dear.' He grinned at me. 'That doesn't sound very exciting.'

'It is,' I protested. 'I like the place I work.'

'Better than the Banco de Bilbao, I guess.'

'I don't know,' I said. 'I've never worked in a bank.'

I didn't know why I'd come here. I didn't want to be with Ignacio. I liked him, but I hardly knew him. My head was fuzzy.

'Would you like to go somewhere to eat?' he asked.

I shrugged my shoulders.

'There's a very nice restaurant just around the corner – Mirabelle. Do you know it?'

'No,' I said.

'I used to work there during the summer holidays.' He laughed at me. 'I'm a pretty good waiter – I've been through most of Europe's capital cities with a tray in my hand.'

I smiled at him. 'OK.'

He took me by the hand and we went to dinner.

~

I enjoyed being in bed with him. He did things that I liked. He caressed me and kissed me and ran his fingers over the base of my stomach which made me tingle. He asked me if I was happy, if it was OK for me. We twisted and turned under the single sheet and the sensations were wonderful.

Afterwards, he lay beside me and lit a cigarette.

'I don't smoke,' I said when he offered me one.

'Ah, yes. You told me the last time.'

I stared at the ceiling.

'Do you love me?' asked Ignacio.

'What?' I turned to look at him. He was smiling slightly.

'Do you love me?' he asked again.

'I—'

He grinned. 'Don't worry. I'm not expecting you to say yes.'

'What do you want me to say?'

'I don't know, Isobel. I guess I want to think that you like me. But, to be honest, I don't think you do.'

'Of course I like you, Ignacio.' I sat up and pulled the sheet up to my chin. 'You're – very likeable.'

'But you don't love me.'

'I don't know you.'

He sighed. 'Being in bed with you is very exciting, Isobel. But I am old-fashioned. I don't know how you think, but I like to have a relationship with the girls I sleep with. Are we having a relationship?'

'That's up to you,' I said.

I wasn't sure whether I wanted to see him again or not. It was very strange.

'Then would you like to meet me on Wednesday night? We could go to the movies, eat afterwards?'

'Of course,' I said again. 'Of course I would.'

⁓

So I met him on Wednesday night, skipping my final

language class, and the following Friday and the Wednesday after that. He was good fun, very attentive and nice to be with. But, despite the sex, which was definitely good, I didn't love him and I knew that I never would love him. I tried, I really did. I kept telling myself of all the great things that he did. But there was something missing and I didn't know what it was.

Then Ignacio broke it off with me.

'I'm sorry,' he said. 'I've had some good times with you, Isobel. But I don't think it's working.' He smiled at me to cushion the blow. 'I think you want someone different to Ignacio de Ribera.'

I stared at him. 'No.'

'But, yes, Isobel. Whoever you're looking for, whatever you're looking for – it isn't me.'

'OK,' I said sharply. 'No problem, Ignacio.' I got up and grabbed my bag. 'Nice knowing you.' And I walked home.

↬

I wasn't as hurt as I could have been, but I felt rejected all the same. At Barbara and Bridget's next party I didn't have the enthusiasm to try and find anyone. I sat in a corner and shared my Southern Comfort with a German girl who hadn't a word of Spanish. It didn't matter. After a few drinks neither of us were talking anyway.

But I was at home in front of the TV when Julie phoned.

'How's tricks?' she asked. 'Keeping busy?'

'Busy enough,' I replied as I hit the mute button on the TV remote control.

'What are you doing?' asked Julie.

'Well, right now I'm doing absolutely nothing,' I said. 'I was dumped by my latest boyfriend.'

'What latest boyfriend?'

I hadn't told her that I'd started seeing Ignacio again. She only knew about that first night. I brought her up to speed.

'You don't sound too devastated,' she said.

'I suppose I'm not.' I poured myself another glass of wine. 'It was good while it lasted, Julie, but it wasn't the love of my life.'

'I suppose that's OK.' But she sounded hesitant.

'Oh, it is, honestly.'

'So how's work?'

'Not bad. Quite good, actually. I've been very busy and I'm glad to say that I get on well with Gabriela so everything's working out in that department.'

'Great.'

'And you?' I asked. 'How are you?'

She sighed. 'All right.'

'All right? Not great?'

'Could be better, I guess.'

'Julie, did you ring to chat about you? I've been rubbishing on about me and all the time there's something wrong with you.'

'Not wrong,' she said.

'What then?'

'I wondered if you'd like to come on holiday with me in a couple of weeks.'

'I thought you were saving your holidays for the States,' I said.

There was a blank silence. 'Julie?'

'I don't know whether I'll need them or not,' she said finally.

'Don't tell me it's all off,' I said. 'I thought everything was going well.'

'I thought so too.'

'So what happened?'

'I don't want to talk about it now,' she said. 'But it's why I need to get away.'

'The offer to come here still stands,' I told her. 'I'm due a week off and there's plenty to do. It's pretty hot, though.'

'Actually, I'd something else in mind,' she said.

'What?' I asked suspiciously.

'Des – you've met him, he's the manager in our office – has an apartment in Sitges,' Julie told me. 'He was going to go for a week in a fortnight's time but he's had to cancel. He offered it to me if I was interested. I thought you might like to join me since Sitges is in Spain so you're halfway there already.'

'Halfway is right,' I told her. 'Sitges is at least five hundred kilometres away.'

'That's nothing,' she said. 'Oh, come on, Isobel. It'll be fun.'

I wondered about that. About as much fun as our holiday in Rhodes, given the sound of her voice.

'OK,' I said. 'When is the apartment available?'

She told me and I wrote the details down on the pad beside the phone. I'd ask Gabriela about holidays in the morning.

❧

Julie and I met in Barcelona airport. I arrived two hours before her and hired a bright blue Seat Ibiza for a week. Her flight was on time and she emerged into the arrivals hall in the middle of a throng of eager holidaymakers. I stood alongside the reps from hundreds of tour operators and waved frantically to catch Julie's attention.

'I hardly recognised you,' she said, finally spotting me.

'I haven't been gone that long.' I picked up her case.

It weighed nothing. Julie was one of those people who can make about six different outfits from a plain white blouse.

'But you look different,' said Julie as she kissed me on the cheek. 'You look – thin.'

'You look exactly the same,' I lied.

Julie looked terrible. She was paler than I remembered, the colour was growing out of her hair and her eyes were smudged with tiredness. Her face was gaunt and it didn't suit her.

'Don't be ridiculous,' she said. 'I look like a ghost. I was out until three this morning with one of the girls from the office.'

I grinned. At least it explained the smudges under her eyes.

'Come on,' I said. 'Let's collect the car.'

I was a bit doubtful about the car. I wasn't used to right-hand drive. I was accustomed to the traffic in Madrid as a pedestrian – take your life in your hands and run – but I knew that I'd never have the nerve to drive there. Julie said it'd be no problem, I'd catch on pretty quickly.

I almost turned the wrong way onto the motorway. I slammed on the brakes and swore loudly as a huge articulated lorry bore down on us.

'It's OK,' gasped Julie. 'We're still alive.'

'Sorry.' I reversed the car and started again. 'I think I know what I'm doing now.'

'I hope so.' She took a tissue from her bag and wiped her forehead. 'I may be depressed but I'm not suicidal.'

'Are you depressed?' I released the clutch and eased onto the road. My confidence grew a little and I picked up speed.

'Oh, you know how it is.' Julie fanned herself with

the tissue. 'I don't feel so bad now that I'm away from home.'

She lapsed into silence and I didn't press her to talk. I hate it when people try to make me talk when I don't want to and I wasn't going to force Julie's confidences. She'd tell me all about it when she was ready.

I turned on the car radio and flamenco music filled the air.

'Very authentic,' murmured Julie as she closed her eyes. 'But I hate flamenco.'

I put a Brian Ferry tape I'd brought into the cassette and we hummed along to 'Avalon'. But when he sang 'These Foolish Things' neither of us joined in and, out of the corner of my eye, I could see Julie wiping away a tear. Oh God, I thought. This could be a perfectly horrible week.

&

The apartment in Sitges was a couple of kilometres outside the town centre. The low-rise building was at the bottom of a hill, an olive grove to the back and pine-trees at the sides. I pulled up outside and switched off the engine.

Our apartment was on the ground floor.

'All the apartments are owned by English people,' said Julie as she unlocked the door. 'Des bought it from a bloke he knows in the UK.'

It was a small apartment – tiny kitchen area, living room, bathroom and one bedroom. The sliding-doors in the living room led onto a small, paved patio.

'It's not bad, is it?' Julie dumped her bag on a chair.

'It's fine.' I opened the patio doors and stepped out-side. There was a pool outside, surrounded by sun-loungers, half of which were occupied. Late evening shadows were beginning to fall across the water and, even as I stood there, more people got up from the loungers and walked back to their apartments.

'I know it's old hat to you by now.' Julie joined me on the patio. 'But it's lovely to be in the sun.'

'I thought you were having a decent summer at home,' I said.

'Oh, it's not the same.' Julie dismissed Irish summers with a shake of her head. 'You can't sit around the pool for a start!'

∽

As it turned out, we didn't spend that much time by the pool. We went for a walk that evening and discovered a beautiful cove with soft, cream-coloured sand and clear, warm water. We decided to go there the following morning, so after a breakfast of coffee and croissants, we went there and unrolled our towels in the semi-shade of a spindly tree.

'Why is it,' I mused as I lay down, 'that we've just got out of bed and we're preparing to go back to sleep again?'

'Because that's what you do on holidays.' Julie rubbed cream onto her arms. 'You sleep. You read. You swim. You eat.'

I giggled. 'What about "you dance all night long"?'

'I've gone past all that,' said Julie darkly. 'I'm a mature woman now.'

I snorted and she flicked some *Ambre Solaire* at me.

We lay down on the towels again.

We hadn't talked last night. We'd had a pizza at a nearby restaurant and chatted about our families and about my job in Spain, but we hadn't talked about the things that we both wanted to talk about. I knew that Julie would talk about Andy when she was ready.

She sat up suddenly and poked me in the ribs. 'Look at that.'

A boat had moored in the cove. A big, white boat with dark glass which wouldn't have looked out of place in St Tropez.

'Wow,' said Julie. 'Wonder who that belongs to?'

'Somebody rich,' I said. 'Somebody very rich.'

'One day I'll be rich.' Julie burrowed in the sand with her toes.

'Why?' I asked. 'You planning to rob the estate agent's? Or just marry into it?'

'I don't think I'll ever get married,' she said. 'I don't think I'm the marrying type.'

'I thought you were exactly the marrying type,' I said. 'Hundreds of boyfriends in your wild-child youth. Looking for something a little more serious now. And I thought you might be going to marry Andy.'

'Maybe I'm looking for something more serious.' Julie twisted her hair around her fingers. 'But Andy Jordan isn't.'

'Tell me about it,' I said simply.

She sighed. 'Oh, Isobel, I thought he loved me. I really and truly did. He was so wonderful at Christmas. He kept saying that he didn't want to go home. He told me that he couldn't imagine life without me. He bought me the most gorgeous gold chain made up of tiny interlocking hearts. What was I supposed to think?'

'Sounds pretty definite,' I agreed.

'He rang me loads of times from the States. We talked about the future, but we kind of skirted around it. So last month I asked him what he thought we should do.'

'And?'

'He suggested that I come and live with him in the States.'

'So? What's the problem?'

'Live with him, Isobel. Not marry him.'

'Oh,' I said.

'I told him I wasn't so sure about leaving home to live with him and he said that it was important that we should get to know each other more before making any long-term commitment.'

'He has a point.'

'No he hasn't.'

For a second I thought that Julie was going to cry.

'But you haven't really been together that much,' I said gently. 'Perhaps he feels that it's the distance that's making your relationship so good.'

'I understand all that,' said Julie. 'But think about it, Isobel. I'm thirty years old. He wants me to pack in my job and go to the States for three months and, at the end of it, who knows whether we'll get married or not. It's not as though we'd be spending all our time together there either. He'll be at work most of the time. I'd be rattling around Florida on my own.'

'Can't you look at it as an extended holiday?'

'No, I can't.' Julie slapped some more suncream onto her legs. 'I've got a life to live and I've got a good job at home. If he wants me to chuck it in, he's got to give me something in return.'

'You always said that you hated your job,' I told her mildly.

'Not hated,' she said. 'OK, it's not exactly the most glamorous career but it pays my wages and I like it really. Besides, Des offered me assistant manager of the Drumcondra branch.'

'Oh.'

'So, you see, I'd be giving up promotion and everything. For what? A three-month failed romance in Florida?'

'Maybe it wouldn't be a failed romance,' I said. 'Maybe you'll go to Florida and have an absolutely wonderful time and you'll end up getting married in the Church of the Seven Veils or something in Vegas.'

She laughed half-heartedly.

'I know you don't want me to say that I see his point of view. But it must be different being in love with someone a few thousand miles away. It's not exactly conducive to learning about each other, is it?' I pushed my damp hair out of my eyes.

'I know.' She sighed and burrowed into the sand again with her toes. 'And I can see his point of view too. It's just that – it's not what I wanted.'

It's not what I wanted. I'd said that to Tim when he suggested moving in with him. I knew exactly how Julie felt. And it wasn't that either of us felt marriage was the be-all and end-all of our existence. It was simply that we wanted to be sure that we were loved. To be secure in that knowledge. And without the marriage certificate it didn't seem that either of us could be.

'We're dreadfully suburban,' I said gloomily.

'I can't help it,' Julie muttered. 'I was born and raised in the suburbs.'

A girl appeared on the edge of the boat. She was tall and slender. She pulled her shining black hair into a pony-tail and stretched her arms skyward. She wore a sleek orange bathing-suit which outlined a near-perfect body. She bounced on her toes for a couple of seconds, then dived into the clear blue water sending up a spray of glittering drops.

'Bitch,' said Julie laconically.

'Come on,' I said. 'Let's get in for a dip ourselves.'

'Oh, Isobel.' Julie made a face. 'I've just covered myself in sunscreen.'

'So what?' I grinned at her. 'It'll protect you in the water.'

It was beautifully warm. I floated, my eyes closed, safely

within my depth while Julie swam parallel to the beach. When I opened my eyes and righted myself, Julie was on her return swim and the girl was back on the boat, surrounded by half-a-dozen muscular, tanned men.

'D'you think she's a film star or something?' Julie surfaced beside me.

'Pop singer maybe?' I hazarded.

'All that beefcake! On one girl. Life is so unfair.'

We sighed at the unfairness of life and went back to lie in the sun.

∽

'I met Tim Malone last week.'

We were having after-dinner drinks in the bar. Julie poured the rest of her beer into a glass and avoided my startled glance.

'You what!' It came out as a strangled yelp.

'Met Tim,' she repeated. 'Not deliberately, of course.'

'Where?'

'Grafton Street. On Saturday. He was in front of me in the Banklink queue.'

'Did you talk to him?' My mouth was dry. I gulped some beer and spluttered as it went down the wrong way. I took a puff of my inhaler.

Julie watched me calmly. She'd seen this before. 'A little,' she replied, when I'd got my breathing under control.

'What did he say?'

Julie shrugged. 'Not much. He knew you'd left Delta-Print and gone abroad.'

'Did he ask?'

'What?'

'About me?'

'Does it matter?'

'Oh, Julie!' I glared at her. 'Come on.'

'He asked how you were,' she told me. 'He said that he felt terrible about everything. He said that he missed you.'

'Did he?'

'He said that he hadn't realised how much a part of his life you were and that he'd probably made a dreadful mistake.'

'You're joking.' I'd paled, I knew I had.

'I wasn't going to tell you,' said Julie. 'I didn't know whether it was a good idea or not.'

A waiter put a ceramic bowl of salted peanuts in front of us. I took a handful and began to chew.

'I wasn't talking to him for long,' Julie continued. 'Five minutes, maybe. He wanted to know about your job and how you were getting on. I told him you were doing brilliantly and that you had a new boyfriend.'

'Julie!'

'Well, what did you want me to say?' she asked. 'Anyway it's nearly true. You have got a good job. You were having a relationship even though I didn't know about it. And I can tell you something for nothing – he nearly vomited when I told him.'

'Did he really?'

'Sure did.' She took some peanuts from the bowl. 'It's the best way, Isobel. Tell them you're not interested any more, get someone new and they come running back.'

'He hasn't come running back,' I pointed out.

'No. But I think he'd like to.'

'You're just saying that.'

She laughed. 'Well, maybe I'm exaggerating a little. But he was put out when he heard about Juan.'

'Juan?'

'Your boyfriend, of course.'

'Jesus, Julie! You mean you actually told him something about an imaginary boyfriend?'

'Not a lot,' she told me. 'Just that he was a businessman and that he was crazy about you.'

'You're the one who's crazy,' I said.

'So what?' She shrugged. 'He'll never find out anyway. Might as well make him jealous.'

I laughed. I liked the idea of a jealous Tim.

'He probably knew you were spoofing,' I said.

'Hoped I was.' Julie grinned. 'But I know he was jealous. I could see it in his eyes.'

'Maybe I should've made him jealous earlier,' I said. 'Maybe it would have made all the difference.'

Julie said nothing. The sound of disco music carried on the warm breeze from the hotel near the beach.

'How d'you feel about him now?'

I sighed and gazed across the cove. The big boat had left earlier in the day, but a small fishing-boat bobbed gently up and down in the water.

'I don't know,' I said finally.

'If he contacted you now, what would you say?'

'I don't know,' I said again.

'Do you still care about him?'

I bit the nail of my index finger and pulled at the jagged edge.

'Sort of.' I looked at her. Her face was full of concern. 'It's hard to explain. I never fell out of love with him. I hated him, of course, for what he did, but that was different. And then I met him with Laura and I kind of went mad. He says that there was nothing between them and maybe it was true, but it was a question of trust. I didn't trust him, then, I couldn't. And he seemed to think that everything was OK between us. That we could carry on exactly as we had before. But we couldn't – I couldn't. I did something awful, too.'

'What?'

'He was away. California, I think. I still had the keys to his house. I let myself in and wiped his computer.'

'Isobel!' Julie looked at me in horrified admiration.

'He was working on something called Saracen 2. I deleted all the files.'

'My God,' she breathed.

'It wasn't a disaster, I'm sure he had loads of backups. But it made me feel better.'

'I bet it did.'

'I did something else, too.'

'What?'

'There were earrings in his bedroom. They weren't mine. I flushed them down his toilet.'

She looked at me open-mouthed.

'They could have been anybody's earrings,' I said defensively. 'I thought that maybe he was sleeping with someone else.'

'Perhaps he was.'

'You see.' I looked miserably at her. 'That was why it had to be over.'

'Oh, Isobel.' She took my hand. 'We're a pair of crocks, aren't we?'

'Rubbish,' I said briskly. 'We're two single women on holiday. Let's make sure we have a good time.'

∽

We had a good time. I felt more like the old Isobel Kavanagh when I was with Julie. I didn't feel as if I had to be different, as if I had to be the life and soul of the party. And I liked it. We didn't try to get off with any of the chunky and hunky men who lurked around the beach. We went to a different restaurant each night, shared a bottle of wine, had coffees and talked.

We talked a lot. I told her about Barbara and Bridget, about Ignacio, about Stefan and about John in the executive swivel-chair.

She stared at me in disbelief.

'Are you taking precautions?'

'For God's sake, Julie!'

'Well, if you're sleeping around you should be using something.'

'I'm not sleeping around,' I said angrily.

'What would you call it?' asked Julie. 'I know I kept telling you to go out there and immerse yourself in Latin lovers. I didn't think you'd take it quite so literally.'

'I didn't,' I said. 'Only one of them was Spanish. You couldn't call Stefan – with whom, I will remind you, I didn't actually do anything – or John, Latin lovers.'

'I still can't believe it.' She waved at the waiter and ordered two more cappuccinos.

'Why not?'

'It's not exactly you.'

'What *is* me?' I asked.

'I'm not sure. But drinking and partying and sleeping around isn't.'

'I'm not sleeping around,' I repeated angrily. 'Come on, Julie! You're making it sound sordid.'

'I'm sorry.'

'I just want to have a good time,' I told her. 'Julie, I'm an adult. I'm not some stupid teenager.'

'Stupid teenagers can get away with partying all night and going to work the next day,' said Julie.

'It's not every night,' I objected. 'And I can cut it in the office. I told you – I'm efficient.'

'You don't look well,' she said.

'Look who's talking!' I glared at her. 'I hardly recognised you when you arrived.'

'I told you, that was because I'd been out the night

before. And I look OK now. You looked awful when we met. Thin face, thin body.'

'I've lost weight because I don't eat as much here,' I told her. 'Much more fresh vegetables and fruit and a lot less meat. So, quite a healthy diet in fact.'

'A diet of veggies and booze isn't much good,' said Julie.

'Stop lecturing me, Donegan,' I said. 'I don't need any more lectures from you. God, it's not as though there's much you can lecture me about. You're here to get over the creep Jordan. I'm here to get over the creep Malone. I don't think there's that much difference between us.'

'I'm not trying to get over him,' said Julie. 'I'm just trying to put a perspective on things.'

'Yes, and that's exactly what I've done too,' I said. 'I've put a perspective on my life.'

'Right,' said Julie.

'Right,' I said.

It was just as well that she was going home the next day.

∽

'I'm sorry,' I said as we stood in the airport terminal.

'It's OK.' Julie was still annoyed with me.

'I mean it,' I said. 'I'm sorry.'

'Is it so hard to get what we want out of life?' asked Julie. 'I mean, I thought I had everything worked out with Andy. I really did. I thought it was all going great, even though he's American and I'm Irish and most of the relationship has been conducted over the phone! And then, suddenly, he comes up with this "live with me" suggestion. And I'm too old to decide that I'll take a couple of years out and do just that. I want to be married and to have kids and all that sort of thing.

I don't want to be footloose and fancy-free any more.' She grimaced. 'That sounds so boring, doesn't it?'

I shook my head. 'Not to me. I wanted all those things too. I always did.'

'Why?' asked Julie.

I shrugged. 'I'm not sure. Maybe it was because of my parents.' I brushed an imaginary fleck of dust from my sleeve. 'They got married very young. Mum was pregnant. She lost the baby.'

'Oh, Isobel!' Julie stared at me. 'I didn't know that.'

'It's not something my mother talks about a lot,' I said wryly. 'Anyway, I was conceived fairly soon afterwards so they had their baby after all. Sometimes, though, I think she resents the fact that I wasn't the first baby. You see, they felt as though they had to get married – well, I guess back then single motherhood was still something you didn't talk about that much. So they got married and they lost the baby, which was the reason they got married in the first place, and then I came along, but I wasn't the right baby. And I think they have always resented me.'

'Well, I think that's absolute rubbish,' said Julie firmly. 'Your mother is nuts about you. About all of you.'

'Perhaps,' I said. 'But I always felt as though I could do it better than her, Julie. I could get engaged and get married and have children and it would be perfect. Not like her.'

Julie stared at me. 'That's crazy, Isobel.'

'I know,' I said. 'But it's how I felt. So, when it all went pear-shaped, I guess I just lost my head completely. I wasn't better than her after all.'

'But it's not a question of being better than anyone,' said Julie. 'It's not a competition, Isobel.'

'I know,' I said again. 'But I always felt it was.'

'You nutter.' She grinned at me, then hugged me.

'You'll find someone, Isobel. And, I suppose if you're having fun in the meantime, you'll enjoy waiting.'

'Yes.' I smiled back at her. 'And you'll find someone too, Julie. Better than Andy Jordan.'

I waved goodbye to her and went home.

Chapter 15

Woman Struggling to Attain the Unreachable
(Joan Miró, 1954)

There was pandemonium in the office. I could hear Gabriela shouting at someone as I stepped out of the lift. It was very unlike Gabriela to shout. She got heated sometimes and her words poured in a torrent of incomprehensible Spanish, but she rarely lost her temper with any of us.

I sat down at my desk just as she stormed out of her office.

'Oh, Isobel,' she said, her voice dripping with sarcasm. 'So nice of you to turn up.'

I stared at her, my mouth open. I was five minutes late.

'It's wonderful to think that I am not the only person, the one person in this office who realises that we need to be here to make money. That if we are not here there is no business.' She stalked down the corridor.

'What on earth is wrong with her?' I asked Magdalena, who had followed Gabriela out of the office.

'José was in a motorbike accident last night,' said Magdalena. 'He broke his leg and he's in hospital. Maria has the flu. Sofia rang in to say that she has food poisoning.

And we've just discovered that the hotel where tomorrow's conference was supposed to be wasn't booked.'

'Oh.' I made a face at Magdalena. 'Is José OK?'

'He's fine. Not a scratch, apart from the leg.'

'That's good. But not so good about the conference.'

'Not so good at the best of times,' she said. 'But a nightmare this week because of the trade exhibition.'

I'd forgotten about the trade exhibition. A gathering of Spanish manufacturers all showing their goods in a major exhibition that would have the hotels full and space at a premium all week.

'But didn't we confirm the booking with them?' I asked.

'Normally we do,' said Magdalena. 'Luis is supposed to do it. I don't know what happened. It wouldn't matter so much, there'd usually be somewhere else even at this short notice, but this week it's a disaster.'

'Don't we have space here?'

'Not enough,' she told me. 'You know our biggest room only holds twenty. There are fifty people booked in for our conference.'

'No wonder Gabriela's thrown a fit,' I mused.

'She'll throw more than a fit if she has to cancel,' said Magdalena glumly. 'She already blames all of us. Especially José, who was in charge of the thing, but since he's in hospital there isn't much she can do. Luis was supposed to do the confirming, but not the actual booking. He hasn't arrived yet so she's doubly annoyed.'

'Have we tried alternative venues?' I asked.

'She's already been on to a dozen hotels, but none of them have availability,' Magdalena said.

Just then, Gabriela walked back into the office. I could see that she was barely keeping her temper in check.

'Well?' she asked, looking at Magdalena. 'Any bright ideas?'

Poor Magdalena looked miserable. First into the office this morning, she'd taken the brunt of Gabriela's anger.

'I have an idea,' I said tentatively. 'A hotel that might have space.'

'Well, don't stand there,' snapped Gabriela. 'Check it out.' She went into her room and slammed the door behind her.

'Time of the month,' said Luis who'd just walked into the office.

'Oh, Luis, that is a terrible thing to say.' Magdalena looked at him furiously. 'And you won't be saying it when she's firing you because she has to cancel the presentation tomorrow.'

'What!' Luis was aghast.

'I rang the hotel this morning to query something. It turns out that you never confirmed the booking. That's your job, Luis. If we don't find an alternative venue quickly, you'll be surplus to requirements,' said Magdalena. 'And I won't be crying for you. You spend too much time chatting up the girls in the office and not enough time doing your job.'

She flounced off to her desk and left me standing in the middle of the office while Luis rummaged frantically through the filing cabinet.

I sat at my own desk and looked up the number of the Hotel Lux. I hadn't been there for a few weeks. I was trying to see less of Barbara and Bridget and their crowd because, no matter what resolutions I made, I always got drunk when I was out with them. Since my holiday with Julie, I'd decided that I'd gone a bit too far in the reinvention of Isobel Kavanagh and that I should be more sensible. Sometimes it seemed the right thing; at other times (like when I was at home on my own) it seemed stupid.

I skimmed through the phone book. Advanta had never

used the Lux before, but there was always the chance it might have a room.

'I'm not sure that we have a room to suit you exactly,' said Señor Murillo, the manager, when I finally got through to him. 'But we do have a function room and it is available tomorrow.'

'Don't book it for anyone else,' I said. 'I'll be there in fifteen minutes.'

I jumped up from the desk and popped my head around Gabriela's door. 'Don't panic just yet,' I said. 'I'm going to check out a place. I'll be back in an hour.'

'Isobel, if you find me somewhere, I'll give you a raise.'

'I hope you mean that,' I said.

I got a taxi outside the office and reached the Lux in a few minutes. It was silly to feel that I had to run up the flight of steps into the hotel, but I did anyway.

Señor Murillo shook my hand. 'It is an emergency, yes?'

'Yes,' I said.

'We will see if the Lux can help you.' He looked at me curiously. 'I have seen you here a number of times before, have I not?'

I smiled at him. 'I drink in the bar sometimes.'

'Ah, yes.' He nodded. 'You have a friend who is a friend of Tomás Medina.'

'That's right.' I was surprised that he knew. But maybe that's why he was the manager.

He led me along a narrow corridor. 'Don't be worried that you are being brought into the worst part of the hotel. This leads to an annexe we had built two years ago.'

'No problem.' But I was worried. The businessmen wouldn't like to think that they were being shunted into the basement.

'Here we are.' Señor Murillo opened a double door. 'Will this suit you?'

It wasn't perfect, but it would certainly suit. There was just about room for fifty people. Chairs were stacked neatly around the walls.

'Do you have projection equipment?' I asked. 'And microphones?'

Señor Murillo nodded.

'And would you be able to provide lunch?'

He looked at me quizzically. 'What sort of lunch?'

'Nothing complicated,' I assured him. 'Cold meat salad, perhaps?'

He looked at his watch as though every second counted. 'We can manage something.'

'It's important that it's good quality,' I said anxiously. 'It doesn't have to be extravagant, but not poor quality.'

'The Hotel Lux never compromises on quality,' he told me pompously.

'OK.' I looked around the room again. It would be all right. 'Can I phone my office to confirm?'

'Certainly.'

I took my mobile phone from my jacket pocket. 'Gabriela?' I'd rung her direct line. 'It's me, Isobel. I have a place for us.'

'Really?' I didn't think she believed me. 'With enough space? With everything we need? With catering?'

'Yes, yes and yes,' I said.

'How much will it cost?' she asked.

'I haven't discussed that yet,' I said. 'I wanted to know what your limits were.'

'You know how much it usually is,' she said. 'I'll leave it up to you.'

'OK. I'll be back shortly.'

'Isobel?'

'Yes?'

'Well done.'

'You can say that after I find out the price.'

Señor Murillo had walked to the end of the room while I made the phone call.

'Señor?'

He turned to me.

'How much will you charge to hire the room all day and to provide me with a projection screen, perhaps a projector, microphones and a lunch for fifty people?'

'You expect me to tell you that straight away?'

'Not straight away,' I said. 'But I need to decide very quickly.'

'And if you don't decide very quickly?'

'Señor, you know and I know that I'm not in a strong bargaining position. But I am also in the position that I have other business I can do with your hotel. If you are interested.' I shrugged to show that I didn't care about the other business. 'It might not be of interest to you, I understand. But . . .' I left the sentence hanging in mid-air.

He grinned at me. 'Come to my office. We will see what we can work out.'

It took twenty minutes to arrive at an acceptable price. It was more than we would normally pay for a venue and lunch, but not horrifically more. I thought that Gabriela would be pleased.

She was. She put her arms around me and told me that I was worth more than anyone else in her office. That the day she had decided to employ me was the best decision of her life. That I was the most sensible person that she had ever met. That I had intelligence. I would go far. If I applied myself – who knows?

'Thank you,' I said, when I had finally extracted myself from her embrace.

'No, it is important that I tell you these things,' she

said, her hand still resting on my shoulder. 'I know I am sometimes difficult to work with. I know that, Isobel. But you continue to work for me and I will reward you.'

I cleared my throat. 'You mentioned something about a rise.' I tried to sound offhand.

'Yes, I did.' Gabriela nodded vigorously. 'There will be extra in your salary this month.'

'Thanks,' I said again, although I wondered exactly how much the extra would be. Still, I felt a great deal of satisfaction knowing that it was me, Isobel, who'd sorted out the crisis. It proved that I was able to do things, that I was as good at business as the rest of them.

Luis took me to lunch. 'To thank you,' he said. 'She would have fired me. It was all my fault.'

'These things happen,' I said as I dipped my chicken into some mayonnaise. 'Although I'm sure it shouldn't have.'

'I thought I'd confirmed with them,' he said. 'I was sure I had. I thought I'd even seen the fax.' He shook his head. 'But it was a mistake.'

'Never mind,' I comforted him. 'It's sorted out now.'

'She absolutely chewed me up,' he said morosely as he picked at his fish. 'She doesn't like it if things go wrong.'

'Can't blame her,' I said. 'And with so many people off work this week, things were even worse. Plus the trade exhibition.'

'I know.' He sighed. 'I thought I was going to be fired.'

'Cheer up.' I laughed. 'You just have to do something wonderful to redeem yourself.'

He rubbed his forehead. 'If she ever trusts me again.'

'Don't be so melodramatic,' I said. 'Of course she'll trust you again.'

'It was a genuine mistake.'

'Luis.' I put down my knife and fork. 'Can you just shut up about it now? Everything is OK.'

We went back to the office. Gabriela was at a meeting. Magdalena grinned at me as I walked to my desk. 'Congratulations,' she said.

'Congratulations?'

'You've saved the day, Isobel! Gabriela was singing your praises earlier.'

I was uncomfortable. 'I just thought of a place,' I said. 'It wasn't anything great.'

'You thought of the right place,' said Magdalena. 'Well done.'

'Thanks.'

I still felt uncomfortable. I'd felt clever earlier, but, in reality, all I'd done was book a hotel. It wasn't exactly brilliant stuff. Still, I supposed, if it meant that Gabriela was happy, it was a good thing. I pulled a file towards me and started to work again.

∽

'It'll be fun,' said Barbara on the phone to me that evening. 'Come on, Isobel, we haven't seen you in ages.'

'I know,' I told her. 'I've been busy in work.'

'It's not a party,' she said. 'Not on a Thursday night. We're just inviting a few people around for drinks. It'll be more sophisticated than falling around the apartment drunk as skunks.'

I laughed. 'OK, what time?'

'About nine.'

'See you then.'

∽

There were about twenty people in the apartment when I

arrived. 'Great to see you.' Barbara kissed me, continental style, on each cheek. 'You're looking fantastic.'

I knew I looked better. I was still eating loads of fresh fruit and vegetables, but I'd had a lot of early nights since I'd come back from Sitges and I'd cut back on my drinking. I was wearing an old pair of jeans that had been slightly tight around the waist a couple of years ago but were now nicely loose, and my silk top was cropped so that my nicely tanned, flat stomach was on display.

I handed over a bottle of Southern Comfort.

'D'you want some of this, or will you have wine to start?' asked Barbara.

'I'll stick to the Southie,' I told her. 'Don't want to mix my drinks!'

She laughed and poured a measure. 'Do you know everyone?'

I knew some of them. I sat on the sofa and chatted to a girl who gave art appreciation classes at the college.

When I'd finished my drink, Tomás handed me a cocktail which I eyed suspiciously.

'I made it myself,' he said. 'You'll like it.'

I did.

❧

'Ladies and gentlemen.' Barbara stood on a coffee-table. 'Can we have a bit of silence for a moment.'

The hum of conversation ceased. 'Thank you,' she said. 'Most of you are probably wondering why we have gathered here tonight. If it had been my choice, it would have been tomorrow night but, unfortunately, Señor Medina is working tomorrow night. And he is the one who has an announcement to make.' She smiled at Tomás. 'It's all yours.'

'*Señors y Señoras.*' Tomás cleared his throat. 'As you

know I have been going out with a wonderful lady for the past few months. It suddenly occurred to me that I was very lucky to have her. And I didn't like the idea that one day she might decide to go back to England. So, I thought, what can I do about this? And the answer was very simple – marry her! I asked her how she felt about it, and she said that it sounded a pretty good idea to her.' He grinned at us all. 'And so, tonight, I want to tell you all that Bridget and I are engaged to be married.'

We clapped as he took a jewellery box out of his pocket.

Bridget stood beside him and he slipped the ring onto her finger. I felt a lump the size of a tennis ball in my throat. We clapped again. Everyone clustered around them to give them good wishes and Bridget held out her hand so that we could see the sparkling diamond on her finger.

'I'm really pleased for you,' I croaked. 'And the ring is lovely.'

'Isn't it?' She beamed at me. 'D'you want to make a wish, Isobel?'

'Oh, I don't—'

'Go on!' She handed it to me. 'Only not for a husband, you know.'

'I know.' I grinned unsteadily at her. 'I'll wish for a rich mother-in-law. That's the form, isn't it?'

She laughed. 'Regretfully, Señora Medina isn't rich. But I love Tomás just the same.'

'I'm glad.' I slid the ring onto my finger and turned it anticlockwise three times.

I didn't wish for anything.

∽

I drank a few more of Tomás's prize-winning cocktails

and then left. It was around midnight and the streets were still teeming with people. The city deserved its reputation as an enjoyed city, I thought, as I crossed the street. Everybody in Madrid liked to have a good time.

Tomás and Bridget. I hadn't imagined that they'd get engaged. I thought Bridget was like Barbara – enjoyed partying and meeting people and having a good time. I didn't think she was the settling-down sort.

Maybe we all are, I thought. Deep down, maybe everyone just wants to find someone and set up house. Despite all the opportunities to do other things. To have great careers. To travel the world. Maybe it's just inbuilt in us.

I shivered even though the air was warm. Oh God, Tim, I thought, why don't you love me any more?

I was going to cry. I didn't want to cry. Not for Tim, not for anyone. But I couldn't help it.

'Isobel?'

I looked up.

'Isobel?'

I wiped away the tears. Of all the people I didn't want to meet, Luis was as high up on the list as it was possible to be.

'Hello, Luis,' I said.

'Are you all right?'

'I'm fine,' I said. 'Honestly.'

'You seemed upset.'

'Not really.' I smiled weakly. 'A friend of mine got engaged. That's all.'

Luis laughed. 'And are you crying because she is engaged to be married or because you are not?'

That was a bit close to the bone. I winced.

'Isobel?'

'I don't know why I'm crying, Luis. It's a woman thing.'

238

'You are crying because you do not like your life in Madrid,' said Luis. 'And you know you should do something about it.'

'There's nothing wrong with my life in Madrid,' I said spiritedly. 'Just because I don't want to fall into bed with you.'

'Why not?'

'Because I work with you.'

'So? Why is that a problem?'

'It just is.'

'That's not much of an answer.'

'It's all you're getting.'

I shook my head. The cocktails, despite their apparent innocence, had made it fuzzier than I thought. I stumbled. Luis caught me by the arm. 'I'm fine,' I told him. 'Leave me alone.'

'If you tell me why you were crying.'

'It's none of your business, Luis.'

'Oh, come on, Isobel.' He held my arm more tightly. 'We are friends. You saved my job. Why were you crying?'

'Because—' I sighed. 'Because I was once engaged to be married myself and because we decided – no, Luis, *he* decided to call it off.'

'Oh.'

'Exactly.'

'And you are upset because now your friend is engaged and you are not.'

'I don't know,' I said irritably. 'I don't know why I'm upset.'

'Come back to my apartment,' said Luis. 'I will make you some coffee.'

'I don't need coffee.'

'But you might need company.'

'I don't think so.'

'Humour me,' said Luis.

~

I hadn't realised how close by me he lived. The block was older and the apartments more spacious. Luis lived on the third floor.

'Sit down.' He waved me towards a battered old sofa. 'Make yourself comfortable.'

I sat down.

'You can turn on the TV or the music centre if you like,' he called from the kitchen.

But I liked the silence. I closed my eyes.

'Isobel?' Luis's voice came from miles away 'Are you all right?'

'Mm?'

'Are you all right?'

I opened my eyes. His face was close to mine, his eyes dark and concerned. I reached out and touched him. 'Mm,' I murmured. 'I'm fine, Luis.'

'Good.' He didn't move as I pulled him closer to me.

'Come here,' I complained. 'How can I kiss you if you're so far away?'

'Do you want to kiss me?' asked Luis.

'I do,' I told him.

'Sure?' But he was closer to me now.

'I want to kiss you.' Our lips were only millimetres apart. 'Oh, Luis, I want to kiss you.'

'I guess I was wrong when I thought you might only like women,' murmured Luis.

~

Luis Cardoso made everyone I'd ever slept with until now seem like an amateur. We kissed for what seemed like

240

hours. Then he lifted me onto his shiny teak dining-table and made love to me. After that, he carried me into his bedroom and made love to me again.

'*Oh, Isobel, mia Isobel,*' he murmured as he held me close to him. 'You are the best, the most wonderful, the most loving.'

'So are you.' I nuzzled close to him. 'So are you, my darling, wonderful, gorgeous Luis.'

～

I woke up at half-past seven. Luis's arm was wrapped around me. My head was pounding, my mouth was dry.

And I knew I'd made another, terrible mistake.

Chapter 16

Personages in the Night (Joan Miró, 1949)

I got out of the bed as quietly as I could. Luis mumbled something then rolled onto his side. I stood beside the bed, holding my breath in case he woke up. But he didn't. I exhaled slowly.

I couldn't believe it. I'd gone to bed with Luis and that was the last thing in the world I'd wanted to do. I had to work with Luis. I had to see him every single day. I couldn't just walk away from him and pretend it hadn't happened.

What on earth had I been thinking of? What had possessed me (apart from Luis in an utterly fantastic way)? I needed my head examined. I tiptoed around the bedroom, picking up my clothes from where I'd thrown them in wild, abandoned passion the night before. I retrieved my bra from the wall-light – I don't know how it had got there. I remembered tiptoeing like this around Ignacio's apartment a few months ago. Julie was right. It was sordid.

I would be late for work. Luis would be late too unless his alarm clock went off pretty soon. I understood now how it was that he arrived looking such a mess. He obviously left getting up until the last possible moment.

The alarm still hadn't gone off by the time I sneaked out of the apartment and ran down the stairs. An army of pile-drivers marched through my head. I felt sick.

I hoped Luis wouldn't wake up for ages, that I'd manage to get into the office before him, that I'd have thought of what I was going to say to him. I'd no idea what I was going to say to him.

The creaky, useless old lift in the Edificio Gerona was out of order again. I'd get fit, I thought, running up and down the stairs of Madrid's apartment blocks. I undressed as I moved through my apartment, into the bathroom and under the (cold) shower.

My nipples stood out like little doorknobs as the icy water cascaded over me. I shivered. It serves you right, I told myself. You stupid, stupid bitch.

I liked Luis. You couldn't help liking Luis. But I didn't love him and, despite the wonderful sex, I knew I'd never love him. This wasn't the kind of situation that works so well in the movies – where the unkempt, casual friend who's always around when the heroine needs him turns out to be the love of her life – a fact she never realises until the final frame even though the rest of us have known it from the moment he's walked onto the screen. It just wasn't like that with Luis.

And, oh God, everyone else in the office would know about it and I didn't want them to. Luis would boast about me the way he boasted about everyone else. I wondered, fleetingly, what had happened to his girl-friend, Maria. But I didn't care about Maria, I only cared about me.

Isobel the idiot. Isobel the fool that had joined the list of Luis's conquests. Isobel Kavanagh, the girl without a brain.

If I hadn't drunk those bloody cocktails I might have been OK. What in heaven's name was in them? I rubbed the towel vigorously over my body. One minute I'd felt fine. The next, I was an emotional wreck. And then I'd turned into some kind of rabid nymphomaniac. I blushed as I remembered crawling over Luis's body, doing things with him that I'd never done before. I groaned and pulled a comb through my hair. No time to dry it. I rummaged through my wardrobe. It'd have to be my red linen suit and white blouse. I hadn't done any ironing in ages and the white blouse was the only one left. And I hated the white blouse.

Gin, I remembered suddenly. There'd been gin in the cocktails and I'm one of those people who normally get depressed when they drink gin. There must have been an anti-depressant in there too. I certainly hadn't been depressed when I sat astride Luis on top of his polished, teak dining-room table.

My head was still thumping. The metro was crowded. I was nearly half an hour late for work.

'Good morning, Isobel.' Luis was at his desk, hair uncombed, suit crumpled.

'Good morning, Luis.' I felt the colour stain my cheeks.

'How are you this morning?'

'Fine. Thank you.' I marched past him, stopped at the water dispenser and filled a paper cup, then sat down at my desk.

'Hi, Isobel.' Magdalena dumped an armful of green folders on my desk. 'You're late.'

'I know.' I glanced involuntarily at my watch. 'Was Gabriela looking for me?'

Magdalena grinned. 'You're lucky. She's at the Lux looking in on the conference and deciding how much of a raise to give you.'

'Good.'

'Where were you last night?' she asked.

'Last night?' I felt the blush start again and had to

force myself not to look in Luis's direction. 'Oh, my friend Bridget got engaged. You know the girl from the college?'

'The one who is going out with the barman from the hotel?'

I nodded. 'That's the one. So we had some drinks in her apartment to celebrate.'

'I wish I could drink as much as you and still make it into the office,' said Magdalena. 'If I'd been out drinking last night I wouldn't be arriving only half an hour late today.'

'I didn't drink that much!' Did everyone in Advanta think of me as a lush? I'd cut down on my drinking, for God's sake. And I'd never really drunk that much in the first place.

'You'd had quite a few when I met you.'

Magdalena turned at the sound of Luis's voice. 'You met Isobel last night?'

'Yes,' said Luis. 'And she wasn't terribly steady on her feet.'

'Oh, I was fine.' I couldn't meet his eyes. Just couldn't.

'Were you? You could have fooled me.'

'I probably fool you all the time,' I said sharply, and Magdalena laughed.

She'd guess, of course. If she hadn't already guessed. I opened my desk drawer to get some paracetamol but the little bubble pack was empty. I rubbed the side of my nose and closed my eyes.

'Here.' Luis stood beside me and offered me a couple of capsules.

'Tylenol,' he said. 'Go ahead.'

'Thanks.'

He sat on the edge of the desk.

'I'm busy,' I said. 'I was late in today.'

He grinned. 'So I noticed. I wasn't.'

'I had to go home and shower.'

'I didn't bother,' said Luis. 'So much more memorable that way.'

'Luis!' I knocked over the remainder of my water. It spilled across the desk and dripped onto the floor.

'Oh, fuck!' I cried.

The others in the office looked up in surprise. Luis said nothing but began to mop the water with a tissue. I looked up and caught Magdalena gazing at us speculatively.

'Clumsy this morning.' Luis threw the sodden tissues into the wastepaper bin.

'Tired,' I said.

'I'm not surprised.'

'Luis,' I said. 'Would you please go away?'

'But why?' He smiled at me. 'Gabriela, the slave-driver, is out of the office. I am not busy. I have time to sit and talk to you, *mia Isobel*.'

'I don't have time to talk to you,' I snapped. 'And I'm not your Isobel.'

'*Oh, mia Isobel!*'

'Luis. Please.'

He shrugged. 'What is wrong, Isobel? If I said nothing to you then you would complain that Luis Cardoso doesn't care about you. That he is happy to get you into his bed but—'

'Luis, for God's sake!'

Magdalena was still watching us. One or two of the other staff were watching us too.

'Luis, I'm sorry, but I don't have time to discuss this now,' I said loudly. 'Perhaps you could talk to me about it after lunch?'

'Anything you wish, *mia Isobel*,' said Luis. 'Anything you wish, anytime you wish.'

He walked back to his desk again and I opened one

of the green folders. But I hadn't a clue what any of the paperwork was about. It was just as well there wasn't a seminar today. I could sit at my desk and stare empty-headed at files and it wouldn't make much difference.

Oh God, I thought, what had I done with my life? I didn't feel like me any more. I didn't feel like the Isobel who cycled along the seafront, letting the wind tangle my hair and bring colour to my cheeks. I didn't feel like the Isobel who made wedding dresses for friends and who'd hand-sewn four hundred and twenty pearls onto her own dress. I didn't feel like the Isobel who ate tea and toast with her sister at midnight while we talked about her career prospects. I felt like a stranger.

And wasn't that what you wanted? I asked myself fiercely as I drew a line through a memo. You wanted to be a different Isobel and you are a different Isobel.

So what's the bloody problem?

I rubbed my temples. My head felt as though it was going to explode.

'Isobel?' I looked up. Magdalena stood in front of my desk holding a cup of coffee. 'I thought you could do with this.'

'Oh, Magdalena, thank you.' I took the cup from her. 'You're right. It's just what I need.'

She pulled up a chair and sat down. 'Are you all right?' she asked.

'Apart from the headache, I'm fine.'

'You look awful, Isobel.'

'Don't you start.'

'Pardon?'

'People are always telling me I look awful.' I smiled at her, but my smile didn't reach my eyes. 'They tell me I'm too pale, or too thin, or that I've black bags under my eyes.'

'Do they?'

'Sometimes.'

'You're pale today,' said Magdalena. 'But you've been thin since I've known you. And, yes, you have black smudges under your eyes.'

'A true friend.' I sighed. 'I know I must look terrible today.'

She pulled the chair closer. 'Isobel?'

'Yes?'

'I know it's rude of me to ask. But did you and Luis—?'

'You're right,' I said. 'It's none of your business.'

She flushed. 'I'm sorry.'

I said nothing.

'I'd better get back to work,' said Magdalena eventually. 'But if you need to talk about anything . . .'

'Why would I need to talk about anything?' I closed one file and opened another. 'There's nothing to talk about.'

She sat in silence for a moment then got up and walked away.

&

My headache grew worse. My eyes hurt. I read endless reports on lecturers and seminars and didn't understand a word of them. At twelve o'clock I got up from my desk and went to the ladies'. My stomach was churning and, although I was hot, I was shivering too. I wondered if I was actually sick, whether I was getting the flu or something which might explain why I felt so bad. I leaned my head against the coolness of the wall-tiles and then, suddenly, lunged for the nearest cubicle and threw up.

Being sick makes me wheeze. It's because you're

coughing and spluttering and you can't breathe properly. For a moment or two, I thought I was going to die. But there was no point in using my inhaler yet, because I knew that I hadn't finished throwing up. My stomach was still on a roller-coaster.

The door to the ladies' opened just as I vomited again.

'Isobel!' Gabriela was beside me in an instant. She'd arrived back at the office a little earlier, delighted at how the conference was going. 'Isobel! Are you all right?'

I couldn't speak. I wished it had been anybody but Gabriela.

She ripped some paper towel from the container and handed it to me. 'I'll get you some water.'

I'd finished being sick. I flushed the toilet, put down the lid and sat down. Now my head was pounding worse than ever and my hands were shaking. I was fighting for every breath too.

Gabriela returned with a paper cup of water. I took a sip and then gasped at her, 'Can you get me my handbag? I need my inhaler.'

She nodded and disappeared again. I rinsed my mouth out with water.

When she came back with the bag I took a couple of puffs of the inhaler and, almost immediately, began to feel better.

'Is this a bad attack?' she asked, her voice full of concern. 'I did not realise you had asthma, Isobel. I didn't think it made you ill like this.'

It was a great excuse, but there was no point in excuses.

'It's not the asthma that made me sick,' I said. 'Being sick has made me wheeze.'

'And what has made you sick?' she asked. 'Have you

249

been feeling unwell for a while? Was it something you ate?'

She was being very tactful, I thought. 'No, Gabriela.' There was no point in lying to her. 'I'm really sorry,' I said. 'Really, really sorry.' And then I started to cry.

I didn't mean to cry. Gabriela said nothing, she just tore off some more paper towel.

'Do you want to talk about it?' she said, after the tears had stopped and I'd blown my nose.

'Oh, no. It's OK, Gabriela. Honestly. I'm fine now.'

'Don't be absolutely ridiculous,' she said sharply. 'You are not well, Isobel.'

'But I am,' I said.

The door to the ladies' opened and both of us looked up. Sofia stared at us in amazement.

'Can you use the toilets on the other floor?' asked Gabriela.

Sofia nodded wordlessly and closed the door again. Oh God, I thought, it'll be all around the office in a minute. Isobel Kavanagh is crying in the toilets and Gabriela is watching her. And Luis would hear about it and he'd think it was because I'd fallen for him or something. Oh God. Oh shit. Oh fuck, fuck, fuck.

'Would you like some more water?'

'No thanks, Gabriela. I feel OK now.'

'I think you'd better tell me about it.'

I shook my head slowly. The pain bounced around my skull.

'Isobel?' I looked up at her. 'I want you to tell me.'

It wasn't any of her business, I thought furiously. It was nothing to do with her.

She waited patiently.

'I'm sorry,' I said again. 'I shouldn't have come in today.'

'Not if you felt this ill,' said Gabriela.

I wasn't going to tell her, but suddenly I did.

'I've made such a mess of things,' I said. 'Oh, Gabriela, I'm such an idiot.'

'Isobel.' She looked at me carefully. 'Are you pregnant?'

I stared at her. I'd never thought that anyone would think of it as a possibility. But of course here I was, head down the toilet and wailing that I'd made a mess of my life. In her shoes, I'd have probably thought the same. But I knew I wasn't pregnant. I'd made sure of that.

'No.' I smiled wanly at her. 'I'm not pregnant.'

She sighed, and I realised it was with relief. 'I just thought—'

'I realise what you must have thought. I'm sorry.'

'Well, it can't be that bad, can it?'

I supposed not. God, if I'd been pregnant – it was too much to even contemplate.

'So, do you want to talk about it anyway?' asked Gabriela.

I smiled again, a little less wanly this time. 'Not really.' I pushed my damp hair out of my eyes. 'Or maybe I should.'

'I think you should,' said Gabriela firmly. 'I've noticed that you haven't looked well lately, Isobel. I thought maybe it was just a lot of late nights, you know. But it's more than that?'

'It's a lot of stupid things,' I said. 'You'll think me a horrible person, Gabriela.'

'No, I won't.'

'You will. Because I am a horrible person.'

'Tell me why.'

I sighed. 'When I came to Madrid, I thought I would be a different person. When I was younger and living at home I had lots of boyfriends but I was a sensible sort of girl. Then I met Tim. I was crazy about him, Gabriela.

251

I couldn't wait to marry him! So when he called it off – I was devastated. I thought my life had come to an end.' I was silent for a moment. Gabriela watched me, but said nothing. 'I was so unhappy at home that I think everyone was sick of me. Barry Cleary was sick of me. It was Sharon who thought I should work abroad. I think it was because I was driving Barry insane. So I came here, Gabriela, and I thought that I could be different. That I should go out every night and have a good time and nobody knew anything about me. And that's what I did. I met a guy in a bar near the apartment and went out with him for a while. I went to lots of parties with the girls from the college. I know I drank too much but I felt better when I was drinking. More lighthearted. Last night I went to an engagement party. I drank cocktails. I never drink cocktails. I got upset – stupid, I know, but I kept thinking about Tim and our wedding and everything and I left the party because I knew I was going to cry. So I was walking home and I met Luis.'

'Luis?' she interrupted me. 'Luis Cardoso? Our Luis?'

'The very one.'

'Oh, Isobel!'

'Don't say "oh, Isobel".' I made a face at her. 'He was so nice to me, Gabriela. He brought me to his apartment and made me coffee and he was – oh, nice and kind and—'

'—you went to bed with him?'

'I couldn't help it,' I said. 'It just seemed the right thing to do.'

'And you've been sick because—?'

'Because I drank too much and because he came and sat on my desk and called me "*mia Isobel*" and because I know everyone in the office will know about it and I feel like such a fool.'

Gabriela shrugged. 'Claims about Luis are exaggerated,' she said. 'Yes, he has been with some of the girls in the office. He seems to be the sort of person who can get away with it! Everyone stays friendly with him afterwards.'

'Very continental,' I said.

She laughed. 'We are, perhaps, less analytical about it. Anyway, maybe you'll want to go out with him again.'

'No,' I said. 'I like him, Gabriela. But he's not my type.'

She made a face. 'Alfredo wasn't my type. But I still knew that he was the one I'd marry.'

'You knew it straight away, you said. But I don't feel that with Luis.'

'Not everyone knows,' said Gabriela.

'I like him,' I said. 'But that's all. And it's not one of these likings that suddenly turn into mad passion. Besides – he's slept with half of Madrid.'

Gabriela chuckled. 'He'd like you to think that.'

'Even so.'

'Are you feeling better now?' she asked.

'I guess so.'

'You shouldn't have come in today. You could have stayed in bed.'

'In Luis's bed?' I said.

'Perhaps not.'

We both smiled.

'But you should go home now, Isobel. There is nothing exceptional scheduled for today. Go home and have a good sleep and you'll feel better by tomorrow.'

I stood up. My legs were shaky.

'I'll order a taxi,' said Gabriela. 'Don't bother going back to your desk. Go into my office and wait there.'

'Thank you,' I said. 'You've been really good to me, Gabriela.'

'What are friends for?' She smiled and gave me a hug.

~

I crawled into bed. My head was thumping, my legs shaking and my breathing was ragged. I'd taken too many puffs of my inhaler and my heart was racing. I felt awful. I wished I was at home in Sutton, where Mum would be sympathetic and bring me cups of weak tea (although, to be honest, I wouldn't have been able to keep it down), and would fetch me cool, damp towels for my aching head. I would have killed for a cool, damp towel right then. The apartment was like a furnace because I didn't leave the air-conditioning on during the day.

I alternately baked and shivered under the sheet. Maybe I *was* getting the flu. Maybe it was nothing to do with cocktails and Luis and humiliation. But I knew that it had everything to do with cocktails and Luis and humiliation.

Eventually I fell into a dreamless sleep.

I was awakened by the sound of the apartment buzzer. I sat up slowly in the bed and shook my head experimentally to see how the headache was. Almost gone, which was good, and I didn't feel sick any more either. Although my legs were still shaky.

I padded into the living room and pressed on the intercom. 'Who is it?'

'It's me, Luis.'

'Luis!'

'Yes. Can I come up?'

'Oh – um – yes, Luis. Of course.'

What else could I say? I pulled on a pair of jeans and a T-shirt and ran my fingers through my hair. I just about had time to wash my mouth out with Listerine when he knocked at the door.

'*Hola*, Isobel. How are you feeling?' His eyes showed nothing but concern.

'Hi, Luis. Come in. I'm much better, thanks.'

'What was it?' he asked. 'Something you ate?'

I shrugged. 'More likely something I drank.'

'Were you very drunk last night, Isobel?'

'I think so.' I smiled faintly. 'I didn't realise it at the time.'

'Poor Isobel.'

'It's my own fault,' I told him. 'I should have had more sense.'

'And maybe more sense than to have come to my apartment?'

'Definitely more sense than that, Luis.'

'I knew you'd been drinking, Isobel. And I'm sorry. I shouldn't have gone to bed with you.'

'As far as I recall it wasn't just the bed,' I said dryly, although the memory of making love on the table was making me squirm.

'It was very good nonetheless.'

'Luis!'

'It's true,' he said. 'You are a very exciting, sexy woman, Isobel.'

'Please, Luis.'

'So what is the problem?'

'I shouldn't have slept with you, Luis. I don't love you.'

'That's not much of a reason.'

'It is for me.'

'But you have slept with other men since you have been in Madrid.'

Oh, God, I thought. Exactly what does he know about me?

'I—'

'No matter, Isobel.'

'Luis, I'm sorry. Honestly.'

Why was I apologising to him?

'It doesn't matter, Isobel. It was a great experience.' He grinned. 'For you too, I hope.'

I blushed. 'Yes.'

'And we are friends?'

'I suppose so.'

'In that case, tell me about it.'

'About what?'

'About the man you ran away from. The Irishman.'

'Does there have to be one?'

'Oh, come on, Isobel. Everyone knows that there was something!'

'Did Gabriela—?'

'Gabriela said nothing. But we're not stupid.'

So much for the Isobel with no history. And so much for my reinvented self – the self I didn't much like anyway. I told him about Tim and me and the wedding. And I didn't care that he regarded me with sympathy afterwards.

'I am not surprised you came to Madrid,' he said. 'We are much nicer men here!'

I laughed, although it hurt my head. 'You are.'

'Isobel, I will not try to get you into bed again. Maybe, in time, you might wish to. If so, I will be here. But I will leave it up to you.'

'Luis, please don't get offended when I say that it'll be a long, long time before I get into bed with anyone again. As long as it'll be before I drink alcohol again.' I stood up and went to the cupboard under the sink. There were six bottles of Rioja in the cupboard. I put them into a cardboard box, along with a bottle of Southern Comfort and a bottle of vodka. 'Take these, please,' I said as I handed him the box. 'I really don't even want them in the apartment any more.'

'You don't think that you have become a little extreme over this?'

'No,' I said. 'I came here to be a different person, Luis, and I became a different person. But I don't like her very much. So if I get rid of these, I get rid of her. Do you understand?'

'I understand,' he said. 'And I hope you get better soon, Isobel.'

'So do I,' I said.

And, when I closed the apartment door after him, I sat down and began to get better.

Chapter 17

Combinations (Salvador Dalí, 1931)

It had been a beautiful day in Madrid. I didn't really want to leave but I'd promised to come home for Ian's birthday in October and I didn't want to break my word. Not that Ian would have cared either way, I suppose, but I knew Mum would be disappointed if I said I wasn't coming. And part of me wanted to see them all again even though another part of me dreaded it.

The plane had begun its descent into Dublin airport. We'd already been told that it was cold and raining and now we were being bumped around as we flew through the heavy clouds. I clutched my armrest and wished that I liked flying.

We shuddered our way downwards, eventually landing with a welcome thud on the runway. The rain splattered against the windows of the plane.

'*Bienvenidos à Dublin*. Welcome to Dublin,' said the stewardess.

'Right,' I muttered as I undid my seatbelt. 'Welcome home, Isobel.'

The airport was crowded. I'd never seen so many people in it before. I looked around for Mum or Dad, but it was impossible to identify anyone in the throng.

'Isobel!' I heard my name before I saw my sister. She was waving frantically at me. I pushed my way through the crowd and hugged her.

'Welcome home,' said Alison. 'I was afraid I'd never be able to see you.'

'I didn't see how I'd pick out anybody in this lot.' I pushed her away from me. 'And I wasn't expecting you.'

'The central heating packed up at lunchtime,' she said. 'Dad is at home supervising the repair-men.'

I shivered at the thought of the house without central heating.

'They've promised it'll be fixed,' said Alison, 'although I don't hold out much hope.'

'You'll certainly feel the cold a lot more,' I told her, 'with your hair like that.'

She grinned at me. 'D'you like it?'

'It's wonderful,' I said. 'You look great.'

She did. She'd had her hair chopped short at the back and full at the front and looked a hundred times more sophisticated than she'd done the last time I'd seen her. She wore black jeans, black boots and a black leather jacket with a smoke-grey fur collar.

'And you've learned to drive too,' I said.

She shook her head. 'Haven't got that far yet. I was going to get lessons but the evenings were too dark and it was raining too much so I thought I'd wait until the spring.'

'Then how are we going to get home?' I asked.

'Peter's driving,' said Alison simply.

'Peter?'

'My boyfriend.' She looked defiantly at me.

'Great,' I said calmly although I couldn't wait to see a boyfriend that Alison deemed worthy enough to drag to the airport on a wet and windy autumn night.

He was waiting for us near the exit. He was tall and fair-haired, with piercing blue eyes.

259

'If you had his children people would think you were Scandinavian,' I murmured when she pointed him out to me.

'Isobel!' She punched me gently in the side. 'I'm not having his children. Don't be stupid.'

She walked up to him and kissed him on the cheek. 'This is Isobel.'

'Hello,' I said.

'Hi.'

Alison linked her arm to his. 'Sorry we took so long. There were thousands of people in there.'

'So I see.'

Taciturn, I thought. It was hard to imagine Alison staying with someone taciturn.

'Would you like me to take your case, Isobel?'

And chivalrous. Well, that was a definite advantage.

'That'd be great.'

'I wouldn't offer,' said Alison. 'She packs bricks in her case.'

'It's OK.' Peter picked it up. 'No problem.'

I was impressed by him. The case weighed a couple of tons.

The rain pelted against the walkway in sheets of water.

'Where did you meet him?' I asked as he paid for his parking ticket.

'Works with me,' said Alison.

'You're not serious!'

'Of course I am.'

'An office romance!' I laughed. 'Alison Kavanagh, the feminist champion, in an office romance.'

'It's not a romance,' she said sharply. 'It's a relationship.'

'That's OK then.' I smothered a smile but Alison didn't notice. She was watching Peter.

He hauled my case into the boot and I clambered into the back seat.

'When did you get your hair cut?' I asked Alison. 'You seem to have left rather a lot of it back here on the seat.'

Peter laughed and Alison giggled.

'That's not hair,' she said. 'At least, not from me. Peter has a Labrador. She sheds.'

'Oh.' I picked clumps of golden fur from my tartan jacket.

'I'm sorry,' said Peter. 'If I'd known I was going to be giving you a lift I'd have cleaned it out a bit. But Alison sprang it on me.'

'Oh, Alison.' I sighed. 'I could've got a taxi, you know.'

'It's no problem,' Peter assured me. 'We were going out tonight anyway.'

'I don't think you would have chosen a night at the airport,' I remarked.

'You'd never have got a taxi tonight,' said Alison. 'Not in this weather.'

I pulled my jacket more tightly around me. I was cold. And the sound of the rain against the windows made me shiver. I thought of my friends in Madrid and how they'd be crowded into Leon's Tapas Bar or eating dinner in one of the millions of cheap and cheerful restaurants they frequented and I missed them.

∽

The central heating was fixed. The hallway was warm. Not very warm, but warm enough. Mum rushed at me almost before I'd crossed the threshold and folded me into her arms.

'Welcome home, darling!' She patted me on the head like a baby. 'It's wonderful to have you back.'

'Thanks,' I mumbled into her blouse 'It's nice to be back.'

'I was afraid your plane would be delayed,' she continued. 'The weather is so awful.'

'It was a bit late,' I admitted. 'But it was good of Peter and Alison to hang around for me.'

'That's OK.' Peter stood in the hall.

'Come in and have a cup of tea, Peter,' said Mum. 'Isobel's right. You were very good to pick her up.'

'I didn't mind,' said Peter.

'Well, take off your jacket and warm yourself inside,' said Mum. 'The heating's been on for about an hour. I was very worried about it. I thought we'd end up wrapped in blankets and eating our dinner in front of the oven for warmth.'

∽

It was strange to be back under their roof. Odd not being in control of my own life. Not being able to lounge around in a T-shirt and nothing else. Not feeling as though I could grab the remote control and turn on whatever programme I liked.

Ian's girlfriend, Honey, called around later that night. She was every bit as beautiful as her photographs suggested, and very intelligent. Ian was besotted by her and I could hardly blame him.

Alison was equally besotted by Peter Gaffney. It was funny to see her face flush whenever his name was mentioned and to discover that she had an entire new wardrobe of sophisticated clothes that she wore when she went out with him.

Ian in love with Honey. Alison in love with Peter. And me, the older sister, far too wise to be in love with anyone.

∽

Ian's party was much better fun than I expected. He'd hired out a room in the local pub and a live band which played seventies hits.

'They're humiliating me,' groaned Alison, nodding in the direction of our parents. 'Dad thinks he is John Travolta.'

'They're having a good time,' I said. 'I think this was a great idea.'

'Oh, Ian's into everything retro these days.' Alison giggled. 'Actually, you're right. It is a good idea. The songs are hilarious!'

'Having fun?' asked Ian as I knocked back a bottle of Ballygowan.

'I haven't had as much exercise in ages,' I told him. 'I'm danced off my feet.'

'You look great.' He grinned at me. 'Alison said you looked like shit when she went to visit.'

'She exaggerated,' I told him.

'She said that you were miserable and that you were drinking too much and eating nothing.'

'She exaggerated,' I repeated.

'Really?'

I sighed. 'I was a bit dodgy for a while, I suppose. I guess I just felt sorry for myself and miserable about everything. But I'm back on track again now. And I'm fine, Ian. Honestly.'

'I believe you,' he said quickly. 'I told you – you look great.'

I was wearing a pair of black jeans that fitted like a second skin and a gold-coloured top that I'd made the previous week. I'd had my hair done before I left Madrid and I knew I looked good. It had been very important for me to look good.

'Ian!' Honey waved at him. 'Come and dance. It's Abba!'

He smiled at me and followed her onto the dance floor. They were a perfect couple.

∽

I sat down at a table near the bar and watched Ian and Honey, Alison and Peter, Mum and Dad as they gyrated to the music. I was glad they were having a good time. Especially Mum and Dad. It was a long time since I'd seen them out enjoying themselves. If I ever thought about my parents' marriage – and I rarely did – I guess I just thought that they cared enough about each other to stay together. I remembered them having a row when I was small. I was in bed, supposed to be asleep. But I hadn't been able to sleep. And then I'd heard raised voices downstairs and I'd tiptoed onto the landing to listen.

'I married you, wasn't that enough?' Dad had demanded. I shivered and pulled my pyjama top around me. I couldn't hear what Mum replied.

'It wasn't my fault,' he said, and his tone was halfway between anger and concern. 'It could have happened to anyone.'

And then I heard my mother and her voice was a wail. 'But it happened to me! I lost my baby. It happened to me.'

I'd run back to the bedroom and pulled the covers over my head. I hadn't known about the lost baby then, about the reason they'd married. And when I found out, years later, I knew that I'd get it right myself. When I got married it would be to the right man, the man who loved me for myself.

∽

'You OK?' Dad sat down beside me.

'I'm fine.'

'You're looking wonderful.'

I smiled. 'Thanks.'

'We've been worried about you.'

'Why?'

'Oh, the way you left, Isobel. Because you were unhappy.'

'Not with you,' I said.

'But unhappy.' He put his arm around me. 'I hated seeing you so miserable.'

'I didn't like it much myself.' I snuggled up to him. 'But I'm over it now, Dad. It's all behind me.'

'And do you like the new job?'

I sat up straight again and nodded. 'They're really good to me. Gabriela's so kind. And the others are friendly.'

'When will you come home?'

'I don't know,' I said. 'Eventually, I suppose.'

'There's no one over there, is there?'

I shook my head.

'Not like you,' he said.

'What d'you mean?'

'Not like you to be without a boyfriend.'

I grinned at him. 'I'm enjoying it.'

'Really?'

'Really.' I kissed him on the cheek. 'I've discovered that I don't need a boyfriend to feel cared about.'

'Of course not,' he said, 'we care about you.'

'I know.' I leaned my head on his shoulder and we sat in companionable silence while the band played 'Mama We're All Crazee Now'.

~

I rang Julie the next day.

'How was the party?' she asked.

'Pretty good. We didn't get home until four.'

'How's the head?'

'Fine.'

'Fine?'

'Absolutely fine. I had a couple of beers and then went on to Ballygowans. So I was OK this morning.'

'That's good.'

'Julie,' I said. 'I mean it. I'm fine.'

She laughed. 'I believe you. When are you calling around?'

'Tonight?'

'Tonight is great.' She cleared her throat. 'There's just one thing, Isobel.'

'What?'

'I'm not on my own.'

I looked at the receiver in puzzlement. Of course she wasn't on her own. At the very least her parents were there too.

'Your parents?'

'I don't mean them, you dope!' she exclaimed. 'God, Isobel, sometimes you're thick.'

'Well, I don't—' Suddenly the penny dropped. 'Andy?'

'Who else?'

'When did he arrive?'

'The beginning of the week. He arrived on the door-step, Isobel.'

'Completely unexpected?'

'Completely. I couldn't believe it.'

'And did he expect you to welcome him with open arms?'

Julie laughed. 'Not exactly. He was sheepish about it really. He brought me a teddy-bear.'

'A teddy-bear!'

'Yes. A huge one. It had a box attached to it.'

'And what was in that?' I asked.

'Another box.' She giggled. 'And another, and another. Until down to the smallest box.'

'Julie!' I knew what was coming.

'It was the most beautiful ring, Isobel. So I tried it on.'

'And are you still wearing it?'

'Of course I am,' she said. 'I love him.'

❧

She looked absolutely radiant. Her hair, nut-brown, almost her natural colour, gleamed in the hall light. Her dress was black silk.

'Looking sharp,' I said. 'Here.' I presented her with some handmade chocolates I'd bought in the Duty Free.

'Oh, Isobel, thank you.' She kissed me on the cheek. 'Come on in.'

'Let me see it.' I grabbed her left hand.

The engagement ring was beautiful. It was a solitaire diamond and it glittered and sparkled on her finger. It was almost as beautiful as my engagement ring had been.

'It's gorgeous,' I breathed. 'Absolutely gorgeous.'

'Thanks.'

'So where is he?'

'In the living room,' said Julie. 'We were watching TV.'

Andy's shoes were upturned carelessly on the carpet and he was half-sitting, half-lying on the sofa. There was a glass of beer and an open newspaper beside him. He swung himself upright when I walked into the room.

'Isobel! It's lovely to see you.'

'Hi, Andy.' I smiled at him. 'Congratulations.'

'Thanks, Isobel. I think I'm very lucky.'

'So do I,' said Julie.

'What made you decide?' I asked.

'I couldn't live without her,' said Andy simply.

Julie beamed.

'Oh, Andy,' I said. 'That's incredibly corny.'

'I know. But it's true.'

'And when did you realise that?'

He thought about it for a moment. 'In work one day. I was sitting at my desk working on a paper and I couldn't concentrate. I kept thinking about Julie. And I knew that I'd be mad to let her go.'

Julie beamed again. 'So he came over to get me.'

'I didn't ring because I was afraid she'd argue with me.' He grimaced. 'Our last conversation hadn't been easy. So I thought I'd surprise her and come over. Hell of a job getting a flight.'

Julie took up the story. 'I was doing my hair and nobody else was in. I'd just started to dry it when the doorbell rang – and there he was.'

'Dripping wet and shivering with cold,' added Andy.

'And a huge teddy-bear, also wet and probably cold.'

'I think you felt sorrier for the bear than me,' said Andy ruefully.

'Well,' Julie grinned at him, 'he did look kind of forlorn.'

'I knew you'd be a sucker for the bear!'

She laughed and turned back to me. 'And Andy looked at me – it was like in a book, Issy— He said that he loved me—'

Andy looked embarrassed. Julie gave him a good-natured push. 'Well, you did. And he asked me to marry him.'

'That's the most romantic thing I ever heard,' I said.

'So I stood looking at him and I couldn't speak,' continued Julie. 'And then he handed me the teddy-bear and the box with the ring.'

'Did it fit?' I asked.

'Isobel!' Julie looked pained.

Andy laughed. 'It's a bit loose. We're getting it sized tomorrow.'

'I don't want to give it to them,' said Julie.

'I'm really delighted for you both,' I said warmly. 'When is the happy day?'

'Next summer,' Julie told me. 'Andy's going to Prague for three months in the New Year and he'll be back and forward to the States for a while after that, so June or July will be the earliest we can reasonably do it.'

'You could always nip in to the register office before then,' I said.

'Isobel Kavanagh! Can you imagine my mother's face if I didn't have a huge, white, fairy-tale wedding?'

'I guess she wants the works?'

'Of course she does,' Julie said. 'She's been waiting for my wedding since I was born! Besides, Andy's family are Greek, after all. They're into big, family affairs.'

'Are they all coming over to Ireland?' I asked.

'I don't know,' said Andy. 'I haven't told them yet.'

'What!!'

He looked sheepish. 'I've told my parents – they expected me for Thanksgiving and I won't be back by then, and Ari knows too, but not the rest of the family.'

'His parents are disappointed he's not marrying a Greek girl. Or an American girl. But they said that maybe Irish was next best.'

I laughed. 'It'll be a great day.'

'I hope so,' said Julie. 'Sit down, Isobel, for goodness sake. Do you want a drink?'

'Southern Comfort would be nice,' I replied. 'A small one, Julie, with lots of ginger.'

She made a face. 'Ruining a good drink.'

'Where's the rest of the family?' I curled up in the big armchair near the fire.

'Visiting Danielle,' said Julie. 'You know what she's like – loves entertaining. She's been watching one of those TV cook programmes and she wants to experiment on them. I'm in her bad books because I said that you were calling around. I told her that Andy and I would visit later in the week. I just couldn't cope with the idea of my parents, my sister, three brothers and their assorted families in one house.'

'Would have been a good introduction for you, Andy,' I remarked.

'I wouldn't have minded.' His tone was brave. 'I like families.'

'So do I,' said Julie. 'But *en masse* the Donegans can take a bit of getting used to.'

We sat back and she turned up the volume on the TV. *True Lies* had just started. It was one of my favourite Arnie movies. And Andy said that Jamie Lee Curtis had the most perfect body in the world.

I sipped my drink and helped Julie demolish the top layer of a box of Ferrero Rocher while Arnie saved Jamie Lee and possibly the free world as well.

'Brilliant,' pronounced Julie when it was over. 'Totally implausible, of course—'

'Never.' Andy grinned at her.

'Not Arnie,' she said. 'Nor the plot. I'm talking about Jamie Lee's stomach. No woman can have a concave stomach after the age of about seventeen!'

'I didn't even have one then,' I muttered. 'And I've blown any chance of looking concave by eating all those chocolates.'

'In that case a slice of fruit cake won't do any more damage,' said Julie. 'Come into the kitchen with me,

Issy. I'll make some coffee. You'll be OK here on your own, won't you, Andy?'

'I'll simply count the moments until you return,' he told her solemnly.

Julie spooned Costa Rica into the filter. The diamond glittered in the kitchen's spotlights.

'It's a fabulous ring,' I told her. 'Really it is.'

She smiled with self-satisfaction. 'I know. I'm so lucky, Isobel. I can't really believe it.'

'You didn't think of saying to him that you had to think things over?' I asked.

'Are you mad?'

'Because you said that to me when we were in Sitges. "If that shit ever calls me again I'll get someone to tell him that I need to think about talking to him".'

'He didn't telephone,' she reminded me. 'He came in person.'

I took three cups out of the cupboard. 'I suppose he did.'

'And I do love him.'

'I can see that,' I said. And I could. It was in all the little things. The way they shared a look, a private understanding, the way they thought of themselves as one unit. I'd felt like that when I was with Tim. I knew what she meant. The pain grabbed me so suddenly that I almost cried out.

'I'm just nipping up to the loo,' I said.

'Sure.' She placed slices of cake onto a gold-rimmed plate.

I sat on the toilet seat, bent over, my head resting on my knees. The pain that I felt wasn't the pain of losing Tim, it was the pain of jealousy. I couldn't believe that I felt like this. Jealous. Of my best friend. Jealous because she loved someone and he loved her and because I was alone. It was so stupid. So childish.

I was over Tim. I was over all that stuff. I shouldn't feel like this.

But I couldn't help it.

If it had worked out then maybe by now I would have had a child of my own. We would have been a family. Tim and Isobel Malone and our baby. You fool, I told myself, sitting upright. A child of your own and you're behaving like a baby yourself. Snap out of it, Isobel.

Someone once told me that envy was the most wasteful of emotions. I reminded myself of that as I sat down with Andy and Julie and tried to make myself not care.

Chapter 18

Pierrot & Guitar (Salvador Dalí, 1924)

I sat under the shade of a tree in the Retiro Park and leafed through *Hola!* I read *Hola!* to improve my Spanish, not for the gossip and the pictures of the Infanta Elena on the beach in Corsica. If there were pictures I was interested in, they were the ones of Leonardo Di Caprio, looking tanned and healthy as he went to a film première. He's too young for you, Isobel, I told myself mournfully. Too young and too far away.

I yawned. I'd been out with Barbara and Bridget the previous night and it had been late when I got back to the apartment. I didn't go out with them very often any more, but we still got together occasionally and last night had been to celebrate Bridget's pregnancy.

Pregnant, I thought. This time last year she didn't even know Tomás and now she was having his baby. Tomás and Bridget lived in an apartment on the other side of town. I'd been there a few times since they'd married. It had been a shock the first time I'd gone. I'd been used to the chaos that was the apartment she'd shared with Barbara – dirty dishes piled into the sink, mounds of ironing heaped into an armchair and knickers hanging over the shower-rail to dry. But her apartment now was absolutely gorgeous. It had polished wooden floorboards, brightly coloured rugs that she'd brought back from their honeymoon in Mexico and modern furniture that could have looked out of place in the old-fashioned building, but somehow didn't. Every time I came back to my apartment I felt as though I'd stepped into some tacky time warp. The furniture was too big and too heavy, the floor tiles were old and needed to be replaced and I didn't have any meaningful knick-knacks lying around that would underline my sense of style and sophistication.

The apartment was boring.

Barbara had suggested I move in with her when Bridget got married, but I'd declined. There weren't as many parties these days, but I didn't think it would be a good idea to live with Barbara. Besides, I was used to living on my own now.

A warm breeze rustled the leaves on the tree. Quite suddenly, winter was over and the cold air had given way to the unexpected warmth. The Madrileños were still bundled up in coats and hats, but I wore jeans and a sweatshirt and didn't care that they probably thought I was a tourist.

The park was crowded. Everyone had taken advantage of the warmth to get out into the air. Balloon sellers and popcorn sellers, guitarists and flautists, families and couples all jostled for position on the pathways.

I lay back on the dry grass, put the magazine behind my head and closed my eyes.

I felt very peaceful. I wasn't wishing to be somewhere else, or wishing I was someone else or wishing that my life had turned out differently. I listened to the sounds of the guitar and the laughter of the children and felt the warmth of the gentlest of breezes caress my face, and I felt completely and utterly at ease. It was as though my whole life had been working towards that one moment when everything was exactly as it should be and nothing could be more perfect. I smiled to myself and drifted into half-sleep.

When I sat up again, the guitarists had stopped playing and the children had gone. It was after four but still warm and I was thirsty. And hungry too, I thought, as my stomach rumbled in a very unladylike way and reminded me that I hadn't had anything to eat since eight that morning.

I got up and brushed the grass from my jeans. I ran my fingers through my hair and made my way out of the park. There was a small café near one of the exits. I hadn't felt the slightest bit hungry all day – now, in sight of the café, I felt as though I'd faint if I didn't get some food inside me quickly.

I sat down at a terrace table and ordered coffee and tortilla. Very few other souls were hardy enough to sit outside but I wanted to get the last of the sun. Crazy when, in a few weeks, I'd be doing my best to stay out of it!

The waiter brought the coffee and the tortilla. I took *Hola!* out of my bag and glanced through it again.

I finished my coffee, ordered another, and sat back in the chair. The feeling of peace and tranquillity was still with me. I hadn't felt this good in weeks.

A couple of middle-aged tourists stopped outside the café and unfolded a huge map of the city. They twisted and turned the map until they were satisfied that they knew where they were.

'I *told* you, Gerard.' The woman, thin and angular and wearing a shocking-pink trouser-suit, looked at him impatiently and tapped the earpiece of her sunglasses against her teeth. 'We should have turned *left* when we came out of the park. Now we've gone miles out of our way.'

'Well, it seems bloody silly to me.' Gerard's face was flushed. 'Why did the sign point *this* way to the art gallery?'

'It probably wasn't the same gallery,' said the woman.

'Oh, for God's sake!' Gerard puffed out his chest. His stomach ballooned over his pale grey trousers. 'How many art galleries can they have? The bloody Prado, whenever you think of Madrid you think of the bloody Prado.'

'You're putting me off going to see it,' said his companion.

'Don't be stupid,' said Gerard as he rearranged his camcorder more comfortably across his shoulder. 'We're here, so we'll go and see it. But I bet it's no great shakes. All these places are the same. People talk about them as if they matter, but they don't really.'

Gerard dismissed one of the world's most famous art galleries with a wave of his arm as he and his female companion walked purposefully down the street. If it's Saturday, it must be Madrid, I thought.

I glanced at my watch. I'd been sitting in the café for almost an hour and I supposed that I should do the decent thing, pay my bill and leave. I opened my bag to get out my purse.

I'd brought my deep, capacious duffel bag and it was almost impossible to find things in it. I couldn't find my purse. At first I panicked, visualising myself having to tell the waiter that I'd no money and imagining my now colloquial Spanish deserting me completely as he decided to report me to the police. But I knew that I was being silly – my purse was in my bag, nestling in the folds of the denim fabric.

Only it wasn't. I took out a dog-eared book, my bottle of *Allure*, my keyring, my bottle of Factor 6, my lip salve and some old postcards that I'd bought when I first came to Madrid but had never sent to anyone. There was no sign of my purse.

I clamped down the feeling of panic. All I had to do was remember exactly what I'd done that afternoon, where I'd put the purse. I hadn't needed any money for the metro because I had a multi-journey ticket. I hadn't needed any money in the park either because I'd simply sat under the tree. But I must have brought my purse with me. I never left it behind.

Underneath the bag, I thought suddenly. Maybe I'd slipped it into the little compartment at the base of the bag. I did that sometimes, to keep things safe. I didn't remember doing it with the purse, but I could have done. I unzipped it frantically but the only thing the compartment under the bag contained was a bright pink Tampax container. No purse.

Shit, I thought. Shit, shit, shit.

I put my belongings back into the bag but rummaged around fruitlessly for another couple of minutes before thumping it to the ground in annoyance.

'*Perdone.*'

I looked up. The man standing beside me was smiling slightly. '*Hay un problema?*'

'No.' I smiled brightly at him. '*No problema.*'

He furrowed his brow. 'You are English?'

'No,' I said again.

'*Española?*' He looked at me in surprise.

'No.' I really didn't want to be involved in this conversation.

'*Americana?*' He grinned.

'No,' I said firmly. '*Soy Irlandesa.*'

'Oh.' He smiled at me. 'I have been to Ireland. It is a nice place.'

God, I thought wearily, not now.

'Yes,' I replied. 'It is a nice place.'

'And you are on holiday here?' He sat down on the seat opposite me.

'No,' I said. 'I work here.'

'Really? Do you like Madrid?'

'Very much,' I replied. I wished he would go away. 'If you'll excuse me,' I continued. 'I have to go.'

'Where?' said the Spaniard. 'You don't have the money to pay your bill.'

I stared at him in dismay.

He laughed at me. 'But of course you don't. I see you making the pantomime. The pieces out of your bag. Your book. Your perfume – nice perfume. Your keys.' He shrugged. 'It is not difficult to see that you have no money.'

'I must have lost my purse.' It sounded feeble, even to me.

'But of course.' He smiled. 'No girl would come into a café and order a meal for which she cannot pay.'

I gasped. Did he think that I was actually some sort of criminal? Did he think that I made a habit of going into places and running off without paying?

'I assure you, I thought I had my purse with me.' I sounded like an old maid.

'Easy mistake,' he said. 'And I'm sure the owner will understand.'

I bit my lip. I was sure that the owner wouldn't.

'So.' He smiled at me again. 'You have a problem.'

'I can explain it to the owner,' I said helplessly. 'It isn't so much money after all.'

'But the tourists, they try this all the time,' said the Spaniard.

'Don't be ridiculous.' I looked angrily at him. 'They don't.'

'All the same.' He shrugged again. 'Perhaps you should let me pay your bill and save some unpleasantness.'

I'd guessed that was coming. 'It's quite all right,' I said pertly. 'I can give *el Señor* my name and my address and I will come to him tomorrow with the money.'

'I suppose so,' he said. He raised an eyebrow. 'But it would be easier for me to pay for you.'

I sighed. 'I couldn't possibly allow you to do that.'

'Why not?'

'Because I don't make a habit of allowing strange men to buy me things,' I said sharply.

He laughed. A real laugh. The laughter made him seem less threatening and more like a helpful stranger. I realised that he was younger than he'd first seemed – his early thirties perhaps? It was hard to tell for certain. His eyes were hidden by a pair of fashionable sunglasses. His skin was olive, his hair black and he was certainly attractive. Not quite my long, lean man, he was too broad-shouldered for that – but there was something about him . . . I blinked to stop myself thinking about him like that. He wore jeans, a sweatshirt with a print of a Joan Miró painting, and had a tan leather jacket around his shoulders.

'You sound like someone from a nineteen-sixties movie,' he said. 'Audrey Hepburn perhaps. Although you do not look fragile enough for Audrey Hepburn. But you have the same kind of eyes.'

I almost smiled. 'Don't be stupid.'

'I'm not being stupid,' he said. 'You are the one who's being stupid. Come on.' He raised his hands expressively. 'Let me pay for your snack and you can go home. *No problema*.'

'I really don't think—'

'I know I'm a strange man.' I knew he was mocking me. 'But I will properly introduce myself to you and then I will not be so strange.' He held out his hand to me. 'Nicolas Juan Carlos Alvarez,' he said. 'But my friends call me Nico.'

I took his hand and shook it. His grip was firm and decisive, his palm dry.

'It's very nice of you to make the offer, Señor Alvarez. But I really think—'

'Don't think,' he said. 'Just act.'

I looked at him doubtfully. 'I would repay you, of course.'

'Of course. But quite unnecessary.'

'I didn't do this deliberately.'

'Why would you?' he asked. 'You could not be sure that someone like me would be at hand.' He took off his sunglasses and his brown eyes twinkled at me.

It was like a jolt, the sudden surge of physical attraction that hit me. I felt my stomach heave as though I was in a lift that had suddenly gone down. My mouth was dry. I couldn't believe that this was happening to me. I swallowed a couple of times and looked down at the table.

'So, it is OK. I will pay for you.' His voice seemed to come from miles away.

'OK,' I croaked.

He motioned to the waiter who, eyeing me curiously all the time, brought my bill.

'Is that it?' Nicolas looked at me in amusement. '*Dos cafés y una ración de tortilla?*'

'I wasn't very hungry.' I glanced at him, unwilling to look him in the eye.

Suddenly he was serious. 'You *are* working here?' he asked. 'You are not a student with nowhere to go?'

'Of course not,' I said impatiently. 'I'm telling you the truth when I say that I forgot my purse. Or lost it, perhaps, in the Retiro Park.'

'You were in the park today?' he asked.

I nodded.

'Me too,' he said.

'Good for you.' I wished that the waiter would take the money so that I could leave.

'So.' He sat back in the seat and looked at me appraisingly. 'What is your name, *Irlandesa*?'

'*Me llamo Isobel*,' I told him.

'*Isabella*.' He rolled the name around in his mouth, making music out of each syllable. '*Isabella*.'

'No,' I corrected him. 'Isobel.'

He smiled slightly. '*Isabella* is prettier, *Irlandesa*.'

'Whatever.' I shrugged

'OK,' he said. 'And what are you doing here in Madrid, *Isabella*?'

The waiter returned and I sighed with relief. Nicolas took out a wallet and overtipped hugely.

'I must be going,' I said. 'It was very good of you to help me out like this, Señor Alvarez, and I'm extremely grateful. I'll send the money to you here.'

'Don't be absolutely ridiculous,' he said and his voice was angry. 'I don't want you to repay me. It is only a portion of tortilla after all!'

'OK.' I didn't want to argue. 'Then can I say thank you very much and goodbye?'

He looked at me for a moment and then smiled. 'Of course. It was very nice to meet you, Isabella.'

'And I'm glad you were here to save me from being arrested,' I said. I slung my bag over my shoulder. 'I must get home now. *Adiós*.'

'*Adiós*.'

I walked down the street without turning back. But I knew that he was watching me. I could feel his eyes on me until I turned the corner into the shade.

～

The purse was sitting on the darkwood table. I still

didn't remember leaving it there. I shook my head at my absentmindedness and opened it to check that I actually had money in it. A small bundle of notes was squashed into the front compartment.

I filled the coffee pot with water and lit the gas. Now that I was at home, alone, I felt safe from any sudden surges of physical desire and I thought that perhaps I had been rude to Nicolas Alvarez. But it was because he was so attractive, because I'd been so surprised by my own reaction. So I'd lashed out, even though there was no need. Because he wasn't trying to pick me up – there was no need for me to flatter myself like that. He'd seen me obviously distressed, having lost my purse. He'd assumed I was a tourist and he'd decided to help.

And I'd behaved childishly. Because I was attracted to him. Not in the way I'd been attracted to the men I'd slept with in my early days in Madrid. Not even in the way I'd been attracted to Luis Cardoso. But in a mind-numbing, electric-shock, scary kind of way. The way I used to be attracted to men. The way I'd first been attracted to Tim Malone.

I shivered. I wasn't interested. Really I wasn't. Nor was I ready. In fact, I didn't think I ever would be ready again. And I was right not to be ready. I had my career to think about. My high-flying career with Advanta Training.

Gabriela had been negotiating to buy a computer company. The owner, Alejandro Juncosa, was still running the company, but Gabriela had assigned Luis and me to work with him. We had a great deal of freedom and responsibility and I loved it. I wasn't going to blow it all on the first man that made me go weak at the knees.

I turned on the TV and flicked through the stations until I reached Sky News. The weather forecast for Spain was warm and sunny. Of course it was warm and sunny. It was that time of year.

He was attractive, though. I could see him quite clearly in my mind's eye. I felt my heart thud again.

No, I said out loud, I wasn't really attracted to him. I was just lucky that he got me out of a tight spot.

I wondered if he went to that café often, if he spent much time in the Retiro Park. He'd been there today, at the same time as me. I wondered what sort of things he liked. Music, perhaps. Did he enjoy the sounds of the classical guitar like I did? Books – but he wouldn't be the sort of man to enjoy gothic tales like *Rebecca* or the very English Jane Austen. He'd like heavy metal and Dean Koontz. Or maybe not. There was the Miró sweatshirt to consider. A man who wore Miró emblazoned across his chest might be an artist at heart himself.

Isobel, I told myself, you are completely insane. Anyway, Miró's art was modern. Nicolas Alvarez could like Miró and Meatloaf.

I went to bed early that night. I decided that I needed my sleep. The strain of working late every evening because we were currently so busy was obviously beginning to tell.

🙝

Every Monday we had a meeting. Gabriela, Magdalena, Alejandro and either Luis or myself got together in the light wood-panelled board room back on the Castellana. Luis and I took it in turns to go to the meeting. When it was about accounts, Luis went; when it was about future courses, I went along.

This morning it was my turn. We went through the courses scheduled for the summer, talked about the successes and failures of the spring agenda and discussed the advertising strategy for the rest of the year.

'Oh, and there's another thing.' Gabriela gathered her

283

papers together. 'We have a table at the industry awards on Friday week. So keep that date free in your diaries.'

I tapped it into my personal organiser. Since buying out Alejandro's firm, we'd become more technology-minded, and we all had electronic organisers. Sometimes I wished I could have kept my battered Filofax, but I had to admit that the organiser was more useful. I could download information from it into my personal computer in the office and I didn't have to thumb through pages and pages of scribbled writing to find things. But I was slower at keying in information than I'd be at simply writing it down.

My diary was getting full for this month. Social butterfly, I told myself as I snapped the organiser shut.

I wondered if I'd have time to make myself a dress for the awards night. I usually made my own evening clothes because at five-foot-one so many off-the-peg dresses didn't fit me properly, but I'd be under a lot of time pressure. I wanted to look good for the dinner, though. It was important for the company.

⁓

I went shopping for material the following evening. Because of the siesta during the day – and even though the department stores stay open the whole day through – many shops stayed open until eight or nine in the evening. After work I hurried along to a fabric shop where I was now quite well known, and bought myself a swathe of deep red, almost maroon, silk.

'It will look wonderful on you,' the sales assistant assured me as she wrapped it in tissue paper.

'I hope so,' I said.

'Oh, absolutely.' She slid the material into a carrier bag. 'And I hope you have a good time at your dinner.'

'Thanks.' I took the bag and walked into the evening sunlight.

'Hi, Isobel!' It was Barbara, laden down with shopping.

'Good God,' I said. 'Buying up the city?'

'New season,' she explained. Barbara was a shopaholic. She couldn't pass by anything that said new without at least trying it on.

'What did you buy?'

'Oh, nothing much. Couple of Mondi skirts. Lovely Max Mara trousers. Fabulous Fendi cardigan.' She was also a designer-label freak.

'Fancy a coffee?' I asked her. 'I was going to catch the last of the sun in the Plaza Mayor and listen to the guitarists.'

'Lovely,' she said, so we headed off for the square.

'*Dos cafés*,' ordered Barbara as she sat back in her chair. 'Oh, God, Isobel, my feet are killing me.'

'What d'you expect?' I asked severely. 'You're walking around in totally unsuitable shoes.'

She laughed. Her shoes were high-heeled and designed for style rather than comfort. 'I know. Still, one must look good, you never know when it might be important.'

'You never know when you might need to sprint down the road either,' I said.

The waiter put two black coffees in front of us.

The Plaza Mayor was filling up. A swarming crowd of football supporters, wearing the rival strips of Madrid's two big clubs, Atletico Madrid and Real Madrid, surged into the square. They were hurling good-natured insults at each other and waving flags. The guitarists, outnumbered, abandoned their music.

'I'd forgotten about this game,' commented Barbara. 'Although how I could when the newspapers have been talking about nothing else for weeks is beyond me.'

'Real will win,' I said confidently. 'Two nil.'

Barbara sighed. 'I couldn't care less.'

'You should go to a match,' I told her. Magdalena, who loved football, had brought me to see Real play a couple of times, and – to my surprise – I'd enjoyed myself.

'The only team I'd ever watch is Liverpool,' said Barbara. 'And even then it's a sacrifice.'

We watched the brightly coloured throng surge through the square.

'*Isabella!*'

I looked around.

'*Isabella!! Qué tal estás?*'

I sat up straight in the chair. Barbara looked at me curiously.

Nicolas Alvarez was carrying a guitar. He wore dusty jeans, the Miró T-shirt and a pair of worn leather shoes.

'You know him?' Barbara eyed me speculatively.

'Not really.'

He stood in front of me. 'How are you?'

'Fine,' I said. 'Thank you.'

His eyes flickered to Barbara who smiled at him.

'This is a friend,' I said. 'Barbara Lane.'

'Pleased to meet you,' he said. 'Nico Alvarez.'

'Pleased to meet you,' said Barbara. 'Would you like to join us? We were just about to order a beer.'

'Thank you.' He pulled up a wicker chair and sat down beside us.

'Are you going to the football?' I asked.

He shook his head. 'No. But there's no point in continuing to play when the plaza has been invaded.'

'Was that you playing the guitar?' asked Barbara. 'It was wonderful.'

'Not just me,' he told her. 'There are three of us. We play sometimes here, sometimes in the park. Sometimes we are very lucky and play at a party or in a hotel.'

I wondered how many times it was him I'd heard play in the park.

'Brilliant,' Barbara said. 'I'd love to be able to play an instrument. And I must have heard you and your pals hundreds of times.'

'Probably,' he said ruefully. 'We play a lot.'

'Isobel, why haven't you introduced me to Nico before now?' Barbara looked innocently at me. 'You know I'm crazy about guitar music.'

I knew nothing of the sort.

'I only met him recently,' I said. 'And I didn't know that he was a musician.'

'Not all the time,' he told me. 'Unfortunately I have also a day job. I work in a pharmaceutical company.'

'That's OK,' said Barbara. 'No musician should have to starve for his art these days.' She beamed at him again. I was getting tired of her beams.

'So did you find your purse?' asked Nico.

I nodded. 'Yes, I'd left it at home. And I'm glad we met because it gives me the opportunity to repay you.' I pulled some money out of my purse.

'Not at all.' Nico waved the proffered notes away. 'You can buy me the beer instead.'

'But—'

'I insist. It was my pleasure to rescue you.'

'Rescue?' Barbara looked at us.

'I was in one of the cafés near the park,' I explained. 'I'd forgotten my purse. Nico paid for me.'

'How chivalrous,' murmured Barbara.

'That's me.' Nico grinned, showing perfect white teeth.

'So tell me.' Barbara moved her chair closer to his. 'Do you give lessons?'

'Pardon?'

'Music lessons. Do you teach people how to play?'

'Oh, no. I don't think I would be good at that.'

'You could be,' she said. 'If you've never tried—'

'I don't have the patience,' he told her.

'That's a shame.' She looked disappointed. 'I would have asked you to teach me.'

I looked at her in astonishment. Barbara learn the guitar! I couldn't believe her.

'If you want to learn I will find out about a teacher for you,' said Nico.

'That's very good of you.' Barbara smiled again.

I wished I could think of something to say but my mind was a complete blank. I'd been totally taken aback by Nico's sudden appearance, and I was shocked to find that, even though he looked hot and scruffy and quite unlike the suave Madrileño of before, I still felt the surge of physical attraction.

'You have been shopping?' His question was directed at both of us.

'Yes,' Barbara answered. 'Spending too much money, as always.'

'And you, Isobel?' He looked at me. 'You had your money with you this time?'

'Yes,' I said.

'What did you buy?'

'Nothing much.' I shrugged. 'Material for a dress I'm going to make.'

'A dressmaker.' He raised an eyebrow. 'I didn't think you were a dressmaker.'

'Only sometimes,' I said. 'Like you only play music sometimes.'

The corner of his mouth twitched. 'And is the dress for you or for someone else?'

'For me.'

'A special occasion?'

'Not really. Work.'

'Where do you work?' he asked.

'A training company,' I answered. 'Nothing very exciting.'

'And you?' He turned to Barbara.

'I teach English at a private college,' she told him.

'Your Spanish is excellent,' he said.

'It should be.' She grinned. 'I feel as though I've lived here for ever.'

'Where do you live?' he asked.

I wondered whether Barbara should tell him. After all, we knew nothing about him. Mum's warnings about crime-filled foreign cities suddenly echoed in my mind. But Barbara had already given him her address. 'Why don't you call in and have coffee sometime?' she asked.

'That's very kind,' he said. 'Do you live there also, Isobel?'

I shook my head.

'Where do you live?' he asked.

It would be rude not to tell him, but I still wasn't sure. 'Edificio Gerona.' The name of the apartment block was suitably vague. There were probably hundreds of Edificio Geronas in Madrid.

Nico glanced at his watch and finished his beer. 'It was very good of you,' he told us. 'But I must go.'

'Don't forget, call in to see me,' said Barbara.

'Of course.' He smiled at her.

I sighed.

'What a gorgeous man,' she breathed as he disappeared into the crowd. 'Why didn't you tell me about him before?'

'Because there was nothing to tell,' I said. 'I bumped into him. He paid my bill. He was very nice. That's it.'

'Isobel!' She looked at me in exasperation. 'I know you've been a bit on the quiet side these last few months but I can't believe you'd pass that one up.'

'Oh, come on, Barbara. He's a scruff.'

'You don't mean that,' she told me shrewdly. 'You're just saying it. You must know that he's the sexiest man to walk the streets of Madrid.'

'I admit that he's attractive,' I said. 'But I think you're getting carried away.'

'I hope I am,' she said. 'In those arms. No problem.'

I laughed. 'You're mad.'

'Not at all,' said Barbara. '*You* are for letting me meet him. I think he's absolutely fantastic.'

'Barbara, you've only spoken to him for about five minutes,' I objected.

'I only need five seconds. And that's rich coming from the girl who—'

'Barbara, please!' I interrupted her.

'Oh, come on, Isobel. Admit it. You're thinking about what it would be like with him!'

'I'm thinking nothing of the sort,' I said sharply.

She made a face but said nothing. I drained the cold dregs of my coffee.

'*Do* you fancy him?' She looked at me questioningly.

'He's attractive, I admit that.' I tried to grin at her. 'But I'm off men at the moment, Barbara. I'm much too busy in work.'

'Oh, work,' she said dismissively. 'There are much more important things in life than work!'

❧

There was no point in being interested, I told myself, as I lay in bed that night. I didn't want any more one-night stands. And a man as attractive as Nicolas would have had hundreds of one-night stands, I was certain of that. The next time I got involved with someone I wanted to be sure it was for ever. And, since nobody could be sure, I wasn't ever going to get involved.

It was easier that way. Much easier.

Chapter 19

Still Life with Bread and Fruit Bowl (Pablo Picasso, 1909)

The good thing about my office in the building where Luis and I worked since the takeover of the computer company, was that it had a tiny bathroom en suite. This meant that I could have a shower in the middle of the day when it got uncomfortably warm or that I could shower and change before going out in the evenings whenever I was working late.

I worked late on the day of the awards dinner. We all did, because it was the last day of a three-month course which had been hugely successful.

I stood in the blue and white bathroom and wrapped my towel around me. I should have been thinking about the dinner but I was thinking about Nico Alvarez. I was annoyed with myself for thinking about him, as though I was sixteen again with a crush on someone totally unsuitable. But I just couldn't get Nico out of my head. Maybe it was just pique because Barbara had thrown herself at him. Maybe I just wanted to see if I could still attract men. But that was stupid and childish and thinking that way made me more annoyed than ever.

I was fastening the clasp of my pearl necklace when Luis knocked on the office door. 'Are you dressed?' he called.

'Of course.'

'Shame.' He poked his head around the door. 'Oh, Isobel, you look lovely.'

'Thank you.' I turned around to show him the dress. I was pleased at how it had turned out. The deep red silk fell in gentle folds around me and the colour flattered my skin tone.

'I know that I'm not much good at clothes,' he said. 'But that's very pretty.'

'I'm glad you like it.'

'I wish my clothes looked half as well,' Luis complained. 'I can't seem to get anything to hang right on me.'

'Idiot,' I said, and straightened the jacket of his tux so that it didn't look as though he'd just slung it on.

'Thank you,' said Luis. 'Shall we go?'

We walked out into the warm evening air. It seemed a pity that we would have to go inside again.

We were late arriving at the hotel. Gabriela was in the foyer, wineglass in her hand, chatting to a number of men.

'Sorry we're late,' said Luis as she caught his eye. 'We took a taxi and the traffic was terrible.'

'You should have walked,' said Gabriela. She detached herself from the group and we strolled further into the hotel. 'I was so bored listening to them! Where's Alejandro?'

'He had to go home first,' I told her. 'He said he'd be here soon.'

'OK.' Gabriela tapped on the edge of her glass. 'You all know the people at our table – Juan Perez, Alberto Martinez, Stefano Santiago and Salvadore Costa. They're our best clients so I want you to be very nice to them.'

'Of course we will,' I told her. 'And I promise not to say a word when Alberto tells me that I have breasts like soft round peaches.'

'Isobel! He didn't say that, did he?'

'Not to me personally.' I grinned at her. 'He was on the phone to someone in his office and I heard him say it. He mentioned the *Irlandesa pequeña* so I knew it was me he was talking about.'

Luis laughed and Gabriela smiled hesitantly. Just then, Alberto arrived and I had to struggle to keep a straight face.

Alejandro and Magdalena arrived just as we were getting ready to go in for dinner. Like Luis, Alejandro wasn't much of a man for business suits, but unlike Luis his tuxedo fitted him perfectly and he'd gelled his black wavy hair so that it stayed neatly in place instead of flopping around his face as it normally did.

'He looks great, doesn't he?' I hissed at Magdalena as we were sitting down.

'Yes,' she said primly.

'I didn't notice how attractive he was before. Very sexy!'

She flushed and unfolded her napkin.

I stared at her, realisation dawning. 'Magdalena! Are you and Alejandro—?'

'Not exactly.'

'Then what, exactly?'

'Isobel!' She looked pleadingly at me. 'I don't know. He asked me if I'd meet him for a drink before the dinner. I said OK.'

'You little witch.' I grinned at her.

'It might be nothing.' Magdalena shrugged but her eyes twinkled.

What was it about working in an office, I wondered, that made people throw themselves at each other? At least I'd never gone out with anyone I'd worked with. Luis didn't count. That night had been a total aberration. And besides, he was still going out with Maria Turo.

It was a boring evening. I listened to the speeches and heard people congratulating themselves and each other and I thought that I'd fall asleep.

Then they announced the winner of the 'Businessperson of the Year' award and we were all amazed to hear Gabriela's name.

She was too. I always thought that people knew they'd won awards in advance so that they had time to prepare a speech and thank everyone in the company, but Gabriela was completely taken by surprise. She blinked a couple of times and looked around as though there might be another Gabriela Suarez in the room. Then everybody at our table started to clap and Gabriela walked up to receive a magnificent cut-glass bowl.

'I am honoured,' she said, her voice shaking. 'And this award is so totally unexpected.' She grew in confidence as she stood there. 'I started my company fifteen years ago and I employed one other person. Now, we have over twenty people working with us full-time and we have many others on seasonal contract work. I am delighted that the hard work of all these people is being recognised and that the name of our company is so well respected. It gives me great pleasure to accept this award on behalf of everybody connected with us. Thank you very much.'

We all stood up and applauded her again. It was very emotional, even though a few minutes earlier I'd been thinking what a load of rubbish all these awards were. Photographers took pictures of Gabriela shaking hands with the mayor and with other business people and she was beaming with pride when she came back to the table.

'Congratulations!' Our clients were thrilled to be at our table.

'Well done, Gabriela!' Luis kissed her on each cheek.

'Wonderful,' I said.

'You are superb,' Magdalena told her.

She put the glass bowl in the centre of the table. I was pleased to discover that it was Waterford crystal.

A waiter appeared with a bottle of Dom Perignon and fluted champagne glasses. We toasted Gabriela and the company and our clients and ourselves and I was proud to be part of it all.

⁓

'I'm just sorry that Alfredo couldn't be here,' said Gabriela later that evening as we sat around the table relaxing. Most of the clients had gone home, a few still hung around the bar. 'He would have been so proud.'

'Why didn't he come?' asked Luis.

'He hates this sort of thing,' she replied. 'He hates wearing suits and dressing up and being nice to people.'

'Don't blame him really.' Luis had undone the top button of his shirt and his bow tie hung around his collar. 'It's unnatural to get dressed up like this.'

'But I'm sure he'll be disappointed when you get home and he realises he missed it,' said Magdalena.

'I guess so.' Gabriela refilled her glass with champagne. 'Yes, you are right, Magdalena, he will be disappointed.'

'That's why it's better to go out with someone in business yourself,' said Magdalena. 'So that they know how things work.'

I caught her eye and she looked away in confusion while Alejandro sipped champagne, completely unperturbed.

'Alfredo knows,' commented Gabriela darkly. 'That's why he doesn't come.'

'I suppose you don't go to vets' conventions,' said Luis.

'He's never asked me.' Gabriela sounded amused. 'And he's never invited his patients to dinner either!'

We laughed at the thought of cats and dogs sitting around Gabriela's highly polished mahogany dining-table.

'Oh, I am so tired!' Magdalena leaned back in her chair and closed her eyes. 'It has been a very busy week.'

'You're right,' Alejandro agreed with her. 'Tomorrow night I'll be sitting in front of TV and nothing will make me move.'

'Me too,' said Gabriela.

'I'm cooking dinner for Maria,' said Luis. 'But then I think we'll just watch a video. If she's expecting a lot from me she'll be very disappointed.'

'She won't be the first girl you've disappointed.' Magdalena grinned and nudged him in the ribs.

'That's very unfair,' said Luis. 'I've never had a complaint!'

'What about you, Isobel?' asked Gabriela. 'Have you anything exciting planned for tomorrow?'

'I need to go shopping,' I said. 'We've been so busy lately I've been living on frozen dinners from the supermarket. And the apartment is a mess. So I'll be very domesticated and tidy it up.'

'How awful for you!' Luis made a face at me. 'Shopping and tidying your apartment.'

'I know it's dull,' I said. 'But it has to be done.'

'Thank goodness I have someone to do it for me,' said Gabriela. 'I really couldn't face wandering around the house with a duster and polish after a night like tonight.'

I grinned at her. She'd drunk lots of champagne as people came up to the table and toasted her again and again. Her face was pink and her eyes were bright.

'So you can sit back and savour your fame,' I said.

'I can't exactly sit back.' She made a face. 'I'm taking the children to see their grandparents tomorrow. My brother will be there with his children too. It will probably be manic.'

'Poor thing,' teased Magdalena.

'That's what you get for being married with children,' I said lightly.

'Oh, I don't know,' said Alejandro. 'I think it might be nice to be married with children.' He glanced at Magdalena and she knocked back her glass of wine.

I looked at my watch. 'I think I'd better go,' I told them. 'I'll see you on Monday. Congratulations again, Gabriela.'

She smiled at me. 'Have a nice weekend, Isobel. And part of the congratulations go to all of you too. I wouldn't have won without your support.'

～

I'd been tired at the hotel but now I was wide awake. I opened the patio door and stood on the balcony of my apartment. The city was almost quiet – I could hear the hum of cars in the distance and the occasional shriek of laughter that wafted on the night air. I wondered who was laughing, what was funny.

I thought of Gabriela and how pleased she'd been about the award, even though she'd tried to be non-chalant about it. It must be wonderful, I mused, to be so successful. So talented and beautiful and happy and brilliant. And to have a husband that adored her and children that she loved. If anyone could have it all, Gabriela did.

I wished I could be like her. I wished I had her determination and her drive. I wished I knew the secret of her success.

∽

I pulled a shapeless white T-shirt over loose emerald-green jersey shorts and slipped into a pair of flat canvas shoes. I looked at myself in the long mirror in the hallway of the apartment. I wasn't at my best this morning.

I'd drunk very little at dinner the night before. A few glasses of wine and a glass of champagne. And lots of water. I'd even had more water before I'd gone to bed. But I'd slept badly and had woken up at six in the morning wheezing and coughing. The wheezing had eased after a couple of puffs on my inhaler, but I hadn't managed to go back to sleep. And now I looked tired. I should make the effort, I thought. I should change into something smarter and then I'd automatically feel better. Slap on a bit of make-up too, maybe, even though I never wore make-up on Saturdays. But I couldn't be bothered. It was only the supermarket after all.

I grabbed my inhaler and shoved it into the pocket of my shorts. My breathing was OK now, but I still didn't feel quite right and I didn't want to get caught out gasping for breath on the side of the street. I never thought about my asthma until it bothered me. And it had bothered me so rarely since I came to Madrid that now, when I wheezed even a little, I noticed it more than ever. Come on, I told myself as I picked up my bag, get on with it.

'*Hola, Isobel!*' Señora Carrasco waved at me as I walked out of the apartment. '*El ascensor – no funciona.*'

I groaned. The lift was always breaking down. And the fifth floor was just that little bit high for trekking up and down the stairs. I took it slowly and my breathing was OK.

Once I was outside I felt better. I walked on the shady

side of the street to the corner shop where I always did my shopping. I liked the corner shop. It was a little family-owned supermarket and the husband and wife were very friendly. Señora Ferrer smiled at me as I walked in.

It was blissfully cool and dark inside. I'd made out a shopping list but, typically, I'd left it sitting at home on the table. I wandered along the aisles, putting things into my wire shopping basket at random, trying to remember what I actually needed. Bathroom stuff, bread and water, I had to get water. That was important. I put a couple of litre bottles into the basket. I stopped at the fruit and vegetable display. My consumption of fresh fruit had gone down lately. Fruit was a good idea. And vegetables. I could make myself pasta and vegetables tonight and have some fruit for dessert.

I picked up a shiny purple aubergine and turned it around in my hand.

'*Hola, Isabella.*'

I turned around so quickly I made myself dizzy. I stumbled for a moment and Nico Alvarez caught me by the arm. 'Are you OK?'

'Yes,' I said. 'Yes, I'm fine.'

'Are you sure? You are very white.'

I smiled at him, a feeble smile. 'Only because I've been out late.'

'Oh,' said Nico. 'Anywhere nice?'

I put the aubergine into my basket. 'Dinner.'

'I see.'

'With the people from work. It was a business dinner.' I wondered as I talked why I felt the need to explain to him.

He nodded. 'And *you* had a good time?'

'It was OK,' I said.

I added peaches, plums, a bunch of black cherries and

a huge green watermelon to the basket. It was too heavy to hold.

'Let me,' said Nico.

He put the fruit into brown-paper bags and weighed it.

'Are you going to eat it all yourself?' he asked.

'Not tonight,' I said faintly, shuddering at the thought.

He grinned at me. 'Just as well.'

I queued at the checkout. I wished I hadn't bought toilet rolls and deodorant. They were such personal types of purchases it was embarrassing to see them moving slowly along the little conveyor belt.

I packed my shopping into my straw basket. The watermelon didn't fit.

Nico took the basket and the watermelon from me.

'I can't ask you to carry them,' I protested.

'You did not ask,' said Nico. 'I'm carrying them anyway.'

I didn't object. Anyhow, I wasn't sure I wanted to. I trailed behind him as he walked back to the apartment. He knew exactly where he was going.

'Edificio Gerona,' he said as we arrived.

'The lift – *no functiona*,' I said. 'And I live *en el quinto piso*.' I was gibbering.

'I'll bring them upstairs.' Nico had already started to climb them and, once again, I followed him.

Señora Carrasco was polishing the number on her apartment door. She beamed at me and at Nico. I was sure that she'd launch into conversation but she said nothing beyond an interested hello.

I pushed open the apartment door. Nico stood outside.

'I suppose you should come in,' I said. I knew I didn't sound very welcoming.

'It's OK.' Nico put my shopping in the tiny hallway. 'I will be going now.'

'Thank you for carrying the things for me.' I didn't know how to behave, that was the problem. I didn't know what to say, what to do.

'It was no trouble,' he said.

'All the same—'

'I got you at a weak moment.' He smiled at me.

'I – maybe.'

'Anyway, you have everything you need?'

'Yes. Thank you.' I smiled feebly at him. 'I'm glad I bumped into you.'

'Bumping into me twice was accidental.' He grinned. 'A third time? I don't think so. I came looking for you.'

'Looking for me?' I stared at him.

He pushed his hands into the pockets of the loose trousers he wore. 'You were already halfway down the street when I saw you. I called, but you didn't hear me.'

'Sorry,' I said. 'I was in a dream. Why did you come looking for me?'

'I thought, perhaps, you might like to come out with me.'

I blinked. He'd come looking for me. To ask me out. I swallowed hard. I couldn't go out with him.

'It's very nice of you, but—'

'But what?'

'But I'm not going out with anyone right now.'

'That's convenient,' said Nico. 'It means you can come out with me and not feel badly about it.'

'No,' I said. 'I mean, I'm not going out with anyone at all.'

'Why?' he asked.

'It's just – I don't think – I'm not ready to go out with anyone.'

'You're not ready?' He looked at me curiously. 'In what way are you not ready, Isabella?'

I didn't know what to say. I couldn't say I wasn't ready

because I didn't want to get involved with someone. Least of all him because I was attracted to him. It sounded ridiculous.

'Oh, Isabella, I won't bite, you know. Perhaps you would like to come to dinner with me. Or we could go to the movies together. Or have coffee. Would you like that? Just coffee?'

I swallowed. I wanted to say yes but I was afraid.

'What is the matter?' he asked gently. 'What are you afraid of?'

'Nothing,' I said. 'Nothing. I'm not afraid.' I laughed. 'Why would I be afraid? I'd love to have coffee with you.'

'This evening?'

'I can't this evening,' I said hastily. 'I've things to do. Not this evening.'

'Tomorrow then?'

I stared at him.

'That is OK?' he asked.

'Yes,' I said. 'Tomorrow is OK.'

'Perfect.' Nico Alvarez smiled at me. 'I will pick you up tomorrow. Eight thirty?'

'Yes,' I said. 'Eight thirty.'

'Excellent. I will go now, Isabella, and leave you to unpack your shopping. Unless you wish me to help?'

'No,' I said hastily. 'No, I can manage. Thank you. I'll see you tomorrow.'

'*Hasta pronto*,' said Nico and kissed me, quickly, continental-style on both cheeks.

I stood in the centre of my apartment, surrounded by shopping, and held my hands to my burning face.

Oh God, I whispered to myself, please let me not make another mistake. Please.

Chapter 20

The Enigma of Desire (Salvador Dalí, 1929)

The girl in the Irish pub was singing 'Nothing Compares 2 U' in the haunting style of Sinéad O'Connor. She held the mike so close to her lips that I could hear each intake of her breath. The melody plucked at my heart and sent shivers down my spine.

'Are you cold?' asked Nico.

I shook my head. 'No. I'm fine. Thank you.'

He smiled at me. 'OK. What would you like to drink, Isabella?'

'A fruit juice would be nice,' I said. 'Orange.'

'*Zumo de naranja*? Are you sure?'

'Yes. Absolutely.'

'OK.' He went up to the bar and left me sitting at the wooden table in the corner.

The pub was crowded. Old metal Guinness signs decorated the walls alongside ads for Tullamore Dew and Jameson. Pottery jars and glass bottles, cream, brown and green, were ranged on high shelves and one wall was given over to a mural of the Lakes of Killarney. The atmosphere was vibrant and the crowd was young.

'I like this place.' Nico placed my glass of juice carefully on the table in front of us.

'I've never been here before,' I said.

'No?' He looked at me in amazement. 'But it is very popular with the Irish people.' He laughed. 'With the Spanish people too!'

'I don't know many Irish people here,' I told him. 'And I usually go to a tapas bar or pavement café with my friends from work.'

'I see.' He took a sip from the pint of Guinness he'd brought back for himself.

'Do you like it, Nico?' I asked curiously.

'Yes,' he said. 'I've been here a number of times before. And I always drink the Guinness. I must have Irish blood, Isabella.'

'My name is Isobel,' I reminded him.

He was silent for a moment and I couldn't think of anything to say to fill the gap.

He'd picked me up from the apartment half an hour earlier and we'd caught the metro to the pub. We'd hardly spoken on the journey. He'd said that I looked beautiful (which was an exaggeration because I was wearing my black jeans, a black cotton top and a light jacket and looked neat, not beautiful); I'd said that I was pleased to see him. And then we travelled in silence to the pub.

Silence didn't seem to bother him. He hadn't made any effort to talk to me then and he wasn't rushing to speak now either. I wondered if he was already regretting his invitation.

The girl finished singing and everyone applauded.

'She was very good,' said Nico. 'A wonderful voice.'

I nodded my agreement. 'It would be nice to have a voice like that.'

'Do you sing, Isabella?'

I laughed. 'No. I can empty a room in ten seconds when I sing.'

'Do you play an instrument?'

I shook my head. 'The only thing I can play is my CD.'

'That's a pity.'

'I like music,' I assured him. 'I'm just no good at it myself.'

'Who is your favourite composer?' asked Nico.

My favourite composer, I thought wildly. I didn't know any composers. I knew bands – Oasis or Blur or the Cranberries – but I couldn't differentiate between Beethoven or Bach. In fact I couldn't think of a composer's name besides Beethoven or Bach.

'Isabella?'

'I don't really have a favourite composer.'

'I will compose something for you, then I can be your favourite.'

I smiled uncertainly. 'Do you compose a lot?' I asked.

'Not exactly.' He ran his fingers through his hair. 'I'd like to be a really good composer, but I don't think I ever will be. And I will admit this to you, *mia Isabella*, but please don't tell anyone else – I compose to make money.'

'But I thought you had a job,' I said. 'You told me before you worked in a pharmaceutical company.'

He nodded. 'The music is a hobby.'

'So you compose songs for your hobby?' I looked at him with interest. 'And you get paid for it? Modern songs?'

He looked uncomfortable. 'No. Not songs.'

'What then?'

'Music for advertising.' He made a face. 'You know, for TV or radio.'

'You mean jingles?'

He nodded. 'Yes. Jingles.'

'Really?' I was intrigued. I'd never thought about anyone sitting down and writing an advertising jingle before. 'Would I have heard them? Are they famous?'

'I cannot say famous,' he said. 'But you have probably heard one.'

'So, Nico, which? Which did you compose?'

He sighed. 'The one for Cocoramba coffee.'

I stared at him. 'Really?'

'Yes.' He looked at me and rubbed his chin. 'You see, not very good.'

'I wouldn't say that,' I told him carefully. 'It certainly sticks in your mind.'

'You see.' He sighed. 'You don't like it.'

I grinned. 'I suppose there's a different set of rules for advertising jingles, Nico. I'm not supposed to like it. Just supposed to remember it. And I do. When I hear it in the morning I can't get it out of my head!'

'I know,' he sighed. 'It was like that when I wrote it. But the company liked it. I have done another one.' He looked at me hopefully. 'I think it is better.'

'Do I know it?' I sat back.

'It's for a perfume,' he said. He cleared his throat, closed his eyes and hummed. The tune was sweet and light.

'That's lovely,' I said.

'Thank you.'

'I mean it. It makes me think of – oh, summer and flowers and birds swooping through the air.'

He smiled. 'I am glad you said about the birds. The perfume is called *Drina*. Short for golondrina.'

'There you are.' I looked at him triumphantly. 'You've succeeded as a composer. I thought of the images you intended. Your music's exactly like a swallow in flight.'

'And what about you?' he asked. 'What do you like to do, Isabella?'

I shivered suddenly. I didn't know what I wanted to tell Nico Alvarez about myself.

'Oh, there's nothing exciting about me, Nico. I don't

do anything creative like play the guitar and write advertising jingles.'

'But you are here in Madrid, not at home in Dublin,' he said. 'Why are you here? For work only? Because you like Spain? Do you have a boyfriend here? Or is there someone waiting for you in Ireland?'

'A lot of questions,' I said.

'You don't have to answer them.' He drained his pint. 'Would you like another drink or would you like something to eat?'

I glanced at my watch. It was nine o'clock. Far too early to eat dinner in Madrid. And I hadn't agreed to go to dinner.

'Another juice would be nice,' I said.

'You would not prefer a glass of wine?'

I shook my head. This was a date, sort of. I didn't want to drink wine and suddenly become mellow and relaxed and start thinking that it would be nice to drag Nico into bed. I didn't trust myself not to think like that when I'd been drinking.

'OK, no problem.'

~

'Here you are.' Nico returned with the juice and another pint of Guinness.

'Thank you.'

He sat beside me, closer to me this time, but forced closer because the pub was even more crowded now.

'Is this really like pubs in Ireland?' he asked.

I looked around and nodded.

'And which do you prefer? This or a tapas bar?'

I shrugged. 'At different times I like them equally.'

'Do you ever get homesick?'

'Why would I get homesick?'

'Family, friends?'

'I talk to my family on the phone,' I said. 'And I've plenty of friends here.'

'It is not easy to find out about you, Isabella.'

'What do you want to find out?' I asked. 'I'll tell you anything you want to know.'

Suddenly he leaned towards me and brushed my hair from my eyes. I jumped.

'I want to know who has treated you so badly that you react like that.'

My heart was hammering in my chest.

'Nobody,' I said. 'And you startled me.'

'I startled you?' He looked at me. 'I moved a piece of your hair, Isabella. I didn't do anything to startle you.'

'Well, you did.' I was shaking and I could feel my lungs begin to tighten. I picked up my bag and took out my inhaler.

'You have asthma?'

'What do you think?' I said tartly, when I'd taken a puff and released my breath slowly.

He grinned. 'I'm sorry. That was a silly question.'

I couldn't help smiling myself, even though I still felt shaky.

'It is bad, the asthma?'

I shook my head. 'Not really. And much better since I came to Madrid.'

'So that's why you are here,' said Nico. 'A health cure.'

'It's not that at all.'

'OK, Isabella. I will stop asking you about things you don't want to talk about.'

We sat in silence. Neither a companionable silence nor a cold silence. Just the absence of talk. I listened to the female singer begging someone to 'Unbreak her Heart'.

Other people had suffered real pain in their lives. Other

women had been beaten by their husbands or betrayed by them. Other women had a right to be unhappy or to recoil when a man pushed hair out of their eyes. I was simply being silly.

'Would you like to go somewhere to eat?' asked Nico.

'Now?' I asked.

'I'm hungry now,' said Nico. 'But if you don't want to, it's not a problem.'

I wanted to but I was afraid to.

'Perhaps not tonight,' he said as I remained silent. 'Perhaps we can leave it for another evening.'

'Perhaps,' I said.

He smiled at me. 'Come on, Isabella. I will take you home.'

The evening air was warm but the breeze was cool. I shivered slightly and buttoned my jacket.

'Soon it will be summer,' Nico remarked, 'and you'll be longing for a cool breeze.'

'I know.' I felt better in the open air. 'But I love the heat, Nico.'

He grinned. 'It's the dry air that's good for your asthma.'

'Actually it's hardly troubled me at all lately,' I said. 'Only if I drink too much.'

'Is that why you drink orange juice?'

I shook my head. 'I just didn't feel like drinking anything stronger tonight.'

'Why?' he asked as we turned onto the main road. 'Were you afraid of what I might do to you if you drank too much?'

'No,' I said. 'I'm not afraid of you.'

'That's something.' He caught me by the hand and dragged me across the street. Horns blared as we reached the opposite pavement. 'Afraid of me now?' he asked. 'Since I nearly got you killed?'

'Terrified.'

He turned towards the metro station.

'I thought I'd walk home,' I said.

'Are you sure?'

I nodded.

'OK.' He fell into step beside me.

'You don't have to walk with me if you don't want to,' I told him. 'I mean, I'd like you to walk with me, but not if it takes you out of your way.'

'I want to walk with you,' he said. 'And I can get a taxi home.'

'Where do you live?' I asked.

'Near the Atocha station.'

'Oh, Nico, that's miles out of your way.'

'It's no problem, Isabella.'

⤴

I liked being with him. People looked at him, I could see that. Women looked at him. He was incredibly attractive. And I couldn't help feeling attractive beside him. I wondered what it would be like to make love to him. Better than the nights with Ignacio. Better than with Stefan. Better than on the swivel-chair with John. Better than Luis. Better than Tim?

I felt myself flush as I thought of Tim. How was it that when I least wanted to remember him, I couldn't help thinking about him? And hating him. And still wishing that I'd married him.

'Edificio Gerona.' Nico stopped outside the apartment building.

'Thanks for walking with me,' I said.

'My pleasure.'

I couldn't ask him in for coffee. I just couldn't.

'Do you think you'll catch a cab easily?' I asked.

'I'm sure I will,' said Nico. 'Or I can get the metro. There's a station just around the corner.'

'Yes,' I said. 'I know.'

We looked at each other in silence.

'Thanks for a lovely evening,' I said.

'Would you like to meet again?' he asked.

'If you like. Yes.'

'I would like to see you, Isabella. When would suit you?'

I needed time. Time to sort out how I felt about this. 'Next week?'

'OK,' said Nico. 'Next week. Only this time I will take you to dinner.'

'All right.' I smiled at him.

'Give me your telephone number,' he said. 'And I will call you.'

I opened my bag and took out a business card.

'*Isobel Ka – van – agh.*' He struggled with my surname. '*Administration Manager.*' He grinned at me. 'An important person, Isabella?'

'It sounds more important than it is,' I said.

He laughed. 'And this is my card.'

'*Nico Juan Carlos Alvarez,*' I read. '*Sales Director.* That sounds very important.'

'We are all sales directors,' he said. 'So I am not very important either.'

'But you are a composer,' I reminded him. 'Not really a sales director at all.'

'And I will compose a song for you,' he told me. 'I promise.'

'Promise me one thing,' I said.

'Anything, *mia Isabella.*'

'Don't compose anything like the jingle for Cocoramba coffee.'

He laughed. I laughed. And we laughed together.

⌒

Everyone from the computer division of Advanta had now moved back to the offices on the Castellana. I liked it there, although I'd grown used to the freedom that working away from Gabriela had brought. Still, it was more convenient to be in the same building. I picked up some reports and brought them into her office.

'I've brought the September lists.' I put the papers on her desk. 'It looks good. But we overlap by one day here—' I pointed it out to her, 'so I think the best thing to do is to get Alejandro to do that day in the office and let Manuel do the course with Crédit Agricole.'

'Have you spoken to Alejandro?' asked Gabriela.

'Not today,' I replied.

'I have.'

'Oh?' She was annoyed about something, I could see that.

'He is leaving us,' she told me.

'What!' I stared at her.

'He feels too constrained here.' Her lips were thin lines of fury. 'He thinks that we are too organised! That it is too planned! I tried to tell him that we are a big company, that we have to be organised, but it is falling on deaf ears with him. He wants to go and write new programs or something silly like that.'

'I see.'

'I thought I was doing him a favour keeping him with the company,' she said. 'Even though he was not always the best person for the job. I know that he prefers doing to training. But his company was a training company! I don't understand it.'

'Maybe he just needs to work on his own,' I told her. 'Maybe that's the sort of person he is.'

'Bah!' She shook her head. I hid a grin. Gabriela's anger was legendary around the company but it rarely lasted. She was the sort of person who got into a complete fury for a while and then forgot about it. She never harboured a grudge, it wasn't in her nature.

'Anyway,' she said more calmly. 'It is not necessarily a bad thing. It gives me the opportunity to change things around again which is something I wished to do.'

'Good,' I said.

'So how do you feel about being the manager of our computer-training division?' she asked.

I stared at her. 'Me? You want me to be the manager?' My voice came out as a squeak.

'Why not?' she asked. 'You know about it. You get on well with people. The clients like you.'

'But me—' I opened and closed my mouth.

'Yes, you.'

'But what about Sofia, or Magdalena, or Luis?' God, I thought, Luis would be furious.

'Isobel, I have chosen you,' said Gabriela. 'Now it is not the usual thing when you have been offered a job to tell the boss that there are three other people in the company who would do it better.'

'I didn't say they could do it better,' I said hastily. 'I just thought . . .' My voice trailed off.

Gabriela smiled. 'I think you will do a good job,' she said. 'And I know that the others will be pleased for you.'

I certainly hoped so. I didn't want to be stabbed in the back.

But when Gabriela made the announcement later in the day, they all congratulated me.

'You deserve it,' said Luis and he sounded as though he meant it.

'Congratulations.' Magdalena kissed me on both cheeks,

although it was Magdalena that I'd been most worried about. I always considered her to be Gabriela's right-hand woman.

'You don't mind?' I asked her privately later.

She smiled at me. 'Not at all. I like working with someone, Isobel, but not being the person in charge. With you, I think it is different. You like telling people what to do.'

Did I? I hadn't noticed. I'd never told people what to do in Delta. Sometimes I'd had to tell them what Barry wanted them to do, but that was entirely different. I hadn't made any decisions myself. But Magdalena was right. I enjoyed working on my own initiative. I grinned to myself as I thought about that. I now had the one key attribute that all employers want – *Must be Able to Work on Own Initiative*. I liked knowing that the ultimate responsibility for getting things right ended with me. I was happy doing things my way.

God, I thought, maybe I've turned into a career woman! Isobel Kavanagh, who'd only wanted to get married and have children, had turned into somebody else without even realising it. I'd reinvented myself after all, but not in the way I'd thought.

❧

I moved into Alejandro's office, changed the pictures to Picasso and Miró, bought some fresh flowers for the vases and sat behind his desk. Power, I thought madly. Power at last!

The strangest part of all was having my own personal assistant. Well, Nina wasn't exactly *my* personal assistant, but she was an office worker who was assigned to computer training and who took my messages when I was out and checked with me before she did anything. So it was almost like having someone looking after me. Nina brought me cups of coffee during the day, although I never asked her to. I didn't like the idea that she felt she should make me coffee. But when I said that to her she told me not to be stupid, she was making some for herself too.

It was Nina who put through the call from Nico.

'It's a man,' she said, 'with a lovely sexy voice, Isobel! And he said it was personal.'

I waited for a moment before I took the call. '*Isobel, dígame.*'

'Hello, Isabella. It's me. Nico.'

'Hi, Nico.'

'I am calling to see if dinner on Saturday night would be OK?'

It sounded pretty good to me. Saturday nights were often lonely nights.

'Where will I meet you?' I asked.

'I will collect you, Isabella.'

'Please don't bother,' I said. 'It's a long way for you, Nico. Tell me somewhere in the centre of the city and I'll meet you there.'

'I'll meet you at Sol metro,' Nico said. 'What time would you like to eat?'

I hadn't quite got into the habit of eating as late as some of the Madrileños. 'Would ten o'clock be OK?'

'Of course,' he said. 'I will see you then.'

'OK,' I said. 'Thanks for calling, Nico.'

'My pleasure, Isabella. Ten o'clock. Saturday.'

'*Adiós,*' I said.

I sat and stared at the computer screen in front of me. My screensaver was a picture of George Clooney. Nico Alvarez made George look plain.

❧

'Hi, Isobel.' Magdalena walked into my office and sat down. 'Are you busy?'

I shrugged. 'Not really. I've got lots of things to do but I can't seem to get to grips with any of them.'

'I know what you mean,' she said. 'I feel very carefree this afternoon.'

'Because Gabriela is in Barcelona.' I grinned at her and she made a face at me.

'Not entirely.'

'Do you want something in particular?' I asked. 'Or just a chat?'

'Nothing special,' she said. 'But I wondered, would you like to come out with us for Sofia's birthday? I thought it would be nice to have a girls' night out. She'll be thirty – she says it's a crisis birthday.'

I laughed. 'Once you get past twenty-one, they're all crisis birthdays. When did you plan to go out?'

'Saturday is the only night we can all make it.' She sighed. 'Everyone seems to be doing so many things these days.'

'But I can't go on Saturday,' I said blankly.

'Can't go?' Magdalena looked at me in astonishment. I was always complaining that my weekends were boring. 'What are you doing on Saturday, Isobel?'

'I – I'm going out already.' I felt my cheeks begin to redden as Magdalena watched me. 'I have a prior commitment.'

'A prior commitment? Like what?'

'I'm going to dinner,' I said.

'Isobel!' Her eyes sparkled. 'With a man?'

'Well, yes, with a man.'

'What man? Who?'

I couldn't help smiling. 'His name is Nico Alvarez. He works for some drugs company and he plays the guitar in his spare time.'

'And is he attractive?'

I thought about Nico, about his black hair and his almost black eyes and his square-cut jawline.

'Oh, yes, Magdalena. He's attractive.'

'Why didn't you tell us before?' she demanded. 'Come on, Isobel. Tell me about him.'

'There isn't much to tell.' I sat back in my chair. 'I met him in a café. Then I met him accidentally in the Plaza Mayor. And he asked me out.'

'And this is your first date?'

'Actually no,' I admitted. 'I went for a drink with him last week.'

'For goodness sake! And you told no one.'

'What was there to tell?' I shrugged. 'It was just a drink.'

'Oh, Isobel, you are so – so Irish! You could have told me about it. I could give you tips on how to be with Spanish men. How to make them love you.'

I laughed. 'I don't want him to love me, Magdalena!'

'But why not?' she asked. 'Everybody wants someone to love them.'

'True,' I said. 'But I want the right person to love me.'

'Maybe this Nico is the right person. You'll have to tell me everything about Saturday night. Where are you going?'

'I don't know yet,' I said.

'Well, don't go to Fernando's because that is where we'll be with Sofia. It wouldn't do to have us cramping your style.'

'Indeed it wouldn't,' I agreed as the phone rang and I picked up the receiver. 'Indeed it wouldn't.'

Chapter 21

Ma Jolie (Pablo Picasso, 1914)

I woke up early on Saturday morning. The sun was barely creeping from behind the building opposite, spilling weak light into the apartment. I pulled the sheet around my head and tried to go back to sleep but it was impossible. I kept thinking about Nico and our date.

I rolled out of bed and pulled on a long white T-shirt. Now that the nights were warmer, I didn't wear any night-clothes in Spain. I poured myself some orange juice and walked out onto the balcony. I loved standing on the balcony, looking out over the city. I wondered if Nico was awake. I leaned over the rail and peered in the direction of the Atocha station, as though there was the remotest chance I could see it!

There was the entire day to get through. I told myself I should just laze around and be relaxed and lovely by ten o'clock that evening, but I wasn't able to laze around. I attacked the apartment, cleaning it so thoroughly that every surface shone. But the smell of disinfectant and wood-polish made me sneeze so violently that I had to go out for a while simply to clear my head.

The city was vibrant and awake. Tourists and Madrileños strolled around the streets and sat out beneath the striped awnings of pavement cafés. It felt good to be alive and good to be part of it.

I window-shopped as I walked, enjoying the feeling of the sun on the back of my neck. I was glad to be here.

I turned a corner and stopped in shock. I had almost walked into a wicker chair outside a café, and, looking inside, I could see Luis Cardoso sitting opposite a stunning blonde. And while I watched, Luis leaned towards her and brushed her cheek with his fingers in a gesture that was both intimate and provocative.

I glanced at my watch. It was only ten o'clock.

Luis looked out of the café window and saw me. I flushed with embarrassment as he raised his hand in a wave and gestured me to come inside. I shook my head. He spoke quickly to the girl in front of him and came out to see me.

'Isobel, this is a surprise!'

'More of a surprise for me,' I said tartly. 'Who's that?'

He looked at me. 'My companion, you mean?'

'Yes, your companion!' I almost spat the words at him.

'Isobel, what on earth is the matter with you? I am with a friend. There is no need for you to react like this.'

'What about Maria?' I asked. 'Does she know you're with a friend?'

'I am no longer seeing Maria,' said Luis evenly. 'So I am perfectly entitled to see whoever else I choose.'

'Oh, Luis.' I felt my face redden again. 'I'm sorry.'

'You know, Isobel, you have the strangest ideas about men and women.' Luis sighed. 'You seem to think that we should all be joined to each other by the hip. And if we have a relationship with someone, then it must be for ever or else it is a personal tragedy. I went out with Maria for a time. It was a choice whether we would stay together or not. We decided not. *We* decided, Isobel, not *I* decided. And so I am now going out with Anna.'

'Is she Spanish?' I looked over his shoulder to where the blonde was lighting a cigarette.

'No.' He grinned at me. 'She is Danish. And she is gorgeous, is she not?'

'She's incredibly gorgeous,' I said.

'So I am a lucky man.'

'Again,' I said.

He laughed. 'Oh, Isobel. You take it all so seriously.'

'I didn't once,' I reminded him.

'Yes, you did.' He smiled at me. 'You, Isobel, were serious even when you tried to have your fling. You did it with such determination.'

'You are a bastard, Luis.' But I said it with amusement in my voice.

'And you are a lovely person, Isobel. But you still need to relax a bit. Take life as it comes—'

'I know, I know,' I interrupted him. 'You've made your point, Luis.'

'Good,' he said. 'So I can go back to my lovely Anna now?'

'Absolutely,' I told him. 'Have fun.'

'We've had that already,' he said calmly as he walked back inside the café.

❧

Was Luis right? I wondered as I showered that evening. Did I take everything too seriously? Had I taken it all too seriously – Tim and me and everything that followed? Did it matter so much, after all?

❧

321

There was a green canopy over the door of Quixote with the name written in gold – a huge, flourishing Q and the rest of the letters trailing after it. The restaurant had been open for about six months and was the sort of place where you looked at the prices and then checked again because you couldn't believe that food could cost so much. I'd never eaten here before, just peered at the menu in its little glass case on the wall outside. I wished Nico had chosen somewhere cheaper and less formal. Thank God, I thought, that I'd decided against my bright pink denim dress and had worn the soft cotton in muted browns and burnt sienna instead.

The *maitre d'* met us at the door and smiled at Nico. 'Nice to see you,' he said and I wondered how often Nico entertained here. We followed him down a steep flight of stairs into the basement of the building.

There were only ten tables in the room, each in a small alcove beneath the vaulted ceilings. In each alcove was a mural of a Spanish building – the cathedral at Seville, the royal palace at Madrid, Gaudì's house in Barcelona. We were led across the highly polished marble floor to sit beneath a picture of the train station at Atocha.

The waiter handed us menus. I looked at mine and suddenly wasn't hungry at all. I was nervous again and annoyed at myself for being nervous.

'Pardon?' Nico looked up at me.

'Nothing,' I said. 'I was just thinking out loud.'

'What will you have to eat?' he asked.

'I think I'll have the Caesar salad to start,' I told him. 'And the *pollo asado*.'

'I hope you like anchovies,' said Nico, 'because the Caesar is laced with them.'

'That's OK,' I said.

'Good.' He smiled at me. 'I'm an anchovy fan too, but you'd be surprised at how many people hate them.'

'What are you going to have?' I asked.

'The *gambas mimosas* are nice,' he said. 'They are cooked in a slightly hot sauce. And I will have the *pollo con almendra*.'

We closed the menus and almost immediately the waiter returned to the table.

'How are you, Nico?' he asked. 'When will we see you here again?'

A bit rich, I thought, considering he was here now. I wondered, again, how often Nico came here. They were treating him like an old friend. Maybe the jingle-writing sideline made him a lot more money than I'd thought.

'I'm not sure, Tonio,' said Nico. 'How is the new guy doing?'

'He plays the piano.' The waiter nodded towards the instrument in the corner of the room. 'But, to be honest, I think Guillaume prefers the guitar.'

'I hope so,' Nico grinned. 'Perhaps he'll give me a call again soon.'

'He will be here later tonight,' said Tonio. 'He had to leave for about an hour, but he'll be pleased to see you, I'm sure.'

'I won't go until he returns,' said Nico. 'So, if he's late it will cost me in wine.'

Tonio laughed. 'What can I get you to eat?'

Nico gave our orders while I mulled over the conversation he'd had with the waiter. So Nico played the guitar here sometimes. How many jobs did he have? The pharmaceutical company, the jingle-writing, playing the guitar in the Plaza Mayor – and maybe in restaurants too! It was a wonder he'd found time to take me to dinner at all.

'I played guitar for them at weekends when this place opened first,' said Nico when the waiter had left. 'Fridays and Saturdays. It went well, I think, but then I had to go to the US for a month on business and the owner brought in a piano-player. This is the trouble with the entertainment industry! You've got to be available all the time.'

'But you think he might give you the guitarist's job back?'

'Maybe.' Nico took one of the soft bread-rolls from the basket in front of us. 'It would be nice.'

'You like playing the guitar in public?'

'I'm a show-off, yes?'

'No,' I shrugged. 'But I must have heard you so many times and not known it was you. In the park, in the square—'

'I hope you enjoyed it.'

'It was beautiful,' I said and suddenly felt embarrassed.

'Thank you,' said Nico simply.

'I don't know where you get time.' I began to butter a roll. 'With your sales job and your jingle-writing – it seems impossible.'

'You're right,' said Nico. 'One day the time will come when I must choose between them all.'

'And what will you choose?'

'I don't know yet,' said Nico. 'I don't know what the most important thing for me is.'

Tonio, the waiter, reappeared with the wine that Nico had ordered and filled our glasses.

'Cheers,' said Nico, in English.

'Cheers.'

The wine was cold and I shivered.

'Are you cold?'

'No,' I said. 'I'm fine.'

'So.' He smiled at me. 'How long do you think you will live in Madrid?'

'I don't know.' I shrugged. 'I've been here over a year now and the time has flown by – I haven't decided.'

'But you will definitely return to Ireland?'

'Sometime. It's my home.'

He nodded. 'You have a big family?'

I told him about them. Strangely, talking about them to somebody else seemed to make me appreciate them more. I didn't say that my mother drove me crazy, or that Dad didn't understand me; nor did I tell him that Alison and I sometimes fought like cats and dogs or that I'd once ripped up Ian's homework in a fit of rage. I made us sound idyllic.

'It would be good to have family like that,' he said as he took another bread-roll.

'Tell me about yours.'

'Oh.' He picked at the roll. 'My family are doctors. My mother is a doctor at the Sta Maria Hospital, my father is also a doctor there. My sister is studying to be a doctor. My brother qualified last year.' He laughed shortly but there was no amusement in it. 'I am the odd one out.'

'But you work in a pharmaceutical company,' I said. 'So you have an interest in medicine too.'

Tonio arrived with our starters.

'*Gracias*,' I murmured as he slid the plate in front of me.

'I trained to be a doctor,' said Nico when Tonio had left. 'But it wasn't what I wanted to be. I thought it was – well, with a family of doctors you nearly always think like that – but it just wasn't what I wanted to do. So I quit.'

'And how did your family react?'

'How do you think?' His eyes were dark. 'They were not amused.'

I grinned at him. 'None of us ever do things the way our parents expect. They've got over it now, though, I suppose. And they must think that the jingle-writing is great!'

'That's a joke, yes?' He looked at me curiously. 'You do not mean that.'

'Of course I do,' I said. 'You wouldn't have been a good doctor. But you are a good musician. And you're still doing something in the medical world too. They must be pleased.'

'They don't exactly see it like that,' said Nico. 'They think I am wasting my time and my brain. And they hate the fact that I am working in a pharmaceutical company!'

'Oh.' I looked blankly at him.

'They think I should be a doctor and stop wasting my training for profit.'

'I suppose that happens in families where there is a tradition of one profession,' I mused. 'But they'll get over it.'

'I don't think so,' said Nico. 'I am the eldest. They think my life is unsuitable.'

'That's stupid,' I said. 'Wait until you're a famous musician. Then they'll be thrilled to pieces.'

He smiled. 'Thank you. I don't think I will ever be a famous musician, but it's nice that you think so. Tell me about you.' He ground black pepper over his food. 'Have you made many friends?'

'Yes,' I nodded. 'I went to a language class two nights a week when I came here first and I made some friends there. The people in the office are nice too. We go out together sometimes.'

'But you miss your family,' said Nico.

'You're big into family,' I said.

'It's a continental thing.' He shrugged.

'My sister came to visit me. We had a good time.'

'And have you seen our art galleries and our museums and our palaces?' he asked.

I laughed. 'We traipsed around everything when she came. And I go to the Prado sometimes.'

326

'Have you gone to the bullfight yet?' he asked.

I looked at him in horror. 'I certainly have not. I couldn't possibly go to a bullfight. I'd be on the side of the bull!'

He laughed at that and filled my glass with Rioja. 'Very foreign.'

I felt more comfortable with him now. I liked the way his eyes crinkled when he smiled and the way his mouth twitched at the corner when I said something that amused him. I liked the way he put his head to one side when he was considering a point and the way he shrugged in a very continental manner when he was dismissing something. I felt myself relax in his company, as though I'd known him for a long, long time.

❧

We didn't have a dessert – I was too full of roast chicken and mushrooms and baby peas. The owner, Guillaume, came to our table and spoke to Nico about playing guitar again some weekends and then he sent over some sambuccas which we knocked back in one mouthful.

I was vaguely light-headed by the time we left the restaurant. The streets were still full of people. Nico took my hand and I moved closer to him, enjoying the feel of his body beside me.

'Have you ever been there?' he asked as we walked past the Convento de las Descalzas Reales.

'The Convent of the Barefoot Royal Nuns.' I smiled at him. 'How could I not go there? It sounded so intriguing.'

'And did you like it?'

'It made me think,' I said, 'that back then women had a lot more power than they have now. Secret passages to the royal palace. Goodness knows what sort of plots they were involved in. And all those paintings and icons!'

Nico laughed. 'You're not meant to think like that. You're supposed to be surprised that it is still a real convent.'

'It *was* interesting,' I said. 'But I bet the past was much more exciting.'

'Would you like another coffee?' he asked.

'If I have more coffee I'll never be able to sleep tonight,' I said. 'But a hot chocolate would be nice.'

'The San Gines?'

I smiled. 'It's a weakness of mine.'

The Chocolateria San Gines was one of my favourite places in Madrid, tucked in among the narrow cobbled streets of the old part of the city. Once, the nuns made the heavy chocolate drinks, now the people behind the counter were probably students, but the quality of the chocolate was superb and chocolate was one of my greatest weaknesses.

I asked for a cup of chocolate and Nico grinned when it was placed in front of me with a pastry stick to dip in it. The liquid was thick and syrupy and clung to the pastry stick. I made appreciative sounds as I ate it while he looked at me in amusement.

'I haven't been here in ages.' I looked at him defensively.

'Such a pity when you seem to like it so much.'

'I know.'

'Why have you been depriving yourself?'

'None of my friends like it as much as me.' I wiped away the chocolate that I'd somehow managed to get onto my nose.

'Your chin also.' Nico picked up the white paper napkin and wiped it away.

'Thank you.' I looked into his eyes as he did it.

'My pleasure.'

I almost said 'No, mine' because I'd liked the way he'd done it – gentle and possessive all at once. I liked him. My heart thudded deep in my chest. I liked him a lot.

He looked at his watch. 'Perhaps I should take you home now,' he said.

I looked at my watch too. 'It's getting late.'

'Sure,' he said. 'Let's go.'

We were quiet in the taxi. I couldn't think of anything to say, and he didn't seem to want to talk. We reached the apartment much too quickly. We got out of the taxi and Nico paid the driver.

'Would you like a nightcap?' I asked, conscious that I was nervous and that my voice sounded shaky.

He smiled. 'Not tonight. Maybe another time.'

I blinked at him. 'Are you sure?'

He nodded. 'We have had a good time, yes? If I come to your apartment now, it might not be such a good time.'

'I—'

'But I would like to see you again, if that's OK.'

'Yes,' I said. 'That's OK.'

'I will telephone you later in the week perhaps.'

'I'd like that.' I scrabbled around in my bag for my keys. 'I had a lovely evening.'

'I too.' He put his arms around me and kissed me.

His kiss was different from Tim's. His skin was smoother and I didn't feel the rasp of a growing beard. His touch was firmer – he held me so tightly I thought I might break. He broke off and looked at me.

'I'll call you next week,' he said.

'OK.' I smiled at him. 'Thanks for a lovely night.'

'Thank you too, Isabella.'

∽

I sat on the balcony and looked over the lights of the
city. I couldn't sleep. I'd had a wonderful time with Nico.
He'd been warm and caring and courteous. He hadn't
wanted to hop into bed with me. (Although a tiny part
of me wondered was that a good thing or not.) I'd liked
being with him. He'd been – comfortable. I touched my
lips where he'd kissed me and wondered if I could fall
for him.

∽

He called on Monday and we met for lunch. He'd like
to meet me that evening, he told me, but he couldn't
because he was playing the guitar with his friends at a
birthday party. This was paid work, he said, not like
busking in the Plaza Mayor, and they never turned down
real, paid work. It made them feel like genuine musicians
and they loved it.

We went to the movies on Tuesday night, to dinner
again on Thursday, we met for lunch on Friday and
he brought me to the Prado on Saturday – so that I
could see the more wonderful works of art and not
get lost.

He held my hand as we walked through the lofty
rooms together, surrounded by history and feeling at
peace. Afterwards we went to the Retiro Park and he
took me out in a boat. I trailed my hand through the
water and pretended that the lake wasn't crowded with
shrieking teenagers hell-bent on capsizing someone. Then
we went for tapas and he took me home. I nearly invited
him in but I didn't and he didn't say anything. He kissed
me on the cheek and said he'd call.

～

Gabriela knew that there was someone. She said she could see it in my eyes and in the way that I smiled. She had watched my smile taking me over day by day, she said, and she was happy to see it.

'You have fallen in love with him?' she asked one afternoon as I went through a report with her.

'Not exactly,' I told her. 'I can't fall in love with someone in a week.'

'No?' She looked quizzically at me.

'Come on, Gabriela,' I said. 'It's all very well for people to fall in love straight away in books or in the movies, but it doesn't work like that in real life.'

'Oh, I don't know.' She shrugged her shoulders. 'I met Alfredo on a Friday night and I knew by the Monday morning that I wanted to marry him.'

'I don't want to marry Nico.' I laughed. 'But he's done great things for how I feel.'

'In that case, I am glad.' Gabriela smiled at me. 'I like you, Isobel. I want you to be happy in Madrid.'

'I *am* happy,' I said and meant it.

～

I went to my favourite fabric shop and bought the material for another dress. Julie and Andy were getting married in six weeks' time and I wanted to wear something special. She'd asked me to be a bridesmaid, but I refused.

'I'm far too old,' I objected. 'You're supposed to get young, virginal things as bridesmaids.'

Julie chuckled. 'If it comes to that, I'm far too old to be getting married in a long – *long*, Isobel – white dress and a veil. But Mum wants it and I suppose I do too, in a way.'

'What about Danielle?' I imagined Julie's older sister would want to be involved.

'She's going to be matron of honour,' said Julie. 'Oh, Isobel, are you sure you wouldn't like it? I think it'd be fun.'

'I'm sure it would. But I'd feel a bit of a moron in a peach and pink creation with silk flowers in my hair. Julie, you know I'd do anything for you but—'

'I understand,' she said. 'Just don't say I didn't ask.'

I'd never say that, she knew. But I couldn't have been a bridesmaid for Julie, walking up the aisle after her. As it was, I dreaded her wedding. I tried not to think about my abandoned nuptials but I couldn't help it. I could see my dress again, the four hundred and twenty pearls glistening, but I resolutely put the picture to the back of my mind.

❧

I picked a deep mauve for my dress. The colour suited me and the material was rich and easy to work with. I kept it plain and fitted with a skirt that finished just above my knee and I knew that it looked simple but elegant.

'That is beautiful,' said Magdalena one evening when she saw it hanging on my dressmaker's dummy. 'It will look so lovely on you.' We were going to the movies later.

'Thanks.' I tidied up my threads and put them away.

'Your friend will go to live in America?'

I nodded. 'We talked about it the last time we met. I'm glad we're still friends, even though we're so far apart.'

She nodded. 'You will have a good time at home?'

'Oh, I hope so.' I grinned at her. 'We'll go out and have lots of fun and make exhibitions of ourselves.'

'And what about Nico?'

'What about him?' I asked.

'He will not go with you?'

I flopped onto the sofa beside her. 'I didn't ask him, Magdalena. And it would be reading something into things with him that just isn't there.'

'I thought you loved him, Isobel.'

I shrugged. 'What's love? I don't know. I like him a lot but I don't want to bring him back home and parade him around as though we're next on the marriage machine.'

'Oh, Isobel, you make it sound awful.'

'I'm sorry.' I stretched my arms above my head. 'I didn't mean to. It's just that people misinterpret things and I don't want that to happen. And I don't know Nico very well yet either.'

She looked at me curiously. 'You have not been to bed with him?'

'Magdalena!'

'It's a fair question.'

I blushed. 'No, I haven't.'

'Why?'

'I don't know.' I stared at the ceiling. 'I suppose mostly because he hasn't suggested it.'

'You could suggest it,' said Magdalena.

'I don't want to,' I said. 'I don't want to be the one to change things.'

'You don't like him in that way?' she asked.

I thought of him, his lean body, his strong arms and his dark, dark eyes. Of course I liked him in that way! I'd be insane not to.

'It's not as simple as that,' I said lamely.

'I think it's odd, Isobel. Is he gay?'

'Magdalena!' But then I thought of the incredibly good-looking Ari Jordan, soon to be Julie's gay brother-in-law.

'It's a reasonable question,' she said. 'You've been out with him a dozen times and he hasn't even suggested going to bed. I'd be worried, Isobel.'

'I'm not worried,' I said. 'And I'm perfectly happy the way things are.'

⌒

Barbara Lane was very pissed off about my relationship with Nico. She complained that she'd been the one to say that she fancied him and that I'd more or less told her to go ahead and meet him if she wanted. And the next thing she knew, she said accusingly, it was me, Isobel, who was dating him. I told her not to be silly and took her and Bridget to hear him play. It was a tourist show at one of the hotels and I warned them in advance that it might not be exactly the sort of thing they'd like. But I promised that Nico, Emilio and Juan were worth listening to. The girls were scathing about the flamenco dancers, they liked one of the singers, they thought that the magician was very good but – like me – they were enthralled by the guitar music.

'They're wonderful,' whispered Barbara as she poured mineral water into her glass. 'Really good.'

'The piece they're playing now was composed by Nico,' I said proprietorially. 'He's a brilliant composer.'

'It's pretty good,' agreed Bridget. 'Pity there isn't really a commercial market for music like this.'

'I know.' I shelled some pistachio nuts. 'He doesn't think they'll ever make it as musicians, but he's thrilled to get this work. He asked his parents to come and listen but they wouldn't.'

'Why not?' asked Barbara.

I told her about Nico's family of doctors and their

belief that he was wasting his talent fooling around with the guitar and writing commercial jingles, despite the job with the pharmaceutical company.

'But he has talent as a musician,' protested Bridget.

'And as a jingle-writer,' I giggled. 'He did the tune for Cocoramba coffee.'

'Oh, not that awful thing!' exclaimed Barbara. 'If you hear it first thing in the morning it's stuck in your head all day long!'

'That's the one.' I laughed. 'But he's done the jingle for *Drina* perfume as well.'

'That's not bad,' she said. 'But he's lucky I don't stand up and announce that he's to blame for the coffee ad.'

'Please don't,' I begged her, because it wasn't outside the bounds of possibility that she might. 'They'd never get another night's work.'

Barbara made a face at me. 'Oh, OK. But only because this music is nice and your Nico is an absolute hunk.'

I blushed. 'He's not my Nico.'

'You mean he's free?' She looked at me archly. 'I can make my move if I want to?'

'I didn't mean it quite like that,' I said.

'You see.' She smiled triumphantly. 'Your Nico.'

'I wouldn't mind someone like that,' said Bridget. 'He's the best-looking bloke I've seen in ages.'

'Oh, come on.' I grinned at them. 'I think you two are getting carried away. Besides,' I looked accusingly at Bridget, 'what about Tomás?'

'What about him?' She shrugged her shoulders and shifted in the seat. 'I love him. He's the father of my child. But he's not as desirable as Nico.'

'Don't be ridiculous. Tomás is fantastic.' I stared at her. 'And look at Nico! He's tall, I'll grant you that – and it's not exactly an advantage for a five-foot-one girl going out with a six-foot-tall man – but he's too thin to be a hunk and his face isn't exactly right.'

They looked at me in silence. 'Isobel,' said Barbara. 'You know exactly what we mean. He oozes sex.'

'Do you think so?' I asked, because I thought so too.

'Stop pretending,' said Bridget. 'You know he does. So,' she sipped her drink, 'how is it?'

'What?'

'The sex.'

I stared into my drink for a moment. 'I don't know yet,' I admitted as I looked up again.

'Isobel!' They both looked at me as though I had two heads. 'You haven't slept with him yet?'

'Good God,' I said sharply. 'I don't have to sleep with every man I meet.'

Barbara arched her eyebrows. 'Really?'

'Give me a break,' I said. 'Things were different then.'

'They certainly were,' she said lazily. 'A man a night, I thought, Isobel.'

'It wasn't like that.'

'Close, though.' She sipped her drink and looked at me appraisingly. 'Does Nico know about your past life?'

'Oh, don't be bloody silly,' I said. 'And you're making it sound sordid.'

'It was a bit, though, wasn't it?' asked Barbara.

'I can't believe you're saying things like this.' I was furious with her. 'I just can't believe it.'

'Leave her alone, Barbara.' Bridget put her hand on her friend's arm. 'Don't tease.'

'Who's teasing?' But Barbara smiled at me. 'Sorry, Isobel.'

'It's OK,' I said but the night was ruined. I felt uncomfortable when Nico came and sat beside us. I was annoyed by the way Barbara simpered and smiled at him while Bridget watched her in amusement. I was cranky and offhand with Nico when he took me home. And I knew I wouldn't ask Barbara or Bridget to come out with me ever again.

Chapter 22

The Signal of Anguish (Salvador Dalí, 1936)

Nico rang me at work. I hadn't seen him in over a week. Both of us had been busy, both working late. I was tired but I hadn't minded the work. He was both tired and irritable because he hated working late in the company since it curtailed his music time. He'd only rung once since the night I'd brought Barbara and Bridget to hear him play and I was afraid that he'd gone off me. I was surprised at how desolate that thought made me feel.

'Isabella?' He never called me anything else. At first I'd wanted him to call me Isobel, but Isabella was warmer, more loving. Although, I thought, as I rested the receiver between my shoulder and ear so that I could continue updating computer files while I talked, although why I wanted him to be loving was a mystery. I wasn't ready to be loved.

'Hello, Nico.'

'How are you today, Isabella?'

'I'm well.' I made a face at the computer which had managed to lose next month's lecture roster. 'And you?'

'I'm well too,' he said. 'Except I'm afraid I cannot go to the cinema with you on Saturday night after all.'

'Why?' I asked. 'Do you have a job?'

'Yes, but not guitar. I've been asked by the company to spend some time in our office in Seville.'

'Seville!' I stopped searching the computer for the lecture roster and held the phone receiver properly. 'Seville! For how long?'

'I'm not sure, *mia Isabella*. A few weeks. I have to be back here by August anyway. After that, who knows?'

'Do they want you to move there permanently?' I was surprised at how disturbed I felt about that.

'No. At least, I don't think so. There is a temporary position there and they want me to fill it. It's at a more senior level than I am now.'

'So they're talking about promoting you. That's great, Nico. But I didn't realise you cared so much about your job! I thought music meant more to you than work did.'

'Isabella, I have to be realistic. I've made some money out of music but not much. This is a good opportunity for me. I have to go.'

'And you'll be back in a few weeks?'

'*Claro*. I'm sorry, it was unexpected. I will miss you, Isabella.'

'But why do you have to go before the weekend?' I knew I sounded petulant.

'I start there on Monday morning. I need to check into the apartment there. Get myself organised.'

'Well, have a good time,' I said. I was surprised about this sudden move and uneasy at the way he'd sprung it on me.

'Would you like to come out with me tomorrow night?' he asked. 'We could have dinner at Quixote perhaps?'

'If you like.'

'Isabella, if you are busy that's fine. Don't trouble yourself on my account.' His voice was cool.

'Nico, I'm sorry.' I was annoyed with myself. 'Of course

I'd like to have dinner with you tomorrow night. And it's not so bad. I'll be in Ireland for some of the time you're away.'

'Of course,' he said. 'At your best friend's wedding.'

'So I'll have lots to do,' I told him.

'And you won't miss me at all,' he said.

~

Alison picked me up at Dublin airport again. She wore a lightweight linen suit and looked very efficient.

'Came from the office,' she explained. 'We had a meeting with some county officials today. Usually I wear jeans and a jumper to work.'

'You look great,' I told her. 'Is Peter with you?' She was still going out with Peter – it was her longest-lasting relationship ever.

She shook her head. 'He's gone to the pub with the officials.'

'Sorry if I dragged you away.'

'No problem.'

I followed her to the car park. She was driving Peter's car.

'He lent it to me,' she explained. 'I'm on his insurance so you don't have to worry.'

'I wasn't worried,' I said as I heaved my bulging suitcase into the boot. 'Though I think it's very sweet that he has you on his insurance.'

'Sod off,' she said companionably and slid into the driver's seat.

Mum was delighted to see me. You'd think I'd been away for years instead of months. She hugged me and kissed me and held me away from her so that she could make critical appraisal.

'You look well.' She sounded surprised.

'Thanks.'

'No, Isobel, I mean it. You've put on some weight since Christmas.'

'I put on some weight *at* Christmas,' I told her darkly. 'All that pudding and cake.'

'Well, I thought you needed it,' she said. 'You were very pale.'

'No, I wasn't.'

'Girls, girls.' Alison put her arm around our shoulders. 'Little birds in their nest shouldn't quarrel.'

'We're not quarrelling,' I said. 'We're debating. How's Ian?'

'Out,' said Alison.

'With Honey?'

She made a face. 'Not sure. It's got a bit ropey with Honey these days.'

'That's a pity,' I said.

'Ian's far too young to tie himself down.' Mum filled the kettle and took cups out of the cupboard.

'True,' I said. 'Men aren't mature enough to get married until they're in their thirties.'

There was an awkward little silence. Marriage hadn't been discussed in the Kavanagh household since my ill-fated nuptials.

'And what about you, Alison?' I asked lightly. 'Any chance of you tripping up the aisle?'

She blushed furiously and shook her head. I said nothing. I wondered whether she'd ask me to make her a wedding dress.

⤳

Julie was in a panic. Her room was a disaster area – clothes, books, half-opened boxes and black refuse sacks littered the floor. I picked my way through the debris.

'It's not debris,' she told me. 'It's my stuff. And wedding presents.'

'Are you bringing all that to the States with you?' I pointed at the heap of boxes stacked against the wall.

'Some of it.'

'Julie,' I peered inside one of them, 'this is full of stuffed toys.'

'Of course it is.' She looked defensively at me. 'It's Yellow Teddy and Raggy Doll and Walrus.'

'Yellow Teddy and Raggy Doll and Walrus?' I raised an eyebrow.

'I have to bring them, Isobel. I've had them since I was a baby. I couldn't possibly sleep if they weren't in the room with me.'

'And this?' I took a small green beret out of the box.

'It was part of my first school uniform.'

'And you want to bring it with you?'

'Why not?'

'No reason.' I grinned at her. 'I don't have my first school uniform and I certainly didn't bring any of it to Madrid with me.'

'I like keeping things,' she said. 'I can't help it.'

I sat on the edge of her bed. 'How's everything going?'

'Oh.' She ran her fingers through her newly styled copper curls. 'It's a nightmare. You've no *idea* how much preparation—' Her voice faltered as she looked at me. I'd tried not to let my expression change but something of my thoughts must have been mirrored in my face.

'I'm sorry, Isobel,' she said. 'That was so thoughtless of me. I didn't mean—'

'It's OK,' I said. 'It doesn't matter.'

'But—'

'Honestly, Julie. Besides, there's another man in my life now. I couldn't be happier.'

'Really?'

'Really.'

'The bloke you told me about? The musician bloke?'

I nodded.

'Have you gone out with him much?'

'A fair bit,' I admitted.

'So tell me about him.' She moved a pile of half-folded jumpers from the bed and sat down beside me. 'What's he like?'

I didn't know what to say. 'He's nice,' was all I could come up with.

'Nice!' She said it with derision. 'You don't say "nice" about a boyfriend. He can be a lot of things – hunk, sexy, attractive, intelligent, a bastard – but not nice.'

'But he is, Julie. He's kind and considerate and brings me to places I like . . .' I shrugged. 'He treats me well.'

'Doesn't sound like it's a very passionate relationship.'

I thought of the night before Nico went away and the chaste kiss that he'd planted on my forehead even though, at that moment, I'd wanted to pull him into my arms and keep him there. Julie was right. It wasn't a very passionate relationship.

'I'm not ready for passion,' I told her.

'Oh, Isobel.' She looked anxiously at me. 'Is it my fault? I know I said some awful things about the fact that you'd been to bed with other blokes, but—'

'Julie, it's nothing to do with that,' I said. 'Honestly.'

'But if there's no passion, why do you go out with him?' she asked.

It wasn't passionate now. But there could be passion. If we wanted it.

'Oh, he's easy to be with. Easy on the eye too.' I laughed.

'As long as you're happy.' But she sounded doubtful.

'When does Andy arrive?' I changed the subject.

She forgot about Nico. 'Tomorrow,' she said. 'I told

him it was silly to arrive the night of my hen party, but he said he'll stay in and watch TV.'

'Where's he staying?'

'With Danielle.' Julie got up and began packing more clothes into the cardboard boxes.

'Are you looking forward to it?' I asked.

'Which?' She put one box on top of the other. 'The wedding or the move?'

'Both.'

'I'm excited about the wedding,' she admitted. 'I can't believe that I'm actually going to do it. I keep thinking that something terrible might happen—' Her hand flew to her mouth and she looked at me aghast. 'I'm sorry,' she said again.

'It's OK,' I assured her. 'And nothing will happen to spoil your day. Unless we manage to get you completely drunk tomorrow night and chain you naked to a lamppost or something. Andy might change his mind if something like that happened.'

'You wouldn't,' she said.

'Wouldn't I?' But I laughed.

∽

There were ten of us at Julie's hen night, although I only knew her sister Danielle, and two mutual friends of ours, Siobhán and Christine.

We went to Thunder Road. It was like being in the Hard Rock Café in Madrid. We ate burgers and drank pitchers of beer and were all a little drunk by the time we left.

Temple Bar was crowded. It was a warm night and most people wore T-shirts and shorts or jeans. I was the only person in a sweatshirt. It wasn't warm enough for me to go bare-armed.

'Where to now?' asked Christine.

'I'm going home.' Danielle looked at her watch. 'It's nearly one o'clock.'

'Early!' Julie was scathing.

'For you, maybe, but I can't keep my eyes open,' said Danielle. 'I'm exhausted. I was up at five this morning with Elaine. I need my rest.'

'OK.' Julie kissed her on the cheek. 'Will you get a taxi all right?'

'Oh, sure,' said Danielle. 'If I can't get one, I'll call Ray. I have my phone with me.'

'OK,' said Julie again. 'I'm glad you came.'

'Goodnight,' said Danielle. 'Don't do anything too outrageous.'

'Who does she think I am?' asked Julie plaintively. 'The whore of Babylon or something? We're just out for a good time.'

'Well, let's get on with it,' said Siobhán. 'How about Eamonn Doran's? That's supposed to be a good spot.'

'OK.' Julie didn't care. She followed Siobhán slightly unsteadily down the street.

I wasn't too steady myself. I caught the heel of my shoe in a loose paving-stone and almost ripped my foot off. Shit, I thought as I tried to wrestle my expensive Spanish leather shoe free.

'Allow me.' Although I couldn't see him, I knew him instantly. I gave the shoe another tug and it came free. I fell backwards, landed with a thump and looked up into the surprised face of Tim Malone.

We stared at each other for a moment.

'Isobel!' he said finally. 'What on earth are you doing here?'

'What does it look like?' I asked. 'Rescuing my foot-wear.'

'I thought you were abroad,' he said. 'Spain, I heard.'

'I'm home for a week,' I told him. 'I'm going to Julie's wedding.' I slid the shoe back onto my foot. 'Remember Julie?'

'Of course,' he said. 'I met her not so long ago.' He eyed me speculatively. 'And she's getting married.'

'Yes,' I nodded. 'An American guy. She's moving to Florida after the wedding.'

'The emigrant society is back,' said Tim. 'You and Julie both.'

'Don't be silly.' We stood looking at each other for a moment. 'I'd better go,' I said briskly. 'We were headed to Eamonn Doran's.'

'They didn't wait for you,' said Tim.

'That's because they didn't notice,' I told him. 'But I'd better catch up with them now.'

'I'll walk with you.' He fell into step beside me before I could say anything.

It felt strange to have him so close.

We walked in silence. He didn't seem to want to talk and I couldn't think of anything to say. I was confused. I couldn't believe that Tim, my Tim, was beside me. He'd been in my mind for so long, sometimes to the front of it, lately pushed to the back of it, but he'd always been part of me. A part I thought had gone for ever. How could he be here now?

We turned into Crow Street. I saw Christine disappear into the pub.

'They'll be looking for me.' I broke the silence.

'No they won't,' he said confidently.

'They will. I'm going into the pub.'

'Fair enough.' Tim caught me by the arm. 'I'll come in for you in fifteen minutes.'

'Don't be silly,' I said.

'Isobel.' He was still holding my arm. 'Isobel, I need to talk to you.'

'There's nothing to say, Tim.'

'Maybe you don't want to listen to me, but I need to talk to you, Isobel.'

I wanted to talk to him. Of course I did.

'OK,' he said. 'You go ahead into the pub. I'll come in shortly. You don't have to come with me.'

I stood looking at him. 'Go on,' he said.

I walked away from him and into the pub.

It was crowded. I pushed my way down the stairs where the music pounded and bodies gyrated. Dry ice pumped from vents in the walls.

The girls were clustered around the bar.

'What happened to you?' demanded Julie over the noise of the music. 'We looked everywhere for you.'

'My heel caught in a paving-stone.' I wasn't going to tell her about Tim. Not yet.

'What d'you want to drink?' she asked.

'A beer. Any beer.' I looked around. Would Tim follow me here? Would I want him to?

'Wake up.' Siobhán prodded me in the side and handed me a bottle of Miller.

'Thanks.' I took it absently. What did he want to talk to me about? There wasn't anything he could say to me. I wished the music wasn't so loud. Time was when I liked it to be very loud, all-encompassing, blocking out everything but the sound, but I wanted to think now and I couldn't think.

The girls had started to dance. Julie's eyes were closed as she moved her head from side to side. She probably wouldn't notice if I left. I moved in time to the music and drank beer from the bottle.

He appeared fifteen minutes later. He might have been there longer, I didn't know.

'Isobel.' I couldn't hear him over the noise but I knew what he was saying. 'Are you coming with me?'

I couldn't see Julie, she was at the centre of a throng of people. I looked around. The girls were all engrossed in the music and themselves. They wouldn't notice if I left.

'Well?' Tim mouthed.

I nodded. I wanted to know what he had to say.

'Come on.' He put his hand on the small of my back. 'There's a coffee house open down the street. We can talk there.'

It was quieter outside but the street was still thronged with people. It was more like half one in the afternoon than half one in the morning.

'When is Julie getting married?' asked Tim.

'On Friday.'

He steered me around the corner and into the coffee shop. It was small, only half a dozen tables with red and white checked oil-cloth on the tables and rickety wooden chairs which rocked when you sat down on them.

'Cappuccino,' he told the waiter who hovered beside us. 'Isobel?'

'The same.'

It wasn't as nice as the chocolate at the Chocolateria San Gines, but it was hot and comforting. I looked closely at Tim.

His hair was shorter, neater. His face was slightly fuller. He wore a denim shirt and jeans. But he hadn't changed much at all.

'You look wonderful,' he said.

'Thank you. So do you.'

He laughed. 'I look wrecked.'

'No,' I said. 'No, you don't.'

He dropped two cubes of brown sugar into his cup. 'I was out with some friends tonight. Last thing I wanted, really. I'd been looking forward to an evening in front of the telly.'

'That's not like you,' I said.

'Oh, it is really.' He stirred his coffee. 'I spend more time in front of the telly now than I used to.'

'Why?'

'Age.' He grinned at me. 'I'm in my thirties now, Isobel. I've got to be sensible.'

I smiled. 'You'll never be sensible.'

'I suppose you're right.' He continued to stir his coffee. I wished he'd drink some of it. The stirring was driving me crazy. I spooned some of the froth from mine and sipped it.

'So what have you been doing with yourself, Isobel?' He finally put the spoon in the saucer. 'I couldn't believe it when I heard you'd gone abroad.'

I shrugged. 'I was bored here. I'd been thinking about changing jobs for a while, then the opportunity in Madrid came along, so I took it.'

'I never imagined you'd do anything like that.'

'Like what?'

'Move away from home. I always thought you were such a home bird, Isobel. I really was surprised.'

'You didn't know me very well after all.' I stared at him.

'I thought I did,' he said.

I said nothing.

'Tell me about the job.' He smiled at me. 'Is it very interesting?'

'It's not bad. We're a training company. We do seminars and training courses for middle and senior management. We organise in-house training schedules for big companies. I work in our computer-training division. I'm the manager, in fact!' I could barely keep the triumph out of my voice.

'I never thought you had it in you.'

'Neither did I,' I confessed. 'But I'm glad I had.'

'So I did the right thing,' said Tim.

'Right thing?'

'When I suggested that we postpone the wedding.'

'You broke my heart,' I said shakily. 'You know you did.' I gulped at the coffee.

'I'm sorry,' said Tim gently. 'I truly am, Isobel. If I could have changed anything I would have.'

'Oh really.' My eyes were bright. 'What would you have changed?'

'I would have married you,' he said.

It was one of those moments when time is suspended. The waiter walked across the room in slow motion. A girl laughed at one of the other tables and the sound seemed to hang in the air for ever. My heart flipped over in my chest.

'Don't be silly.' My words were a croak.

'I'm not being silly,' he said. 'I'm stating a fact.'

I picked up my bag and rummaged around in it. I grabbed my inhaler and took a puff.

'How's the asthma?' he asked.

'Not bad most of the time,' I replied. 'The air in Madrid suits me better. It's drier than here.'

'I thought, perhaps, it was me made you wheeze,' said Tim.

'No.'

'I meant what I said.' He drained his cup and signalled to the waiter for a refill.

'I don't understand,' I said.

He leaned back in the chair. 'Remember when I wanted the wedding postponed? I told you that it had all got too much for me. And it had, Isobel. I was in a heap over it. It seemed like every single day there was something else to do, something else to worry about, something else to distract me. And I kept thinking "Will it be like this for ever? Will Isobel always be running my life?" I panicked, Isobel. That's all.'

'You told me that you felt trapped.'

'I did,' he said. 'I felt as though I had no control over anything any more. It was awful.'

'But if you loved me—' I broke off, unable to finish the sentence.

'I *did* love you,' he said. 'I lost sight of *why* I loved you, that's all. When we finally decided it was over, it was like a weight off my shoulders.' Tim looked apologetically at me. 'I was so relieved. I felt that I'd got my life back again. And I had a good time. I went out with my friends, I went out with the people from work, I stayed up all night whenever I wanted to keep going with a project and I didn't have to worry about how you felt or that I was meant to be seeing you or anything like that. So everything was great for a while.'

'And then?'

He ran his fingers through his hair. 'And then – then I missed you. At first I thought it was simply because I'd run out of things to do. I thought that I was being stupid. I knew that you wouldn't want to have anything to do with me anyway. So I went out with a few girls. Nothing serious. But none of them was you, Isobel. And I got more and more upset about what had happened and how I'd treated you. I couldn't believe I'd done what I'd done. It was as though I was a different person. So I rang your office one day, and they told me that you'd left.'

'That must have surprised you,' I said.

'I was astonished,' he admitted. 'I couldn't believe it. I assumed you'd have stayed with Delta. So I asked them where you were and they said you'd gone abroad. I couldn't believe that.'

I smiled faintly. 'It was hard to believe myself.'

'I didn't know what to do. I decided that you'd obviously made a serious decision about your life but

I couldn't believe that you wouldn't want to come back some day. I rang your house.'

'Did you?' I looked at him in surprise. 'Nobody told me.'

'They wouldn't,' he said wryly. 'I spoke to your sister.'

'To Alison?' I was amazed. 'She never said.'

'I didn't think she would,' said Tim. 'She told me that you had a fabulous job in Spain and that you wouldn't have the slightest interest in hearing from me and that you'd made a great life for yourself and would I kindly hang up because she was expecting a call.'

'Wow.'

'She was pretty adamant,' said Tim.

'She didn't breathe a word of this to me.'

'Well.' He made a face. 'She never liked me anyway. I suppose she thought I'd try and lure you back from Spain or something.'

I laughed. 'You'd have a hard job.'

'Would I?' he asked.

I fiddled with the catch on my bracelet. 'I like Spain.'

'I suppose it's much more exciting living there than here.'

'Nothing to do with excitement,' I said.

'And have you made friends there?' asked Tim.

I looked at him. 'Of course I have. I'm not a hermit. The people I work with are a great bunch, and I made some other friends from a language study course.'

'Boyfriends?' he asked with studied casualness.

'On and off,' I replied, equally casual.

'Julie told me you had a boyfriend. I met her ages ago. I thought she enjoyed breaking that piece of news. But I suppose it's to be expected. A girl like you wouldn't be without one for long.'

'A girl like me?'

'Attractive, beautiful, desirable.'

I laughed. 'You're getting carried away, Tim.'

'A bit, perhaps.'

'A lot.' I drained my coffee and looked at my watch. 'It's getting late.'

'I suppose so.'

'My eyes are closing,' I told him.

'There wasn't any other woman, you know,' he said.

I coughed. 'What?'

'You thought it had something to do with Laura Hart, didn't you? It hadn't, Isobel. I swear it.'

'I believe you.' I could see her again, sitting in his back garden, in the pink T-shirt, looking beautiful.

'Honestly. It's like I said. It was the whole wedding thing.' He took my hand and I jumped. He held it more closely, twined his fingers between mine. 'It had become a nightmare. Who to ask, who to leave out. Hotels, menus, bands. All that sort of stuff. And it seemed so crazy.'

'It's OK, Tim. It doesn't matter any more.'

'But it wasn't just that.' He sighed. 'I felt as though I was being used.'

'What!?'

'I know, it sounds stupid. But you talked about the house and the things you wanted to do to it, and how easy it would be to get to work from Donnybrook and how we could still live there if we had a child – and I thought – this girl doesn't love me, she just loves the things I can give her.'

'Tim!' I freed my hand from his grasp and stared at him in horror. 'You can't believe that.'

'I believed it at the time,' he said.

'No.' I was aghast. 'I never felt as though you were a provider of things, Tim. I loved you.'

He held up his hands in a gesture of despair. 'I just wasn't sure any more.'

'You make it sound terrible,' I said. 'Maybe I *was* terrible. I didn't mean to be. I suppose I did talk about the house. I wanted it to be our house, not just your house. I never meant—' Suddenly I couldn't talk any more. A tear rolled out of my eye, down my cheek, and landed on the table.

'Oh, Isobel.' He reached out to me. 'I'm so sorry.'

I took a tissue from my bag and blew my nose. 'It's OK.'

'It's not OK,' he said. 'I've ruined our lives.'

I wiped my eyes. 'Don't be silly,' I said shakily. 'My life is fine, thanks.'

'But you're not married to me,' he said. 'And I regret that very much.'

'Do you?' I didn't think he meant it.

'More than anything.'

I swallowed. 'It's a bit late now, Tim. I have a job abroad.'

'You were right to take the job,' said Tim. 'But I wish you'd stayed.'

'And pass up the chance of a Spanish lover?' My tone was light but inside I was a mess. I couldn't believe that I was here, with Tim, having this conversation. I couldn't believe that, after working so hard to rebuild my life, to change everything, I was sitting face to face with him and he was able to make me feel exactly as I'd done when I first went out with him. I wasn't free of him, despite what I'd hoped. There was still something between us. I closed my eyes.

'Thinking of him?' asked Tim.

'Who?'

'Your Spanish lover?'

Isabella, querida. It was as though he'd just whispered the words into my ear. *Isabella, querida.* Passion that was there but unshared. Barely spoken.

'No,' I said tautly.

'Good,' said Tim. He paid the waiter and grinned at me. His boyish, devil-may-care grin. 'So what are we going to do now?' he asked.

'I'm going home,' I said. 'I told you I was tired. I'm going to fall asleep any minute.'

'I didn't mean now, this minute,' said Tim. 'I meant – now, generally.'

'I don't know,' I told him. 'I'm going back to Madrid after Julie's wedding. Lots of work on my plate. And I bet you've got some hot-shot project coming up.'

'Isobel, it was important, us meeting like this.'

'Oh, Tim, maybe it was, but things are different now.'

'But do you feel differently?' He touched my cheek. 'Or do you only think you do?'

His fingers burned into my cheek. I was immobile. The waiter placed the bill on the table.

'We need to meet again,' said Tim.

'Yes,' I whispered.

'We've got to talk.'

I nodded.

'We have to make sure that we reach the right decisions.'

'I know.'

'I've never stopped loving you, Isobel.'

Oh God, I thought, maybe I'd never stopped loving him either.

Chapter 23

The Beautiful Bird Revealing the Unknown to a Pair of Lovers (Joan Miró, 1941)

Julie and I went to the Berkley Court for breakfast on the morning of her wedding. We arrived there at nine o'clock, dressed down in jeans and T-shirts and probably doing nothing for its five-star reputation. It had been Julie's idea. She thought it would be a good way to start the day. We ordered bacon, sausage, eggs, tomatoes, toast and croissants.

'I'll burst out of my dress,' said Julie mournfully, as she dipped toast into the runny yolk of her egg. 'But I'm so hungry and it'll be ages before we get anything else to eat.'

I was hungry too, and amazed at Julie's casual approach to the big day.

'But what's left to do?' she asked when I said so. 'I have to turn up at the church at three o'clock. That's six hours away. My hair appointment is for noon. I'm doing my own make-up. This is a nice, restful way to start the day.'

I agreed with her. 'Has everyone arrived safely?' I asked.

She nodded. 'Mr and Mrs Jordan got in last night. They're staying at the Marine. So is Ari. There's a cluster of other relatives and friends of the Jordans but most of them have made their own arrangements for staying and I don't know much about it. Nor,' she added as she popped some sausage into her mouth, 'do I care.'

'I wish I'd been as laid-back as you,' I told her.

'But I wasn't a few days ago,' said Julie. 'Remember when you called to the house? I was in a total panic then.'

'Still—'

'Still, what?' She looked at me curiously. 'What's the matter with you, Isobel? You've been acting funny all morning.'

I buttered some toast. 'Nothing.'

'Is it the whole wedding thing?' Her voice was full of concern. 'Maybe I shouldn't have involved you so much. Maybe it was wrong of me to ask you to do a reading. Maybe—'

'Julie!' I forestalled a litany of maybes. 'It's nothing to do with your wedding. Honestly.'

'All the same,' she said. 'I can understand how you might feel – upset about it.'

'I'm not upset.'

'Well, there's something wrong.'

I gazed around the dining room. Mostly businessmen having power breakfasts, I guessed. Dressed in sharp suits and neat ties, briefcases by their sides. Sometimes I had breakfasts like that, in the Lux or the Sheraton or the Hilton. Not very often, but sometimes.

'Isobel?' Julie looked at me. 'What's the matter?'

'I met Tim,' I told her.

She stared at me. 'Tim?'

'Tim. Tim Malone. My ex-fiancé. Remember him?'

'I know who you mean.' Her voice was sharp. 'When did you meet him? Why did you meet him?'

'The night of your hen party. By accident.'

She put her knife and fork on her plate. 'I knew you'd disappeared. We were looking for you. I thought you'd just got tired but I couldn't understand why you hadn't said goodnight.'

I felt uncomfortable. 'I know. I'm sorry.'

'But, Isobel. *Tim*.'

'It was an accident,' I assured her. 'When we came out of Thunder Road I caught my heel between a couple of paving-stones. He was there.'

'How was he there?' she demanded. 'How did he know to be there?'

'He didn't know,' I said. 'Of course he didn't know. It was one of life's little coincidences.'

'Oh, Isobel.' She sounded even more concerned. 'What did you do?'

'Nothing,' I said calmly. 'He asked me out for a cup of coffee. I didn't really want to go, but he was very insistent.'

'Is that where you were when everyone else was in Eamonn Doran's?' she demanded.

'I *was* there for a while. But he said he'd come and get me. And he did.'

'So you had coffee. What did you talk about?'

'This and that,' I told her. 'My job. Spain. Things like that.'

'It's good that you had lots of great things to tell him,' said Julie. 'Did you tell him about Nico?'

I shook my head. 'No point.'

'Isobel! Of course there was a point. At least that way he knows he can't just waltz back into your life.'

'He wasn't waltzing back into my life,' I protested.

'I hope not. So did you tell him to sod off?'

'I didn't say anything like that, Julie. I listened to him.'

She looked grimly at me. 'Listened to him?'

'He apologised for everything,' I said. 'He felt badly about it all. Did you know he rang the office looking for me? And the house?'

'Of course I knew,' she said. 'Alison told me.'

'Alison did?' I stared at her.

'She was worried he'd try to contact you,' said Julie. 'So we promised each other not to tell him exactly where you were.'

'Oh, for God's sake!' I looked at her in anger. 'What did you think I was? Some sort of Victorian heroine who'd swoon at his feet or something? How dare you decide something like that?'

'We were thinking about you, Isobel,' she said. 'Honestly.'

I couldn't be angry with her for long. Besides, I probably would have done the same. 'You might have told me.'

'We thought – well, you were getting better, Isobel. We didn't want you to be messed up by a phone call from Tim Malone.'

'I wouldn't have been.' I pushed my plate away.

'So what are you going to do?' asked Julie.

'Do?'

'About Tim.'

'Nothing much.' I was offhand. 'I might meet him before I go back to Spain. I don't know.'

'Be careful, Isobel.' She looked worried. 'He made mincemeat out of you before. Don't let him do it again.'

'I won't.' I smiled at her. 'You're getting all steamed up over nothing, Julie. Honestly you are.'

But she didn't look convinced.

❧

The church looked wonderful. So did Andy Jordan, as he

stood at the altar, tall and handsome in a black tux. Ari was beside him, whispering into his ear. Julie's brother Joe showed me to a pew on the bride's side. I smelt the familiar smell of the church, the polish, the flowers, the religious smell, and felt almost peaceful. It was hard to think that a couple of years ago it would have been my wedding. It should have been Tim waiting at the altar, it should have been posies of peach and white at the end of each pew instead of the red and yellow which were there now. It should have been the Conrad instead of the Marine. It should have been the pearl-covered dress that had taken so long to make and had ended up in ribbons. Alison had discovered it under the bed after I'd gone to Madrid. This morning she'd told me that she'd bundled it up with the rubbish and thrown it away.

'I felt really bad about it, Isobel,' she said. 'But what else could I do? And I didn't want Mum to find it and start sobbing about how that bastard had ruined her daughter's life.'

I shrugged but it was hard to think that all my work and all my dreams had ended up on a rubbish tip.

Alison poked me in the side. 'You'd never guess he was gay, would you?' she whispered in a carrying tone that made the people in the pew in front of us turn around.

'They'll think you mean Andy.' I shook with laughter. 'They're horrified already.'

'It's such a waste,' she said mournfully. 'They're both so good-looking.'

'I know.'

'Is he going out with someone?'

'I don't know,' I said. 'But he's definitely gay, Alison, there's no point in you thinking you could change that.'

'I'm not thinking anything of the sort,' she said. 'Besides, I have my own love life worked out, thanks very much.'

'You and Peter?'

She shrugged. 'We get on well together. We like the same things. We laugh at the same jokes. Why not?'

'Will you marry him?'

'I might.' She looked at me defensively. 'I'm not sure yet. We won't rush into anything. I might live with him first.'

'God.' I thought about Alison living with Peter Gaffney. 'Can you imagine how Mum'll react?'

'That's what's holding me back,' she said glumly.

There was a stir at the back of the church and Julie arrived wearing a long, white, frothy dress that took up half the aisle.

'She's certainly gone for it,' murmured Alison.

But she looked lovely. I tried not to feel jealous as she walked serenely by, I tried not to feel somehow less of a person when she smiled at me. I tried to be joyful and happy when she exchanged vows with Andy and I did the second reading in a strong voice, confidently speaking about love and devotion as though I knew what it was all about.

When would Tim phone me? Since I'd met him two days before, I'd jumped each time the phone had rung so that Mum looked at me strangely and asked who I was expecting to call. I'd said Gabriela, that there had been a problem at work just before I left, but I knew that she didn't believe me.

I hadn't told them about meeting Tim. I hadn't even intended to tell Julie. I glanced at Alison. She'd have a fit if she thought I'd met him. She'd go absolutely berserk.

Julie and Andy signed the register and we all went out into the sunlight. It was a perfect day, the kind of day I'd wanted. People wished them well, kissed Julie, shook Andy's hand. Cherry-blossom floated down from the trees and caught in her hair.

'Hi, Isobel.' Ari Jordan came over to me. 'How are you?'

'Very well, thanks. And you?'

'I'm well too.'

'How's the chiropractic going?'

'Great,' he said. 'I was at a course in Australia a couple of months ago. Learned a lot of good stuff.' He winked at me. 'Met an absolute hunk of a lifeguard on Bondi Beach.'

'Ari!'

'It was a short-lived thing,' he said.

'Is there anyone long-term in your life now?' I asked. He shook his head. 'But I'm hopeful. How about you?'

'No,' I said, trying to keep the thoughts of Tim out of my head.

'Did you ever hear of what happened to the shit who dumped you?'

'Oh, Ari,' I protested, 'he wasn't that bad.'

'Worse, from what I recall,' said Ari. 'You were distraught on that holiday in Rhodes. I felt so much for you.'

'That was nice of you.'

'Andy tells me you moved to Europe.'

I nodded. 'I'm working in Madrid now.'

'Any nice men there?'

'Lots.' I grinned at him.

'I meant for you.' He looked offended.

'I know,' I said. 'And yes, I've dated as you'd put it, a couple of times.'

'Only a couple?'

'A couple of guys more than a couple of times.'

'That's good.'

'Yes,' I said.

'Any of them serious?'

I thought of Nico as he waited in the reception area of the office for me. Leaning against the wall. Dressed in a suit because he was meeting other suits, as he put it. Tall, dark, handsome. Oozing sex, as Barbara put it.

'No,' I said.

'Good,' said Ari. 'You need to get around a bit.'

'Hi there.' My sister joined us. 'You must be Ari. I'm Alison.'

'Wonderful to meet you,' said Ari and turned his charm on her.

I wandered around the church grounds. When I'd thought of Nico I'd experienced the pain of missing him. But Tim crowded my thoughts too. I wasn't sure how I felt about them both. I tried to tell myself that it didn't matter, that I wasn't involved with either of them, that it was all academic. But I couldn't believe myself. I sat on the stone wall and watched as the photographer did his work.

~

Our table was top-heavy with women. Siobhán, Christine, Alison, myself, a girl called Natalie from Julie's office and only a couple of men, both from her office too. Their names were Mark and Jim and they insisted that they were thrilled to be surrounded by women.

'I'm sure they are,' whispered Alison. 'What about us? That's more to the point.'

'You shouldn't be eyeing up men,' I scolded. 'What about Peter?'

'What about him?' She grinned at me. I must have looked surprised because she made a face. 'I'm only joking, Isobel. My God, but you've lost your sense of humour.'

'No, I haven't,' I said crossly. 'I just—' I sighed. Maybe

she was right. I couldn't find anything to be light-hearted about today. I tried all the time. I'd done my best at the church and afterwards when we were having drinks – but I couldn't get into the spirit of things and my mind was a mass of contradictions.

During the ceremony I'd thought about Tim. I'd visualised us standing in this church together, exchanging vows and I'd shivered inside. But outside, in the glow of the afternoon sun, I'd thought of Nico and wished that he wasn't in Seville. And that I'd given in to passion before he'd left.

I hated them both for making me feel like this. I hated myself for being a fool.

~

I sat at the table and took a puff of my inhaler. I'd been dancing for half an hour without a break and I was exhausted. The girls were still going strong, but I needed to sit down and catch my breath. Besides, my feet were sore. I didn't mind sitting there on my own, I needed the rest. But Julie saw me and hurried over.

'Are you OK?' she asked.

'Of course.' I slid the inhaler back into my bag. 'I'm knackered, that's all.'

'Are you enjoying yourself?'

'It's a great day,' I told her. 'Really great.'

'It's going well, isn't it?' she said in quiet satisfaction. 'Wasn't the church lovely?'

I nodded.

'I thought Dad's speech was a bit long.'

'No it wasn't.'

'He shouldn't have said that about the night of my Debs'.'

'Julie, you never told me that you'd asked two men to your Debs'.' I laughed at her.

'I didn't,' she said vehemently. 'Dad was exaggerating. It was a mix-up, that's all.'

I laughed again. 'At least Andy now thinks you're some kind of hot stuff.'

'He knows I'm hot stuff.' She dissolved into laughter. 'And I'll be even hotter when we get to the States.'

'Are you looking forward to it?'

She nodded. 'Yes, I am. I know I'll probably get homesick, but I think I'll be able for it. After all, Isobel, if you could do it, so can I.'

'Madrid is closer to home than Florida.'

'None of it is that far away these days.' She smiled. 'And you have to come and visit. Very soon.'

'I will.'

She got up. 'I'd better circulate. There's loads of old aunts that I haven't even talked to yet.'

'Go ahead,' I said.

'Sure you're all right?'

'Of course.' I waved her away. 'Besides, here comes Jim from your office. I can chat to him. Now go. Circulate.'

She kissed me on the head. 'Talk to you later.'

Jim sat down on the chair she'd vacated. 'She looks great, doesn't she?' he asked.

'Fabulous,' I said.

'Such a nice girl, too,' he said. 'Des was very disappointed when she handed in her notice.'

'I didn't see him here.'

'He's at a different table. One with couples.'

I grinned. 'I'd noticed we were at an unescorted table. And that you guys seemed to have got the better part of the bargain.'

'Only if we get the best girl.'

'I'm disappointed in you.' I grimaced. 'Very sexist.'

'Not at all,' he said with injured innocence. 'A statement of fact.' He drained his glass. 'Can I get you a drink?'

'No thanks. I'm fine.'

'Well, would you like to dance?' He looked invitingly at me.

The music was slow now. The band was playing 'Moonlight Serenade'.

'Why not?'

Jim wasn't a good dancer. He stepped on my toes twice in as many minutes.

'I'm sorry,' he said after the second time.

'It's OK.'

'I've never been much good at this. My mother says I've two left feet.'

'Don't think about it,' I told him. 'Just move with the music.'

'So you're living in Spain,' he said.

'Yes.'

'Do you like it?'

'Yes. Madrid's a nice city.'

'Good place to live?'

'I think so.'

'Would you ever come back?'

I shrugged within the circle of his arms. 'Maybe.'

'Are you going to dance with him all night or can I butt in?' Mark tapped me on the shoulder.

'I don't mind.' I looked from one to the other.

'My turn,' said Mark.

Jim grinned at me and disappeared towards the bar.

'You wouldn't want to believe anything he tells you,' said Mark.

'Why?'

'He's a pathological liar. Does it to impress women.

Has he told you he's the one that really runs the office yet?'

I looked up at Mark. 'I thought Julie was the one who really ran the office.'

He laughed. 'You're probably right.' He held me closer to him. 'You're a good dancer.'

'So are you.' He was better than Jim, anyway.

'And you live in Madrid?'

I nodded.

'Like it there?'

'Yes.'

'Ever think of coming back?'

'Sometimes.' I smiled. 'Not often.'

'That's a shame,' said Mark. 'When do you go back?'

'Day after tomorrow.'

'Would you like to come out with me tomorrow night?'

I stopped and stared at him. 'Me?'

'Yes, you.'

'Tomorrow night?'

'Yes, tomorrow night.'

'But you don't know me.'

'I talked to you over the meal. Julie's talked about you before. And I'd like to get to know you.'

'It's very kind of you. But I don't think so.'

'Just a drink, something to eat?' He looked hopefully at me.

'No, Mark. Thanks all the same. But I've things to do tomorrow.'

'Oh, well.' He shrugged. 'It was worth the chance.'

The music speeded up again and I said that I wanted to sit down. He left me at the table and disappeared in the direction of the gents. I shook my head as I thought of a date with Mark. I couldn't understand why he'd asked me.

It was warm in the hotel. I needed some air.

It was still warm outside too. Other couples wandered around the hotel gardens, or sat in clusters on the grass. I walked along the gravel path towards the sea, then sat on the edge of the grass and watched a ship slowly cross the horizon.

I was lonely. I ached inside and I didn't know why. I wanted to cry when I should have felt glad for Julie and for Andy. I was sick at myself for the envy that I knew I felt. I got up and walked back to the hotel but I couldn't go back inside feeling like this.

I walked through the grass, leaned against a huge tree and closed my eyes. If only I was back in Madrid.

'Mark McCrory, someone will see us.'

'No, they won't.'

I recognised Mark's voice and opened my eyes again. I couldn't see him, or Christine (whose voice I also recognised), but I saw the leaves of the huge rhododendron bush rustle slightly and heard a giggle.

'Mark!' It was a suppressed cry.

I slid down into a sitting position behind the tree trunk. I was afraid to walk away in case they'd see me.

'Oh, Mark! Yes!'

Bloody hell, I thought. He's not doing it with Christine in the bushes. He can't be.

'I've always wanted to, Christine. You know that.'

He *was* doing it to her in the bushes.

'Oh, Mark.'

'I mean, why haven't we got together before?'

She groaned.

'God, you're beautiful,' he said.

I was glad he'd got over the disappointment of me turning down his date.

'My God, you're huge.'

I had to get out of here. Even if they did see me.

Anyway, they wouldn't see me. They had far greater things on their minds.

～

Mrs Donegan cornered me as I walked inside.

'It's great to see you again, Isobel.'

'You too. Doesn't Julie look wonderful?'

'She was always a pretty girl.' Mrs Donegan looked mistily at her daughter. 'I hate to think of her going so far away.'

'It's not that far,' I said.

'America.' Mrs Donegan sighed. 'People used to go to America and never come home.'

'That was a long time ago,' I reminded her. 'And it's only a six-hour flight these days. Besides, you can phone. Or fax. Or e-mail.' I grinned. 'Any of those wonderful ways of modern communication.'

'I can't even use the microwave properly,' said Mrs Donegan ruefully. 'So I don't think I'll get very far with the e-mailing. However that works.'

'You need a computer,' I told her.

'Well, there you are then,' she said. 'We certainly don't have one of those. And even if we did, I'd be afraid to switch it on. I'm not technology-minded.'

'You don't think you are,' I said, 'but computers are all around us. Electronic thermostats, your video recorder—'

'That's another thing I can't use,' she said. 'I'll stick with the phone, I suppose. Tell me, Isobel, how are you getting on in Spain? Do you miss home?'

I suppose she wanted reassurance that Julie would miss home, but that she'd cope.

'Sometimes,' I admitted. 'But it's good fun being abroad.'

'Do you get lonely?'

'Of course,' I said. 'But not all the time. I've lots of friends.'

'I'm glad,' said Mrs Donegan. 'I'm glad you worked things out after that terrible time you had.'

There was a lump in my throat. I wished people weren't always so sympathetic. Even now. 'Oh, I got over that a long time ago,' I told her cheerfully.

'That's good.' She patted me on the shoulder and looked around the room. 'We must find a new man for you, Isobel.'

'Oh, no,' I said hastily. 'I'm happy.'

'The very person.' She beamed at Mark McCrory who'd just walked into the ballroom. He was on his own. I kept a straight face with difficulty.

'Mark, Mark, this is Isobel.' Mrs Donegan waved at him.

'It's OK, we've met.' I smiled briefly at Mark. 'I'm sorry, I must go and powder my nose. See you later, Mrs Donegan.'

I fled into the foyer. The band began to play 'I Will Survive'.

I hated weddings. Truly I did.

Chapter 24

The Persistence of Memory (Salvador Dalí, 1931)

I didn't sleep very well that night. My breathing was uneven and I lay on my side while thoughts whirled around in my head like paper in the wind. I thought of how lovely Julie had looked, of her obvious delight in Andy Jordan. Of Mark and Christine. Of Alison and Peter Gaffney. Of Luis. Of Nico. Of Tim. I took another puff of my inhaler. My asthma was much worse since I'd come home.

I tried not to think of Tim but I couldn't help it. I despised myself for suddenly allowing him to take over my semi-conscious mind, for being so close to me again. I heard the dawn chorus begin at five o'clock and the milkman arrive at six. I lay in bed, eyes open, and stared at the tear in the wallpaper where I'd once stuck a poster of Michael Hutchence. I grieved for what had happened to him and I ached for the girl I'd once been.

I got up and wrapped my dressing-gown around me. I went downstairs, put on the kettle and played around with a bowl of cereal. I wasn't hungry.

I didn't do much that day, just sat in the garden and read Mum's Agatha Christie books. I'd read them all when I was younger and I still remembered whodunnit which made a mockery of my engrossed reading.

Mum joined me for a while. It was peaceful sitting there and I should have been able to allow the warmth of the sun and the powerful fragrance of the roses to lull me, but I couldn't. When the phone rang, I jumped a mile.

But Mum had already got up to answer it.

'No one,' she said when she came back out with a glass of orange juice for me. 'We've had more wrong numbers in the last two months than you'd believe. We reported it, but it's a waste of time. We've got the same number as some shop in Cork, but people keep forgetting to put the area code in front of it.'

I finished *Murder on the Orient Express* and started *Death on the Nile*. Alison wandered out with a cushion and her Walkman. 'Don't wake me,' she instructed, as she slid the headphones over her ears. 'I'm exhausted.'

The phone rang before she sat down. 'It's probably Peter,' she said. 'I'll get it.'

It was a wrong number too. 'I'm not getting up if it rings again,' she warned. 'Peter will have to learn that I need my sleep.'

It rang again about half an hour later.

'I'll get it this time,' I said. 'I need to fetch another drink anyway.'

∽

'Thank God you answered at last,' said Tim Malone. 'I really didn't want to hang up again. Your mad mother would have decided that it was a nuisance call and phoned the police.'

'That was you earlier?'

'Of course it was me,' he said. 'Who else would it be?'

'I don't know,' I said. 'I'm sure lots of people ring this house. Alison has a good social life, Ian has friends, so has Mum. And Dad. Not that many people ring here for me.'

'Don't be facetious,' he told me.

'I'm merely stating a fact.'

'OK, OK. I rang to find out what time you can meet me tonight.'

'Meet you?'

'Of course, Isobel. I meant what I said the other day. We need to talk.'

'Why?'

'Because there's a lot of things we need to say.'

'I thought you'd said it all.'

'Well, I did,' said Tim. 'But I need to know how you feel, Isobel. I need to meet you. Please.'

He'd never said please to me before.

'Oh, Tim, what's the point? It's too late.'

'The point is that there are things in our lives that need to be sorted out. It's never too late.'

'My life is sorted out,' I said desperately.

'Maybe,' said Tim. 'And if it is then I promise to leave you alone and never contact you again. But we have to be sure, Isobel. We owe it to ourselves.'

'Do we?'

'Yes,' said Tim firmly.

My hands were sweating. I wiped each palm on my denim shorts. 'What do you suggest?'

'I'll be in town tonight. There's a new pub on Dawson Street. It's got atmosphere and, if you don't like me, at least there are other good-looking men swarming around.'

I laughed. '*Other* good-looking men?'

'Good-looking men,' he said. 'Not me.'

'Modesty was always one of your strengths,' I told him.

'Not this time,' he said and I could almost believe him. 'Honestly, Isobel. Not this time. Not about this.'

'I don't want to meet you in a pub,' I told him. 'We always used to meet in pubs. Besides, I don't know the new pubs anymore.'

'What would you like to do?' he asked.

I was silent.

'Tell you what,' he said. 'To prove how serious I am about this, I'll pick you up. I'll face the lion in its den, ring your doorbell and pick you up.'

I shuddered at the thought of Tim ringing the doorbell.

'No,' I said. 'Don't do that.'

He thought for a moment. 'I'll meet you in Fitzers. We can go for a drink afterwards if you like.'

'OK.'

'Eight o'clock.'

'OK.'

'See you then, Isobel.'

I still couldn't believe I'd agreed to meet him.

❧

'But I thought you'd stay in tonight.' Mum was upset. 'It's your last night.'

'I promised some friends I'd meet them,' I told her. 'I didn't realise it mattered to you.'

'Of course it matters,' she said sharply. 'You're my daughter. I like having you here.'

I put my arm around her. 'I'm sorry. But I've made the arrangements now.'

'Oh, it doesn't matter,' she sighed. 'You young people have to do your own thing. Not hang around with doddery old women like me.'

'Mum!' I looked at her in exasperation. 'You know it isn't like that.'

She looked sulky.

'And I'm not a young thing,' I reminded her. 'I was thirty this year.'

'You don't look a day over twenty,' she said spiritedly.

'Oh, thank you.' I hugged her again, and kissed her on the face. 'There are times when I love you, Mum.'

'You can't placate me like that,' she said, although there was amusement in her voice. 'Go on, have a good time with your friends.'

'See you later.' I picked up my bag and hurried out of the house.

❧

I was early. I decided against going to the restaurant straight away because I didn't want to sit there waiting for Tim. He was dreadful about time-keeping. He rarely turned up on time for any of our dates, usually arriving fifteen to twenty minutes late, with no real excuse. I wasn't going to let that happen tonight. I would be late myself.

I sat overlooking the cricket pitch at Trinity College and allowed the evening sun to warm my shoulders. When I closed my eyes I could almost imagine being in the Retiro Park. Someone was playing a guitar. I opened my eyes again. It was a young girl, chestnut hair tumbling around her shoulders. Not Nico. I laughed at myself, then shivered as I thought of Nico. I was going insane, I knew I was.

❧

Tim was already at the table when I arrived. I sat down opposite him and smiled tentatively.

'You look lovely,' he said.

'Thanks.' I hadn't worked that hard at it tonight. Jeans,

a white blouse and a blue jacket. No make-up, just a touch of mascara and some lip-gloss. Simple jewellery. Nothing that screamed at him that I'd spent ages thinking about what to wear, how to look.

'Would you like something to drink?' he asked.

I shook my head.

'Sure?'

'Positive.'

I hid behind the menu and looked at the jumble of letters.

'What do you want?' asked Tim.

'Penne.' I said the first thing I could see.

'Nothing more substantial?'

'I like pasta,' I said.

'OK, fine.' He signalled the waiter who hovered near the bar.

'Thanks for coming out tonight,' said Tim, when he'd given the order. 'I wasn't sure that you would. I'd have understood if you hadn't, Isobel, but I needed to talk to you.'

I picked the leaves off the rose in the vase in front of me.

'I said it the other night and I meant it.' Tim frowned. 'I made a big mistake, Isobel. The biggest.'

I swallowed the lump that had come into my throat.

'Afterwards I wondered what had happened to me. I was so happy with you. I loved you. I wanted to marry you.' He shrugged. 'I can't explain it other than what I've already said. I panicked.'

I didn't know what he wanted me to say. I tore the rose leaves in half.

'If I could change it, I would,' said Tim.

'You can't change things,' I said. My voice echoed around in my head as though someone else had spoken. 'Things are different now.'

'How different?' asked Tim.

I blinked a couple of times. 'I have a new life. A new country. New friends. New job.'

'Does that mean you've turned your back on everything here?'

'No.' I cleared my throat. 'But you can't expect me to want to give up everything I've worked for.'

'And what is that exactly?' asked Tim.

'I told you. I've a responsible position in our company. I'm well-paid, Tim, and I have an interesting job. I have a good life in Madrid. It's a nice city. I've made a lot of friends.'

'Is there someone special?'

'I have a boyfriend,' I said, hating the word which sounded so young and childish. 'He treats me well.'

'What does he do?'

'He's a musician.'

'Isobel!' Tim stared at me. 'For God's sake! What does a musician earn?'

'He also works in a pharmaceutical company.'

'I suppose that's something,' said Tim. 'But a musician, Isobel. One of these refugees from the sixties types? Or a Nigel Kennedy clone?'

'He was born in the sixties,' I told him. 'Hardly a refugee. And Kennedy plays the violin. Nico is a guitarist.'

'Then it's flower-power nostalgia,' said Tim. 'Honestly, Isobel.'

'What?' I glared at him. 'Just because he doesn't fit your ideal of what a man should be? A techno whiz-kid or a company clone?'

'No. Nothing like that.' He looked apologetically at me. 'I didn't mean to imply – I'm sorry, Isobel.'

'Nico is a decent, caring bloke and I'm very fond of him.'

'But do you love him?' asked Tim.

'I don't know,' I said finally.

'Then you don't love him,' said Tim decisively. 'If you did, you'd know. You knew that you loved me, didn't you?'

'I thought I loved you,' I said. 'But then again, I thought you loved me.'

'*Touché*,' said Tim as the waiter placed our food in front of us.

I swirled my pasta around in the cream and mushroom sauce. There were so many things I shared with Tim. I couldn't just forget about them all, forget about him. The time when we'd been caught in a thunderstorm and we'd stood on the beach at Sandymount clutching at each other while the rain pummelled the sand and the waves crashed onto the shore. The time we'd gone to Galway and got a puncture and Tim had let go of the spare wheel which took off down the road so that he'd had to sprint after it. The time his mother told me that she didn't think I should wear such a see-through blouse and Tim had told her not to be such a silly old cow and that I was absolutely gorgeous. And the ordinary times. Watching TV together. Walking down the street together. Being part of each other's lives.

'Isobel, I loved you more than I ever loved anyone before.' Tim put down his fork and looked straight into my eyes. 'And I was the worst kind of asshole to do what I did to you. I can understand if you absolutely hate me and never want to see me again. I *know* all of that, Isobel. I know I'm a selfish, self-centred, opinionated fool. I *know*. I know I let things get so out of hand that I made an idiot out of you as well as myself. I appreciate how you felt, even though you might never believe that. All I'm asking now is that you give me a chance. You don't have to commit to anything. Just give me a chance, that's all.'

'A chance at what?' I asked. 'We can hardly have a relationship while I'm two thousand miles away.'

'Think about me,' he said. 'I could come to Madrid for a few weeks. You know how it is – I can bring my laptop and work just about anywhere. I wouldn't impose myself on your life, Isobel. I just think we had something really special and I don't want to let it go without being absolutely sure that it's already dead.'

His eyes glistened. I'd never brought a man to the brink of tears before.

'Let me think about it,' I said after a while. 'I'm very confused, Tim. I don't know how I feel.'

'I understand that,' he said. 'Absolutely.' He beamed at me. 'I care about you a hell of a lot, Isobel.'

'I care about you too,' I said.

〜

We went for a drink in the latest trendy pub afterwards. It was crowded, hordes of people spilling onto the pavement with their bottles of beer. It reminded me of Spain. We sat on the edge of a terracotta planter and observed life as it went on around us. Our shoulders touched. I could feel the heat of Tim's body through my blouse and it was achingly familiar. Every so often I trembled and I didn't know why. Each time, Tim asked me if I was OK and each time I said yes, fine thanks.

'My bum is sore,' he said after we'd been there for about half an hour. 'We'll have to go somewhere else.'

I looked at my watch. 'I'd better go home,' I told him. 'My flight is in the morning.'

'Plenty of time.' Tim grinned at me. 'Come on, a night-cap and then I'll drive you home.'

'I don't want another drink here, Tim.'

'I wasn't thinking of here,' he said. 'I thought we could go back to my place.'

I stared at him. 'No.'

He caught me by the hand. 'Do you hate me that much?'

'It's not that.' I bit my lip. 'Be realistic, Tim. If we go back to your place, sooner or later – well, sooner or later—' I broke off.

'I'll try and have my evil way with you?' he supplied.

'Sort of.' I looked at him. 'I can't imagine that you wouldn't, Tim.'

'You've a lot to learn about me,' he said. 'I've changed. I truly have. And of course I want to make love to you, Isobel. From the moment I saw you tonight I wanted to get you into bed. But I won't. Because I want you to believe in me. And I'm not going to mess up what little trust you might have left for the sake of a quick—'

'Tim, please!'

'So come back,' he said. 'I'll be a model of good behaviour, have some coffee to make sure that I can drive you home safely, and then you can see that I'm a reformed character.'

'I wish you'd stop talking about yourself as if you were some dissolute bastard,' I said in irritation. 'You'd swear that you went around doing nothing but breaking girls' hearts. It wasn't quite like that, was it?'

'I just feel so badly about things,' he said. 'I keep thinking that you must hate me.'

'I'd have hated you more if you'd gone through with it and then decided that it was a big mistake,' I told him.

'Really?'

'Of course.' I spoke decisively although it was the first time I really believed it myself. 'It would have been much worse, wouldn't it? We'd have been married and it would all have gone wrong and we'd have been twice as miserable.' I smiled at him. 'God, Tim, I would have hated to get married and have it all go wrong.'

'You're an incredible person, Isobel Kavanagh.'

'I know.' I drained my bottle of beer.

It was easier in Tim's car somehow. We didn't speak, but he put a tape of classical music into the deck and I let the soothing sound wash over me, relaxing me. I wondered if he'd chosen that tape specially for me. Tim's taste was more heavy metal than Vivaldi and I couldn't believe he'd changed that much in a couple of years. It showed that he'd made an effort though – when we'd gone out together before, the window would have been down and Led Zeppelin would have blared from the speakers. I leaned my head against the edge of the seat and closed my eyes.

'Tired?' asked Tim.

'Not really.'

'Sure?'

'Just – chilling out,' I said.

It was very strange to walk into his house again. I'd never expected to be there, to sit on the well-remembered sofa with my legs curled up in front of me while Tim went into the kitchen to make coffee. It felt odd. Right and yet – not right. I shook my head.

The engraved silver picture-frame caught my eye and I got up to look at it. I remembered the night that the photograph had been taken – the night of our engage-ment. I looked self-satisfied then, I thought, my eyes smiling into the camera, my arm possessively around Tim's shoulder and my ring glittering on the third finger of my left hand.

'I didn't like to hide it away.' Tim walked back into the room carrying two cups of steaming coffee. 'I hope you don't mind?'

'It seems funny to remember it now.' I took a cup from

him and sipped the coffee. 'I got pretty blitzed that night as far as I remember.'

'You and me both.' Tim smiled ruefully. 'And Greg phoned at an ungodly hour the next morning for me to go in to the office.'

'Poor you,' I teased.

'I was sick three times,' he told me.

'I remember,' I said. 'You called around to the house that evening and told me that it was as well you only got engaged once.' I bit my lip as soon as the words were out.

'I'm sorry.' Tim placed his coffee cup on the mantelpiece and put his arm around me. 'I'm really sorry, Isobel.'

I didn't know whether to let him hold me. Part of me wanted him to – part of me ached at feeling his arm around me again. But I was afraid. Afraid that the emotions would come back and no matter what Tim said, I just couldn't fall in love with him again. It would be too easy and it would hurt too much.

He kissed my hair. 'I keep saying and doing the wrong thing, don't I?'

I lifted my head to look at him. 'It's too much, Tim. I can't cope. Not now.'

'Sometime?'

'I don't know.'

'You have to let me prove to you that I love you.'

'Why?'

'Because I'll never forgive myself if you don't.'

I leaned against his chest as I'd done so many times in the past. It was wonderfully normal to be with him again. And it gave me a huge sense of – satisfaction, I suppose, to realise that the man who'd dumped me at the altar still loved me. I'd gone away, I'd rebuilt my life, I'd put him to the back of my mind, and now he wanted me again. It was a feeling of power that I'd never experienced before. But I was still afraid. I broke free from Tim and sat on the sofa again.

He sat beside me and hit the remote. Sky News was showing us the weather – high pressure over Europe, projected temperatures of 24° in Dublin, 34° in Madrid.

'It must be like a cauldron there,' said Tim.

'Sometimes,' I admitted.

'But you like it?'

'It's home.'

He reached out and took my hand. 'Really?'

'For now.'

'You know, this should have been your home,' he said. 'If I hadn't been such a jerk.'

I swallowed. 'But it's not.'

Tim squeezed my hand. 'It still could be.'

'No, it couldn't.' I slipped my hand from his and stood up. 'It couldn't, Tim. I have to go.'

He handed me my jacket and picked up the keys of his car.

∽

The porch light was still on when I got home. I opened the front door as quietly as I could and walked gently into the kitchen. Ian and Alison were sitting at the table, a pot of tea and an apple-cake in front of them.

'Midnight feast?' I asked lightly.

'No,' said Alison.

'Can I have some?'

'If you like.' Ian took a mug from the wooden tree and filled it for me.

'Thanks.' I sat down.

'Did you have a good time tonight?' asked Alison.

'Not bad.'

'Where did you go?'

'Something to eat. Then for a drink.'

'Who with?'

I stared at her. 'Is this some sort of inquisition? I get the impression that you're being a mother surrogate here. What's the problem?'

'I just wanted to know who you were out with tonight,' she said. 'That's all.'

'Why?'

'I didn't realise it was a secret.'

We glared at each other.

'It isn't a secret,' I said.

'It was him, wasn't it?'

'Him?'

'You bloody well know, Issy.'

Ian broke into the conversation. 'It was that shitbrain Malone.'

I stirred my tea. 'I met Tim, yes.'

'For God's sake, Isobel!' Alison looked at me in despair. 'What on earth are you doing going out with him?'

'I wasn't "going out with him",' I said. 'At least, not in the way you're implying. I met him for something to eat and a drink. That's all.'

'But, Isobel, he broke your heart!'

I smiled serenely at her. 'When you're a bit older you'll understand that time is, as they say, a great healer.'

'Oh, cut the crap,' she snarled.

'Look,' I pushed my cup away, 'I met Tim a couple of days ago and he invited me out. It was a no hard feelings thing, that's all. So I don't see what you're getting all het up about. If it didn't bother me, it shouldn't bother you. And I don't know why you feel the need to question me about it. And how the hell did you know I was meeting him anyway?'

'Julie.'

'Julie!'

'She told me you'd met him.'

'Jesus wept.' I sighed. 'You and Julie spend far too much time worrying about me and not enough worrying about yourselves. On her wedding day too! The fact that I met Tim Malone and have arrived home in a perfectly sane and healthy manner should, I hope, reassure you that I haven't lost my mind or anything. It was a perfectly reasonable and rational meeting. Old friends. That's all.'

Alison looked disbelievingly at me. Ian didn't look at me at all.

'That's all,' I repeated.

'I don't want him to upset you,' muttered Ian.

'It's very good of you to care, but there's no need.'

'Yes, there is,' he said. 'You're my sister.'

'Mum would love to hear all this.' I laughed. 'Her three children looking out for each other. I seem to recall that she would have enjoyed a little sibling harmony when we were younger.'

Ian smiled slightly. Alison stabbed at the apple-cake.

'Honestly,' I said. 'I'm fine.'

'Don't let him mess you around, Issy,' Alison pleaded.

'I won't,' I told her. 'Nobody will mess me around. I promise.'

Chapter 25

Landscape with Two Figures (Pablo Picasso, 1908)

'Pretty good.' Gabriela closed the brochure and put it into her folder. 'The winter courses should be well booked up this year.'

'We've had advance bookings already,' I reminded her. 'And a lot of the people who did the beginner's courses with Alejandro a few months ago are booking in for intermediate courses now.'

'I'm very pleased with the way things have gone,' said Gabriela. 'And I'm particularly pleased at how hard you have worked, Isobel.'

'Oh, I enjoyed it.' It was true. Although my personal life had become more confusing by the day, my professional life was great. I was very happy working with Gabriela, much happier than I'd been at Delta. I liked coming up with new ideas for courses, or ways of making old ones more up-to-date and interesting. I loved meeting people and my job gave me more than enough opportunities to do that.

'Would you like a quick drink before going home?' Gabriela glanced at her watch.

'Sure. Let me just check my voice-mail.' I went into my office and listened to my messages. The third was from Nico.

'*I am going mad, not being able to talk to you,*' he said. '*I am tired of speaking to your machine, Isabella. I know it is more than a month since I came to Seville and I'm sorry that the job is taking so long. But I will be home soon. I miss you.*'

I miss you too, I thought as I gathered up my belongings and put on my lime-green jacket. I miss you a lot. I hadn't realised how accustomed I'd become to Nico being around. To having coffee with him in the Plaza Mayor. To going boating in the Retiro Park. To strolling around the shops with him while he clucked disapproval at the prices of clothes and then urged me to buy the most expensive thing anyway. And especially to sitting with him in the Chocolateria San Gines while he watched in amusement as I tackled the almost solid cups of chocolate.

Gabriela and I strolled downstairs together and into the newly-decorated reception area – all shiny marble tiles and a fountain in the centre. A man got up from one of the modern metal seats.

'Tim?' I looked at him in astonishment.

'Hi, Isobel.' He wore a light-coloured suit, white shirt and olive-green tie. 'How's it going?'

'Tim,' I repeated, not quite believing it was him.

'Yes, it's me.' He grinned at me and kissed me formally on each cheek. '*Buenos días.*'

'What on earth are you doing here?' I asked.

'Waiting for you,' he said.

'This is a friend?' Gabriela was watching us.

'Yes.' I turned to her. 'I'm sorry. I should have introduced you. Gabriela Suarez, Tim Malone. Gabriela is my boss, Tim. Tim is a – an old friend, Gabriela.'

'Tim,' she repeated. She raised an eyebrow at me. '*Tu novio?*'

I nodded. '*Sí.*'

'It is good to meet you.' She shook Tim's hand. 'I have heard about you. I was just leaving. I will see you tomorrow, Isobel.'

'But, Gabriela—'

'Don't worry,' she called over her shoulder. 'I'm catching the metro.'

Tim and I stood in reception and stared at each other.

'I can't believe it,' I said again. 'What are you doing here, Tim?'

'Is that any way to treat your long-lost fiancé?' he asked. 'I told you. I came to see you.'

'But here?'

'I had to come to Madrid anyway,' he explained. 'Well, Greg Roberts could have done it but when I heard Madrid . . . I had to come, Isobel. Obviously.'

'Obviously.'

Tim put his hand around my shoulder and steered me out into the street. I blinked in the fierce light of the sun and scrabbled around in my bag for my sunglasses.

'I've never been here before.' He looked around. 'Nice, isn't it?'

'I like it.' I put on the sunglasses and felt better now that Tim couldn't look directly into my eyes. 'How long are you staying?' He'd picked up a grey canvas bag at reception which I guessed contained clothes.

'Until Sunday. Tonight, tomorrow night and then a flight home Sunday morning. I wanted the afternoon one but it was full.'

'Where are you staying?'

He made a face. 'I didn't book anywhere. And don't look at me like that, Isobel – it was just I wasn't sure where to stay. You can recommend somewhere to me.'

'The Lux is handy,' I told him. 'It's near the centre of things.'

'The Lux it is then,' he said cheerfully and swung his bag over his shoulder.

I could have asked him to stay. Maybe it would have been the right thing to do. But how could it be when I only had one bedroom and one bed? I wasn't ready for anyone to share that bed.

'You OK?' he asked.

'Yes.'

'Have I ruined your weekend?'

'No. Not at all.'

'How about the Spanish boyfriend? I won't mess that up, Isobel.'

'He's not here,' I said absently.

What would I have done if he was? I cursed Nico for being away.

'Thanks for replying to my messages,' said Tim.

I laughed. He'd sent an e-mail every day since I'd returned to Spain. I usually replied before I went home. This morning's message had been jokey, light-hearted, with no hint of his impending visit.

'What were you planning on doing here?' I asked him.

'It depends on you,' said Tim. 'I want to take you out. Wine you. Dine you. Do all the things that I've wanted to do with you. Just be with you again, Isobel.'

'But if I've already got plans?'

He shrugged. 'No problem. Do your own thing. I can always meet Mario and Felipe. I'd prefer not to, but there's plenty for me to do if you're busy.'

'I'm not busy,' I said.

'Good.' He smiled at me. 'Let's have a great time this weekend.'

I brought him to the Lux. Señor Murillo was standing in the foyer. '*Hola, Isobel.*' He shook my hand and kissed me. 'How are you?'

'Very well, thank you.'

'Are you here for business or pleasure?' he asked.

'I'm not quite sure.' I indicated Tim. 'This is a friend of mine. I wondered if you would have a room for him. Until Sunday morning?'

'But for you, of course, Isobel. Let me see what we can do.' He checked the computer on the desk in the corner. 'A single room?'

'Yes,' said Tim.

'No problem. If you will give me some details then we can code a key for you.'

I sat down while Señor Murillo organised a room for Tim. I still felt guilty that I hadn't asked him to stay with me. But it would have been too much.

'Room fifty-five.' Tim came over to me with the plastic keycard. 'I'll just sling my gear there and then we could go somewhere?'

'Tim, I need to get home first. Change. You know.'

'But—' His eyes met mine. 'Of course. I'm sorry, Isobel. Do you want me to pick you up later?'

I shook my head. 'I'll meet you here. Say – an hour and a half?'

'Jesus – what are you going to do?' He grinned broadly. 'Dye your hair? Have liposuction?'

'Do you think I need it?'

'God, no.' He looked horrified. 'That was a joke, Isobel. Honestly.'

I smiled. 'I know. I'll see you back here. There's a little bar just to the left.'

Tim nodded. 'Come here often, do you?'

'We use it for conferences,' I said.

'See you later.' He kissed me only this time it was less formal.

'Yes.' I rubbed my cheek. 'See you later.'

❧

I walked back to the apartment. I couldn't believe he'd come here. Not Tim. Not chasing after me. Tim had never chased after me. As far as I could remember, I was the one who'd always done the chasing. From the night I'd met him in Howth until the day I'd handed back the ring, I was the one who'd gone looking for him. I was the one who'd sat beside the telephone willing it to ring. I was the one who'd seethed when his job took him to the States or the UK or Japan while I waited at home. I was the one who'd always been there whenever he wanted. But this time he'd had to come to me. I smiled to myself as I walked up the stairs to the fifth floor.

I was like a teenager on her first date. I tried on and discarded my pink dress, my blue dress, my green dress and my red dress. I put on my tight denim jeans and a bright yellow top but decided that, if we went to eat anywhere, I'd explode out of the jeans. I put on a pair of wide cotton trousers and a matching top but I thought they made my hips look too expansive. I tried my green skirt and cropped blouse, but I'd put on weight since the last time I'd worn that outfit and a ridge of skin poked out of the gap between the blouse and the skirt. They'd said I was thin when I'd first come to Spain, but I wasn't thin now! Fifteen minutes before I was to meet him I was still standing in front of the mirror in my bedroom wearing nothing but my bra and pants. The phone rang. I swore softly.

'*Isabella, querida.*'

Oh, shit, I thought. Not now.

'Isabella, I haven't once managed to talk to you.' Nico sounded peeved. 'I have called but you have not replied.'

'That's not true, Nico. I called back the number you left, but it's a mobile phone – sometimes there was no signal, sometimes it was in use.'

'Bloody Carlos,' snapped Nico. 'He keeps borrowing it.'

I grinned. 'Well, I did call you.'

'It's so long since we talked, Isabella. Not since you went to Ireland. I needed to hear your voice.'

'It's good to hear you too, Nico.' I glanced at my watch.

'How was your friend's wedding?'

'It was fun,' I said. 'It was like all weddings.'

'Not much fun,' said Nico. 'I hate weddings. All fuss.'

That sounded chillingly familiar.

'I had a good time,' I told him.

'And your family?'

'They're fine.'

'But you will not go back to Ireland yet? You will stay in Madrid?'

'Of course,' I said.

'I am glad.' His voice softened. 'It is lonely here without you, Isabella.'

'Is it?'

'Yes. There is nobody to sit with in the evening. No one to talk to. No one like you.'

'You're probably having a great time without me!' I laughed.

'No,' he said seriously. 'I am not. But the work is good, I enjoy that.'

'I'm glad.'

'So what are you doing tonight?' asked Nico.

I cleared my throat. 'I am going out with some friends,' I lied. 'With Barbara and with Bridget.'

'Oh.' He paused for a moment. 'Anywhere nice?'

'I don't know,' I told him. 'We're meeting in the Lux. Actually, Nico, I'm a little bit late.'

'I'm sorry,' he said. 'I didn't mean to make you late.'

'No. That's OK.' Suddenly I didn't want him to hang up. 'Really, Nico. I'm glad you called.'

'I am glad I called. I thought you might decide you were an *Irlandesa* after all.'

'I'll always be an *Irlandesa*, Nico. But I'm a *Madrileña* too.'

He laughed. 'Take care of yourself, *querida*. I will be back next week.'

'Take care of yourself, too, Nico.'

'*Buenas noches*.'

'Goodnight.'

I replaced the receiver. I was shaking. Then I looked at my watch again, pulled on the green dress which was the nearest, and hurried out to meet Tim.

~

I don't know why I felt so guilty. I met him in the Lux's tiny bar and we walked to Cactus Charlies, a burger and beer restaurant which I frequented with the girls when we didn't go to the Hard Rock Café. I didn't want to go to the Hard Rock with Tim.

We sat at a corner table and ordered burgers and chips. Burgers and chips were my favourite comfort foods and I felt the need for comfort. Tim insisted on ordering wine too, although I didn't want to drink alcohol.

'Oh, come on,' he urged. 'It won't kill you.'

'It's not that. I'm tired. Wine will make me sleepier. You don't want me to fall asleep on you, do you?'

'That's not in the game-plan.' He grinned at me.

What *was* in the game-plan? I wondered. What, really, did Tim think could or would happen between us? And what did I want to happen?

'—in the end he agreed that I was right and we changed the configuration and it worked.' Tim beamed at me as he finished the story I'd been half-listening to.

'You got your own way,' I said.

'I always get my own way,' said Tim.

'Do you?'

'Always.' He looked me straight in the eye. The waiter put the food on the table.

'So, that girl I saw you with is your boss?' Tim poured a fountain of salt onto his chips.

I nodded. 'Gabriela Suarez.'

'Great legs.'

'Tim!'

'Well, she has. Good-looking woman for her age.'

'What age is she?'

'Forty-ish?' He looked at me quizzically.

'Fortyish.' I smiled. 'Her husband's a vet and she has two gorgeous children.'

'Do you still want children?'

The question stunned me. I gulped some wine. 'Sometime. Not yet.'

'You told me once that a woman should have children before she's thirty.'

'I think it was my mother who said that.'

'I don't think I was talking to your mother about parenthood.'

'Anyway, not yet,' I repeated.

'But you still want them?'

'Of course.'

'I thought maybe you'd changed your mind.'

'Why?'

He shrugged. 'So many changes, Isobel. Your life, your job. Everything about you is different. Especially here.'

'What's different?' I asked.

He sat back in the chair. 'You're better-looking—'

'Oh, Tim!' I interrupted him. 'That's a ridiculous thing to say.'

'But true,' he continued. 'Maybe it's the weather or something. But you look healthier – I haven't seen you use your inhaler at all yet. At home you'd have squirted it at least once by now. You're more confident—'

'Huh,' I interrupted him again.

'More decisive.'

He hadn't seen the ritual of choosing what to wear.

'More – desirable.'

'Tim!'

'It's true,' he said.

'You keep saying all this stuff to me.' I pushed my unfinished food away, 'as though there's some reason that I should fall into your arms and say "Great, I've reached your standards" and everything would be OK.'

'I'm sorry,' he said. 'I didn't mean it like that. And although I think you've changed, it's only in some ways. You're still the same Isobel. And still the Isobel I fell in love with.'

'And out of love with,' I reminded him.

'No,' he said. 'I never fell out of love with you. I just wasn't sure about everything. That's completely different.' He refilled his wine glass. 'Women seem to think that men don't feel anything. That we make decisions simply because it's convenient to do something at a particular time. But I felt a lot of things for you, Isobel, and I didn't just switch off when you decided that you wouldn't wait for me.'

I said nothing. Rocky Racoon blared out of the loud-speakers.

'Do you want to go?' asked Tim.

I nodded.

I let him pay the bill. We walked out onto the crowded streets.

'Would you like to go for a drink?'

I shook my head.

'A walk?'

'No, thanks.'

'What would you like to do?'

'Nothing.'

'Isobel.' He turned me to face him. 'Don't be mad at me.'

'I'm not,' I said. 'Really I'm not. I'm just – confused.'

He put his arm around me. 'Don't be,' he said. 'Don't be.'

We strolled back to the Lux. I thought he might want to walk me back to my apartment and I didn't know what to say, but instead he ushered me into the hotel and into the bar.

'One drink,' he said. 'And you can have mineral water if you like.'

I ordered a Southern Comfort.

We sat in the uncomfortable armchairs – low, rounded, straight-backed. Tim picked the dry-roasted peanuts out of the Bombay Mix on the table.

'Will you come out with me tomorrow?' he asked.

I laughed. 'You sound like a kid asking a friend out to play.'

'Will you come out to play with me tomorrow,' he asked mockingly.

'If you're good.'

'Of course I'm good.'

'Where d'you want to go?'

'I suppose you're bored with touristy things, are you?'

'No.' I grinned. 'I've only seen some places. But there's lots to see if that's what you want to do.'

'I'll let you choose,' said Tim. 'I'd like to spend the day with you.'

'Sure.' I drained my glass. 'But I'd better go now.'

He reached out and caught me by the hand. 'You don't have to.'

I didn't move. I could feel a pulse beating at the base of my throat.

'I do,' I said.

'You could stay here,' said Tim.

I slid my hand out of his. 'No, I couldn't.'

'I'm not forcing you,' he said.

'Good.'

'I just want you to.'

'Maybe.' I stood up although my legs were shaking. 'But I can't, Tim.'

'Somebody better at home?' He laughed but his eyes were serious.

'No.'

'Sure?'

'Certain.'

'I'll walk you back to your apartment.'

'I'd rather you didn't,' I told him. 'It's not far but I'll get a taxi. There's a rank outside the hotel.'

'I'd really rather go with you. That is, if you insist on going in the first place.'

'I insist on going and I insist on going alone.' I smiled at him. 'You're right – I am much more decisive. I'll call you tomorrow.'

'OK,' said Tim. 'But I'll see you to your cab.'

There were plenty of taxis lined up outside the hotel.

'See?' I said. 'Easy.'

'Take care, Isobel.' He kissed me, very quickly, very gently, on the lips.

'Goodnight,' I said as the taxi pulled away from the kerb.

I hung up all my dresses when I got home. I cleansed, toned and moisturised my face. I sat on my balcony, wearing an ancient T-shirt, and I stared across the jumble of buildings at the neon sign that said *Hotel Lux*.

⁓

I rang him early the next morning.

'What time is it?' he asked sleepily. 'God, Isobel, it's only eight o'clock.'

I laughed. 'Up early, to bed late – but a siesta in the middle of the day, Tim. That's how it works here.'

'But I didn't have a siesta yesterday,' he complained.

'You will today,' I promised. 'It's going to be scorchingly hot. You won't be able to do anything but sleep by midday.'

'Want to bet?' he asked.

'I'll meet you in an hour,' I told him.

'OK,' he said. 'Why don't we have breakfast together?'

So we did. Orange juice and croissants in the Lux's dining room. The waitress fawned over Tim although I couldn't understand why. Then he smiled at her and I did understand because when he smiled at me like that I went weak at the knees.

'Have you planned our itinerary?' he demanded.

'I didn't want to make it too difficult for you,' I laughed. 'You've got to go to the Prado and you've got to see *Guernica*. If you don't, people will think you're a complete philistine. And you have to have a drink in the Plaza Mayor. And then we can go to the royal palace – you'll like that, Tim. There's an old armoury and dispensary there. Also,' I looked at him, 'if you want a busman's holiday there's a computer software exhibition you could go to.'

'Ah.' He looked at me guiltily. 'I knew about the exhibition. That's why Greg said I could come. Softsys is showing Crusader, Saracen 2 and Grail. I don't have to go as an exhibitor, but I said I'd drop in and see how the guys here were getting on.'

'I guessed,' I told him. 'What time?'

He shrugged. 'Doesn't matter.'

'Would you like to do that first?'

He looked sheepish. 'If you don't mind. Get it out of the way.'

I kissed him on the forehead. It was completely natural, spontaneous, and he grinned at me. 'I can read you like a book,' I said.

Actually the exhibition was interesting. I left Tim at the Softsys stand while I wandered around some of the others. I picked up leaflets on a whole range of new software ideas and some nifty little office gadgets too. I spent ages looking at a clothes-design program and wondered if I should buy it for myself. I realised that I was now very computer literate and I could understand Tim's fascination, although I couldn't imagine how anyone could actually sit down and write a program that could cope with such a wide range of tasks. They had computer games too – so realistic that you could almost believe you were flying a fighter jet or piloting a submarine.

After about an hour I collected Tim and dragged him along to look at paintings. I was pleasantly surprised when he, too, looked at *Guernica* in shocked amazement and told me that he always thought it was in colour.

'Mad as a hatter,' he proclaimed as he looked at the smaller, detailed sketches of the painting that Picasso had done. 'How could you think up something like that?'

'It's no different to you dreaming up a complicated software package,' I said. 'Creative, artistic.'

'You're mad as a hatter too.' Tim put his arm around me and pulled me closer to him.

It was hot by the time we reached the Plaza Mayor. We sat down under the shade of a yellow umbrella and I stretched my feet out in front of me.

'It's the shuffling along that makes them tired,' I said as I wriggled my toes. 'Walking at a decent pace doesn't do half as much damage.'

'I do quite a bit of walking these days,' said Tim. 'Hill walking mainly.'

'Good God.' I looked at him in surprise. 'I thought the most energetic thing you did was walk to the Chinese takeaway.'

'You underestimate me,' he said. 'Always willing to try new things, that's me.'

I smiled and closed my eyes. The square was crowded with tourists – this time of the year the Madrileños disappeared out of the city. But the tourists were here in force, clicking their cameras and soaking up the sun.

A guitarist was playing 'Sad Lisa', the notes of the melody drifting through the still air. I opened my eyes. But it wasn't Nico sitting in the square plucking at the guitar strings. I don't know why I thought it might be.

'When does everything close down for siesta?' asked Tim.

I looked at my watch. 'Fairly soon.'

'Do the bars and restaurants close too?'

'Don't be silly,' I told him. 'Not when there are tourists around.'

'It's nice here, isn't it?' He leaned back in the cane chair and put his hands behind his head. 'Peaceful.'

'Yes.'

'I don't think I could live here, though.'

'Why not?'

'Too hot,' he said. 'Too bright. Too dusty.'

'Oh, Tim. That's ridiculous.'

'No.' He sat up straight again. 'I'd miss the unpredictability of the weather at home. The days when it starts out horrible and cold and then the sun suddenly breaks through the cloud and it's beautiful.'

'Dank, misty, grey Novembers,' I said.

'Crisp, clear, multi-coloured Octobers,' he returned.

'Dank, misty, grey Augusts,' I grinned.

'Sitting in St Stephen's Green watching the ducks.'

'I'll bring you to the Retiro,' I said. 'Although that's more like the Phoenix Park really.'

'Come home, Isobel,' he said suddenly.

I didn't reply. We sat in silence for a while.

'You were probably right about the siesta,' he said eventually. 'My eyes are closing. I should get back to my room for a while.'

'OK.'

We caught the metro to the Lux. I wanted to stay on for my station but Tim dragged me with him.

'Don't worry. I'm not going to do anything to you.' He kept a firm hold of my wrist until we were inside the hotel. 'A siesta means resting, doesn't it? Come with me.'

'With you?'

'To my room,' he said.

'Oh, Tim.' I picked at the edge of my bag. 'I don't think—'

'Nothing will happen,' he told me.

'It's not that.'

'What then?'

I shrugged. 'I don't know.'

'Please, Isobel. It's not really a single room. There are two beds, you can lie on one, I'll lie on the other. But we've only got today and I want you to stay with me.'

I knew it was stupid but I went upstairs with him anyway.

The rooms in the Lux were surprisingly big and beautifully decorated. Tim's had mint-green carpet, matching curtains and contrasting bedspreads.

He lay down on the bed nearest the window and closed his eyes. I lay on the other one.

'Come here,' he said.

'No.'

'Isobel, please.'

'Tim, what's the point?'

'I want you near me.'

I sighed and got onto the bed beside him. He put his arm around me and I flinched.

'Isobel.' He sounded hurt. 'I won't eat you.'

'Sorry.' I moved closer to him.

He stroked my hair, the side of my face, the base of my throat. I knew I was crazy, I knew where it would lead, but I couldn't help myself. Tim was my ex-fiancé, after all, it wasn't as though I'd come up to the bedroom of a complete stranger. It wasn't like other times, completely meaningless. Tim was familiar, comforting. We had shared so much together. He pulled me still closer to him.

'Remember the time in your house?' he murmured as he undid the buttons of my light summer blouse.

I giggled. Everyone had been out. We'd been in my bedroom. I hadn't bothered to lock the door, I knew that nobody was expected home. Then, just as I was beginning to be swept away by the joy of making love to Tim, the door had creaked open. I'd frozen, mid-groan. Tim – well, it wasn't Tim's finest hour either. And then Sooty, next-door's cat, had stalked across the bedroom floor, his tail a damn sight more erect than Tim was right then. I'd burst out laughing, but Tim hadn't found it funny. At the time. He was laughing now as he remembered.

'No cats here,' he whispered.

He kissed my neck, moving down between my breasts.

'I thought you said you wouldn't eat me.' I was trembling with desire.

'I lied,' said Tim.

⁓

I went to the airport with him the next day. He kissed me, hugged me, told me he'd be in touch. I said, great, I'd wait to hear from him. I waited until he'd gone through the departure gate before I left.

I wished I hadn't slept with him. In a long list of stupid things, it was the stupidest thing I'd ever done. Part of me had loved it – being back with him, hearing him say my name over and over again, knowing how to bring him to the brink and then moving back – having power over him. And as he'd made love to me, I'd thought that he was mine again and I felt incredibly powerful.

But now I wasn't sure. That was Tim's legacy to me – never to be sure. I didn't know if I loved him all over again, or whether it was just a physical thing. He said he loved me, he told me hundreds of times, but I couldn't be certain. He'd told me that two years ago.

Yet I'd felt so at home with him. The way he moved. The way he did things that I loved. Everything about him.

And when I was at home again I could still smell Tim's smell and hear Tim's voice and I felt incredibly alone and unbelievably guilty.

Chapter 26

Night (Joan Miró, 1957)

The e-mails from Tim were there most mornings when I got into the office. He told me he sent them from his home computer just before he went to bed. So that you're my last waking thought, he'd said.

Today's message was a poem. I looked at it in astonishment. A poem! From a man whose favourite reading was *PC User* and whose favourite books were by Robert Ludlum!

> *Come live with me, and be my love,*
> *And we will some new pleasures prove*
> *Of golden sands, and crystal brooks,*
> *With silken lines, and silver hooks.*

I remembered it from school. It was John Donne and I'd never expected that anyone would send it to me in later life, so proving our English teacher right when she said that poetry was useful. Useful to Tim, perhaps, but I didn't know how to feel about having poetry sent to me, least of all by Tim. Come live with me and be my love – I'd been down that path already!

I looked at the words on the screen for a moment then simply typed *thanks* and sent that as my reply.

When I got home that evening I changed into a T-shirt and shorts, opened a bottle of San Miguel and sat on the balcony. I'd no plans to go out, I wanted to be on my own for a while. I read my book while the sun slid lower in the sky and the lights came on in the apartments around me.

The phone rang. I didn't want it to be Tim. I couldn't cope with Tim right now.

'Isabella.'

'Nico.'

'How are you, *querida*?'

'I'm fine. How are you?'

'I'm at home. I arrived an hour ago. I would like to see you.'

'That would be nice.' I'd wondered when Nico would reappear, wondered how I'd feel.

'It's OK if I come to your apartment? Say – half an hour?'

I hesitated.

'Isabella?'

'Yes, Nico. Of course.'

'I will not stay long. I have lots of things to write up. But I cannot go to bed without seeing you, Isabella.'

'OK,' I said.

'Isabella – everything is all right?'

'Of course,' I told him. 'Everything is fine.' I replaced the receiver and leaned my head against the patio window.

It was exactly half an hour later when he called. I'd changed into a cotton top and trousers.

'Hi.' I opened the door and let him in.

He crushed me into his arms. 'I thought I'd never get home.'

'You're squashing me.' But I laughed.

'Sorry. It seems so long since I've seen you.'

'A month.'

'A lifetime,' he declared. 'Here is a present for you.' He handed me a bottle of wine and a box of handmade chocolates.

'Oh, Nico, thank you.'

'I thought of you without anyone to take you out for chocolate and so I had to do something about it.'

I hadn't brought Tim to the Chocolateria San Gines. He didn't like chocolate anyway.

'Thank you, Nico,' I said again.

'So.' He held me at arm's length. 'You look tired, Isabella. You have black circles under your eyes.'

'Have I?'

'Yes. And you are pale.'

'I feel OK.'

'Sure? It is not the asthma? Or hay fever?'

'No,' I said.

'Good.' Nico kissed me gently on the lips.

What's happening to me? I asked myself, as I returned the kiss with an intensity that truly shocked me. How can I kiss Nico like this when I've just slept with Tim? This was all wrong.

'Do you want some wine?' I asked breathlessly when we came up for air.

'If you like.'

'I'll open this.' I picked up the bottle he had given me. 'I like Faustino.'

'OK.' Nico sat down. 'It's good to be back.'

I watched him for a moment, then I opened the bottle and poured the wine into glasses.

'You're supposed to say it's good to have me back,' he said.

'Of course it is.' I handed him the wine. 'Would you like a chocolate?'

'No, Isabella. They are for you.'

I sat on the sofa beside him.

'What have you been doing while I was away?' he asked.

'Well, I went home,' I said. 'That was a week. And I worked.'

'No play?'

'Oh, I went out a few times.'

'Anywhere nice?'

I shook my head.

'Did you miss me?' asked Nico.

'Naturally,' I replied.

'We are playing guitar tomorrow night,' he told me. 'Do you want to come along?'

'If I'm not working late.'

'Working late! Oh, Isabella, don't say that you have to work late. I thought we were both finished with working late.'

'Not yet,' I said. 'We're extremely busy right now.'

'The committed career woman,' he said. 'Try and come, *mia Isabella*.'

'Of course I'll try,' I said, more gently. 'Where are you playing?'

'The Meridien. Nine o'clock. We've never played there before – Juan and Emilio were very worried in case I wouldn't be home in time! Why don't you bring your friends?'

'Maybe.'

He reached out for me and held me close to him. He ran his fingers gently down my arm. I couldn't believe the way I was feeling. I looked up at him. The passion was there, easy to read. He slid the cotton top from my shoulders.

'From the moment that I left, I wanted to come back,' he told me. 'I have never felt about a woman the way I do about you, Isabella.'

I swallowed. I didn't love him. I *couldn't* love him.

He kissed me so gently. Tenderly, his lips soft, his body hard. Should I say yes to this? I wondered wildly. Or should I think of Tim and remember that he said he loved me.

'Are you all right?' asked Nico suddenly.

'I – I'm – of course.'

'And this is OK with you?' He moved his fingers from the base of my throat to the swell of my breasts. Desire exploded within me. And suddenly I wanted him for no other reason than he was there and he loved me and I wanted him to love me.

~

He was a wonderful lover. Part of me had thought that he wouldn't be, and that was why he hadn't tried to get me into bed before now. I didn't compare him with anyone as he covered my body in kisses. I couldn't even think when he moved inside me. I had never before abandoned myself so utterly to another person. My mind was completely blank and the only thing that mattered in the world was the closeness of him, the scent of him, the feeling of him.

Afterwards I didn't feel guilty. I didn't feel as I had after any of the others. It had been too great an experience for that. But I had no idea of where I went from here.

~

'Are you busy tonight?' I asked Magdalena next morning.

'Not really.' She laughed. 'I was going to go to my exercise class. But if you have an excuse to put it off, that's great!'

'You don't need to exercise,' I said. 'You're fine the way you are.'

'Thank you, Isobel. But I have put on nearly half a kilo in the last few months and I want to lose it.'

'Abandon your class tonight,' I said. 'And come with me to hear Nico play.'

'Nico!' Her eyes glinted. 'He is back in Madrid, your Nico?'

'Of course he's back in Madrid,' I said irritably. 'That's why I'm going to hear him play.'

'And have you seen him yet?'

I blushed. I couldn't help it. I could feel the colour start in my cheeks and rush to my forehead.

'Isobel!' Her eyes glinted even more.

'What?'

'When did you see him?'

'Last night.'

'And did you give him a warm welcome?'

'What do you think?' I asked.

'I think you must have given him a very warm welcome indeed to look like that.' She grinned at me.

'Oh, Magdalena,' I sighed. 'I didn't mean to, you know.'

'Does it matter?' She looked at me curiously. 'Is everything all right, Isobel?'

'To be honest, I don't know.'

The phone on my desk rang. 'Señora Mantilla. How are you? Can I help?'

Magdalena made a face at me. Señora Mantilla was one of our most difficult clients. 'Good luck,' she mouthed and slipped out of the office.

❧

I was busy all day. Gabriela had gone to Barcelona again

409

but had managed to leave one of her computer disks behind. Although she was good at running the company, our boss was not the world's most computer-literate person. Eventually we managed to download the disk onto her computer, but not before she'd done her best to try and wipe her presentation from the hard disk.

'I don't know why I bother sometimes,' I muttered to Luis, who'd prepared the disk Gabriela had left behind. 'I think she does it to make life more difficult.'

'Of course she does,' he said seriously. 'It's a test, every time.'

'It bloody better not be,' I told him. 'I don't need her testing me.'

'You're very irritable,' said Luis.

'I'm sorry,' I sighed.

⤙

I wanted to sit back and listen to the music that night but Magdalena insisted that I tell her everything that had happened with Nico. And with Tim. Gabriela had told her about Tim's arrival in Madrid.

'To be honest,' said Magdalena, 'I thought you'd tell me about it, Isobel.'

'I would have,' I said. 'But it didn't seem important.'

'But your ex-fiancé.' She looked at me. 'It's something worth telling, Isobel.'

'I wanted to forget about it,' I said.

'Why?'

The audience clapped as Nico, Emilio and Juan walked onto the tiny stage. They looked great in their flowing white shirts and skin-tight black jeans.

Magdalena nudged me. 'Who is that one?'

'Emilio,' I told her. 'He's nice.'

'But your Nico is the best-looking of all, no?'

Of course he was. Easily. My Nico. I shivered.

'I wish I could play like that,' said Magdalena enviously. 'It's so lovely.'

Haunting, I thought. I watched Nico as his fingers moved over the strings of the guitar. As they had over me, I remembered, and it had been so wonderful. I felt the desire fizz up inside me again. It was as well that nobody could read my thoughts or see the images that ran through my head.

When they finished they received a rapturous applause. They smiled at the audience, bowed once and retreated behind the tiny stage.

'Will they join us?' asked Magdalena.

'I think they play again a little later,' I said. 'And then they'll join us.'

'So tell me,' she topped up our glasses from the bottle of wine, 'what is the story about you and Nico?'

'There's no story,' I said. 'Honestly.'

'How can you say that, Isobel. I saw the way you looked at him.'

I flushed. 'And how exactly was that?'

'As though you belonged to him.'

'Well, I don't. And he doesn't belong to me. If I've learned one thing over the last few years, it's that people don't belong to each other.'

'But you love him?'

'God, Magdalena, I just don't know.' I looked miserably at her. 'I don't trust how I feel about anything any more.'

'Maybe you think about it too much,' she said. 'Maybe you shouldn't try to analyse how you feel.'

'I think I have to,' I said. 'I left Ireland because of Tim. You know the story, Magdalena.' (Everyone in Advanta knew the story by now.) 'And when I came here first I just wanted to have a good time. Although I didn't really enjoy having a good time! Then I met Nico. And he's one of the nicest people I know. But I didn't think he loved me. Cared for me, yes. But love – it's a different thing. So I went home for my friend's wedding and I met Tim again.'

She sipped her wine as she listened to me. Her eyes never left my face.

'And he told me that he loved me and that everything had been a mistake and that he wished he'd married me.'

'Isobel!'

'And I told him that it was far too late, that I had a new life. But he sent me messages. And Nico was in Seville.'

'Oh, Isobel.'

'And then Tim arrived in Madrid. He was like a limpet. He was with me all the time.'

'So you slept with him?'

I nodded. 'I didn't want to. Well, maybe I did. That's the whole thing, Magdalena, I just don't know any more. So he went back to Ireland and he rings all the time and tells me he loves me. Then Nico came back from Seville and he arrived at my apartment with wine and flowers and—'

'You slept with him,' said Magdalena in a matter-of-fact tone.

'God, Magdalena, I feel awful.'

'But you have slept with other men in Madrid.'

'How much do you know about me?' I asked her. 'I mean, is my entire life the subject of office gossip or something? Does everyone know every mistake I've ever made?'

'Luis told me,' said Magdalena.

'Luis. I might have known.'

'He cares about you a lot,' she said.

'Oh, really.'

'Yes. He likes you. He thinks you have courage.'

'Why?' I laughed harshly. 'Because I did what he did? Slept with people I didn't care about?'

'That's unfair,' said Magdalena.

'Why are you defending him?' I asked.

'I'm not defending him,' she said. 'I'm defending you. Who says you didn't care about the people you slept with?'

I stared at her and suddenly wanted to cry.

'Come on, Isobel,' she said. 'It's not so bad.'

'It feels like it is,' I said.

'You don't have to care about anyone if you don't want to,' she said. 'You can sit at home every evening and watch TV if you like. There's no rule that says there has to be a man in your life.'

'I know,' I said glumly. 'But I can't seem to keep them out of it.'

~

Nico and the others played once more, then came to the table and sat with us. I introduced him to Magdalena and she told him that the music had been magical. Then, unashamedly, she turned her attention to Emilio.

'Did you enjoy it?' asked Nico.

'The music? I always enjoy it,' I told him. 'You have an incredible gift, Nico.'

'*Gracias.*' He smiled mockingly.

'I mean it. You should chuck the company and take up music full-time.'

'But I cannot do that, Isabella. I have to earn my living, you know.'

'And you don't think you could earn it from music?'

'I don't think so.'

'In spite of the jingles?'

He made a face. 'The jingles are not music.'

'But with them and with the nights you play—'

'I still would not make enough, Isabella.'

'For what?' I asked. 'You're an independent person. You don't need to make a lot of money.'

'Perhaps.' He looked at me oddly. 'But perhaps one day I will need the money. When I have a family of my own.'

I could feel myself shaking. I wanted to get out of this conversation. Quickly.

'Oh, musicians don't settle down,' I said as lightly as I could. 'Everybody knows that.'

'Isobel, would you like another drink?' Magdalena rescued me.

'A *café solo* would be nice,' I answered gratefully.

'And you, Nico?'

'*Un vaso de vino tinto, por favor.*'

'Do you want something to eat?' I asked.

He shook his head. 'I'm not hungry. I'll have *tortilla* when I go home.'

'OK.' I felt snubbed even though he'd been perfectly friendly.

I sipped my coffee while the others laughed and talked. I felt as though I wasn't really here, as though I was watching myself. Isobel Kavanagh, in Spain. With friends. Trying to say the right thing. But did she really fit in?

'Are you all right, Isabella?' Nico turned to me.

'I'm fine,' I said. 'Why?'

'You seem distracted.'

'A little,' I told him. 'It was a busy day today.'

'Would you like to go home?'

If I said yes, would he want to come with me? Would he want to make love to me again?

'Maybe I should,' I said finally. 'I can hardly keep my eyes open.'

'Come on.' Nico stood up. 'I will talk to you guys tomorrow. And it was wonderful to meet you, Magdalena.'

'You too.' She smiled at him. '*Buenas noches*.'

'*Buenas noches*,' said Nico and I together.

~

We walked in silence to the Edificio Gerona. I couldn't think of a single thing to say. Nico didn't seem to feel the need to say anything.

The lift was broken. I was breathless when we got to the fifth floor and had to fish around in my bag for my inhaler. Nico watched as I puffed at it.

'Is it allergic, your asthma? Or psychological?'

'Both, I suppose.' I unlocked the apartment door.

'And you have had it all your life?'

'Yes.'

'Anybody else in your family suffer?'

'Not in my immediate family,' I told him. 'But my mother's sister, Rachel, wheezes too.'

'It doesn't affect you too badly.'

'Only when I'm under pressure,' I said. 'If I've had to rush. If something smells very strongly.' I shrugged. 'It's not important.'

'What is important to you, Isabella?'

'Nico, stop acting like a doctor. Would you like me to make you some *tortilla*?'

His dark eyes glinted. 'How domesticated!'

'I will make some if you're hungry.'

Why did everything we said sound as if we were talking about something else? Why did I feel so off-balance tonight?

'OK, Isabella.' Suddenly he smiled. 'I will risk your homemade *tortilla*.'

I broke some eggs into a bowl and began to whisk

them. Nico turned on the TV. They were showing *ER*. I heated some oil in a pan and poured the eggs into it.

'That smells great,' said Nico.

I flipped the omelette over, sprinkled it with basil and oregano, then slid it onto a plate.

'*Tenga.*'

'*Gracias.*'

I spooned coffee into the cafetière. I'd never be able to sleep tonight, I thought. All this caffeine running through my body.

The phone rang and I jumped.

I picked up the receiver.

'Did you like my poem?' asked Tim Malone.

I glanced at Nico who was eating the omelette and reading the newspaper. 'Very unlike you,' I told Tim. 'But yes.'

'I'm trying to be unpredictable,' he told me. 'I want you to be surprised by me.'

'I was always surprised by you.' I smiled slightly.

'I just rang to say that I miss you,' he said. 'And that the sentiments in the poem – well, it's how I feel.'

'Oh, Tim!' I hadn't meant to say his name but I couldn't help it.

Nico glanced up from the paper.

'I want you to know how much I love you,' said Tim. 'And how much I miss you. And how much I want you to come home.'

'I really don't think it's a good idea to talk about this now.' I moved away from the sofa, closer to the window.

'Why not?'

'It's late.'

'Am I boring you?'

'No.'

Nico was reflected in the glass. His head was bent over

the paper as though he was concentrating deeply on the news. But he couldn't have been. I know I'd have been eavesdropping if I was him.

'You must know how I feel, Isobel. And you know you feel the same way. You know you do! Otherwise you never would have come to the room with me and—'

'Tim!'

'What are you hiding from?' he asked. 'God, I know I treated you badly. I've spent the last couple of years realising that. But that doesn't mean that I can't make up for it, Isobel. Honestly.'

'I know,' I said, although I knew nothing of the sort. 'But I don't want to talk about it now.'

'All right.' He sighed. 'I'll phone you tomorrow.'

'OK.'

'Sleep well, Isobel.'

'You too.'

'I'll be thinking about you.'

'Really?'

'I'm always thinking about you.'

'Goodnight,' I said and put the receiver down.

I poured out the coffee and handed a cup to Nico.

'*Gracias,*' he said. 'Who was on the telephone?'

I shrugged. 'An old friend.'

'Is this an old male friend?' asked Nico casually.

'Yes.'

'A good friend?'

'Once.'

'I see.' He sipped his coffee. 'Did you see in the newspaper that there will be a strike on the metro next week? That will be trouble, don't you think?'

'I didn't notice it,' I said. 'When will it start?'

Nico rustled through the paper. 'Monday morning. I will have to get up early for work.'

'Me too,' I said brightly. 'I'm going to see some clients

on the other side of the city. I must leave myself plenty of time.'

Nico drained his cup. 'I must go,' he said. He looked at me for a moment. 'You are tired, Isabella?'

'I – yes.'

'That is a pity.' He reached out and touched my face, very gently. 'Perhaps you need a good night's sleep.'

'Perhaps.'

He kissed me on the lips, but it was a casual kiss. 'I will telephone you.'

'Yes. Please.'

'Take care, *querida*.'

'You too,' I said.

Chapter 27

Girl Seated Seen from the Rear (Salvador Dalí, 1925)

It was a bad-hair day, one of those days when lots of little things conspire against you so that you feel as though God has singled you out for special, irritating attention.

My alarm clock didn't go off so I was late getting up. My hairdryer cut out with a loud bang, a flurry of dust and blew the fuses in the apartment. I missed the metro by seconds as I clattered into the station, my still-damp hair swinging around my face.

It didn't stop in the office either. Nina rang in sick, I lost the file of our October students and I knocked over a cup of coffee and ruined the memo I'd just printed. I was cursing grimly to myself when Gabriela walked in.

'Hi, Isobel.' She looked flustered. 'Sorry to barge in on you, but I'm having a crisis.'

'You too?' I finished mopping the coffee from my desk and threw the tissue into the bin.

'Rosa has chicken pox,' said Gabriela. 'And I think Julio will get it too. I came in because I had a meeting this morning, but I've got to get back home again. Rosa is feeling sorry for herself and I have to stop her scratching her spots.'

'Poor thing,' I commiserated.

'But I need you to do me a favour.' Gabriela put a folder on my desk. 'I was supposed to go to Barcelona tomorrow – you know, the conference on corporate training? I can't go now. I'd like you to go instead.'

'Oh.' I looked at her blankly.

'Is this a problem, Isobel?'

I shook my head. 'Not at all.'

She smiled with relief. 'I was afraid that you were going to refuse.'

'How can I refuse?' I grinned at her. 'You're the boss.'

'Yes, but—'

'It's OK, Gabriela. Honestly.'

'You will like Barcelona,' she said. 'It is a pretty city.'

'I won't have much time to see it.' I glanced at the schedule for the conference.

'Oh, you can stay for the weekend if you like,' said Gabriela. 'I was booked in for tomorrow and Thursday, but if you want to stay for Friday and Saturday, that's OK.'

'Perhaps.'

'Whatever you like. I've really got to go.' She looked anxiously at her watch. 'Silvia is looking after them but they can be hell if they're sick.'

'Go,' I said. 'Don't worry about anything.'

She smiled at me and disappeared. I wiped a spot of coffee from the keyboard.

Two days in Barcelona would be nice although Nico would be pissed off at me. We were supposed to be going to dinner tomorrow night. He wouldn't be all that understanding if I cancelled.

Since the night we'd made love our relationship had changed. Of course it had to change, but it hadn't changed for the better. I felt guilty for having slept with him even though I desperately wanted to sleep with him again. But I was still getting the e-mails from Tim and I kept thinking of Tim every night when I went to bed. And Nico didn't try to make love to me again. I think – but I'm not sure – that I was offended by that! It was as though I hadn't been good enough for him.

There was a barrier between us and it wasn't entirely of my making.

I sighed and reached for the phone.

'Alvarez.'

'Hi, Nico, it's me. Isobel.'

'*Hola, Isabella.*' He was casual.

'I called because I can't go to dinner with you tomorrow night.'

'Why not?' It sounded as though he was only half-listening to me.

'I've got to go to Barcelona for Gabriela.'

'Lucky you,' said Nico.

'It's only for a couple of days. I'll be back by the weekend.'

'Whatever you like.'

'I'm sorry,' I said. 'I was looking forward to dinner.'

'Were you?'

'Of course I was.'

'It doesn't matter,' he said. 'You can call me when you get back.'

'Nico?'

'Yes?'

I sighed. 'Nothing.' I replaced the receiver. It had been a very unsatisfactory telephone call.

∽

The conference finished on Thursday afternoon. Despite Gabriela's assurances that there would be no problem in staying over, I wanted to leave Barcelona. For an unknown reason I was caught in a black depression and I didn't have the heart to go sightseeing. So I stuck to the original timetable and caught the seven o'clock flight back to Madrid.

The arrivals hall was crowded but I saw Nico straight away. Tall and dark and with an indefinable something that made him stand out from the crowd. My heart contracted as he smiled at me.

'What are you doing here?' I asked. 'How did you know I was coming back tonight?'

'I rang your office,' he said simply. 'Nina told me.'

'It was good of you to come.'

'I wanted to.' He lifted my bag from my shoulder. 'Allow me.'

I was glad to let him take it. It was getting heavier by the second.

'I brought the car,' said Nico.

He rarely drove his car; Madrid was not the type of city you drove in for pleasure.

'Come on.' He opened the door for me. I moved a dozen CDs and a sheaf of music out of the way and got in.

'Did you enjoy the conference?' Nico drove like all Spaniards – fast.

'Yes.' I clutched at the arm-rest in the door as we hurtled around a corner.

'I thought it would be very boring.'

'Mostly it was,' I admitted. 'But there were some interesting bits.'

'Worth missing dinner for?'

'Don't get at me, Nico.'

'I'm sorry.' He sped through amber lights and I closed my eyes tightly.

'Here we are.'

I opened my eyes again. We weren't anywhere near my apartment.

'I thought we could have dinner tonight instead,' said Nico.

'Where are we?'

'This is my home,' he said as he got out of the car.

We were on a tree-lined avenue. Small villas and low-rise apartment buildings stood side-by-side.

'This block is where my apartment is. I am on the top floor.' It was only three stories high. Brightly coloured flowers climbed the whitewashed walls and each balcony was dotted with terracotta pots bursting with blossoms.

I followed him up the cream and brown marble stairs to his apartment. The interior walls of the building were hung with reproduction Picassos and Mirós. On each stairway a huge cactus plant thrust out of a glazed urn.

'At least the apartment hasn't burnt to the ground.' Nico unlocked the door. 'Come in.'

The living room of Nico's apartment was at least twice the size of mine and his balcony reached around two sides of the building. The interior walls were apple-white and covered with old theatre prints. The table in the dining area was pale wood and a huge blue and red porcelain bowl of fruit was in its centre. The apartment was surprisingly stylish for a man who lived on his own. I couldn't help comparing it with the mess that had been Tim's house. I doubted very much that Nico had ever left an empty takeaway carton on the beautiful dining-table.

'I'm not the best cook in Madrid.' Nico stood beside me. 'But I do my best for you, Isabella. There is a chicken cooking in the oven – I hope – and I have prepared vegetables also.'

'Oh, Nico, thank you,' I said.

'When I eat for myself, I usually send out for food.' He smiled sheepishly. 'Not good, healthy food. Pizzas and burgers usually.'

'Very nutritious,' I said.

'But I have made a special effort for you,' he promised. 'I hope you like it.'

'Of course I will.'

Tim had never cooked for me. Tim had never made a special effort for me. Maybe the new Tim had a *cordon bleu* qualification and would slave over a hot cooker for me whenever I wanted. I pushed thoughts of him to the back of my mind.

Despite his protestations, Nico was a surprisingly good cook. I enjoyed the meal and I was almost content lying in the curve of his arm on his comfortable grey sofa afterwards.

'You are very special to me, Isabella,' he whispered as he curled my hair between his fingers. 'Very special.'

He kissed me. I loved the way Nico kissed me. I followed him into his very masculine bedroom and we made love with a strange kind of desperation that matched my mood and that made him hold me tighter than he ever had before.

'Stay the night with me,' he murmured. 'There is no need for you to go back, is there?'

There wasn't. I didn't have to go into the office the next day if I didn't want to. I would, of course, but I didn't have to be at my desk at the crack of dawn. And I wanted to stay with Nico. I wanted to burrow into the bed beside him and lie in the warmth of his arms. I wanted so much, yet I didn't know exactly what I needed. And, yes, when we were locked together, then I felt special.

∽

He was already out of bed when I woke up the following morning. I could hear him whistle to himself as he clattered around in the kitchen. I slid out of bed and grabbed a discarded T-shirt which hung over the back of a chair. I looked at myself in the mirror. My eyes were dark smudges in a pale face. Nico's T-shirt, smelling of *Polo*, was long and almost reached my knees.

The aroma of freshly brewed coffee enticed me into the kitchen. Everything was clinically clean here too. The worktops were grey stone, the sink was polished chrome and the cooker was a very businesslike unit built into the pale wood surrounds.

'*Café solo?*' He handed me a tiny cup.

'*Gracias.*' I sipped the coffee and looked around with interest. There was a photograph on the wall of the kitchen and I moved closer to it.

It showed Nico standing in front of a detached two-storey villa. His parents were on one side of him. He had his arm around the girl on his left and she looked up at him, adoration in her eyes. She had creamy skin, a perfect face, and long black hair that almost reached her waist.

'Who's she?' I asked casually.

'That's Carmen,' he said, equally casually.

'Is she a relative?'

The question was so silly that I was surprised he took it seriously. He shook his head. 'She was a friend of mine.'

'A close friend?'

'She was a girlfriend, Isabella. We went out with each other for a long time.'

'And did you love her?' I asked.

He was silent for a moment and sipped his coffee carefully. 'Who knows?'

'Either you loved her or you didn't.' My tone was petulant.

'I loved her for a time,' he said.

'You look very happy in that photograph.' I peered at it more closely. 'When was it taken?'

'Last year,' said Nico.

So last year, when I had been nursing a broken heart, Nico had been in love with the girl in the photograph. Carmen. Maybe he'd made love to her in this apartment, in the same bed as he'd made love to me. Perhaps he'd cooked her *pollo con ajo*, as he'd cooked it for me. I supposed he'd whispered '*Carmen, querida*' to her as he'd murmured '*Isabella, querida*' to me.

And why shouldn't he? I hadn't known him then; God knows I'd had a love of my own to worry about. And yet I felt a sudden stab of jealousy and its intensity shocked me. I'd never expected to feel like this. The coffee was bitter in my mouth.

'Why did you split up?' I asked.

'For goodness sake, Isabella!' He looked at me in annoyance. 'It's only a photograph.'

'I know what it is.'

'Well, then.'

'But it's a photograph of your ex-girlfriend.'

'So what?'

'There's something odd about a man who keeps a photo of his ex-girlfriend hanging in his house.' Suddenly I thought of Tim and our engagement photo on his mantelpiece and I blushed furiously. But Nico didn't notice my flaming face.

'Isabella, you're being silly.'

'I'm not.'

'Yes, you are. I don't like it when you act like a child.'

'Don't talk to me like that.' I glared at him.

He turned away and rinsed his coffee cup. I watched

him, angry and upset. He took a diary from a shelf and looked through it. It was clear to me that he didn't want to talk to me. That the subject of Carmen – *Carmen querida* – was too sensitive.

'Do you mind if I have a shower?' I asked finally.

He glanced up from the diary. 'Go ahead.'

I stalked into the bathroom. The water in the shower was so hot that I nearly lost a layer of skin. I got dressed and walked back into the living room. Nico was flicking through some brochures.

'I'd better go to work,' I told him.

'OK,' he said. 'I'm meeting some clients, I won't be in the office today.'

'Thank you for dinner last night.'

'*De nada.*' He barely looked up from his work.

'Will you call me?'

'I'm playing in Quixote tonight. Tomorrow perhaps?' He turned over a page.

'Sure. Tomorrow.' I picked up my bag. 'I'll get the metro to the office.'

He stood up. 'I'd carry it for you, but I am late already.'

'It's OK.'

He smiled slightly. 'Have a good day, Isabella.'

'Sure.'

He kissed me on the cheek. 'I'll call you.'

&

I stood in the metro station, jostled in every direction by *Madrileños* hurrying to work. I was hurt by Nico's sudden indifference and upset by the evidence of his previous girlfriend. And I didn't know why I was so upset. And I didn't know what to do next. And I didn't know what I wanted to do next.

❧

Friday night in Madrid. I sat on the balcony and listened to the sound of the traffic, the sudden blaring of a car horn, people calling to each other. I went inside and got my briefcase. I took out the notes I'd made at the conference. I read about training schedules, conference organisers, hotel facilities, in-house programmes, expert lecturers. I sat with the sheaves of paper on my lap and I didn't move, even when my stupid tears smudged the print so that I couldn't read any more.

❧

The telephone woke me the following morning, dragging me from the fitful sleep I'd finally fallen into. A headache pounded at the top of my head.

'*Hola,*' I croaked.

'Isobel? Is that you?'

'Alison.' I blinked a few times and looked at my watch. 'What are you doing out of bed at nine o'clock on a Saturday morning?'

'It's only eight here,' she said. 'I had to phone you. It's awful news. Granny Behan died last night.'

'What?' I blinked again.

'Last night,' repeated Alison. 'Granny Behan died.'

'How's Mum?'

'Oh, OK – ish,' said Alison. 'You know.'

'What happened?'

'Heart attack, I think. Her next-door neighbour always calls in on Friday nights. When Granny didn't answer the door she got worried and phoned. Dad went over. Granny was dead in her armchair.'

'Oh, God.'

'The funeral's on Monday.'

'I'll be there,' I said. 'Is Mum up yet?'

'No,' said Alison. 'She was very upset last night. Dad made her drink some brandy and she's asleep now.'

'I'll phone later,' I said. 'I'll let her know about my flight.'

'I can't believe she's dead.' Alison sounded suddenly bewildered. 'One minute she's alive and one minute she's dead. It doesn't seem possible.'

'No.'

'I'd better go. I've got to do things. I'll wait to hear from you later.'

'OK,' I said. 'Thanks for ringing.'

'Sorry to muck up your weekend.'

I hung up and sat on the sofa.

We weren't a very close family. We'd visited Granny Behan when we were children, of course, but she wasn't a story-book granny – she wasn't plump and welcoming with grey hair and glasses. Granny Behan had been a tall, angular woman whose bones had stuck in you. She wasn't the sort of granny who'd play chasing around the back garden or allow you to mess up her furniture. Granny Behan had treated us like miniature adults and, when we were in her house, that was how we behaved. But whenever there was anything wrong, when we'd fallen or hurt ourselves, or when Mum needed to go somewhere, Granny Behan had always been there to look after us.

'Those dreadful children,' she'd say, looking at us from soft brown eyes that belied her stern appearance. And she'd bandage us, tell us not to be silly, no need for tears and give us her encyclopaedia to look through.

I hadn't seen Granny Behan the last time I was in Dublin. I regretted not having made the effort now. Caught up in my own world I hadn't thought of her. Poor Gran. Poor Mum.

I reached out for the phone. I needed to talk to Nico. He'd understand. He'd comfort me.

But I only heard the shrill ringing at the other end. Nico wasn't there.

Chapter 28

Weeping Woman (Pablo Picasso, 1937)

The sky was blue and cloudless but a cool breeze rustled through the leaves of the trees in the graveyard and I pulled my cotton jacket more tightly around me as we prayed for Granny Behan.

Mum threw clay onto the coffin, a dull thud followed by the sound of pebbles sliding on the polished wood. We turned away and walked to the cars.

'She had a long life,' said Mum later, as we dispensed tea and sandwiches back at her house. 'And she'd be glad to go quickly.'

People always said that. Maybe it was true.

'I wish I'd seen her again.' Rachel stood beside my mother. She was pale and subdued, quite unlike her usual cheerful self.

'She knew you were thinking about her,' said Mum.

'But I wasn't.' Rachel stirred her tea. 'I wasn't thinking about her at all.'

'Of course you were,' said Mum determinedly. 'You just had her to the back of your mind, that's all. With family, you're always thinking about them. They're with you all the time.'

Mum was a great believer in family.

'It's just so hard to believe.' Rachel's eyes watered. 'So quickly.' She took her tea and walked out to the garden.

'Always dramatising.' Mum handed me a cup. 'Drink this, Isobel, you look shattered.'

'Headache,' I muttered.

'Take something for it.'

'I did.'

Mum looked at me quizzically. 'You all right?'

I nodded. 'I'm OK.'

'Working too hard,' she said.

I smiled wanly. 'No, not really.'

Tessa Blaney, one of Mum's friends, joined us. 'Why don't you have a nice cup of tea yourself, Helen,' she said gently. 'You could probably do with it.'

'I will, when I see to everyone else.'

'Let me worry about them for a while. Go on, Helen. Have a bit of a sit down.'

She nudged Mum away from the teapot and made her take a cup of the steaming brown liquid. 'It'll do you good.'

'I suppose so.' Mum went and joined Rachel in the garden.

They looked very alike sitting on the low stone wall together. Mum's hair was greyer, but they had the same features, the same expressions, the same way of half-raising an eyebrow when they were talking to each other. Family.

'And how are you, Isobel?' asked Tessa. 'I hear you're doing really well over there in Spain.'

'Not bad, Mrs Blaney.'

'Are you having a good time?'

'Oh, yes. Fine.'

'Job's going well?'

'Yes.'

432

'And tell me, have you met any nice young man over there?'

I smiled at her. 'There's lots of nice young men over there.'

'Any one in particular?'

There had been, of course. But Nico hadn't answered his phone at all on Saturday. And I wasn't going to go to his apartment and start ringing the bell.

'Sometimes,' I compromised.

'Well, isn't it great to be young and have men dancing attendance on you?'

'I wouldn't know,' I said.

Tessa Blaney laughed. 'Don't lie to me, Isobel Kavanagh. I can tell there's someone.'

I smiled again and my head hurt. I wished Tessa would go away. I wanted to be on my own.

'Isobel!' Ian beckoned to me across the room. I excused myself from Tessa. 'Thought you were looking particularly trapped,' he said.

'I was.'

'Are you OK?' he asked. 'You look dreadful.'

'Thanks!'

'I don't mean it like that.' He shrugged. 'You're awfully pale, you know.'

'I'm fine,' I told him. 'Headache, that's all.'

'This bloody thing would give anyone a headache.' He looked around. 'All these people! Who'd have thought Granny knew them all?'

'I don't suppose she did,' I said. 'Lots of them are Mum's friends. They've come to offer support.'

'Support!' He snorted. 'Support in eating sandwiches and drinking tea. Or whiskey.' He nodded in the direction of Tessa's husband who held a crystal glass filled with an overgenerous measure.

'Why not?' I asked. 'They came to the funeral. Probably

433

the last thing they wanted to do today. The least we can do is give them something to eat and drink.'

'Are you getting sensible?' asked Ian. 'Or have you just become a bit of an old woman?'

'Sod off,' I said companionably and he put his arm around my shoulder and squeezed me.

Ian's Honey had come to the funeral Mass but she'd gone back to work directly afterwards, explaining that she hadn't been able to get a stand-in to take her appointments.

It was all back on again with Honey, apparently. 'Can't seem to live without her,' Ian had told me. 'Something about her, Issy.'

'The fact that she has legs up to her armpits,' I had teased gently.

Alison and Peter sat side-by-side. They looked completely natural together and right for each other, two fair heads bent close, engrossed in their own world.

'Are you sure you're OK?'

I'd sighed without realising it and Ian was looking at me anxiously.

'I wish people would stop asking me that,' I said crossly. 'There's nothing wrong with me.'

'Mum says that they work you like a slave in Madrid.'

'What would she know?' I asked. 'And they don't. Besides, I like it.'

'Alison told me that you had a boyfriend there.'

'On and off,' I said.

'Not serious then?'

I looked at my brother. I'd never discussed relationships with him before. Not really. I'd always thought of him as too young, even when he'd sympathised with me about Tim and then later, when, with Alison, he'd warned me about getting involved with him again.

'Not serious,' I said.

'But you look – sad.'

'We're at a funeral, Ian. It's supposed to be sad.'

'Not this bit,' said my brother. 'This is where people laugh and tell stories.'

'You're dreadful,' I told him. 'Really dreadful.'

But he was right. Under the influence of the whiskey and the tea, people were chatting easily, smiling, even joking a little. Mum and Rachel were talking animatedly now, Rachel using her hands to illustrate some point and Mum mimicking her.

Why did I feel as though I was frozen inside? Why did I want to go home to Sutton, throw myself on the single bed and wrap the duvet around me as I'd done when I was a teenager? Surely the ache that I felt now, that indescribable ache for no reason, surely that was a relic of teenage angst and had no place in the life of someone who was thirty?

A successful, career-woman thirty.

With no one to put his arm around her as Peter did around Alison. Or no one to confide in as Ian did with Honey. Or no one to laugh with as Andy and Julie did.

Don't be so bloody stupid, I told myself viciously. You are an independent woman. Being married is no longer the aim of your life. And if you need a hug and a kiss right now you only have to call Tim Malone. He'd be happy to oblige. You wouldn't even have to ask.

The hum of conversation continued. I still felt as though I was trapped in my own world, cocooned from everyone else. I talked to people I hadn't seen in a long time – Ursula Walsh, Gran's next-door neighbour, who'd always seemed very old to me but now, inexplicably, looked younger than her fifty-five years; Paddy Reynolds, who owned the butcher's shop in Sutton, the only place Gran ever bought meat and the only place Mum ever bought it either; Cliona Hughes, the lecturer at the

English literature evening class that Gran attended. I hadn't known Gran was going to English literature classes – she was seventy-seven, what more could she learn? But Cliona Hughes said that Gran was a wonderful woman – sparky – and an inspiration to the class. She would have been sparky, I supposed. She'd always been more sparky than comfortable.

It was stupid to miss her now, when I hadn't seen her in so long. I washed cups and plates and stacked the dishes neatly in the pine cupboard beside the sink. Then I poured myself a Southern Comfort from the bottle on the table. I'd introduced Gran to Southern Comfort, five or six years ago. She'd loved it. I gulped back the drink and allowed it to warm me.

I wanted to go home. I was tired of being surrounded by people. I needed some quiet.

'Go ahead,' said Ian when I muttered to him that I could do with a bit of solitude. 'I'll keep an eye on Mum.'

'Do you mind?'

He shook his head. 'You look really tired, Issy. And you've got to go back to Spain tomorrow night.'

I smiled feebly at him. 'Jet-setting, that's me.'

'Go and have a sleep,' he advised. 'I won't tell Mum you've gone.'

'Thanks.' I kissed him on the shoulder which was as high as I reached on Ian these days. 'See you later.'

I walked back along the seafront, not caring that the breeze was still cold. I was nearly knocked down by half-a-dozen children rollerblading at high speed along the cycle track. I thought of the rollerbladers in the Retiro Park who didn't go for speed, just intricate jumps and spins and loops. But for the first time ever the thought of sitting in the park didn't cheer me up. All I wanted was to fall asleep and be somewhere apart from the day-time world.

But I couldn't go to sleep. I lay in my bedroom and counted sheep but I stayed wide awake. I tried breathing slowly and evenly but only induced a fit of coughing. I pulled the quilt around my shoulders and burrowed under the pillow but I could still hear the birds in the tree outside the window and the sound of children laughing as they played on the road outside.

I got out of bed again and went downstairs. I took the washing in off the line. I sat in the garden. I pulled a few weeds. Then I went inside and phoned Softsys.

'Just a moment,' said Shauna brightly when I asked for Tim Malone. She'd hesitated for a second, trying to place my voice, but couldn't remember me. I didn't give my name, said it was a personal call.

'Hello.'

'Hello, Tim?'

'Isobel? Isobel, how lovely to hear from you.'

'Thanks.'

'Are you OK? You sound a bit funny.'

'I'm at home, Tim. I came home for my grandmother's funeral.'

'Oh, Isobel. Your mum's mother?'

'Yes.'

'I'm sorry.'

'Me too.'

'Is your Mum OK?'

'Oh, I suppose so.'

'How long are you staying?' he asked.

'Not long,' I told him. 'I'm going back tomorrow afternoon.'

'That's not much of a break.'

'It's all I have time to take.'

'You sound fed up,' he said.

'I am.'

'Where are you now?'

'At home.'

'Your mum's?'

'It's the only home I have.'

'Do you want me to come out?' he asked.

I hesitated.

'Would you like to meet me?' he amended.

'Yes.'

'Well, do you want me to come out there, or will you come into town?'

I didn't know what I wanted.

'I'll come out there,' said Tim. 'You're obviously in shock, Isobel.'

'I shouldn't be in shock,' I said. 'She was my grandmother, after all. It's not as though it was Mum or Dad.'

'It's a shock all the same,' said Tim firmly. 'I'll be out in half an hour.'

Half an hour. Nobody would be back from Granny Behan's in half an hour. I washed my face and put on some foundation. I couldn't meet Tim looking pale and wan although it seemed somehow irreverent to apply eye-shadow and mascara, even if the eye-shadow was terracotta and the mascara colourless.

I waited in the front room until I saw his car pull up. I went outside straight away.

'Hi there.' He held out his arms and folded me to him.

'Hi.' I leaned against his shoulder. The comfort I wanted. The comfort I needed.

'Come on,' said Tim. 'Let's go.'

He drove up the hill of Howth and parked at the summit. He didn't speak during the drive, didn't try to ask me anything.

'Here.' He handed me a waxed jacket from the back seat of the car. 'It's chilly.'

'What about you?' I asked.

'I've got a jumper.' He grinned at me. 'Besides, I'm a man. We don't feel the cold.'

We walked precariously through the gorse and furze until we came to a clear patch and sat down overlooking the sea.

'It's beautiful, isn't it?' Tim's words encompassed the glittering water, the bright blue sky, the golden flowers around us and the wheeling, screeching gulls overhead.

'Yes.'

'More beautiful than Spain?'

'Different,' I said. I shivered.

'Are you cold?'

'Not really. This jacket's lovely.'

'Do you miss this in Madrid?'

'What?'

'The sea. The smell of it, the taste of it in the air.'

'Tim!' I looked at him. 'That's very lyrical.'

'I like the sea,' he said defensively. 'I'd hate to live somewhere land-locked.'

I smiled. 'I know. I like it too, although I've never quite got to grips with it like lots of the people around here. I don't do yachting or racing or even swimming very much.'

'It must be strange in Madrid, to know it's so far away.'

'If you go to the Palacio Real you can look over the approach to the city,' I told him. 'On a hot day it shimmers and shifts so that you can almost believe it is the sea.'

'Not quite the same thing,' said Tim.

'No.'

'And what other ways do you fool yourself in Madrid?' he asked.

'What!'

'I'm sorry.' He didn't really sound it.

'Don't get at me, Tim. I'm not in the mood.'

He hugged me. 'I didn't mean to get at you.'

'No?'

'No.'

I leaned against him again and closed my eyes. He was right about the sea. I missed it. I missed places that I'd known all my life, places that had meaning for me, where I'd grown up, learned about growing up. Madrid had been an escape for me, but had it served its purpose?

'Do you like my messages?' he asked.

'You must have to do a lot of work to send me poetry,' I murmured lazily.

'You inspire me,' he said.

'Don't be bloody stupid.' But it was nice to hear him say things like this. I wondered if he really loved me. It was as though he did, but – never sure, I thought to myself, never sure with Tim.

'I love you, Isobel.' He broke into my thoughts. 'Truly I do.'

'Oh, Tim.'

He kissed me. Slowly, surely, exploring me as though he'd never kissed me before. He ran his fingers through my hair, caressed my cheeks, held me tight.

'I want to be with you.' He held me away from him. 'I want to put my mistake right.'

I stood up. The wind buffeted me. Tim jumped up and steadied me.

'I was OK,' I told him. 'I'm not going to be knocked down by a gust of wind.'

'How do I know that?' he asked.

'I'm not that fragile,' I replied.

We stood side by side.

'I mean it, Isobel,' said Tim. 'I love you. I want you to marry me.'

He looked so earnest, so loving, so sincere. He was here with me when I needed him. He understood how I felt.

'Why?' I asked.

'Because we were meant for each other.'

I raised an eyebrow.

'And I've missed you.'

'Have you gone out with other people?' I asked.

He looked uncomfortable.

'I don't care,' I said hastily. 'I've gone out with other people myself. I just want to know.'

'A few girls,' he said. 'They didn't mean anything.'

'Did they know that?'

'Pardon?'

'Nothing.'

'We're a good team, Isobel. We can make it work.'

I stared out over the sea. 'What if it all gets too much for you again?' I asked.

'It wouldn't,' he said.

'How d'you know?'

'I just do.'

The sun sparkled off the water below us.

'Are you sure?'

'Of course,' he said.

'I'd have to get a job here,' I mused.

'You can have babies if that's what you want.'

'Tim!' I looked at him. 'I never wanted to marry you just to have babies.'

'But you want them?'

I thought of Gabriela's black-eyed children. 'Yes,' I said.

'So do I,' said Tim. 'I've thought about that a lot. When you talked about it before, it made me feel even more trapped. But now I feel differently.'

'Do you?'

'Absolutely. I reckon I'd be a good dad. Pretty nifty at the computer games, anyhow.'

I grinned at him. 'Competitive git.'

'We'll have wonderful children,' he told me.

Tim was giving me my life back. The one I always thought I'd have. I wanted it now. I really did.

'OK,' I said.

'OK what?'

'OK, I'll marry you.'

'Oh, Isobel.' He hugged me so hard that he squeezed all the breath out of me and I had to take a puff of my inhaler.

～

I didn't say anything to my family that night. It wasn't the right time. But I caught the DART into town next morning and met my fiancé.

'I hope this is OK.' He took a blue velvet box out of his pocket.

'Tim!' I opened it cautiously. My engagement ring sparkled at me. My first engagement ring.

'I kept it,' he said. 'I couldn't bring myself to go back to the jeweller with it and I—' He shrugged.

'Thought it might come in useful one day.' I slipped it on to my finger and watched the sun glitter against the stone.

'No,' he said.

'You weren't keeping it for me.'

'I don't know why I kept it,' he said honestly.

I smiled at him. 'It's lovely. It was lovely two years ago and it's lovely now.'

'I couldn't think of a more appropriate one. I wondered if it was quite right, giving you the same ring again, but I reckoned if you didn't like it you'd throw it back at me and we'd be back to square one again.'

I laughed. 'I never threw it at you.'

'You probably wanted to.'

'Maybe.'

He kissed me. 'I've got to get back to work. I know it's not the thing when you've just got engaged for the second time, but I do have a project bubbling and Greg is going mad for me to finish it.'

'All right.' I didn't mind. 'Do you want to drop me at the airport later?'

He hesitated for a second.

'It doesn't matter if you can't.'

'No. I want to. What time?'

'Four.'

'D'you want me to pick you up at home?' He looked apprehensive.

'I have to tell them,' I said. 'We might as well get it over with.'

'I wish you didn't have to go back today,' he said irritably. 'We can't talk things over properly. And we should get it all organised.'

'You sound like I used to.'

'*Touché.*'

'But you're right. We've just decided on this without thinking it through.'

'We don't need to think it through,' he told me firmly. 'We'll get married as soon as you tidy things up in Madrid. A winter wedding would be nice, don't you think?'

'I'm imagining me with goosepimples in a white dress,' I said. 'It's not a very attractive picture!'

'You'll be beautiful no matter what time of the year. I think the best thing would be for me to come to Madrid in a few weeks' time. Help you pack your stuff, that sort of thing. Have a pre-wedding holiday. We can settle on things then.'

'OK.' I was happy to let him take over.

'OK.' He kissed me again. 'I'll have to go, Isobel. I'm really sorry. I'll pick you up at four.'

'Fine. I'll go home and break the happy news.'

'Don't look so glum about it!'

'I'm not glum.' I smiled at him. 'I'm very, very happy.'

∽

My family's reaction was more muted than I'd expected. Well, there was only Mum and Dad to react – Alison and Ian were at work.

Mum was sitting at the kitchen table looking through the sample memoriam cards that had flooded through the doorway as soon as Gran's death had been announced. I thought it incredibly ghoulish and intrusive of companies to send them, but it seemed to give Mum a focus. She was reading the rhymes out loud.

'I know this probably isn't the best time,' I said as I sat down beside her. 'But I have some news.'

'News?' Her eyes were still far away.

'Good news,' I said brightly.

'I could do with good news.' She shuffled the cards together as though they were playing cards.

'I'm getting married.'

She stared at me.

'I'm engaged,' I said.

'Engaged? Who are you engaged to?'

I moistened my lips. 'Don't get mad at me.'

'I'm not mad.'

'Tim Malone.'

'What?' She blinked a couple of times. 'You're engaged to Tim Malone?'

'Yes.'

'But, Isobel—'

'I know what you're going to say and you're right. I had my doubts too. But I met him when I came home for Julie's wedding and I've been in touch with him ever since. We both realise that we still love each other and we want to get married.' Why did I sound so defiant?

'Well, Isobel, if it's what you want.' She looked more bewildered than ever.

'It's what I want.'

'But what about your job in Spain? I thought you loved that job. I thought you loved Madrid. I thought you had a boyfriend in Madrid.'

Isabella querida. But not when I needed him. And how come my mother was suddenly so enthusiastic about my life in Spain?

'Not a serious boyfriend,' I told her. 'And, yes, I like my job. But I need to think about my future. It's not in Madrid, Mum. It's here. Living here in my own house and raising my own family. That's what I want.'

'And you think you'll be happy with him?'

'I know I will.'

'You thought that before.' She looked anxiously at me.

'I know. And we got it all wrong.' I put my arm around her. 'But we'll get it right this time, Mum. I know we will.'

'I only want you to be happy.' Her eyes filled with tears. 'It's important, Isobel.'

'I know.' I held her close to me while she cried for her mother and I felt more grown-up than I ever had in my life before.

∼

Tim called at exactly four o'clock. He looked nervous.

'Come in.' I opened the hall door wide.

'Your dad isn't standing there with a hammer, is he?'

I shook my head. 'They're in the kitchen. Ian and Alison are at work.'

'I can't say I'm sorry to miss Alison,' he said.

'Don't be so scared.' I squeezed his arm. 'She doesn't mean to snap.'

'I'm not convinced about that,' he said darkly.

He followed me into the kitchen.

'Hello, Mr Kavanagh. Mrs Kavanagh.'

'Hello, Tim.' Dad stood up. 'I wasn't expecting to see you in this house again.'

'To be honest, I wasn't expecting it either,' said Tim. He looked very boyish. 'But I'm glad I came to my senses and I'm glad Isobel understands me.'

'I hope she doesn't have to do too much understanding!'

'Not at all.' My fiancé was extremely polite. 'I think we've worked through our difficulties and I'm really looking forward to settling down with her.'

'Just don't hurt her again,' said Dad gruffly.

'I'll never hurt her again,' said Tim.

'When are you going to get married?' Mum had asked me this already.

'Isobel will decide,' said Tim. 'She has to go back and sort things out in Spain and when she's ready, I'm ready. But I don't want to rush her.'

'I hope you're doing the right thing.' Her glance took in both of us.

'I know we are,' said Tim.

'We'd better go.' I picked up my bag. 'It wouldn't do for me to miss the flight.'

I kissed my parents goodbye and followed Tim to the car.

'Nightmare,' he breathed as we drove away.

'What d'you mean, nightmare?'

'Meeting them. I was afraid your dad might kill me.'

'They're not that bad.' I laughed.

'Who knows?' asked Tim. 'They probably blame me for everything.'

'Tim, it *was* all your fault.'

'You see?' But he was smiling. 'I knew you'd blame me.'

It was lovely to have him kiss me goodbye. To have someone who didn't want me to go. To feel the warmth of his embrace, the scratch of his five o'clock shadow as I sat on the plane. To know that he was waiting for me.

It was wonderful to know that he was waiting for me again.

Chapter 29

Girl Standing at the Window (Salvador Dalí, 1925)

I stood in the queue at the taxi rank outside the terminal building and felt a trickle of sweat slide down my back. The sky was blue-grey, thunder growled in the distance and the air was humid, difficult to breathe. I shook my inhaler and sucked on the mist. It didn't help all that much – it was like being in a sauna and I could never stay in a sauna for more than five minutes.

The taxi was air-conditioned. I sat back and gratefully breathed in the cool air. I had a headache again, made worse by the oppressive humidity. I rubbed my temples and closed my eyes. The taxi driver took the long way around to my apartment but I didn't care. Sometimes I'd argue with taxi drivers who took the long way around, but not today. Today I was too happy to argue, despite my headache and despite my wheezing lungs. Today was the beginning of the rest of my life. I held out my hand and turned it so that the diamond ring caught the sudden shaft of sunlight that had filtered into the taxi. Isobel Malone, I said to myself. Exactly as it was meant to be.

The thunder was closer. I paid the fare and hurried into the apartment building. The lift – working – glided up to the fifth floor.

Señora Carrasco was painting her front door.

'*Hola, Isobel.*' She waved the paintbrush in friendly greeting. 'Where have you been?'

'I was at home,' I told her. 'In Dublin. My grandmother died.'

'Oh, Isobel.' She placed the paintbrush carefully on the tin of paint and came over to me. 'I'm so sorry.'

'It's OK,' I said. 'She was old.'

Señora Carrasco hugged me. 'But it is a sad time, nonetheless.'

'Yes.' I took my keys out of my pocket.

My neighbour eyed me curiously. 'Are you all right, Isobel? You look very pale.'

'It's the weather,' I said.

'Yes.' She grinned. 'I do not like the storms. That is why I am painting inside.'

I laughed. 'I do. But only when it starts properly – thunder, lightning, rain!'

'We need some rain,' agreed Señora Carrasco.

'Well,' I smiled at her. 'I'd best get inside, tidy up.'

'Isobel!' She caught me by the hand. 'Isobel – you are wearing an engagement ring!'

'Yes.' I smiled at her again. 'I'm engaged to be married.'

She stared at me. 'I did not know. That is wonderful news – your friend is a very sexy man.'

I blushed, then shivered. 'I think you are mixing things up, Señora. You have not met my fiancé.'

'But—'

'I am marrying an old friend from Ireland.'

'I am surprised.' She regarded me thoughtfully. 'Your other friend spent so much time with you.'

I blushed and said nothing. Neither did she.

I opened my apartment door. 'I've got to go. I've things to do.'

'OK.' She walked back across the hall. 'No problem.'

'I—' But she'd picked up the paintbrush again. I shook my head. It didn't matter to me what she thought. Nothing mattered to me other than the fact that I was engaged to Tim again. And that I knew that he loved me.

I had a lukewarm shower and wrapped a robe around me. It was almost dark in the apartment now, the clouds overhead heavy and dark.

The phone rang and startled me.

'Hello, Isobel,' said Tim.

'Hi.'

'How're you doing?'

'Fine, thanks.'

'I just rang to say that I miss you.'

'Oh, Tim. And I miss you too.'

A clap of thunder broke almost overhead and I jumped.

'What was that?' asked Tim.

'Thunder,' I said. 'There's going to be a massive storm tonight. The sky is almost black and I can hardly breathe.'

'You're all right though?'

'Of course.'

'Well, I just rang to say I'm thinking of you.'

'And I'm thinking of you too.'

'Take care, Isobel.'

'You too, Tim.'

I hung up and walked onto the balcony. A flash of lightning lit up the sky, tearing it in half as it cut its way earthwards. A moment later peals of thunder rolled one after the other, crashing overhead. The lightning struck again. I stepped back towards the shelter of the apartment. I loved thunderstorms but I'd never seen anything like this before – huge, jagged bolts of lightning and thunder so loud that it seemed to surround me. God moving furniture around, Mum had told me when I was small, and I believed her until one day I asked, if he was God, why didn't he lift it instead of dragging it across the sky and making such a noise?

The next lightning flash was almost on top of the Hotel Lux. The next peal of thunder seemed to be overhead. Then, suddenly, an eerie silence. It seemed as though the whole city was waiting for something, holding its breath. And then the rain came. Cascading out of the sky, falling in great sheets of water, like a tidal wave hitting the beach. There were no individual drops of rain, just one flood of water, pouring onto the balcony so that I was soaked; there was far too much water to be drained away through the little outlet in the concrete surround. I reached behind me and closed the patio door. I was wet through already so I might as well stay where I was but there was no need for the apartment to be flooded. I leaned over the balcony and watched the water race in torrents down the street, crashing into cars and swirling around lampposts. It was wonderful.

I thought I heard a knock on my apartment door but I wasn't sure. The noise of the storm was so great that it blotted out everything else. I went back into the apartment and peered through the spy-hole in the door.

Nico stood outside, a bunch of flowers in his hand. I caught my breath and stood, immobile, dripping rain-water onto the tiled floor. How had he got in? I wondered. There was a security system in place so that people couldn't come in the entrance door without somebody buzzing them in. But someone had let Nico in. And he must know that I was here. I bit my lip. I wasn't quite ready to face Nico yet. To tell him about Tim.

He rapped on the door again. He knew that I was here; he would be able to see the light. I had to let him in. I opened the door.

'Isabella!' He strode inside. 'Isabella, where have you been?' He almost embraced me, but didn't. I was too wet for anyone to hug.

'On the balcony,' I said lightly. 'Watching the storm.'

He stared at me. 'I didn't mean just now. I meant for the past few days.'

'I had to go home,' I told him. 'My grandmother died.'

'So it was true,' he said.

'What d'you mean – it was true?'

'I rang your office, of course. But the girl who told me said it in such a way that I thought, perhaps, she was lying.'

'Oh Nico, don't be so bloody silly.' I shivered in the wet robe.

'You are cold.'

'Of course I'm cold,' I said. 'I was standing in the rain.'

'Why would you do that?'

I shrugged.

'Are you all right, Isabella?'

'Absolutely.' I shivered again. 'I'll get dressed.'

'Not because of me.' He smiled and my heart skipped a beat. He had a wonderful smile.

'I'll get dressed.' I walked into the bedroom and closed the door behind me.

I was freezing. I pulled on a pair of jeans and a cotton jumper. My hair hung in rats' tails around my face. I rubbed it with the towel and ran a comb through it. I sprayed *Allure* behind my ears, then replaced the bottle on my dresser with a bang. What was I thinking of? Perfume for Nico! Why?

My ring was on my bedside locker. I left it there. I would tell Nico tonight, of course, but I didn't think it would be a good idea to waltz into the living room flashing my diamond at him.

He'd left the flowers on the table and opened the

patio door again. It had stopped raining, but the balcony was still awash with water. Nico stood at the door, looking out.

'Hello again,' I said.

'Why did you bother?' he asked.

'Bother?'

'The jeans, the jumper. I liked you the way you were.'

'I was cold.' I undid the cellophane wrapping from the flowers.

'Is everything all right, Isabella?' He stepped back into the apartment and wiped his feet on the mat. 'Were you very close to your grandmother?'

'I liked her,' I told him. 'It was a shock to hear that she'd died.'

'You should have called me,' he said.

'When?'

'When you heard the news.'

'I did,' I said shortly. 'You didn't answer.'

'Poor Isabella.' He put his arms around me and I could feel the beating of his heart. 'I'm sorry. I should have telephoned you before now.'

'No.' I pulled away from him. 'I'm glad you called around, Nico. I wanted to talk to you.'

He held me at arm's length. 'To talk to me?' He laughed. 'That sounds very serious, *mia Isabella*.'

'I suppose it is,' I said. I sat down on the sofa and he sat in the chair opposite me, looking at me from big brown eyes that, tonight, were almost black.

'I met a friend when I was back in Dublin,' I began nervously. 'An old friend.'

Nico raised one eyebrow but said nothing.

'We'd been friends for a long time,' I said. 'We loved each other.'

Nico sat back in the armchair and looked at me speculatively.

'Well, to be honest, Nico, we were engaged to each other.'

'Engaged?'

'To be married. Obviously.'

'Obviously.'

'But we split up. That's – why I came to Madrid, really. To forget about him.'

'But you did not forget?'

'I – put him to the back of my mind,' I said.

'You did a good job,' said Nico. 'I never realised that there was someone at the back of your mind.'

'Nico, I—'

'When we made love together, I didn't know that you were trying to keep your fiancé to the back of your mind.'

'Nico—'

'When we went out together, I didn't know that I was there to help you forget.'

'Nico—'

'When I called you *querida* I didn't realise that it meant absolutely nothing to you because there was someone else.'

'Nico, it wasn't like that.'

'Oh?'

'No.'

We glared at each other for a moment.

'I care for you a lot,' I said lamely.

'Thank you.'

'But – well, where was it going, Nico? It wasn't as though we were going to get married or anything. It wasn't as though it was for ever.'

'Why?'

'Oh, come on,' I said. 'Sure, you called me *querida*. Sure, you made love to me. Sure, we were together and it was wonderful. But I was never the person you really cared about. I'm an *Irlandesa*, I'm not the girl you'd marry!'

'Since when has marriage become so important to you? What about your job – your great career?'

'It's not the most important thing.'

'You told me it was.'

'No, I didn't. I said it was important to me. But I wanted to get married someday. I was ready to get married before, but it didn't work out. I'm ready to be married now.'

'But not to me.'

'You don't want to marry me,' I said. 'I know I'm not the girl you want. Or the girl your family wants. Try Carmen.'

'Carmen!' He stared at me. 'I do not love Carmen.'

'You loved her,' I said. 'I could see that. You probably still love her. Why else would you keep a photograph of her in your apartment?'

'Don't be absolutely ridiculous.' He stood up. 'You are upset about a photograph! I can't believe I'm hearing this, Isobel.'

He'd called me Isobel. He never called me Isobel.

'I'm sorry,' I said. 'I like you a lot, Nico—'

'I'm flattered.'

'—but it isn't for ever, is it? And with Tim it will be for ever.'

'Tim,' he said. 'He has phoned you, hasn't he? He phoned you one night when I was here. So you didn't just meet him when you went home, did you?'

'It's a bit more complicated than that,' I said.

'I did not believe you were this kind of girl,' said Nico. 'You go out with me, make love to me, share things with me. And then you tell me that you are going to marry someone else!'

'If I'd thought it mattered—'

'What?' he asked. 'If you'd thought it mattered – what? You allowed me to care for you and to make love to you. If a man had done this to a woman – had told her it was over and he was going to marry someone else you would think he was a pig. But it's OK for you to go out with me when you feel like it and then decide that you want to go home and marry this, this – Tim.'

'Oh, stop it!' I cried. 'You're twisting things around!'

'Am I?'

'Yes. And you never once acted as though you wanted anything more permanent. We were friends, that's all.'

'Is that what you think?'

I said nothing. I was close to tears.

'Is it?' he demanded. 'Is that the way I have treated you?'

'Please, Nico.'

'Oh, do not start to cry.' He looked at me in disgust. 'It is a thing women do, cry. When things are happening that they don't like – they cry.'

'Nico—'

'And I am supposed to say that it doesn't matter, because of your tears. Well it does matter, Isobel. It matters to me. I cared about you, I loved you, I thought you loved me. OK, so I was wrong. But don't cry to pretend that you are hurt. Don't insult me like that.'

I bit my lip.

'So it is over between us,' said Nico. 'I am sorry, Isobel. Perhaps I should have dragged you to bed on our first date together. Perhaps that would have put things into context for you. Perhaps you would have felt better about it that way. But I didn't think you were ready. I thought there was *something* – I didn't realise it was *someone*. I wanted to make love to you so much, Isobel. And I didn't. But when we did – it was wonderful. I thought it meant as much to you as it did to me. I'm sorry if I was wrong.

I'm sorry that I didn't know I was only a substitute for the man you want to marry! You were ready to sleep with me, though, when you felt like it. It is a strange thing for a man to feel used. Still, no matter. You have got what you want. You have made him jealous enough to marry you!'

'It wasn't like that.' I almost choked on the words. 'I swear it wasn't, Nico.'

'I admire you,' he said. 'I admire the way you can suddenly switch from one person to another. It is a wonderful talent you have, Isobel.'

'Nico, I told you I was engaged to Tim before,' I said desperately. 'But we didn't simply split up. There was less than a month to go to the wedding. He got cold feet. We postponed the wedding. Then we decided that we wouldn't get married at all. He was afraid of marriage then. I came to Madrid to forget about it – start all over again. And you helped me. I care about you a lot. But I can't be sure about how I really feel with people any more. Or how they feel about me. Not one hundred per cent, absolutely sure. Except Tim. I can be sure of Tim because we've been there already. So I know everything will be all right. He won't let me down a second time.'

'Isobel.' Nico rested his hands on my shoulders and I jumped. 'What are you saying? That you are marrying this man because he dumped you once and you can be sure he won't do it again? That is the craziest thing I've ever heard.'

'But I loved him,' I said. 'I still love him.'

'Are you sure?'

'Absolutely.'

'One hundred per cent?'

'Yes.'

He let me go again. 'I do not understand,' he said.

'You're a man,' I told him. 'How can you understand?'

He shook his head. 'You are marrying someone who has treated you badly before. Are you out of your mind?'

'No.'

'Isobel – would you change it if I asked you to marry *me*?'

'Nico, please don't say things you don't mean.'

'How do you know I don't mean it? Do you want me to change my mind now? Would that make things easier? You are being very silly, *querida*.'

'*Don't* call me that,' I said sharply.

'I am sorry,' he said. 'And I am sorry you want to end it like this.'

'Me too,' I whispered. 'Truly, I am. But, Nico, let's face it. You're a good-looking man. You can pick any girl you want. Barbara Lane, for instance. She's crazy about you. Magdalena told me that you were the sexiest man she'd ever seen. Women will fall at your feet, Nico.'

He stared at me. 'Do you think that is the person I am?' he asked. 'That I want for women to fall at my feet? Do you understand me at all?'

I felt terrible. 'I'm sorry.'

'You are so caught up with how *you* feel, Isobel, that you haven't thought a single bit about how *I* feel. You think that because you have fallen in love with your Tim again that I can just forget about you by going out with someone else. It worked for you, of course.'

'Please stop, Nico.' I pushed a strand of damp hair from my forehead. 'I didn't mean—' But I'd run out of words.

We stood looking at each other. The water gurgled on the balcony. The thunder still rumbled, faintly, in the distance.

'I will go,' he said finally. 'I hope that you will be very happy, Isobel.'

'Thank you,' I said faintly.

He stopped at the door. 'If I had thought you wanted

to be married – if you had once made me think that way – I would have asked you, Isobel. Perhaps it is as well I did not.' He went out and slammed the door behind him.

I stood in the centre of the room. My head was pounding and I could hardly breathe. I wrapped my arms around me and hugged myself tightly. That was the worst scene of my life. Worse than when Tim had dumped me. Worse than telling people that the wedding was off. Worse than anything. Because I'd hurt someone I never wanted to hurt.

Nico had told me he loved me. But what else does a man say when he has just taken you to bed? I like you? You're OK? Hey, you were wonderful? They don't all tell you that they love you, but it's one of the phrases. Tim had told me that he loved me after the first time. I hadn't believed him then. It takes more than a roll in the sheets after all.

I picked up the flowers from the table. Roses. Nico liked bringing roses. Red were his favourite. These were orange, bursting with colour and with scent. But my asthma was still troubling me and I was afraid to sniff them.

I walked onto the balcony, still with the roses in my hand. There was no sign of Nico.

It's not fair, I thought. He didn't understand. I cared about Nico. Maybe I loved Nico. But I had to marry Tim. That was the way things were. I looked at the flowers. He always brought me flowers. He was a very generous man. But he talked nonsense and he knew what to say to make me feel bad. I wished, now, that I'd never met him. My fingers tightened around the roses then I suddenly hurled them over the balcony into the darkness below. I leaned over and watched them as they were washed away, faint splashes of colour in the blackness of the rainwater that coursed down the street.

Chapter 30

Illumined Pleasures (Salvador Dalí, 1929)

I got up early the next morning. I dusted my face with powder – there were dark circles under my eyes and my cheeks were pale. I wondered if I had a serious illness. The headache was still there, not as blinding as it had been, but enough to make me wince in the glare of the morning sun. There were traces of the thunderstorm in the city – the leaves that had been ripped from the trees were now in sodden masses at the side of the road and murky puddles lurked in the gaps between the paving-stones. But the air was clear and I didn't need my inhaler to ease my breathing.

I walked into the office building, very conscious of the glittering ring on my finger, but I didn't meet anyone on my way into my room and I was glad about that. I felt slightly uncomfortable at the thought of telling them about my engagement. Mostly, I felt uncomfortable about telling Gabriela. She was more than just a boss to me, she'd taken an interest in me, given me opportunities that I'd never had before, and I hated the idea of repaying her by leaving.

Our morning meeting was in the boardroom. I brought a notebook and a folder although I didn't need either of them. We sat around the circular table while Gabriela, having offered her condolences about my grandmother, talked about next year and the new courses she had in mind. We'd landed a contract for a telephone company which had recently changed all its computer software so she wanted me to draw up a plan for their in-house training. I nodded. She hadn't noticed the ring yet – nobody had because I'd kept my hand under the table.

She handed around new brochures. 'Let me know what you think.'

It was my moment. I reached out and took one. The lights reflected off the diamond and it glittered furiously.

It took a few seconds for people to react.

Luis noticed first. 'Isobel! You are engaged!'

Even though I was ready for it, I blushed.

'Isobel!' Gabriela stared at me. 'You never told me.'

'It was a bit sudden,' I explained.

'But when did you do this?' she demanded. 'You were in Dublin the last couple of days. Where did you get the time?'

'I met him while I was there.'

She looked at me blankly. 'But I saw Nico yesterday morning. He was in the Plaza Mayor.'

I stared at her. 'I'm not engaged to Nico.'

'What?' Luis looked at me, his face showing puzzlement.

'I'm engaged to Tim,' I said.

'Tim?' It was Magdalena's turn to look blank. 'Tim?'

'Your ex-fiancé!' Gabriela still stared at me.

'Not ex any more.' I giggled nervously.

'But what about Nico?' asked Luis.

'Nico knows about it,' I said.

'I thought you were still going out with him,' said Gabriela.

I said nothing.

'Does this mean you're going back to Ireland?' Magdalena asked.

'I – eventually – yes.'

'When?' Gabriela sounded businesslike.

'I'm not certain.'

'When do you plan to get married?'

'We didn't set a date. It was all rather sudden.'

'Certainly it was sudden,' said Luis. 'I can't believe it, Isobel.'

'Why not?'

'I thought you hated him.'

'Not hated,' I said.

'But – he was so bad to you.'

'That's in the past. And he was right to do what he did. Maybe not when he did it, but these things happen.'

'All the same—'

'Please,' I interrupted. 'I'm engaged to be married to Tim. I hope you'll all come to the wedding.'

Gabriela smiled at me. 'Of course,' she said. 'But we'll be sorry to lose you, Isobel.'

'I'll be sorry to leave,' I said as I bent my head over the new brochure.

~

'I meant that,' I told her later as we sat in her office. 'I feel really bad about leaving the company.'

'If it's what you have to do,' she said.

'I think it is.' I twirled the ring on my finger. 'I love him, Gabriela. I can't help it.'

'So what are your plans?'

'He wants to get married as soon as possible. But I wanted to sort things out here first. Stay with you until you are sure who you want to replace me. I think we'll get married in January.'

'Three months, more or less,' said Gabriela. 'That is not far away.'

'No.'

'And your Tim, he would not like to live in Madrid?'

I shook my head. 'He wouldn't like the weather. He likes four seasons, not two.'

Gabriela laughed. 'I understand. I hope you'll be very happy, Isobel.'

'I hope so too.'

She clipped some papers together. 'I didn't realise you and Nico had split up.'

I blushed. 'We hadn't exactly,' I admitted. 'Although things had become a little uncomfortable between us.'

'So – he didn't know you were seeing Tim?'

'Gabriela, you're making it sound as if I was doing something terrible. I know it seems as though I was stringing Nico along, but it wasn't like that, honestly.'

'He must be feeling hurt.'

'I should have done things differently,' I said. 'But he'll get over it. It's not as though I was the only girl in his life.'

'There was someone else?' Gabriela looked surprised.

'Not exactly.' I shifted in my seat. 'But he still has a photograph of his previous girlfriend in his apartment and I'm sure he still cares about her.'

'That doesn't mean he didn't care about you,' said Gabriela.

'It wouldn't have worked,' I told her. 'Honestly, Gabriela. I know it was great at first, but we've had some awful rows in the last few weeks. I've made the right choice.'

'I didn't know it was a matter of choice between them.'

I shrugged. 'It wasn't. But, Gabriela, Tim was there when I needed him. When Gran died and I felt so badly, Tim was there to comfort me and care for me.'

'And where was Nico?' she asked.

'I don't know,' I told her. 'I phoned to tell him, but he wasn't around. We had a very easygoing relationship that way.' I smiled at her. 'Now I'd better go and phone Felipe Caruana. I promised him I'd call about his in-house training programme.'

'OK.' Gabriela pulled a brochure from the pile in front of her.

I was halfway to the door when her voice stopped me. 'Isobel?'

'Yes?' I turned around.

She looked anxiously at me. 'Don't take this the wrong way. But are you sure you're doing the right thing?'

~

Was I doing the right thing? It was easier to be objective about it in Madrid. And I knew I was being objective. Tim loved me – he'd proved that he loved me. Nico said that he loved me but that didn't mean anything. Marriage was more than love, it was a partnership. Tim and I could be that partnership because we'd been through trust and mistrust and we understood each other. I didn't always understand Nico. He looked at life in a different way to me. It was part of his foreignness, part of what attracted me to him, but you couldn't build a life on differences. And we were very different. At the end of the day, despite the pharmaceutical company, despite the jingles, despite saying that he'd marry me, I knew that Nico was a free spirit. He wasn't the marrying type. I thought maybe it was more his pride that was hurt when I told him about Tim. A macho man like Nico – even a sensitive, guitar-playing, art-loving macho man – wouldn't be all that pleased about being dumped by his girlfriend.

I turned onto the Calle Don Alvaro. The days were getting shorter. The streetlights glowed in the dark.

Back in the apartment, I sat down in the armchair and pulled the phone toward me. Julie would understand.

∽

'Tim Malone!' Her voice squeaked. 'You're marrying Tim Malone!'

'Why not?'

'Isobel, he treated you like shit!'

'No, he didn't,' I protested. 'He wasn't ready to marry me and he said so. I wouldn't call that treating me like shit.'

'You're out of your mind!'

'No, I'm not.'

'You said once that you could never be sure of him again,' she said.

'You said once that you never wanted to speak to Andy Jordan again,' I pointed out.

'I know.' She sounded worried.

'Don't worry about me,' I told her. 'I know what I'm doing.'

'Do you?'

'Absolutely.'

'When's the wedding?' Her tone was lighter.

'January, I think.'

'And what about your job?' she asked.

'I'll try to get something when I go home,' I said. 'But Tim and I want to start a family.'

'Is this what it's all about?' she asked. 'Having children?'

'No, it's not.' I twirled the ends of my hair. 'But I've

always wanted a family, Julie. And Tim is ready now. He wasn't before.'

'So now that he's ready he'll marry you.'

'Kind of.'

'But your life has changed,' she said. 'You're not the same person.'

'Of course I am.'

'Last time we talked you'd been promoted and you said that you were a businesswoman and proud of it!'

'I was. I am. But there's more to life than work, Julie.'

'I know.' She still sounded worried. Why was everyone so damned worried about me? Why did they think that I didn't know what I was doing?

'What happened to Nico?' she asked.

And why did they all ask about Nico? It wasn't as though we'd been going together for years. It wasn't as though Julie had even met him!

'Nico's fine,' I told her. 'We just weren't for ever, that's all.'

'Why?'

'I don't know why,' I said. 'I just know.'

'If you're sure.'

'I'm sure.'

'That's OK, then.'

'Will you be at the wedding?' I asked.

'Of course,' said Julie. 'I wouldn't miss it.'

'Thanks, Julie.'

'What are you thanking me for?'

'I thought you might not be able to come.'

'Are you out of your mind?' she asked comfortably. 'It's your wedding, Isobel. I would have been there the first time so I'll definitely be there the second. How could I miss it?'

'Will Andy come?'

'If I tell him to,' she chuckled.

'How is he?'

'Wonderful,' she said.

'Everything OK in the USA?'

'I love it here,' she said. 'I love the people and I love the life.'

'Are you working yet?' She hadn't been last time I called.

'Not so's it counts,' she admitted. 'I'm doing some part-time work in a car salesroom. Not exactly me, but it keeps me occupied. To be honest, Isobel, we're hoping to start a family soon ourselves.'

'Really?'

I could almost see her shrug. 'Gotta start sometime.'

'Good luck.'

'Thanks.' She laughed. 'We're having fun trying anyhow.'

'I bet you are.' I thought of Andy Jordan, lean and muscular.

'It's funny.' She laughed again. 'All the times I desperately hoped that I wasn't pregnant and now I want to be.'

'Well, don't let me keep you from it,' I told her.

'He's at work,' said Julie. 'But don't worry, I'll hop on him when he comes in.'

'You're lucky,' I said. 'You and Andy are so perfect for each other.'

'We work at it,' she said. 'We're not always perfect, Isobel. Nothing is.'

'Rubbish.' I laughed. 'Tim and I will be perfect. I promise you.'

'I hope so.'

'We will,' I said. 'I'll give you a call when we've got a definite date for the wedding, Julie.'

'OK,' she said. 'Thanks for ringing. And congratulations – again.'

'Thanks.'

'Take care.' She rang off.

❧

I turned on the TV and picked up my book. Even though I didn't want to watch TV, I liked having it on for company. It was lonely living by myself. I'd done it and I'd learned a lot but I missed having people around me. It would be nice, when we were married, to sit side-by-side with Tim on the sofa watching TV in companionable silence. Sharing things. That's what it was about, after all. Sharing. And one day we'd have our own children sitting with us. I grinned to myself at my suburban dream. A perfect family. Whereas what would probably happen would be that we'd have two kids who wore rings through their lips or belly-buttons or whatever the current fad would be, while they complained to each other that we didn't understand them. But it was nice to dream the dream anyhow.

❧

I went shopping at the weekend. I bought six pairs of shoes in a small shop off the Serrano because I could never find shoes in Dublin to fit me. The sales assistant thought all her bonus days had come at once when I brought them all over to the cash desk. One of the pairs was white, the softest of leather with a spindly heel. I thought that, whatever sort of wedding dress I eventually got, the shoes would look wonderful with it. I bought a newspaper and went into a small café where I skimmed through the stories and ate luscious pastries. I intended to diet when I got back to Dublin, but I wasn't going to start now.

'Hello, Isobel.' I glanced up from the paper. Barbara Lane stood beside my table.

'Barbara!' I hadn't seen her since the night she'd come to hear Nico play. 'How are you?'

'I'm fine.' She pulled out a chair. 'Mind if I join you?'

'Not at all.' I'd been furious with her that night but now it didn't matter at all. My life had changed and what Barbara thought or did made no difference to me whatsoever.

'Any news?' I asked as she sat down.

She shook her head. 'Life's been very boring lately. You?'

I smiled at her and held out my hand.

'Oh, Isobel.' She gasped. 'It's absolutely gorgeous.'

'Thanks.'

'When did you—?'

'Last week.'

She smiled ruefully. 'I always knew it. You said you didn't fancy him, that it was just a fling, but I always knew it wasn't.'

For a wicked moment I thought of letting her believe that I'd got myself engaged to Nico Alvarez. But common sense took over.

'I *did* fancy him but it *was* just a fling,' I said. 'I'm engaged to Tim.'

'Tim!' She stared at me in astonishment. 'Tim – your boyfriend? That Tim?'

I grinned. 'That Tim.'

'But – why?'

'Why do most people get engaged?' I asked.

'It's just that—' She broke off and signalled a waiter. '*Dos cafés, por favor.*'

'I love Tim,' I said simply. 'And I want to marry him.'

'But what about Nico? When did you split up? Because I was sure I saw you with him only a couple of weeks ago. In the Plaza Espana.'

'You might have done.' I shrugged.

'So—'

'It's quite simple. *Gracias*,' I said to the waiter who put the cup of coffee in front of me. 'I had to go home. I met Tim. We decided we still loved each other. I got engaged.'

'I'm shocked.' She dropped a lump of brown sugar into her coffee. 'I really am.'

'Why?'

'I just thought that you and Nico – oh, I suppose I was making a mountain out of a molehill. It's just that you were different with him, Isobel. And,' she looked at me from beneath her fringe, 'I was jealous of you.'

'Jealous?'

'Oh, don't pretend.' She stirred her coffee vigorously and splashed the table.

'OK,' I said. 'I won't. You fancied Nico. You were pissed off at me for going out with him. It's all right, Barbara. It doesn't matter.'

'Obviously not,' she said. 'You look great.'

'Thanks.' So at least the make-up worked. I'd looked awful that morning – still pale as a ghost and still with huge black circles under my eyes. I didn't know why I looked so dreadful because I felt all right. I still had the occasional dregs of my headache, but paracetamol kept that at bay.

'So when are you getting married?' asked Barbara.

'January, I think.'

'Back in Ireland?'

'Obviously.'

She sat back in her chair. 'I'm still amazed.'

'Don't be.' I grinned at her. 'Just think of me back in

dreary old Dublin, up to my neck in housework, while you're still having a great time here.'

'Have you got a job?' she asked.

'Not yet.' I made a face. 'I'll get one, but I'm not going to try until after Christmas. Doesn't seem any point.'

'It's funny but I can't imagine you as a married woman up to your neck in housework,' said Barbara. 'I can only see you as you were with us – on the party trail.'

'Yes, well.' I sipped my coffee. 'That was a period in my life that I'd just as soon forget.'

'You had a good time,' Barbara reminded me.

'Oh, sure I did. But it wasn't really me, you know.'

'You don't think so?'

'I was under pressure then,' I said. 'I'm different now.'

She smiled at me. 'I hope you'll be very happy.'

'Thanks.'

'Really I do.'

'Would you like another coffee?' I asked.

She nodded and I ordered two more *solos*. I was pleased to have made my peace with Barbara. Even if she'd never realised that I'd gone through a period of disliking her intensely.

'How's Bridget?' I asked.

'So-so.'

'So-so?'

'She's OK,' said Barbara. 'But she's feeling a little under pressure herself.'

'Oh?'

'Tomás is out a lot,' said Barbara. 'Bridget is left at home with Christopher. She's not very happy about it.'

'I hope it gets better,' I said. 'Tell her I said hello.'

'Sure.' Barbara laughed shortly. 'Once the three of us went out every night of the week. Now you and Bridget are boring, married women.'

'Not quite married yet,' I told her. 'And I've had a slip-up on my way to the altar before.'

'You don't think it'll happen again, do you?' She sounded so horrified that I burst out laughing.

'Of course not! I was only joking. He wouldn't have the nerve to dump me a second time.'

'I think you're great to give him a second chance!' said Barbara.

'I don't look on it as a second chance,' I said. 'I feel it was always meant to have been this way.'

'I'm glad it's worked out for you,' she told me. 'Honestly.'

'Thanks, Barbara.'

She tapped her fingers on the handle of her coffee-cup. 'Can I ask you something?'

'Of course.'

'Would it bother you if I contacted Nico?'

'Contacted Nico?'

'Yes.' Barbara blushed slightly. 'Asked him out to dinner.'

I stared at her. 'You want to ask Nico out?'

'Yes,' she said. 'That's right.'

'Well, there's no reason for it to bother me,' I said, squashing the sudden spurt of – jealousy – that had rushed through me. Not jealousy, I couldn't be jealous of anyone going out with Nico. But it felt odd to think about it all the same.

'I know,' she said blithely. 'It's just that I'd feel awkward calling him without telling you first.'

'You go ahead and call,' I said. 'I'm sure he'd be delighted to hear from you.'

'You're a good friend, Isobel,' said Barbara. 'And I wish you the best of luck with Tim.'

'Will you come to the wedding?' I asked the question on impulse and wished I hadn't.

'I'd love to.' She beamed at me. 'Get you safely up the aisle this time.'

'Great,' I said. 'It'll be fun.'

~

I thought about them that evening as I arranged my six pairs of shoes at the bottom of my wardrobe. Barbara and Nico. They were probably more suited than Nico and I ever were. Barbara had no desire to move back to England. She'd look after Nico in a way that I hadn't.

I wondered if he'd accept her invitation to dinner.

Chapter 31

The Circus (Joan Miró, 1937)

'These are the follow-up files.' I double-clicked on the bright yellow folder at the top of the computer screen. 'The follow-ups are all labelled yellow. Green for the active folders and red for the completed ones.'

Nina nodded.

'All the standard letters are in the stationery folder.'

'I know, Isobel,' she said gently. 'I access them on the network.'

'Of course you do.' I pushed my hair back from my face. I was growing it longer for the wedding and it was driving me crazy. 'I'm sorry, Nina. I know I'm repeating myself.'

'It's OK.' She grinned at me. 'I'm making allowances because of the stress you're under.'

'I'm not under any stress,' I told her.

'Of course you are.' She smiled. 'You're packing to go home. You're trying to organise everything here. You want to be with your fiancé—'

'Oh, God!' I looked at my watch. 'I have to pick him up at the airport.'

'You've plenty of time,' said Nina. 'Don't panic.'

But I couldn't help panicking. The last four weeks had

been absolute chaos as I tried to streamline everything for my successor. I wanted to be sure that there was no chance of things going wrong because of anything I'd done, or failed to do. I had Nina driven demented.

Luis was taking over my job. I was glad it was Luis, that it wasn't a stranger. Which was silly, but it was how I felt. I hadn't talked much to Luis about it because I didn't want him to think I was trying to tell him how to do things. It was up to him to find his own way.

We'd gone for beer and tapas the previous night and that was the closest we'd got to a business meeting. We sat on the high barstools and shared *patatas a la romana* while the windows of the tapas bar dripped with steam.

'I'll miss this place,' I sighed. 'It was the first tapas bar I ever came to, and it's the best.'

'I'll miss you,' said Luis.

'Oh, Luis.' There was a lump in my throat. 'I'll miss you too.'

He took me by the hand. 'You're a good person, Isobel.'

'Don't be silly.' But I left my hand in his.

'You've been good for the company. You've been good to me.'

'And you to me,' I said.

'It might have worked between us.' His brown eyes twinkled.

'It would never have worked between us,' I said.

'But that night was wonderful,' said Luis.

'I get the impression,' I said, as I removed my hand from his, 'that you specialise in wonderful nights.'

He laughed. 'I enjoy making love, Isobel.'

'And you're good at it!'

'*Gracias.*' He grinned wickedly.

'But we would have been hopeless together.'

'*Por qué?*'

'I don't know why,' I said. 'We just would.'

'And now you are going to marry the man who made you too unhappy to go out with me,' he said.

'It wasn't because of Tim I wouldn't go out with you.' I made a face at him. 'It was because I couldn't sit in a restaurant with someone who thought it was OK to wear a red shirt and a yellow tie.'

'That's not fair!' He looked down at his chest. 'The tie was a present from Anna.'

'Why do they all buy you ties?' I asked. 'Maria was always buying them for you.'

'It's a female thing,' said Luis. 'You think of it as a leash!'

'We do not,' I said firmly.

'Well, I knew it was time to split with Maria when she'd bought me a dozen of them,' he said seriously. 'Talk about a noose around my neck.'

I giggled. 'That's outrageous, Luis.'

'Have you ever bought a man a tie, Isobel?'

'I bought Tim one for his birthday,' I admitted. 'But I also bought him a zip drive.'

'It's an ownership thing,' said Luis. 'Trust me.'

'Do you want another beer?' I asked.

'Why not?' He kissed me on the cheek.

～

I hadn't been drunk in a long, long time. Not like this, anyway. Not so drunk that I couldn't focus properly.

Luis helped me out of the taxi.

'I'm fine now,' I told him. 'Really I am.'

'I'll see you up to your apartment,' he said. 'I don't want to be responsible for you falling down the stairs or getting stuck in the lift.'

'I wouldn't.' But I stumbled up the steps.

'Oh, Isobel, I'm sorry.' He caught me under the arm. 'I shouldn't have made you drink the sambuccas.'

'I shouldn't have drunk them,' I said. 'I'm going to be so ill tomorrow.'

'I'll get you inside the apartment and make coffee,' said Luis.

I fell over the threshold and flopped onto the sofa. 'It wasn't even that much alcohol,' I moaned. 'Just a few beers and the sambuccas. That's all.'

'I like the posters,' said Luis, as he looked around.

I'd hung Miró posters on the walls, since he'd last been in the apartment.

'They look like I feel,' I said. 'Shaky.'

Luis laughed. 'You rest, I'll make coffee.'

It was nice to lie on the sofa and let someone else do all the work. And the good thing was that I felt safe and secure with Luis. Despite everything, he was the one man I knew who was like an ordinary friend to me. It was as though our night of mad passion had happened in another life.

'Here you are,' he said, just as I was dozing off. 'A good blast of caffeine should help.'

'Oh, thank you.' I sat up and sipped the coffee. 'I'll miss you, Luis.'

'And I'll miss you,' he said. 'Even if I never really got to understand you.'

'You don't need to understand me,' I told him.

'I'll miss our conversations,' said Luis.

'Me too.'

'And arguing with you about courses.'

I sipped the coffee, more cautiously this time because the first mouthful had burned my tongue.

'I'll miss lots of things about Spain,' I admitted.

'But you'll have a new, more exciting life back home.'

'Will I?'

'Isobel!' He looked at me in astonishment. 'Are you having second thoughts?'

'Oh, don't be silly.' I put the cup on the floor. 'It's just that I wonder what it'll be like, that's all.'

'What do you think it'll be like?' he asked.

'I don't know.' I shrugged. 'I'm scared I won't get a job, Luis. That I'll be dependent on Tim.'

'Does that matter?'

I tucked my legs beneath me and rested my head on his shoulder. 'It wouldn't have,' I said. 'A few years ago I wouldn't have cared. But I do now. I've worked so hard to be independent.'

'You'll get a job,' said Luis confidently. 'But you might decide to chuck it in and have babies, Isobel.'

'Gabriela has two children and she still works.'

'Yes.' He raised his eyebrows. 'But she also has a nanny and a housekeeper!'

I laughed. 'And I suppose I'll be the nanny and the housekeeper.'

'Not if you get another executive position like with Advanta,' said Luis. 'Then you can hire them yourself.'

'We'll see.' I yawned. 'Oh, God, Luis – I'm sorry, I'm just so tired.'

'I'll let you go to bed,' he said. 'All alone, Isobel.'

'I wouldn't be much use to you anyway,' I said. 'I'm far too tired to do anything.'

He laughed. 'Goodnight, Isobel. Sleep well.'

'Goodnight, Luis.'

I thought about getting up to go to bed but I didn't. I lay on the sofa with my eyes closed, and the next thing I knew it was the following morning and I had a hangover.

∽

I looked at my watch again. There was nothing left to

do. The files were organised. Next week's schedule was printed. My presentation for AutosReal was ready for Luis to use. I had finished work. I'd plenty of time before I had to be at the airport.

Gabriela tapped at my half-open door. 'Can I come in?'

'Of course.'

She smiled as she looked at my empty desk. 'Finished?'

I nodded.

'So.' She sat on my visitor's chair. 'It is complete for you. Your time in Spain.'

'Mm.'

'You have enjoyed living here?'

'It's been wonderful,' I told her. 'I've loved it. This company is the best I've ever worked for – and you're the best boss I know.'

'Thank you.' She leaned back in the chair. 'I'm sorry you're leaving us.'

'I'm sorry to go.' I pushed my irritating hair out of my eyes. 'But I know I'm doing the right thing, Gabriela.'

'I never said you weren't.'

'No,' I agreed with her. 'But some people are afraid I'm making a mistake. I'm not making a mistake, Gabriela. I love Tim. I've always loved him.'

'And your friend Nico?'

I sighed. 'I cared about him a lot,' I told her. 'Maybe I loved him too, Gabriela. I don't know. Maybe he loved me. Although I don't think so. Not really. I think it was because I was a foreigner. He found me different. He was getting over a long-term relationship when he started to go out with me and I think I was what he needed at the time. But it was – oh, I don't know.' I stared into space as I thought about Nico. 'It was like one of those movies where they show a couple through a misty lens as they stroll hand-in-hand along the beach, or run through flower-filled meadows. It wasn't real, Gabriela.' I was silent. 'It was always a holiday romance. And when we argued we never had a proper argument. Maybe it was because we didn't know the words!' My voice was shaky. 'OK – I cared about him. But it wouldn't have worked.'

'Why not?' She fiddled with her beautiful emerald earrings.

'Because we're from different backgrounds. And I know that one day I'd want to go home.' I made a face. 'In a year at least, Gabriela. It came to me when I was in Barcelona. I didn't want work to be the most important thing all my life. I wanted to go home to a husband and a family. And that's what I'll have in Ireland.'

She said nothing.

'I'll be happy,' I told her.

'Of course you will.' She stood up. 'What time are you meeting Tim?'

'His flight's due in at eight.'

'Plenty of time. Can you come into my office for a few minutes?'

'Of course.'

Today was my last official day at work. A Thursday. Gabriela had brought forward the annual Christmas party and turned it into a combined Christmas, going-away and getting-married night. Tim would be there too. I was looking forward to the party and to introducing my fiancé to my friends.

Gabriela pushed the door of her office open. They were all gathered there – Magdalena, Sofia, Nina, Luis, José—

'We wanted to say goodbye to you,' said Magdalena. 'And good luck.'

'Thanks.' I couldn't think of anything to say. There was a lump in my throat.

'We will have the party tomorrow,' Gabriela said. 'But everyone wanted to wish you well today.'

'And to say that we hope you'll be very happy.'

'And that we'll miss you.'

'And we wanted to give you this, for yourself, to remember us.' Nina stepped forward and handed me a small, gift-wrapped box.

'Oh.' I took the box. I was going to cry. I knew I was. I fumbled at the red and gold paper, trying not to tear it but failing miserably. I'd assumed (cheekily, I suppose) that they'd get me a wedding-present. But I hadn't expected anything like the beautiful gold bracelet that nestled on the cotton wool in the box. 'It's beautiful,' I whispered, blinking the tears from my eyes. 'Really lovely. Thank you all.' I looked up. They were watching me, pleased expressions on their faces.

'This is for you, Isobel, and not for your house,' explained Magdalena. 'We wanted something so that you could think about us anytime, not just when you were in the kitchen!'

'I'll never forget you,' I told them fervently. 'Never. You're the nicest people I know.' Then I burst into proper tears, sobbing convulsively and laughing at myself while I did so. They gathered around me, hugged me, told me that they'd always remember me. It was far more emotional than my departure from DeltaPrint had been.

'So.' Gabriela finally broke up the gathering. 'We will see you tomorrow night, Isobel. At my house.'

'It's very good of you,' I said. 'Really good of you, Gabriela.'

'I enjoy it.' She beamed at me. 'I like having people to my house. And we'll have a great time tomorrow. Besides, we all want to meet the wonderful Tim.'

I looked at her suspiciously. Was she, even gently,

teasing me about him? But her expression was guileless, her eyes wide and clear.

'You'll have your chance tomorrow,' I said. 'And he's looking forward to meeting you all too.' I fastened the bracelet around my wrist. The gold glinted warmly in the office lights. I wanted to cry again. I was hopeless at these sorts of scenes. I brushed at my damp cheeks.

They lined up to kiss me, each taking it in turn to plant multiple kisses on my face. Then we hugged each other. The hugging and kissing went on for at least ten minutes before I finally managed to tear myself free and make my way out of the office building into the night.

The cold was rasping, the pavements dusted with a light covering of rarely-seen snow. I shivered, pulled my suede jacket tightly around me and shoved my hands deep into the pockets. I'd miss them all, I thought, as I clattered down the steps to the metro. They'd become so much a part of my life. And, because I had no family in Madrid, they'd become like family to me. I squeezed myself into the train that had just arrived. No more metro. Back to the grind of driving through Dublin's chaotic city traffic. Or not, of course. Maybe I'd get a job near Donnybrook so that I could get the bus to work. Or walk. I walked to work in Madrid sometimes. I leaned my head against the window. Maybe I wouldn't be able to get a job. Were there too many people equally, if not better qualified than me, already looking for jobs? I sighed. Of course I might get pregnant. Working might not be an option. I scratched my nose. My bracelet slid along my arm.

Señora Carrasco was at the letterboxes in the hallway. '*Buenas tardes.*' She nodded at me.

'*Buenas tardes,*' I replied.

'How is your packing going?' she asked as she took four white envelopes out of her letterbox.

'Not bad.' I unlocked my own box. It was empty.

'You will have to send me a photograph of your wedding.'

I grinned and pushed the button for the lift. 'Of course.'

'We all want to see you on your wedding day.'

'I'm sure I'll have plenty of photos.'

The lift doors opened and we got inside. As we glided gently up to the fifth floor I was suddenly overcome with terror that it would get stuck between floors, that we'd be there for a couple of hours while Tim waited – patiently, impatiently? – at the airport for me to arrive. Impatiently. He wasn't a patient person.

But the doors sighed open and we stepped out onto the fifth floor. I said goodnight to Señora Carrasco as I unlocked the door to my apartment.

It was quiet. That was the thing I both liked and disliked most about living alone. The peace when I wanted peace; but the terror of silence when I needed company. It would be different living with somebody. I wondered whether I'd be a pain in the neck to live with, so used to dropping my clothes wherever I liked or leaving half-read books and magazines lying around the place. And then there was my washing-up obsession – no plate, no cup, no pot allowed to wait around in the sink. It had to be washed immediately.

Of course Tim had lived on his own much longer than me. Untidy, easygoing Tim would probably be driven demented by my insistence on having jars and cans stacked neatly in cupboards with their labels facing outwards.

I shook my head. I'd never had these kinds of thoughts the first time we got engaged. The strain was definitely getting to me.

I changed into soft black trousers and a red chenille

jumper. I pulled on my shiny black boots and my padded black jacket. The festive look, I thought as I checked my appearance in front of the mirror. I was too pale, I decided – the black made me look like a ghost. I wrapped my red woollen scarf around my neck and instantly looked better. It was important to look right. To look perfect for Tim.

The flight had already touched down when I arrived at the airport. I looked around anxiously in case he might have already made his way to the arrivals area, but there was no sign of him. I stamped my feet on the tiled floor to warm them up.

Then he emerged through the glass doors and looked around.

'Over here!' I called as I waved at him. 'Tim! Over here!'

He saw me and his eyes lit up. I was glad that I had that effect on him.

'Isobel!' He dropped his suitcase and hugged me. 'Good to see you again.'

'Good to see me?' I teased. 'You're supposed to say that you've thought about me night and day.'

'I have,' he said. 'Didn't you get my messages?'

The e-mails had arrived every day. 'Sure did.'

'You probably didn't realise that I had the soul of a poet.'

'Yes, well—' I grinned. 'The last message wasn't very poetic: *Have lots of food in stock, I'm famished.*'

He smiled. 'I'm a growing man.'

'Come on.' I caught his hand. 'I made goulash last night. We only have to heat it up.'

'That's my girl,' he murmured as I led him outside to a taxi.

We sat in the back seat and he put his arm around me. 'It's bloody cold.'

'I know. Colder than usual for the beginning of December.'

'It isn't this cold at home.'

'Don't you remember your geography?' I said. 'A continental climate – hot, dry summers, cold, dry winters. That's what we get here.'

He pulled me closer to him. 'Good job I know lots of ways to keep warm.'

I snuggled into him. 'Good job I like them.'

〜

He looked around the apartment with interest. 'I thought it would be smaller, more cramped.'

'It's small enough.' I stepped over a box full of books.

'I thought it would be like a studio.'

'Oh, no. I like having a separate bedroom. I couldn't have lived in a studio.'

'It's in here, I presume.' He pushed open the bedroom door.

'The bed squeaks,' I told him.

He sat on the edge and bounced up and down a couple of times. 'So it does. But I won't let that bother me if you don't.'

'You get used to it.'

'And did it get much use at squeaking?'

I felt myself blush. 'No.'

'Sure?' He got up and put his arms around me.

'Absolutely.'

'Nobody else got used to the squeaks?'

I gulped. 'I don't think so.'

'You don't think so!' He held me away from him and looked into my eyes. 'How many men have you gone out with since you came here? I thought there was only the one.' His tone was light but the question was serious.

'Hardly even one.' I smiled at him and returned his look.

'Oh, all right.' He pulled me to him again. 'I won't ask. It's not fair. But I hope none of them was better than me.'

Isabella querida. It was as though Nico was in the room.

I shivered, then I hugged Tim tightly and kissed him.

'Isobel.' His voice was husky.

'Tim.' I unbuckled the belt of his trousers.

'Isobel.' He slid my jumper over my head.

'Tim.' I unbuttoned his shirt.

'Oh, Isobel.'

It was frantic and quick. The bed squeaked loudly and I had to stop myself giggling each time it did. Tim held me tight, and was so fierce that it almost hurt. I wrapped my arms around his neck and clutched him.

'God, I've missed you,' he panted. 'I kept thinking and thinking about this moment and it's been driving me crazy.'

'I hope it was worth it.'

'It's always worth it.'

'Good.' I smiled up at him.

He closed his eyes and lay across me. He was heavy, squashing the breath out of me.

'Tim?'

'Mm?'

'Sorry. I need my inhaler.'

'Oh. OK.' He rolled off me. 'Are you all right?'

'Yes, more or less.' I took a puff. 'All this frantic activity.'

He laughed. 'Come back to me, Isobel. I'll show you frantic activity.'

'I thought you wanted something to eat.'

'Yes.' He looked darkly at me. 'You, Isobel.'

So we made love again and this time it was slower, less urgent, more pleasurable. And this time I closed my ears to the squeaking springs.

&

We went shopping the next day. I brought him to a furniture store near the Plaza de Colon and he looked at the heavy, darkwood table and chairs and asked me exactly how I thought we were going to get them back to Dublin.

'I wasn't thinking of these,' I told him. 'I just brought you to show you what they were like.'

'They're nice, I'll admit that.' He ran his fingers over the highly-polished surfaces. 'But they wouldn't go in my house, Isobel. That table's far too big.'

'I know,' I said. 'But we mightn't live there for ever. I want to put new ideas into your head.'

'New ideas about what?'

'I don't know.' I shrugged. 'Decor, furniture, all that sort of thing.'

'Please don't tell me you want to redecorate everything,' he begged. 'I've only just had the bathroom redone.'

'Have you?'

'Yes. And it's very nice, all green and gold, you'll like it.'

'I'm sure I will.'

'But you can mess around with the living room if you like,' he said.

'Thanks!'

'It needs to be redecorated,' he admitted. 'The wallpaper's peeling off the walls.'

'Why? The house isn't damp, is it?'

'No.' He shook his head. 'But I think the paper was

put up before the walls dried out properly or something. It's the original paper, I've never had it replaced.'

'Don't worry,' I told him. 'I'll do it for you. I want to make things – well, a bit different.'

'Why?'

'So's it's not just your house,' I said. 'I want to feel like it's partly mine.'

'It will be.' He looked puzzled. 'Once we're married it's automatically half-yours.'

'I know,' I said. 'But I want to *feel* that it is. By changing things.'

He smiled but I knew he didn't understand. 'Whatever you like, Isobel. Whatever makes you happy.'

He'd changed so much, I thought, as we strolled hand-in-hand down the Calle de Serrano and peered in the windows of the clothes shops. A couple of years ago he wouldn't have said 'Whatever makes you happy'. A couple of years ago it was whatever made *him* happy. It was great to know that he cared so much about me. That he loved me. I squeezed his hand and he looked at me. 'What?'

'Nothing. I love you.'

'Good,' he said and put his arm around me.

~

We took a taxi to Gabriela's house that evening. We'd almost come to blows earlier as we got ready – Tim spent hours showering and shaving and then he'd left the mirrors steamed up so that I couldn't see properly to do my make-up.

'You don't need make-up,' he said. 'You're fine the way you are.'

'Don't be stupid.' I rubbed the mirror with the damp towel and peered at my face in the smeared circle while Tim stood in the doorway and blocked the light.

'Honestly, Isobel. You've been working with them for over a year. They must know what you look like by now!'

'Of course they do.' I rubbed foundation cream onto my face. 'But we're going out, Tim. I always wear make-up when I'm going out. And I usually wear it into the office too.'

'You never used to.'

'That was because I didn't think I needed to.'

'Why do you need to now?'

'I meet more people. I like to look good.'

'That's rubbish!' He tucked his shirt into his trousers. 'You always look good.'

'Thanks,' I said impatiently. 'But I need to do my face. Now if you're finished in here would you mind giving me a bit of room?'

'Oh, have it your way!' He stalked out of the doorway.

'Oh, sod off,' I muttered sotto voce.

'I heard that.'

'And?'

'Not very nice, Isobel. To the man who's travelled two thousand miles to be with you.'

I was suddenly contrite. It wasn't Tim's fault that I was used to spending as long as I liked in the bathroom. It wasn't his fault that the mirror had misted up. I was just tetchy.

'Sorry,' I said.

'Oh, it's OK.' He put his head around the bathroom door. 'I guess I forgive you.'

❧

It didn't seem like almost a year since I'd last been at Gabriela's house. We crunched our way up the gravel path and stood outside the door.

'Nice place,' commented Tim.

'Wait until you go inside,' I said. 'It's fabulous.'

'Come in, come in!' Gabriela held the door wide. 'It's wonderful to meet you, Tim.'

'We have met already.' He turned all the charm of his smile on her. 'When I called into the office to meet Isobel. Do you remember?'

'Of course I remember.' She smiled back at him. 'How could I forget?' She led us through to the living area. 'And how are you finding Madrid?'

'Colder than the last time I was here.' Tim rubbed his hands together. 'And Isobel dragged me around shops all afternoon so I was practically frozen.'

'Isobel!' She grinned at me. 'Tim does not look to me like a man who will spend much time in the shops.'

'Depends on the sort of shop,' I told her. 'Computer shops – can't get him out. Clothes shops – can't get him in!'

We laughed.

Most of the others had already arrived and were sitting in front of the log fire drinking red wine.

'For you?' Gabriela looked at us enquiringly.

'Wine is perfect,' I said.

'Beer?' asked Tim hopefully.

'Of course.'

Gabriela went to get the drinks while I introduced Tim to my ex-colleagues.

'He is most handsome,' muttered Sofia to me in Spanish. 'Very masculine. Very attractive.'

'Thank you.'

'Not as attractive as me, of course,' said Luis and I started to giggle.

'What?' asked Tim. 'What are you laughing at?'

'Nothing,' I assured him. 'They were just telling me what a good catch you are.'

Tim couldn't speak a word of Spanish but nearly everyone had passable English and they did their best to speak English all the time.

'Tell us about the wedding, Isobel,' begged Nina. 'What date is it? What will you wear?'

'We haven't set the date exactly yet.' I turned to Tim for confirmation. 'In January sometime, but I'll organise that when I go home. And I haven't decided on the dress either yet.'

'Will you make it yourself?' asked Magdalena.

'I don't know,' I replied.

'Oh, you should!' she cried. 'You made such a beautiful dress for me.'

I'd made her a dress for a black-tie function she'd gone to during the summer. It had been one of the nicest dresses I'd ever made – I'd found some white silk with almost invisible silver threads running through it and made a calf-length dress with shoestring straps. On Magdalena, with her almost black eyes and creamy complexion, it had looked absolutely stunning.

But I wasn't sure about making myself a wedding dress. I thought it might be unlucky. I'd done it once, after all, and I really wasn't sure I should do it a second time.

'Of course she'll make her own dress,' said Tim. 'She makes them for everyone else so the least she can do is make her own.'

'Will you make it long?' asked Nina. 'With a huge train and a veil?'

I couldn't see myself in a dress like that. Even my first one hadn't a huge train. 'I don't think so.'

'Oh, Isobel! You should.'

'It's not quite me,' I explained.

'What's you?' asked Luis.

'Not long trains and veils,' I told him.

'You have to have a veil!' Tim looked horrified. 'I like the bit where the bride comes to the church with the veil over her face and then lifts it back.'

'You've been watching too many movies.' I laughed. 'That doesn't happen much these days.'

'All the same, Isobel.' His voice was pleading. 'It'd be nice, don't you think?'

'Maybe.' I wasn't convinced.

'More wine?' asked Alfredo.

He refilled all our glasses, then Gabriela put on a party CD and we got up and danced. Then Tim and José (whose English was almost as good as Gabriela's) got into a conversation about computers. Luis and Anna were engrossed in conversation. I sat down in one of Gabriela's huge rose-pink armchairs and stretched my legs out in front of me.

'I probably shouldn't have spent so much time shopping,' I told Magdalena. 'My feet are killing me. And these shoes don't help.' They were lovely shoes in soft black leather, but they were a pair of the new ones I'd bought recently and I was getting a blister on my heel.

'Tim is a very nice man,' she said. 'I thought he would be more – no – not so very nice.'

'Of course he's nice,' I retorted. 'Why d'you think I'm marrying him?'

She shrugged. 'I do not know. I was surprised at the news, that is all.'

I smiled at her. 'I know that everyone thinks I'm crazy, but I've known Tim a long time and I love him.'

'I thought you did not love him any more. I thought you were in love with Nicolas.'

'Oh, Nico.' I dismissed him with a wave of my hand. 'A passing fancy, Magdalena! Someone to while away the time.' But I felt disloyal as I uttered the words and I wished I hadn't said it.

'He also was a very nice man,' she said dreamily. 'And also very good-looking. How do you manage that, Isobel? It is very unfair for you to grab all the good-looking men.'

'Must be my fatal charm.' I laughed. 'My good looks, my wonderful cooking!'

'Probably the wonderful cooking,' agreed Magdalena. 'My mother always says that cooking is a good way to get a man.'

I grinned. 'I think mine does too. And what about you, Magdalena? Any men on the horizon for you?'

She blushed. 'I am seeing Alejandro.'

'Alejandro!' I looked at her in amazement. 'I didn't realise that you were going out with Alejandro. I thought you said it was just a once-off thing.'

'It was,' she admitted. 'And then he phoned me, Isobel. Asked me to dinner. So I went.'

'How long has this been going on?'

'Four weeks and four days,' she told me.

'Does Gabriela know?'

'Not yet.' Magdalena bit the corner of her lip. 'I do not want to tell her yet, Isobel. She wasn't very happy when Alejandro left and—'

'I can guess.' I ran my fingers through my hair. 'So maybe you'll be inviting me to your wedding one day, Magdalena.'

She laughed. 'Maybe. But not yet, Isobel. We are taking it easy. No rushing into things.'

I smiled at her. 'Sensible Magdalena! But I wish you all the best.'

'Thank you,' she said. 'And for you I wish everything good too.'

❧

Gabriela brought around some tiny vol-au-vents and slices of tortilla. Alfredo filled our glasses again. I danced with José and with Luis. Tim (despite his dislike of jigging around as he called it) danced with Gabriela and Nina. Then we danced with each other.

'I like your friends,' he told me.

'They like you too.'

'I can see why you enjoy working with them.'

'They're nice people.'

He kissed me on the cheek. 'But you'll be happier at home with me.'

I closed my eyes. 'I know.'

∼

Later on we played Trivial Pursuit and the team of women easily beat the team of men.

'It's not fair,' said Luis. 'You girls got all the easy questions.'

'Rubbish!' Gabriela threw a cushion at him. 'We're just more intelligent.'

'It's called *Trivial* Pursuit,' said Tim. '*Trivial*. Not more intelligent.'

'Just because you lost,' I said lazily. 'And we had plenty to spare. You hadn't even got the pink wedge.'

'Huh.' Tim looked huffily at me and I laughed.

Alfredo filled our glasses again. Gabriela went outside and then reappeared with a huge gift-wrapped present. Another present, I thought. These people were far too good to me. She stood at the window and clapped her hands to get our full attention.

'I only want to say a few words. Isobel came to us nearly two years ago. Since then she has been a hardworking and responsible member of our company. She has been a good friend to all of us. We are very sorry to see her go.' She smiled at me and I blushed. 'But we are glad that she is going to marry Tim and be even happier than she was with us. And we wish her every success in her future. And we want to give you this, Isobel, as a memento of working with us here in Spain. We hope that you will come and visit us often.'

They clapped. I swallowed a couple of times, got up and stood beside Gabriela.

'Thank you all very much.' I looked at them all sitting in front of me, smiling at me. Suddenly I couldn't say anything else. My throat constricted and my eyes filled with tears. 'I'm sorry to leave you,' I croaked finally. 'I've loved being here.' I wiped the tears away as Gabriela hugged me and everyone else clapped.

'Sorry,' I said.

'Open your present.' Gabriela smiled at me.

I tore off the gift-wrapping. It was a magnificent reproduction of the Dalí painting that hung in my office. The girl looking out of the window. 'It's wonderful,' I said. 'Thank you all very much.'

'Luis wanted the Miró,' she told me. 'The lady walking the dog. But I thought this would be nicer.'

'You couldn't pick one I'd like better,' I said sincerely. 'Thank you, Gabriela. Thank you for everything.'

⌒

I was still strung out by the time Tim and I got back to the apartment in the early hours of the morning. I climbed into bed and put my arms around him, but I didn't want to make love.

'Why not?' he whispered as he ran his fingers along my thighs.

'Not tonight,' I said. 'I can't tonight.'

'Just as well I'm bringing you home,' he said. 'You're getting far too emotional over here.'

But he kissed me on the lips to show that he was teasing.

Chapter 32

Cat Catching a Bird (Pablo Picasso, 1939)

We slept late the following morning. I woke up at noon and didn't know where I was. I stared at the ceiling and struggled out of my sleep-filled haze. Then I turned in the bed and saw Tim lying on his back, eyes closed and snoring almost imperceptibly. I put my arm around him and he grunted but didn't wake up. I lay against his shoulder and closed my eyes again. Thank God it's Saturday, I thought, and then I suddenly remembered that it didn't matter to me what day it was. I'd left my job.

When I woke up on Monday I could roll over and fall asleep again if I wanted. No need for me to drag myself, mentally kicking and screaming, out of bed. There was no job for me to go to. I was dependent on Tim. The thought overwhelmed me. I'd never been dependent on anyone since the day I left school. I shivered and burrowed down beneath the duvet.

Tim didn't wake up, even when I got out of bed and made breakfast. He slept on, untroubled, dead to the world. I had a shower, washed my hair and was drying it before he stumbled out of the bedroom, rubbing his eyes and yawning.

'You woke me up,' he said.

'What?' I switched off my brand-new hairdryer.

'The noise. Woke me up.'

'I'm so sorry.' I made a face at him. 'Just as well something did, though, you'd have slept until tomorrow.'

'I know.' He yawned again. 'I was exhausted.'

'Poor thing. Here.' I threw a towel at him. 'The people in the building opposite can see into the apartment. We wouldn't want them to be driven into a frenzy by your magnificent masculinity.'

'Isobel!' But he wrapped the towel around his naked body all the same. He poured himself some coffee and bit into one of the croissants I'd left out on the table. 'I liked your friends.'

'Thanks.' I unplugged the hairdryer and left it on the sofa. 'They're nice people. Gabriela especially. She's been really good to me.'

'Classy lady,' he agreed. 'And she likes you.'

'We seemed to click.'

'Sorry to be leaving them?'

'Of course not.' I sat on his lap. 'Why should I be?'

'No reason. Isobel!' He almost choked as I undid the towel. 'Isobel, that's lovely but what about the people in the apartment opposite?'

'Let them watch.' I grinned at him. 'They might learn something.'

⁓

I'd booked a table in Quixote for that evening. When Tim had originally organised to come to Madrid we'd expected he'd be able to spend a week or two in the city, but he was very busy in work and we were going back to Ireland on Monday evening. So I thought it would be nice to go somewhere exclusive and romantic together before we went home. Besides, I wanted to impress him.

We took a metro into town and strolled to the restaurant. The city was crowded with people.

'This way.' I dragged him across the road and almost under the wheels of a Seat Ibiza being driven at high speed.

'Jesus, Isobel! Why did you do that?'

'We'd be waiting ages otherwise,' I explained. 'And you weren't in any danger.'

'Oh, really.' He tut-tutted at me. 'Just remember, you're not in the will yet.'

I laughed and turned down the sidestreet. The heavy wooden door of the restaurant was closed.

'Have we got the right day?' Tim looked at me doubtfully.

'Of course. I booked it.' I rang the bell.

The *maitre d'* answered the door and ushered us inside. We followed him down the steep flight of stairs into the basement of the building.

We were led across the highly polished marble floor to sit beneath a picture of the train station at Atocha. Fleetingly, I thought of Nico.

'A bomb went off there a few years ago,' I told Tim who looked at the painting with interest.

'While you were here?'

'No, well before that.'

'Good,' he said. 'I don't like to think you were in danger.'

'My hero.'

The waiter handed us menus.

'This is costing a fortune,' said Tim as he looked through it.

'It's my treat,' I told him. 'And it's worth every cent.'

We ordered *gambas mimosas* and *pollo cataluna*.

Tim smiled at me and yawned.

'Tired?'

He shook his head. 'Not really. Relaxed if anything. It's nice to get away for a couple of days.'

'It'll be hectic when we get back,' I said. 'Christmas, then the wedding.' I looked anxiously at him. 'You don't think it's all a bit much, do you? Maybe we should have the wedding later. March, or April.'

'Oh, Isobel, better off having it early. Anyway if we had it late people would say I was dithering again.'

'And are you?'

'What do you think?'

I smiled.

'You know I love you,' he said.

I nodded.

'I was a fool a couple of years ago. An absolute fool.'

'That's what I was thinking about,' I admitted. 'Rushing around for Christmas and then straight into the wedding – I thought, maybe—'

He smiled at me. 'Don't be an ass, Isobel.'

'OK.'

Tim ordered a Penendes white wine and we toasted each other before drinking it. 'To us,' he said.

'To us,' I echoed.

The restaurant was about three quarters full. I loved it here, the way the waiters seemed to glide rather than walk, the subdued hum of conversation, the clink of crystal glass and, in the background, the soft strumming of a guitar.

I'd jumped when the guitarist began to play but he wasn't Nico Alvarez, just a man in his twenties whom I'd never seen before. 'You OK?' asked Tim. 'You're in a trance.'

'No, sorry, I'm fine.' I looked up just as the waiter arrived with our prawns.

The food was wonderful. We didn't speak while we ate.

'It was good?' asked the waiter, and we nodded.

'You'll have to do a cookery course,' said Tim. 'Learn to produce things like that.'

'You should be so lucky.'

'I'll expect my dinner on the table every evening by seven.'

'You probably won't be home by seven.'

'Of course I will. Home and starving.'

'I thought your favourite food was a Big Mac and chips.'

'Almost,' he admitted. 'But if you started throwing *gambas mimosas* at me I might change my mind.'

'And what else do you want?' I teased. 'Your socks washed, your shirts ironed, your furniture polished?'

He laughed. 'There'll be a divison of labour, of course. But until you get a job—'

'Hopefully I'll get one right away,' I told him. 'I can't see myself sitting at home somehow.'

'I can't either,' he said. 'Although I could have. When we were engaged before.'

'Maybe,' I said. 'But I'm a different person now.'

'You still want a family.' It was a statement not a question.

'Of course. And you?'

'I'm sure we'll have the most beautiful children,' he said. 'Your eyes and my cheekbones.'

'What's wrong with my cheekbones?' I demanded.

'Nothing,' he said. 'But you always told me that you envied mine.'

The *pollo cataluna* arrived and the waiter refilled our wine glasses. Tim ordered another bottle.

'I'll be drunk. Again,' I said.

'Don't worry, you'll lead a life of total abstinence as Mrs Malone.'

Mrs Malone. I tried not to let myself think of being Mrs Malone. Whenever the name hovered at the edge of my consciousness I pushed it away, as though by thinking of it, letting it come into my head, it would somehow make everything go wrong. Mrs Malone. Isobel Malone. I couldn't believe that it was actually going to happen.

'This is fantastic.' Tim waved a forkful of chicken in front of me.

I cut a piece of my own and nodded. 'Delicious.' But I couldn't taste it. I wondered if I was getting a cold. My sense of taste always disappeared just before I started to sneeze.

'We'll go out at least once a week when we're married,' Tim told me. 'It's important that we should go out together and have fun, not just sit in night after night watching TV. Even after we have kids we'll have to make sure that we get time to be with each other.'

It was like talking to a different person these days. He never would have said things like that before.

'How long do you want to wait?' I asked.

'For what?'

'Before we have children?'

'That's up to you, Isobel. You're the one that'll have them.'

'But they'll be yours too.'

'I know. But whatever makes you happy.'

A completely different person, I thought. I drank some wine and it went down the wrong way.

'Are you all right?' asked Tim and I coughed and spluttered and my eyes watered.

'Fine,' I gasped. 'Just catching my breath.'

He watched me anxiously. 'Sure?'

I nodded. 'In a second.'

I took a puff of my inhaler. I hated doing that in public.

'OK now?'

'Yes,' I replied. 'I'll just go to the loo and repair my face.'

'It looks OK from here,' said Tim, but I wanted to be sure that I hadn't streaked mascara all down my cheeks in my fit of coughing. It was the sort of thing that Tim wouldn't actually notice.

The arched ceilings were in the ladies too, along with more murals of Spanish buildings and art deco mirrors surrounded by coloured mosaic. I redid my eyes and my lipstick and checked my dress. Not one I'd made myself, this evening. It was a pink wool I'd bought recently and it clung to every contour of my body.

I shivered. I didn't know why. It wasn't cold. I checked my tights for ladders, tucked my hair behind my ears and walked back to the dining room.

Nico and Barbara were sitting at the table directly in front of me. He was laughing at something she said, his eyes bright, his smile genuine. She leaned forward and touched his hand.

I stood rooted to the spot. Nico and Barbara. Here. Together. I didn't know why I was so shocked. She'd said that she was going to ask him out and she obviously had. So it shouldn't have surprised me. But I was surprised to see them here.

He saw me. The smile left his face, his eyes darkened and our eyes met. I couldn't see anything in them. Not hurt, nor accusation, nor even dislike. There was nothing. I swallowed and took a step towards them.

'Hi Nico, Barbara,' I said as I reached their table.

'Isobel!' The look Barbara shot me was triumphant. 'How are you?'

'I'm great.' The words came out but as though someone else was speaking them.

'What are you doing here?' she asked.

'Having dinner.'

I thought Nico smiled ever so slightly.

'It's Nico's birthday,' she told me. 'We're here to celebrate.'

'*Feliz cumpleaños*,' I said.

'Thank you.' He didn't look at me.

'So who are you with?' asked Barbara.

'Tim,' I said uncomfortably. 'I'm going home with him on Monday and I thought it would be nice to come here.'

'Monday?' This time Nico's glance flickered in my direction.

'Yes.'

'I thought you were staying until the middle of December,' said Barbara. 'That's what you told me, wasn't it?'

'I know,' I said. 'But Tim has to get back to work and there didn't seem much point in staying.'

'So have you set a date for the wedding yet?' She looked beautiful tonight, I thought. Beautiful and elegant and sophisticated in a way that I'd never seen her look before. Her eyes sparkled as she looked at me.

'January sometime,' I said. 'I'll be sending you your invitation, of course.'

'I can't wait,' she said. 'How about you, Nico?'

I looked at him, aghast. He couldn't possibly even consider coming to my wedding. Could he? Would he seriously think about showing up with Barbara?

'I would love to come,' he said, sending my heart plummeting to my shoes, 'but I do not think I can attend. I'm sorry, Is—'

'It's OK,' I interrupted. 'No problem. It's fine.'

Barbara looked at me in amusement. 'And where's lover-boy?'

'We're over there.' I indicated our table where Tim was reading the dessert menu with the look of someone who hasn't yet had anything to eat.

'God, Isobel, he's very good-looking.' Her sophistic-ated air slipped a little. 'I didn't realise—' She looked at me, then back to Tim, then at Nico. 'You certainly pick them.'

'Thanks.' I flushed with embarrassment.

'Will you introduce me?' she asked.

'If you like.'

'Isobel! I'm your friend! Of course I want to meet him.'

'OK.' I looked helplessly at Nico but he was studying the mural of the marina at Marbella.

'It's OK,' he said without looking at either of us. 'I will wait here for you, Barbara.'

She grabbed me by the elbow. 'I hope you don't mind about Nico,' she hissed. 'But you said you wouldn't care if I asked him out.'

'Of course I don't mind. Why should I mind?'

'Well, you know . . .'

'It doesn't matter. I was surprised though. I didn't realise you and he—'

'It's only our third date,' said Barbara. 'And the other two were at the Lux evening show so they don't really count. I thought it would be nice to bring him here as a treat.'

'It's lovely, isn't it?'

'And romantic.' She giggled. 'I'm hoping – well, you know.'

I wished she'd shut up.

'Hi, Tim. Look. This is another of my friends, Barbara Lane. She's one of the girls from the language college I told you about.'

'Barbara.' Tim's greeting made it seem as if he'd waited his whole life to meet her. 'Lovely to meet you. I've heard a lot about you.'

'All good, I hope.'

'None good.' He laughed and winked at her.

'So you're the man that broke Isobel's heart.'

He didn't bat an eyelid. 'And mended it again.'

'You think?' She grinned wickedly at him.

'You mean I didn't?'

'Well—' She smiled. 'Let's just say that there was a queue of people wanting to have a go.'

'Lucky that I managed to get her back then,' said Tim.

'Lucky indeed.' She smiled again. 'Lucky for me too.'

He didn't understand and I didn't enlighten him.

'I've invited Barbara to the wedding,' I told him. 'And Bridget too, of course.'

'I hope I can come,' said Barbara. 'I haven't been to a wedding in ages. I always cry.'

'So do I,' I said drily.

'I'd better get back,' she said. 'I don't like to leave him too long in case someone pinches him.'

'I know what you mean,' I said evenly.

'Where are you sitting?' asked Tim. 'Would you like to join us for a drink?'

I felt myself begin to wheeze again.

Barbara smiled. 'We've only just started dinner,' she said. 'But thanks, anyway.'

'We'll be here a little longer if you change your mind,' said Tim.

Barbara kissed me on the cheek. 'Don't worry, I won't,' she whispered and walked back to her table. Tim watched her go. From where he sat he could only see the back of Nico's head.

'Nice girl,' he said.

'Good friend.' I sat down and breathed more easily again.

'Going out with a local?'

I nodded.

506

'Will she marry him, d'you think?'

'I don't know.' She couldn't. Not Barbara. Not Nico. It wouldn't last.

And how the hell would I know? Maybe Barbara was exactly the sort of girl he needed. I pushed my escaping hair back from my face again. Maybe I'd get it cut. It was all very well to want elegant tresses for my wedding but it was driving me insane.

'Isobel?' Tim looked at me curiously.

'Yes?'

'You were miles away.'

'Was I?'

'Yes,' he said. 'I asked what the *Suprise Quixote* was likely to be.'

∽

The apartment was bare. Not of furniture, of course, it had come furnished. But it was empty all the same. There were no flowers in the big pottery vases on the sideboard, there was no fruit in the multicoloured bowl on the table. The wardrobe was cleared, the bathroom shelves emptied. It was awful. I felt – bereft. I stood at the front door, reluctant to close it for the last time while Tim struggled with two of my cases and a box of Lladro ceramics that I was bringing home to Mum.

Señora Carrasco opened her door. She'd called over the night before and we'd shared half a bottle of port while she told me that I was one of the best neighbours she'd ever had and informed Tim that he was a lucky, lucky man and that he'd been fortunate to prise me from the arms of other (perhaps less scrupulous) men. And she looked knowingly at me and nodded sagely.

'Everyone keeps telling me I'm lucky,' muttered Tim as we climbed into bed that night. 'Come on, Isobel –

time to prove it.' He pulled me to him and I snuggled into the warmth of his body. We were both lucky, I told myself, as he gently stroked my thigh. Lucky Tim. Lucky Isobel. Lucky at last.

Chapter 33

Seated Woman (Joan Miró, 1938)

I was never very good at Christmas shopping. I'm not sure that many people are – crowds, jostling, and blank space where the ideas for presents should be. I suppose some enjoy the cut and thrust of it all, and some relish the last-minute panic of rushing out on Christmas week with a list full of people to buy for, but it's not me. Besides, I wheeze in a crowd. I was wheezing now, in the middle of Brown Thomas, surrounded by a mist from sample sprays for expensive perfumes that men were recklessly buying for their wives or girlfriends or mistresses. I tried not to breathe as I struggled through the throng. I was buying Tim a briefcase for Christmas. He'd told me about it in such a way that I knew it was the present he wanted, even though it seemed hopelessly unromantic and far too practical a gift.

'Maroon,' he said. 'Very dark. Not shiny.'

And I could see it now, in the centre of the display, understated in its elegance but (surely) overstated in its price. I peered at the label to make certain that the decimal point was in the right place. Oh well, I thought, next year it'll be woolly socks and thermals for him. We'll have settled into our domestic rut by then. In a year's time a briefcase will probably seem like a dangerously exciting present.

I knew that I was being cynical but I couldn't help it. I'd been in town since early morning. It was nearly one o'clock now and I hadn't even bought anything yet. I'd looked everywhere, of course, I'm a great looker, but I'd suddenly become hopelessly indecisive. I'd dithered between a blue angora jumper or a green silk blouse for Mum and bought neither. I'd made a mental note to buy a chunky jewelled costume bracelet I'd seen earlier for Alison, but hadn't bought it yet just in case there was something else I thought she'd prefer. I hadn't a clue what to get Dad. Or Ian. Or Jemima, Honey's replacement. Honey, it seemed, had got tired of Ian not asking her to marry him.

'But he's too young to get married,' I told Alison when she imparted this news.

'I know that and you know that,' she'd replied. 'But Honey loves him.'

When I asked Ian about it he simply said that she'd become too clingy. 'Wants to know where I am all the time. She doesn't bloody own me.' The words sounded very familiar. So did the sentiment. I hoped that Honey had found someone else.

I brought the briefcase to the sales desk. An assistant wrapped it lovingly in tissue paper before sliding it into the striped carrier bag. 'It's very nice,' he told me. 'Very popular this year.'

'Thanks.' I slung the rope handles of the bag over my shoulder and nearly took the eye out of a tired-looking woman waiting to pay for a soft leather wallet.

'Sorry,' I said. 'Really.'

'It's OK,' she said. 'If this is the closest I get to danger I'll be doing well this year. Last year I was mugged waiting for a DART. Nearly lost a tooth. I hate Christmas.'

'Oh.' I felt as though I was in the middle of *A Christmas Carol*. I left her to it and pushed my way into the main body of the store again.

I felt better now that I'd bought something. As though I belonged in the crowd. The bag marked me out as a shopper at last. I took the escalator upwards, walked around in a daze. I was really hungry now and feeling almost lightheaded. I'd put on weight since I'd come home. Lounging around with nothing much to do had seen me raid the fridge more often than I ever had before. In Spain I rarely snacked and if I did it was always fresh fruit. Except, of course, when Nico had brought me to the Chocolateria. I'd have to diet like mad after Christmas so that I'd look thin and beautiful when I married Tim. As always, when I thought of marrying Tim, my heart lurched and I felt the tingle of anticipation run through me. Isobel Malone. Finally.

Maybe it was thinking about my wedding that directed my footsteps, but quite suddenly I was standing at the bridal department, gazing at the truly incredible dress that was on display. It was a dream dress, the sort you imagined as a child when you pretended to be a fairy princess. Pure, dazzling white, with a skirt that took up incalculable yards of shimmering satin. An intricate pattern of white velvet rosebuds twined around the bodice and drifted onto the skirt. I'd made some dramatic dresses in my time, but this one simply took my breath away.

'Would you like to try it on?' The sales assistant was watching me.

I shook my head. 'It's beautiful, but it's too much. I couldn't possibly wear anything like that.'

'It'd look great on you,' she said. 'With your colouring. Absolutely stunning!'

I smiled at her. 'Maybe. But I couldn't wear it. Honestly I couldn't. Besides,' I made a face, 'I'm sure it's much too expensive.'

'It's the most important day of your life,' said the sales assistant. 'And you want to look perfect.'

I supposed she was right.

'Try it on, why not?' She grinned at me. 'It's quiet here today. People are buying Christmas presents not wedding dresses. And it would look great on you.'

I hesitated.

'Go on,' she said again.

'Oh, all right.' I followed her into the changing area and put Tim's briefcase on the floor beside a spindly chair.

'It's one of our most popular dresses.' She disappeared into another room and returned with my size. 'Everyone says that they feel like a princess when they put it on. Most of them end up buying it.'

'I promise you I won't end up buying it,' I told her as I slipped out of my jeans and jumper, thankful that I was wearing a really pretty set of underwear that I'd bought in a shop on the Calle de Serrano – cream and pink in soft cotton.

'Here you are.'

I stepped into the dress. She eased the zip upwards, pulled at the sleeves and rearranged the skirt. Then she stood back, looked at me and smiled. 'I told you,' she said. 'Like a princess.'

I wanted to say that looking like a princess wasn't any guarantee of a happy marriage but I couldn't speak. The dress was more than the sum of its parts, it had looked beautiful if over the top on the display, but wearing it – wearing it was a different story completely. I stared at the reflection of the lightly tanned, long-haired girl in the mirror and I hardly recognised myself. If I bought this dress, or if I made one like it, Tim would keel over at the altar.

'It suits you,' she said. And it did. I didn't think it would. I thought that acres of satin would look stupid on a woman of thirty. But I didn't look thirty. I looked young and eager.

'The dress is so important for every bride.' The sales assistant's voice seemed to come from miles away. 'It's a statement, of course. And that dress makes a very powerful statement.'

Isobel Malone. That was the statement I'd be making. Isobel Kavanagh loves Tim Malone and wants to be with him for ever. There was a lump in my throat.

'It gets some people that way.'

The sales assistant was looking at me understandingly. 'To be honest, it gets to me too.' She sniffed. 'You all look so wonderful.'

I smiled. 'Do we?'

'Oh, yes.'

'I suppose we should.'

'Why not? You'll only do it once.' She grimaced. 'Hopefully.'

'Hopefully,' I repeated. I blinked at my reflection again. 'I look – incredible.'

'Yes.' She looked at me critically. 'You do.'

'But I can't buy it. Not today anyway.'

'That's OK. I like seeing different people in it. And when you're ready to buy, even if it's not this dress, please visit us again. I'm sure we'll have something that you'll like.'

'I like this.' I turned around again. 'I really do. But it wasn't what I had in mind, you see. I wanted something simple.'

'Oh, simple,' she said scornfully. 'Why have simple when you can have utterly extravagant.'

I laughed. 'I'll come back.'

She unzipped the dress. 'I look forward to seeing you.'

It was a bit of a come-down getting back into jeans. I thanked her and retrieved Tim's briefcase. There was still the rest of the Christmas shopping to do.

But I was revitalised. I bought a couple of Mars Bars to sustain me, then stalked up Grafton Street ignoring the crowds and bought the green silk blouse for Mum, the bracelet for Alison, a jumper for Ian, and a hip flask for Dad. I bought a book on dogs for Peter Gaffney and perfume for Jemima. Then I bought myself a pair of black leather boots and a leather jacket.

Mum would go mad, I knew. She'd look at the boots and jacket and tell me that I should wait for the sales. But I wouldn't have time to shop in the sales – I'd be busy with wedding details. I stood at St Stephen's Green and waited for a taxi. I hoped that it would be warmer than this by then.

There were hordes of people waiting for taxis. I stamped my feet to keep them warm and wished that I'd worn a hat and gloves. I'd managed to lose my grey fake-fur hat in the move back to Dublin and I'm the sort of person who can't hold on to a pair of gloves for more than a couple of days. I cupped my hands and blew into them to warm them while my shopping formed a barrier around me.

Eventually a taxi arrived. I gave the driver the address and leaned back in the seat. Tim had wanted me to move in with him when I got home. He'd been surprised and, I thought, hurt when I said that I wanted to live with my parents.

'But we're getting married, Isobel,' he'd protested. 'And you practically lived with me before.'

'But I didn't,' I reminded him. 'I wanted to marry you. I still want to marry you.'

'And I want to marry you,' he said. 'I just think that we might as well be sharing the same house.'

'It's only eight weeks. You can wait for eight weeks, can't you?'

'It's not a question of waiting,' he said. 'It's a question of wanting you close to me all the time. Now that I have you,' he added, 'I don't want to let you go.'

'You say the nicest things.' I cuddled close to him. 'That's why I love you.'

But I hadn't moved in with him and I was glad I'd been firm about it.

The taxi drew up outside the house. I stood at the gate and looked at the necklace of yellow lights snaking their way around Dublin Bay, reflecting on the blackness of the sea. The sight was one of the advantages of living on the coast. I'd missed it while I was away.

'Tim rang,' said Mum as I walked in the door. 'He says that he'll meet you directly at the Chilli Club. He'll be going there straight from work.'

'Oh, bugger,' I said.

'Isobel!' Mum looked angrily at me. 'You know I hate that expression.'

I smothered a grin. 'Sorry.'

'As well you should be.'

I followed her into the kitchen. 'Did he say what time?'

'No.' She filled the kettle. 'What time are you supposed to be meeting him?'

'Eight.' I opened the fridge door and unwrapped a lump of cheddar cheese. 'Early.'

'It's late,' said Mum. 'Late to be eating a full meal. I don't know how you don't lie awake with indigestion every night.'

'I don't know either.' I nibbled on the cheese. 'But we didn't eat until much later in Madrid.'

'Foreigners are different.' She sniffed and arranged pork chops on the grill. 'Do you want one?'

I shook my head. 'Better not. This is Tim's pre-Christmas present to me – a romantic night out. Wouldn't do if I couldn't eat any of it. I'll make a sandwich. I didn't eat anything in town. I'm ravenous.'

'Your eating pattern is all out of sync,' said Mum. 'That's what going abroad does for you.'

'Don't be daft.' I kissed her lightly on the cheek.

'When you've finished that sandwich will you set the table for me?' she asked.

'Sure. Are you expecting everyone home for tea?'

'Yes,' she said. 'A rare occurrence in this household.'

'In every household,' I told her. 'Don't you read anything, Mum? It's all snacking and grazing now, not family meals.'

'There'll always be family meals in this house,' she said grimly as she sliced tomatoes.

'I'll keep that in mind when I'm in Donnybrook,' I said. 'Whenever I can't cope I'll come running home.'

'But you will cope, won't you?' She put the knife down on the worktop and turned to me. 'You'll be all right with Tim, Isobel?'

Her eyes were worried, her brow furrowed.

'Of course I will.' I smiled at her. 'We'll be fine, Mum. Honestly.'

'I don't like to interfere,' she said. 'It's all very well having my own ideas but I don't want to run your life. I've never tried to do that, Isobel.'

I raised an eyebrow. 'What about Barry Dillon?' I asked. Barry had been my second boyfriend. Mum hadn't liked him and he hadn't lasted very long. She'd made sure of that.

'Who?' She looked surprised.

'Never mind.' I smiled at her. 'It doesn't matter.'

'I don't remember any Barry Dillon.' Mum wiped her hands on her blue and white striped apron. 'But then you had so many boyfriends, Isobel. I never knew who you'd turn up with next.'

'That was me. Miss Popularity.'

'You were popular. You were – are – a good-looking girl. That's enough to make you popular when you're sixteen.'

'It's not a bad thing when you're older either.' I grinned.

'I know. And you're lucky, Isobel. You're still pretty.'

'Thanks,' I said.

'And it's hard for me to think of any of you as other than babies.'

'I suppose not.'

I thought, suddenly, of the baby she'd lost. Of the way it had all gone wrong for her.

'So I want what's best for you. I want you to be happy. I want you to have everything you want from life.'

'I am happy,' I assured her. 'I'm getting exactly what I want.'

She picked up the knife and began chopping mush-rooms. 'It's not that I don't believe you—'

'But . . .' I supplied.

'There's no "but".'

'It sounded like a "but" coming on.'

'No. Really. It's just—' She turned around again. 'Are you absolutely sure this time?' Her voice was shaky. 'Are you certain that he's the one, Isobel?'

I put my arms around her and held her tight. 'I'm certain. Absolutely certain.'

❧

Ian gave me a lift into town. He'd borrowed Dad's car to drive to Jemima's house which was in Rathgar.

'A southsider,' I teased as I fastened the seat belt. 'Honestly, Ian, I'm surprised at you.'

'She's nice,' he said defensively. 'She likes me and I like her.'

'Sounds intense.' I turned on the heater.

'It's – restful.'

'Restful?' I glanced at him as he pulled out into the main road, his eyes narrowed against the glare of the oncoming headlights. 'What on earth would you want with a restful relationship?'

'God, Isobel, we're not all voracious party animals, you know.' He accelerated along the coast road. 'I like to sit with a girl and just – rest.'

'That's fine,' I told him. 'No problem. I wish I'd had a boyfriend like you. None of them ever wanted to sit and rest. Sit and struggle more like.'

'I told you, we're not all animals. Maybe you just go out with the wrong sort of man.'

I glanced at him again. 'And who have you in mind?'

'Nobody.'

'Sounds to me like you do.'

'Don't be stupid.' He braked at the lights and swore under his breath.

'So Jemima likes to be restful, does she?' I switched the topic back to his love life.

'Yes, she does. Honey always wanted to do things. She couldn't sit still for more than five minutes. She exhausted me. "Ian, we must do this. Ian, we should go here. Ian, we have to meet these people. Ian, stop lounging around in front of the TV".' The lights turned green and he eased the car forward. 'Then, when she phoned, it was "Where are you going, what are you doing, who are you seeing?" It drove me nuts.'

'When I came home for Gran's funeral you said you couldn't live without her,' I reminded him.

'I was used to her,' he said. 'It's not exactly the same thing.'

'And are you in love with Jemima?'

He laughed. 'No, Isobel, I'm not. But I like her a lot and we have fun together and it's very, very unpressurised. Honey wanted to get married, you know.'

'Alison told me.'

'I'm too young to get married. It would have been a disaster. It's different for girls.'

'Is it?' I asked.

'Yes,' he said definitely. 'There's something about girls and being married.'

'Married women have a higher depression rate than married men,' I told him. 'In fact, I think married men are the most contented people there are. So there's something wrong about your theory.'

'Rubbish,' he said. 'I haven't yet met a girl who secretly didn't want to waltz down the aisle with some unfortunate sod.'

I smiled. 'I'm sure there are loads.'

'Name one,' he said.

'You see?' said Ian when I'd been silent for a couple of minutes. 'I rest my case.'

'We must all be mad then,' I said wryly. 'It's not the be-all and end-all of everything.'

We stopped at another set of lights. In the car beside us a girl, wrapped up in a black leather coat with a fur collar, snuggled against the man who was driving.

'And what do you think?' asked Ian. 'Really and truly?'

'Really and truly I don't know.' I leaned my head against the headrest. 'I want the companionship and the love and the stability, I suppose.'

'And for that you're going to marry that shithead.'

'Ian, you don't have to call him that. And there's more to it. I just don't have the words.'

'Or maybe you don't have the feelings.'

I shot a dark look at him but he was concentrating on the road ahead. 'I love Tim,' I said. 'And I don't see that I should have to keep justifying myself to everyone.'

'I didn't ask you to.'

'You didn't need to.'

He let me out at Trinity Street. Town was still crowded with people hurrying around with shopping or dressed up for Christmas parties. Much as I'd hated it earlier when I was shopping, I was now drawn into the festive mood of the city. People were in better humour now. The shoppers had finished searching for the perfect present and had decided to reward themselves with a drink in O'Neills or the Old Stand or anywhere else they could get in. Most of the pubs were jammed full, as though the beer was free. I cut through Exchequer Street, and across Grafton Street, where this time I noticed the animated display in the Brown Thomas windows and took time to look at it with a childish delight.

I remembered being brought to see Santa as a child, queueing for ages outside some city store (although I couldn't remember which). Then, when I finally came face to face with him and he'd put his arm around me, I screamed for my mother. I couldn't have been more than three or four. I didn't remember Alison being with us, even as a baby.

Nostalgic idiot, I told myself, as I rang the bell on the door of the restaurant.

'Malone for two?' The waitress smiled at me. 'In the corner. Your companion hasn't arrived yet.'

That was nothing new. Although he had tried, very hard, to be more punctual. 'I know how much you hate me being late,' he'd told me the second night I was home. 'So I'll do my best to be on time for everything from now on. Although,' and he'd smiled, 'if you just come and live with me now, you wouldn't have to worry about it.'

But I hadn't changed my mind.

'Can I get you something to drink?'

'Mineral water, please.'

She returned with a glass of sparkling water and a couple of menus. I sipped the water and read the menu, prounouncing the Malaysian words to myself and wondering exactly how they should be said. I always ordered the easy things, like *rendang beef* or *green curry*, simply because I was too embarrassed to get the names wrong.

I glanced at my watch. Only ten minutes late. That wasn't bad really, anything could have made him ten minutes late. I looked up at the sound of the doorbell and arranged my face into a smile, but it wasn't Tim.

It was a group of men and women, laughing and chattering as they made their way to a table in the corner. An office party by the sounds of things – they were ripping the reputation of someone called Vivi in accounts to shreds. Something to do with Jim in investments and Paul in finance. I hoped that Vivi could last the pace. I eavesdropped unashamedly, enjoying the office gossip. I missed office gossip. I missed my job. And where the hell was Tim?

I closed the menu with a snap and knocked over the glass of water.

The waitress flurried around while I apologised over and over again and she told me that it didn't matter and that there was no harm done and that it was only water, it wouldn't stain. Then she went off to get another tablecloth while I sat in my chair and tried to ignore the furtive glances of the other diners and pretend that this wasn't happening to me.

A new tablecloth was brought, the table was reset and I was given another mineral water. I said thank you and buried my head in the menu again. I wished Tim would hurry up. People were still looking at me, they'd realised now that I'd been sitting here on my own for twenty-five minutes. They'd be muttering to each other that my date had stood me up. I stretched out my left hand on the table so that the engagement ring sparkled in the light. Let them know that I had a man, a man who'd made a commitment to me. If he was a little late, it didn't matter. But I wished fervently he'd hurry up and arrive.

It was five minutes before he did, bringing with him a waft of raw night air mingled with stale smoke and beer. He sat down beside me and took my warm hand in his freezing one.

'I'm really sorry,' he said. 'Honestly, Isobel. I tried and tried to get here on time. I've come from work.'

'Work via the pub?' I hazarded.

'I had to,' he said. 'Everyone was going and I couldn't just walk out. I only had one.'

I said nothing.

'Well, two,' he amended. 'But I swear to God that's all, Isobel. I didn't even enjoy them, I left a full pint behind.'

I believed him. There was a sense of injured innocence about him that it was hard to doubt. Besides, Tim's eyes always went a delicate shade of pink after three pints, and they were still clear, if slightly hazy.

'I was having the most terrible time with Greg,' he continued as he released my hand so that he could open the menu. 'He wants me to finish another phase of this project we're working on before the end of the week. I asked him was he out of his mind – there's another three weeks of work there. But you know Greg, deadlines, commitments, all that sort of stuff.'

I nodded.

'So I told him that it'd be finished when it was finished and I was working flat out as it was.'

'And that was OK?'

'He huffed and he puffed but he gave in eventually.'

'That's good.'

'As long as it's finished before the wedding that'll do,' said Tim. 'Greg is like that. He sets an impossible deadline so that you end up promising something only barely achievable.'

I smiled. 'I hope you won't be tapping away at that computer on our wedding night.'

'Don't worry.' Tim grinned at me. 'I intend tapping away at something far more interesting.'

'Tim!'

'Sorry.' He squeezed my hand. 'I love you, Isobel.'

'Why?'

'What sort of question is that?'

'Why do you love me?'

'For millions of reasons. But mostly—' he leaned forward, 'because you're the sexiest thing on two legs in the whole universe.'

I smiled. We ordered food. I sat back in the chair and gazed around the room while Tim revisited his conversation with Greg about the project they were working on. I wasn't really listening to him, just the drone of his voice. All the stories about work were the same – Greg wanted too much, Tim delivered. Eventually. After a huge argument.

'So I'll have to go in on St Stephen's Day,' he said.

I looked at him. 'That's a bummer.'

'Oh, better get it finished. It wouldn't do to have him ringing me up on the morning of the wedding screeching for me to come in.'

I smiled. 'No.'

'How've you been getting on with things?' he asked. 'Everything under control?'

'Yes.' Because I wasn't working, I had time to organise everything. Much more time than on the previous occasion, although the closeness of the date made things awkward.

'Hotel booked, band booked, church booked—'

'Tim, everything is booked,' I said firmly.

'I just want things to go perfectly,' he said.

'Thanks.'

'So that when we're old and grey you can't complain about it.'

'I won't.'

'The honeymoon is more of a problem than I thought,' he said lightly.

'Oh?'

'I can only get a week off work.'

'Oh, Tim!'

'Well, what did you expect?' he asked. 'I took time off to come to Spain—'

'A few days!' I interrupted.

'I had some time off earlier in the year.'

'What for?'

He ignored me. 'And since our leave goes from April to April, I don't have much leave left.'

'So what are you saying?'

'That we'll go somewhere for a week.'

'Better than nothing, I suppose.' I made a face. 'And I guess I'll be aching to get back to work.'

'You don't have to,' said Tim.

'I do,' I told him. 'Like I said before, if we have children it'll be different. But I couldn't stay at home unless we had a family. What would I do all day?'

He shrugged. 'Paint? Knit? Sew?' He nodded. 'You could do that, Isobel. You could do dressmaking full-time.'

'I couldn't,' I said.

'Why not?' He smiled at the waitress who placed *satay chicken* in front of him. 'You like making clothes.'

'I know,' I said. 'But not full-time.'

'But you once thought of it.'

'Not seriously,' I told him. 'I wouldn't do it all the time. I wouldn't enjoy it.'

'Are you enjoying your time off?' he asked as he gently slid the delicate chicken from the wooden skewers. 'It must be nice not to have to get up in the morning.'

'Nice but strange,' I said. 'I keep thinking I should have something to do.'

'You have got something to do,' objected Tim. 'You're the chief wedding organiser.'

'That's me.'

'Have you started on your dress yet?' he asked.

I shook my head.

'You'll look gorgeous,' he told me. 'Everyone says so.'

'Do they?' I could feel myself blush. Not a deep, scorching blush, but a creeping pale-pink one.

'Of course,' said Tim. 'Dave thinks you're the sexiest girl he knows.'

'Tim!'

'It's true. He said that you were easily the most beddable thing at the Christmas party.'

Softsys's party had been the previous weekend. I'd worn the maroon dress I'd made for the dinner where Gabriela had been voted businessperson of the year.

'He said he could hardly keep his hands off you,' continued Tim.

I was blushing again.

'He said that if you weren't engaged to me, he'd have a go at you himself.'

'He did not!' I looked at Tim in horror. I hated the idea of them talking about me like this.

'He'd had a couple of pints at the time,' Tim reassured me.

'All the same.' I pushed my plate away. 'I don't like being discussed as though I was some sort of commodity.'

'You're not a commodity,' said Tim, 'and we didn't talk about you as if you were.'

'Even so. The idea of Dave having a go at me, as you so delicately put it!'

'He didn't mean any harm.' Tim's tone was defensive. 'And I'm proud that he feels like that about you.'

'Why?'

'Because it means that I made the right choice, doesn't it?'

'Does it?' I stared at him.

'Of course,' he continued blithely. 'It's great to know that the girl you're about to marry is the object of desire of so many people! I like knowing that you're mine and that there's nothing anyone can do about it. It makes me feel good.'

'Well it makes me feel like a piece of meat.'

'Oh, Isobel, don't be stupid.'

'I'm not.'

'You are. You're taking me up all wrong.'

'Tim, I'm not something you own, you know.'

He grabbed my hand again. 'Of course not. But I'm glad you're mine.'

I didn't reply. It was too complicated. But I hoped that Dave wouldn't be at our wedding. It would be too embarrassing to meet him and know he'd said the kind of things he'd said to Tim. Was I overreacting? Probably. I knew men talked like that to each other. I'd heard them in Delta. 'She's a looker, that one.' 'Hot for it.' 'Wouldn't mind a piece of that!' And they didn't mean anything by it. Not really. It was just the way men were.

I wondered if the men in Spain had talked that way. I'd never overheard them, but I supposed they must have. And Bridget had once said that Tomás treated her like a possession. Maybe it was just men. Maybe they never grew out of thinking of women like that. I didn't want to be a possession.

'What are you thinking about?' asked Tim.

'Nothing important,' I answered as I stirred my coffee. 'Nothing at all.'

Chapter 34

Basket of Bread (Salvador Dalí, 1926)

I didn't make my wedding dress. I bought it.

I'd gone into town to look at material. I'd decided to make myself something simple because I thought that I was too old for airy-fairy concoctions that bore no relation to the kind of person you were. So, nothing cute and puffy like the first dress I'd made. A plain dress, I thought, with a short jacket to go over it. And, despite Tim's wishes, I'd forget the veil and just wear flowers in my hair.

But somehow, without meaning to, I found myself in BT's and staring at their wedding dresses again. I told myself it was to rob ideas, but it wasn't. I just wanted a last look at the impossible dress I'd tried on before Christmas.

The same assistant was there. She smiled at me. 'You were here before.'

'Yes,' I admitted. 'I thought I'd take a look again. But I'll probably end up making my own dress.'

'You're a dressmaker?'

'Sometimes,' I said. 'I've made wedding dresses for other people and they've never complained!'

'Do you want to try one on?' she asked.

'Oh, I don't think so. I just want to get the feel of things.'

She smiled again. 'That's OK.'

'Did you sell the other dress? The one I tried on before?' I asked as I looked around.

She shook her head. 'Not yet.' Then she laughed. 'We have four of them in stock. Would you like to try it on again?'

I bit my lip. 'I told you I probably won't buy it.'

'I don't mind,' she said. 'Were you a twelve or a ten?'

'I don't know what size the one I tried was,' I said. 'Most of me is a ten, but I get occasional twelve days.'

She laughed. 'Come on, let's see what we can do.'

I hadn't put on as much weight as I thought. The ten fitted perfectly.

I stood in front of the forest of mirrors and looked at myself from every angle. It was still a fabulous dress.

But I didn't need a fabulous dress to marry Tim. I'd made a fabulous dress! I could still remember sewing all those bloody pearls on it. Stupid to have cut it up in a fit of temper.

I sighed.

'I thought you might like to try this with it.' The assistant handed me a veil and headdress. 'It goes really well, I think.'

'Does it?'

'Absolutely.'

I looked fantastic. I knew I did. It didn't look silly, or flouncy or over-the-top. It looked just right.

'You look wonderful,' said the sales assistant. 'Really wonderful.'

If I made a dress would I look this wonderful? I could copy it, I knew. But it wouldn't be quite the same thing.

'When's the wedding?' she asked.

'The end of January,' I said idly as I gazed at my reflection.

'The end of January and you still haven't bought a dress!' She looked at me in horror. 'Are you crazy?'

'Why?'

'Don't you think it's important to get the exact right one?'

'I think,' I said as I took off the veil, 'that it's more important to get the right man.'

I got dressed again and turned from Isobel Kavanagh, thing of beauty, into Isobel Kavanagh, girl with unmanageable hair.

'How much is it?' I asked the assistant.

'The dress or the veil?'

'The whole lot.'

She told me and I tried to look nonchalant. The price of the dress was almost as much as our week-long honeymoon.

'But worth every cent,' she said. 'For a day to remember.'

I could afford the dress. It just seemed like an incredible waste of money.

'Of course, it is reduced by ten per cent,' added the sales assistant.

'That makes a big difference.' I grinned at her.

Did I want to be Isobel Kavanagh, fairy princess? When everyone came to the wedding, what kind of Isobel did they expect to see? Someone revelling in the whole razzmatazz of getting married – like Julie, or someone in a sensible white dress and jacket? And if I was sensible, would they think that I was only being sensible because of what had happened the last time? Did I care what anyone thought?

The sales assistant watched me silently.

'It's such a lovely dress,' I said eventually.

'And it looked perfect on you.'

I smiled. 'You'd have to say that, wouldn't you?'

'Not at all. If you looked like the back of a bus I'd suggest something else.'

'I should make my own,' I told her.

'In less than a month?'

'It's not that difficult.'

'But you've other things to do, I'm sure.'

I didn't, really. I'd lots of time to slope off and do exactly what I liked. Even making my wedding dress and Alison's bridesmaid's dress, which would be time-consuming all the same.

'Could I try it on again?' I asked. 'I mean, would you mind?'

She shook her head. 'Try it on as many times as you like.'

∽

The dress, when packed, took up the entire back of the car. It was a mountain of froth.

∽

Alison was lounging in front of the TV, her legs dangling over the end of the sofa.

'Going out tonight?' I asked.

She shook her head. 'Peter's playing football with the guys from the office. They go for a few pints afterwards and I wouldn't dream of meeting with him then.'

'Good,' I said. 'I need to measure you for the bridesmaid's dress. And I want your opinion on mine.'

'My opinion?' Alison looked at me curiously. 'Have you made it already?'

'And how could I have done that?'

'Isobel!' She followed me up the stairs. 'Don't tell me you bought it!'

'OK, I won't.'

'Oh, my God!' She stared at the dress which I had hung over my dressmaker's dummy. 'It's the most gorgeous thing I've ever seen.'

'Thank you.'

'It's – wonderful.'

'I know.'

'You'll look absolutely stunning in it.'

I laughed.

'Where did you get it?'

'BT's.'

'How much did it cost?' She fingered the material.

'Lots.'

'Well, it was worth it.'

I laughed again. 'I hope Tim thinks so.'

'He'd have to be blind not to think so,' said Alison. 'And, whatever else he is, he isn't blind.'

'Give it a rest, will you.' I sat on the bed. 'If I've got over the last time, why can't you?'

'I've got over it,' said Alison as she sat down beside me. 'I didn't have much getting over to do, after all. But he was so bloody rotten to you, Isobel. And I just feel that he could be again. I'm sorry. I know you're not supposed to say things like this about people's boyfriends or girlfriends. Whatever. I know that I'm supposed to like him for your sake. But I can't forgive him.'

'Oh, Alison.' I put my arm around her shoulder. 'You're not the worst sister in the world.'

'I'm the best,' she said. 'Believe it!'

⌒

The phone rang at eight o'clock. Ian jumped out of the armchair and rushed into the hall to answer it. He came back a moment later looking rueful. 'It's for you,' he told me. 'It's someone from Spain.'

'Spain?' I looked up from *Irish Bride*. My heart had begun to beat faster. 'Who from Spain?'

Ian shrugged. 'Dunno. Didn't ask.'

'You're useless.' I put the magazine on the coffee table and walked slowly to the phone. 'Hello,' I said. 'It's Isobel.'

'Hi, Isobel.' I was surprised and somehow disappointed to hear Barbara.

'Barbara! How are you?'

'Not bad,' she replied. 'And you? How are the great wedding preparations going?'

'Oh, all right.' I laughed. 'That sounds terrible. They're going fine, Barbara, I'm just worn out, thats all. I'm fed up with lists of people and menus and all that shit.'

'Poor you,' she sympathised. 'I feel *so-o-o* sorry for you.'

'Shut up,' I said, amused. 'What have you been doing with your life since I left?'

'This and that,' she said. 'I've been very busy in work. We've got extra classes and I'm working two nights a week.'

'You mustn't get out much,' I said.

'Enough.'

'Is it cold there right now?' I asked.

'Yes,' said Barbara. 'But not as bad as last year. The frost melts very early. What about Ireland?'

'Not too bad,' I said. 'Misty.'

'Wish you were here?' she asked.

'Nope. My fiancé is here.'

'Ah, sweet love,' she teased.

'Speaking of sweet love,' my tone was light, 'how's Nico?'

'He's fine.'

'Keeping well?'

'Absolutely.'

'Still playing music?'

She paused. 'Not as much.'

'Why?'

'He's got a new job.'

'New job,' I echoed. 'He never said anything about looking for a new job.'

'He only got it recently,' she told me. 'He was headhunted.'

'Headhunted! Nico?'

'Why not?'

'It doesn't sound like Nico.'

'He's become very career-oriented lately,' said Barbara.

'Really?'

'Yes.' I could almost see her nod. 'He's taking life more seriously.'

'You must be having an effect.' My laughter was forced.

'I hope so,' she said.

'Are you seeing much of him?'

'When I can. He's so busy.'

'It definitely doesn't sound like him,' I said.

'He's changed,' she said. 'I think he's sort of matured.'

'Matured?' The echo was back.

'I've matured him.' Barbara laughed.

'Congratulations,' I said.

'Maybe not,' she conceded.

'I'm glad you're getting on together.'

'Oh, yes. Absolutely. He's a wonderful person, isn't he?'

'I – yes.'

'Attractive. That helps, of course. But he's a decent person too.'

'Yes,' I repeated.

'So warm, so sexy.'

'Barbara!'

'Well, he is, isn't he?'

'I – yes.' I didn't seem to be able to say much else.

'It's working well,' she continued.

'You don't mind?' I asked.

'Mind what?'

'That I went out with him first.'

'Isobel, Isobel! Bitchy.'

'Sorry.'

'I don't mind.' She giggled. 'It's me he's with now.'

'Yes,' I said. 'It's you.'

'Anyway,' her voice was serious again, 'I rang to say that I can't come to your wedding after all, Isobel.'

'Oh, Barbara. Why not?'

'Because of Nico, really. We're going to Seville. Un-expectedly.'

Seville. He'd told me he'd take me to Seville. Not that it mattered.

'That's a pity,' I said. 'I'll miss you not being there.'

'I'll be sorry to miss it myself,' she told me. 'Wanted to see you safely married off, Isobel.'

'Will Bridget still be coming?' I asked.

'Yes,' said Barbara. 'And Tomás! Didn't she send you a card?'

'Yes, she did. I just thought that maybe it didn't suit her.'

'We don't see that much of each other these days,' said Barbara.

'I suppose things change.' I clutched the receiver in my right hand.

'Of course,' said Barbara. 'Look, Isobel, I really am sorry I can't come.'

'At least Bridget can,' I said. 'And I'm glad one of you will make it. You were both very good friends to me.'

'Oh, Isobel.' Suddenly she sounded uncomfortable. 'Thank you. We had some good fun, didn't we?'

'Yes,' I said. 'We did.'

'Anyway,' she said brightly, 'I hope you have a wonderful day.'

'Thanks.'

'And a wonderful life.'

'Thanks again. You too, Barbara. And have a good time in Seville.'

'Absolutely.'

'Bye then. Keep in touch.'

'Sure,' she said.

But I knew she wouldn't.

❦

The next day was 6 January. *Cabalgata* in Spain. I thought of Gabriela's children checking their shoes to see if they'd been filled with sweets and I felt a sudden wave of homesickness for somewhere that had never truly been home. But they'd been so good to me. All of them. And I missed them. I thought of Barbara and Nico going to Seville together.

But I was going to Venice, with Tim.

❦

Mum asked me to do some shopping for her. When I agreed, she handed me a list a mile long. The supermarket was crowded and I grew more and more irritable as I pushed a trolley with a mind of its own up and down the aisles.

I was back at the car when I realised that I'd forgotten the washing powder. Mum had called after me as I got into the car. She hadn't put it on the list but she needed it anyway. Non-biological. The other sort brought Ian out in a rash.

I unloaded the plastic bags into the boot and went back into the supermarket. It seemed such a waste for one packet of washing powder. I stood in the express queue.

I had a sudden horrible vision of spending my life in supermarkets. Doing domestic things. Washing and cleaning and looking after Tim. I shivered involuntarily. But it wouldn't just be that. I was being silly. There would be the things I craved. The love and the companionship. The understanding. And, eventually, the children.

The woman in front of me had twelve items in her basket. The express queue was for ten or less. I wanted to say something but thought the better of it. Life was too short. There were more important things to worry about.

It was drizzling as I got back to the car. I wondered what the weather would be like in Venice. Hardly all that warm at this time of the year. Venice had been Tim's idea and I'd fallen in with it, but I wondered if I should have insisted on somewhere further away, like Barbados. I'd always wanted to go to Barbados. In fact, I thought, as I opened the car door and slid into the driving seat, I should have asked Tim if he'd like to get married there. That would have appealed to his new, romantic nature.

Too late now, Isobel, I told myself. You should have thought about it before. Besides, if I'd opted for a Caribbean wedding we wouldn't have been able to invite all our friends and I wanted my friends to be there.

Even if one of my friends would be too busy having days and nights of unadulterated passion with Nico Alvarez in Seville.

Three weeks to go, I told myself, as I started the car. I wondered where the nearest shopping centre to Donnybrook was. I'd never thought about that before.

Chapter 35

Dream (Salvador Dalí, 1931)

I was wearing the dress I'd made. The four hundred and twenty pearls glistened in the morning light and the skirt billowed around me, tugged by the breeze. The sky was stained pink from the morning sun which was peeping above the horizon.

Tim stood beneath the apple-tree. His suit was silver-grey and he carried a top hat. He smiled at me as I approached.

Father O'Brien had an old missal in his hand. It was a heavy prayer-book, bound with mother-of-pearl. He looked solemnly at us.

'Tim, do you take this woman to be your lawful wedded wife? To love and to cherish from this day forward, for richer for poorer, in sickness and in health as long as you both shall live?'

'I would,' said Tim. 'I intended to, Father, but look at her.'

Father O'Brien looked at me.

'How can you seriously expect me to marry her when she's dressed like that?'

I gasped in horror at his words then looked down at my beautiful dress and cried aloud. The pearls were falling off, one at a time, dropping around my feet and nestling

*in the lush green grass. And the dress itself was changing,
dissolving before my eyes until suddenly I was wearing the
net curtains – curtains that I knew Mum had thrown out
years ago.*

*'She couldn't be bothered to make the effort,' said Tim.
'Why should I marry her if she can't even wear a decent
dress?'*

'You have a point,' said Father O'Brien.

*I wanted to say that it was a mistake, that I had the
perfect dress to wear, but my vocal cords were paralysed
and I could say nothing.*

*Barbara Lane stood beside Father O'Brien. She was
wearing the Brown Thomas dress and she looked wonderful
in it. 'It's OK,' she said. 'I'll marry him. Don't worry, Tim.
Everything is going to be all right.' And she kissed him on
the lips while I was powerless to stop her.*

*'In that case,' said Father O'Brien, closing the mother-
of-pearl missal, 'what God has joined together, let no man
put asunder.'*

My voice returned. 'No!' I screamed. 'No!'

∽

I sat up in the bed, my heart thumping against my ribs. I
was shaking. The dream had been so real, so vivid. I smiled
feebly. But it was only a dream. I wrapped my arms around
myself. I really shouldn't be suffering from nerves, but I
must be to dream that kind of dream again. I hugged
myself for a couple of minutes. 'It wasn't nerves,' I said
out loud as I threw back the duvet and got out of bed. It
was eating sweet and sour chicken at eleven o'clock the
night before.

All the same I wished that the damn wedding was
over and done with and that I was safely married to Tim
Malone with nothing to worry about any more.

Alison pushed open the bedroom door. 'You awake?'
I faked a casual yawn. 'Just about.'

'Hurry up. Dad says he'll give us a lift into town if we're ready by nine.'

'OK.'

We were going shopping again. There was so much shopping to do I could hardly believe it. Each time I thought there was nothing left, I suddenly thought of something else. But today's shopping was important. We had to buy shoes for Alison and a going away outfit for me.

I'd finished her bridesmaid's dress the night before – that was what had me eating Chinese late at night – I hadn't wanted to stop earlier. I'd made the right decision, I knew, because her dress looked wonderful. It was red velvet, with long sleeves and a scooped neck. She'd tried it on when I'd finished and I'd slipped into my wedding dress and both of us had cried.

'It'll be you in a few months' time,' I said as I stepped out of my dress.

'I know.' She smiled at me. 'I'm really looking forward to it.'

'Well, it's a lot of hassle,' I said. 'I should've insisted we got married in Madrid.'

'Do you miss it?' she asked.

'Sometimes.' I hung the dress carefully on its padded hanger. 'I miss the job and the people at the office . . .' my voice trailed off as I thought about them and what they might be doing at that moment.

Gabriela and Alfredo sitting on the sofa in front of their widescreen TV while their children slept upstairs.

Magdalena and Alejandro having dinner.

Luis and Anna. Or Maria. Or Carlotta. Or Conchita. Or – well, Luis and anyone, I supposed.

Bridget and Tomás trying to make their marriage work.

Barbara and Nico planning for Seville.

'Do you regret coming back?' Alison's words broke into the picture of Barbara and Nico strolling hand in hand through the streets of Seville.

'No,' I said firmly, shutting out the images. 'But I wish that everything didn't seem to be so rushed.'

~

'Where do you want me to leave you?' asked Dad as we turned onto the quays.

'Anywhere will do, Dad. Which way are you going?'

'Doesn't matter. Through Dame Street.'

'Leave us opposite the Central Bank. We can cut through to Grafton Street that way.' Alison took a small mirror out of her bag and examined her face. 'I think I'm getting a cold sore.'

I looked at her critically. 'I don't see anything.'

'No. But my lip is starting to tingle.'

'We'll nip into a chemist. Get something to put on it.'

'Bloody hell,' she said crossly. 'It'd be just my luck to have a whopping great sore on my lip. I'll look horrible in the photos.'

I grinned at her. 'Don't worry, dearest sister. People won't be looking at you. They'll be looking at the radiant bride instead.'

Dad dropped us off, we bought some cream in the chemist and Alison smeared it over her lip. 'Hope this works.'

'It will,' I told her confidently. 'The pharmacist was very sure.'

'Peter hates cold sores,' she said.

'I'm sure he loves you warts and all,' I said sympathetically.

'Thank God I haven't got warts.' She stopped outside a plate-glass window and examined her reflection again.

'Come on, Ali,' I said impatiently. 'We'll never get anywhere if you don't speed things up a bit.'

I didn't think it would be difficult finding shoes for Alison because, unlike me with my stupid size threes, she's a nice, average five. But I reckoned without her quest for perfection.

We'd brought some of the fabric from her calf-length bridesmaid's dress with us and Alison insisted on getting a perfect match.

'It'll never be perfect,' I said, after she'd rejected another half-dozen pairs of shoes and we were entering yet another shop. 'I don't care if they don't match the dress. You can wear black shoes, Alison.'

'Don't be utterly ridiculous.' She marched up to a sales assistant and waved the red velvet fabric under her nose. 'It's not that difficult a shade.'

I was getting a headache. Probably because of eye strain. When I'd waltzed home with the shop-bought dress, Mum had decided that I had time to make her outfit too. So I'd been cutting and sewing non-stop for the past week.

'What about these?' Alison slipped on a pair of bright red shoes and posed in them.

'They're fine,' I said.

'Isobel! You're not even looking at them.'

'I am. Honestly. They're fine.'

'I'm not sure.' She stood in front of the mirror. 'They're brighter than the fabric.'

'It doesn't matter, Alison. Nobody will notice.'

'Of course they'll notice. People notice everything at weddings! And I know you think that they'll all be entranced by you in that divine dress, but they'll notice if my shoes are pillar-box while the dress is more cherry.'

She was right, of course. They weren't perfect. They were far from perfect. I couldn't understand why I didn't care more.

'Are you all right, Isobel?' She looked at me anxiously. 'You're terribly pale.'

'I'm OK,' I said. 'I just have a bit of a headache. That's all.'

Alison looked at her watch. 'Why don't we grab a coffee or something. It's nearly one. You're probably just suffering from caffeine deprivation.'

'Good idea,' I said. 'I could do with sitting down. My feet are killing me.'

I was wearing a pair of navy court shoes that I'd bought in Madrid. They were work shoes, utterly unsuitable for walking around town and I had no idea why I'd worn them. It wasn't as though I was going to be trying on shoes today. But I hadn't been thinking clearly this morning.

'Fancy a burger?' asked Alison. 'I don't know about you, but I'm starving.'

I made a face. 'I'm not hungry. And I'm on a diet.'

'A diet!' She looked at me scornfully. 'You weigh about seven stone. What are you dieting for?'

'I weigh eight stone,' I said. 'And I'm trying to purify my system.'

'No wonder you've a bloody headache.' My sister looked disgusted. 'Purify your system. That's a load of rubbish.'

'I need it,' I told her. 'I've been eating nothing but junk since I've come home. I used to eat healthy stuff in Madrid. Fruit and vegetables and pasta. Now I'm eating Mum's efforts at home cooking and Chinese takeaways at Tim's.'

'Well, I'm getting something to eat,' she said firmly. 'And if you just want to sip hot water, that's fine by me.'

There was a queue for burgers. I stood beside Alison and rummaged in my bag to see if I'd brought some paracetamol with me. Maybe Alison was right, maybe it was the detox diet that was doing it to me. Maybe I should eat something, even though I wasn't hungry.

'Hamburger and coffee, please,' I said.

The sales assistant, whose name badge said 'Betseigh', looked at me. 'Would you like cheese on the burger?'

I stared at her. 'No.'

'Would you like fries with that order?'

'No?'

'Anything else?'

I felt like Michael Douglas in *Falling Down*. If I had a gun I would have blasted it over the stupid girl's head.

'Burger and coffee,' I repeated. 'Hamburger. No fries. No cheese. No anything else. Just burger and coffee. That's my order, *Betseigh*.' I said the name in disbelief. Why did people find the need to spell their names in ridiculous ways? What was wrong with plain Betsy?

'OK, OK.' Betseigh made a face at me. 'I'm only doing my job.'

'You could add my order on to that.' Alison nudged me. 'Since you've obviously decided to eat, have you forgotten about me?'

I rubbed my temples. 'I'm sorry. I'm sorry.'

Betseigh stared at me, her finger poised over the register. 'There's more?'

'A double cheeseburger de luxe, large fries and a Coke,' said Alison.

The girl smiled. 'Would you like to upgrade that?'

'Nope.' Alison grinned at her. 'That should sort me out for a while.'

Betseigh went to fill the order and Alison turned to me. 'Are you all right, Isobel? Because I think you're starting to crack up or something. You were so rude to her and it's not like you.'

'I'm perfectly all right,' I said. 'Honestly. It's just so crowded.'

There was concern in Alison's face. 'If it bothers you we could skip this and go somewhere else.'

I nodded. 'No, it's fine. It's just stuffy in here. I'll be OK after the coffee. You're probably right. I need the caffeine.'

'Enjoy your meal,' said Betseigh as she put our order in front of us.

'Sure,' said Alison. 'Thanks.'

We sat down at a table. Alison pushed the chips at me.

'No thanks,' I said automatically.

'Isobel! Eat some.'

'I'm not hungry.' I unwrapped the burger. 'At least, I don't want chips. If I'd wanted chips I'd have ordered them from Betseigh!'

Alison grinned. 'Poor girl. You terrorised her.'

'I know it's not her fault,' I said contritely. 'But it drives me mad. If you ask for a burger, they want to know if you want chips. If you ask for a burger and chips, they try to sell you Coke. If you ask for all three, they want you to "upgrade" your meal – whatever that means. Why can't they just let you order what you want and leave you alone?'

'Sales techniques?' Alison hazarded.

'I suppose so.' I took one of her chips absentmindedly and ate it before I realised what I was doing.

'Have another,' she offered. 'It'll do you good.'

⌒

We stood outside the final shop and I took a squirt of my inhaler.

'Asthma at you?' asked Alison.

'Stress-related.' I grinned at her although my headache was pounding behind my eye and it wasn't being helped by my wheezing.

But we hit pay-dirt on the shoes. They were red suede, a shade darker than the dress. I held the fabric against the shoe and nodded. 'It's great. Are they comfortable?'

Alison slipped the shoes on again and walked up and down the shop. 'OK,' she said. 'A bit high.'

'That doesn't matter,' I told her. 'You won't fall off them, will you?'

'No. But I'll tower over you.'

'No, you won't,' I said. 'The shoes I brought from Madrid have a high heel. It'll only be your natural height that'll make me look like a midget.'

She laughed and hugged me. 'I'm looking forward to your wedding, Isobel.'

'So am I,' I told her. 'And it's a trial run for you.'

'At least I'll know which relatives to leave out.' She grinned. 'If Dad's cousin Cáit makes a total show of us, I'll feel quite justified in leaving her off the guest list.'

We only saw Cáit at weddings and funerals. She was a huge woman, big in every direction, whose personality matched her body shape. She wasn't even a blood relation, just some kind of connection by marriage. But she turned up at everything. She'd been at Granny Behan's funeral, sobbing as though her heart would break. She'd be the life and soul of my wedding, though.

Alison took off the red suede shoes and slipped back into her own. 'Come on, Issy. Will I take these?'

I nodded. 'Absolutely.'

❧

'Thank God,' I told Alison as we walked towards Tara

Street to catch a DART. 'I was beginning to think you'd be wearing a pair of flip-flops.'

'They're nice.' She peered into the bag. 'Very elegant.'

'They're lovely.' I peered in too. 'I'm glad that's over with.'

We got on the train and I sat down with relief.

'Am I wrong, or are you getting fed up with the whole thing?' asked Alison.

I grinned at her. 'Just a little.'

She frowned. 'Why? Surely you should be enjoying it.'

'I am, in a way.' I made a face. 'It's just doing Mum's outfit and everything. It took more time than I thought. And I hate fussing about all the details.'

'I always thought you liked fussing, Isobel.'

'To a point,' I said. 'Right now, I wish it was all over.'

She was silent. The train sped through Fairview and Clontarf. I leaned my head against the window and closed my eyes.

I didn't realise I'd fallen asleep until Alison shook me on the shoulder to tell me that it was our stop.

~

Tim had organised a night out for both sets of parents. I hadn't wanted him to. It was too close to the wedding and, after the words that had been spoken between Mum and Denise Malone a couple of years earlier, I couldn't believe that they would sit down together and have a meal. But Tim thought it would be a good idea.

'Are we supposed to be there too?' I asked.

'Of course.' He looked at me in surprise. 'Why not?'

'I just wondered. Thought maybe it was just for them.'

'It's for all of us,' he said. 'We're all one family.'

'Tim, I've never heard such crap from you before.' I pulled gently at his hair. 'All one family! When you know your mother doesn't like me and my mother doesn't like yours and God knows what our fathers think!'

He smiled. 'Don't take it all personally, Isobel. They'll get on fine.'

'Will they?'

'Of course.'

⌒

I ached to have a night in front of the TV, but I sat in the restaurant while Mum and Mrs Malone tried to outdo each other with stories of their youth and Dad and Mr Malone chatted easily about the possibility of Manchester United doing the double again.

'It's an all-round team,' said Mr Malone as he poked at a sliver of beef. 'They've got the right balance between defence and attack.'

'Couldn't agree with you more.' Dad eyed his beef suspiciously. 'You know, I asked for this well done. It's still got pink in it.'

'Dad, please.' I put my hand on his arm. 'It's a French restaurant. They do everything rare here.'

'Huh.' Dad stabbed the beef. 'I don't care how the French do it, I asked for it well done.'

'Dad—'

'Would you like me to send it back?' asked Tim.

Dad turned it over as though it might get up from the plate and walk.

I sighed.

Tim called over the waiter and asked if the men's beef could be cooked a little more.

'No problem,' said the waiter.

'Thanks, Tim,' said Mr Malone.

'That's what I like in a man.' Dad grinned and thumped Tim gently on the back. 'Decisiveness.'

Decisiveness, I thought bleakly. Dad got over things quickly.

'Are you OK?' whispered Tim.

'Of course.' I swirled my risotto around on the plate.

'I can't help feeling that you're—' He sighed suddenly. 'Do you *want* to get married, Isobel?'

My heart thudded in my chest. Not again, I thought, despairingly. Don't tell me he's doing it to me again. The wall opposite me came in and out of focus and I felt my breathing stop.

'Isobel,' hissed Tim. 'Are you all right?'

I blinked a couple of times. The wall stopped shimmering. I took my inhaler out of my bag.

'Are you OK, love?' Mum looked anxiously at me.

'Yes,' I said. 'I'm fine.'

'You sure?' asked Mr Malone.

I smiled faintly at him. 'Yes.' I took a sip of water.

'What was all that about?' whispered Tim.

'I don't know. I – you asked me if I wanted to get married. I thought perhaps you'd changed your mind.'

'I asked *you* if *you* wanted to get married,' said Tim. 'There's nothing in there about *me* changing *my* mind.'

'I'm sorry,' I said. 'It's nerves.'

Tim smiled at me. 'I know. I get nervous myself sometimes.'

'Tim?'

'Yes?'

'Why are you marrying me?'

He sighed. 'Because I love you.'

'Why do you love me?'

'God alone knows.' He kissed me on the side of the cheek and turned to talk to my father.

I wanted to talk to him but this was the wrong place. I

couldn't understand why I was so nervous, why I couldn't relax. But I couldn't. I couldn't understand why I was becoming such a basket case. Everything was organised. All the replies had come back to the invitations. The tickets to Venice had arrived that morning. My dress was hanging up in the wardrobe at home. I'd booked an appointment for a manicure for the day before the wedding. I needed one false nail to replace the natural one I'd bitten in a moment of tension the previous week. I was going to get them painted blood red, to match Alison's outfit. There was nothing left to panic about, yet I still felt on the verge of hysteria all the time. I hadn't been like this last time. I knew I hadn't.

Maybe it was because I was still afraid that Tim would call it off again. Even though, deep down, I knew he wouldn't. It was the trust thing. I trusted him, I knew I did, and yet there was one little part of me that felt he could still do something completely unexpected and ruin my life.

He leaned over to me and nodded towards our mothers. 'They seem to be getting on quite well now.' They were exchanging recipes.

'It's definitely superficial,' I muttered and he laughed.

The waiter cleared the table and put desserts in front of us. Everyone was having a good time. I just wished that I didn't feel as though I was floating above them all, looking down on everything.

'It's going to be a lovely wedding,' said Denise Malone suddenly. 'And I'm delighted that these two young people have finally got their act together.'

'So am I,' said Dad. 'Although, Denise, I have to tell you that if your son leaves my daughter in the lurch a second time, I'll thrash him to within an inch of his life.'

'Dad,' I muttered.

'Fair enough,' said Brendan Malone. 'And if your daughter leaves my son in the lurch, I'll do the same to her!'

Everybody laughed. Tim put his arm around me. 'You can rest assured that there's no chance of this wedding not happening,' he said. 'I love Isobel and I know that she loves me. And we might have had a turbulent past, but that only makes our future together even stronger. When Isobel went to Madrid, I realised that I'd nearly lost the person who means the most in the world to me. When she agreed to marry me – for the second time – she truly made me the happiest person in the world.'

Mum wiped a tear from her eye.

'So here and now I want to thank Isobel for putting up with me and for understanding me, and I look forward to a long and happy life with her.' Tim smiled broadly at me.

'You've used up your speech for the wedding,' I said.

'Nope.' He grinned. 'I have another one for that.'

'Good grief.' I grinned back even though smiling actually hurt my head at the moment. 'Will you be producing a book? You know, Tim Malone's guide to a wedding speech for every occasion?'

They all laughed. Dad ordered some more wine. Tim kissed me.

I'd never felt more loved and wanted in all my life.

Or so terrified.

Chapter 36

Daybreak I (Joan Miró, 1946)

I hardly recognised Julie when she called around to the house. She'd always been pretty, but now she looked sensational. Her hair was lighter, her skin was clear and her eyes sparkled. She looked like someone who was very happy with life. I was conscious of my own lank hair (I hadn't washed it that morning) and the spots that had appeared on my face due to the fact that I was back on the detox diet. The spots would be gone before the wedding, I knew, but I was acutely aware of the one just under my right eye because I could see it out of my peripheral vision. Julie had no spots. I don't think she'd ever had a spot.

'How are you?' She hugged me tightly. 'I've missed you, Isobel.'

'Me too.' I grinned at her. 'It seems a lifetime since last summer.'

'Not to me,' said Julie. 'To me it's all gone in the blink of an eye.'

We went into the front room where three toasters were neatly stacked against the wall. I shivered and turned on the radiator.

'Mum's on one of her economy drives again,' I explained.

'It's lights off, radiators off once you step out of a room these days.'

Julie laughed. 'It seems weird to have radiators again. I'm used to air-conditioning now.'

'Lucky thing.' I opened the sideboard. 'D'you want a Southern Comfort or have you turned to some other American drink?'

She shook her head. 'Something non-alcoholic please, Isobel. Tonic or Ballygowan would be fine.'

'Are you sure?' I asked. 'I'm not trying to force drink on you, but as a celebration?'

'I want to celebrate with you.' She smiled. 'But I'm just not drinking alcohol at the moment.'

It took a second for the penny to drop. 'Julie! Are you pregnant?'

She beamed at me. 'It's early days, Isobel. Very early. So I haven't told anyone yet. But yes, I am.'

That explained the sensational look, I supposed, although I wasn't sure how sensational she'd feel in the sweltering heat of Florida.

'Congratulations.' I smiled at her. 'When's it due?'

'Not until July,' she told me. 'It was only confirmed a couple of weeks ago. I sort of thought I might be, but I was afraid to check. I couldn't have stood it if the doctor had just told me I had a stomach bug.'

I poured her a glass of mineral water and filled a glass with Southern Comfort for myself. 'Cheers.'

'Cheers.' She sat down on the sofa. 'You look tired, Isobel.'

'I am.' I nodded. 'It's been a bit of a rush and there always seems to be some last-minute thing going wrong. I'm deciding that they're lucky omens though. Nothing went wrong the last time!'

'And you're happy?' She sipped the mineral water.

'Oh, yes. I know I'm doing the right thing.'

'I couldn't believe it when you phoned,' said Julie. 'It was the biggest shock I'd ever had.'

'Sorry.' I smiled at her. 'It's all your fault anyway. I wouldn't have met him if it hadn't been for you and Andy getting hitched.'

'I know.' She frowned. 'I feel responsible.'

'Don't look so depressed about it! You should be pleased.'

Was Julie going to give me a lecture? I wondered. I couldn't bear the idea of someone else asking me if I was doing the right thing, if I'd thought it through properly, if I was sure – absolutely sure – that Tim Malone was the one for me. God knows, I'd thought about it often enough myself. It wasn't as though I'd simply seen him and decided that I still loved him and that was that. I'd agonised over it. Even, one day, written down a list of whys and why nots. Nobody could be more sure about their wedding plans than I was.

'I *am* pleased,' said Julie, after a pause. 'I'm delighted for you, Isobel. You deserve to be happy.'

'I will be.'

'So are you completely organised yet?'

I grimaced. 'Almost. I was prancing around in the shoes I'm supposed to wear – which I brought back specially from Spain – when the bloody heel broke! I couldn't believe it.'

'Oh no!' Julie laughed. 'Did you get them repaired?'

'Of course. But it was just something I could've done without.'

'It's not a real wedding until you've had a couple of near disasters.' Julie grinned at me. 'As long as *you* don't get hassled, that's the main thing.'

It was good to be with Julie. Of all the people I knew, she was the one who understood me the most. And she was helping me to relax by not taking the shoe thing seriously. I'd been absolutely furious when it happened – almost mute with rage. I'd thrown the shoe across the bedroom where the nail jutting out from the heel had torn the wallpaper that Dad had put up only two months earlier. I'd stuck it back and it didn't look too bad, but I felt terrible about it. Then Stella, the soloist we'd booked for the church, had phoned to say that she had a throat infection and that she wasn't sure about singing at the wedding.

'Tell me you're joking,' I begged, but she croaked that no, she wasn't, but she was on antibiotics and hopefully it'd clear up soon.

'And what if it doesn't?' I asked.

'There's a girl I know,' she whispered. 'Her name's Bernadette. She'll do it for you.'

But I didn't know Bernadette and I didn't want a complete stranger singing at my wedding. I didn't know Stella either, she was a friend of a friend of Tim's, but we'd heard her singing and she was good. This Bernadette could be utter crap for all I knew and the first I'd hear of it would be when she butchered the *Panis Angelicus*. No, I didn't want Bernadette.

But I might not have an option. I told Stella to keep in touch on the throat front.

'I'll say a little prayer,' said Mum when I told her. I didn't think prayers were what we needed. Stronger antibiotics might do the trick.

'What are you thinking about?' asked Julie.

I told her about Stella and Bernadette. 'So, as of now, I have absolutely no idea who'll be singing at the wedding.'

'It doesn't matter,' said Julie. 'They're all the same, these wedding singers.'

'No they're not,' I told her. 'When I went to my Cousin Linda's wedding about five years ago, the soloist was absolutely awful. She was Harry's sister-in-law and apparently had offered to sing and Linda didn't have the nerve to say no. But she said that every false note was like a dagger through her heart! The congregation were in fits of giggles every time she opened her mouth.'

'Oh, well, nothing like that will happen to you.'

'I hope not,' I said fervently. 'I keep telling Alison I don't want everything to be perfect, but trauma-free would be nice.'

'My trauma was that the underskirt of my dress caught on a nail or something at the top of the stairs,' said Julie. 'I heard a ripping noise and I nearly freaked out altogether. It wasn't that bad, just a small tear, but I thought I was going to faint all the same. And then Dad kept patting my hand in the car, telling me it was the proudest moment of his life.'

'I wonder why that is?' I mused. 'Surely they should be more proud of you when you leave school or graduate. After all, that's something that you've done all by yourself. Getting married is more luck really.'

'God, Isobel, you're a great advertisement for romance.'

'I am,' I protested. 'It's just – oh, never mind.'

I refilled the glasses. 'Anyway, let's talk about something else for a while. I'm sick to my back teeth of weddings. Tell me about Florida.'

'It's great,' said Julie. She settled back more comfortably in the sofa. 'I was lonely at first, and everything was very different. You know, even the English is very different – all that stuff about faucets and diapers and skillets. You don't realise how many words are different until you're there. And people are different too. So – enthusiastic about everything.'

I grinned. 'What about your house?'

'I brought photos.' Julie opened her bag and took them out. 'I know it's a boring thing to look at other people's photos, but I brought them anyway.'

'It's not boring at all!' I pored over a picture of the Jordans' home. It was a whitewashed, red-roofed villa, built three sides around a small courtyard. There was a fountain in the courtyard which was crammed with pots of brightly coloured flowers.

'Oh Julie, that's lovely,' I said.

'I know.' She flicked through the photos. 'This is the back.'

'Julie! I know you told me you had a pool, but this is huge!'

'It's not really. It's just the angle. It's quite close to the house.'

'It's fabulous.'

'Thanks. I keep wondering about what to do when the baby is born. You can't cover it up – you couldn't live there without having a pool. But I'm terrified of the idea of the kid wandering into it. You know the way they do.'

'Not really,' I said. 'But I'll take your word for it. Julie – this kitchen is incredible!!'

It was the last word in hi-tec – stainless steel and marble surfaces, softened by huge vases of different coloured flowers. Except for the flowers, it reminded me a little of Nico's kitchen. Except for the flowers and, of course, the photo of Carmen.

God, I thought. How could I have let Nico creep into my head like that? Nico and bloody Carmen. And it wasn't Carmen any more either. It was Barbara. Nico and Barbara in Seville.

'This is the bathroom,' Julie giggled. 'I know it's naff to bring photos of your bathroom, but I thought I'd show it to you anyway.'

'Is that a jacuzzi?!'

She nodded. 'It's Andy's favourite place.'

'You lucky, lucky thing, Julie Jordan.'

She smiled at me. 'I love it when people call me that.'

'Julie Jordan,' I repeated.

'I know it's stupid. I know I should be more mature about it. But whenever I hear it I kind of hug myself and thank God that I met Andy. Because I'm cracked about him.'

'I'm really pleased, Julie. You deserve him.'

'Thanks,' she said and showed me a photograph of their dining-room table.

⤙

I went to the doctor's the next day. I was still suffering from headaches which I suspected were brought on by stress, but no matter how relaxed I tried to make myself be nothing seemed to work.

Dr Byrne made me lie on the couch while she did a complete check-up on me.

'You're OK,' she said, 'but a little run down, Isobel. Are you eating properly?'

'I've been dieting,' I admitted.

'Well stop,' said Dr Byrne. 'You certainly don't need to lose weight.'

'It was more a detox thing,' I told her. 'To purify my system.'

Dr Byrne sighed. 'You're perfectly healthy. You don't need to do anything like this, Isobel. Eat sensibly and you'll be fine. Fresh fruit and vegetables would be good.' She pulled a pad towards her and started to write. 'These will shift the headache. And for goodness sake try to relax. I know getting married is a stressful time, but you don't need to get into a complete knot over it.'

'I know,' I said meekly.

She looked up from the pad. 'Is everything else OK?'

'What do you mean?'

She shrugged. 'Just that. There's nothing else bothering you, is there?'

I grinned at her. 'Only how to keep my mother and Tim's mother on civil terms until after the ceremony.'

She laughed and handed me the prescription. 'Have a few early nights,' she advised. 'And enjoy yourself on the day.'

⤳

The phone was ringing as I got home and I grabbed the receiver.

'Hello?'

'Hello, can I speak to Isobel Kavanagh, please?' It was a female voice, one I didn't recognise.

'Speaking.'

'Isobel, this is Marianne Leahy. I'm the personnel director of the Eastmann College. You applied for the position of administrator with us.'

'That's right.'

'I know this is somewhat short notice, but I was wondering if you could come in for interview tomorrow morning. Say ten o'clock.'

'Absolutely. Of course I can.' An interview! I'd applied for half-a-dozen jobs since I'd come back and this was the first interview. All of the others had sent back standard letters telling me that there were hundreds of suitable applicants and that they'd be in touch. Actually, I vaguely remembered that the Eastmann College had sent back something very similar.

'Do you know where we are?' asked Marianne.

I frowned. 'Merrion Square?'

'That's right,' said Marianne. 'I look forward to seeing you, Isobel.'

'I'm looking forward to it too,' I said.

I was surprised at how pleased the prospect of an interview made me feel. Even though my days were full of wedding preparations I'd felt as though something was missing. The idea that I might soon have a job again was more exciting than I'd imagined.

I went upstairs. My room was a mess. I was bringing some clothes over to Tim's that afternoon so that I'd have a basic wardrobe there for when we came back from Venice. Tim liked the idea of me leaving my clothes there. I planned to stay for the evening and cook him dinner. He liked that idea even more.

I stuffed several pairs of jeans, a few skirts, half-a-dozen tops and a selection of shoes into a suitcase and squeezed it closed. Dad had left me the car so I heaved the suitcase into the boot and drove across town to Donnybrook. Although Tim had given me the keys to his house the day I'd come back to Dublin I hadn't been in it on my own since my return. In fact, the last time I'd been in Tim's house on my own had been the day I'd wiped his computer files and thrown the earrings down the toilet. I'd have to confess that to him sometime, although I wasn't sure how I'd pluck up the courage to do it. It would be easier to explain the computer files than the earrings. I wondered whose they were. I hadn't thought about them in ages.

I let myself in the door and switched off the alarm. Still the same entry code, which was just as well because I hadn't thought to ask Tim if he'd changed it. I lugged the suitcase upstairs to the main bedroom. The bed was made, the dark blue and yellow duvet stretched carefully over the bed and the pillows, with their matching blue and yellow pillowcases, neatly plumped up. Tim had become terribly domesticated.

I opened the suitcase and laid my clothes out on the bed. It seemed creepy somehow, to be leaving things in his house. I wished I could get the feeling that it belonged to both of us, but I couldn't. The decor was all Tim. Sharp, definite colours. No pastel shades – even the yellow in the bedroom was a very vivid yellow. And it was clearly a man's bedroom. His dressing-gown, black and white stripes, hung on the back of the bedroom door. The shelves in the en-suite bathroom were laden with Gillette shaving foam, Paco Rabanne aftershave, and Imperial Leather soap. In Spain, my bathroom had had jars of pot-pourri on the shelves, along with pots of Clarins creams, Lancôme make-up and a selection of half-full perfume bottles. It had been tiled in pink and grey – feminine, even if that had nothing to do with me. Tim's bathroom was green, with a border of gold tiles.

I opened the chrome bathroom cabinet. Razor blades, Alka-Seltzer, Panadol, dental floss, athlete's foot powder (ugh!) and a half-full bottle of *Belles di Ricci* perfume.

I picked up the gaudy bottle and sprayed the perfume onto my wrist. Whose was it? I wondered bleakly. And why was it in Tim's bathroom cabinet?

I went back into the bedroom and sat on the bed. Was it going to be like this all the time? Was I always going to suspect the worst of him? And why, in heaven's name, should I be suspecting anything right now, when I knew that he'd come running back to me and that, more than ever, he was the one who wanted to get married? He wasn't sleeping with someone else. I knew that.

And if he'd had relationships while I was in Madrid – well, who was I to get upset about that? My God, if Tim only knew about the things I'd done in Madrid . . .

But the niggling feeling of distrust stayed with me so that I bit my lip as I hung up my clothes in the space he'd emptied for me the previous night. I wished that I didn't feel the way I did. I wished that I could trust Tim completely and utterly as I once had.

I made myself a cup of tea. Mechanically, opening the right cupboard door, taking out the tea caddy, taking out the mug with the picture of the Plaza Mayor that I'd brought back from Spain. I didn't have to think where any of those things were – I knew. And surely, I thought, desperately, surely that meant something. There were messages on his answering machine. I stared at the blinking light – four messages, popular bloke. I knew that I shouldn't listen to them but I couldn't help myself.

And none of them was a heart-stopping message from some secret lover. They were all simple work-related things. Which, I thought, just went to prove that I was hopelessly paranoid and that the sooner I actually married Tim the better.

⌇

'Honey, I'm home!!' Tim peered around the kitchen door and I jumped with fright. I hadn't heard the hall door open, I was immersed in a Robin Cook medical thriller which I'd found on Tim's bookshelf.

'You scared the living daylights out of me,' I told him.

'Sorry.' He kissed me. 'How was your day?'

'Is this practice for when we're married?' I asked.

'Sort of,' said Tim, 'but I won't always have these for you.' He produced a box of Belgian chocolates from a bag.

'Oh, Tim. Thanks.' I kissed him this time. 'They're great.'

'I thought you could forget about the diet for a couple of days,' he said as he dumped a pile of books onto the kitchen table. 'They have to be eaten within a week.'

I thought about the strict detox diet and Dr Byrne's advice. So I ate the biggest, creamiest chocolate of them all.

'Your dinner is ready,' I said with my mouth full. 'Are you hungry?'

'Even if I'd eaten a horse at lunchtime I'd tell you I was hungry,' said Tim. 'That smells delicious.'

'You didn't have a big lunch, did you?' I asked.

He laughed. 'No. How could I when I knew you were slaving away over a hot cooker for me?'

'Just as well,' I said. 'Go on, sit down.'

I put the plate of steak, vegetables and scalloped potatoes (another find in the freezer) in front of him. 'Eat up.'

'What are you having?' He eyed my plate of vegetables with distrust.

'Corn, peas, aubergine and red pepper,' I said. 'It's a mix you had in the freezer with a best-before date of next week.'

'Really?' He looked horrified. 'I tend to throw things in there and forget about them. Why aren't you having any steak? Or potatoes?'

'Not that hungry,' I said, and had a fit of the giggles when Tim put the box of chocolates onto the side of my plate.

We watched TV together afterwards. It was cosy and natural and I felt suddenly peaceful.

'Happy?' he asked, as I leaned my head on his shoulder.

'Mmm.'

'This time next week it'll all be over.'

'Don't say that.'

'Why? Don't you want us to be married?'

'Of course.' I looked up at him. 'It was the way you said it – it'll all be over – as though once we were married, everything would be different.'

'Everything will be better,' he said confidently. 'And I'm wrong anyhow. This time next week we'll be walking over the Rialto in Venice.'

I smiled. 'It sounds great.'

'I'm sorry it's only for a week,' said Tim. 'Truly I am. I'll make it up to you, though. We'll go somewhere really special for the summer.'

'Where?' I asked lazily.

'Mexico, Jamaica, Pattaya Beach, Langkawai, The Seychelles—'

'Keep talking,' I said, 'they all sound great.'

'We'll go anywhere you want,' Tim told me. 'I just want you to be happy.'

I snuggled closer to him. 'Tim?'

'Yes?'

'Can I ask you something?'

'Of course. What sort of something?'

'It's stupid.'

'So?'

'I don't want you to think I'm paranoid.'

'I know that already.' He ruffled my hair. 'What's wrong?'

'Nothing. It's just—' I took a deep breath. 'I was in your bathroom today and I opened the cabinet. There was perfume in it.'

'And?'

'And I wondered why.'

There was a brittle silence. He sat up straight and looked at me. 'What d'you mean – you wondered why?'

'Why there was a woman's perfume in your bathroom cabinet.'

I stared at the floor, my face red, feeling guilty.

'Isobel, you are an awful fool,' said Tim. 'That's been there for ages.'

I glanced up at him.

'It's Laura's perfume,' he said and I felt my heart thud in my chest.

'She stayed here one night.'

I swallowed.

'We were working late and she stayed here. She did that a couple of times.'

I said nothing.

'It was perfectly platonic,' said Tim. 'She looks too much like you, Isobel. I couldn't possibly have taken her to bed, even if I wanted to.'

'Why?'

'I don't know,' he said irritably. 'There's probably some perfectly decent psychological reason, but I couldn't. And I didn't. Which, I think, I've told you before. More than once.'

I bit my lip.

'For God's sake, Isobel.' Tim looked angry. 'I can't believe you're actually upset about this.'

I looked down at the floor to hide the tears that were about to fall. 'I don't know,' I whispered. The tears fell. They slid down my cheeks and dripped onto the green carpet, leaving dark spots where they landed.

'Do you think I'm having some sort of relationship with her?' he asked. 'Do you?'

'No,' I muttered.

'Well, then. Why the tears?'

'I don't know.'

He pulled me to him. 'You're being silly, Isobel. Really silly.'

'I know.'

He sighed. 'I don't know what it is about Laura. I knew you were upset about her before. But honestly, I never slept with her. I never even kissed her.'

'I'm sorry.' I wiped away the tears. 'I don't know what's the matter with me, Tim.'

'Come here.' He pulled me into his arms. 'I love you, Isobel.'

It was good to hear him say it. He stroked my hair. I closed my eyes. Then I remembered something.

'I want to ask you a question.' I opened my eyes and looked at him.

'Another one?'

'Please. It's not an easy question.'

He stared at me. 'What?'

'Did Laura – well, did she – did—'

'Isobel!' He looked exasperated. 'What?'

'Did she ever leave earrings here?'

'Earrings?' He looked at me as though I was completely insane. 'Earrings? Why would she—' He broke off and stared at me suddenly. 'Gold ones. With rubies?'

I nodded.

'One afternoon, when we were working, she was using headphones and the earrings were digging into her. She took them off and then went home without them – or so she thought. She asked me about them. I thought I'd put them away somewhere, but I could never find them. Isobel – what about her earrings?'

It had been a secret that had weighed on me for a long time. 'I flushed them down the toilet,' I told him miserably.

'You flushed them down the toilet.' He stared at me. I wanted to curl up and die. 'You flushed them down the toilet.' Then suddenly he started to laugh. 'Oh, Isobel. You're quite mad! I think that's why I love you.'

'Are you sure?'

'I've never been more sure of anything.' And he folded me into his arms again.

I stayed the night in Tim's house. We made love twice.

Chapter 37

Daybreak II (Joan Miró, 1964)

I woke up at eight o'clock, just before Tim's alarm went off. I had to get home, Dad needed the car. And I'd forgotten, until I was almost asleep, about my job interview. I needed to get home, have a shower and dress in something more suitable than baggy jeans and a sweatshirt. I slid out of the bed.

'Where're you going?' mumbled Tim sleepily.

'I've got to go home,' I said. 'I promised Dad I'd have the car back. He needs it today.'

'Come back to bed.' Tim stretched his arm out over the duvet.

'I can't, Tim. I'm in a hurry.'

'Your dad doesn't need the car at eight in the morning.' Tim was awake now.

'No, but I want to get home and have a shower. I've an interview today.'

'A what?' He sat up in the bed. His hair stood spikily on the top of his head.

'Interview.' I pulled my sweatshirt over my head. 'At ten o'clock.'

'What sort of interview?'

'Job interview,' I said. 'What other sort is there?'

He didn't say anything. I brushed my hair and fastened my watch around my wrist.

'Why didn't you tell me about it last night?'

'I forgot.' I leaned forward and kissed him on the head. 'I was carried away by you and it completely slipped my mind.'

'Tell me about it,' he demanded.

'There isn't a lot to tell.' I sat on the edge of the bed. 'The ad said administrator. It's for a place called the Eastmann College. They're in Merrion Square.'

'Never heard of them,' said Tim.

'Neither did I before I read the ad.' I yawned. 'I sent off my CV before Christmas. I didn't really expect to hear from them.'

'It seems a bit crazy going for an interview today.' Tim was grumpy.

'Why?'

'Isn't it obvious?' He stared at me. 'We're getting married next week!'

'They'll hardly expect me to start next week,' I told him. 'They're probably interviewing lots of people. I'd say it'll be at least a fortnight before I know. Plenty of time.'

'All the same.' He sounded aggrieved. 'You should have told me.'

'I would have told you,' I said. 'But I already said. I forgot.'

He sighed and threw back the duvet. 'I suppose now that you've woken me I might as well get up.'

'You'll be on time for once.' I grinned at him. 'I'd better go, Tim. You know Dad. He'll be hopping up and down wondering if I've forgotten. And he won't ring to check. All that'll happen is that his blood pressure will soar.'

'I'd hate to be responsible for landing your dad in hospital,' said Tim. 'I'll give you a buzz later.'

'OK.' I kissed him again, only this time it was a proper kiss.

'Take care of yourself.'

'You too,' I said and ran downstairs.

As I suspected, Dad was pacing up and down the hallway when I arrived home.

'Plenty of time,' I told him as he looked at his watch. 'Don't fuss, Dad.'

'You should have been here last night,' he said.

'Oh, Dad.' I hugged him. 'Don't be such a fuddy duddy daddy.'

He didn't smile. I made a face at his back as he let himself out.

Mum was in the kitchen, reading the *Irish Times* and sipping tea. Alison was doing her make-up at the kitchen mirror.

'Morning,' I said brightly.

'Uh.' Alison outlined her lips.

'Good morning,' said Mum. 'You took your time in getting home.'

'You knew I was staying with Tim last night,' I said as I buttered a slice of toast.

'I don't like it,' said Mum. 'It isn't right.'

'Oh, God.' I sighed. 'Don't give me a hard time now, Mum. I'm in a hurry.'

'What sort of a hurry?'

'The sort where you don't linger around the place,' I said through a mouthful of toast. 'I've got an interview this morning.'

'A what? I wish you wouldn't speak with your mouth full.'

I swallowed. 'An interview.'

'Interview? Who with? What for?'

'With some woman for the job of administrator in Eastmann College,' I told her.

'A job interview?'

Sometimes my mother could be very dense.

'Yes.'

'Isobel, you can't go to a job interview when you're getting married next week.'

'Do you know that you sound just like Tim?' I demanded. 'Of course I can. And I have to get a move on. It's at ten o'clock and I need to shower.'

'Good idea,' muttered Alison from the other end of the room.

'Oh, shut up,' I said.

Ian had obviously been the last person in the bathroom. The towels were scattered on the floor, across the sink and across the toilet cistern. His razor was still in the sink and he'd left a scum of bristle around it.

It took ages to dry my hair and even then I wasn't happy about it. I used handfuls of mousse to try and keep some sort of shape on it but the final result was still too curly.

I took my Louise Kennedy suit from the wardrobe. It was three years old, I hadn't brought it to Spain, but it still fitted me and it still looked smart. It was olive green with bronze buttons on the jacket. For one horrible moment I thought I'd taken my plain-black court shoes over to Tim's last night, but I found them at the bottom of the wardrobe, under a black refuse-sack full of socks and well-worn jeans.

I wiped them with some tissue, then decided that I'd better polish them properly, then got polish on the cuff of my cream-coloured blouse so that I had to change it for a white one, which I didn't think went with the suit half as well. Maybe Tim and Mum were right. Maybe I was off my rocker going for an interview today.

It was drizzling by the time I was ready. I took Dad's golf umbrella from under the stairs and walked to the bus stop. I really, really missed the metro.

The bus was late and the traffic was appalling. By the time I reached the Eastmann College building it was exactly ten o'clock.

It was a Georgian building with a fanlight window over a shiny black painted door. A gold plaque on the wall said *Eastmann College – founded 1977.* I pushed the door open and walked inside.

The entrance hall was impressive. A chandelier hung from the high ceiling. The walls were painted primrose yellow and were hung with portraits – Oscar Wilde, George Bernard Shaw, Seamus Heaney, Edna O'Brien and Mary Robinson. A girl whom I guessed to be in her early twenties sat behind an almost antique desk. She looked enquiringly at me.

'I'm here to see Marianne Leahy,' I told her. 'My name is Isobel Kavanagh.'

She looked in a red appointments book. 'Yes. Can you wait a moment, please.'

I nodded and sat down on one of the velvet upholstered chairs. I knew nothing about Eastmann College but they didn't stint on the furniture. The students must be pretty mature, I thought. The chairs wouldn't have lasted a minute in the Madrid college where I'd done my Spanish classes. Of course, it had been a very different place. The building had been old, as this was, but completely modernised inside. I rather liked this. It was very beautiful.

'Can you go up to the first floor?' asked the receptionist. 'Marianne is the first door on the left.'

I nodded and went upstairs.

I tapped on the door marked *Administrator* and walked inside.

For some reason I'd expected Marianne Leahy to be a clone of Gabriela. But she wasn't. Marianne looked to be in her late forties or even early fifties – although I might have got that impression from her iron-grey hair which was cut very short. She wore very little make-up, and no jewellery. Her suit was navy blue. I hadn't felt nervous until now, but suddenly I realised that my mouth was dry and my palms sweating.

'Isobel.' She smiled and I felt better. It was a genuine smile, reaching her eyes and softening her stern features.

'Hello,' I said.

'Take a seat.' She opened a folder and took out my CV. 'I'm glad to meet you.'

'Thanks for taking the time,' I said.

'You've an excellent CV.'

I nearly said, no, not really, but then I realised that I could blow the job instantly if I was stupid. So I said 'thank you' again.

'Tell me about your career.' Marianne sat back in her leather chair while I talked about DeltaPrint, Advanta and the work I'd done.

She listened carefully, asked occasional questions and made notes. She raised her eyebrows when I told her that I was getting married the following week. Then she told me a little about Eastmann College and the sort of work I'd be doing if I got the job. She only came in to the college a couple of times a month so the entire responsibility for running things would be mine. It sounded exciting.

'It was very nice meeting you,' she said. 'Obviously, I've other candidates to talk to. So I won't be able to give you an answer this week.' She smiled. 'In fact, not before you're married! But I will give you a call as soon as I can.'

'Thank you.' I stood up and shook hands with her.

'I hope you have a lovely wedding,' she said as I left the room.

It had been OK, I thought, as I walked to Pearse station. I'd answered her questions readily, and nothing she'd talked about seemed out of my capabilities. I was hopeful.

I wanted that job. The more I thought about it, the more interesting it became. I wished I didn't have to wait for two weeks to find out whether or not I'd been successful. I wished she'd given me some hint straight away.

The train slid into the station and I hopped on. Merrion Square would be handy enough for Donnybrook. I could walk it in the summer. I enjoyed walking to work, it gave you time to plan your day. I hoped I'd have lots of planning for Eastmann College.

∼

Mum was hoovering the hall when I opened the front door.

'Why on earth are you doing that now?' I asked.

'I opened the door and that little runt of a dog from next door ran in,' she said furiously. 'He'd been digging in the flowerbed, the dirty little beggar. He got muck all over my hall.'

'Oh dear.' I smothered a smile.

'It's nothing to smile about.' She switched off the hoover. 'As you'll no doubt find out yourself.'

'They don't have a dog next door to Tim,' I said. 'And if they had it'd be too scared to run in. He doesn't like dogs and he'd give it a boot up the bum before it knew where it was.'

'I wish you wouldn't use language like that,' complained Mum.

'I've used a lot worse.' I made a face at her.

'Not at your interview, I hope.'

'What d'you think I am?' I took off my coat and hung it over the banister.

'How did it go?'

'Not bad, actually.' I followed her into the kitchen where she filled the kettle. 'It sounded like an interesting job.'

'But what about Tim?' asked Mum.

'What about him?'

She looked uncomfortable. 'It's just that I thought you were getting married to have children.'

'Mum!' I looked at her in despair. 'I want to. Sometime. Not this year, though. And I need a job in the meantime.'

'I just thought it'd be good if you got yourself something nice and easy,' she said. 'Answering the telephone or something.'

'Helen Kavanagh! Answering the phone can be very stressful. Do you realise that it's being at the bottom of the pile that can stress you? Not having any control over what you do or when you do it? Worrying about being five minutes late for work? *That's* stress.'

She sighed. 'Well, you know what you want.'

'Yes, I do.' I spooned instant coffee into two cups. 'And by this time next week I'll have it.'

❧

Although we'd wanted to get married on a Saturday, we had to settle for Monday. It had been absolutely impossible to book a hotel for a Saturday wedding with the amount of notice that we'd been able to give them. Because it was a Monday I'd been doubtful whether any of the people from Spain would be able to come. I'd imagined that they might all discover reasons why they couldn't – like Barbara. But Luis, Gabriela and Magdalena arrived on Saturday afternoon as promised and I'd booked the El Paso in Howth for ten o'clock that night. Peter and

Alison and Julie came along too. Despite all my longings to have more nights in, this was a night out I'd looked forward to for ages.

The restaurant was full and buzzing with conversation when the four of us arrived.

We ordered a pitcher of beer and Julie asked for mineral water.

I hadn't told either Alison or Peter about her pregnancy but Alison looked at her in the knowing way that women look at each other and Julie blushed. Alison grinned and said 'congratulations' and Peter looked at us as if we'd gone crazy.

Gabriela, Luis and Magdalena arrived at the same time as the beer.

'Gabriela!' I called. '*Aquí*!'

'Isobel!' She swept towards me. 'Isobel! *Cómo estás?*'

'*Muy bien.*' I hugged her and kissed her. 'And you?'

'I'm very well also.'

'*Hola, Isobel.*' Luis got in on the hugging act.

'It's lovely to see you,' said Magdalena.

'And all of you,' I said. 'I've missed you so much.'

And I had. It was only seeing them all again that made me realise quite how much. I introduced Peter, Alison and Julie.

'We have heard a lot about you,' said Gabriela as she sat down. 'Isobel told us lots of stories about her life in Ireland.'

'She probably lied,' said Alison. 'Made herself out to be an angel.'

Gabriela laughed. 'Only sometimes.'

'Did you have a good flight?' I turned to Luis who was looking very well tonight in jeans and a denim shirt. For once nothing clashed.

'It was OK,' he said. 'We were delayed a little at Barajas but we made up the time.'

'And your hotel?'

'It is near the sea. On the other side of the river. I have a wonderful view of Dublin Bay from my bedroom window.'

'Yes,' Magdalena chimed in. 'Me also. The sea is fantastic. I have never seen it that colour before. And the white tops of the waves!'

I could understand her amazement. I'd felt equally amazed the first time I'd seen the azure calmness of the Mediterranean.

'Have you got everything ready, Isobel?' asked Gabriela.

I nodded. 'Nothing left to do but turn up.'

'And you can always change your mind about that!' Magdalena blushed the moment the words left her lips. There was a frozen silence and everyone looked at me.

'No fear of that,' I said as I filled my glass with beer.

Everyone started to talk at the same time then, chattering about the first thing that came into their heads. I looked at the menu and tried to ignore the desperation in their voices.

We ordered chicken wings and tortillas, and an assortment of main courses. The atmosphere lightened a little when the food arrived and everyone got their fingers messy with the chicken wings.

'How is business?' I asked Gabriela.

'Very good,' she replied. 'We have signed a contract with Amicar Insurances for two years and I am making a presentation on Thursday morning to one of the banks. It's been a good start to the year.'

'How about you, Isobel?' asked Luis. 'Have you been enjoying your time of leisure?'

'Actually, I was at an interview today,' I said.

'An interview!' Julie looked at me in amazement. 'I didn't know you were going for an interview.'

'It was sudden,' I told her.

'Where?' she asked.

So I told them about Eastmann College and Marianne Leahy and how I hoped I'd made a good impression. 'I gave your name as a reference, Gabriela,' I added.

'You know I will give you a good reference,' she said. 'In fact, if you ever want to come back to Madrid there will always be a job waiting for you.'

I swallowed the lump that had suddenly appeared in my throat. Gabriela had been so good to me and she was still being good to me. 'Thanks,' I said.

'It's not quite the same without you.' Luis laughed. 'There is no one going around the office singing.'

'Very funny.' I joined in their laughter. Anytime I even hummed a bar of a song in the office people ran for cover.

'Tell us about America.' Luis turned his charm on Julie. 'What is life like there?'

She talked for a while about Florida and about Andy and his work and their house. I noticed that she spent a lot of time talking about the house. I wondered if I'd become like that when Tim and I were married. Would my priorities change completely? Would having a chrome bathroom cabinet instead of a gold one be one of those life or death questions?

'I like gold myself,' said Gabriela. 'But only in a big room. It takes over a small one.'

'That's what I think,' Julie agreed. 'And the en-suite bathroom is very small.'

I caught Peter Gaffney's eye and we both started to giggle. Alison wanted to know what was so funny but I shook my head. 'Nothing, nothing.'

We stuffed ourselves with *enchilladas* and *fajitas* and then we ordered margharita cocktails.

'I shouldn't drink this,' said Julie, who'd asked for one made very, very weak.

'Oh, don't worry about it,' Alison advised. 'It's probably good for you.'

'The trouble about being pregnant,' murmured Julie, 'is that you think of absolutely everything relative to the baby. You completely forget that you're a person yourself.'

'Don't drink it if you don't want to,' I said. 'But if you do, please don't go into paroxysms of guilt.'

She grinned. 'I'll drink a little.'

Julie sipped at her weak margharita while we ordered another round. And another. I was feeling happier than I'd done in ages.

'What are you going to do tomorrow?' I asked as I put another empty glass on the table.

'We will go into the city,' said Magdalena. 'I have a guide book.'

'Some of the shops will be open,' Alison told her. 'You can do a little shopping if you like.'

'Really?'

Alison nodded. 'From about one o'clock. It's a nice time to look around. Not too crowded.'

'Not shops,' groaned Gabriela. 'I have had a bad month with my credit card.'

'Did you buy that with it?' I asked. She was wearing an amber-coloured suit which looked wonderful on her.

'Yes,' she said. 'And I bought jeans and trousers and shoes and jumpers. Alfredo said that if I bring any more clothes into the house he will divorce me.'

'You keep that in mind.' Peter hugged Alison. 'If you ever go on a spending spree like that – it's curtains for our marriage.'

'Dream on, honey.' She grinned at him.

Luis ordered more cocktails.

'Oh, no, Luis. Please don't,' I begged. 'If I drink

any more I'll have a hangover tomorrow and I have things to do.'

'I thought you said everything is done,' he protested.

'I have to bring some presents to Tim's house. And I want to polish my nails. It's hopeless trying to do that on Monday morning. All that'd happen is that I'd smudge them or get nail polish all over my dress.'

'How about an Irish coffee?' he said.

I sighed. 'All right. But that's absolutely it.'

We had the Irish coffees – except for Julie who just had ordinary coffee. The alcohol had made me mellow; I sat back in my seat feeling very relaxed and very at peace with the world. These were my best friends. It was good to be with them.

'We'd better go,' said Alison as she checked her watch. 'It's nearly one o'clock.'

'I'm tired,' admitted Julie.

'Me too.' Gabriela yawned and set us all off.

I paid the bill, waving away Luis's protests and his attempts to pay instead. Then we walked outside into the cold night air. The moon shone frostily down onto the black sea and a wind whistled across the bay. Julie shivered.

The steel wires of the boats clanged in the wind. Just as they had done the first night I met Tim. Almost here, in fact. When he'd put his arm around me and we'd walked along the pier and afterwards he'd kissed me and I'd said 'wow'. I stared unseeingly across the bay and felt as though I had fallen back in time. It was as though it were that night again, as though the last few years hadn't happened, had been merely a vivid dream.

'Are you OK, Isobel?' Alison nudged me.

'Of course.' I returned to the present with a jolt.

The Spanish contingent climbed into a taxi and waved goodnight.

'See you on Monday!' cried Gabriela as their car disappeared down the road.

Alison, Peter, Julie and myself got into a second taxi. I leaned back in the seat, suddenly tired. I was asleep before we reached the house.

⌒

I wasn't too bad the next morning. I had a slight headache but it was an ordinary hangover headache, not the pounding ones of a few days ago. It disappeared almost immediately when I took a couple of Dr Byrne's tablets.

In the afternoon I bundled up the remaining bits and pieces that I wanted to leave at Tim's house. Although, I told myself as I turned into his road, I'd really have to start thinking of it as my house too. Perhaps once I'd moved in permanently, I'd be able to feel differently about it.

Tim was drinking coffee when I walked in.

'Afternoon,' he said. 'Have you got all the stuff?'

I nodded. 'I'll put it in the spare room and we can rummage through it later.'

'OK.' He drained his cup. 'Help yourself to coffee or tea if you like. I've got to go out for a while.'

'Oh, Tim. Where to?'

He looked embarrassed. 'I'm meeting Greg and the lads for a few drinks.'

'Tim!' I looked at him in horror. 'I thought you were going out last night!'

'I was,' he said. 'But my folks had invited some old fogey relatives over to dinner and they wanted me to make an appearance. So I told the guys I'd meet them tonight instead.'

'Tim Malone, whatever you do, don't get blitzed tonight.'

'Of course I won't.' He put his arms around me. 'I'll

probably have one or two too many, but don't panic. I'll be there tomorrow. On time. Waiting for you.'

'I'll be on time too,' I said. 'You know me. Always punctual.'

He kissed me gently on the lips. 'I know. Honestly, Isobel, I'll behave myself. It's not like we're a bunch of kids, you know. We can be sensible.'

I looked at him in disbelief. I couldn't imagine, in a million years, a group of men in a pub being sensible.

'Honestly,' he repeated as he nibbled at my left ear. 'And I won't let them do anything awful to me.'

'They wouldn't, would they?' The thought was dreadful. I could see Tim stark naked, chained to a railing. Or Tim, his drink spiked, being bundled into a taxi and sent to Kerry. Or Tim, passed out, having his head shaved.

'Isobel!' He laughed. 'I told you. We're mature adults.'

But I had an awful sense of foreboding as I drove back to Sutton. I wished that he hadn't told me he was meeting his friends tonight.

∽

There was a taxi parked outside our house.

Mum was in the hallway and, much to my surprise, so was Bridget Evans-Medina.

'I was just going,' she explained when I said that I hadn't expected to see her before tomorrow. 'I wanted to leave a gift for you, that's all.'

'Oh, Bridget, thanks. Wouldn't you like to stay for a cup of tea or anything?' I peered at the taxi. 'Is Tomás with you?'

She shook her head. 'He couldn't come. He's at home with Christopher. But I'm staying with some friends in Monkstown so I don't mind.'

'How are things with you and Tomás?'

She smiled. 'A bit better now, I think. It was hard at first, Isobel. It wasn't what I expected. But we've both changed.'

'What did you expect?' I asked curiously. 'How was it different?'

'I don't know.' She made a face. 'I think I expected him to be as romantic when we were married as he was beforehand. And, of course, it can't be like that. Not when you're with someone every minute of the day. And I got pregnant too quickly. I thought he just wanted me chained to the house, you know.'

I smiled sympathetically at her.

'And he does have a bias towards me being at home and looking after things.' She sighed. 'We compromised.'

'I'm glad,' I said. 'I'm glad it's working.'

'So am I.' She smiled at me. 'Do you know, at first I just wanted to walk out. But then I realised that I loved him. That he was important to me.'

'I know how you feel,' I said. 'Well, it's nice to know we're all getting sorted out. You and Tomás, me and Tim, Barbara and Nico.'

'Barbara and Nico?' She looked at me in amazement.

'They've been going out,' I told her. 'Didn't you know?'

'I know that she asked him to dinner one night,' said Bridget. 'And that she went with some friends to hear them playing in the Lux. But they're not going out together.'

I stared at her. 'They're going to Seville this week-end.'

'No, they're not.' She shook her head. 'Barbara is in Liverpool. She's been there for the last week.'

'Are you sure?'

'Of course I'm sure. I rang her last night. I wondered

582

if she was coming over for the wedding. I know she told you she couldn't because she was doing a course, but I thought she might just make it.'

'She never told me anything about a course,' I said slowly. 'She told me she was going to Seville. And I thought it was with Nico.'

Bridget grinned. 'Maybe she just wanted to be sure you were over Nico. You know Barbara. Maybe she was afraid that if you thought he was footloose and fancy-free you'd have second thoughts about your wedding!'

'That's ridiculous,' I said.

'Of course it is.' Bridget smiled. 'But Barbara was never very rational about Nico, I'm afraid. She really thought she'd get something going with him. And she was pissed off at you, Isobel, both for going out with him and then for dumping him!'

'Silly,' I said dismissively.

'Oh, well.' Bridget shrugged. 'It doesn't matter. Anyway, as far as I know, Nico's fine. Tomás told me that he doesn't play in the Lux any more.'

'He doesn't?'

'No. Apparently he got some promotion in work. So he's incredibly busy. Working evenings, Saturdays – you name it. I don't think he's been in the Lux for weeks.'

'He probably still plays in the Retiro Park,' I said.

'In December?' Bridget laughed. 'He might be mad, but not that mad, Isobel.' She looked at her watch. 'I'd better go. I'm supposed to meet the girls soon.'

'OK, Bridget,' I said. 'Thanks for calling.'

'You're welcome.' She smiled. 'It was great seeing you. And I can't wait for tomorrow!'

'Neither can I.' I hugged her. 'By this time tomorrow night, we'll both be married women.'

'Absolutely.' She kissed me on both cheeks. '*Buenas noches*, Isobel.'

'*Buenas noches*,' I said as she walked down the garden path.

Chapter 38

Hair Dishevelled by the Fleeing Constellation
(Joan Miró, 1940)

I left the milk bottles outside the front door before I went to bed and shivered in the raw night air. The white smudge of the Milky Way cut through the dark night sky and made me feel small and insignificant. All those stars, perhaps with planets of their own. And maybe people like me living on them, worrying about the fact that their fiancé was off with a bunch of blokes the night before his wedding. I prayed that nothing awful would happen to him. It would be a complete nightmare if we discovered in the morning that they had played some trick that had gone horribly wrong and that he was stranded in the depths of the countryside, totally unable to get back to Dublin.

I imagined what Mum would say. And Dad. I almost smiled at the thought of it. 'We told you,' they'd mutter grimly. 'He was never right for you, Isobel.'

I shivered in the cool night breeze that came in from the sea and closed the front door. I put on the latch and drew across the safety catch.

Everybody was home. Ian was listening to CDs in his room. Alison was lying on the sofa. She'd plastered a skin-purifying, high-moisturising, turn-you-into-a-sex-goddess face mask over herself.

'Any luck?' I asked.

'Huh?'

'Has it turned you into a cross between Sandra Bullock and Sharon Stone yet?'

'Sod off,' she said. 'You'll want me to look the part tomorrow.'

'I have every confidence in you,' I told her. 'But I'm working on the basis of beauty sleep. I'm going to bed.'

'That's a good idea.' Mum was filing her nails. 'You should get some rest, Isobel.'

'Absolutely.' Dad looked up from Ian's copy of *Four-Four-Two*. 'Get your rest now.'

'OK,' I said. 'Goodnight, everyone.'

'Goodnight,' they echoed.

I went up to my bedroom and closed the door behind me. I wasn't sleepy but I needed time to be alone. All evening the family had talked about the wedding, about getting our hair done, about the church, about the soloist (Stella's antibiotics hadn't worked, it was the untested Bernadette tomorrow!), about the champagne reception, about the band, about the hotel – they went on and on until I was sick of it. And when I didn't answer Mum's ridiculous question about whether or not I should have had a smoked salmon starter, she asked me if I was feeling all right, if I had a headache, a temperature, anything at all?

'I have a temperature,' I'd snapped. 'But it's normal.' Then Mum looked hurt and I felt terrible.

'Nerves,' Ian had muttered and taken himself off to his room.

I could hear the rhythmic thud of guitar through the bedroom wall but it was comforting not annoying. I sat in front of the mirror and went through the cleanse, tone and moisturise ritual that I'd started the day I got my first spot. This time tomorrow, I said, as I wiped away the cleanser, this time tomorrow I will be Isobel Malone. I will be married. I will be Tim's wife. Isobel Malone, I mouthed at my reflection. Is-o-bel Ma-lone.

Isabella querida. Isabella.

Would this have happened anyway? I asked myself savagely. If Bridget hadn't shown up and told me that Barbara and Nico weren't an item and that Nico had turned into a workaholic? Would I have thought of Nico tonight?

It wasn't as though he'd left me for Barbara. I'd left him. For Tim. And I knew I was doing the right thing. I was certain. But I couldn't help thinking about him. *Isabella querida.*

I'd have probably thought about other boyfriends if Tim and I had married when we were supposed to. It would have been Alan Davenport or any of them. Whispering, oh Isobel!

I closed my eyes tightly and summoned up a picture of Tim. Tim looking handsome and wonderful in his black tux, a carnation in his buttonhole. Tim smiling at me as I walked up the aisle to him. Tim's face as he saw me in my ridiculously extravagant dress.

I opened my eyes again. The dress wasn't ridiculously extravagant. It was perfect. My heartbeat slowed down and the raggedness in my breathing abated. Everything would be all right. It was normal to have nerves. I would be OK.

The bed was cold. I hadn't got used to sleeping in a single bed since I'd come home. I hated the way I couldn't pull the duvet right around me, under my chin, turning it into a cocoon. The bed in my apartment in Madrid had been a double bed. Just as well, really, given the amount of time Nico had spent in it.

Not Nico again, I screamed silently. Not Nico, not now. Nico was over and I'd kind of loved him and he'd kind of loved me but it wasn't the getting married sort of love and what Tim and I had was.

Isabella querida. I didn't even. *want* to think about him. *Hadn't* thought about him. Not for ages. So why now? Why tonight? When I needed to be calm and relaxed. When it was Tim I was worried about, Tim who could (even now) be handcuffed to a lamppost in Donnybrook!

I loved Tim and he loved me. He'd told me at least a thousand times since I'd come home: I love you, Isobel. I need you, Isobel. You're the only one for me, Isobel. This time Tim loved me with the same need as I'd loved him. This time it was Tim that wanted all the trappings of a big wedding, it was Tim that talked about redecorating the house, it was Tim that couldn't wait until our wedding day.

So I didn't have to worry that he wouldn't show up and I didn't have to imagine how I'd react if he rang me to say he was sorry, but he'd changed his mind. It wasn't going to happen. Everything was fine. Everything was sorted out. All I had to do was get a good night's sleep and look my radiant best in the morning.

I heard the rest of the family come to bed. Mum called in to Ian to turn off the CD. He lowered it down but I could still hear the bass. Alison poked her head around my door and whispered goodnight. I grunted back at her. She was really looking forward to tomorrow. The dress I'd made looked fabulous on her and she loved it. Mum's suit looked great too. We'd all look great tomorrow. It would be fine.

It was around two when I fell asleep. And I dreamed the dream again, the one about Father O'Brien and wearing net curtains instead of a dress. I woke up at three, sweating. I fumbled for my inhaler, knocked it off the bedside locker and under my bed. I hated it when that happened. I hated feeling around for it under the bed. When I was small I'd believed that there were spooky creatures underneath. I knew there weren't any spooky creatures there, but I still didn't like waving my hand under it. Childish. Immature. Silly Isobel. I took two puffs and felt better. I hoped I wouldn't be wheezy tomorrow. My bouquet was of fresh flowers and if I didn't deliberately sniff them I'd be all right. It was very traditional: red and white carnations surrounded by gypsophilia. My other bouquet, the one for the first wedding, had been roses.

I lay down and closed my eyes but I was wide awake and couldn't go back to sleep so I turned on the light. I could read, I thought, but I knew I couldn't concentrate long enough to read anything properly. Three o'clock is a horrible time of the night to be awake.

Eventually I went downstairs and made myself a cup of tea. I was as quiet as possible, but Alison walked into the kitchen just as I was pouring milk into the cup.

'I thought I heard something,' she said.

'You shouldn't have come downstairs.' I took a second cup from the rack and filled it for her. 'What if I'd been a burglar? I could've smashed your head in.'

She laughed. 'Risk I had to take. Besides, I heard the fridge door opening. I don't think burglars would be bothered about the contents of our fridge.'

'Probably not.' I sat down at the table and sipped my tea.

'Can't you sleep?' asked Alison.

'D'you think I'd be sitting here drinking tea if I could?'

'I suppose not. I wonder will I be the same?'

'I don't know,' I replied. 'Maybe it's par for the course.

You lie awake and you wonder if you're doing the right thing, and you think back over your life and you hope that the future's going to be OK.'

Alison nodded. 'I understand.'

'It's not that I don't want to marry him,' I said. 'It's just that you hope that everything turns out the way you want, that's all. And you realise how final it is.'

'Not really.' She grinned. 'You can always get a divorce.'

'But nobody thinks like that going into it,' I protested. 'You don't stand in the church and think that it doesn't matter because you can get a divorce. You want it to work.'

'So – are you having second thoughts?' She added some more milk to her tea.

'No,' I said. 'Just thoughts.'

We sat in silence. The hands on the kitchen clock suddenly whirred around the face in a frenzy. It was a radio-controlled clock – the manic spinning of its hands meant it needed a new battery.

'You don't have to marry him,' said Alison blandly. 'If you don't want to.'

'Oh, don't be bloody silly.' I got up and rinsed my cup under the tap. 'He went out with the blokes from his office tonight. I'm worried in case he's too hungover to turn up tomorrow!'

'Isobel! Not really?'

'No.' I sighed. 'Not really. He'll probably be hungover though.'

She grinned. 'And his eyes will be pink.'

'Do you notice that too?' I asked. 'That his eyes go pink?'

'Most people's do.'

'But he doesn't have to drink very much.'

She laughed. 'And when they send back the photos

590

they'll have a little comment about how to avoid pink eyes! By standing further back when you use the flash!'

I laughed too. 'And avoiding all alcoholic drink the night before.'

Alison yawned. 'I'm tired. I think I'll go back to bed.'

I was feeling tired myself now. 'Me too,' I said and followed her upstairs.

∽

It was an absolutely beautiful morning. The sun shone from a cloudless blue sky and the breeze – miraculously – was from the south so that it was almost warm.

The house was in a state of chaos. Mum had commandeered the bathroom; Ian, trying to be helpful by ironing for the first time in his life, had singed a hole in his shirt; Alison derided him for not knowing that the three dots on the iron meant hot and Dad wandered around the house looking for the notes for his after-dinner speech.

I remembered Julie's idea of going to the Berkley Court for a pre-wedding breakfast and I wished I'd followed her example. I hadn't fallen asleep until nearly five o'clock, there were black bags under my eyes and, despite everything, a spot had chosen today of all days to reappear on my forehead. I dabbed Clearasil on it in the hopes that it might dry out before I got around to doing my make-up.

Alison and I went to the hairdresser's at eleven. We were both wearing our hair the same way, although hers was now long enough for the style and mine only just made it.

'As soon as I get back from Venice I'm going to get it chopped off again,' I told Tanya, the hairstylist.

'It suits you like this, Isobel.' She stood back and

admired her work. 'You should be patient, let it grow a little longer.'

'Patience was never one of my stronger points.'

'We'd better put some spray in,' she said.

I nodded and took a deep breath. Hairspray made me sneeze and wheeze. I held my breath until a few seconds after she stopped spraying and the tiny molecules had stopped floating around the air in front of me. But I sneezed anyway.

'Are you OK?' asked Alison.

'I will be.' I sneezed eight times in a row and tears ran down my cheeks.

Tanya giggled and I made a face at her. When I finally stopped I paid her and we left the salon. Usually I walked to the hairdresser's but today we'd driven, on the basis that the breeze might whip up into a wind and ruin Tanya's good work before we got home again. But it was still mild and warm as we got into the car and drove home.

'It's exciting, isn't it?' Alison smiled at me. 'It's the one day when everyone does exactly what you want.'

'It's the one day when nobody wants to upset you,' I amended. 'And that's not a bad thing.'

Peace had been restored at home. Dad had found his notes, Mum was doing her make-up and Ian had managed to iron another shirt, this time without ruining it.

'Your hair is lovely,' said Mum. 'Really pretty. You look very young like that.'

'Thanks.'

'I've just made some soup and sandwiches,' she said. 'Don't forget it'll be late before you get anything to eat.'

'I'm not hungry,' I said.

'I'm starving,' said Alison. 'Lead me to it.'

'You have to eat something,' Mum told me. 'Even

if you don't think you're hungry now. You'll be hungry later.'

I didn't think so. My stomach was in a knot and every so often a wave of adrenalin shot through me, sending acid into my tummy and making me wince with pain.

But she almost force-fed me with chicken soup and ham sandwiches and I supposed she had a point.

'By the way, Tim rang when you were in the hairdresser's.'

'Did he?' I looked anxiously at her.

'He said that he was tucked up safely in bed by midnight and that he'll be waiting for you at two o'clock.' She beamed at me. 'I must say, Isobel, I had grave doubts about you marrying him. I really had. But I think it's all worked out for the best. He wasn't mature enough before. He's changed and that's a good thing.'

'I've changed too,' I said.

'But you were always mature,' she said confidently. 'Girls are.'

⁓

The only thing left was the veil. Alison helped me to secure it onto my head, then we both stepped back from the mirror.

'Oh, Isobel.' Her lip quivered. 'You look beautiful.'

'Thanks.'

'And the veil is wonderful.'

I made a face. 'I didn't really want a long veil. It was Tim that wanted that.'

'Why?'

'I think he has some male fantasy about virginal brides or something.'

She chortled. 'Well he's barking up the wrong tree there.'

'Alison Kavanagh!' I shoved her gently. 'That's a terrible thing to say to me.'

'Truth hurts,' she said blithely.

I adjusted the veil.

'You *do* look wonderful,' she said. 'And the dress is perfect.'

Mum knocked on the door. 'Are you ready yet?'

'Yes,' I said.

She came in and started to cry. I hugged her and told her that I loved her but she kept her face buried in my shoulder and I was afraid that her make-up would rub off on my dress.

'It's OK,' she sniffed. 'And I haven't ruined your dress.' She dabbed at the sleeve with a tissue.

'Don't worry,' I said. 'Everything's fine.'

'Your dad wants to take a photograph in the garden,' said Mum.

'The garden!' Alison threw her eyes to heaven. 'What's he thinking of? It's bleak in the garden.'

'He wants to,' said Mum defiantly.

'I don't mind,' I said.

We trooped downstairs. Dad took a photo as we walked into the kitchen.

'Oh, really, Dad!' Alison made a face at him.

'Come on,' he said. 'A nice family photograph.'

He set the camera on timer and we stood under the bare branches of the apple-tree, Mum and Dad, Ian, Alison and me. The camera whirred into action and took the photo.

'That'll be lovely,' said Dad. 'Just the five of us.'

We went inside again and Mum peered out of the front window.

'The cars are here.'

'OK,' I said.

'I'll be going, then.'

'See you there.'

'You'll be OK?'

'Of course.'

Dad went with them to the door. I stood in the kitchen and gazed out at the back garden. It was nice to have thirty seconds to myself.

❧

Dad held my hand all the way in the car. He didn't talk and I was grateful to him for that. But Dad wasn't a chatterer. And he understood me more than Mum.

The photographer bustled around with his camera. He made me get out of the car twice because he said I'd bent my head at the wrong moment the first time.

'Look up!' he cried. 'Come on, Isobel.'

I looked up, he got his photograph and then we walked into the church.

It was the strangest sensation. I stood at the end of the aisle and it had never seemed longer. The red carpet stretched into infinity in front of me and the guests in the pews seemed to be insignificant dots miles away in the distance. But I could see Tim at the top of the church. He was there, as he'd promised. Relief flooded over me, so strong that I felt myself shake. Dad squeezed my hand again and I felt better. I wished that I'd taken a squirt of my inhaler before I'd come into the church, but I'd forgotten. I knew it was only nerves that was making my breath come in short gasps.

The organ wheezed into life. Dad and I walked slowly up the aisle. I was lightheaded, but I didn't know whether that was from hyperventilating or whether it was the sense of occasion getting to me.

The little posies of red and white flowers, tied with white satin ribbons, looked very elegant at the end of each pew. The red and white flowers on the altar were magnificent.

I recognised people as I walked by. Christine and Siobhán. Greg Roberts. Mum's sister, Rachel. Dennis, holding Sorcha by the hand. Luis. Magdalena. Gabriela, dabbing at her eyes with a tiny handkerchief. Julie. Her sister, Danielle. Other relatives. Mum. Denise Malone. And, finally, Tim. He smiled at me. His eyes were pink.

The congregation sat down. People cleared their throats. Someone coughed. I wanted to sneeze. I wriggled my nose to stop it.

It seemed very solemn all of a sudden. Very solemn and very religious and very final. I kept my breathing slow and easy.

Father O'Brien smiled at us and I looked down at my dress to make sure it hadn't turned into net curtains. Tim squeezed my hand, already sore from all the squeezing Dad had done in the car.

The priest started to talk about love. And marriage. He reminded everyone that Tim and I had had our ups and downs. But that we'd grown through that adversity and become stronger people as a result. People who were now committed to living a Christian marriage and a Christian life.

Because we were older, he said, we had past experiences to help us. I thought of some of my past experiences and bit my lip. Ignacio. Stefan. John. Luis. I almost smiled when I thought of Luis. At least I'd been able to look him in the face again. Eventually. And I thought of Nico.

Father O'Brien smiled at us again and then, unexpectedly, because I hadn't even been listening to what was going on, he was saying to Tim: 'Do you, Tim, take Isobel as your lawful wedded wife?' It had happened before I realised it was going to happen and the suddenness of it all made me hold my breath.

Tim was saying the words: 'For richer for poorer, in sickness and in health, as long as we both shall live.'

I gasped.

Father O'Brien smiled at me. 'Do you, Isobel, take Tim as your lawful wedded husband?'

The words echoed around the church, bounced around in my head. 'Sickness, health, richer, poorer, as long—'

I stared at him. He smiled encouragingly at me. This was it, then. This was my dream come true.

I cleared my throat. 'I, Isobel—'

I stopped.

There was a ripple of laughter from the church and Tim grinned at me. Father O'Brien smiled again too.

I cleared my throat again. 'I, Isobel—' And there was thunder in my ears and a mist in front of my eyes and a feeling that time was standing still. I could sense everyone as though in a movie still, watching me, listening to me, waiting for me to say the words. But the words were stuck in my throat and they wouldn't come. I wanted to say them. They were there, somewhere inside me. But I couldn't get them past my lips which remained stubbornly closed.

Tim was looking anxiously at me. Father O'Brien watched benevolently. The crowd waited expectantly.

And suddenly the bubble burst, time moved forward again and I looked at Tim and at Father O'Brien and gasped, 'I'm sorry. I can't.'

Then I dropped my bouquet on the steps of the altar, picked up the skirt of my dress, and ran as fast as my spindly heels would allow out of the church.

The chauffeur was leaning against the car door smoking a cigarette. He looked at me in complete amazement as I came flying down the steps.

'Start the car,' I commanded as I jumped into the back seat, yanking the dress in with me. 'And drive.'

'What?'

'Don't argue, just do it,' I snapped.

He did what I said. I suppose he was too terrified by my manic look to refuse. As we drove down the road I looked back through the rear window and saw the crowd of people appear in the church door and I was both appalled and relieved at what I had done.

'Where to?' asked the driver.

I wondered whether this had happened to him before. He was remarkably relaxed.

'The Summit,' I said clearly. 'Howth Summit.'

He said nothing but drove at a steady forty miles an hour. It only took a few minutes to reach the summit.

'What now?' He stopped the car and looked around at me.

'Wait here,' I said.

I got out of the car and walked to the edge of the hill.

Suddenly the driver was beside me. 'Don't do anything stupid,' he said, his eyes full of concern. 'For God's sake, girl. Nothing is that bad.'

I turned to him and laughed and it was a real laugh, full of joy. 'I'm not doing anything stupid,' I said. 'I've just saved myself from doing something stupid. Honestly. It's OK. Wait for me.'

He stayed where he was while I picked my way uncertainly through the rough, damp grass. The end of the dress would be stained green. I didn't care.

The breeze was much stronger here. It pushed me and pulled at me so that I struggled to keep my balance on my high-heeled oyster-white shoes.

I stood and looked out to the horizon where the blue of the sky and the green of the sea met. My breathing was better now, helped by the freshness of the air.

I closed my eyes. I had done a terrible, terrible thing.

People would say that I'd done it to get my revenge on Tim and, I supposed, lots of them would believe that. But I hadn't. Up until the moment that Father O'Brien had asked me the question, I'd intended to marry Tim. I'd gone through a night of doubts and fears and I'd woken up certain that I was doing the right thing. Even walking up the aisle, though I'd been nervous, I was still certain that I was doing the right thing.

And thinking of Ignacio and Stefan and John and Luis I was sure I was doing the right thing.

And thinking of Nico . . . When I thought of Nico, I wasn't sure of anything any more.

Yet I still would have gone through with it. But when Father O'Brien said the words out loud, when he asked me whether I wanted Tim as my husband – then it was like a bolt of lightning, like an electric shock. *I didn't.* And at first I didn't believe it myself. My body tried to say the words but my mind wouldn't let it. And I couldn't believe it.

But I knew that I'd made the right decision. Even if I'd left it very late in the day. I felt as though a huge weight had been lifted from my shoulders and, for the first time in weeks, I didn't have a headache and I didn't need to puff my inhaler.

The wind tugged at my veil and whipped it around my face. I reached up and untied it. I held it out in front of me and it stretched out, long and white, like a banner in the air.

They'd never forgive me. Never.

Then I let go of the veil and the wind took it, spinning it around and around before carrying it high off the hill and out to the blue-green sea.

Destinations

Sheila O'Flanagan

First Maeve Binchy brought us to *Dublin 4*, now Sheila
O'Flanagan takes us to new *Destinations* . . . enjoy the
ride!

Destinations reveals the inside track on the lives of
ordinary commuters. And uncovers the hidden links
that lie beneath the surface of 'anonymous' city lives.

Two eavesdropping passengers learn more than they
bargained for; an office-party fling has unforeseen
consequences; a suburban housewife is forced to face
her estranged mother – and her thorny past; an office
worker finds her commute to work livened up by the
daily sightings of a handsome stranger; a hot date with
the office stud gets off to a disastrous start . . . is there
light at the end of the tunnel?

Destinations – tales that go the distance with you, from
one of Ireland's best-loved story-tellers.

Praise for Sheila O'Flanagan's bestsellers

'The Sheila O'Flanagan guarantee is a pretty powerful
one' *Irish Independent*

'Highly readable' *Express*

'Hugely enjoyable' *Best*

'Another fantastic book . . . a must-read' *Irish News*

0 7553 0761 5

headline

Now you can buy any of these other bestselling books by **Sheila O'Flanagan** from your bookshop or *direct from her publisher*.

FREE P&P AND UK DELIVERY
(Overseas and Ireland £3.50 per book)

Destinations	£6.99
He's Got to Go	£6.99
Caroline's Sister	£6.99
Isobel's Wedding	£5.99
My Favourite Goodbye	£5.99
Far From Over	£6.99
Suddenly Single	£6.99

TO ORDER SIMPLY CALL THIS NUMBER

01235 400 414

or visit our website: www.madaboutbooks.com

Prices and availability subject to change without notice.